THE WITCH QUEEN

THE THAYAR CROWN
BOOK I

ALEXANDRIA
ARDEN

CONTENTS

For all the women who had to shoulder too much at an early age —
I see you.
And you are not alone.

CONTENT & TRIGGER WARNINGS

The Witch Queen is an adult fantasy romance book, intended for audiences 18+. The violence and romance are often incredibly explicit. The content and trigger warnings below are intended to prepare readers for what they will experience. Some of these trigger warnings may provide minor spoilers for the book.

- Parental loss

- Explicit sexual activity

- Mention of sexual assault/ sexual harassment (not on the page)

- Very close call with sexual assault (but it is stopped before it happens)

- Brief reference to past suicidal ideation

- Mature language and cursing

- Violence – this is a fantasy book about war

- Explicit/ Gory Torture

- Depiction of a panic attack

- Death of loved ones

- Sexist/ patriarchal culture – none of the MCs share these beliefs

- Homophobic culture – none of the MCs share these beliefs

Please read responsibly. If you have any questions about these content and trigger warnings, please don't hesitate to contact me via email or social media.

alexandria.arden.author@gmail.com

@alexandriaardenauthor (I am most active on Instagram and TikTok)

GLOSSARY

People

Laurel Elestren (lau-rel eh-less-tren) — Queen of Thayaria; The Witch Queen

Hawthorne Vicant (haa-thorn vie-kant) — Prince of Velmara; The Shining Prince

Mazus Vicant (ma-zes vie-kant) — King of Velmara; The Golden King

Nemesia Nestern (neh-me-see-uh nes-turn) — Chair of the Council of Advisors of Thayaria; former General of Thayaria

Silene Kalmeera (si-leen cal-meer-uh) — betrothed and best friend of Prince Hawthorne

Fionn Solanum (fee-on soh-lan-um) — best friend and guard of Prince Hawthorne

Carex Callaway (care-ux cal-uh-way) — captain of the Thayarian Royal Guard; former lover of Queen Laurel

Admon (ad-mohn) — advisor to Queen Laurel

Krantz (crants) — leader of the Sons and Daughters of Thayaria

Lobelia (lo-bee-lee-uh) - Queen of Delsar

Places

Thayaria (thay-r-ee-uh) — the kingdom within the Four Kingdoms with the most ley lines crossing it; the only place where the thayar flower grows

Velmara (vel-mar-uh) — the largest kingdom in the Four Kingdoms; known for it's extensive collection of texts called the Velmaran Archive

Delsar (del-sarr) — the smallest of the Four Kingdoms; known for it's fearsome female warriors

Reshnar (resh-narr) — the only kingdom within the Four Kingdoms with a human ruler and a democracy

Arberly (r-ber-lee) — the capitol of Thayaria

Arnia (r-nee-uh) — the capitol of Velmara

Nivan Desert (nigh-von) — a large stretch of land in Velmara where no ley lines cross, making it very challenging to channel the magic of the aether; both a magical and topographic desert

Echosa (eh-ko-suh) — a port town in Thayaria; the closest port to both Velmara and Delsar

Eless (el-us) — an estate named after the Elestren family, built in the region most populated by humans in Thayaria and near the location where Laurel's mother was raised

Oakton (oak-tun) — a village in Thayaria, south of Arberly

Rusthelm (rust-helm) — a village in Thayaria, west of Arberly)

Miscellaneous

Aether (ay-thur) — the magical force of the world; magic users must channel it through a conduit in order to practice magic

Leylines (lay-lines) — concentration of aether that run like magical rivers across the Four Kingdoms

Aerstep (air-step-ing) — similar to teleportation; the act of using aether to disappear from one place and reappear in another. Can also be used to summon objects. The distance a magic user can aerstep is based on their magical strength.

Aether-heart (ay-thur hart) — the source of magic in a magical being; similar to a soul

Leymaster (lay-mas-tur) — an expert magic user; someone whose mastery over leylines and their own magic lends them the skills and knowledge to teach others

Aethermancer (ay-thur-man-ser) — a derogatory term referring to someone who conducts magical experiments or practices unsafe or even unsavory magic

Aether-voice (ay-thur voyse) — the ability only sitting monarchs in the Four Kingdoms possess to lace their voice with aether, allowing them to bend others less powerful than them to their will

Abscission (ab-si-zhen) — a two week period unique to Thayaria that starts the day of the Winter Solstice, where all the trees and other plants drop their leaves immediately and remain bare until the period is over. It is considered the coldest time of year in Thayaria and custom dictates that Thayarians relax and rest during this time period.

MAP

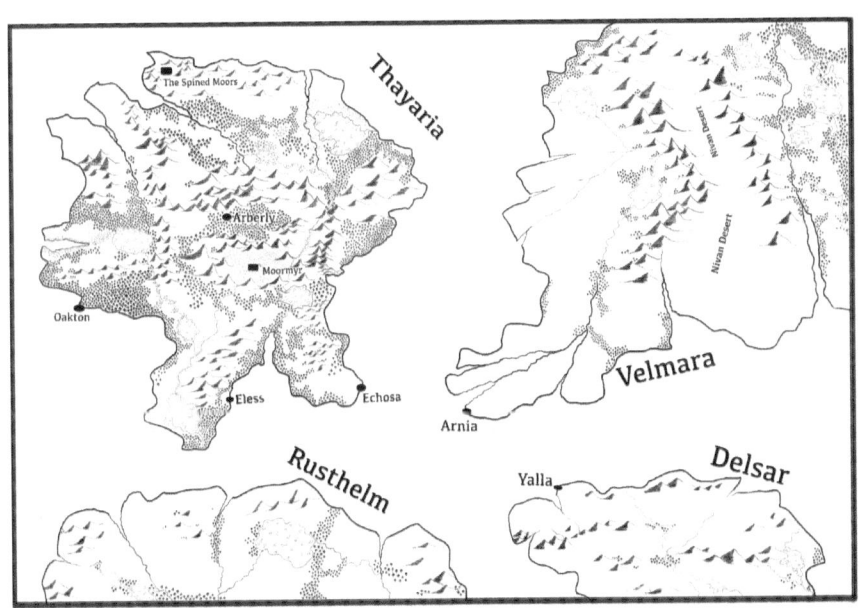

hand drawn by the author

PROLOGUE

"Get your ass up and be the Queen your people deserve," a familiar feminine voice commands over the clinks and grunts of the battle below. "You don't have the luxury of falling apart, not when your people are dying to protect *you*."

Nemesia, my General and the only person who would dare address me so curtly, crouches down beside me and places her calloused warrior's hand on my back. Voice softening, she adds, "I know you're tired. I know you're grieving. We all are. But if we lose this battle, it might be the end. Our only option is to keep pushing forward. We need a plan, Laurel."

I stand and look down upon the battle from the hilltop where our command is set up, desperation and fear threatening to consume me. Fae soldiers clad in armor fight in the Valley of Moormyr below me, surrounded by snow-capped mountains, the wild thayar flowers crushed beneath their feet.

Just five years ago, my parents brought me to a festival held in this very valley. Now, the crimson petals and dark green leaves are indistinguishable from the blood, mud, and other gore of a three-day long battle. No one prepared me for the stench of war, or the mess of it, and I've learned the hard way in the last two months what endless skirmishes, raids, and battles do to the once picturesque landscape of my kingdom.

Grief stabs my insides, sending me to my knees again as I remember my parents and the festival that was their favorite event in Thayaria. Tears run down my face as I crumple, curling myself into a ball. I'll never be able to finish this war, will never live up to the legacy of my parents. They ruled Thayaria for three hundred years, providing our kingdom with three centuries of peace and prosperity—how could I possibly replace them? I'm nowhere near ready to rule, not at only twenty years old. I was supposed to have centuries of training and preparation before I inherited their throne. With the long lives of the fae, my parents should have lived long enough to pass the throne to me gradually, staying on as advisors until I was ready to rule on my own. Now I'm alone, with no one to guide me or tell me how to end this war.

"Pull it together, Laurel," Nemesia hisses, though not unkindly, breaking through my inner turmoil. Nemesia's hand doesn't leave my back as I stand again, knees weak and limbs uncertain. With a deep inhale, I turn to face the closest person I've ever had to a sibling, her hazel eyes staring back at me with deep set resolve. She's barely out of fae adolescence herself, our centuries-long lives extending what humans consider early adulthood well into our fourth decade. At forty years old, she's what humans consider early twenties, while I'm practically a teenager. Despite her age, Nemesia was the only person I considered appointing General of my armies when the time came to choose her mother's replacement. "We need a plan. And I will not make it without you," she repeats, her tall, lithe body—so unlike my own—towering over me. Tendrils of white-blonde hair escape her braid as the wind caresses her sharp and angular features. Dark tawny skin ripples with muscles in a tense stance.

"We need a plan," I repeat, nodding in acknowledgement of all the things Nemesia isn't saying aloud. *We need my magic.* Magic that I'm barely capable of wielding and that no one understands, myself included. Magic that my parents insisted—demanded—I keep secret. They gave their lives trying to protect me, trying to keep the full extent of my powers and my lack of control over them locked away. But I knew this moment would come. No matter how hard my parents fought to keep my magic—to keep *me*—a secret, I knew it wouldn't work. Part of me wonders if that's why Mazus launched this war to begin with. He wanted me to reveal the secrets of the prophecy-blessed heir, now ruler, of Thayaria.

Nemesia gives me an encouraging smile, lips cracked from weeks of sun and wind exposure.

I can't allow myself to dwell on the prophecy, not now, not when it has completely and utterly destroyed my life. A fated love that will unite realms is what I was apparently destined for, though in much more flowery language than that. My entire life I've been lauded and praised for all the good I would eventually do, envied for the fate that awaited me. But the prophecy is nonsense. All I have is magic I can't control, the blood of my people on my hands, and an impossible choice. I squeeze my eyes shut and deeply inhale, then center myself within the current of the aether flowing around me. I hold my breath for three seconds, then slowly exhale—just like I was taught by the leymaster my parents brought in when I started displaying abnormal magical powers at the age of nine.

Opening my eyes, Nemesia still stares back at me, eyes wide with expectation.

"What if there is no plan, Neme? What if—what if I don't have enough magic to stop this?" I ask softly, my voice trembling.

Nemesia takes my hands in hers, looking deep into my eyes and seeing through me, like she always does. "I've seen you tap into the aether deeper than anyone ever has, Laurel."

I sigh, dropping her hands. Her belief in me is both fortifying and suffocating. I look back down at the battle. My armies have dwindled to a few hundred soldiers, while Mazus has battalions still waiting in his army camp just outside the valley who have yet to join the fight. My eyes lock onto a female Thayarian soldier battling three massive Velmaran males, and my body tenses with recognition. She was once assigned to my personal guard. Though outnumbered, she drives forward with her sword, stabbing one Velmaran soldier in the stomach and parrying to slash the arm of another. For a moment, there's a flare of hope in my chest that she may be able to take them—before a fourth soldier comes up behind her. He knocks her to the ground and swiftly slices the back of her neck. She slumps to the ground and doesn't get up again.

Bile rises in my throat, but I force myself to stay standing. My shoulders slump in shame—I cannot remember her name.

Resolve hardens in my chest. My magic will not be enough—not with how unpredictable my control is. Night after night of this war, I've practiced, trying to use my aether gifts consistently. But each night, my empty hands remind me of all I've lost. No, there's no plan, no scenario where we win this war. I decide on what a part of me always knew was inevitable.

"Send a message to Mazus," I whisper to Nemesia, not wanting to say the words aloud but having no other option. "I want an audience with him. And a temporary respite from the battle while we... *negotiate*." Nemesia gives me a hard look, the angles of her expression creating a sharp line from her jaw to her pointed fae ears. "Until then, we hold the line in case he doesn't agree to the ceasefire."

"What are you planning?" she asks warily.

"He asked for my hand. And like a fool I turned him down, believing myself destined for something greater because of that damned prophecy. Believing I didn't have to marry a centuries-old male who makes my skin crawl." I will not allow fanciful dreams to kill my people for another minute. "Send the message." The last words are firm and final, the whispering uncertainty gone from my voice. I give her a look that once upon a time she would have told me was my *queen* look, eyes hardened and lips pursed. Then, we would have laughed at the idea that I'd one day be a queen. Now she only nods, hesitating briefly before striding back to the tent. I hear her shouting orders to her commanders, firm and brokering no argument. Several fae leave the war tent to send out the message to hold the line and not retreat. Not yet, at least.

It was always going to lead to this. I've given up on the idea of fated mates and destinies. Those dreams died with my parents.

Thayarian soldiers—my soldiers—battle two and three opponents at a time while we wait for what feels like ages for a response from Mazus. They're tired and faltering. Then, I hear it: horns blaring and the order to fall back from the Velmaran commanders echoing across the valley. The Velmaran soldiers dutifully depart, eyes on my soldiers and weapons still up as they back away from the line of fighting. The brows of my soldiers furrow in skepticism, unsure what's brought the fighting to such an abrupt halt.

My eyes immediately find Nemesia when I walk into the war tent. Her hardened eyes and the tense shoulders of her lieutenants make my heart drop from my chest. Reaching the huddled group, I ask, "What are his terms?"

"We can't accept them, Your Majesty," Nemesia quickly answers. "We're preparing a missive now with our counter proposal."

"What are his terms?" I demand this time, using the voice laced with the aether that compels any who are less powerful than me to obey my orders. I once loved hearing my mother use this voice.

Nemesia sighs. "He wants you to meet him in his personal tent. Alone. He asks that you bring no weapons, no advisors, and no guards. It's an outrageous demand."

"I'll accept."

"But—"

"Tell him I'll be there in an hour," I interrupt, then turn away, unable to meet Nemesia's eyes. I know what she's thinking. That I can't do this. That this is everything my parents fought for and gave their lives to prevent. But I'm not willing to sacrifice my people in a selfish pursuit of love or magic.

An hour later, the crimson silk of my empire-waist dress swirls around me as I scan the Velmaran encampment across the valley, a spring storm building that makes the air dance with electricity. This is the same place I stood three days ago as this battle began, with the hope of a decisive victory filling my chest. Now all I feel is cold resolve.

"Are you sure—" Nemesia tries to say.

"I'm sure. Be ready for anything."

I stride down the hill and cross the expanse between the two war camps. Fallen fae litter the landscape, impossible to distinguish friend from foe. As I walk, the noxious mud squelches beneath my feet with blood and other gore. I try to avoid getting the bottom of my dress dirty, slowly picking my way through the maze of severed limbs and abandoned weapons. Halfway across the expanse, I realize that it's pointless, and Mazus should see what walking across the battlefield he created causes, even if it's just a ruined dress.

As I approach, Velmaran soldiers break out in hisses of "witch," and my cheeks heat with shame. Mazus was the first to use the word, and it's taken off in the last few months of war. Narrowed eyes and pursed lips greet me when I finally reach the edge of their encampment, the soldiers on guard wary of me. Air channelers probe my body for weapons using wind, and when they're satisfied I've complied with the terms, they nod to a guard standing outside what must be Mazus's personal tent.

I feel a tingle of Mazus's magic along my shoulders and tense, knowing what's about to happen and yet still unprepared for the jolt of aerstepping magic that brings me face to face with the Velmaran King. Internally rolling my eyes, I look up at the man who declared war on my kingdom, labeled me a witch, and claimed he had to defeat *me* for the good of the Four Kingdoms. As if my very existence threatened the safety of our world.

Mazus Vicant embodies his moniker—the Golden King, he's called. Tall and tanned, he towers over me as his handsome face pulls into a glowing smile. Olive, green-brown eyes stare down at me, like a forest at twilight. Such an unusual shade that I'd know them anywhere. Despite his otherworldly beauty, the way he carries himself and the hollowness of his expression, like he's chiseled from stone, make my skin crawl when I'm in his presence.

"I would have aerstepped you across the battlefield," he says with a look of disgust on his perfect face, surveying the bottom of my dress. "I simply assumed you would use that deep well of power you keep hidden to avoid the filth now covering the bottom half of your dress."

I clench my jaw. *Play nice, you're trying to marry him after all.* "I only wanted to ensure you knew I was coming and for your guards to adequately search me," I say with sickly sweetness.

"You need not lie to me. I know you have little control over your magic, *witch*." I try to hide my flinching at his words, but I'm unsuccessful. He notices and gives me a menacing grin. "If only you'd agreed to marry me. I could've counseled you, and we might have been able to avoid the tragic *accident* that led to your parents' deaths. Committed by one with too much power and too little guidance." My fists ball, and I feel magical energy begin to pulse through me. I try to speak, to scream at him the truth of his treachery, but he cuts me off. "No, there's no need for lies between us. I know why you're here, why you sent your pleading message to call for temporary peace and a meeting with me. You want to surrender. Want to beg me to wed you as a last desperate attempt to get me to agree to end this war."

It takes all the willpower in me to hold my tongue. *He just needs to stroke his own ego first. Let him get it out. This doesn't change your plan.*

"And since I'm demanding no lies from you, I'll hold myself to that same standard. I'm the Golden King, after all. Driven by honor and duty and all the things my people believe me to be." He grins, flashing his bright white teeth in what feels more like a snarl than a smile. "The truth is, I don't need to marry you. Not anymore. I don't need to end this war in a peace treaty. I'm winning. *Decisively.* And considering you aren't even half as beautiful as my first wife, and certainly more trouble than she ever was, I have no desire to shackle myself to you in marriage when I can take what I want so easily."

My chest tightens, panic rising. "Mazus, Your Majesty, please—my people—"

Disgust crosses his expression as he cuts me off. "Laurel, begging like this is beneath you. And certainly doesn't make me want to marry you. *Weakness is repulsive.*" He practically spits the last sentence, but I barely comprehend what he's saying. The distinct buzz of magical energy from the aether builds in my body. *No, not right now. I need to stay in control.* Sweat gathers on my brow from the effort of pushing the magic down. "As we speak, my soldiers are picking off the pitiful remaining army you have. I've sent my best assassin after your *General*," he spits the word, as if the idea of a young female general disgusts him. *No. No, no, no. Not again. I can't lose another person.* The buzzing intensifies, and this time I can't dampen it. It shakes my bones and churns my organs. I'm consumed by rage and so... much... energy... "I will take you back to Velmara to experiment on. Thayaria will be absorbed into Velmara, and we can forget all about this pitiful excuse for a war."

He takes a step toward me, and I react instantly. His body freezes, eyes widening in shock and horror as he realizes I've stopped his ability to move. I stare at my own hands, unsure what magic I've used and how to undo it. Looking at Mazus again, determination settles across his expression. He grunts, breaking my magical hold on him, then calls for guards to bring in iron shackles. I vaguely sense the guards arrive, distracted by my fury and the effort of keeping my magic under control. If I let go and unleash it, I'll have no ability to direct it, not in this emotional state. Not to mention the years-long plan to keep the true depth of my power hidden, the plan my parents *died for*, will be ruined.

Soldiers grab me and pin my arms to my sides, their grips so tight it makes my arms ache. I scream in fear, but there's no one coming to save me. My parents are dead, thousands of my soldiers have already fallen, and Nemesia... the only person left in this world who I love is probably already dead. Mazus steps toward me, a dagger and several vials in his hands. He slices down my arm and a whimper of pain escapes me. Tears collect in my eyes and blur my vision. I try again to break out of the soldiers' hold, whipping and contorting my body in any position I can think of to break free, but to no avail.

Collecting the crimson blood that seeps from my skin, Mazus grins at me with malice. I panic, unsure of what's happening. Iron shackles clamp around my wrists, and then Mazus is speaking with his aether-voice, able to compel me because of the iron, even though I have more power than him.

"Laurel, use plants to slice your wrists," he commands, and my magic rises to follow his command, even as my mind pushes against the order. If I don't get out of here, I won't survive what he plans to do with me. Of that I'm sure. I grunt, and with every ounce of magical prowess I possess, I ignore the compulsion. His eyes widen in a lethal fury as his hand wraps around my throat, squeezing tightly. I try to bring my hands up to pry him off me, but they remain shackled at my sides. My eyes water, and my nose runs. He issues the command again, and I manage to fight it off, but just barely. The iron is quickly draining me of my power. I have to get out of here.

I can't move my hands, can't breathe, can't even thrash my body, so I close my eyes and focus on the only thing that might save me—magic. My skin buzzes with more intensity than I've ever felt. With barely the whisper of a thought, I stop the aether from flowing through Mazus's veins again, an awareness of how to use the magic washing over me. Before the guards can react, I've halted them as well, and I easily duck out of their grasp. The iron on my wrists melts away. With an explosion of light, I take one step forward in the tent and the next is on the grass of my war camp. My arm still drips with blood from Mazus's cut.

The bodies of my slaughtered soldiers are everywhere. Only a few remain, desperately trying to fight off the Velmaran soldiers sent to decimate my forces. I want to help them, but my thoughts are on the war tent and Nemesia. Without thinking, I'm aerstepping again through a pocket of magical current and then I'm in the tent. A soldier has Nemesia pulled tight against his chest, dagger poised at her throat and ready to slice.

The buzzing inside of me builds to an unbearable level. I can't breathe, and the world around me becomes fuzzy as my sight diminishes. All I feel is the jostling of the magical current as it rises, unchecked, within me. The tent shakes, steel poles bending towards my orbit. The soldier holding Nemesia looks up for a brief second, hostility flickering across his expression. With barely another thought, I find the magical current flowing around the soldier, then focus in on where it collects around his heart. I wrap my power around his magical source and *squeeze,* willing the aether to stop flowing through him. He drops.

Relief fills my lungs as Nemesia gasps for breath. Before I can reach her, another dagger whips through the air. I turn, realizing too late that the King said he sent his *best assassin* for Nemesia, not a soldier.

I can sense the magic being channeled through the steel of the tiny blade as it whips towards Nemesia's heart.

It will not miss.

The pressure inside of me builds and builds—filling my stomach, my lungs, and my throat with sizzling, burning magic—until I *erupt*. With a screeching bellow, I force magic into and then out of me in massive amounts, thinking only that I want this all to be over. That I want my people safe and the Velmaran soldiers *gone*. That I want King Mazus to suffer like he made me suffer, and that I want him defeated. With a final, hoarse yell, all the magic within me pours into those desires. I won't be able to hide the truth of my power after this, but I don't care.

When all the magic drains from my veins, I collapse in a heap on the ground, relieved that death will finally take me.

Witch Queen, Witch Queen—Leave me be
Witch Queen, Witch Queen—Set your sights away from me
Witch Queen, Witch Queen—Terrifying and fierce
Witch Queen, Witch Queen—My heart don't pierce

Velmaran Children's Nursery Rhyme

Three Hundred Years Later

"It's time to wake up, *sweetheart*," a soft feminine voice whispers in my ear. I grunt, not ready to wake. She persists, gently shoving me, and giggles brightly when I throw a pillow blindly at her. "As your betrothed, I must insist that you wake so we can leave these chambers together, Hawthorne Vicant." Silene's warm amber eyes stare back at me with absolute mischief dancing in them.

"Why do you *insist* on waking me *so* early?" I groan. Silene only grins, then rolls out of the bed and begins taking off her cloak, leather leggings, and soft tunic. I avert my gaze even though she couldn't care less what I see. Taking a dress from the wardrobe in the corner by the bathing chamber, she laces it up with expert precision.

Glancing down at me still lying in bed, she says, laughter in her voice, "I rise early because I can't bear to be stuck in these chambers with your stinky arse for even a second longer than necessary." Then she throws me a damp towel, and I use it to wipe the sleep from my eyes before drawing the water out of it with my magic and shooting it towards Silene. She ducks out of the way.

"I do not smell! My hygiene is excellent, and you know it." I stand, stretching my arms above me to release the tension from my shoulders and back from another night of poor sleep. "How was your night?"

"Fine. Nothing out of the ordinary," she says with a shrug of her shoulders that makes my eyes roll involuntarily.

"Are you ever going to tell me what you actually *do* when you sneak from my room on the nights we're pretending to be madly in love?" I tease. Silene merely gives me a look that says it's none of my business. Raising my hands in surrender, I study her closely. The dark circles beginning to form under her eyes tell me she's clearly exhausted and trying to hide it.

At only forty years old, Silene is very young for a fae. She's short by both fae *and* human standards, barely reaching my shoulders. Her black hair tumbles down her back to her waist in tight curls, and her deep, golden tan skin reveals muscles from training as a warrior in secret. Females are discouraged from fighting in Velmara, from doing anything that would put their childbearing capability at risk. Those customs chafe at Silene as tightly as the dresses she's expected to wear.

After dressing quickly, Silene and I exit my bedroom hand in hand. We enter the sitting room attached to my chambers, where servants with watchful eyes prepare a breakfast for us. I squeeze Silene's hand, then don the mask of doting fiancé and rakish, irresponsible prince.

Lifting her hands to my lips and lavishing kisses atop them, I murmur, loud enough for the servants to hear, "I will miss you today, love." She flashes me a blushing, demure smile, one so unlike the real Silene. It breaks my heart to see her forced to play this role. Silene is effervescent, a force of nature, with a mind that rivals the King's best strategists and the warm personality of a beam of sunlight. She doesn't blush, doesn't lower her eyes from anything.

"I'll be waiting for you in the bedroom tonight to help you forget the stuffy meetings you have to attend," she coos. I pull out a chair for her before sitting in my own, my gaze hungry with lust I do not feel for the female I consider my little sister.

"Leave us," I command the army of servants my father insists I keep. "I wish to dine with my betrothed in peace."

The servants hesitate, clearly nervous to disobey what are likely orders to stay and report anything interesting back to my father's spymaster. I plaster a magnetic grin on my face. "Oh, come on," I say with a loveable whine. "Give us a little privacy. You can tell Citus that we ate our breakfast quietly. You know Silene is shy. Wouldn't want her to blush herself to death when I inevitably say dirty things to her. I can't help myself." I give them a wink, while Silene plays her part perfectly, her gaze looking down in mock embarrassment. The head servant softens, her own lips quirking even as she pretends to roll her eyes in mock annoyance.

"Come, let's leave the two lovebirds alone," she urges the other servants. On her way out, she gives me a knowing look, and I make a point of looking sheepish to cement the ruse. When they're gone, Silene slumps in her chair, the picture of perfect nobility nowhere to be seen in her posture.

"Thank the aether they're gone. I would have vomited all over this breakfast table if I had to pretend to be seducing you for another moment," she jests, filling her plate with eggs, meat, potatoes, and fruit.

"Seducing me? I assure you it takes much more than pretty smiles and insinuation to seduce me." She murmurs something that sounds like *hardly* under her breath before she stuffs her face with food. "Whatever you did last night," I start. Silene looks up and scowls. "That you aren't going to tell me about," I add, holding up my hands in surrender, "must have been... exhilarating, if you're that famished." She only rips another bite of sausage off the link she's holding, chewing aggressively, then gives me a wink.

A year ago, my father, King Mazus of Velmara, and Silene's parents, some of the wealthiest and most influential Velmaran nobles, announced our betrothal to the kingdom via pamphlets delivered across the realm. *Announcing Prince Hawthorne, the Shining Prince, and his Kalmeera Bride*, the headline read. Receiving our own pamphlet was the first time either of us had heard anything about it. I'd fought hard against the match, insisting Silene was too young for marriage and that I had no interest in the institution. My father and his advisors, including her parents, only conceded that we'd have a long engagement.

Neither of us has any intention of following through. I hate that my father forced me into a betrothal with a female I don't have those kinds of feelings for, nor does she have them for me. But I'm lucky she's one of the two people in this entire kingdom I fully trust.

"I have to go," I tell her as I stand. "Stay here and finish breakfast. No need to rush out on my account."

"Oh, I plan to stay here all day and have a little nap in your *massive* bed, then I'll take my time sampling all the fancy soaps you keep in your bathing chamber."

I smile, happy to give her access to a comfortable space away from her family and the expectations of the noble females of Velmara.

After sitting through several hours of meetings, I finally sneak away.

Fionn, my best friend of the last three hundred years and the second person I wholly trust in this kingdom, waits for me by the gates to the city. Leaning against a wall, his towering frame is instantly recognizable—at nearly seven feet tall, he stands a head above everyone in the courtyard, myself included. Fionn pulls his shoulder-length blonde hair into a knot at the base of his neck and scratches the scruffy beard he tries to keep neat but never quite manages, scowling at the other guards who gape at him. He spots me and prowls over, and everyone lingering near him practically trips over themselves trying to get out of his way.

"Are you ready to go?" he asks, bronze eyes looking down at me.

I clap him on the back, then say, loudly, "Yes, my friend. Thank you for agreeing to escort me through the city to shop for a gift for my fiancé. This close to the Forum meeting, we can't be too careful." My father has eyes and ears everywhere, so Fionn acts as my *guard*. As one of the greatest warriors in Velmaran history, it's a good guise, but we both know I don't need his protection.

The gate guards open the side door for us, and we step into the capital of Velmara. The city of Arnia sprawls across the entire southern peninsula. As a seaside capital, the people here are on the water nearly as much as they're on land. The Floating Market, the city's largest shopping district, is nestled in a cove and sits atop the water, held up by ancient magic. Fionn and I head there to meet with our contacts for updates on the recent shipments of thayar flower.

As we walk, evidence of my father's effective propaganda machine is on full display. His eyes stare at me from drawings plastered across walls and buildings, with headlines like *Golden King Heads to Forum of Royals* typed in bold ink. My own image is also present, stories about the *Shining Prince* just as popular as those about the Golden King. Fionn chuckles when we see an advertisement for an exclusive interview with a fae female claiming to be my long-lost mate. The masses will believe anything—especially stories about mythical mates. At least a dozen females a month show up to the palace gates demanding to see me, claiming they suddenly feel a bond with me that hasn't been seen in our world for millennia, if it ever existed at all. I always send Silene to them with a bag of gold, knowing only the most desperate would attempt anything like that.

Fionn and I continue to duck and weave through the throngs of fae and humans. They notice as I pass by, pointing and whispering, telling their companions whatever recent story or rumor they've heard about my exploits. Fionn's looming presence is all that keeps them from swarming me. The people of Velmara know me as a fun-loving drunk, the Prince who has no interest in ruling and spends his days gambling, drinking, and flirting with women, despite being engaged to the most desired female in the entire kingdom. Of course they want to get close to that version of me. I play it up when I'm in public, the mask a protection from letting anyone, my father included, get too close to the real version of me.

As we pass by an open-air stand selling sweet treats, I lean over to pinch the bottom of the raven-haired shopkeeper, who I visit regularly to trade flirtatious barbs with. She lets out a flirty giggle and slaps me across the arm. I only wink at her as I keep walking, her laughs lost in the noise of the market. We pass another stall, this one selling various tinctures and ointments, run by a widower and his daughter. She's as tall as I am, her long legs lean and golden. She doesn't see me approach, wrapped up in restocking a shelf.

I lean in to whisper in her ear. "Hi, Kareena." She jumps, nearly dropping the jar in her hand.

"Hawthorne! You can't just sneak up on me like that," she chides half-heartedly. I smirk, and she rolls her eyes flirtatiously. I wrap my arm around her waist and spin her in my arms as she laughs in protest, before setting her down and whispering in her ear again.

"Any news for me?" I ask, this time my voice low and serious. She shakes her head subtly, so I give her a kiss on the cheek and sweep away from the shop, Fionn on my heels. We continue in this way as we make our way through the Floating Market. I stop at each of my contacts' shops, using my magnanimous charm as cover for my real mission—gathering information about my father's and the noble's movements. There's little news for me today, only confirming my suspicions that with the upcoming Forum of Royals, my father is being extra careful about what might leak.

A gangly adolescent fae has the courage to approach us and hands me a thick trifold of parchment before quickly darting away as he calls out the topic of the missive. "The Witch Queen of Thayaria will be at the upcoming Forum. Read all about how the once prophecy-blessed Queen turned vile and became the phantom we all fear! Witch Queen news you don't want to miss!" People swarm him, eager to get their hands on the government sponsored material.

I scan the parchment for any new information before dropping it on the ground in disgust. My father pays orphans to walk the streets and stir up commotion about the Queen of Thayaria every few years. They hand out *informational pamphlets*, as my father calls them, telling people they need to read whatever new story he's uncovered to keep their families safe. As a result, the people of Velmara are terrified of the *Witch Queen* across the sea, afraid she'll swoop onto our shores at any moment and steal their children in the night. The common enemy keeps them from turning their sights on their true oppressors—my father and his greedy nobles.

In reality, we know very little about what Queen Laurel Elestren has actually been up to for the last three hundred years. Thayaria and its reclusive Queen have been sequestered away behind a thick wall of mist since the war my father launched against them three centuries years ago. But my concern lies with my people, not with those hidden behind mist an ocean away.

"What information are you hoping to gather?" Fionn asks once we've cleared the dense thoroughfare and are walking down a quiet side street of the Floating Market.

"I *hope* the thayar shipments are reaching the Nivan Desert, and that Ragnor tells us our fears haven't been realized. The people of Eastern Velmara need the goods the merchants ship across the desert. And the kingdom needs trade to be flowing to keep the economy bolstered."

"But..." Fionn continues for me, sensing my hesitation.

"But I don't think that's what we're going to hear," is all I say, lips tight. Fionn only nods.

We reach our destination, a jewelry store in the Floating Market known for magically enhanced adornments. The building is painted red, the chipped paint standard for the shops that constantly battle salty winds. When we enter, a beautiful female greets us with a frown, shoulders squared and hands on her hips. She tosses her long honey-blonde hair over her shoulders in a huff and narrows her bright blue eyes on me.

"Thorne Vicant, what have I told you about conducting your little *business* in my shop without giving me warning that you're coming?" she admonishes, though there's amusement in her tone.

I quirk my lips in a half smile, instantly turning on the charm that's become second nature to me. "Oh, come on, Enessa, don't be cross with me. We both know you love being in on all my schemes." I give her a wink, and she leans into my body. I wrap my arm around her waist and plant a kiss on her cheek while she pretends to bat me away. Fionn only stands near the doorway, bored. "Tell me, Enessa, what whispers have you heard since my last visit?"

I place my head in the crook of her neck so that my warm breath tingles across her ear, though I'm careful that's all I do. A peck on the cheek or a quick pat on the ass is as far as I'll allow my actual affections to go with those I'm playing pretend with. They may think it's more, or wish it so, but there are lines even I will not cross to get what I want.

"You know the only people who visit my shop are wealthy nobles purchasing gifts for their mistresses. They're the only ones who can afford me," she says, voice low and seductive with innuendo as she pulls me tighter into her.

"And that's exactly why you're the best informant I have." Another smile, another wink, and she's melting in my arms, telling me everything I want to know. I'd sigh with the mundanity of it all if I weren't so practiced at this point.

"The nobles are still angry with the King for cutting their supply of thayar. With me, they talk boldly of their plans to remind him of their influence and how much he needs them, though I imagine it's another story with the King around instead of a pretty face."

Enessa also knows how to get information using her good looks and charm. I only nod before releasing her. She pretend pouts but tilts her head in the direction of the back room, hidden from view by a thick velvet curtain. "They're back there," she whispers. I teasingly slap her backside with a look of pure mirth before parting the curtain to enter the hidden space beyond, Fionn on my heels.

There's a small worn worktable with two males seated at it. They're both dressed in the light layers of merchants who travel the Nivan Desert. When I enter, they stand and bow quickly.

"Your Royal Highness," the taller of the two says.

"Ragnor, please, we're beyond those formalities." I smile, then clap him on the back. He gives me a grin, and we sit at the table. Fionn and the other male Ragnor introduces as his son sit on either side of us. Enessa busies herself polishing jewelry, though I know she listens despite pretending not to care. "Thank you for meeting. I know it's been a long journey. How are things?" I ask.

Ragnor hesitates before speaking, choosing his words carefully. "It's been a challenging few months. Fewer shipments of the thayar flower are making it to the desert. You know we need to use the tea we brew from the flower to enhance our magic enough to channel wind. We're having to resort to manual labor more often. Pulling sand ships across the desert with ropes is back-breaking work. Without the flower, none of our channelers are strong enough to access their air magic, and we have no way to fill the sails with wind. It's hurting our ability to get supplies to the far reaches of the kingdom. Not to mention, everything we get we have to use, so we haven't been able to add at all to the stores you asked us to create."

I frown. "That doesn't make any sense. Imports have increased threefold in Arnia, but supplies here have also been limited. My father's advisors are telling the nobles and the people that magic is getting even harder to channel in the desert, so Velmara is sending more of its shipments there. If you aren't receiving it either, where is it going?" I lock eyes with Fionn before returning my gaze to Ragnor. Ragnor's eyes narrow and his lips purse. "What is it?" I prompt.

"There are rumors..." he says slowly, "rumors that there's a massive stockpile locked away in the mountains northwest of the desert that the King himself oversees. We haven't been able to confirm or deny the rumors, nor can we find anyone who's seen the stockpile firsthand. But the people of the desert believe the King is hoarding the flower for himself."

My stomach drops. This is the third merchant I've heard it from. There's nowhere else the shipments of magic-enhancing flowers could be going. But for what end?

"Thank you, Ragnor. I'll do what I can to divert more shipments to the desert. Send word if you learn anything else."

Once Ragnor and his son are gone, Enessa leads us to the front of the store and hands me a small, wrapped parcel.

"Your alibi." She winks. "Silene will love it."

"Add it to my father's account, and charge him double," I tell her with a grin. While I'm careful who I reveal the full depth of my intentions to in this kingdom, I've built a network of trustworthy allies who share my contempt of my father. Enessa and I have a complicated relationship. We flirt, shamelessly, and pretend we're having a poorly hidden affair to provide cover for what's really going on. Most of the court, my father included, think she's my mistress, and that she provides expensive jewelry to my betrothed. I can't think too hard about it, deeply uncomfortable that I'm perceived as someone who would do that to my fiancé, even if it's a marriage neither of us intends to enter into.

"Will you come see me again soon?" Enessa whispers in my ear on the front step of her shop, pressing her body to mine in a seductive arc that pushes her breasts right into my line of sight.

Some days, it's hard to know if Enessa wants more. We're outside, where there are eyes watching, so she could be playing her part to maintain our cover. Not to mention she too is as practiced at this as I am, having been my spy with the nobles for decades. But the way she clings to me, body pushed firmly against mine, makes me question how much is pretend for her. Either way, I can't afford to lose her as an ally, so I squeeze her tightly. I bury the shame I feel at using her, then lean down to her ear and let my breath send shivers up her spine.

"I'll send word next time before I come. I promise." She grins satisfactorily. Then I'm pulling away, her arms lingering to get one last touch, leaving her staring after Fionn and me as we make our way out of the Floating Market.

"Do you think you'll ever actually take a lover? A real one?" Fionn asks, his assessing gaze seeing everything as usual.

"I could ask the same of you," I challenge with a smirk. He merely nods, and we continue our walk out of the Floating Market in silence. Once we exit the pier that marks the end of the market, Fionn heads in the opposite direction of the palace. I stop him.

"Silene needs to be with us when we debrief. She's got more brains than us both combined."

"That's why I told her to meet us there," he says with a cocky smirk, nodding toward our favorite gambling den.

I grin wide. "In that case, lead the way."

The Salty Saloon is dark inside despite the bright Velmaran daylight, its windows covered with light-blocking curtains. Despite it being the middle of the day, the wobbly wooden tables are all filled with patrons drinking tankards of the golden ale and gambling away their savings.

Once we're settled into a dark corner, away from prying eyes or listening ears, Silene says, "It makes sense with everything we've heard that the King is stockpiling thayar in the Northern Mountains, despite intense political pressure about declining supplies. I overheard my parents discussing plans with another noble house to coerce him into restoring their stores. He doesn't often deny them something like this. He's got to be planning something big." We sit in silence for a few moments, lost in our thoughts. "So, here's what we know," Silene starts. My lips quirk up in a smile at what Fionn and I tease is her catchphrase. When she faces a problem she can't sort through, she goes back over the facts methodically. "We know supplies of thayar in Arnia are limited. We know the nobles are pissed about this."

"Because they are impotent, sniveling rats who rely on its magic-enhancing properties to stay in power and oppress the people of this kingdom," Fionn interjects.

"Yes, Fionn, we know how you feel about the noble houses. Your commoner birth is showing, and you're not helping," Silene remarks, then sticks her tongue out at him.

He gestures in mock offense. "Just trying to add to the list of things we know. We know the nobles are losing their shit because they know what will happen if the people see how weak their magic has become from centuries of inbreeding."

"As I was *saying*," Silene continues as she tucks an unruly coil of hair behind her pointed ear, "the nobles are pissed, because they need the flower supply to maintain control." She gives him a look that says, *Satisfied?* He nods. "We know the story being told in Arnia is that the imports are being diverted to the Nivan Desert. We know the Nivan

Desert is also seeing fewer and fewer thayar shipments, which they need to power their air channelers to ship goods across the desert. And we know most of the desert merchants believe the thayar is being secreted away to the Northern Mountains..." She fades off, stopping where we always stop.

"He has to be stockpiling it for a magical purpose, right?" I say. "Maybe another one of his experiments?"

"That is one big fuckin' experiment," Fionn adds. He's not wrong. The amount of thayar that's disappeared could power the kingdom's trade for centuries.

"All we can do right now is wait for more information to reach us," I finally say. "With the upcoming Forum, what my father negotiates with Thayaria and the other kingdoms will be illuminating. Until then, we sit tight."

They both nod their agreement while I push down my feeling of uneasiness for what must be the tenth time today alone. I need to do something to stop my father. And soon.

A Queen shall rise whose strength matches the powers of old. Born to a daughter of mortals under the blood moon bloom—unbounded, limitless, her might will see no equal. Blood-to-Blood, the Queen and her fated love will unite what has been torn apart.

The Prophecy of the Thayarian Queen

The light filters in through the curtain on the balcony as wet, scratchy licks pepper my face. Groaning, I roll away from Lunaria and hide my eyes under the silken sheet of my bed. Undeterred, the large feline nuzzles my neck, purring so intensely it vibrates my vocal cords.

"I'm getting up. You can stop fretting over me," I grumble back at her. Slowly blinking in the light of the morning sun, I stare up into the intelligent, golden eyes of the wolf-sized cat I consider my pet but who absolutely considers herself my keeper. She leaps from the bed, satisfied that I won't go back to sleep. I want to do just that to annoy her but instead fling my feet off the side of the bed. Lunaria has always had a keen understanding of my needs, and today's early wake up is no different.

The air is brisk and biting. I left the doors to the balcony wide open last night so Lunaria could prowl outside before collapsing into bed. It's early autumn in Thayaria, and the nights are growing colder and colder. Slipping on a robe, I quickly attune myself to the aether pulsing strongly around me, willing the floors to heat and the air to warm.

With another thought, the fireplace across the room is roaring, and I sigh in contentment. Much better.

My large bedroom is all soft throws and comfortable leather chairs. The bed is covered in almost as many blankets as pillows, and the pillows take up half of the bed. In the corner is a large palette for Lunaria, though she usually sleeps in the bed with me or on the balcony. Her sleek black body prowls to the curtains blowing in the light morning breeze, and she pauses to invite me to follow her before walking outside.

I part the curtains and step onto the balcony, looking down upon Arberly, the capital city of Thayaria. It's early, so the city is still yawning awake, only a handful of citizens buzzing in the soft morning light. Beyond the city, the rolling hills of Thayaria glisten with dewdrops, the dark green mounds dotted with swaths of deep crimson and rust from the last months of the thayar flower bloom. This far from the coast, Thayaria is hazy from the barrier of mist I accidentally erected around the kingdom during the war with Velmara, but not so hazy that visibility is impacted. I take a deep inhale, appreciating the smell that only comes with autumn mornings—pine and petrichor, with sweet notes of dew. With one final glance across the pink-hued sky, I turn back to my chambers.

Somehow, Amaryll has already drawn my bath and laid out a breakfast tray, the stealthy housekeeper always one step ahead of even Lunaria. On my way to the bathing chamber, I take the steaming cup of tea and add in a heaping pour of cream.

The large space is one of the few luxuries I allow myself as Queen of Thayaria, with a large sunken tub nestled next to a set of floor-to-ceiling windows, overlooking a view of more of Thayaria's rolling, misty hills. A plush rug covers most of the floor, and there are pipes to pump water into the tub and a small basin tucked against one wall. After undressing and sinking into the steaming water, I sip my tea while watching the verdant hills slowly lighten in color as the sun fully rises.

Twenty minutes later, the water sluices down my wide hips and luscious thighs as I leave the bath. Wrapped in a towel, I gingerly step into the attached closet, looking at the gowns and tunics lining the walls. Choosing a black velvet gown that accentuates my figure, I will the water in my hair to evaporate into the already humid room, then set about braiding my wavy, auburn hair into a single braid down my back. Amaryll will be angry that I didn't call for her to send in attendants to fix my hair, but most days I prefer it pulled back from my face in a simple style and don't need servants to do things like braid my hair. I line my eyes with dark kohl and paint my lips a deep red. Returning to my breakfast tray, I refill my mug with more tea and make myself a plate. An awareness washes over me, like a quick prick of a needle to the back of my neck.

Someone is trying to leave Thayaria.

With a sixth sense I still don't fully understand, I instantly know that they aren't a port worker attempting to cross the barrier that surrounds Thayaria to haul in goods from a merchant ship. If they had been, I would extend my will and allow them to leave. The mist that has surrounded my kingdom for three hundred years after my accidental surge of power at the Battle of Moormyr has a consciousness to it, representing me while also being separate from me.

I close my eyes, focusing on the western coast where I feel the disruption. The mist perks its head up at my magical gaze and whispers to me. *Rebel. Bad Intentions. Kill.* The person attempting to shove their way through the barrier is wrapped in a blanket of dew and hauled into the center of the hazy wall. I hesitate for a moment, considering whether to give whoever this is a second chance. But the mist insists, practically screaming in my head the need for justice. While I may not know what this person has done, I trust the mist's judgement, even if I can't explain why. With a deep inhale, I unleash my fury, their bones and organs evaporating instantly. The mist settles, content and humming once again, and I bring my consciousness back into my body.

Anger courses through me as I finish my breakfast, and I use it to bury any guilt I may feel from my merciless decision. *How dare someone attempt to breach my mist.* A rebel, no less, and when I was having a relaxing morning. I rip apart the sweet bread in my hands with more vigor than usual. Remembering the rebels currently sitting in chains far below me, I aerstep to the palace dungeons.

The Thayarian palace is built into the side of a mountain named Verdeshorn, and our holding cells are buried deep below its peak. The damp and earthy space is dark and ominous, and I use the water in the air to gather an eerie mist around me, then dim the lights emanating from the torches on the wall. I will the temperature to drop—I want the prisoners to know I'm coming. Most fae can't use their magic down here because of the iron the floors and walls are made with, but those rules don't apply to me, and they'll be all the more terrified because of it.

"Your Majesty." The guards on duty see me and bow deeply. "We didn't realize you were coming today." Their eyes are wide in apprehension at my surprise appearance. "Would you like us to send someone for the Captain?"

"That won't be necessary. Captain Carex is busy with other duties. Please, bring the prisoners to the interrogation room."

When the first prisoner is brought in, a fae male with blonde hair, I direct the guard to chain him to the wall before dismissing him. My steps echo as I prowl closer to the prisoner, eyes unblinking in a stare meant to make him squirm.

The male spits at me. "I won't tell you anything, *Witch.*" I only smirk.

"Now, now, surely you can come up with a better insult than that," I murmur. "My moniker is the *Witch Queen,* after all. It's hardly even an insult. But, no matter, I will overlook your unremarkable intellect and get right to the point. Tell me who you take your orders from and what the rebels' plans are. Why are you trying to get out of Thayaria?"

He only glares at me, and I sigh. I could force the confession from him, could use the aether-voice that commands any fae with less power than me—which, in my case, is *every* fae—to do as I command. One order to tell the truth and he'd be spilling all his secrets. But it's a skill I use infrequently, uncomfortable with the idea that I have the power to remove someone's agency and free will, especially considering what's been done to *me* with this power by other monarchs. Not to mention, I do enjoy a little bit of torture.

"Fine, we'll do it the hard way." I tap into the aether around me, letting it guide me to the ivy growing along the stone walls. The vines creep toward the rebel, then wrap up and around his body, covering his mouth and eyes. They squeeze him tightly. At the same time, I force the air from his lungs. He struggles against the bindings, choking sounds filling the room. After a few moments, I release him slightly. "Ready to talk?" He remains silent.

The vines burrow into one eye socket, piercing and then crushing the eye within. His screams grow louder. For good measure, I send one tentacle snaking down his throat, gagging him, before ripping the air from his lungs once again. His knees collapse, and he dangles from where he is chained against the wall. When his body begins to convulse, I release the magic. With a snap of my fingers the light in the room vanishes except for an unearthly glow around me. As I approach him, the smell of piss wafts over me.

"We've only just begun, and already you've pissed yourself. Surely you knew the risks of *angering* the Witch Queen. Surely your leaders told you what would happen if you were caught unleashing a magical bomb in my kingdom that injured *dozens* of innocents." I practically growl the words, my fury rising. With clenched fists, the control I have over my magic slips slightly, and I feel the room quiver around me.

The Sons and Daughters of Thayaria have been around for about fifty years, challenging my rule and spreading the same propaganda of the Golden King—that I'm a witch, that Thayaria's isolation is due to my own need for power and control, and that I deny Thayarian citizens the safe harbor Velmara offers. It's a small subset of the population, but those who believe in the rebellion's narrative are certain a better life awaits them in Velmara, if only I would surrender to the Golden King. If I didn't know that Mazus was as barred from Thayaria as the rest of the world, I'd think he had started the rebellion himself to undermine me. For most of their history, I was content to leave the rebels to their ideology and peaceful protest, believing in the right of my citizens to free speech and belief. But over the last five years, they've turned violent, and that I will not tolerate.

The male is blubbering now, blood running from his eye socket and vomit on his chin. "I don't know anything else that's planned, I swear," he whimpers. "My only contact was captured with me. He'll know more."

I narrow my eyes, trying to determine if he's telling the truth. His body shakes, and something like regret flashes across his eyes. I release him and open the door, motioning the guard to come in as I walk away from the prisoner.

"Remove him. He'll stand trial for his crimes tomorrow. If he's found guilty, he'll be executed." The male begins to sob and plead, but I cut him off, looking over my shoulder to speak to him. "Be grateful I provide swift executions for those found guilty of treason. Bring in the next prisoner."

My morning continues in this way, torturing fae after fae in increasingly creative ways. The male who organized the attack was a powerful plant channeler and somehow used the ivy to slit his own throat before I could question him despite the dampening of fae power in these cells. No others were able to provide any real information, and I leave the cells even more frustrated than when I entered them.

"Now to everyone's favorite topic of the decade—the upcoming Forum of Royals," Nemesia says to my Council of Advisors. After cleaning up from *questioning* the prisoners, I had to attend a meeting with my advisors. The Council chamber is a large room with floor-to-ceiling windows overlooking the city of Arberly. Being only a few feet down from my rooms, it's the same view I see every day when I wake. Late afternoon light illuminates the massive round table where over thirty fae and humans sit. Papers and tea mugs litter the tabletop. "We need to discuss which advisors will accompany Her Majesty to Delsar for the conference and what the security detail will look like," Nemesia continues.

I sigh, knowing exactly what she's going to propose, and knowing exactly what my response will be. We have this argument every ten years when the decennial meeting of monarchs and other kingdom leaders occurs. It's still called the Forum of Royals, despite the fact that the Republic of Reshnar implemented a democratic government over two hundred years ago.

"What are the parameters?" Admon, one of my advisors, asks. The old fae male was an advisor to my father, and even grandfather, and is the leymaster my parents brought in to teach me to use my magic all those years ago. He's tall and sturdy looking, with blue eyes that sparkle when he knows he's telling you something you need to hear. His hair and beard are both gray and long. For a fae to look that old, they have to have been alive for over a thousand years, maybe more.

"Two advisors and four guards," Nemesia informs the room. "As Her Majesty's Chair of the Council of Advisors, I'll obviously be accompanying her. We must discuss and vote on which additional member of this Council will attend. My proposal is—"

"You aren't the obvious choice," I interrupt. "This is the twenty-ninth Forum of Royals in my time as Queen, and not once have I agreed to nor even suggested that you attend with me, as you well know. Your history with the King of Velmara—"

"Is nothing compared to your own, Your Majesty," Nemesia adds.

I give her a pointed stare before adding, "That may be true, but my presence is, unfortunately, required. Yours is not."

The rest of my advisors look on in boredom, many of them witness to this exact argument several times over, knowing that Nemesia will insist, and I'll rely on my station as Queen to overrule her. It's one of the rare instances where I do it, and the guilt eats me alive every time. Even my oldest friend and most trusted advisor feels the shackles I've placed on my people with the mist and the tension between Thayaria and the rest of the Four Kingdoms. I can't help but wonder who she would have become, with her brilliant mind and penchant for politics, had she grown up in a world where Thayaria wasn't isolated. But I won't—can't—allow Nemesia to be in King Mazus's presence, especially with so few guards. Even three hundred years later, the sting of grief is fresh when I recall how I felt thinking that blade was going to land in her heart during the Battle of Moormyr.

"This year is different, Laurel, and you know it," she adds with a quiet intensity.

Now the advisors' eyes widen in shock, staring between Nemesia and me. Admon's eyes twinkle, alone in his lack of concern. Nemesia may not shy away from giving me direct and honest feedback but using my given name and not my title during a formal Council meeting is unheard of.

Nemesia stands tall, hazel eyes burning with a fire I haven't seen in her since she was the General of my armies. Her jaw clenches and unclenches, and her hands are balled into fists.

After the Battle at Moormyr, Nemesia abandoned life as a warrior, unable to fight or even spar for many decades after. She blamed herself for our loss. Instead, she devoted herself to politics, philosophy, and helping me put the pieces of my kingdom back together. She's the most learned scholar in all of Thayaria, and her mind for political strategy is a valuable asset to me. Despite the centuries since that awful battle, Nemesia's scars and guilt remain. And while she keeps her fighting skills sharp, she has sworn to never lead armies again.

"Make your case, Nemesia," I concede, gesturing for her to continue. She nods in silent gratitude, then stands before the round table.

"With the thayar flowers in decline, and us being no closer to understanding why or uncovering a solution, it's critical that I go." A fresh wave of guilt and fear wash over me at the reminder of the danger my kingdom is in. But I don't let it show on my face, keeping my calm and unwavering demeanor firmly in place as I listen to Nemesia's speech. "We need to assess—carefully and delicately—whether any of the other kingdoms have experienced their own magical irregularities and if the rulers have ideas as to why this could be happening. I'm the most knowledgeable on the subject, not to mention my skill as a courtier, and we need this information. We don't have another ten years to wait for the next Forum." She looks at me, pleading in her eyes. I give her a slight nod, indicating I understand what she isn't saying, though not willing to concede just yet. "Laurel," she whispers quietly. Something about the desperation in her expression softens my resolve. I know she cares as much about the people of Thayaria as I do. If she's letting her own fear show, she's serious. I let out a huff of air and wave my hand.

"Fine. What do others think?" I ask, searching the eyes of those around me. Only nods and soft murmurs of agreement greet me. "If none are opposed, then I'll follow the Council's guidance. Nemesia will accompany me," I decide. "Are there nominations for the second advisor to attend?"

Several advisors speak up offering a few names of seasoned diplomats. Carex, one of my youngest advisors and the current Captain of the Royal Guard, advocates strongly for himself. Nemesia's eyes narrow. She's never forgiven Carex for the failed romantic relationship with me, even though it ended mostly amicably after decades of courting. He has swayed a large contingent of advisors to his side when Nemesia offers another name.

"Admon should come as our second advisor. He's attended many times, and his familiarity with the other kingdoms will prove useful in gathering information," she says. I wonder how much of her suggestion is driven by her genuine desire to have Admon there and how much is to protect me from traveling for several weeks with a former lover.

Admon is an interesting choice. While he has attended many times in the past, he's the eldest advisor on the Council, and doesn't leave the capital, or even his rooms, often. More than half of the advisors nod their heads in agreement. Carex fidgets in frustration, eyes filled with annoyance he doesn't try to hide.

"Admon, are you willing to go?" I ask.

"It would be my honor, Queen Laurel." His warm smile softens something inside of me. I look around the room, offering the Council ample opportunity to disagree or challenge the decision.

"Your Majesty," Carex starts. "I believe I'm an excellent choice. Not to mention I'll be a fifth guard for you. I think you should consider—"

Nemesia cuts him off. "While I appreciate your enthusiasm, Carex, you're new to this Council, and very new to foreign relations. This is not a decision we should make lightly. We'll vote." She has a point. Carex has only been on the Council one year, while most of the other advisors have served for decades or even centuries.

"Those in favor of Admon?" Nemesia asks the room. At least two-thirds of the room raise their hands.

"Then it's decided," I say. "Nemesia and Admon, please work with Carex to bring me a shortlist of guards who should accompany us."

They both nod, and Nemesia adds, "It will be to you by the end of the day." Carex only fumes. I'm sure the two of them will battle it out again over who the guards will be, Carex insisting he attend himself as a guard. What I would give to watch that verbal sparring match...

Nathaniel, a towering and lanky fae male who has served for thirty years, clears his throat. His dark black eyes lock on several other advisors, as if he's seeking their support for what he's about to say. I notice several heads nod almost imperceptibly. This is planned, then.

"I'd like for us to discuss the matter of the barrier," Nathaniel says, voice wavering slightly, likely because he knows this is a sensitive subject. I stiffen, not wanting to get into this conversation now. Several heads now nod enthusiastically in agreement with Nathaniel, encouraging him to continue. When he speaks again, his words are steady. "Surely after three hundred years, it's time to lower it. The people want to be able to leave Thayaria. Our isolation causes unnecessary fear."

"I'm not discussing this matter with the Council," I say firmly and with all the queenly command I can muster. "This is my decision. It's not time."

Tension fills the air, the unsaid remarks as loud as if they'd been yelled. The Council has advocated strongly over the years to drop the mist—it's the only topic we regularly disagree on. But they don't know—can't know—why the mist won't come down any time soon.

"If you won't drop it entirely, then perhaps we should allow more people to leave. You have the ability to let small groups cross the barrier. Surely, we can let those who'd like to leave do so without dropping the barrier entirely," he adds. More murmuring and head nods make their way through the Council.

I resist the urge to sigh. This is yet another thing I can't be fully honest with my advisors about. Yes, I can grant entry to small groups or merchants entering and exiting the mist, but it's draining. Not to mention it makes me feel a little like I'm losing a part of myself every time I do it. The mist is an extension of me, and I think when I part it, I'm somehow altering or slicing open some magical source deep within me. But it's hard to explain to a room of advisors that I fear allowing mass crossings might have negative impacts on my psyche. Instead of admitting all this, I give the hollow excuse I've given hundreds of times before.

"As I've explained multiple times, I'm not capable of allowing more than a few crossings a day, and we need to reserve those for dock workers bringing in shipments." The looks of skepticism turned in my direction make me inwardly squirm, but I keep my expression unwavering.

"We have no more topics for today's meeting," Nemesia offers quickly, saving me from questions I can't answer. Wary eyes study me, but I ignore them, despite the angry side conversations I know the dismissal of this topic will cause once the meeting adjourns.

After nodding to the Council to dismiss them from the session, they slowly filter out of the room, conversing amongst themselves. I stand back from the group, locking eyes with Nemesia and giving her a pointed look. Then I sweep out of the chamber and back down the short hallway to my suite. She follows, understanding my desire to continue the conversation in private. We walk into my sitting room turned makeshift office, Nemesia collapsing into her favorite chair. I settle into a worn leather sofa that's seen too many conversations like this one, its supple leather familiar and comforting despite being older than most of the other furniture in the room.

"Out with it," Nemesia says. "I know you're going to try and convince me not to go, but I have more reasons I did not share in the Council meeting."

"Do those other reasons have anything to do with Mazus Vicant? And a fear that he's somehow behind the disappearance of the thayar?" I ask.

She smiles conspiratorially, a grin I'm so familiar with after three centuries of friendship. "So, you share my concern? If that's the case, I don't understand your hesitancy to bring me with you to the Forum. It's on Delsar this cycle, and you know Velmara won't try anything there. Their relationship is too tenuous." Velmara and the kingdom closest to them, Delsar, located just south of Velmara's capital city, have almost as bad a relationship with one another as Velmara and Thayaria.

I sigh. "I agree that we need to use everything at our disposal to uncover the truth, even you. It doesn't make me any less nervous for your safety, but as you once told me, sometimes I have to be the Queen my people deserve." I smile. The tension falls away from Nemesia's body. "Why do *you* think Mazus is behind our declining flower population?"

She walks to the bar cart I keep along the back of the room and pours herself a glass of amber whiskey. "I don't have any conclusive evidence, just a gut feeling. There's been nothing in any of our archives to suggest that this has ever happened before, or that any of the scholars of the past were even worried about something like this happening.

"But I've been corresponding with a scholar located south of us, in Reshnar. I didn't tell him the flowers are declining. I said that we—well, you, since I thought telling him the *Witch Queen* wanted this information would terrify him into helping—want any information the Reshnar archives have on the thayar. He probably thinks you're planning to use them in a spell or some other evil ritual people make up in their minds." Nemesia pours a glass of wine and then hands it to me. "He confirmed everything we already know—the flowers only grow in Thayaria, are somehow connected to the magic of the leylines, and are likely the result of so many leylines flowing through and converging here. He suggested he'd love to learn more about the extent of their magic-enhancing properties, but I didn't engage in that conversation. The only information Reshnar had that we didn't is a unique drawing of the flowers from an old text."

She hands me a sheet of parchment. My eyes scan the sketch, and I frown as I study it. It's a depiction of the thayar flower, done with painstaking detail and perfect accuracy. The top third of the stem looks like it's been dipped in crimson paint, with dozens of soft fuzzy petals arcing out from the deep green stalk. But the drawing is titled, '*Depiction of the thayar flower found in Velmara.*' My eyes return to hers, searching for a clue about why the flower that only grows in Thayaria is labeled as found in Velmara.

"The Reshnar scholar believed it was a mistake when the book was transcribed from its original. He asked me to confirm whether we have the same book and whether the drawing exists with this label or not."

"And do we?"

She nods slowly. "Yes, we have a copy of the book and the drawing. But it's labeled correctly." She pulls a large tome from her bag, flicking to a page before handing it over to me. The same crimson and green drawing is depicted, but the label now says, '*Depiction of the thayar flower found in Thayaria.*'

"But..." I prompt her to continue.

"But," she adds, "his copy is older than our copy. Typically, scholars would assume the oldest copy is the more accurate, as there are less opportunities for translation mistakes. It could just be an error, but we shouldn't overlook the possibility that it's correct. If the flower did grow in Velmara, Mazus might've found information in Velmara's archives that explains how it disappeared from Velmara. I'm worried he's somehow using that information to influence its decline here."

Silence lingers around us as I process the information. For the last hundred years or so, the magic-enhancing flower has had fewer and fewer blooms. In the last five years, the change has been dramatic. It's part of the reason the rebels have turned violent and why their recruitment efforts are now more successful. The people are scared what will happen with less access to our most important resource.

"It's a stretch, but I wouldn't put it past Mazus. We certainly can't rule it out," is all I tell her, not willing to let my own fear show, not even to my closest friend. "We need to see if there are any opportunities to learn more during the Forum. We'll have to be careful, but I can't deny this year's gathering is a good opportunity. You and Admon should see what you can uncover about this while we're there." I intentionally leave out my own reasons for suspecting Mazus, as some secrets are too big, even for Nemesia. "And what of the Sons and Daughters of Thayaria?" I ask. "Are you any closer to finding their leaders or intercepting their plans?" Nemesia tenses, avoiding making eye contact. "Neme... tell me," I command. She sighs, taking another sip of her drink as she returns to her favorite chair.

"They're growing. This year seems to be a tipping point. People are worried about the declining thayar populations, and the rebels are stoking those fears with claims that *your* magic is affecting the flowers." It takes the centuries of practice I've had at hiding my emotions to stay silent at that comment, too close to the truth of my own fears. "They're saying it's true you practice witchcraft, citing the *blood-to-blood* line in the prophecy. There are murmurs that you, and by extension Thayaria, are being punished by the gods." She pauses, waiting for my reaction. I only nod, my mask of cool indifference firmly in place, gesturing for her to continue. "I had hoped to keep this from you until I found more information, but..." She trails off. I look at her expectantly, tension coiling in my gut. "The Sons and Daughters have been telling new recruits that you used a group of powerful plant channelers to try and help the thayar grow, and that it was unsuccessful."

I still, the tension in my gut expanding to my shoulders and neck. My mind races, realizing the implications at the same time as Nemesia says, "We have a mole." Nemesia is tense, eyes staring at mine with fury and fear.

"We were so careful. Only a handful of advisors knew what we were planning, and even they didn't know the dates or which channelers we used," I say. My frustration begins to boil over, and I feel the aether building around me. I inhale, locking down the current with practiced control.

"It could have been one of the plant channelers, but they were all loyalists from before the War. Not to mention, I've had them all watched by my spies since, and not a single one of them has done anything out of the ordinary. I believe it must be someone on the Council," she says with grim determination.

"Until we know more, we have to proceed as if the Council is compromised. And we *must* ensure no one at the Forum knows or finds out about the rebellion or the mole," I command. Nemesia nods.

"I know you don't want to consider this, but it might be worth revisiting the rebellion with the Council of Advisors. Even though it's compromised, the discussion might reveal information about who could be the mole. And not every advisor has betrayed us—there are smart people on the Council who will have good ideas about how to deal with the rebels," Nemesia suggests, shoulders squared for my reaction to yet another conversation we've had many times.

"No. The rebels are after me. This is *my* problem to solve," I say with no argument in my voice. I won't ask the Council to fix the results of *my* failures, *my* shortcomings as a leader. Not to mention, if there is a mole, I don't want to give them *any* additional information to pass along to the rebels.

Nemesia looks at me, eyes churning with worry. "I know what you did this morning," she says softly. "I may not be the Captain of the Royal Guard, but many of them are loyal to me and tell me everything." When I only give her a challenging look, she sighs. "Did you at least uncover something useful?" My throat tightens, holding back the frustration and pain clawing my insides. I shake my head. Nemesia nods again, standing to leave. She pauses at the door, looking back at me. "I know you blame yourself, El. This isn't your fault. You are, and have been, a good Queen. The majority of your people know that."

I say nothing. Guilt and anger surge through me. Regardless of what Nemesia believes, I know that my people wouldn't be in this situation if it weren't for me. At the heart of the rebellion's fears is Thayaria's isolation from the rest of the world, and that is all on me. I may not have swung the metaphorical blade, but the leader who gives the order is just as culpable.

Those who channel the aether through water are considered a lower order of magic users, though this prejudice is unfair to the many practical applications of water channeling. Trade between the four kingdoms would stagnate without their ability to hasten travel by ship or calm raging seas. The strongest of this order can even heal injuries with only the smallest amount of liquid.

The Unabridged History of Magical Orders, Volume I

We make the journey to Delsar for the Forum of Royals in four days—one to travel by horseback from Arberly to the port town of Echosa, and three to travel by sea to the arid and mountainous kingdom of Delsar. The trip would normally take closer to eight days to complete, but with six water channelers, our ship was propelled through the water quickly.

The night we spent at my favorite tavern in Echosa, The Emerald Shell, highlighted for me how much the rebellion has impacted the rural regions of my kingdom. When I'd entered the tavern common room, very few citizens had stood to bow to me—most had instead looked on with skepticism and even loathing. Not that I require my people to fall on their knees in front of me. In fact, I'd prefer they don't. But this was a reminder that I need to deal with the rebels soon.

Yalla, the shining white capital city of Delsar, gleams as we approach the port. Nemesia sidles up beside me, tension rolling off her body in waves so thick I can sense each time she clenches and unclenches her jaw. Words of comfort won't help, so I simply point out landmarks I remember from previous visits to help ease her nerves. The white stucco buildings, distinguished by their harsh lines and angular features, are so different from the architecture of Thayaria, where we build into and around the environment. All of Delsar is a desert, and the red cliffs and soil make the city and its white skyline stand out brightly. By the time we dock in the massive port, the smell of fish and brine thick in the air, Nemesia has relaxed and is back to ordering the guards and speaking in hushed murmurs with Admon.

As we disembark from the ship, dock workers all stop and stare. *"The Witch Queen,"* they whisper as I pass, pointing to me with fear in their gaze. *"Stay back." "Don't let her look directly in your eyes." "Hide the children."* I've heard them all, and after three hundred years of whispers, I can ignore the barbs, even if they still sting in a place I keep buried beneath my icy exterior.

A tall, bronze woman clad in strips of flowing gossamer fabric in varying shades of pink awaits us. Her eyes are mahogany, with midnight black curly hair framing her face and stopping just above her shoulders. She's beautiful and severe, the epitome of the fierce warrior the Delsar people are known for. As I approach, she bows respectfully, though her muscles are clenched tightly.

"Welcome, Your Majesty," she says with forced confidence, "my name is Diaskia. I'm your guide during your stay on Delsar and will do my best to assist you with any requests you may have. Servants are unloading your belongings and will bring them to your rooms in the palace. Your advisors have each been provided with rooms close to yours, and your guards will have sleeping quarters on the same floor. I'll escort you to the palace."

"Thank you, Diaskia," I say, and she stiffens, eyes unable to hide her fear of me. Nemesia takes over the coordination with her. Whether to protect Diaskia or to protect me, I'm unsure.

Diaskia turns to a large cart, carved with colorful depictions of the Delsar landscape and topped by a delicate silk sail. She gestures for us to sit with stiff movements, her fear still written clearly in her body language. When we're all settled, she raises her hands and channels aether through the air to create a wind that fills the sails and slowly moves the cart along the dusty streets toward the palace. As we travel, she points out architecture or notable buildings. Nemesia's eyes widen at the training yard and officer's quarters for the all-female army Delsar is known for. Despite swearing off fighting and military leadership, Nemesia's a warrior at heart.

When we reach the bleached white palace, massive and embellished with gold and silver accents that top its many towers and spires, Diaskia escorts us through a wing on the western side. Inside, it's bright and airy, sparsely decorated except for the detailing carved directly on the stone. Battles are depicted alongside festivals and even births, marking a tapestry of Delsarian life. Servants pass us, their eyes widening in shock and then fear when they see me. Some bow before moving away, while others simply keep their head down and walk as quickly away from me as they can.

We reach a massive marble staircase, white but glittering when sunlight from the skylights above hit it. On the fifth floor, we turn left, walking toward a set of double doors inlaid with gold and silver. Diaskia opens them, walking through with my party of advisors and guards following closely behind.

"You should recognize these rooms, Your Majesty," Diaskia says. "You were given them the last time the Forum of Royals was held in Delsar."

"I'm sure they'll be as comfortable this time as they were before," I say with a smile, hoping to put the warrior at ease. But a few smiles and kind gestures won't undo centuries of propaganda about the Witch Queen and her dark magic, especially because of my own decision to lean into the persona when it serves me. Diaskia tenses, her desire to leave apparent in the tight posture and darting eyes.

"If your guards and advisors will follow me, I'll escort them to their rooms and sleeping quarters," Diaskia says in clipped tones.

My entourage follows her out, leaving me alone for the first time in days, and I can't help the sigh of relief that escapes me. Weary from travel and little sleep, I make quick work of cleaning myself and return to the bedroom. Pouring myself a glass of Delsarian wine, I curl up on the bed. Despite my nerves for the next day, the wine and exhaustion lull me into a light doze.

The sleep doesn't last. The usual nightmares I face in the lead up to seeing King Mazus again wake me before the sun rises. Those haunting green eyes replay in my mind, making me shiver. Even three hundred years later, I still viscerally remember the utter feeling of desperation, fear, and lack of agency as Mazus's guards pinned me down while he ordered me to slit my own wrists. Still remember the panic of not being in control of my own magic—of knowing that there was no one coming to save me. I take a few deep breaths, taking time to remember that I saved *myself*, saved my entire kingdom, all alone. I let that thought bolster me like it always does and whisper affirmations that have become routine.

You are the last defense against Mazus. No one is coming to save you. You must save yourself.

Once the fear and panic pass, I use the extra time to take detailed care of my appearance, braiding my hair into a complex weave that circles the top of my head and doing my makeup with expert precision. The deep emerald dress I select looks almost black until the light hits it just right. It brings out the color of my eyes and pays homage to the verdant landscape of my kingdom. Embroidered with thayar flowers, the flowing layers are designed to keep me cool in the warm climate of Delsar.

I inspect my appearance in the mirror, my bright green eyes staring back at me. Ivory skin stands out starkly against the dark dress and makeup, and I adjust a few auburn coils of hair before delicately placing the crown of gilded laurel and thayar flowers atop the intricate coif.

I can't keep my mind from wandering to one of my earliest memories. Seated in front of my mother at her own vanity, she had delicately combed the knots out of my hair before braiding it away from my face. Then she placed a real laurel wreath atop my head.

"My sweet Laurel," she said as she adjusted the wreath. "You're named after the Thayarian crown. It's made of gilded laurel as an homage to the foliage that grows so abundantly here. I wanted to give you a name that was worthy of the beautiful and magical life I knew you would live." Her soft fingers brushed against my cheeks, and she smelled like lavender and sea salt as she leaned down to kiss the top of my head.

The fresh laurel wreath, a Thayarian symbol of spring and the innocence of childhood, felt so light that day. I had worn it proudly, head floating in the clouds with dreams of one day wearing the real thing as I skipped around the palace, showing off my wreath to anyone who passed me by. Now, the crown is yet another reminder of the loss of parents who should have lived another thousand years, a constant sign that I haven't lived up to their legacy.

Taking several deep breaths, I look at myself in the mirror until I see a queen staring back, fearless and ready to play the role of the terrifying and mad Witch Queen. A role that has kept my people safe from interest in the shrouded, misty kingdom these last centuries.

A knock at the door pulls me out of my deep focus. Nemesia and Admon enter, both dressed in emerald green pant suits that compliment my dress. We make an imposing triad clad in dark clothing and stacked with weapons. Diaskia appears at the door, shoulders tense, and we follow her into the western wing of the palace, the four guards following closely behind.

The hallway is lined with open alcoves overlooking the sea, the blue sparkling against the white framing arches. The chambers the Forum will be held in are on the first level, and soon we enter a large room with a massive circular table in the middle. There are four equally impressive chairs spaced evenly around the table, with smaller chairs on either side for the advisors.

"It appears you're the first to arrive," Diaskia says, and she gestures to the closest set of chairs. "You may take a seat when you're ready. Your guards are to stand against the wall or in the hallway beyond." With that, Diaskia leaves us.

Nemesia immediately takes charge, ordering two guards to stay in the room and the other two to remain outside and on alert. Admon looks my way and gives me an encouraging smile, his blue eyes twinkling.

"Here we go, Your Majesty," he jests, and I return the smile, though I imagine it doesn't reach my eyes. The wounds of the war have scabbed over, but that doesn't mean I enjoy being forced to make nice with the male who invaded my kingdom and the leaders who did nothing to stop him. Admon's eyes suddenly harden, and I know who's entered behind my back. I steel myself, turning cold eyes upon Mazus Vicant.

He hasn't aged a day since the Battle of Moormyr, that perfectly crafted appearance still as flawless as ever. None but his closest circle know his true age. He was born centuries before even my parents, potentially even before Admon. And yet—he looks as if he could be just out of his adolescence. Yet another mystery of the Golden King.

"Laurel, it is always such a rare *pleasure* to see you," he says with a plastered-on smile. I tense for an instant before recovering, noticing his use of my given name and not my title.

Not allowing him to get under my skin, I respond smoothly and cooly. "I wish I could say the same, *Mazus*." Now he stills, clearly irked by my own lack of formality and groveling. One of his advisors, an ancient graying male who looks as old as the Four Kingdoms, glances between us, then quickly looks to Admon, before returning his gaze to his King.

"How is Thayaria?" Mazus asks with fake interest. "Still shrouded in mist? Are you ever going to let anyone in or do you intend to isolate yourself for the rest of your long life?"

I bare my teeth in a contemptuous smile. "Why don't you try to cross the barrier and find out?"

Mazus eyes me coldly, tension roiling in the air between us. Before it can snap, the Queen of Delsar enters, chortling at the scene before her and cutting through the strain instantly. Lobelia Bantsum's tall frame matches those of the Delsarian warrior women. Her hair is fully gray, though the rest of her bronze body remains strong and toned, the muscles of her arms and abdomen on display in the turquoise cropped, sleeveless top she wears with matching flowing pants. "It's only been five minutes, and the Witch Queen and Golden King are already at odds. What a surprise," she says with a twinkle in her eye.

I've never known what to think of the Delsarian Queen. She always has an air of knowing more than everyone else in the room, and she probably does, considering she too is over one thousand years old. Age is a closely guarded secret amongst fae. It's difficult to know which leaders knew one another as adolescents, and Mazus and Lobelia are no different. It's well known that she loathes the Velmaran King, and the two are always renegotiating trade agreements between their nations, each attempting to get the upper hand on the other. She did not come to Thayaria's aid during the war, but neither did she aid Velmara.

From my perspective, she's as culpable as the rest of them. The centuries-long alliance Thayaria once had with Delsar ended the day she decided not to get involved when Mazus invaded my kingdom unprovoked.

I settle into the role she and everyone else expects of me, adding sarcastically, "Your Majesty, you know I can't resist ruffling Mazus's feathers a little. Since I can't practice my *dark magic* here, I must resort to cheap insults and petty gestures." Lobelia grins, that knowing look in her eyes once again.

"Ah yes, the dark magic of the Witch Queen, seen by Mazus himself and proclaimed by his messengers across the Four Kingdoms. Too powerful to be left unchecked, he claimed. The reason for his so-called war. How do your witchly pursuits go, Queen Laurel?"

"A witch never reveals her secrets," I add cheekily before taking my seat, ignoring Mazus's cold gaze.

Mazus stalks to his chair, taking the one across from me and staring me down with a smug look, and I resist the urge to unleash my actual power on him. I will the room to shake for just a moment to taunt him, and he sends a quick burst of air at my face in response. My eyes narrow and I bare my teeth.

Before things can escalate more with Mazus, the Reshnar leader enters, and all eyes quickly turn to him. Clem Carther is the first human to attend a Forum of Royals. He was elected to the highest leadership position by the Reshnar people three years ago. Mazus glares at him with unguarded contempt, while Lobelia looks at him like she wants to devour him, though in what way I'm unsure. He bows to each of us, before saying, "Your Majesties, it's my honor to be here for this *historical* Forum of *Leaders*." My eyebrow quirks up.

Clem walks to the open chair to my left and sits, his two advisors—one human, one fae—sitting beside him. All three of them give me a wide berth. The Reshnar human pulls out several rolls of parchment, quills, and even a few books. He's short and wide, his belly bulging out from his waist-length tunic. The loose trousers and riding boots he wears look like they were purchased just today, the sheen of the boots so bright I can see Admon's reflection in them. His brown hair is kept short, and he looks to be in his late fifties. While he appears at first glance to be laid back, his brown eyes are sharp and focused. He looks at the three royals around him, then says, "Well, shall we begin? I for one have an unending list of topics to discuss."

I groan internally. The next three days are going to be dreadfully dull.

"Queen Laurel, if you want to continue receiving grain from Delsar with such low taxes, I'm sorry to say you're going to need to offer us more shipments of the thayar flower," Queen Lobelia tells me, the irreverent and mischievous persona from before replaced with a no-nonsense negotiator.

We've been discussing Thayaria's grain imports for the last hour, one of the few high-stakes topics of this meeting. Because of Thayaria's isolation, we rely on trade and barter agreements to ensure we get the food we need. Despite our lush environment, cultivated agriculture is very difficult to maintain—the wild plants take over almost any plot of land unless there is careful tending. Thankfully every other nation requires thayar in some capacity, giving us the upper hand in negotiations.

"The amount of thayar you've requested, and with *zero* taxes, I'll add, is a non-starter. Give me another number, or I'll turn my attention to President Carther and secure my grain from Reshnar, despite our centuries-long agreement," I respond coolly. President Carther looks like he wants to disappear rather than negotiate with me.

Lobelia hisses. "You know as well as I that Reshnar has little use for thayar flower, since over eighty percent of its population is human. You won't get favorable grain prices there. Your only other option is Velmara." Her eyes dart to Mazus, who looks at me with contempt and glee.

"And *you* know that with my control over the entire supply of thayar flower, I have a lot more power in this negotiation than you want to admit. Give me. Another. Number." I use my aether-voice, reminding every single leader at this table that I'm more powerful than them all combined. Both Mazus and Lobelia wince. If I wanted to, I could force them to their knees. When crowned, every fae monarch receives the ability to speak with aether in their voice, granting them control over those less powerful than them. It's a convenient way to measure the magic of those in power.

"I would be happy to provide Thayaria with the grain you seek," Mazus sneers. "Velmara relies on thayar for most of our kingdom's trade, as you know. Any increase in our imports would be met with favorable trade terms." His eyes sparkle. He knows I need the grain, but also knows I refuse to trade with Velmara. Out of necessity, we sell them thayar at an inflated price and use the funds to purchase what we need from one of the other two kingdoms. Unfortunately, the prices barely make a dent in their deep coffers.

"That won't be necessary," I respond icily before turning my attention back to Lobelia.

Despite my calm exterior, I was worried this would happen. Thayaria's supplies of thayar are decreasing dramatically. If we don't find a solution soon, we won't be able to keep up with our existing commitments to the other three kingdoms, much less any changes to those terms. Not only will our revenue decrease to almost nonexistent, prohibiting us from purchasing what we need to survive in isolation, the other kingdoms will surely uncover what's going on and become more fervent in their own research to get past the barrier.

"Fine," Lobelia says. "You can receive a fifteen percent increase in grain, and in return you'll provide equal amounts of thayar. If you want twenty percent more, we'd be happy to do that deal as well."

I suspect this is the agreement she wanted all along, and by presenting it this way, she appears fair and reasonable. An even trade. But thayar is worth much more than grain, and she knows it. Fifteen percent more grain is equal to less than five percent more thayar. Even if it was fair, Thayaria doesn't currently have enough thayar production to increase Delsar's share so dramatically.

"Now, far be it from me to step in where I'm not wanted," Mazus begins, and I struggle to keep from rolling my eyes, "but that does seem like a fair agreement. Thayar grows abundantly on Thayaria, surely your people can shoulder such a small change to their thayar access." His eyes twinkle knowingly, and my stomach drops. *He knows about the declining blooms.*

"I don't remember asking for your input," Lobelia hisses. He only raises his hands as if he's simply trying to help.

"Fifteen percent increase in grain for a seven percent increase in thayar. Same taxes as the last agreement. That's my final offer, and you know it's more generous than I could be," I tell Lobelia. Nemesia tenses beside me, aware that Thayaria won't be able to honor even these terms if we don't find a way to stop the declining blooms.

"You have a deal, Queen Laurel," Lobelia says with a smirk. "And I believe that was the last topic for this year's Forum. We can—"

Mazus clears his throat, interrupting Lobelia. "There is one other final matter that I'd like for us to discuss before adjourning." My blood turns to ice, dread clenching in my gut as I quickly exchange glances with Nemesia and Admon.

"Well, spit it out, Mazus," Lobelia says dryly, clearly as ready to be done as I am.

He smirks at her, then looks directly at me. "I'd like to propose that Thayaria and Velmara exchange emissaries."

The room breaks out in hushed murmurs, even the highly trained Delsar advisors and guards are unable to keep from voicing their shock. Mazus's own advisors look at him with their brows furrowed. They clearly didn't know about their King's plans.

I raise my hand to quiet the room. "Emissaries?" I ask. "You want to send ambassadors to Thayaria?"

"Yes, Your Majesty," he replies, using my title now that he wants something. "Ambassadors. For too long our kingdoms have been isolated from one another, and I know I'm partially to blame for that. After three hundred years, I grow weary of the tension. I want us to take steps, albeit very small ones, to repair our two kingdoms' relationship."

"*Partially* to blame?" I ask, incredulous. "*You* attacked *my* kingdom—"

Admon cuts me off. "Your Majesty," he says, voice careful, "I believe we should hear him out." I look at Admon, my eyes blazing. He drops his voice, whispering so I barely hear him. "There may be much information to gain by testing his reasoning for this proposal. It's strategic for him to have brought this to the Forum, in front of the other leaders, instead of sending a letter to you or even having his advisors bring it up with Nemesia and I first to gauge your reception. Something is afoot. I suggest we hold our tongues and discover what it is."

My cheeks heat. Even after three hundred years, Admon's wise counsel still feels like the reproach of a parent. I nod, then turn back to Mazus, who's grinning so wide I grow nauseous at the sight.

Mazus continues. "As I was saying, I would like to repair our kingdoms' relationship, and I'm prepared to send my only child, Hawthorne Vicant, the Shining Prince of Velmara, as my emissary."

My eyes narrow in suspicion. Mazus can't believe I'd be foolish enough to allow his son to come to Thayaria as a spy for him. But I only say, "And why would you send the *Crown Prince* of Velmara to a country where you cannot reach him once he steps foot on my soil, where he will have no allies or friends to call on should he find trouble?"

His eyes drop in mock resignation. "I confess I have a secondary motive for sending my son. Thorne, as he's called by those who love him, needs to take more interest in the ruling of his country. For too long I've allowed him to shirk his responsibilities, wasting away his life in brothels and taverns. I will not live forever, and I wish to leave my kingdom in capable hands when that fateful day comes. I feel he needs a new environment to be able to flourish."

I don't believe a single word out of his mouth. I doubt anyone in this room does. Instead of voicing this, I simply ask, coldly, "Why now?"

"It's weighed heavily on me for many years, Your Majesty. I fear I have no answer for you other than I've finally determined to take action. The weight of my past is too much to bear any longer." Clem looks like he's eating this up, his eyes glimmering with hope and his mouth ticked up in a soft smile. He believes the Golden King to be a shining beacon of light. All of the people of Reshnar do, their alliance with Velmara as solid as ever.

Before I can respond, Nemesia surprises me by saying, "What else are you prepared to give us should we agree?"

My eyes cut to hers, exasperated that she's entertaining this nonsense. But I don't undermine her, not here. I've learned that lesson the hard way too many times. I return my gaze to Mazus.

"What is it that you require to *bribe* you into diplomatic relations?" he sneers.

The audacity. A wind whips around the room, my power seeping out in my fury. Queen Lobelia is feral with delight, and Clem looks like he wants to crawl under the table, his features pulled into a grimace. Nemesia puts her hand gently on my arm, lowering me back to my seat. I hadn't even realized I'd stood.

"To even consider this, we would need more favorable thayar prices and access to Velmara's archives for the emissary we send. We will adjourn to another room to discuss while you think over what you're prepared to offer," Nemesia says, her voice strong and clear.

"Your *bribe*, as you say, better be worth my time," I hiss, turning on my heel and slamming a wind into Mazus's advisors that knocks them over.

The people of Thayaria are known to be powerful plant channelers. While the ability exists outside of Thayaria, nowhere else has such a large population, and most of the notable plant channelers throughout history have been Thayarian. Magical historians and philosophers alike agree that Thayarians' affinity for plant channeling stems from the numerous leylines that cover the kingdom. Plant channelers are best known for their ability to coax the landscape to their will, though their control over the plants around them take many by surprise as they find themselves ensnared in a trap of vines.

A Brief History of Modern Thayaria

"What the *hell* are you doing?" Laurel asks sharply once we're secluded. "I will not allow that bastard's *son* into my kingdom!" The room practically shakes with her power.

"El, listen to me," I say with my calmest voice, attempting to deescalate the situation before she blasts me with her power. "We can gain access to the archives, can ask for better thayar prices. You don't even have to interact with the Prince, just relegate him to the Council and give him busy work."

"And who would we even send?" Laurel spits out. She's lethal. I've never seen her this angry, especially not with me. I pause, knowing what her reaction will be when I reveal the plan I came up with the moment Mazus threw out this insane proposal.

"Me." I keep my eyes locked on Laurel's. She physically convulses for just a moment, so quick that few would catch it. Then she locks down her emotions in the vault she's too practiced at using. The Queen emerges, and she dons a mask of cool indifference that I hate seeing. "I know you don't trust him. I don't trust him either. I know this is some farce and that we haven't yet determined the game he's playing. But we have to put our best pieces on the board and play the game. And *I'm* our best piece," I say, squaring my shoulders and keeping my eyes on hers. "If he agrees to give me access to the archives, I might finally find information that can help us."

"You know as well as I that he'll hide any books that are of relevance to us," she says dryly.

"I know he will *try*," I respond, confidence in my voice. "But I'm capable of finding information in the most irrelevant of books. I see what others don't see. I can find information in those archives that no one else can. And I'll come home at the tiniest whisper of trouble." I sense Laurel becoming more open to the idea, the mask of Queen receding, so I press on. "I'm out of ideas, El." My voice wavers. "I have no more experiments to try, or books to read, or elder fae to talk to. The flowers are declining, and we don't know why or what impact it will have on the kingdom. Admon and I both tried finding answers here from the other advisors, and that was a dead end. Even if this is another one, we *must* try. There could be real answers in Velmara." I lock my eyes on hers, pleading with unspoken words. She looks away.

"Admon, what do you think?" she asks the elder fae. He frowns, the deep lines on his face shifting with the movement.

"I've known both of you all your lives," he says thoughtfully, kind and wise eyes darting between the two of us. "I was there the day you were born, Laurel. I was the one who received the missive that the Valley of Moormyr had bloomed under the blood moon. I delivered that news to your parents and watched them connect it to the prophecy and realize the implications. I've seen you both shoulder more than your fair share of tragedy and trauma. You've matured gracefully under immense pressure." My throat aches with tears I don't dare shed. I glance at Laurel. She must feel the same, though she would never show it, even better than I at concealing her emotions. "So I also know," Admon continues, "what it will cost the two of you to be separated. But I do believe Nemesia is the best person to send. She knows every book in our own archives back to front and is smart enough to make connections where others may not. She can also protect herself with her magic if it comes to it."

Laurel's resolve falters, eyes softening and brow unfurrowing. Laurel's a good Queen. She's a fair and honest ruler, who truly listens to the advice of her counselors. She may put up her own wall of mist between herself and the world, but underneath she's just as beautiful and lush as Thayaria.

Laurel sighs. "I'm wary of Mazus's true motivations. He's up to something. This is not some altruistic gesture…"

"El, we know—" I start to protest, but she cuts me off.

"But I see the sense in sending Nemesia to Velmara," she says, finally meeting my eyes with a look of open vulnerability. Relief courses through me. "We should ask Mazus to agree to pay more for Velmara's imports of thayar," Laurel continues. "We know that our supply is going to decrease soon. With decreased supply, we'll have no choice but to raise prices to keep our revenue stable. That could signal to the other rulers that something's amiss. If Mazus pays more now, it will cover the shortfall in revenue and keep our secret longer."

I'm delighted but not surprised by Laurel's line of thinking.

"If Mazus knows about the declining thayar already," I add, following Laurel's logic, "he'll have to agree to this, because he knows that prices will go up inevitably once our supply runs low. His kingdom relies so heavily on thayar imports for their trade across the Nivan Desert, he can't afford to let Thayaria send future limited supplies to the highest bidder. This lets him secure the flower and might tell us what information he has."

Admon sits thoughtfully, looking between the two of us. "It's a good plan. If Mazus agrees readily, we'll also know how desperate he is to send his son to Thayaria. We won't know why, but we'll have more information regarding his intentions."

Mazus and his decrepit advisors whisper in a corner as we enter the chambers, returning to their seats when they spot us. Mazus gazes coldly at Laurel, then asks, "So, what have you decided to ask for? I confess we're not eager to make the first move. We've agreed to give you access to the archives. That feels sufficient to us."

Laurel stands, every inch the powerful and confident Queen I've seen her become over the last three hundred years, so different from the female I had to peel from the ground during the Battle of Moormyr. Her shoulders are set, back straight, eyes hard with resolve. She gives Mazus a haughty look that scares even me, so unused to this version of her.

"Let me remind you that *you* are the one who seeks this arrangement," she says, and the room quivers. "I am perfectly content to leave things as they are. Nevertheless, in addition to access to the archives, should you wish to burden me with your incompetent and imprudent son, you're going to have to pay me for it. I want a thirty percent increase on the export tax you pay for thayar flowers. In exchange, Thayaria will source our grain exclusively from Velmara."

The room erupts in chaos once again. Lobelia hisses while Mazus's advisors look aghast, hands raised in outrage. It's a smart plan, though I'm unsurprised at her expert political maneuvering. The Council of Advisors fights every time about who to send with Laurel to the Forum of Royals, but the reality is she doesn't need anyone to accompany her. She's fully capable of running her kingdom and negotiating with the other leaders. She's the only one who doesn't see the fearsome and capable ruler she's become.

Mazus and Laurel stare one another down. I practically hold my breath, waiting for Mazus's response. He raises a single hand, and the room quiets. "You have a deal, Queen Laurel," Mazus says, eyes bright. I let out an inaudible sigh, tension leaving my body, while Mazus's advisors suck in a breath. Laurel only grins.

"And what about Delsar?" Lobelia asks, though not with the anger I would have expected from her.

"You can still purchase thayar from us at the same quantity of prior years, and I'll reduce the export tax by fifteen percent," Laurel responds. Lobelia only nods, and I can't understand why she isn't more upset at this turn of events.

Despite my confusion, I nearly laugh at Laurel's brilliance. She's played the game well. The arrangement secures Thayaria grain without increasing thayar shipments by a single stem. We'll make more coin on the shipments we do produce, a resource we'll desperately need in the future if I don't uncover a way to stop the declining magic. Plus, it gets us out of the agreement with Lobelia that we absolutely would not have been able to honor, while covering the real reason for us agreeing to trade with Velmara after three hundred years of embargo.

Laurel remains stoic, staring Mazus down with a self-satisfied smirk. Mazus sneers at her in return, the two of them locked in a battle of silent wills. The tension coils in the room, and once again the Delsar Queen has to step in to cut the tension. The room practically takes an audible breath in at the release.

"While I'm disappointed to have lost the trade agreement to Velmara, I for one am happy to see Thayaria and Velmara taking steps to become what they once were—allies," Queen Lobelia says. Something prickles at the back of my mind at her use of the word, but I shove it aside for another time, too relieved and thrilled with the outcome of events to worry about anything else right now.

After the Forum concludes, Laurel and I sit in her suite together in comfortable silence. I prepare a generous pour of red wine for her, and an even more generous pour of whiskey for myself, handing her the glass before taking my seat on a sofa next to her.

"So," I say, "I'm going to Velmara." The enormity of what I'm about to do hits me, but I push down my reservations.

"You're going to Velmara," she repeats. "I'm not sure I'm prepared to rule Thayaria without you. We haven't even discussed what to do about the Sons and Daughters of Thayaria." She rubs her hands across her face. Laurel looks exhausted and worn down. Her always-on composure and control make it easy to overlook the pressure she puts on herself to be the perfect leader. Glassy eyes stare back at me. She likely hasn't slept well in weeks.

"I've already spoken with Admon and given him direction for the Sons and Daughters, though I didn't tell him about the mole," I tell her gently, hoping to ease her concerns. "I counseled him to have the advisors spread whispers telling the truth of this arrangement—that I'm going to Velmara to seek answers about the thayar and that we are dipping a toe in the water of reconciliation with Velmara. I also instructed him to mention we'll be getting increased revenues for our exports. This should quell their recruitment efforts and take away the full power of their narrative." Guilt and shame at not being able to stop the rebel attacks before leaving for Velmara churn within me.

"Who are you going to take with you?" she asks me, and I once again hesitate to tell her my plans, knowing how she'll feel about them.

"Well..." I start slowly. I take a deep breath, steeling myself. "I think I should go alone."

"Absolutely not." Laurel's expression leaves no room for argument. I groan.

"El, you've got to stop saying no to everything that puts me at the slightest amount of risk."

"I don't, actually. I get to do whatever I want, and what I want is to keep you, my sister in every way that counts, safe. And this isn't a slight amount of risk. Going alone to Velmara is insanity. Surely you know that."

"Of course I know the risk. I've been through everything you have," I snap, unable to keep the frustration from my voice. I immediately regret it when I see Laurel's face shutter. Sighing, I rub a hand across the back of my neck. "I only mean, I'm just as aware as you are of what I'm walking into. And I've weighed the benefits and risks. Trust that I wouldn't put myself in danger unless I had a good reason."

Her bright green eyes search mine. "And what is this good reason?"

"There are several. First, if I go alone, Mazus will underestimate me. You know how fucked up his views are about females. It will be easier for me to fly under the radar if there isn't an entire Thayarian entourage with me. Second, there are very few individuals

I would trust enough to bring with me, and I need all of them to stay with you. You'll have Velmarans snooping around your court, not to mention the rising tensions with the rebellion. I want every possible advisor and guard with you." Laurel rolls her eyes and tries to protest, but I interrupt her and keep going. "Third, if it's just me, it's a lot easier to get out if things go south. If I bring multiple people with me, I'll feel responsible for their safety, and I can't guarantee it. I won't put others at risk." I stare her down, hoping my gaze expresses what I cannot say. The wounds of the war have not healed for me. My own guilt at leading thousands of soldiers to their deaths still haunts me. The idea of taking even a single other person with me who might be killed because of me ignites a grief I cannot bear.

She sighs. "Are you absolutely certain this is what you want? Of course I trust you. You know you can do whatever you want after I protest a little first." We both chuckle. "I just want you to be safe."

I squeeze her hand. "I'm sure. I'll be safe, and it'll be easier to get out alone. Like I said, I promise to come home at the first sign of trouble."

She takes a long sip of her wine and sighs. "Fine. What else do we need to sort out before you leave?"

"Carex can take over my spy network, loath as I am to give him that role." Laurel smiles knowingly. "If my spies uncover any of the rebel plans, they'll report it. But... we haven't been able to infiltrate them so far."

"You should be nicer to Carex. He means well," Laurel says, and I have to stop myself from rolling my eyes.

"Despite what you may think, I am capable of putting my feelings for him aside when making decisions about the kingdom. As the Captain of the Royal Guard, he's the right choice as my replacement for our intelligence efforts. Plus, he's so in love with you he'll do anything to keep you safe."

Laurel snorts and rolls her eyes. "We can agree to disagree on that front. *He* was the one who decided we weren't right for each other. But you've covered everything, as usual. I'll have to hope I can find something to stop the rebels while you're gone."

"You should stay on alert," I warn. "Things could change with the rebels at any moment. They may be attacking small villages now, but they could easily escalate to larger targets, even the palace. Be careful who you discuss any plans with while I'm gone. The mole is of more concern to me than the rebels. Don't tell anyone of our suspicions."

Laurel nods in agreement. "So... how excited are you really to read all those books?" she asks with a genuine grin, changing the somber mood in an instant.

I laugh. "Truly, I think I might squeal when they first bring me to the archives. Other than this trip, it's been a long time since I've left Thayaria, so I can't help but be a little excited to see something new too." Laurel winces, so quickly most wouldn't catch the small movement, but I do. I know she feels enormous guilt for the mist, though I still don't understand why she won't drop it. It's the one subject she won't discuss with me. There's more to her unwillingness than a fear of the outside world, but I haven't discovered it yet. I quickly change the subject to ease her pain. "To see another kingdom's history and research is amazing, but to see Velmara's... it's a once in a lifetime opportunity. Even if I'll have to occasionally interact with Mazus the Moldy."

She scrunches her nose, then bursts out with a deep belly laugh. "I forgot we used to call him that," she says through her heaving laughter. "If he gets too pompous, just drop that little moniker and then put up the strongest plant defenses you can muster." Grinning, my heart swells with happiness to see her laughing. She doesn't do it nearly enough, if at all, anymore. It's also a relief to discuss Mazus in such lighthearted terms for once.

"I'm going to Velmara to cozy up to old Mazus the Moldy, and you're going to meet the Shining Prince. I hear he's extremely handsome." I give her a wink.

Laurel snorts. "I hear there isn't much more to him than that. They say he spends his days drunk, wooing women only to abandon them the next day. Gambling his father's fortune and then finding the closest brothel to bed into at night. But I've also heard he has light channeling abilities that eclipse even the King's powers. I can assure you I don't intend to take much notice of whether he's handsome or not. I don't intend to take much notice of him at all. He's the son of the worst male we've ever known and is almost certainly being sent to spy on me."

I consider her words, my own suspicions about Mazus's motivations resurfacing. "I'm not convinced he's being sent to spy, actually. It seems too obvious. Mazus wouldn't be so straightforward, though I also think he believes us incapable of determining his real plans with our tiny female brains or whatever it is he thinks makes females so inferior."

She chuckles, though it's more reserved than her earlier laughter. "Why do you think he's sending his son?"

I shake my head in confusion and let out a heavy breath. "It's almost like—like he wants the two of you to meet for some reason. Or maybe he wants his son out of the way in Velmara. Maybe both. I haven't worked it out yet, but those are my two leading theories."

Her eyes narrow as she falls deep in thought. "You may be on to something. Either way, I don't plan to meet him at all. I'll let the Council handle him entirely, like you suggested. He can stay in his chambers, meet with the Council, and gallivant around the city. Arberly has plenty of pubs for him to drink in and find whatever willing females he wants to take to his bed. He'll report back to Mazus only what he can glean from those meaningless interactions."

"You really think you can get away with *never* meeting with him?" I ask, and she shrugs.

"It's worth trying, especially if Mazus has some secret reason for wanting us to meet."

I consider her plan. "You're the Queen, and he'll be in the kingdom of his enemy. A kingdom that none can reach without your consent. I think you can do whatever the hell you want with him. It's a good plan." She breaks into a smirk.

"And if he finds out more than he should? If he somehow sees something that puts Thayaria at risk, or discovers the declining thayar? What should I do then?" she asks.

"You should kill him."

Light channelers are considered the highest order of magic users, and for good reason. Their power is considered the closest to the raw power of the aether, as both light and aether are currents that can be directed and shaped. Light channelers can brighten or dim the light around them, the strongest able to cast large areas in complete darkness in the middle of the day. Few take this risk, however, as most light wielders are greatly weakened or even completely powerless once darkness descends.

The Unabridged History of Magical Orders, Volume I

I enter my father's Council chambers at his summons, the smaller ones he uses for intimate meetings. *At least I won't have the entire kingdom watching whatever news he's about to drop on me.*

The room is sickeningly gilded, nearly every surface shining with some kind of gold plating or other adornment. There are no windows, making me feel even more confined. A small rectangular table commands the middle of the room, only three people sitting at it. My father sits at the head, his presence imposing even when he isn't crowned or wearing his regalia. He's dressed rather informally, though his tunic is still embroidered with gold and purple thread, intricate suns adorning the shoulders and sleeves.

On his left and right are his two closest advisors, Citus and Gloxynia. Both are ancient fae with graying hair who are probably even older than my father, though no one can say for certain. Gloxynia's beady eyes stare me down, lips pursed in a permanent soured expression, and I bristle under her gaze. My eyes shift to Citus, hoping to find something in his expression that tells me what this meeting is about. His blue eyes, milky with age, give nothing away. Unlike Gloxynia, Citus is wrinkled and looks like he may crumble into dust at any moment. With a hunched back and frail limbs, palace courtiers often joke that he was alive when the aether was created millennia ago. They may not be far off.

My father notices me and scowls. "Sit." Always trying to get under his skin, I approach a beverage cart in the corner instead and pour myself a mug of steaming tea, adding in a generous splash of whiskey. The mug is solid gold, giving it a heft that's impractical for its actual use and requires magic to prevent burns from the heated metal. Just another way the Velmaran court is designed to place power at the center of everything it does. Without thayar elixir to enhance their magical ability, many nobles would be unable to use the mug.

My father lets out a long-suffering sigh. "It is seven in the morning, Hawthorne, and you are already drinking." I add another splash of whiskey because I can, slowly stirring the steaming liquid while I feel my father's eyes on my back. With a smirk, I leisurely make my way to the table and sit.

"So," I say, slouching in my chair, "what has led you to call me here at such an ungodly hour? I've barely even gone to bed after my nighttime activities." I wink and revel at the way it makes him clench his jaw. I actually went to bed early last night and feel perfectly rested, but he'll get strategically placed rumors later today reporting that I was seen buying out the city's most illustrious brothel. Whatever it takes to keep him underestimating me. "Going to betroth me to another female? Already have the next one lined up in case Silene has an untimely end like dear old mother?"

It's dangerous, being this errant. But his reaction, or lack thereof, is information. He wants something from me, otherwise he would have dismissed me the moment I showed disdain, or at the very least aerstepped the whiskey bottle to fly at my head. I stare him down and pick at my fingernails, playing the role he expects of me.

"The Witch Queen has agreed to take one emissary from Velmara into her court," he says, matter-of-factly. My jaw drops, and I'm unable to hide my shock for a brief moment. My mind races, wondering why he's told me this information and how in the world he got the Queen of Thayaria to agree to trade emissaries. "Queen Laurel and I have agreed to a mutual exchange of ambassadors as a first step in repairing our sordid history," he continues. "In exchange, she'll buy her grain exclusively from Velmara, and we'll pay an increased cost on thayar imports," he says. Realization dawns on me.

He's sending me to Thayaria.

"The Velmaran representative will need to get close to the Queen and observe her magic," he continues. "I wish to know how strong she's become in the last three hundred years. I also want to know what Thayaria is like, who her advisors are, how the people feel about her, anything that may be interesting to know."

I know the answer to my next question, but I ask anyway. "And who will you be sending?"

My father smiles, wide and feral. "You."

The lights flicker, the only external sign that I'm affected by this information. They flash brightly, dim, then return to normal. Even though I had no intention of drinking the disgusting concoction of whiskey and tea, I consider downing it, just to get my bearings. Instead, I take a deep breath and center myself, not letting my concern show.

"Me?" I ask, incredulous, adding a haughty confidence to my voice that I don't feel. "Why me? As you love to remind me, I'm useless, only good for drinking and fucking. And I have no political skills to speak of. I would make a terrible emissary. Not to mention, I have no desire to live my days in the hovel of Thayaria. I decline." I feign nonchalance, leaning back in my chair once again as if I don't have a care in the world.

My father stills, and as his eyes burn with an icy rage, I know I've gotten under his skin—a rare occurrence. "Leave us," he says to his advisors with a quiet intensity. I dust imaginary lint from my shoulders as they leave, feigning disinterest. "You do not get to decline," my father says with a dangerous edge to his voice. His power ripples off him in waves I can almost feel. If I were anyone else, anyone weaker than him in power, I wouldn't be able to resist the nudge of aether lacing his voice. But I'm stronger than him, a fact that has led to his hatred of me since the day my magic appeared.

"You *will* go to Thayaria," he continues. "Otherwise, Fionn will suddenly find himself on guard duty in the Nivan Desert. And Silene will find herself betrothed to another, someone I can assure you will not pretend to sleep with her every few days so she can go cavort with her other *female* lovers. She will do her duty to her kingdom and produce heirs, with you or someone else, or die trying." Every muscle in my body is tense and alert. I must pause for too long, because he bares his teeth in a menacing smile. "I know all about the little deal you and Silene have struck. I know that she doesn't care at all about the common whore you've taken on as a mistress. *A shopkeeper.* So beneath you, Hawthorne. I've been content to ignore it, knowing that eventually the two of you would have no choice but to marry. And what you do in your bedroom is none of my business as long as a legitimate heir is produced. But I grow weary of your antics, and I've found another purpose for you."

My mind races, trying to find a solution. I could offer him something else, but there's nothing he wants from me. When my father makes his mind up about something, there's no changing it. And while I don't believe for an instant that he truly wants me to spy for him— he would never trust me with something so important—I will play along. For now.

"Fine," I hiss out. "I'll play pretend as your emissary and report back. But Fionn and Silene come with me." I will not leave them here for him to decide what to do with while I'm gone. My father considers for a moment, then nods in agreement. I almost slump from the chair in relief. "Why now? What's made you decide on this arrangement after so much time?"

"My reasons are my own," he sneers. "They do not concern you. I have... allies in Thayaria, so wipe any plans of lying to me or not doing your best to get close to the Queen from your mind. If you slip up, I'll bring you home and deliver on my promise. Thayaria is not as impenetrable as you may think." He gives me a meaningful look, then waves his hand in dismissal before turning back to the pile of documents scattered on the table in front of him. "Make your preparations. You depart in a week."

"What the actual fuck," Fionn says an hour later when I tell him the news. Silene wasn't here when I arrived in the sparring chambers, ready to beat the shit out of anyone or anything that crossed my path, but Fionn was. The moment he saw my face, he ripped off his shirt and picked up a weapon. We fought in silence for several minutes, our swords clashing in a familiar rhythm and echoing off the walls and high ceilings around us. After I'd taken the edge off the furious energy coursing through my veins, I told him about the meeting and our impending diplomatic vacation.

"If you don't want to go..." I say, grunting with the effort of blocking one of Fionn's parries.

"Don't be an idiot. I'm going," Fionn says, not even out of breath. He feints to the right, then twists his body while I lunge so that he can come up behind me, his sword at my neck. "How else will you get any better at using a sword if I'm not there to remind you that I still beat you every time?" He releases me, grinning.

I drop the sword, heaving deep breaths. I'm an excellent swordsman, but Fionn is better, not even needing the metal channeling affinities he has to best me. Although I would never admit it to him, he does in fact beat me nearly every time. We walk to the edge of the ring, replacing our training weapons on the rack.

"Do you think she's really a blood mage?" he asks, concern flashing through his eyes.

I shrug. "I wish I knew. My father has convinced everyone she is, and I don't know how else she would have achieved the barrier magic she's been able to maintain for three hundred years. There's no other explanation for it but spellwork."

"But..." Fionn prompts with his typical prodding.

"But," I say, "if my father swears it's blood magic, that makes me believe it must be anything but that." Fionn nods, brows furrowed in thought. "What of the rumors?" I ask him, teasing in my voice. "Do you believe Thayaria is leached of magic and oozing black from the very ground, or that she tortures her people and steals their blood to fuel her witchcraft? That she kidnaps children from their beds and drains their bodies of blood so she can control their parents?"

Fionn's face drains of color. "I guess we're going to find out," he says with a visible swallow. Despite his casual words, I know his fear of the Witch Queen is rooted in his upbringing as a commoner, who deeply believe my father's propaganda. Though he knows the truth about the Golden King now, some beliefs are hard to shake.

"Find out what?" Silene's voice calls across the cavernous space. She crosses the damp, underground cave that houses four separate sparring rings, abandoned for the training yard my father built several hundred years ago to train his army, making this the perfect meetup place for the three of us.

I hesitate for a moment, not sure how much to tell her about my father's threats. As she reaches us, I decide to only share the details of the trip and not the information he's discovered about her nighttime activities through his network of spies. Information she hasn't even shared with me yet. She should have known better than to test the reach of palace informants, but I understand all too well the need to fight against the constraints placed upon her. "The Queen of Thayaria has agreed to allow an envoy from Velmara to visit, and she'll be sending her own here. I'm to be the official ambassador."

Silene's jaw drops. She looks between Fionn and I, eyes narrowed in suspicion. "We're not messing with you," I say. "It's true. I leave in a week."

She shakes her head in disbelief. "Why? Where is this coming from?"

"According to him, he and the Queen have agreed to this arrangement to repair the relationship between Thayaria and Velmara. He ordered me to get close to her and learn about her magic and the kingdom. Report back to him as a spy. But those can't be his real motivations."

"Of course they aren't," she says matter-of-factly, "but it's an opportunity for us all the same." I look at her, confusion on my face. "I'm obviously going with you, as is Fionn. You'd be freaking out more if we weren't. And this can be a strategic advantage for us if we play it correctly." I give her a wide grin. Silene's always been the political strategist among us, and now is no different. "You know my opinions on the Witch Queen's power," she continues. "I think she has an affinity for every possible conduit, maybe even ones we don't know about. She's not a blood mage, she's just incredibly powerful." Fionn and I roll our eyes at Silene's unbelievable theory. She holds up her hands, acquiescing. "But if she really *does* use blood magic, this is a chance for us to learn more about it and determine if your suspicions about your father are true." I quickly look around, nervous that we'll be overheard, even knowing that no one ventures into this abandoned and musty basement except the three of us.

"She has a point," Fionn adds. "The Witch Queen could help us confirm whether your father also uses... blood magic." He whispers the last two words, as if even uttering them will suddenly unleash untold evil into the world.

"Are you sure you want to come with me? It won't be easy getting close to Queen Laurel. It might even be impossible. And it will be incredibly dangerous, guaranteed. Even if we do get close, there's still my father to deal with. I don't want to wrap you up in whatever scheme he's planning," I say.

Silene rolls her eyes. "We're already wrapped up in your father's schemes."

"She's right," Fionn adds. "I've been helping you undermine your father for centuries."

"No offense," Silene says flippantly, "but everything we've been doing here in Velmara barely moves the needle. I know we've worked hard to build our network, but stealing a shipment of thayar here and there, poisoning a noble or two so they can't vote on initiatives, stealing books from the archives... they're all small actions. It's going to take us *hundreds* of years to make any kind of impact using these tactics. *This* is a real opportunity."

I consider her words, accepting their decision and feeling grateful for their friendship. "There's more," I say. They look at me expectantly. "My father has agreed to pay her a thirty percent higher price for thayar imports. In exchange, Thayaria will buy its grain exclusively from Velmara. It could just be part of the negotiation, but..." I trail off.

"But it can't be a coincidence that something strange is happening with the thayar shipments and your father goes off and agrees to pay more for a good the kingdom desperately needs while only securing a grain monopoly and a single emissary in exchange," Silene finishes for me. "It doesn't add up. Maybe we can learn more in Thayaria. They may have more knowledge of the uses of thayar and what a large stockpile could do in the wrong hands."

A plan slowly forms in my mind. For the last two hundred years, since I began to suspect my father intentionally killed my mother in one of his *magic experiments*, I've wondered whether he practiced blood magic. I've never been able to do anything about it, nor have I ever come this close to having a real plan to confirm my speculation. Fueled by grief and rage, I've been undeterred for centuries, finding small ways to undermine him. But Silene's right—we've barely made a difference with the underground operation we've built. This could be a real chance to not only gather information to expose my father but also build a bridge with a powerful ruler.

"We do exactly as my father asks, and we get close to the Witch Queen to observe her magic and her court," I tell them. "We also keep our ears open for information on the flower. But we do it for our own reasons. If we can make her an ally, that's an added bonus. But either way, we're going to find the information we need to take down the Golden King."

"And how exactly do you plan to get information about blood magic out of the Witch Queen?" Fionn asks skeptically.

I break out in a wide smile. "By doing what I do best. I'll charm her. Seduce her. She's been in isolation for three centuries. She won't see my handsome face coming."

MAZUS

Recent developments are going according to plan. Queen Laurel agreed to my proposal for emissaries, and my worthless son will be in the Witch Queen's kingdom by tomorrow afternoon. The human armies are also growing their numbers rapidly, thanks to my soldier salary program that promises their families two generations of payments in exchange for their service. And the rapidly growing army did not come up once at the Forum of Royals. Not a single person guessed at my true motivations for sending Hawthorne to Thayaria, not even that obnoxious girl betrothed to him who's too smart for her own good.

I place a single petal of thayar flower on the sterile workstation, then wrap it in enough swirling wind to keep it hovering in the air. While I observe the effects, my thoughts drift to my son and the potential for him to ruin plans that have been in the works for centuries.

I chuckle at the thought. Hawthorne is too kindhearted and weak-willed to go against me in Thayaria. That stupid boy cares too much for his friends and will do anything to keep them safe from the punishment I threatened. And his own natural curiosity will likely drive him to learn more about the female he was once told would be his stepmother.

That plan hadn't worked out, and thank the aether for that. Had I culled her magic like I'd intended to, it would've destroyed the only chance I have at seeing my plans through. Not to mention, marriage doesn't suit me. Once Hawthorne was born, I'd left his mother to pursue her own life and told her she was free to do whatever she pleased, as long as she stayed out of my way. But the bitch didn't listen and poked her nose in too many unwelcome places. She was *also* too smart for her own good, and it cost her everything.

With another strong push of raw aether, the thayar flower crumbles into dust, and I sweep the remains into a small pile. Lowering my nose to the powder, I snort it up through my nostrils, reveling in the feel of power jolting through my veins.

My late wife's face crosses my mind. Renowned for her beauty, I'd married her for her family's line of powerful light channelers, hoping she would produce a strong heir. And she had, though Hawthorne's magical abilities are eclipsed by other traits he gets from his mother. He is overly sympathetic, rash and impulsive, pleasure seeking, and loyal to his friends. But the people of Velmara have come to love him. I can't do anything to their *Shining Prince.*

My blood boils thinking of that moniker. Velmara had once been called the 'Golden Kingdom,' named for its yellow hills that produce enough gold to gild every structure in the capital city twice over. When I took the throne from my father, I slowly seeded the moniker 'Golden King' out to the people. A slip to a courtier here and there, a typo in the transcriptions of my speeches. It was the first real success of my propaganda machine. Within one hundred years, I'd become the Golden King, the golden king*dom* forgotten.

But when Hawthorne was born and the Velmaran people realized the strength of his light channeling magic, they had dubbed him the Shining Prince all on their own. The name grates on my nerves every time I hear it.

I shudder, the control I keep in such a firm grip slipping. My eyes turn into slits, vision blurring with a yellow haze. Steam escapes my nostrils, and I feel my skin stretching and hardening. With a deep breath in, I reverse the slip, then take one more inhale to solidify my restraint.

Nicknames can be powerful. The Golden King persona serves me well, and coining the name Witch Queen for Laurel is one of my proudest accomplishments. Even those suspicious of me, like Queen Lobelia, still somewhat believe that Laurel practices the witchcraft of blood magic, not realizing it is I who seeded those beliefs. The people of the primarily human kingdom of Reshnar are absolutely terrified of the Witch Queen and her dark magic thanks to my stories about her, and all the commoners in Velmara fear what she might do to their children if unleashed.

I gave Laurel that moniker before the Battle of Moormyr as a way to justify the invasion of Thayaria. But it really took hold when Laurel released a wave of power so strong it was felt even in the Nivan Desert, every single Velmaran soldier, myself included, killed or aerstepped from Thayaria. The death toll had been in the thousands, sealing her fate as the blood-curdling *Witch Queen.*

People, human and fae alike, are so easy to manipulate. Just pull the right strings, suggest the right messages at the right time, and they'll believe anything. Even easier is getting them to forget their history. For if the people of this world remembered its history, they would know that it's impossible for Laurel to have used blood magic that day, or any day, for that matter.

The least understood of the conduits for magic is that of air. Some aspects of air chan-
neling, like wind manipulation and levitation, are easy to grasp; however, the more
complex aspects of air channeling, such as aerstepping, have confused scholars for
centuries. Some scholars have even gone as far as to suggest there is a separate conduit
for the aether that aersteppers use—space. Since not all air channelers can aerstep, the
argument makes logical sense to many scholars. These debates have raged for centuries,
and the only thing scholars can agree on is that the aether's mysteries have yet to be
fully unraveled.

The Unabridged History of Magical Orders, Volume I

My trunks are packed with all the items I'll need for an indefinite trip to Thayaria—clothes, weapons, books, and two trunks full of wine. I'm not taking any
chances that there isn't any alcohol in the isolated kingdom. Fionn and Silene are also
packed, though they have far fewer trunks than me. We stand together in my chambers,
servants hauling our trunks out on wheels. I scan each room of my suite, looking
for anything valuable or important I may have left behind. Seeing nothing, I slip the
small satchel with my most prized possessions—my mother's family ring, a dagger that
belonged to my mother's brother, and three letters my mother wrote me as a child, the
parchment now worn soft—over my shoulder, steeling myself for what's to come.

As usual, Silene is the de facto commander of our little group. Dressed in a light traveling dress, she directs the servants and even forces Fionn to go wash his hands. "The dirt under your nails will make a horrid impression," she tells him.

He growls. "I have dirt under my nails because I'm a warrior. That is the impression I want to make." But he concedes, quickly scrubbing his hands and under his nails in the bathing chamber.

When all the trunks have been hauled away, the three of us share a moment where we let the fear show on our faces before locking it and my suite away.

"You guys go ahead to the departure ceremony. I don't want my father to be angry with you for being late," I tell them.

"And *you* plan to be late?" Silene asks. I only grin. She sighs, ushering Fionn down the hall as I turn left from my room and make my way toward my mother's chambers.

Pulling a key from my pocket, I unlock the door and step inside the suite, my eyes scanning the room as early morning light illuminates the swirling dust. I take in a deep inhale, desperately wanting to smell her scent lingering but knowing it disappeared from the space hundreds of years ago. I can almost see her spectral figure pacing back and forth, lecturing me on the importance of using my power for good as I practiced conjuring light orbs and releasing them. My lips quirk in a smile.

She was beautiful, known throughout Velmara for both her looks and her kind heart. She hated my father and did her best to keep him away from me when I was young. Her influence, though short-lived, shaped me into who I am today, and I'm so grateful that she kept me out of my father's clutches during my early years.

"I miss you," I whisper, emotion lacing my voice. Not for the first time, I wonder what she would think of the male I've become. Deep down, I worry she'd be ashamed of the flirty, irreverent, unfeeling person I pretend to be. I have so many memories of her teaching me what leadership meant, urging me to be a better ruler than my father. Even at eight years old, she insisted that it was my responsibility to uphold the values that the Velmaran Crown should stand for. I was born to live in the light, she would always say. Now I slink through the shadows, trying to secretly undermine my father while pretending to the Velmaran people that I don't care about them. I feel a sudden need to explain to the room what I'm doing, like somehow whispering my plans to go to Thayaria will serve as atonement to her memory. "I'm going to Thayaria to try and find something to stop father. You always told me it was beautiful there, always said I would visit someday. I can't wait to see it for myself and see your prediction come true." My eyes sting, and I have to pull myself away from the only room that has ever felt like home. "Goodbye, mama."

With my final goodbye, I turn from the room and lock the door behind me again, then create an intricate and invisible knot of magical light to seal it from any unwanted visitors. I let my hand linger on the door for another beat, then pull myself away and toward whatever fate awaits me in Thayaria.

A large crowd has gathered in the throne room, and I internally roll my eyes. *Of course he would make a spectacle of this.* My father sits on his gold throne, embellished with gems and carvings of various Velmaran landscapes. As I approach, his eyes bore into me. When I stand by his side on the platform, he hisses, low enough for only me to hear even as he keeps a smile plastered on his face. "You're late."

"Am I?" I feign. "Guess I forgot what time we were meeting."

He only stands to address the waiting crowd. They hush in reverence. "Thank you all for joining me as I send off my only child with the hope that we can repair Velmara and Thayaria's tenuous relationship. Thank you for sending Prince Hawthorne off to the Witch Queen," he yells loudly, the crowd booing at the mention of the Witch Queen. He holds up a hand and they quiet again. "I know you fear for the Crown Prince at the hands of the Witch Queen, but she has assured me that he will have every protection and comfort his station commands." *Highly unlikely.* "Though I myself have feared the Witch Queen and cowed from her magic, I believe it's time for us to offer her the olive branch of friendship. It is for her to accept, and, hopefully, through her friendship with Velmara, turn away from her wicked witchcraft. Prince Hawthorne and his entourage will be the first people, human or fae, to step foot on Thayarian soil in three hundred years. If anyone can restore Thayaria to what it once was and set the Witch Queen on the right path again, it is Velmara's Shining Prince!" he yells as cheers erupt.

The people are eating up his speech as palace scribes copy down every word to send out a copy to the kingdom. I'm seething by the time he finishes uttering his false pieties and grandstanding. His words from our conversation echo in my mind. *Thayaria is not as impenetrable as you may think*, he had said. What did he mean by that? I'm lost in thought when he calls the three of us forward to be aerstepped.

He pats me on the shoulder, and I want to grimace. Leaning closer to me, he uses his air magic to bring his whisper to my ears only. "Do not forget my threats, Hawthorne. And threats they were. You *will* get close to Witch Queen, or I'll make the lives of the two people behind you miserable in every way I know how."

With a flourish of his hand, tightness squeezes my body for several seconds, tingles dancing across my shoulders and down my back. My eyes briefly close, and when I open them, I'm standing on a wooden pier with a thick, eerie wall of mist rising above me.

Fionn reacts instantly, stepping in front of Silene and me, his hand hovering near the dagger I know hides at his waist. As one of the most powerful metal channelers in Velmaran history, Fionn wouldn't even need to touch the weapon to make it fly forward towards its target. The pier we stand on extends far into the ocean, waves jostling the wooden planks, though the massive wall of mist ahead of us is more concerning. Shimmering blue gray swirls from the surface of the sea and up, even my strong fae sight not able to find where the hazy wall ends. Nothing is visible through it. If I didn't know that a kingdom lay on the other side, I might think this is the end of the world, some line marking the boundary of the Four Kingdoms. I wonder how Queen Laurel manages it. Though I've heard stories about it almost my entire life—being nearly the same age as the Queen—the barrier is even more impressive in person.

All magic users draw their power from the leylines of the aether running through our world and must channel its magic through a conduit. Most fae have an affinity for one, maybe two, conduits. No one knows the Witch Queen's conduit affinity, whether it's one of the five common conduits or something more obscure, and that's what leads so many to fear her mysterious power. Even Silene's theory that she has an affinity for all conduits doesn't explain the mist. My father's official story is that she's a blood channeler, meaning she uses blood to cast spell work, a forbidden form of magic considered evil amongst the fae.

Whatever her secrets, I will discover them and determine what to tell my father later.

The mist stirs, white ribbons moving lazily, before it parts. A group of fae step forward to greet us. An elderly fae with a long white beard and twinkling blue eyes and a tall and severe dark-skinned female stand in front of the group. The female radiates power, covered in weapons and striding confidently toward us. When she approaches, I bow, assuming this to be Queen Laurel. Silene nudges my arm.

"Welcome to Thayaria, Prince Hawthorne," the female says with a menacing smirk. "I'm Nemesia Nestern, the Chair of the Council of Advisors of Thayaria. I will be aerstepped to Velmara as your counterpart shortly, but I couldn't miss the opportunity to greet you as you enter Thayaria." So, this is the famous General who led Thayaria's armies in the war with Velmara. Her reputation for being nearly as fierce as the Witch

Queen herself tracks with the female standing before me. I scan the faces of the females behind Nemesia, wondering which is Queen Laurel and why she hasn't identified herself. I find only stoic expressions staring back at me. "You will not find Her Majesty among us, if that is what you look for. Queen Laurel does not need to be present to extend her will to the mist and allow you and your court to enter Thayaria."

I work to keep my face neutral. If the mist is the result of blood magic, I expected that Queen Laurel would need to be present with blood to cast spellwork to part the mist. We were briefed by my father's aethermasters that she may even require samples of our own blood to allow us to pass. I glance at Silene, wondering if she's thinking the same thing as me. Her face is thoughtful, brows furrowed, and lips pursed.

"Of course," I say with a wide and charming smile. "She must be very busy. Thank you for greeting us in her stead." Nemesia's gaze only hardens, and she squares her shoulders as she crosses her arms.

"Please do follow us through the mist barrier," the male says, his voice a bit kinder. "It's thick for about twenty paces, but once you're through you'll find visibility is rather normal the farther you travel from the coast." With that, the group of Thayarians turn and begin to walk back through the mist. I hesitate for only a moment, then push forward through my trepidation. Silene and especially Fionn need to see my confidence in order to take those steps themselves into the thick haze.

As soon as I cross the misty barrier, visibility is completely gone. I feel Fionn place his hand on my shoulder and hope Silene has done the same behind him. The mist has an *energy* to it I did not expect, almost like it's sentient. It laps at my face and hands, stroking gentle caresses across my skin. As it slides down my back, I relax, *certain* it's safe and won't harm me or my friends. When I reach the edge of the barrier and take my first steps into Thayarian territory, it lingers at my side for just a moment, like the tendrils don't want to let me go, before it snaps back into the barrier that is more wall than mist.

Fionn and Silene return to my side as we gaze at the small town in front of us. It looks just like any port town in Velmara, though with much more vibrant and lush foliage growing around it and the lingering mist that gives it a sleepy feeling. Rather than multiple slips, there's one long pier that extends beyond the mist for ships to dock at while Thayarians quickly unload the goods. Beyond the pier, stone buildings line a single thoroughfare through the center of the town.

Nemesia and the other advisors lead us down this road, several Thayarians carting our trunks on wheeled dollies or levitating them with practiced ease while staring at us with wary looks. We stop in front of a tavern named The Emerald Shell, covered in moss with horses tethered outside. The moss seems to shift towards Nemesia, as if she's the sun and it must turn toward her light. I find myself shrinking back from her imposing presence while she tracks every step with her fastidious gaze.

Nemesia finally introduces the male next to her. "This is Admon. In my absence, he'll serve as the Acting Chair of the Council of Advisors. He's your primary contact during your *short* time in Thayaria." Silene narrows her eyes at the gruff advisor, clear dislike written across her features.

"It's excellent to meet you, Admon," I say with a respectful nod of my head and a vibrant smile in an attempt to break the tension building. He returns the gesture while Nemesia bares her teeth, every inch the warrior whispered about. She looks like she wants to devour us.

"We have horses waiting to begin your journey to Arberly. Since it's still early morning, we'll sleep one night on the road, and should be to the capital by tomorrow evening," Admon informs us.

"We won't be aerstepped by Her Majesty or another air channeler?" Silene asks.

Admon smiles apologetically, the perfect picture of a courtier, while Nemesia sneers. Silene rolls her eyes dramatically in the direction of the General, and I have to smother my laugh. Only Silene would have the balls to roll her eyes at Nemesia Nestern.

"I'm afraid not," Admon soothes. "Our air channelers are all occupied elsewhere, many stationed at port towns like Echosa to make unloading ships easier. I assure you we will endeavor to make your journey as comfortable and swift as possible." He doesn't answer why the Queen is not available.

"Are you too delicate to travel by horse, Velmaran?" Nemesia gruffly asks Silene, eyes stormy with hatred. Silene stares the tall female down, not afraid of her bluster. Neither breaks their gaze, so I step in.

"We'll be glad of the opportunity to see more of this beautiful kingdom," I offer with all the princely charm I can muster. Nemesia turns her attention my way, while Silene keeps her eyes glued on the General, like she can't look away. But for what reason, I'm not sure.

"You would do well to attempt to *see* very little," Nemesia hisses, the threat clear, before turning on her heel and stalking away from us.

There is no word to describe the Witch Queen other than monster. *The Queen of Thayaria feels nothing, too lost in the bloodrage that comes when one starts practicing blood magic. Despite the Golden King's unending attempts to reason with her or appeal to her emotions, she remains unphased. She lusts for more power and is too far gone to see that she has completely destroyed her kingdom. The once picturesque landscape of Thayaria now decays with rot.*

The Witch Queen and Her Treachery

The journey is swift and comfortable, if a bit unnerving. We stay on well-traveled roads lined with trees that feel like they're watching us, the eyes of the Witch Queen trained on the unwelcome guests. Even Silene is affected by the haunting environment, staying quiet and close to either Fionn or me. Every so often, one of us jumps, sure we've seen something move in the forest around us. At one point, Fionn swears the plants are trailing after us. Admon only smiles, neither confirming nor denying Fionn's allegations. Toward the end of the second day, my horse pants with the strain of traveling uphill. We must be making the ascent to the capital city nestled amongst rolling hills and mountain peaks.

When we crest the final peak, the view takes my breath away. At the highest point of the city stands the palace, much smaller than the Velmaran castle. It's difficult to tell the material the residence is made from, as almost every inch is covered in creeping vines and dark blooming flowers. Part of the structure appears to be built into the side of the rounded mountain, with windows peeking out from grassy cliff sides. There are several moss-covered towers, and in the right light I imagine the architecture would simply appear to be part of the rolling landscape. The whole effect is frightening.

We continue to ride along the ridge, and the capital city of Thayaria appears, at odds with the eldritch palace. Arberly is a sprawling city with colorful buildings dotted across the knolls and valleys, surrounded on all sides by larger mountain ranges that look almost navy in the mist, the silver fog adding intrigue to the layers of tree-lined ridges. All manner of plants cover the buildings and roads. The whole city looks like one overgrown garden that effortlessly appears both wild and manicured all at once. Next to me, Fionn and Silene are as awed as I am, their mouths open and eyes wide. This is certainly not the dark and decaying landscape children are warned of when their parents threaten to send them here if they misbehave.

Admon walks to us, and his eyes twinkle with delight. "It truly is a magnificent view. Even I never tire of entering the city from this direction." We're led down a steep, winding road, then up and down several more slopes. The road we travel seems to skirt the city, a direct route to the palace. When we reach tall mossy gates, several guards come out and look through our trunks before grunting to signal us to move forward. "Your quarters will be on one of the lower levels of the palace, so that you may easily enter the city without needing to trek down, and then up, the many flights of stairs this palace is known for," Admon informs us. "You're free to enter the city at your leisure, but you should know the Thayarian people will be extremely wary of you. Very few have left this kingdom or even this city their entire lives, and as you know, we have had no foreigners here for a very long time. Even Queen Laurel herself rarely leaves the kingdom."

With that warning, Admon turns to lead us farther into the palace. We follow him along overgrown garden paths and through a door built into a hill. Inside, the palace walls are a dark gray, the lights dim and flickering. My skin prickles at the steep temperature drop as we trek farther into the heart of the castle. The place has an ominous feel, and I shudder to think what our rooms might look like. After several turns, we stop at two large double doors carved with various flora. Admon opens them, and we walk into a spacious and gloriously warm apartment.

"There are three bedrooms in this apartment," Admon tells us, "all connecting to a sitting room. Each bedroom has a private bathing chamber, and water in the bathing chamber is provided by a system of pipes connected to a hot spring a few miles away. Meals will be served in your sitting room every day, though you're free to find meals elsewhere in the city. The Council of Advisors has scheduled a formal introduction meeting tomorrow afternoon. Until then, I'll leave you to get settled, as I'm sure you're tired from two days of travel." Admon pauses for a moment to see if we have any questions. When we stay silent, he bows and leaves.

"It feels very... cozy," Silene says. The sitting room has a large bay of windows that appear to slide open onto a ground floor patio. In one corner is a fireplace, already roaring. Comfortable chairs are interspersed throughout, with a large table in another corner. Like everything in Thayaria, the space is also lined with plants that trail along the walls, adding to the pleasant ambiance.

Nothing this comfortable exists in the Velmaran palace. It is all gilded chairs that are cold and hard, formal spaces with lifeless decor—even in the private suites. I did my best to make my own suite comfortable, but even after centuries of seeking perfectly worn leather sofas, it's nothing compared to this sitting room.

"Do you think the plants can listen in on our conversation?" Fionn whispers, eyes wide in fear. Silene giggles, and I shake my head no, though I'm not actually confident in the answer.

"Let's get settled. I'm exhausted," I tell them.

Fionn peaks his head in each bedroom, then walks into the one closest to the external doors, ever the protective warrior. "This one's mine," he grunts. I give Silene a look that says she's free to choose her bedroom next.

She looks into the remaining two, then gives me a maniacal grin. "One of these is clearly meant for the Crown Prince of Velmara. Too bad he was stupid enough to give his courtier first pick." She stalks into what appears to be the larger bedroom as I follow. The room is painted gold, as if the Thayarians assumed I would want to keep the color of my country even in my sleeping chambers. The bed is massive, with a gold comforter and lush pillows. It has its own private patio, a table and chairs set there to admire the picturesque view.

I loathe the gold that covers the Velmaran palace and am more than happy to give this bedroom over to Silene. She collapses onto the bed, moaning at the soft bedding. "Thank the aether, these beds are comfortable. I could sleep for *days* after the chaos of last week." With a smile, I leave her to appreciate the bed intended for me.

The last remaining bedroom is smaller, though not by much. It's painted a deep green that relaxes my tense body the instant I step into the room. Had I taken the first pick, I would have chosen this bedroom. It feels warm, the camel leather sofa at the foot of the bed pairing perfectly with the velvet emerald comforter. The desk is a rich oak, and even the bathing chamber is dark and moody. After changing out of my dusty travel clothes, I settle into the comfortable bed and allow my exhaustion to lull me into a deep sleep.

The next morning, Fionn, Silene, and I eat breakfast together in the sitting room. We all slept well somehow, not concerned that it was our first night in a country that killed hundreds of our people the last time Velmarans were on these lands.

"What's our strategy for this Council meeting today? Do you think the Queen will be there?" Fionn asks.

I nod. "I assume she'll formally greet us today. I plan to be observant and do my best to keep my mouth shut."

Silene shakes her head up and down vigorously in agreement. "Yes, Thorne, *keep your mouth shut*, you impulsive rake." Fionn chuckles, and I give Silene a wink. "What of our betrothal? Are we officially engaged here?" she asks.

"What do you think?" I ask, sure she has an opinion.

She frowns, pausing to consider the options. "We let them continue to believe whatever it is they've heard. If they bring up the betrothal, then we're a couple. If they don't, then we get to finally be rid of each other," she taunts, and I laugh before giving her my agreement. If they do think we're betrothed, I'll have to find a way to establish that it's a political arrangement made by my father if my plan to charm Queen Laurel into spilling her secrets is going to work.

A knock at the door reveals Admon.

"If you're ready," he says from the doorway, "I'll show you to the Council chambers." I nod, and we follow him out the door and down the hallway we entered last night. He stops before a large staircase, then looks back at us. "I must warn you," he says, a twinkle in his eyes, "this palace has many floors, and the Council chambers are at the very top. We are in for a vigorous walk. Since we're at a higher elevation than you're unused to, this may be a difficult trek." Fionn puffs out his chest a bit, huffing at the implication that he's not capable of conquering stairs. Silene and I trade glances in silent laughter.

Thirty minutes later, all three of us, Fionn included, are out of breath. Admon seems perfectly fine. "You weren't kidding when you warned us about the stairs," I barely gasp out. Admon only smiles and leads us down another dark and cold hallway and into a large Council chamber.

I'm surprised at the number of advisors here. There must be at least thirty in the room. While my father has many courtiers and nobles, his formal list of advisors is extremely short, holding only two names.

Admon notices my surprise. "Her Majesty Queen Laurel is a ruler who seeks the opinions of many when making decisions. The Council of Advisors is quite large, as you can see. Not everyone attends every meeting, but they have all shown up to meet Velmara's Crown Prince." I only nod, then follow him to the head of the large square table, where four seats have been arranged. He gestures for Silene, Fionn, and me to sit.

Once again, I search for the Queen, and once again, Admon informs me, "Her Majesty will not be joining us. She has delegated relations with Velmara to her Council. You will meet with sub-committees of the Council for various topics throughout your time here." I bristle, feeling somewhat insulted that the Queen is not even attempting to meet me or welcome me herself. Before I can say anything, Admon stands and addresses the room. "As the temporary and acting chair of the Council of Advisors, I am delighted to introduce you to His Royal Highness, Prince Hawthorne Vicant, Crown Prince of Velmara. We are pleased to extend you our welcome, Prince Hawthorne. We are also pleased to meet your betrothed, Miss Silene Kalmeera, as well as your advisor, Fionn Solanum. Welcome to Thayaria."

So much for staying silent on our betrothal. I inwardly sigh. They must have been told by my father when he wrote to Queen Laurel requesting permission for me to bring two advisors along. It seems he's not letting me out of this betrothal, even if it would have made it easier to get her to trust me. The room of advisors claps quietly, an odd reaction to being introduced to the first strangers to enter their lands in three hundred years.

Admon continues. "Today's meeting is an opportunity for the advisors to introduce themselves. Once the room has completed introductions, we'll ask for a list of topics you'd like to prioritize so that we can arrange a series of meetings for your first weeks here."

All thirty plus advisors tell me their names and the sub-committees they're assigned to as they offer their pleasantries and welcomes. I try my best to commit every name to memory but can only keep track of a few. Aria, who leads the small business programs, is an attractive female who bats her lashes at me after I give her a dimple-revealing smirk. Lionel, a human with blonde hair and a red beard, runs the kitchens. Nathaniel, an extremely tall fae with a face that makes him look like he's perpetually keeping a secret, is in charge of infrastructure for the kingdom.

When the Captain of the Royal Guard introduces himself, I attempt to flirt with him, not out of any real interest in the straight-laced male, but to see what boundaries may exist there. He'd prove a useful ally in getting closer to the Queen, especially if I could charm him enough to reveal her guard rotation or schedule. He wouldn't be the first male I've wooed in order to get what I want. Despite my best efforts to wink and make suggestive comments, he only responds awkwardly, like he's unsure what to do with the interest of the Crown Prince of Velmara.

The introduction takes what feels like ages and is not at all what I expected. I assumed the Queen would greet me with veiled threats and tell me to stay out of her way, then show a small bit of power to keep me in line. I certainly didn't expect I'd have to actually work while I was here.

There are dozens, maybe more, sub-committees, all with special topics and agendas. Many of the advisors make their plea to be my priority in the first weeks. One of them, a mousy and matronly looking female fae named Margery who introduces herself as the Minister of Education for Thayaria, makes an impassioned speech about desiring my expertise in light channeling at the school in Arberly. They have several light channelers who are struggling without teachers. That piques my interest, and I make a mental note to make that one of my priorities.

When the last of the advisors is done introducing themselves, Admon looks at me expectantly. I don't know what to do, but Silene steps on my foot to urge me to act. I stand, trying to imitate the way I've seen my father give speeches to his nobles.

"Thank you for the warm welcome. Silene, Fionn, and I are grateful for your hospitality and are thrilled to be here in Thayaria." I flash my most charming grin, and I see it working on several of the younger advisors. Though I was nervous when I first began speaking, my next words surprise me. "I would like to learn more about your magical education system, your trade agreements with other kingdoms, and your programs for supporting small family-owned businesses." I didn't realize I cared about those topics, but I find myself excited at the prospect of learning more.

Silene steps on my foot again. "I'll discuss this with Silene and Fionn and provide a thorough list to you by tomorrow," I add for Silene's benefit, and she relaxes. I've apparently said what she wants me to say.

Admon claps his hands. "Excellent, Your Highness. We'll await your missive and begin setting up the additional meetings." With that, he dismisses the Council, and the advisors all stand and begin to make their way out of the chambers.

"Admon," I say. He turns to me. "When will I meet Her Majesty, Queen Laurel? I expected to have been introduced by now."

"Her Majesty has many other responsibilities. As I said, she has wholly entrusted the Velmaran relationship to her Council. I am to be your primary point of contact."

I don't respond, reading between the lines. They don't intend for me to meet Queen Laurel.

Only the most powerful of light channelers can bend light to mask or cloak themselves and remain invisible in certain circumstances. Even rarer is the ability to bend light around another person or object.

The Unabridged History of Magical Orders, Volume I

"Thank you, Your Majesty," the fae baker says, bowing to me, eyes filled with tears of joy. Today I'm holding court, a monthly open-door session where citizens can petition me or my advisors on any topic. The male currently walking away came because the price of flour has risen significantly, cutting his margins in half. I assured him I would instruct the Chancellor of the food imports sub-committee to look into procuring more grain to increase supply and thus decrease prices for the goods. It should be easy enough to do after the recent Forum negotiations.

The next petitioner is called forward, and I struggle to remain upright and listening. After five hours of this, with another hour to go, my mind wanders often. My parents used to trade off when they held these sessions so that they remained sharp and alert, able to respond to the people with empathy and attentiveness. I don't have the luxury of a partner, so I acutely feel my aching back and foggy attention.

I take a cursory glance over the crowd. The audience is settled on benches in a half-moon shape that take up most of the chamber floor, and a large walkway splits the room in two. At the beginning of the day, the seats were nearly at capacity, filled with companions of the petitioners, guards, and curious onlookers. However, as the day droned on, and the list of scheduled citizens dwindled, so had the crowd. I start to turn my head back to the center of the room, when a silver glint catches my eye. I do a double take, concerned a weapon has been brought into the room. But I find nothing—it must have been the buckle of a belt. *I'm getting tired.*

"Your Majesty, thank you for seeing me," a petite woman I recognize as a seamstress from Arberly says. She looks nervous, hands clasped in front of her and shoulders hunched. "I'm afraid I bring upsetting news. My shop burned down in a fire two weeks ago after my apprentice left a candle burning. Many water channelers aided me in putting out the flames, but all of my fabrics and works in progress were burned. I have no means of procuring additional fabrics to fulfill my current orders, nor can I take any new clients. I am, as they say, destitute. I've come today to ask for a small business loan to purchase new materials. I will of course pay it back. You may not remember, but I've made several gowns for you. I hope the quality of my work shows that I'm fully capable of getting my business back on track." When she finishes, she bows again.

"Of course, I remember your dresses, and your shop, Alyss," I say, smiling at her. Her eyes widen in surprise when I use her name, but I make it a point to remember every single person who has ever worked for me, even if it takes me hours and hours of studying briefs made for me by advisors and servants. After I watched a guard of mine die during the war, and couldn't recall her name, I vowed that I would never forget a name again, and I haven't. "We have the small business fund for situations just like these. If the loan is paid back within three months, we charge no interest. The Chancellor who oversees the program, Aria, will walk you through the terms and assist you through the process. Please, follow her to one of the meeting rooms in the back."

"Oh, thank you, Your Majesty," Alyss says, tears building in her eyes. She wipes them away, then bows again before following Aria. I stretch my neck, then motion for the next petitioner.

While the next person pleads their case, my eyes wander to the specter who has sat in the back of the chambers all day, barely moving, his presence putting me on edge as I wait for him to make a move. While most wouldn't see him due to the light bending around him, the focused and sustained current of aether pooling in one place makes him light up like a beacon in the night to my trained eyes. And once I notice the massive gathering of magic, it's easy for me to peer through it at the person standing within its blaze.

It's been two weeks since the three ambassadors arrived in Thayaria. By all accounts, they've been kept busy by my advisors. And relegating the Thayarian ambassadors to the Council has also kept the advisors busy, giving me more time to search for the mole's identity. So far, I've had no luck, but I'm not giving up. I'll find that mole, even without Nemesia's help.

The specter stretches his arms above his head, bored by the daily workings of my kingdom. Interestingly, it's not the Shining Prince, or at least I don't think it is. The massive male who stands there has bronze eyes and blonde hair, and descriptions of Prince Hawthorne mention the olive, mossy green eyes that match his father's. This must be one of the courtiers the Prince brought with him—Fionn, if I remember the name correctly. I'm reluctantly impressed with Prince Hawthorne's ability to not only light bend around someone other than himself—from another room, no less—but to sustain it for this long. Rumors of his power appear to be true.

The jolt of energy that surged back through me as the Velmaran group entered Thayaria crosses my mind for the hundredth time this week. I don't often part the mist for those entering Thayaria, and I've never done it for outsiders, but I've never felt anything like that. It was as if the magic that makes up the mist was *excited* but also settled and content. I could swear it had whispered to me, words that I don't want to examine too closely.

Admon coughs, drawing my attention back to the petitioner in front of me. This time it's a burly human, stocky, and covered in tattoos. Humans are welcome to attend, and I have several human advisors, but they aren't frequent visitors of these particular court days. Because they often have very different issues than the fae, and because despite all of our efforts, humans and fae have a strained relationship at times, we offer separate court days for humans.

The man recounts the story of a human village fifty miles from here called Rusthelm that has fallen victim to an illness. Almost all the villagers are sick. They're desperate, explaining the human's willingness to appear during the fae court day. As he pleads, I once again notice a shining glint out of the corner of my eye, but when I turn my head in that direction, there's nothing there. My legs grow restless, and I struggle to pay attention to the man, mind wandering and body aching where it meets the hard and cold chair I sit upon.

"Your Majesty, we'd be so grateful if you could send healers to our village. We need to be able to take care of the children, and almost everyone is too sick," he says. "I'm one of the only adults who has not fallen ill."

"Of course," I respond. "Healers will be sent immediately." He bows low, thanking me profusely as I scan the room for the next petitioner.

There's no one left, and my stomach coils with uneasiness. While I'm grateful to finish early, we rarely do. Most court days we have to turn the people away and tell them to come back again later, even after we go hours past the scheduled end time. The lack of citizens gives me pause. Perhaps the Velmaran in the back of the room is planning something, hoping to catch me off guard. Unfortunately for him, I don't plan to wait around and find out.

"And what about you, Velmaran? Do you have anything to petition me for?" I ask as I obliterate the light surrounding Fionn so that he's visible to the whole room. He freezes, eyes locked on me in fear and panic. The warrior clearly did not expect to be seen or have the magic hiding him removed. The room around him is just as surprised, judging by the gasps and murmurs that echo through the space.

I wrap Fionn in vines, pinning him to the wall as I study the crowd's reaction, looking for any threat in the room. Almost everyone has stilled, unsure how to react. A group of several fae males have their shoulders squared off, gazes locked on me with what looks like a predatory gleam. My eyes return to Fionn, sure I'll find him eyeing that group with a knowing look. But he only stares at me in shock, nothing else—not even a glimmer of annoyance or frustration that a plan has gone awry. Another glint of metal catches my attention from behind me, and when I turn this time four fae males stand there with swords and daggers.

How did they get past the guards? Weapons aren't allowed in the palace by citizens, and every person is supposed to be thoroughly checked by the Royal Guard before they are let into these chambers. I'm furious, ready to demand they be removed and the guards be punished for their lapse in protocol, when the ground shakes beneath me. The room goes deathly silent. Even Fionn freezes in his trap of vines.

I scan the room closely, not sure what has caused the shaking. Fionn looks confused, but the fae with weapons only grin. The shaking intensifies as my eyes find Admon's across the room, his own expression furrowed. All the other advisors look concerned and afraid, not a single one of them giving away their own potential involvement.

I barely have time to shield my advisors and myself before the room explodes in bright light and a roaring boom. Despite the magical shield, I'm knocked to the ground, banging my head against the sharp corner of my chair. Ears ringing, I struggle to focus my eyes. Admon slumps in his chair, and at least three other advisors are catatonic next to him. I stumble as I attempt to stand, but a second blast knocks me back down. Unsure what's happened and head throbbing, I can't concentrate on the scene around me. Shapes and bodies blur across my vision while I fight the fogginess of my mind to make sense of them.

High pitched screams finally pierce through the haze of my confusion, and it brings me out of my stupor. I clear away the thick smoke that has gathered in the hall with my magic. Unconscious bodies cover the floor, dark crimson blood sprayed across the walls and ceiling. The sharp metallic scent of blood fills my nostrils as I inhale. Limbs have been severed, and those still conscious moan or scream their pain. Velmara—or whoever is responsible—will pay for their deaths. The combination of sounds and smells transports me back to the war, to the endless bodies that fell and the blood that constantly lingered around the war camp. But I don't crumple in fear—not this time.

Instead, I stand and gather magic around me as I seek out the source of the chaos, sure it's the Velmaran. But he remains immobilized in the back, pinned by vines and fighting to get out of their grip. With a roar, he breaks through the vise of ivy binding him with sheer strength and immediately begins helping people get out of the room. I'm about to kill him, slice through his neck with whatever weapon I can summon, when I notice him pick up a limp Alyss and carry her to safety. Were the Velmarans involved in this attack at all, or is it just a coincidence the warrior was here today? The frustration of not being able to act, unable to identify who to rage against for this violence, nearly tears me apart. My ire builds and builds, until the room shakes with my own magic. A gathering group in the center of the room catches my attention, distracting me from my anger for a brief moment.

A dozen Thayarian citizens, humans and fae alike, march toward me, all armed. The fae gather their magic to them. They've detonated some kind of magical bomb and are preparing to launch another. Before I can confront them, Royal Guards have surrounded the group of rebels with a windy spray of water. Two fae raise their hands and aerstep the guards to the other side of the room. They slam into the stone wall with a crack that makes me nauseous, bodies slumping to the ground. Swords that litter the ground lift and hurl toward the unconscious guards. They're impaled as I scream for healers to help them. Despite my frustration with the Royal Guard's failure today, the guilt of their deaths will haunt me. The blonde Velmaran runs into the fray, fighting the Thayarian attackers with the practiced ease of a well-trained warrior and saving several citizens from their blows. *That's interesting.*

Suddenly, a dagger flies toward me, the hum of the aether-directed blade unmistakable even in the noisy room. I shatter it into hundreds of pieces that fly in all directions. The eyes of a red-haired assailant widen in shock. He's tall, his red hair shoulder-length and framing dark blue eyes. I force the air from his lungs, choking him just long enough to send a message before I release him and leave him panting on the ground.

Using my magic to summon a sword into my hand, I stalk toward the group of assailants. Dewy mist collects around me and a strong wind whips my hair out of its braid. With each step, I pull more magic to me, careful that I only use magic connected to a conduit affinity. Water and light churn in a cyclone that I hurl at the group of fae, trapping them behind a wall of elemental magic.

Pointing the sword at the closest fae to me, I demand, aether barely lacing my voice, "Who sent you?" When they don't answer, I repeat myself, this time with so much magic in my voice that they're forced to their knees, my hesitation to use the aether-voice gone in my fury that they would attack me. Everyone in the room cowers from the commanding magic, and as the terrified expressions of my people reach me, a pang of guilt and shame washes over me. I push it down, determined to deal with my emotions *after* this attack is stopped. "Who sent you? Was it Velmara? Answer me, or I'll kill you where you stand." The room shakes with my power not my voice echoing with an other-worldly reverberation. My eyes cut back to the Velmaran, who has halted in his tracks and gone to his own knees, staring me down with a mixture of fear and awe.

The red-haired male looks at me, hatred burning in his eyes. "No one sent us," he spits out. "We're here for ourselves." He stands and spreads his arms wide. "We're the Sons and Daughters of Thayaria, and we won't be stopped. Your reign of witchcraft is over!" Dozens of swords and daggers rise up around me, the sharp blades cutting through the air with a zing. He's a strong metal channeler. Probably one of the strongest in Thayaria, since the trait isn't commonly found here. The weapons point toward my heart, but I only smile, vicious and feral. *Let him try and touch me.*

The moment the weapons move, I obliterate them with a single thought. No shards are even left behind, a light dust falling to the ground the only evidence they ever existed. I sigh inwardly at the slip in my cover, but move forward, hoping to distract the room from the magic I just displayed with more conduit-based magic. Vines creep through the windows and wrap themselves around the group of rebels, pinning them down in a drapery of green. The tendrils wrap several times around the head of the man who spoke, covering his mouth so he cannot speak.

"Guards," I command the group of Royal Guards who have arrived, Carex at their head. "First, bring all the palace healers in here and help those who are injured. These vines will hold the rebels, so take your time." I smirk. "Then, escort these *traitors* to the dungeon and chain them up. I'll take care of them, in due time. Carex—I expect a full investigation report from you on why the Royal Guards allowed *armed* civilians into this chamber." Carex blanches, but nods as he and his soldiers begin to act on my orders.

I stalk up to the rebel group and lower my voice, so only a few of them sitting closest to me can hear. "You're going to see just what my *witchcraft* can do." With one final pulse of magic, I squeeze the plants harder around them before turning away and pinning the Velmaran spy in place with another web of vines.

As I approach him, his expression betrays his absolute terror. I look directly into those bronze eyes, menace in my hard gaze. "The only reason you aren't dead where you stand is because I saw you helping the injured. Be sure you give your Prince *all* the details of what happened today. I want to make sure he knows who he's spying on." The male's jaw drops, and I revel in the moment as his throat bobs with a swallow.

I prowl closer, stopping just inches away. I lower my voice. "Send Prince Hawthorne my regards and tell him that if I *ever* catch any of you spying on me again, I'll kill you. This is your only warning." With the threat lingering in the air, I aerstep from the room, tightening the tendrils that hold the rebels in place as I go.

Thayarian ale should be carefully consumed, especially by those unused to its potent blend. Because of the recent isolation of the kingdom, Thayarians have had to become inventive to secure the things they used to import, such as alcohol. Their ale is created by water and plant channelers working together to ferment the grain quickly, and the thayar flower is used to amplify the process even further. This results in a unique flavor and the ability to knock even experienced drinkers on their arse with just a few pints.

A Brief History of Modern Thayaria

"She's fucking powerful," Fionn repeats for the third time. He came running back to our apartment, slamming the door behind him and looking at me with a terrified expression I've never seen from the warrior. Silene and I listened in stunned silence as Fionn relayed what happened at court. Some rebel group attacked, but before they could do any serious damage, Laurel stopped them.

"Some of her power made sense," Fionn says. "The first dagger thrown at her exploded into shards, indicating metal channeling. She just broke the blade apart, though she did it quick as a whip. I would have had a fifty-fifty shot of pulling that off. And the wind, light, and water cyclone that circled them also could have been regular channeling, as were the plants that ensnared the group. It would confirm that she has an affinity for all the known conduits. But the way she made those weapons just... disappear... It's unlike anything I've ever seen."

"I would just like to point out that the two of you have always insisted I was crazy for thinking the Queen had an affinity for all five conduits. Looks like I'm right," Silene says with triumph in her voice and a wide grin.

"Fine," I admit. "That does seem to be the case. But you have to agree the idea of that is... It's inconceivable."

"Yes, thank you, I'm incredibly intelligent, I know," Silene says after sticking out her tongue. Both Fionn and I roll our eyes. Despite her flippant and childish demeanor, I can see the gears turning in Silene's mind. "Did she appear to use any blood or speak any spells?"

"Not that I saw. But there was plenty of blood around her from the explosion. I don't know if she needs to physically touch it to channel or just have it around," Fionn answers.

"We just don't know enough about it, and that's the problem," I say with a frustrated growl. "We're not going to find anything out if all we ever do is meet with her never-ending Council of Advisors."

"She made it extremely clear that we shouldn't try another stunt like today, Thorne," Fionn says firmly. "It's too dangerous to attempt to spy on her again. I don't even know how she knew I was there."

"That's what troubles me the most," Silene offers. "Your light bending is impossible to spot. We've used it countless times, even around your father, and this has never happened. Did you slip at some point?"

"No," I say, firmly. "I know I can be a cocky bastard sometimes, but when it comes to my magic, it's warranted." I give them a crooked smile. "I didn't slip. I know I didn't."

"What do we do now?" Fionn asks. All three of us deflate, unsure where to go from here.

It's been *weeks* since we arrived in Thayaria, and all we have to show for it are endless meetings with mid-level advisors. We've listened to them plan how much grain to purchase, where to store it, whether they should subsidize it; sat in on discussions about applications for government-sponsored small business and arts grants; even observed a contentious vote regarding raising taxes in Arberly to fund more scholarships to the magical training school for gifted channelers. On and on the meetings go, never about anything that might give us insight into Queen Laurel's magic, pulling us from room-to-room with little time to rest or strategize with one another on how to get the information we actually want.

Today was the first day we attempted to get closer to the Queen, after one of the advisors let slip in a morning meeting on food security that she had to end early to attend court. It was a testament to how locked away we've been that we hadn't even heard of the public court date yet. We hastily hatched our plan and sent Fionn to listen, deciding it was too risky to send me.

"Let's go to the city tonight and try to learn more about this rebel group that attacked. We should see how the general public feels about today's events," I suggest. Silene and Fionn share a glance, and I sense their hesitation. "Look, very few people actually know what we look like, thanks to the Council of Advisors keeping us locked away. We can wear traditional Thayarian clothing and keep the hoods of our cloaks up. We have no idea how long we're going to be here. I for one do not intend to spend months—or aether-forbid, years—of my life holed up with the two of you in this apartment," I tell them with all the princely command I can muster.

"No way, it's too risky," Silene lectures.

"Come on," I whine, dragging out the last word. "I'm stir crazy in this palace, and if you don't let me out, I'll end up barging in on the Queen and demanding an audience. You know I have no patience and a tiny tendency to be impulsive."

Fionn snorts while Silene chews her bottom lip and narrows her eyes. "Fine. But only because you have a *massive* tendency to be impulsive, and I love a costume opportunity." She gives me a stern look. "But we have to be careful. We stick to crowded pubs. We wear disguises. No fighting, and absolutely *no drinking*." Fionn and I smirk at one another over Silene's head even as we nod our agreement.

As luck would have it, because of the public court day, many fae traveled to Arberly to petition the Queen and the streets are filled with citizens from out of town. An hour later, we're seated in a pub that's packed to the brim, every table crammed with fae drinking copious amounts of an amber liquid that looks unlike any alcohol I've ever seen. A bar maid walks around with a giant pitcher, refilling anyone who has the coin, and musicians are just setting up for the evening in the only space left. I nurse the ale Fionn purchased at the bar, surprised by how good it tastes, earthy and nutty all at once. Silene only rolled her eyes when he returned to the table with a glass for each of us, immediately breaking her no drinking rule.

"I'm surprised at how... high functioning everything in this kingdom is," Silene screams across the table at me, and I nod in agreement. "The sub-committees and the Council—it's all so civilized and organized. And the programs you described from today's court session... Those would never exist in Velmara."

"It's nothing like the stories told about the Queen abroad," I respond as loudly as I can. Fionn looks around, spotting a table that has just vacated tucked away in the back. He nods in that direction, and we follow.

"That's better," Silene's already hoarse voice says.

"I hate to admit it," I continue, "but I'm having... not fun... but I'm *enjoying* being an ambassador. I'm learning more than I ever would have under my father. Even if none of the topics are actually all that important."

"Your father would certainly never run a kingdom this way. He would have to give up too much control," Silene observes astutely.

We drop into a comfortable silence, watching the comings and goings of the pub. Despite the many fae from out of town, there still appears to be a large gathering of regulars in the middle of the room with several tables pushed together so they can play a card game I don't recognize. They greet one another as they enter, calling out and raising hands to indicate where their group has gathered. The space feels just like a Velmaran pub, maybe even a little more lively. For a kingdom rumored to be in squalor, the city of Arberly is thriving.

"So, here's what we know." Silene's catchphrase and sudden interruption of the silence makes me smile, while Fionn groans and rolls his eyes. "The Queen delegates almost all aspects of running her kingdom to an endless hierarchy of advisors and sub-committees. She rarely leaves Thayaria, but we don't really know what she *does* here, since her advisors seem to handle the day-to-day decision making. The kingdom is prosperous, despite being isolated..." Silene says the words matter-of-factly, ticking each item off using her fingers before trailing off.

I chime in. "At least some of her people feel comfortable enough to petition her for help with even minor things like the cost of flour. That means people aren't largely afraid of her. Despite my father's nonsense about being the Golden King, no Velmaran would come to him for help like that."

"But—we also know there's a rebel group opposed to her rule who believe her to be a witch," Silene adds. I nod.

"We know she's *fucking powerful*," Fionn adds, causing my lips to twitch in amusement.

"So we've heard," Silene teases him. "Anything else?"

"The aether is stronger here than anywhere else. I've always heard it was because of all the leylines, but now we know that's true," I add.

"What do you mean?" Silene asks.

"Well, it's hard to put into words..." I say. "When I tapped into the aether, I didn't have to exert as much effort to pull the current through the light. And it bubbled up so quickly

I almost sliced Fionn in half." He grimaces, and I give him a wink. "I was *obviously* able to control it, but it took me by surprise. I didn't notice it until today, though. Every day that I've water channeled it feels the same. Have you guys noticed anything with your magic?"

"I haven't used my magic at all," Fionn says, disappointed. "Not much need to guide weapons into their targets when you're sitting in diplomatic meetings all day."

"Depends on the meeting," I joke.

"My air channeling experience is the same as yours," Silene says. "Have you noticed anything else?"

I'm about to shake my head no, when I remember the mist. "Actually, I can't believe none of us remembered this and brought it up yet. The mist is somewhat sentient." Silene and Fionn look at me in confusion. "It... reacted when we walked into it, remember? It—I don't know—it *caressed* my face, like it was trying to figure me out. And it had an energy to it, like it was welcoming us in."

After a few beats, Silene says, "That didn't happen to me. It was just a thick mist."

"Same here," Fionn says. "Maybe you just have a thing for mist."

"I do not!" I exclaim. "It definitely touched me."

"And *where* would you say that it *touched* you?" Fionn croons, a twinkle of mirth in his eyes.

"Not like that, you bastard!" I yell, pushing him out of his seat. He grins widely at me, then heads back to the bar to get another round of drinks.

Silene furrows her brow, staring absentmindedly in concentration. "We need to learn more about the Sons and Daughters of Thayaria," she murmurs. "Figure out why they think she practices witchcraft, and whether the leaders of the group are genuinely afraid of her or whether they're just using a convenient narrative to take power for themselves."

"Agreed. It doesn't appear the attack has made anyone more fearful," I say, looking around the room at the continuous cheering and conversing of the patrons. "I think it's time we do a little *mingling*. Get to know the locals." I stand just as Fionn returns with a fresh pint of ale.

"Are we leaving?" he asks.

"No," I tell him. "Just going to stretch my legs a little and see if I can make any new friends."

"He's *mingling*," Silene mocks. "And I want to go on the record saying this is a bad idea. You may be many things, Thorne Vicant, but a commoner is not one of them. These people are going to spot you for who you are instantly."

I clutch my chest in mock offense. "I will have you know, I once convinced an entire tavern that I was a merchant from Delsar, exploring the Nivan Desert for new ways to transport goods in hot climates without magic."

Fionn roars with laughter, causing a few heads to turn in our direction. "No, you didn't, you bloody idiot. Everyone knew who you were and just played along because they didn't know what else to do." He and Silene trade looks of amusement.

I blink, genuinely shocked by the information, but recover quickly. "Well, no matter, people here don't know what I look like. It'll be fine. I'll challenge a few people to a drinking game or two, buy some tables a few rounds, and everyone will think I'm just a drunk looking to have a good time."

"You are a drunk looking to have a good time," Fionn and Silene both say at the same time. I only wink at them, then down my pint of ale in one chug.

I drink my way through the pub, making several friends who give me very little information but who enjoy the rounds of drinks I buy for them. A group of females celebrating the last night before their friend is married buy *me* drinks, and when I try to leave, they put up a hearty protest. Silene has to rescue me, and we make our way to another pub, this one a little less rowdy but still accommodating. I finally find a man who's happy to tell me all about the so-called witchcraft the Queen practices, though his description of her activities is wholly limited to sexual acts with willing fae males. Unsurprisingly, he has no reservations or concerns about her witchcraft, and simply hopes she'll call upon him one day to *serve* her.

"Creep," Silene whispers under her breath as she and Fionn drag me away. I protest, but my ale-addled mind can't fight off their combined strength.

At the third pub, at least half the tables are set up for gambling, so it's harder to make casual conversation. I want to join in, but Silene pulls me back, reminding me I don't actually know how to play the game they are calling Skran. Instead, we sit at one of the smaller tables and order a round of drinks. Silene's eyes watch the game with an intense focus that means she's scheming.

"Stay here," she eventually tells us before walking over to one of the tables and joining in on the game. Within half an hour, she's cleaned out all of the patrons. It's a testament to how females are regarded in Thayaria that the protests are jovial in nature. In Velmara, I'd be worried for Silene's safety if she'd bested a group of males out of so much coin.

"So much for staying under the radar," Fionn hisses at her as she returns to our table with a heaping pile of verdes, the Thayarian currency. Her expression is sheepish but proud.

"Well, I didn't *mean* to win so often. I was just trying to learn," she responds, causing both Fionn and me to chuckle. "The game is simple, really. There are five suits of cards, one for each aether conduit, and corresponding tokens. The goal is to trade with others to make as many sets of matching cards and tokens as you can. But you can wager on every aspect of the game—even whether another player's lying or not. You play until someone thinks they have the most matches, and they yell Skran. Then, everyone reveals their hands. The trick is to make people think you're lying and don't have very many matches." We just stare at her. "Come on, let's go to that empty table. I'll teach you both. Might as well have some fun!" We follow her to the table and proceed to lose our own coin to her as she attempts to teach us the local game.

A hooded figure sits down next to me.

"Care if I join you?" a male voice asks. Fionn and Silene stiffen, but I pat him on the back in a welcoming gesture.

"If you're willing to lose all your verdes to this one," I nod at Silene, "then be my guest."

He lowers his hood, revealing a fae with blonde hair, golden eyes, and a scar across one cheek. He grins at us, then places a small pile of the bronze coins on the table. "Deal me in."

We play several hands in silence, and he beats Silene at least twice. She takes the loss in good humor, though I can tell she's wary of him by her quick glances in his direction. Despite his skill, she still manages to rid us all of our initial starting bets.

"Looks like you're as good as they say," he says jovially to Silene. Then he looks at me. Voice low, he murmurs, "You've been inquiring about the Sons and Daughters."

"Is that a question?" I ask with a cocky grin as both Fionn and Silene tense.

"I might have a contact. What makes you interested in them?"

"Guess I just heard about today's events and decided I wanted to learn more," I say, truthfully, allowing him to read his own intentions into the statement. "Do you have information?"

"I might," he says cautiously. "But first I need to know you're serious. What do you think about the Witch Queen?"

I pause to consider my words carefully, choosing to rely on the truth. "I don't know much about her, really, other than what I hear from others. That makes me unsure of her intentions and whether she's fit to rule."

The male eyes me thoughtfully, then smiles. "Buy me into the next round of Skran and my next drink," he says. "We'll discuss some ways you can 'learn more,' as you say."

Silene's eyes are wary, and Fionn looks like he wants to bury a knife in the man's chest, but I only grin and agree to his offer, always the one in our group who's most comfortable around strangers. Silene deals us in again, this time with my own coin sponsoring our new *friend*.

"So, tell me about the Sons and Daughters," I say in a hushed voice after the first hand.

"They're a network of humans and fae who work to ensure the future of the sons and daughters of this kingdom."

"I see," I say, slowly. "And you aren't part of that network, is that right?"

He grins. "Exactly. I just know of them. Nothing more." We both know he's lying, but I don't press it. Silene and Fionn stay silent, listening intently while continuing to place bets on the game, leaving me to navigate the conversation.

"And does this network often target the Queen of Thayaria?" I ask.

"Today was the first act against Queen Laurel herself. Earlier attacks mostly targeted smaller villages across Thayaria. But I've heard there could be more planned. Rumors only, of course."

"Of course," I say, considering his words carefully.

"Skran," the stranger calls. Silene's lips twitch. She knows she's won. "Six pairs," he says.

"Nine pairs," Silene immediately responds, revealing her hand. She scoops the last of his verdes—my verdes—into her pile.

"Well, that's my cue to leave," the stranger says with a good-natured grin. He leans down close to me, and says, voice low, "There's a granary a few blocks from here, painted red. Go there and ask for a fae named Restin." With that, he stands and stalks to the door.

Fionn practically carries me home, Silene keeping a watchful gaze as I sing a bawdy tune all the way to the palace. While we were speaking with the stranger, I drank way more ale than I realized as he continued to wave over the barmaid for refills.

Once inside our apartment, they deposit me in bed and set several glasses of water on the bedside table. "You guys are the bessssssst friends a male could ask for," I slur out. They both roll their eyes, then close the door and leave me to my drunken state.

Thayarian ale must be strong, because while I drank a lot, a night like tonight back home wouldn't have made me this inebriated. The ceiling spins above me as I think about the Queen and the information I've learned. Suddenly, I have an idea and stand from the bed before crashing back down. I take a deep breath, then stand again, and this time it holds. Stumbling to the desk, I pull out a blank piece of parchment and dip a quill into the inkpot. Then I pen a scathing note to none other than Queen Laurel.

Sealing the letter with my signet, I stumble into the common area and lay the missive on the dining table, promising to send it in the morning.

Thayaria is home to a rare species of feline. Comparable in size to a wolf or deer, the sidhe
run wild in the mountains and moors of northern Thayaria. Many myths surround
these ancient and mysterious creatures. One of these tales attributes the sidhe to a circle
of witches who became trapped in the cat-like form after practicing blood magic, and
parents tell their children stories of the spine-chilling apparitions to get them to go to sleep
at night. Many notable monarchs in Thayarian history have kept a sidhe as a pet after
it unexpectedly followed them home and never left.

A Brief History of Modern Thayaria

What an insufferable prick, I think as I throw my magic against the wall of mist off the
northern coast. *A lazy, entitled drunk. Everything I've heard about him is true.*

I was seated at my desk, reading the morning missives, when a servant knocked on the
door. Hands trembling, she handed me a folded piece of parchment with *Her Majesty*
Queen Laurel written across the front in small, blocky script.

"Who is this from?" I demanded. "Why was it not delivered with the regular post?" I
immediately regretted my harshness when the woman stuttered out her apologies. It isn't
her fault that when I go too long without letting out my magic, I get a little testy. And I
was beyond *testy* this morning, sitting there running my mind over everything I needed
to fix. Alone.

"It's from the Velmaran Court, Your Majesty. I found it on their table when I delivered the breakfast tray to them this morning. I showed it to Sir Admon, and he requested I bring it to you straight away. I don't know which of the three wrote it, ma'am," the poor girl had barely whispered out.

"Thank you, you were right to bring this to me. Forgive me, I was unfamiliar with the handwriting." She left, and I ripped the letter open, unable to contain my curiosity.

Prince Hawthorne had written me a letter, demanding that I extend *common courtesy* and meet with him and his court. He'd also written several thinly veiled threats, hinting that if he continued to be pushed aside to advisors, he would write to his father, requesting to leave and citing *Thayaria's unwillingness to take any steps toward reconciliation.* He had concluded the missive with, *After yesterday's upsetting events, I would hate for news of Thayaria's internal struggles to cause my father to doubt the value in paying increased prices for thayar imports.*

I would never allow a letter like that to leave the kingdom, and I have of course been monitoring his correspondence... But there's always the possibility that Mazus has other ways of communicating with his son, and I certainly don't want the King of Velmara finding out about the political tension in Thayaria.

As soon as I read the letter, I aerstepped to the northern coast of Thayaria, generally known as The Spined Moors. It's the only place safe enough for me to practice my magic, especially when I'm this riled up from both the missive and yesterday's attack. Massive, jagged bluffs dot the landscape, the pointed peaks so unlike the soft rolling hills near Arberly, though they're hard to see this close to the coast and the mist barrier. Everything is hazy here, giving it an ominous look. With very few inhabitants, the region is wild, but something about it always feels like home.

The isolated and inaccessible region has been my magical refuge since I was nine years old and started displaying magic never seen before. My parents had lectured me relentlessly about keeping the true depth of my magic a secret, requiring that if I were to truly practice with my leymaster, Admon, we travel here. Admon and I spent countless hours out here, away from civilized society and keeping the secret my parents were so afraid to reveal to anyone.

With an exhale, I dig my feet into the soil beneath me and force myself to home in on the magical current of aether I feel coursing all around me. Most of that magic is concentrated in the leylines that cross the world, though *I* can sense aether in everything. It's why I can tell that the magic of Thayaria is declining along with the thayar. The decreasing blooms of the flower that defines my kingdom is the symptom of a much larger problem that I haven't told anyone about, not even Nemesia. I'm probably the only fae alive who can sense that less and less aether now rolls across Thayaria, and it terrifies me. I don't know what's caused it, but I fear it's my fault. The mist barrier I erected *must* take massive amounts of aether to sustain itself, and I worry it's slowly draining Thayaria of its magic. It's the most logical explanation.

I draw in as much as I can bear to hold, even though I fear that any massive expenditures of magic will further exacerbate the decline. Then I focus my intentions on the misty barrier a dozen yards away off the coast. With a shrill shriek, I hurl magic at the murky wall like I've done countless other times, my thoughts concentrated on permanently lifting its protection. The air around me crackles, the sky illuminating with streaks of lightning. The mist shimmers like I've never seen before, and for a wonderful, exhilarating moment, I think I've finally done it, finally lifted the curse of the mist off the backs of the Thayarian people.

And then the current settles, the magic returns to the leylines of aether running through Thayaria, and my hope is crushed again. I sigh, knowing I should have known better. It's been three hundred years since that fateful day in the war with Velmara, and despite all my efforts, I still cannot lift the mist that may be leeching my kingdom dry of its magic.

I want to sag in defeat and let my body crumple with the shame I feel. Instead, I go through my usual exercises, mostly ones I developed with Admon to help me with control. I gather aether again, my skin humming with the buzz of power, then force myself to release it without expending any of it, directing it back into the leylines around me. Then I focus on leylines as far away as I can sense, forcing myself to ignore the thrum of energy from the nearby threads. I wrench aether across thousands and thousands of miles into my body. With that magic, I call the tiniest spark of fire into my palm and maintain it, only allowing the smallest drip of magic to seep into its blaze. Without training, my magic is like a battering ram or a dam lifted for the first time in decades. On instinct, aether wants to pour out of me in massive amounts, more than most fae can even *fathom*, much less survive channeling. Practicing control and releasing small amounts of aether ensures that when it really matters, when my emotions are heightened and I'm reacting on instinct, I don't blow a massive hole in whatever structure surrounds me, or worse. I train to make absolutely certain that I don't have another incident like the one that erected the mist ever again.

I repeat these exercises, among others, for hours, careful that I limit the aether I let pour into me. I'm afraid that if I go too far, I'll topple whatever delicate balance still exists in the magic around me. I practice until I'm shaking with exhaustion and an icy sweat coats my brow, a punishment for what I've forced my people to endure. Most fae eventually tire when using large amounts of magic—the ability to channel aether is not limitless, even for me. I just have a much higher tolerance than others, able to go hours without tiring. But that's not what makes me so exhausted today. My magic is getting harder to use and even harder to control. Something about it is *heavy* after training all morning. The feeling isn't new—for the last several decades, I've felt the burden of my magic physically, and it's been progressively getting worse. I have this burning *need* inside of me to exert my magic, to take it to its limits and then keep pushing. Yet when I do that, like today, I feel completely broken afterward—like I'm made up of a series of pieces delicately stitched together, and the seams are fraying. Whether that's because something is happening to my magic, or I'm just incredibly stressed and my magic is reacting, I cannot say. But I worry what will happen when those threads that keep me contained burst open.

Drinking deeply from a water skin before sitting down, I pull the letter out of my bag and read it again, trying to parse real threats from grandstanding. What I know of the Prince's rash and raffish personality don't align with the carefully crafted intimidation in this letter. They certainly don't align to the display of power I saw from him during the court session. He's supposed to be uninterested in anything other than drinking and meeting his next conquest, incapable of this level of political maneuvering.

I need to meet him. I huff out a dry laugh. If he wants to meet the *Witch Queen*, then he shall meet her. I gather my things and aerstep myself back to my room, limbs heavy and body aching all over. Sitting down at my desk, I pen a reply to the Prince.

Your Royal Highness, Prince Hawthorne, Ambassador of Velmara,

Allow me to extend my deepest condolences for not meeting your expectations of diplomatic propriety. I fear I have never been exposed to Velmaran customs on the matter of emissaries, as my last and only meaningful encounter with your kingdom was the war between our two peoples. While I do meet with your father the King on occasion as required by the Forum of Royals, I confess those to be unhappy affairs in which the conventions of ambassador relations have never been discussed. When I agreed to this arrangement with His Majesty King Mazus, there were no terms set out regarding my attentiveness. I am highly doubtful that your father meets regularly with my emissary in Velmara. Nevertheless, I will agree to a meeting with you, if only to demonstrate to you my commitment to upholding the spirit of this agreement. When you write to your father, I expect I will see assurances of your happiness in Thayaria when I review such correspondence. My advisors will arrange our audience. In the meantime, please do feel free to alert me if the tediousness of ambassador work proves to be too much for you, and I shall direct my advisors to keep you entertained with more pleasurable activities.

Yours truly,

Her Majesty, Queen Laurel of Thayaria

I fold the parchment, address it to the *Velmaran Ambassador*—not the Prince—then seal it with my signet. I place the envelope in the bin reserved for outgoing messages and push the haughty prince from my mind.

Two days later, I've selected a black flowing dress that dips low between my breasts, revealing cleavage and the soft skin of my stomach. It's low in the back as well, gathering at my waist with a velvet sash that lays delicately over the semi-transparent black gossamer that trails the floor. My thick thighs are on full display through the gauzy material, and I've sheathed a ceremonial dagger on my thigh, visible through the dress. The velvet bodice is embroidered with thayar flowers in deep mahogany, and the thin straps that go over my shoulders resemble twisting black vines. It borders on improper, and I'd never wear something like this to hold court, but for an appearance as the Witch Queen, it will do nicely. The *Shining Prince* will learn he should be careful what he asks for.

I've even allowed attendants to do my hair, and the auburn locks flow in waves down my back under the laurel and thayar crown. My eyes are lined in thick kohl, and I wear maroon lip paint. The female staring back at me in the mirror looks feral, and my lips turn up in a simpering smirk. I even wear a ring that is sharp enough to pierce skin, hoping his eyes are keen enough to see it and assume I use it to draw blood for my *spells*.

Let him think me the Witch Queen, blood mage and terrifying sorceress.

Lunaria stalks over to me, nuzzling her head against my leg. "Want to go with me to terrify some Velmarans?" I ask. Her eyes glow with understanding, as eager as I am to don this mask.

Instead of walking down the endless stairs that I absolutely loathe to reach the throne room, I aerstep myself and Lunaria to the small chamber behind the hulking mass of vines and flowers that make up the Thayarian throne. It's rarely used, as I hate the formality and imposing feel of the space. I hold court days in smaller, less formal receiving chambers. But for this meeting, I'll make an exception. Lunaria stretches her front legs, then her back legs, before turning to me, eyes bright and menacing. Just before I enter, an idea strikes, and I will the massive space beyond to fill with an eerie mist. I dim the lights as well, then enter the throne room.

The magical adjustments have worked, and the space is ominous. Dark green marble floors line the room, glittering in the dim and misty light. The stone walls are covered in ivy, and several potted plants line the walls. I coax the ivy to slither across the floor and will the metal ivy on the throne to do the same. Admon catches my eye from the chairs that have been set up for a handful of advisors and gives me a twinkling look as I prowl toward the throne, Lunaria at my side. She looks terrifying in this environment, her sleek black coat and golden yellow eyes a warning to any who might cross me. I sit on the cold throne, and she stands at attention by my feet, gazing out at the room.

"Bring them in," I order, waving my hand in a dismissive fashion. Two guards open the massive, gilded doors that swing outward to reveal the three Velmarans, who walk in and bow deeply. The Prince stands in front, his onyx hair swept back from his face and perfectly messy. I tense at the sight of his familiar eyes, the same green-brown color that haunts my dreams even still. Searching his face for other similarities to the King of Velmara, I realize he's remarkably handsome, just like his father. He has a strong jawline and full lips, though the effect is alluring rather than off-putting like Mazus. He's tanned, like most Velmarans, and keeps his dark beard trimmed short.

Wearing a fitted suit of deep red, the gold accents shining in the light with what I suspect is his doing, he cuts a striking figure. Tall, muscular, and confident, I understand why he has a reputation for charming females and males—women and men—alike. His posture is effortless, like he belongs in any room he walks into, and something about his presence... energizes me. I shift in my seat slightly at the feeling. His eyes widen in surprise for only a moment before recovering.

He grins with an alluring smile and an air of forced charm, before pushing up his shirt sleeves. The movement brings my attention to his forearms, their flexing the only sign of his discomfort. The tan skin there makes my mouth go dry, and I hate the way I react to him. I scowl to hide the effect he has on me, which only makes him grin wider, accentuating the dimple on his right cheek. I stare at it for a beat too long, mesmerized, then chastise myself for studying him that closely. He takes a single step forward but stops when Lunaria bares her teeth in a hiss.

"Good girl," I murmur to her, low enough so only she can hear. Inexplicably, the Prince must hear me, because his lips twitch with mischief.

The massive warrior from the court day stands behind him—Fionn—honey-blonde hair pulled into a bun at his nape. He wears the leathers of a soldier, the same he wore the day of the attack, and his bronze eyes are wide in fear that he doesn't, or can't, hide. Beside him is a fae female, who must be Prince Hawthorne's betrothed. She's short, with coiled black hair and intelligent eyes. I immediately identify her as the brain of their triad. She doesn't look afraid, not in the way the warrior does, but her expression is wary and studious as she takes in the throne room, Lunaria, and finally, me.

Prince Hawthorne smiles again, then says, "It's a delight to *finally* meet you, Your Majesty."

The Thayarian throne room is as dangerous as it is alluring. With windows open to the vines that cover the palace facade, monarchs have access to a deadly weapon. It is also rumored that the room itself is built atop a carefully maintained thayar greenhouse, providing an extra magical boost to those who sit on the throne of laurel.

A Brief History of Modern Thayaria

My first thought when my eyes land on the Witch Queen is that no one has ever spoken of how beautiful she is. She's also fucking terrifying, especially with all the fog, slithering vines, and dim lights that I'm sure are her doing. Despite the dark makeup, her eyes are bright, piercing and viridescent—her milk-white skin providing the perfect backdrop for the beautiful green to shine. I have to force my gaze away from them. Her figure is all soft features, from the small, button nose to the voluptuous legs on full display in a tantalizing dress that leaves little to the imagination. A dress that exposes too much to keep my eyes from dipping to her chest. My mouth goes dry at her full breasts and curvy figure, and I try to cover it with a wide smile that I know exposes my dimple. Her delicate, heart-shaped lips purse in suspicion, and I take an involuntary step toward her, unable to stop my body from moving closer. Her features sharpen at the same time the enormous black feline next to her stands, arches its back, and hisses. I swear I hear her murmur praise to the hellish beast, and my lips quirk involuntarily. She adjusts herself, causing her long reddish-brown hair to sweep across her breasts, drawing my attention back to them and emptying my mind of all rational thought. I take a deep breath and intentionally move my eyes to the cat that now looks like it will gouge my eyes out with a single swipe of its massive paw. *Get it together.*

When I woke the morning after our pub-crawl with the worst hangover in a hundred years, I panicked the moment I saw that the letter I only vaguely remembered writing the evening before was gone. Silene and Fionn had stared at me in horror as I told them of the drunken missive I'd written, with threats and demands so aggressive we were sure she'd kill us immediately. I'd waited in anticipation all day, my head pounding and my body aching from the ale.

When her reply came, we all read it together, not sure what to make of the cheeky response. It matched the aggression of my letter, maneuvering through her own threats with expert precision and calling me out for complaining about doing the work of an ambassador. But it was also... funny. Or at least, I thought it was. She called her interactions with my father 'unhappy affairs.' It was also more honest than I expected, and that gave me hope I might make a real ally of her.

"It's a delight to *finally* meet you, Your Majesty," I say as I stand in front of the imposing monarch. *Shit, why did I have to stress the 'finally.'* Recovering, I add, "I confess the letter I sent was written in a... compromised state of mind. Your Thayarian ale is more potent than I expected." I try to look sheepish, dropping my eyes to the ground and rubbing my hand on the back of my neck before looking back up at her with my brightest and most magnetic smile. If I have any hope of recovering this situation, I need her to find me unthreatening and attractive. Thankfully, that's my specialty.

"I find that when inebriated, one's truest emotions and feelings come to the surface," she says coolly, not missing a beat. *Fuck, this is going poorly.* Vines inch closer to my feet, not quite wrapping around them, but the threat of her is clearly conveyed.

"While the letter may have expressed the spirit of my emotion clearly, it certainly did not reflect my true intentions. That was the ale talking." I wink. She stares me down, expression unmoved, apparently immune to my charms. After what feels like a lifetime of tense silence, her lips finally quirk, barely visible.

"Thayarian ale is indeed potent, due to the unique way in which it's made," she acknowledges, giving me the smallest bit of slack on the line she's hooked me on, though the vines at my feet don't move away. One of them inches up my leg, and I look at her sharply. This time, a challenging smile full of mirth crosses her lips before the vine returns to the ground. She wants to get a reaction from me, and that thought is more exciting that it should be.

"Indeed," I say, ignoring the threat before I gesture to Fionn and Silene. "May I introduce Fionn Solanum, my close friend and advisor, and Silene Kalmeera." I intentionally don't introduce Silene as my betrothed. Fionn and Silene both bow again but remain silent.

"Welcome to Thayaria, Fionn and Silene," the Queen says. "I trust you've found your accommodations comfortable." They both nod. Then she pins me with a look, all the warmth drained from her voice as she says, "So, Prince Hawthorne, you requested this meeting. What is it you wished to discuss with me?"

Right to the point. I squirm under her calculating gaze, sure she could wink me out of existence like she did the weapons when the rebels attacked. I smile through my discomfort, used to these kinds of interactions from a lifetime living with my father in the Velmaran Court.

"I simply wished to meet the notorious female whose court and kingdom I'm to spend my time getting to know. This arrangement is an extension of friendship, is it not? I'd like to extend that friendship to the monarch herself." I flash another grin, though she seems impervious to them.

"Well, you've met me and have delivered your *kind* words of friendship. If that's all, you're dismissed," she says coldly, then stands. The advisors seated several yards away in the room stand with her.

I tense, knowing this could be the last time I see her if I don't offer her something. "Wait," I rush out. She lifts a single brow. "I discovered interesting... information about the Sons and Daughters of Thayaria while out drinking. I thought you'd like to know what I uncovered." The room shakes slightly with what I think is Laurel's power. *Fascinating.*

Pressure on my legs reveals vines that wrap up my thighs. They squeeze tightly and pin me in place, only inches away from my *favorite* part of my body. I barely have time to consider what castration by plants would feel like before there's a prickling sensation on my neck. A small dagger made of water hovers right near my jugular. She's got me entirely at her mercy, and something tingles low in my stomach at that thought. Am I *attracted* to the Witch Queen? The idea is unfathomable, and yet, I can't look away from her full hips and the curve of her waist.

The familiar zing of a weapon being unsheathed brings me out of my lust-addled haze, Fionn's huff behind me telling me he doesn't like Laurel's antics one bit. The dagger at my neck only presses in harder, shockingly sharp for something made of water. It doesn't break skin—yet—but I have no doubt it could if she wanted it to. I can't stop my heavy breathing, my nerves reaching a breaking point even for me. Within minutes, the meeting has devolved into threats and drawn weapons. Silene appears at my side, though she has the sense not to draw a weapon or call on her magic. The tension in the air is as thick as the swirling mist the Witch Queen conjures around us.

"Easy, Fionn," I murmur to diffuse the tension. He sheaches his weapon, and the vines release their grip slightly. The dagger disappears, though I know she could conjure it again instantly if she wished.

The Queen pauses for a moment, staring me down with those enchanting eyes, then sits again. She studies me closely, and I can't stop the shivers that wrack my body under her assessing gaze. I'm supposed to be seducing her, and yet *I'm* the one who can't look away. The silence stretches as the vines around my legs fully unwind. For a moment, I think she won't respond, that she's waiting for me to speak again.

"Everyone out," she finally commands. Her advisors look surprised, eyes wide and mouths open.

Admon stands. "Your Majesty," he begins, but she cuts him off.

"I said, everyone out. I wish to speak to Prince Hawthorne *alone*." This time, aether laces her voice, and I'm forced to my knees in shock along with everyone else in the room. *She's stronger than me.* The realization is as exhilarating as it is terrifying.

Beside me on the ground, Silene murmurs a heated, "What the hell are you doing?"

"Wasn't going well, had to improvise," I whisper back as the three of us stand again. Her advisors file out of the room, trading wary glances between themselves.

"That order applies to you as well, Ambassadors Kalmeera and Solanum," she says, though her voice is softer this time. At least her ire only seems to be directed toward me. Fionn and Silene hesitate, turning taut expressions and worried eyes to me. I give them a subtle nod that tells them I'll be fine, and they slowly back out of the room, their training keeping them from showing their backs to the threat.

The monstrous cat by Queen Laurel's side stretches its legs and prowls toward me while the Witch Queen and I study one another in silence. The creature slowly circles me, eyes bright and predatory.

"This one doesn't count as *everyone*?" I joke, nodding to her pet. "I wouldn't mind you ordering *it* away." The cat hisses in my direction, and I can't help but take a step back, though I try—and likely fail—to make it look natural.

Queen Laurel doesn't acknowledge the comment or react in any way. She's as controlled as my father. Sitting on the edge of her throne, posture mimicking the sinister feline who now sits directly in front of me, she narrows her eyes. True fear enters my gut now, regretting sending Fionn and Selene away.

"And why, Prince Hawthorne, were you in a position to uncover information about the Sons and Daughters? Did you seek them out?" she asks in a low voice, aether pulsing slightly, and it's all I can do to remain standing. The room trembles around us. Centuries at my father's side have taught me when I'm in real danger, and this moment might be the most at risk I've ever been. Vines slowly inch up my legs again, ready to shackle my wrists and ankles.

"I sought them out, yes" I say slowly, "but only to gather information that might help me better ally with you. I wish for us to build a true friendship while I'm here." I make a point not to wink or smile, trying to convey my seriousness at the situation. Something tells me flirting will not get me through this meeting, and I abandon my plan to seduce her, at least for today. She laughs, cold and unfeeling. Without warning, my lungs collapse, and I try to bring my hands to my throat, but some unseeable force pins them to my sides. The Queen's eyes are bright with malice as I stand there suffocating.

"I don't believe for one second that Velmara and King Mazus desire true friendship through this arrangement," she spits out. Breath returns to my lungs, and I gasp, my body slumping. Her feline companion stalks around me again, eyes aglow in the dark and hazy room. My palms sweat, and I feel the Queen's power pulsing in the thick mist around me. One wrong move, and she'll unleash its fury.

Taking a deep breath, I make a rash and impulsive decision. "I didn't say that Velmara or King Mazus desired true friendship. I said that *I* do." It's a risk to speak this plainly. Queen Laurel could easily tell my father of this conversation. The information could help her negotiate even better trade terms or could get her out of this entire arrangement. But if I'm going to get any information out of her about blood magic and what my father might be planning with the missing thayar, I need her to see me as an ally.

Her eyes widen for just a moment, but she recovers quickly. "And how would a *true friendship* with *you* benefit me, Prince? You're the irresponsible prince of a kingdom an ocean away, the son of my greatest enemy, who could rule for another thousand years. From everything I've heard, your father has cast you aside with this arrangement, and you're unfit to rule. Even when I gave you access to the inner workings of my government, you scoffed at being asked to put in real work and complained that you had not instead been lavished with attention from the Queen."

Her words sting, too close to my own insecurities, and yet so disconnected from who I *want* to be. Frustration rises in response. The light in the room brightens with my magic, and I can feel every droplet of water that creates the hazy fog in the room. It's time to show her I am not some powerless prince she can order around as she pleases. She may be more powerful than me, but only just.

My fear replaced with anger, I snarl at her. "You know nothing about me. I took *offense,* not at the opportunity you provided me to do 'real work' as you call it, but at the lack of dignity and respect offered to me since I arrived. I didn't expect you to lavish me with attention, but I did expect you to *greet* the Crown Prince of the kingdom who now provides you with the lion's share of your revenue. And having me listen in on endless meetings about inconsequential topics isn't 'work'—it's babysitting. So don't pretend to be offended by my displeasure at being farmed out to your least important advisors to fill my days with meaningless activity."

I've lost my temper, and now I can't stop. The light in the room is blazing, the mist completely burned away by my magic. I let her get the upper hand initially, but I'm the closest equal she has across the Four Kingdoms, and she should be reminded of it. Lightning dances across the ceiling above her head, and spears of light rush past her, barely missing striking her, my aim perfect. The Queen's eyes widen in shock, though she doesn't move, only stares at me with what looks like awe written across her expression before she shuts her emotions away again. But I ignore it, too lost in the moment to pause and appreciate the turning of the tables.

"I've offered you information that might help prevent more death and injury of your people, and instead of negotiating for that information, you *insult* me." I spit the last bit out, my voice a sneer. Something about this female gets under my skin. For added effect, I will bolts of lightning to arc out from my palms. Queen Laurel stares at me for a moment, eyes bright with an emotion I can't place. I think she might be so angry she can't speak, and I channel aether into the light and water around me, ready to put up whatever defenses I can against her imposing power.

Her laughter cuts through the thick air, surprising me so much I nearly send a dagger of light hurling toward her before I realize what the sound is. This laugh differs from the lifeless chuff I heard before, a melodious lilt that has me once again almost dropping to my knees, though this time for an entirely different reason. One that I need to bury deep within me so that I don't examine it too closely and allow it to distract me from my purpose here. The sound is so at odds with the persona of the Witch Queen sitting before me, I don't know what to think of it or of her.

"I'm sorry," she says, almost *giggling*. "It's just, here you are, Mazus's son, chastising *me* for not caring about the death and injury of my people. The irony is too great, Prince Hawthorne." I'm not sure what to do, so I dazzle her with my best charming grin, once again returning to the role I'm most comfortable with. That sobers her. Her face settles into a mask of cool unfeeling once again. "I don't take my people's lives for granted. Yesterday's attack was a tragedy—two guards died, and dozens were injured. I have misjudged you and insulted you. I apologize. Please, tell me what you would like in exchange for the information you uncovered on the Sons and Daughters."

Now it's my turn to be shocked into silence. I expected her to lose her temper, to castrate me, or use my blood to turn my organs inside out. At the very least, she should have knocked me to my knees again to remind me she's still more powerful than me and demanded the information. Instead, she laughed, apologized, and moved on. I'm wary of what game she's playing, but I tell myself I'm too unsettled to be anything but truthful, not wanting to examine the motivations behind my honesty with this alluring female.

"I told you what I want. A true friendship and alliance. I... *chafe* under my father's rule," I admit impulsively, immediately regretting the blunt honesty, but I have no choice but to continue. "I don't agree with many of his actions. I'd like to help you uncover the plans of the Sons and Daughters." I'm flying by the seat of my pants now, not entirely sure what words are coming out of my mouth. "In return, give me the chance to show you who I am, without my father's reputation clouding your impression." Her eyes narrow, and the cat returns to her side. "We're nearly the same age," I continue. "My father may seem undying, but he's ancient, and I'm his only child. I *will* take the throne one day. Consider this opportunity the chance to lay real seeds for a better relationship with the future King of Velmara, and not the current one."

I've practically laid myself bare, though I left out my desire to learn more about blood magic and my suspicions about my father. Silene's going to kill me when she learns about this conversation. If Queen Laurel betrays me to my father, can I spin this as a ruse to get closer to her as he requested?

The Queen chews her lip, and I find the gesture... adorable. I shake my head, trying to clear thoughts of her appearance from my mind. This is *not* what I should be thinking about right now.

Finally, she says, eyes narrowed, "I don't trust you, and I certainly don't trust your father. Why did he really send you here? Tell me the truth. If you lie—well, I told your father you'd be in an enemy kingdom with no friends or allies and at *my mercy*. So, consider your words carefully."

I answer quickly and truthfully, no concerns telling her what I know, not after what I've already shared. "He wants me to learn more about your magic. He asked me to assess how powerful you've become, and desired information about the state of the kingdom. But—I don't believe that's his true motivation, though I haven't uncovered the real reason yet. He gave me no way to provide updates to him nor any indication when I might return to Velmara. If he really wanted this info, he'd have found a way for me to communicate with him." This revelation guts my negotiation power. If she knows I can't contact my father, I have nothing to hold over her if things don't go well. Unfortunately, I only realize this after the admission has left my mouth.

She once again chews her lip, and my body tenses, breath catching. I want to run my fingers across those lips, want to... *Stop.*

"I see," she says quietly as she absentmindedly strokes her cat's head, lost in her own thoughts. The room darkens once again, mist swirling around me and the floor quivering with the force of her power. Her gaze hardens, eyes lethal. Vines wrap around my legs again and squeeze tightly in warning before releasing me. "I'll agree to give you the chance to prove yourself to me, but nothing more," she says with an edge to her voice that makes my palms sweat. "But if you betray me, or put my people at risk, I'll kill you and make your friends suffer. Your male warrior has only seen the tiniest tip of the depth of my power. There is nowhere you can go where I won't find you, and I can make you and your friends pay with more than your lives. Do you understand?" Her eyes stare daggers into me, piercing deeper than another person ever has.

Finally, an interaction with a monarch that I'm used to. Threats and grandstanding are my specialty. I give her a cocky smile, the one I give my father when he threatens me and I want to get under his skin. "Understood, Your Majesty. The big bad scary Witch Queen will find me and torture me, blah blah blah. Good thing I don't plan on betraying you."

I think I catch a tick of her lips, but she recovers. "Good. Now, tell me, what information do you have, and how do you propose to discover the plans of the Sons and Daughters of Thayaria?"

"I thought you'd never ask," I say in an exasperated huff before grinning at her again. "I have a contact to ask for at a granary. My plan is to find the contact, join the Sons and Daughters in disguise as a Thayarian commoner, then pass you any information that I hear."

She laughs again, loud and full, and I take another involuntary step toward her, catching myself when the feline eyes me suspiciously. "That's the worst plan I've ever heard, *princeling*. But I can work with it. We do things in Thayaria with careful planning. I don't take a single risk that my plans won't work out." *Silene is going to love her.*

Her laugh and relaxed posture light something up inside of me. I can't stop myself from saying, "Well, then, *witchling*, please do instruct me in how to perfect this plan." I give her a charming wink. It's easy to flirt with her. Either she doesn't notice, or doesn't care, because she returns to her icy, all business exterior, and we discuss her ideas for the infiltration.

The Witch Queen delights in torture, even when her victims don't deserve it. She strings those she falsely accuses of treason up by their feet, letting all the blood rush to their head and extremities. Then she drains them of their blood one tiny slice of their flesh at a time, collecting it in buckets beneath them so not a single drop is wasted.

The Witch Queen and Her Treachery

"I swear, Your Majesty, I didn't know there would be any bombs or explosions. I just thought—they said—I thought we were going to come and scare you. That's all," a terrified and sobbing rebel chokes out. I've been in the prison for hours, my attempt to coax information out of those who attacked me unproductive. As usual, no one seems to know anything about the leadership of the rebellion. "I have a wife and child at home. A little girl. She's only seven. Please." His whimpers are infuriating, mostly because I'm falling prey to them. I sigh as I release the dagger of ice pinned under his jaw.

Everyone I've spoken to is a member of Thayaria's rural population, where the decline is most impactful. This fae lost his livelihood transporting the flower from the refinery in Arberly to the southeastern region where he lives. With less thayar comes less need for it to move throughout the kingdom. While I don't condone their violence, I empathize with my people's fear. Rebellion leadership, whoever they may be, have preyed on that fear and used it to bring people into this who are just looking for a solution. Paired with misinformation and outright lies about the support the Crown has in place for those impacted by the decline, rural Thayaria is a tinderbox just waiting for someone to strike the match.

"For now, you'll stay in the cells until the Council of Advisors decides when your trial will be," I inform the rebel before me, my voice taking on an icy and emotionless tenor. The male collapses, in relief or fear I'm not sure. I don't wait to find out, exiting this room and nodding to the Royal Guards who stand watch outside the interrogation chamber to deal with him. Then I walk to the identical room across the hall where the final rebel waits for my questioning.

The red-headed fae who spoke for the group of attackers is chained to the wall in iron cuffs, his eyes darting around the room in fear. When I approach him, he cries out. "Please, Your Majesty, have mercy."

It's always the same. *Have mercy. Don't kill me. I didn't know.* I wonder if Mazus's prisoners plead their case to him in the same way, or whether those found guilty of treason in Velmara know not to bother. Before speaking, I carefully study the male in front of me, looking for any clues about him. Red hair and blue eyes give him a striking look, a unique set of features in Thayaria. He wrings his calloused hands, his dirt-lined nails catching my attention. He does manual labor. It looks like I've found yet another layperson. As my assessing look travels up and down his body, he trembles, unwilling or unable to meet my gaze.

"You seemed sure of yourself when you had a blade in your hand and a group of rebels at your back," I hiss. The male swallows in fear, eyes darting everywhere but at me. "You spoke for the group. Was it you who organized this attack? Tell me the truth, and I'll consider your request for mercy." My words are a command, though not with the aether-voice. I don't need it to strike fear into the hearts of my people.

"N-n-oo, Y-y-your Ma-majesty." He's shaking so hard now he can barely speak, his words a quiet stutter.

"No? Then tell me who sent you, and don't tell me you don't know. Somehow, you knew when and where to show up with a blade, so I want details about how that came to be." He wrings his hands, his mouth opening and shutting. "Tell me *now*." I will the room to shake a bit, but still, I avoid using the aether-voice to force the confession. I *hate* the power of the aether-voice, knowing exactly what horrors it can force upon someone. It's an abomination, made even more appalling by the fact that it's granted to monarchs who already have unlimited and unchecked power. While I use it occasionally to intimidate or scare, I try to avoid using it to compel.

"There were pa-pamphlets. Th-they told us wh-where to m-meet. It s-said if we were t-tired of our s-situation, that we s-should come and d-demand you li-lift the m-m-mist."

My teeth grind at his words. It's always a demand to lift the mist, the one thing I cannot give them and cannot explain, not without risking Thayaria even further. If Mazus and the other leaders knew the mist was not wholly in my control, there's no telling what they would attempt. Of course, now that he's alone, the confidence and grandstanding are gone.

"And yet—that's not how the interaction played out. You, who took upon yourself to speak for this group that you know so little about, said not one word about the mist, only declaring that my reign was over. Tell me, which is it? Does the rebellion want me to lift the mist, or does the rebellion simply hate my reign and wish me gone?" Without looking in a mirror, I know my eyes are bright with malevolence, and even I wouldn't want to be chained to the wall in this room with me right now.

"I d-don't k-kn-know..." He slumps, his stringy red hair dropping around his face like he's accepted his fate to die, and the smallest twinge of guilt takes root in my stomach.

"What do you do when you aren't rushing off to attack and injure civilians?" I ask, my voice a bit softer but still emotionless. His eyes widen, like he didn't expect the question from the monster standing before him.

"I'm a f-f-farmer. Well, I w-w-was." Of course. That explains the calloused hands and dirty nails. Just another person whipped into a frenzy by leaders who won't show their faces or do the dirty work. Without another word, I leave the room, and the Royal Guards enter behind me to return him into his cells. Making up my mind about what to do with these prisoners, I aerstep to my rooms to prepare for my follow-up visit with the Velmarans.

I bathe and wash the grime of the prison off me. Despite how frequently I visit the cells beneath the palace, I never get used to the way they make my skin crawl afterwards, even as someone who can still access the aether while down there. I can't imagine what it's like for those who lose their power completely to the nulling effects. Walking to my closet, I select a deep plum gown with long bell sleeves and a high slit. I leave my hair in loose waves around my shoulders. Opting to keep up appearances with the Witch Queen makeup, I line my eyes and paint my lips once again, trying and failing to keep my mind from wandering where it absolutely should not wander.

It's been three days since the meeting with the Velmaran entourage, and I can't stop thinking about Prince Hawthorne. Every time I remember his winks and smiles, I'm irritated all over again. I can't seem to reconcile his reputation as the entitled and always-drunk Shining Prince with the dauntless and handsome male I encountered in the throne room. Irritating smiles aside, he's not what I expected. The power he displayed when he was truly angry *impressed* me—he's undoubtedly the most powerful fae I've ever met, potentially second in power to only me. And even though his plans were artless, the political maneuvering he showed was expert. I've gone over our meeting in my mind a hundred times, trying to determine his motivations and whether he's genuine in his desire to build an alliance behind his father's back. *Is that even possible?*

If he is his father's lackey and this is all a ruse, he's playing it well. And if he's not—well, I don't know what that means. A potential alliance with Prince Hawthorne could change everything for my people. Regardless, I can't turn down the opportunity to infiltrate the Sons and Daughters without my Council's—and the potential mole's—knowledge. I'm playing a dangerous game, opening up to the Prince and his advisors even this small amount. They'll certainly uncover information about the declining thayar, and if Mazus didn't already know, he will soon. I sigh and rub my temples as I lean my forehead against the mirror in my closet. I'm juggling too many things—the rebels, the mole, and now whatever this alliance with the Velmaran entourage is. I wish Nemesia were here to help me sort through this mess.

I chuff out loud thinking of my best friend. Nemesia would think it madness I've enlisted the help of an enemy from abroad to foil plans hatched against me by the enemy within my own borders. It probably *is* madness—not only have I broken our agreement to never meet with Prince Hawthorne, I also didn't kill him when he learned too much, and now I'm willingly partnering with him. I'm blindly trusting three strangers more than I trust the thirty plus advisors on my Council, who have an average service tenure of more than one hundred years. *No, not blindly trusting—you're smarter than that.* I won't let them get too close, nor will I truly trust them. They'll get just enough information to help me achieve my goals, and nothing more.

Prince Hawthorne's face flashes across my mind, and my body tingles with the memory. Pressure builds low in my belly at the thought of seeing the Prince again, but I brush away the idea that it's anything other than nerves for pulling this subterfuge off. I cannot—will not—allow him to become a distraction. I'm going to uncover the rebel leaders' identities and then *dispose* of the Shining Prince. In whatever way necessary. Mazus was a fool to send his son here—he won't be returning home, especially not now. Something churns in my gut. Uncertainty? Guilt? I push it down, and with a final glance at Lunaria, whose eyes are too keen for my liking, I aerstep to the ground floor of the palace.

Fionn and the Prince jump in their chairs when I arrive in their apartment with no notice. Their eyes meet mine as they stand quickly, bowing low, and I find myself tracking the Prince's movements with interest. Like the day of our meeting in the throne room, he's well dressed, the perfectly tailored tunic and fitted pants emphasizing the hard lines of his body. He catches me staring and gives me a wink, causing my cheeks to heat involuntarily. Fionn's suspicious gaze stays fixed on me, eyes narrowed. I bare my teeth in a hiss to cement Fionn's fear and distract the Prince *and* myself from the focused way I was taking in his form. Scaring males is my specialty, and even Prince Hawthorne takes a small step back. Satisfaction thrums through me.

"Well, Your Majesty, I'd welcome you to our rooms, but since they are in fact *your* rooms, I'll skip those pleasantries," Silene says with forced cheeriness from my left. She walks out of the primary bedroom, and I freeze for just a moment at the implication. *They're betrothed, of course they're sleeping in the same bed.* I shake away the thought and the twinge of something I can't explain, focusing all my attention on the small female. Her petite and toned frame practically bounces with excitement, and I can't help myself from warming to her lighthearted and exuberant personality.

"Silene," I say, "thank you for receiving me. I trust Prince Hawthorne has advised you of the purpose of today's meeting." Silene nods as she follows me to the other two chairs across from Prince Hawthorne and Fionn. "The Prince informed me of the contact you received for the Sons and Daughters, and of your plan to infiltrate them. I'm still a bit suspicious of your motivations for seeking them out." I pause, letting them feel a zap of energy and the smallest squeezing of their necks with a rope of air. Three sets of wide eyes stare back at me, but they remain silent and otherwise unaffected. Prince Hawthorne smirks, like he *likes it*, and it makes me want to rip the air from his lungs, but I refrain. They're well trained, or at the very least used to veiled threats—I'm sure Mazus is quick to use his power to threaten. "However, it would be foolish of me to pass up this opportunity."

"Thorne didn't give us much information," Silene begins cautiously. "How do you intend for us to pursue this *opportunity*, as you say?" Something about the Prince's nickname gives me tingles down my spine. Ignoring it, I walk them through the high-level details of my scheme.

"Prince Hawthorne's intent to approach the contact himself and remain undercover is... underdeveloped." Silene's mouth drops open. She clearly didn't know about or endorse this foolish idea. I can't resist leveling my own smirk at the Prince, like I've won some game we're both playing. "You should not hide your identity from the rebel group. They likely already knew who you were and targeted the Prince intentionally at that pub. Even if he somehow managed to remain inconspicuous at the pub, he won't remain so for long. Plus, you're more likely to be introduced to their leaders quickly if they know who you are and think you want to help them." Silene nods her agreement, while the

Prince keeps his eyes trained on my face. His expression is calm, but he won't look away, and it's unsettling. I continue the conversation quickly, ignoring the way my blood heats under his gaze. "Silene and Fionn, you'll go to the contact as a confirmation of sorts. They'll expect Prince Hawthorne to send his entourage ahead first. Once the two of you have secured an introduction to their leadership, you'll bring Prince Hawthorne into the scheme." The Prince opens his mouth to protest, but Silene cuts him off.

"I like the plan. Not only is it more *believable* that a prince would send his advisors ahead of him to scope the situation out..." She gives the Prince a pointed look that nearly breaks my trained expression, my lips quirking slightly at the way she can boss him around with just a look. "It keeps him out of danger until we can assess any potential risks."

"I don't need to be protected from a rural group of fae and humans playing at insurgents," the Prince interjects, but Silene merely looks at him with a no-nonsense expression that reminds me of Nemesia, and he shuts up. I like her, and I don't want to. I *can't* allow myself to—not when I'll have no choice at the end of all this but to make them all disappear, Silene included.

"As I was saying..." Silene draws out the phrase with a pointed glance at the Prince, "I think this is the right approach. But how are we going to convince the rebels to trust us? How will we convince them we're on their side? If they're smart, they'll spot the ruse." I smile wide, the final pieces of my plan clicking into place only hours ago as I realized the rebels rotting away in my cells were no more Sons and Daughters leadership than I am.

"Because you're going to offer to break out the group of them I took prisoner after the attack." They did not expect this. Even Silene remains quiet—a quizzical look upon her face.

"Why would you give up the prisoners?" Prince Hawthorne asks, studying me with an uncharacteristically guarded expression.

I shrug. "I've learned what I can from them. They're rural citizens whipped up into a frenzy by zealous radicals. They aren't the real prize. I want to know who their leaders are—what they're planning. The group who attacked don't have any of that information. Better to have you pretend to break them out to gain favor with the rebels than for me to keep them from their families."

Prince Hawthorne's eyes look me over carefully, his gaze traveling up and down my body. I can *sense* the strength of his power as he assesses me, like it somehow calls to my own power and watches what I'll do. Something buried deep inside of me, an awareness not dissimilar to the way the mist feels when it calls on me, stills and focuses wholly on the Prince, making its own assessment. The intimacy of the moment sends shivers through me that I attempt to mask. Those mossy, olive eyes flash brightly and he smirks again, like there's some secret between us. I pointedly return my gaze to Silene, who is thoughtful and oblivious to whatever was just happening between the Prince and me.

"It could work," she says slowly. "We'll need to be careful, but I think we can pull it off. Fionn and I can go to the granary tomorrow and initiate first contact."

I smile, then clap my hands together. "Excellent!" They all jump, a sure sign they aren't as relaxed as they appear. "I'd like to keep meeting here, away from my advisors. For now, let's keep this between us." Silene's eyes narrow, and I fear she's guessed more about this situation than I want her to. I wave my hand, hoping to divert her suspicions. "They over complicate matters like this." Not a lie. Also not the truth. Trusting them with information about the mole on my Council would be foolish. "Endless committees and chancellors make for effective day-to-day governing, but slow things down." I'm not sure I've successfully assuaged her suspicion, but she says nothing. The Prince's eyes sparkle. "Is there something else, Prince Hawthorne?" I ask.

He stands from his chair and bends into a deep bow, keeping his eyes locked on mine. "No, witchling, I'm at your service." My mouth goes inexplicably dry at the way the deep timbre off his voice says 'witchling,' the nickname impacting me more than I want to admit. "Should we expect you tomorrow evening around the same time to debrief Fionn and Silene's first contact?"

"Yes, same time tomorrow," I say with forced iciness to hide the breathlessness I feel, before returning to my rooms and Lunaria's knowing eyes.

Metal channeling is a powerful order of magic use. Strong metal channelers can guide weapons into their mark using the aether, a powerful skill for a warrior. Those of average strength often take roles as blacksmiths, supplying the weapons and armor for kingdoms. Some can even craft blades imbued with aether magic to keep them eternally sharp or to wound more deeply.

The Unabridged History of Magical Orders, Volume I

The next day, I can barely keep my attention focused on the advisors presenting revenue numbers and other operational kingdom updates. Sensing my mind wandering, Carex asks, "Your Majesty, should we have a short recess?" I startle from my thoughts and nod. Carex approaches me where I stand in the corner pouring myself a mug of tea.

"Is everything alright, Laurel?" he asks in a low voice only I can hear. I look at his handsome face, gray eyes bright as he observes me with an awareness that only comes from an ex-lover. It's been twenty years since our three decades-long courtship ended, mostly amicably, but it had been a deep and intense affair before fizzling out. Nonetheless, Carex knows me well and can tell that I'm preoccupied.

"Yes, I didn't sleep well last night. My mind is wandering. I'll have a cup of tea before we resume."

He doesn't believe me. "Laurel, it's not just today. You've been distracted for weeks. I know you must be missing Nemesia's absence. Please, confide in me."

His words echo what he told me when we'd ended our relationship. He had wanted *more*. Wanted to become my partner, wanted me to bring him into my confidence. He had pushed and pushed, until we both realized I wasn't ready. *I can't keep pushing you for more, Laurel. If you can't let me in, how can we ever evolve?* He had said the words with kindness, but we both knew what they meant. The next day, he'd asked if we should end things. I knew it was coming, knew that it was the only way forward, but it still stung. I'd agreed because I didn't know what else to say. I think we both thought we'd eventually resume the relationship, though when and what that would look like neither of us had an answer for.

I consider telling him the truth now, bringing him into my confidence. Consider allowing him to fill the massive hole that Nemesia has left behind her. But I can't trust him, or anyone on the Council, for that matter. With everything crushing in on me now, my preference to shut everyone out has only intensified.

When I don't respond, lost in my thoughts, he presses on. "Let me in, Laurel. You're clearly struggling. I can help."

"There's a lot going on right now. I'm distracted. That's all."

He pushes further. "Laurel, the rebels—" Anger rises inside of me. His tendency to persist until someone gives him what he wants is annoying now that we're no longer together.

"Thank you for your concern, Carex, but you should focus on your own duties. I'm still waiting for a report on how *your* Royal Guards allowed armed rebels into the palace. A lapse in security that resulted in death and injury." Carex flinches, the barb landing as intended. "I would like to drink a cup of tea. If you'll excuse me." With that, I walk away.

The meeting concludes an hour later, and it's finally time to get an update from the Velmaran ambassadors. I had to make up a story about what information Prince Hawthorne has about the rebellion since several advisors heard his initial comments in the throne room. Thankfully, I'd been able to convince them the Prince had heard nothing more than rumors in the pub and had used it as an excuse to meet with me. I return to my rooms to dress in my usual armor of makeup and a scandalous, dark dress before aerstepping to the apartment.

When I arrive, all three Velmarans are sitting near the fire, conversing with the practiced ease of longtime friends. I can't help but smile at the roar of laughter that comes from the Prince after something Silene says. She smiles up at him and grabs his hand tightly before releasing it, her expression so light-hearted and genuine that I can tell there's a real connection between them. And Hawthorne—the laughter makes his face radiant and unguarded in what I think might be a rare moment, reserved only for his best friend and his betrothed. *They'll make a happy couple when they're married.* I don't understand the twinge in my gut I feel at that thought.

Fionn notices my presence first, a serious and watchful expression quickly consuming his face. He fears me more than the others. Silene and Prince Hawthorne turn to face me as well, plastering reserved and somewhat forced smiles onto their faces, no sign of the easiness from before. That too gives me a twinge of discomfort that I don't know how to feel about. I look at them expectantly, jumping right into business to avoid the way their now-guarded expressions affect me.

"How did the meeting go?"

Silene takes the lead in debriefing me. "As expected. They knew who we were and were expecting us. You were right about Thorne being targeted in the pub. They knew exactly who he was that night." I can't help but smirk, feeling like I've won another game between the Prince and me. "We met a fae named Restin. I think he's a leader here in Arberly."

"You think or you know? With a name, you need to be sure."

She blushes and lowers her eyes. "I know. I don't know why I added 'I think.'"

I soften my voice. "It's okay. Never say you think when you know. Be confident in the intelligence you've gathered." I smile gently at her, hoping to undo my harshness from before. She smiles back, and this time the smile is genuine.

"Restin is the leader of the rebellion here in Arberly," she repeats with confidence in her voice. "We made the offer to break out the prisoners as a show of loyalty to their cause. Restin promised to introduce us to leadership once we deliver the prisoners to them. We're meeting at the granary again in a week."

"So…" I say with a smile, "I guess we should plan a prison break. We only have a week." They look between one another, eyes betraying their concern.

"You plan for *us* to actually break them out?" Prince Hawthorne asks with a tone of lazy indifference.

"Of course. The rebels could have spies anywhere, not to mention if I simply handed over the prisoners to you, my Council would have questions. We must enact a plan for you to break them out, but for it to look like it was the rebels themselves to protect your positions here in Thayaria." They look nervous, shoulders tight and unspoken words on their lips. Glances between them confirm what I already suspected: they don't trust me, and I don't blame them. We're reluctant allies at best, from enemy kingdoms, and I'm putting them at risk. "Don't tell me you're afraid of a little skirmish," I tease, trying to lighten the mood. "My guards are well-trained, but I expected the famous Shining Prince and his powerful metal channeler to be capable of taking them on." Fionn's jaw clenches, and I can see that I've ruffled his feathers. I've made the situation worse by saying something that could be interpreted as a threat. I clear my throat. "What I meant was—"

"We're perfectly capable of battling a few palace guards," Fionn interrupts. *Ah, I've hurt his ego, then.* "We can do it with no one even seeing us or the rebels."

"That is precisely what we do *not* want," I say harshly. Silene winces, and I vow to tone it down. They need to trust me, even if I don't trust them. "If the prisoners go missing with no witnesses, the three of you will be instantly suspected or believed to be working with the rebels. My Council—all of Thayaria, really—distrusts you, and are looking for any reason to insist I return you to Velmara at once. You need to break them out with a rebel or two with you and ensure only the rebels are seen."

Fionn looks disappointed, and I wonder how the famed warrior is taking to the life of a diplomat. They don't have access to any sparring rings, and that must be especially frustrating for him. I'll fix that tomorrow. They'll need to train for the breakout anyway without raising suspicions, and it will be an olive branch. I hope.

Silene, ever the strategist, chimes in. "Thorne can use his magic to hide us and make it so that only the rebels are seen. We'll have to convince the rebels to provide fighters and ensure they know they'll be blamed for the breakout. I suspect they won't mind. We'll want to make sure there are enough guards to spot and report the rebels, but not so many guards that it's suspicious only a few rebels can get past them."

"Leave that to me. Prince Hawthorne, would you be able to hide *both* Fionn and Silene from another room?" I ask.

"Of course. I'm not the most powerful light channeler *ever known* for nothing." He winks.

"Rumors of your reputation mention little about your *magical* abilities," I retort.

Catching my subtle innuendo, he smirks. "And what *abilities* did you hear about, witchling?" My legs clench together involuntarily at the sultry tone of his voice, but I won't let him win whatever this is.

"Let's just say your reputation for drinking and—other things—precedes you," I add, eyes focused on the dimple that makes another appearance.

"Sounds like you were really interested in me," he quips, voice low. I swear his body leans in toward me, but I ignore it.

"Hardly," I scoff, though my cheeks heat and I try really hard not to notice the way his shirt stretches taut across his chest.

"If only we'd met sooner, you wouldn't have had to go to such extreme lengths to learn more," he taunts. I find myself rolling my eyes while my lips tighten in an unbidden half-smile. I quickly return my face to neutral. I need to get this conversation back on track.

"Speaking of meeting, after you *demanded* an audience with me and chastised me so thoroughly for the lack of pomp and circumstance for your arrival, I'm suddenly feeling *inspired* to throw a ball in your honor, princeling." I give the last word my most sarcastic bluster, challenging the Prince with my gaze. The plan dawns on him and his face brightens. My breath catches in my chest at the sight of his handsome features pulled into a smile directed only at me, but I don't let that show on my face.

"With the recent rebel attacks, you'll want to increase security significantly for a ball. You wouldn't want the rebels to cause trouble in front of the Velmaran Crown Prince, would you?" he asks in mock concern.

"Precisely," I say, slipping into a cool mask of regal indifference. That doesn't stop us from staring at one another for a second too long, energy pulsing between us. Fionn clears his throat, and my cheeks heat this time in embarrassment. I'm suddenly aware that his betrothed, who I find myself liking more and more, sits next to me. Shame courses through my body.

I can't deny I find the Prince attractive. Any female even slightly interested in males would, with his bright smiles and the dimple on one cheek and the way his dark hair looks so effortlessly swept back from his face and his strong forearms... I shut those thoughts down. I can't afford to let myself get distracted. He's still the *Velmaran Prince*, my enemy, and someone I was literally plotting to kill just days ago. Am *still* plotting to kill. From this point forward, I vow to smother any notice of his *features*. I'm getting the information I need from him, then getting rid of him. I push down the queasiness I feel at the idea of having Prince Hawthorne, or even worse, Silene, killed. I tip my chin higher, determined to stick to the plan and stop getting sidetracked. My people deserve a Queen who puts them first and doesn't get distracted by dimples and winks.

"I'll set the date of the ball with my Council tomorrow so you can inform the rebels of when to prepare for the breakout," I say, the words coming out awkward and stilted.

"And do you have a plan for how to actually get the rebels *out* of the palace?" Silene asks, apparently unaffected by the blatant flirting between the Prince and me. "We might be able to sneak them out of prison without notice, but this is a big palace. It will be challenging to march them through the halls and to a group of rebels waiting for them outside."

"I have a plan. I'll tell you about it in due time." I'm not yet ready to trust them with information about the secret passage out of the prison.

"We need to plan—" Silene starts.

"I said I'll tell you about it at the right time," I say fiercely. For the second time in this conversation, she winces. Guilt swims through my gut, but I push it down, reminding myself that she's the future daughter-in-law of King Mazus. And that I will have to make difficult decisions in the near future about her. As the tension lingers between us, I aerstep away.

When I aerstep the next morning to meet the Velmarans for a tour of their new training room, Carex is with them already. Prince Hawthorne leans against the wall, relaxed and casual like he's grown up in the palace, making small talk and joking. It looks like he's trying to *flirt* with Carex. He gives the Captain a wink and a smirk, which only makes Carex look uncomfortable. I don't understand this male—he seems to flirt with everyone he meets, despite his betrothed standing right next to him. His broad chest is on full display in the form-fitting shirt he wears, and that dimple appears as he makes a joke with Silene. *Stop looking at him.*

I square my shoulders and address the Captain. "Carex, I didn't expect to see you. I planned to give the ambassadors a tour of their new training room." I'm suspicious of Carex's fortuitous timing. He bows low, then stands to meet my eyes.

"I ran into them in the hall in front of the kitchens. I had just finished my final checks on the space. If you'd like, Your Majesty, I'm happy to provide them a tour so you can return to your other work. I'm sure you have more pressing matters to attend to," he says. He's collected, his face holding a calm expression, but something about the encounter doesn't sit right with me.

"That won't be necessary. Thank you for preparing this so quickly. I know what havoc the guards can wreak in their training rooms."

Carex tenses. "Your Majesty," he says in a low voice. Stepping closer, he adds so only I can hear, "Is it wise for you to be alone and unguarded with them? I should come with you to watch your back." I notice he eyes Fionn suspiciously, and he must know of the male's reputation as a warrior and incredibly powerful metal channeler. I consider him carefully, unsure what he'll do if I refuse his protection. Though it irks me, I begrudgingly consent to have him accompany us, not wanting to stir up any suspicion on his part.

The training rooms for the Royal Guard sit in natural caves in the mountain the palace is built into. This makes them all unique—some are small, appropriate for only a pair of sparring partners, while others are enormous. This one is big enough for about a half dozen guards, but no more. The ceiling is high, with mats stacked in the far-right corner. Racks of practice weapons line one side, and ivy crawls up the walls. There are oak buckets of water throughout the room, and torches emit a yellow glowing ember. All channelers will find something in the space for magic practice, though there's also a circle lined in iron to block magic for certain training situations.

While we walk around the room, I explain the iron ring and the conduits available, desperately trying and failing to keep my eyes from watching Prince Hawthorne and his muscled chest closely. I show them how to refill the water buckets from the spigot and inspect the practice weapons. I palm the only dagger on the rack and hide it in my dress sleeve. When we've explored every corner of the room, I turn and look at the Prince.

"Is there anything else you require, Prince Hawthorne?" I ask.

"No, Your Majesty." He bows, and a piece of hair falls into his eyes from the perfectly messy style. I want to run my fingers over the silky locks. *Stop it, Laurel.* "Fionn, Silene, and I train in a similar space under the Velmaran palace, so we're pleased to feel so at home. Thank you for your hospitality. I'm sure Fionn in particular will be relieved to have the chance to wave a sword around my face once again." He smiles, bright and alluring, and that cursed dimple makes another appearance. I clench my fists to keep from reacting to it, only to realize my body has leaned into him. Coughing, I back away.

"Carex, I've just realized there are no daggers available on the weapons rack. Would you mind running to another room and grabbing one? I believe Miss Kalmeera mentioned daggers being her weapon of choice." Silene thankfully doesn't react to the blatant lie I've just told. Smart girl. I knew she'd catch on.

Carex looks the weapons rack over, confusion lining his features. "I could have sworn there was one there," he says. "Of course, Your Majesty. I'll be back *shortly*." He emphasizes the word, giving Hawthorne and Fionn a hard stare as if to warn them off trying anything, then walks briskly from the room.

Prince Hawthorne's eyes twinkle, while Silene's stare at me with an assessing expression. "I too could have sworn I saw a dagger on that rack, Your Majesty," the Prince says smoothly, teasingly, his eyes bright and locked on mine. Suddenly, the weapon hurls away from me. It flies through the room and ends up in Fionn's outstretched hand. He stares at me, challenging me to react. I grin, hoping to put them all more at ease. Prince Hawthorne and Silene break out into laughter, and Fionn's lips even twitch.

"You should have seen your face!" Silene tentatively says. She's testing me, wondering how casual she can be. I widen my smile, and she returns it, bright and beaming. Warmth spreads through my body at being part of their endless teasing of one another, and I find myself laughing with them.

"I asked Carex to leave so I could speak with you," I tell them. "The ball will be in two weeks' time. Two nights before the ball, I'll walk you through the full plan for the escape. Prince Hawthorne, you'll need to attend meetings with myself and the Council to plan the welcome ball."

"I look forward to party planning with you, witchling. I'm told I have an affinity for throwing a raging celebration," he says with a wink.

"Is that right? It doesn't seem like *planning* would be part of your skill set." Silene snorts and Fionn whistles. I honestly didn't even know what words were coming out of my mouth before I spoke them. The Prince grins wide, clearly enjoying this back and forth between us.

"When it comes to having *fun*, I know a thing or two." The innuendo he laces into the words has me breathing heavy.

"So I've heard, princeling. Just remember you have a job to do. It's not a party, it's a distraction." With that, I aerstep from the room, trying to ignore the fluttering in my stomach.

The reputation of the Witch Queen is nothing compared to the reality of her practices. She uses her blackened vines to trap you in a gory and oozing web of treachery. Once she has you pinned down and immobilized, she goes in for the killing blow. She'll slice your throat, then divide your blood in half. One part she drinks to maintain eternal youth, the other she uses to cast spells that advance her infernal cause.

The Witch Queen and Her Treachery

When Laurel leaves the training room, Fionn instantly goes into sparring mode. Throwing me a sword, he advances before I can catch it. Silene finds a table and chairs in the corner, eyes showing she's lost in thought. I barely notice her before Fionn slams the hilt of his sword into my gut, knocking the breath from my lungs. The whoosh of blades are the only sounds as we clash against one another in the underground recess, Fionn's blows growing more aggressive the longer we train.

"What has you so on edge?" I ask. He only grunts and swings the blade again. I block his swipe, then drop my sword. "Seriously, Fionn, what's up?"

"I don't trust the Queen." His shoulders and body are tense, eyes storming. "Something feels off—there's too much secrecy. Why wouldn't she want her advisors involved when they're a part of every other aspect of ruling the kingdom? She's hiding something."

He's right about the secrecy—it's strange. And it makes me wonder whether this is a trap intended to get us in a bad situation we can't get out of.

"I think I know why," Silene says before striding over to us. She places her hands on her hips. "She has a mole." Her posture exudes confidence. She's sure about this.

"What makes you think that?" I ask.

"Here's what we know. The Queen told us to keep our arrangement a secret from her advisors. She tried to play it off as them being too bureaucratic and slowing things down. But letting rebel prisoners go is a *big* thing to keep from them, based on what we've seen about how she rules." She makes a good point. While it wouldn't be unusual for my father to keep important things from his advisors, Laurel's different. There has to be a reason she doesn't want them involved. "And then today, she made up an excuse to send Carex away—the *Captain* of her Royal Guard, no less. Why keep the breakout secret from the Captain of the Royal Guard, unless she was afraid it might somehow get back to the rebels that we're working together? He'd make the breakout much easier to pull off. Even if her advisors would slow something like this down, you'd think she'd at least want Carex to know what's going on. She *has* to have a mole. It's the only explanation."

As usual, Silene has guessed all the players and plays before most of us even knew there was a game afoot. Queen Laurel keeping this information from us stings a bit. I understand she doesn't trust us, but this is critical information to share with potential allies. It's a good reminder of how far we have to go to truly earn her trust, much less become friendly.

"It has to be Carex," Fionn grunts while inspecting the weapons rack. "He's always snooping around. I heard him tell the Queen he ran into us while leaving the training room, but that wasn't true. I clocked him following us from our rooms."

"Why didn't you say anything?" I ask, incredulous.

Fionn only shrugs. "Wanted to see what he was up to before I revealed we knew he was there." And just as Silene knows how to play the game, Fionn knows when to watch and learn. My friends are both too intelligent and good at what they do. I'm just a bloke with a crown and a handsome face. I'd be nothing without them.

Silene scrunches her nose and looks away, uncertainty written across her features. "I agree the Captain seems dodgy, but I'm not so sure it's him. Or if it is him, he's doing a terrible job hiding his interest in what we're doing. He's always around—that seems too obvious." I nod my agreement, while Fionn only huffs. The Captain has found many excuses to follow us around since we've been here, often showing up to sub-committee meetings uninvited with the excuse he just wants to "sit in." Even the other advisors have seemed put off by his presence.

"What do we do now?" Fionn asks. "This ruse has only gotten more dangerous. It was one thing to risk being exposed accidentally through rebel intel, but now that we know there's someone informing them? It makes our situation even more precarious. We could walk into a trap at any point. It would be prudent to abandon this plan." His gruff voice is all commander, a sign of how worried he is, and I don't blame him. We're playing a dangerous game. My eyes dart to Silene, wanting her opinion as well.

"We're trying to trick a lot of people," Silene admits, amber eyes bright and wide as they bore into me. "Your father, the rebels, even the Queen to some extent—we haven't exactly been honest about our motivations for wanting to make her an ally. Someone is bound to find us out."

Nervousness builds in my stomach, but I have no choice but to push it away.

"We're in too deep now to pull out of anything," I admit, my voice somber. "If we tell the Queen we don't want to aid her anymore, I fear what she may do in her suspicion. And it's not like I can write to my father and tell him we've gotten ourselves wrapped up in a scheme we need to get out of. Moving forward is the only option we have." Four eyes stare back at me, concern storming in their gazes. To lighten the mood, I add, "How dangerous can these rebels be, anyway? Against Fionn and me? We'll be just fine." The words are hollow in the cavernous space, but none of us contradict them.

"What do you think the plan will be to get the prisoners out of the castle?" Silene asks. "I don't like that we won't know until a few days before."

"Another reason I don't trust her," Fionn grumbles quietly.

"I don't know, but if I trust anything, it's that the Queen knows how to make a plan. That's enough worrying for one day." I give them a grin. "Let's train. We need to be ready for anything. You too, Silene." She tries to hide her excited smile but doesn't fool Fionn and me. We know better than anyone her desire to be a great warrior, to use her skill with a blade to make up for the average magic most Velmaran nobles have.

We spend the next few hours running through drills with Fionn. The deep tenor of his voice is gentle as he models moves for Silene or corrects my form. Despite the blustering warrior exterior, Fionn is a patient teacher. Without his guidance, I never would have mastered my magic. Silene takes his direction with the dedication of an apprentice, mastering several moves in our short session. My lips can't help the smile that spreads across my face as I watch my two best friends deep in concentration on their training. We're in an enemy kingdom a thousand miles from Velmara, deep underground in the home of the most notoriously dangerous fae to ever live. And yet, it feels like home.

Shit, it's cold. Howling wind whips my hair away from my face, chilling me to my core in the outdoor garden I stumbled upon while exploring the palace. After training, Silene and Fionn had gotten wrapped up in playing Skran, Fionn determined to master the Thayarian game. My body was restless, eager to keep moving despite the grueling exercise Fionn put me through.

I pretended to head to bed early, then snuck back out, cloaking myself with my light magic. As Fionn yelled "Skran!" loudly, I used his loud bellow to slip through our apartment doors and into the palace, unsure of my destination. I'd wandered aimlessly until I stumbled upon a glass door leading to a terrace filled with some of the most stunning trees and flowers I've ever seen.

Despite the cold temperatures, a result of the fast-approaching winter, the garden is still effervescent in its beauty. Draping emerald trees create a canopy across the stone paths, while flowers in crimson, magenta, and lavender mound under the trees. Ivy and moss cover the path in areas, giving the space that now familiar classic Thayarian feel of being perfectly overgrown and luscious. Though I'm freezing, I can't bring myself to turn and head inside, captivated by the harmony of smells that dance through the air and the peaceful quiet under the rising stars. As I round another corner, the same sense of being watched tickles my spine like it did as we traveled to the capital. I keep walking until the path opens up to a stunning view of the mountains behind Arberly, a misty navy portrait in the darkening sky.

"And what exactly are you doing here, Prince Hawthorne, hidden from view?" a cool and hard voice says from the shadows. I jump, searching the dark to my left for the Queen. A laugh sounds from beyond my line of sight before Queen Laurel appears, posture rigid and green eyes assessing. I release the magic cloaking me and bow deeply.

"Apologies, Your Majesty." I hold my hands up in mock surrender. "I snuck from my rooms so Fionn and Silene wouldn't protest my exploring and forgot to remove the magic. I assure you I'm up to nothing nefarious. Just some good old fashion hiding from my friends." My sheepish grin does nothing to break her unwavering expression.

"Why are you *exploring* my palace?" she asks, an edge to her voice. I take a few steps closer to her, practically involuntarily. It reminds me of my ruse to seduce her, so I take another step. Apparently, I have a death wish.

I shrug my shoulders, trying to lighten the mood. "I needed to move—needed to get out of the apartments. I was getting antsy." I stretch my arms above my head for emphasis. "Am I not permitted to wander the palace?" My eyes narrow with a challenge I know she'll rise to.

"I'd prefer you *wander* visible, where others can see you," she responds cooly.

"You saw me just fine," I retort with a cocky smirk. I've somehow miraculously gotten her alone, and I intend to put the opportunity to good use. She gives me a long stare, like she's bored and unfeeling. But here, under the barely visible stars just before twilight, I see it for the mask it is. And this time, I don't back down, my skin itching with the need to unravel her, just a little. I return the stare, not breaking her gaze. We stare at one another until her lips twitch, and she looks away. *Thorne—one, Queen Laurel—too many to count.* But at least I'm making progress.

"*I* saw you because I'm a super powerful *witch*, remember?" she says sarcastically, and it's *almost...* flirty.

I press my advantage and make an exaggerated bow. "I'll ensure I keep my *impressive* magic at bay in my future adventures through the palace, *witchling.*"

She scoffs half-heartedly. "A little light trick is hardly *impressive magic*, princeling." Suddenly, I'm lifted in the air by a strong gale before being set down ten paces away. Queen Laurel pins me with a smirk that's equal parts seductive and terrifying. From this distance, her curvy figure is on full display in leather leggings and a tight-fitting tunic. With her hair pulled from her face in a simple braid and no makeup, there's something vulnerable about her tonight. In three strides, I return to stand in front of her, only a foot away, my body towering over her small stature. I swear her breath catches the tiniest bit, though she reveals nothing in her expression. My lips pull at the corners. "How was your training session?" she asks coolly, apparently unaffected by our closeness, though she doesn't step away.

"Hellish." I close the distance between us by another step, and now I have her *squirming.* Her eyes dilate, and her nostrils flare. I'm desperate to fully crack that icy exterior. "Fionn's brutal in his workouts, and with a month of sitting around, I was out of shape. He's mandated high-intensity drills twice a week. I told him we should just walk up the aethers-damned stairs over and over again. But I think he hates them as much as the rest of us." This time I know her lips twitch in a held-back smile. I *almost* cracked her. So I crowd her body with mine, the need to get a reaction from her overwhelming me. Once again, she doesn't back away, and we're so close that I can lean down and whisper in her pointed ear. "I've never wanted to be an air channeler more than when I walked up to the Council chambers for the first time. Good news is by the end of this ambassador appointment, my ass is going to look even better than it already does." I pull back and wink. That comment gets an actual laugh out of her, and I can't help from smiling at the sound.

"Good night, princeling," she says with a roll of her eyes.

"Good night, witchling," I yell as she walks away, her face in profile. A real smile breaks out across her lips, and my heart skips a beat in my chest. *Success.*

Laurel

While plant and water channelers are the most well-known of healers, light channelers
can also heal injuries. In fact, light healing is said to be the strongest of the healing
abilities, as it requires a stronger concentration of aether to perform and thus passes
that extra aether to the person being healed. However, it takes immense focus and
control to heal via light, and very few light channelers throughout history have
possessed the skill.

A Practical Guide to Magical Healing

"Prince Hawthorne, are you sure you wouldn't like dancing lessons before the ball? Aria is a skilled dancer and teacher. I'm sure she'd be happy to walk you through the waltz we'll open the ball with," I say to the Prince and the room of advisors. We've been planning the ball this last week and decided to open it with a dance between the Prince and me. It's a good opportunity for Silene and Fionn to sneak away, since everyone will be watching us, but I don't want to do it. The Prince annoys me endlessly, always charming everyone with his dimple and his winks, despite being *engaged*. He's a shameless flirt—it's *excessive*. Never mind the way I feel when that flirting turns my way... If I allow him close enough to dance, he'll use his stupidly handsome face to break through the carefully constructed wall I've erected around the Velmarans. The wall that is more difficult to maintain than I want to admit.

"Oh, my dance skills will *measure up* to your *expectations,* I'm sure of it." He somehow makes the statement seem like an innuendo, and my cheeks heat slightly even as my blood boils in anger that he would say something like that in front of a room full of advisors. He truly has no shame as he leans back in his chair, smug and relaxed, clearly aware of how his statement sounds. This at least matches the rumors I know about him—a flirt, a womanizer, a handsome heartbreak. Aria, a young and pretty advisor, doesn't seem to mind. She bats her eyelashes at him, and I want to roll my eyes.

"I would be happy to give you lessons, Your Highness," Aria says with a sickly sweetness that makes something stir in my belly.

"I've been taught the traditional dances from many kingdoms. Even those I never thought I'd visit. I don't need lessons." His eyes shine as they lock on me, paying Aria no attention.

"Suit yourself," I murmur, forcing myself to rip my gaze away from the way his rolled up shirt sleeves show off his strong forearms and large, calloused hands. The fact that his hands are rough instead of soft and smooth, like I'd expect from a Prince who does nothing but drink and flirt, affects me *too* much.

"Your Majesty, Your Highness, should we review the menu?" Lionel, another advisor who manages the kitchens, asks. I nod, grateful to change the subject and get my mind off the idea of waltzing with the handsome—and irritating—Prince. Lionel stands, but before he can continue, Carex bursts into the room.

"Your Majesty," Carex huffs out, a panic in his voice that puts me on edge. "I just received a missive. There's been another rebel attack. On Rusthelm." My heart sinks. I'd just sent two healers there to help with the village-wide illness. Is the attack because of my assistance? How can I protect my people if any action from me spurs the rebels to retaliate?

The guilt and frustration force me into action. I'm immediately on my feet, ready to aerstep there and wipe out the rebel force. The room shakes with my power, and for the briefest of moments, I lose a tiny bit of my awareness, lost in rage and what feels like *madness.* But it's so short I barely register it, too focused on the situation at hand. I scan the faces of every advisor in meticulous detail, looking for the smallest twitch of lips or lack thereof, hoping to find someone who doesn't look surprised at the news and might lead me to the mole. But shocked and concerned faces are all that stare back at me, waiting for my orders. Carex places his hand on my arm, and I jump slightly at his touch.

"We've stopped the attack, and the rebels fled." His lowered voice and attempt at a soothing touch tell me he's trying to comfort me, but nothing can make this reality any better. "But there were many injuries. We need more healers. Quickly."

"Let me help," Prince Hawthorne interrupts before I can respond. "I'm a powerful healer. I heal with both water and light." Carex's furrowed brow matches my own skepticism, though I also can't ignore the shock his ability to heal with *two* conduits brings. I knew he was powerful, but this is rare and unusual.

"I don't think that's a good idea," I say firmly while Carex nods in agreement, though several advisors seem to purse their lips. The Prince has won them over these last weeks. It's infuriating.

"How many were injured?" Prince Hawthorne asks. Carex hesitates. The Prince stands, his towering frame dominating the room. "How many? Tell me," he demands, and I'm taken aback by the seriousness and authority in his voice. It's the voice of a leader, a ruler, brokering no room for argument. He fills the entire room with his imposing presence, and it's no surprise that Carex gives in to his command.

"Dozens, maybe more, is our best guess," Carex admits. Anguish fills my chest. I *must* stop these attacks.

Prince Hawthorne turns back to me. "Let. Me. Help. Your healers can only handle half a dozen people at best before their magic is spent. I can do four times that, maybe more." The Prince is confident, sure of his magic. Olive, mossy eyes plead with me. I want to help the injured, but what if this impacts Hawthorne's ability to persuade the rebels that he's on their side? What if this is some trick by the Velmarans? It's too much to sort out this quickly, especially as my heart beats faster with every second we don't move to action. "Can we speak about this privately?" the Prince asks. Carex interrupts before I even open my mouth.

"You're insane if you think I'm going to leave you alone with Her Majesty," Carex spits. I turn angry eyes on him. I wasn't going to agree, but now I will, just to spite Carex and his protectiveness.

"I decide where I go and with whom I speak, Carex." Before he can respond, I walk away.

Before following me out of the room, I hear the Prince murmur lowly to Carex with thick insinuation, "Don't worry, we can bring you along another time." Did he just imply that we'd have a *threesome*? Right now, of all times? This male is absolutely insufferable.

When we're in the hall outside the Council chambers, Prince Hawthorne smirks as he leans against the wall with a cool confidence that makes me hot all over, though with anger or something else I don't want to admit. How can he be relaxed at a time like this? "Make this quick," I hiss to hide my reaction to his imposing presence.

"I know what's going through your mind, witchling." He reaches for my face, as if he's going to touch it, and I step out of his reach. He drops his hand quickly, trying to cover the gesture by running his hands through his hair. I'm *not* affected by the way the movement makes his hair fall back so perfectly across his handsome features. *I can't be.*

I scoff to hide the awkwardness of the situation. "I highly doubt that."

He leans against the wall again, crossing his arms over his chest casually, eyes sparkling. "You're wondering whether bringing me will hurt our chances to convince the rebels of the ruse. And whether you can trust me. But you also see the sense in another *jaw-droppingly powerful* healer there with you. *And* you're annoyed at how protective Carex has been acting lately. Plus, you can't keep your eyes off my handsome Velmaran face," he says with a grin.

My mouth opens. I want to protest, but he very accurately summed up every thought I've had in the last five minutes. "I wasn't thinking you are jaw-droppingly powerful," I say to spite him, and the words come out more defensive than I want them to. I don't even address the handsome comment. He just keeps smirking.

"Look, if the rebels ask me about it, I'll just tell them you asked me to come, and I had no choice if I was going to keep up appearances with you. And now would hardly be the time for me to betray you, right before we're about to implicate ourselves in a heist that would easily give you an excuse to have me killed if we're caught. I can help."

It's convincing. But what if I'm the one being played? What if he orchestrated the attack, and he wants to go to help the rebels get away, or for some other duplicitous reason? Or, what if this is just a way to get close to me, to build my trust in him so I spill all my secrets? I can't forget that Nemesia thought Mazus *wanted* the Prince and I to meet. There's got to be a reason for that. I study his features. His eyes are pleading, open and genuine. And it *would* be the worst possible time for him to show his hand and betray me. It's a risk, but we're already in this, and I can't deny the injured. But I don't plan to take my eyes off him while we're there.

"Fine," I relent. "But you heal people, and you stay where I can see you. If I suspect you of doing anything other than healing, I will rip the air from your lungs until you suffocate to death." He only grins, the bastard unafraid of anything I say.

"You know, my father makes these kinds of threats all the time, too. Maybe you have more in common than you think."

I pull the air from his lungs instantly, then flood them with water for several seconds. When I release the magic, he chokes, spitting water and gasping for breath.

"Point made?" I ask.

"Clear as ice, witchling," he replies, eyes somehow twinkling with mirth, as if he enjoys my threats.

Now it's my turn to grin, a feral expression that's more bared teeth than smile. "Good."

I aerstep four healers, the Prince, Carex, and six guards to Rusthelm. Thick smoke immediately fills my nose when we arrive, quickly followed by the sounds of groans and screams. Most of the village is on fire and black clouds rise high above into the sky. I steel myself, locking the mask of the Queen in place, ready for anything.

Prince Hawthorne runs into the village the second we appear, gathering a massive orb of water around him and dousing the first building he reaches. Without missing a beat, he drops more water onto the next building, then yells for the healers to follow him. Within seconds, he's disobeyed my order to stay in my sight. I sigh. It's not the time to fight this.

"Guards!" Carex yells. "Four of you should follow Prince Hawthorne and search the buildings that are no longer on fire for any survivors. Bring them here. The other two—stay here and start helping the healers set up a makeshift infirmary." They nod and immediately follow orders. "His power will be helpful here," Carex admits to me, nodding to the Prince. I reluctantly nod my head in agreement, but say nothing, just calmly walk into town to assist with finding the injured.

"Over here," a guard yells, and I aerstep to where he stands in front of a partially burned home before he leads me inside. Huddled together in a corner is a family of fae—two children and their parents. It's incredibly rare for fae to have two children, especially two who are so close in age. They're burned severely, and only the father appears to be conscious.

"Please, help us," the father croaks out, lips cracking as he speaks. These injuries might be beyond even my own healing power. Though I can theoretically heal with any conduit I like, I haven't mastered any of them. It's time to see if Prince Hawthorne is as powerful a healer as he claims.

"Get the Prince," I quietly tell the guard before crouching in front of the family. I hide my cringing at their charred skin. "What's your name?"

"R-R-Russell."

"I'm going to heal you first, so you can help calm the rest of your family when they wake." He nods. I place my hand on his forearm, and he moans in pain. I want to jerk away, but I keep my hand steady. Conjuring cool, healing water, his blistered and cracked skin slowly reforms under my touch. He hisses. "I'll work as fast as I can," I whisper. "Tell me if you need to take a break." He only nods, eyes shut tight against the pain.

"Aethers," Prince Hawthorne says from behind me, voice reverent. Russell's eyes snap open and lock on Prince Hawthorne, and his already tense body locks up.

"Vel-Velmaran," he whispers, fear in his eyes.

"It's okay, Russell," I tell him. "Prince Hawthorne is a powerful healer. He's only here to help." The Prince crouches beside me and reaches for the first child. Russell hisses.

"Here, Prince Hawthorne," I motion him toward me, scooting over to make space for him next to me. "Heal Russell with me. It will go faster, and then he can help us with his family." He nods and sits next to me, his large frame crowding my space. Despite the circumstances, my body reacts to the nearness of him, goosebumps breaking out across my flesh. I'm acutely aware of every line of muscle that presses in against me, of the heat of his body as it wraps around me.

Russell still eyes the Prince with fear, but allows Hawthorne to place hands on his chest, where melted clothing sticks to his skin. Bright, warm light nearly blinds me. I look away, keeping my focus on the water I'm running across blistered skin. Russell gasps, and I look up. The light is gone, and Russell's entire upper body has been healed. It's not perfect, and he'll still need additional treatment, but the skin is deep red instead of black. Water gathers in the Prince's palms, and he briefly closes his eyes in concentration before setting his hands on Russell's chest, allowing the water to soothe and heal the wound once more. When he's done, Russell's chest is pink, like he got a little too much sun.

"That's incredible," I murmur, reluctantly impressed. Prince Hawthorne doesn't even react, just moves to Russell's legs.

"It'll be bright again. Close your eyes," he commands. I do as he says, though he wasn't speaking to me. Even with my eyes closed, I still feel the warmth of the light he conjures, can feel it soothing my own nerves. His body adjusts next to me, pressing him even closer against my side. I sigh contentedly, then immediately cough to hide the noise. When the light fades, I open my eyes to once again look at crimson skin. "How does that feel, Russell?" the Prince asks, his voice soft and kind. A piece of hair falls in his face, and I want to push it away. Instead, I stand, ignoring the squeezing in my chest.

"Th-thank you," Russell says from the ground.

"I'm sorry this happened to you," the Prince croaks out, genuine emotion in his voice. "I'd like to help your family now, if that's okay. Can I help your children?" Russell nods, and the Prince moves on to the first child. I can only watch, entranced by the gentleness of his movements. When her legs are healed, she wakes, screaming in fear and pain. Russell takes her hand while Prince Hawthorne smooths her hair back from her face.

"It's okay, my angel," Russell coos. "This is a Prince, and he's going to heal you." She stops screaming, though tears still run down her cheeks as she stares up at Hawthorne without fear in her eyes.

"You tell me if I need to stop, okay? Close your eyes, and when you open them, you'll be better," the Prince says in a soothing tone. Then he grabs her other hand and light flares, her small frame healing quickly, no need for his water magic. When the light fades, Russell wraps his arms around her, sobbing into her hair, ignoring his own skin. He grabs the Prince's hand, shaking it, unable to say anything else. Prince Hawthorne only smiles brightly, no winks or smirks or disarming dimple in sight, before moving on to the young boy.

Once he finishes stabilizing the family with his magic, I aerstep them to the makeshift infirmary, where they'll receive additional treatment. Before I leave to go back into the village, I overhear the Prince speaking with the little girl. "Are you really a prince?" she asks him in wonder.

"I am," he responds with laughter in his voice.

"What's it like being a prince? Do you have a princess you take care of?"

Prince Hawthorne chuckles. "No. No princess. Though maybe I need to find one. Being a prince comes with a lot of responsibility though. I have to take care of my people, care for them, and worry about them. Just like you probably do with your family."

"Yeah," she says joyfully. "Does that make me a princess?"

"I think it does," the Prince coos.

I have to leave before I overhear more. I don't want to think of the Velmaran Prince as the kind of male who talks to little girls about princesses after healing them with a gentleness I can only dream of possessing. I'm all hard angles and terse words, even when I'm trying my best, while he moves between every situation with ease. If I let him show me more of himself, it will make it too hard to make the right decision later. There may be more to him than the charming grins, but that doesn't change my plans. I will not forget who sired him, and to whom he will have to report back to when this is all over if I let him leave Thayaria.

Diving back into the fray, I find at least a dozen more people to help. Stab wounds, severed limbs, more burn victims. My fury ignites with every person I save. I get occasional glances of the Prince. He works as diligently as me, but quicker, though I don't want to admit it. Gone are his simpering looks and sarcastic smiles. Face smudged with soot and shirt soaked through with sweat, this Prince is compassionate and kind. When I catch him carrying a little girl in his arms with tears running down his cheeks, her limp and pale body telling me everything I need to know about the situation, my chest tightens.

We continue this way for hours until the final count of injured is closer to sixty. Thankfully, the only death is the one child, though any death is catastrophic in my eyes. After we've combed every building for survivors, Prince Hawthorne and I return to the makeshift infirmary, helping where we can.

A man across the field starts yelling frantically. "You," he roars. "You're one of them! You stabbed my wife."

I'm there in an instant, willing the grass to grow and wrap around the suspect. The screaming man breaks into sobs while a healer comforts him. Prince Hawthorne and Carex appear at my side, Carex's sword drawn and the Prince's hands lit up with light, though Hawthorne looks infinitely more at ease than Carex.

"Are you part of the Sons and Daughters rebel group?" Carex demands. I don't expect the accused to admit to it, but he surprises me.

"I am," he spits. "I came here to give you a message."

Fearing he'll hurt the group of injured, I aerstep the rebel, Carex, Prince Hawthorne and myself to the other side of the village with no warning. They all look surprised when we reappear under a massive oak tree.

"*Witch*," the rebel hisses. I only pin his arms to his side with ivy, tying him to the tree, today's events giving me little patience for this nonsense.

"I'm not in the mood. I'm a Witch, you hate my rule, you're going to make me suffer. I've heard it all. What's your message, rebel?" I ask, the cold fury in my voice palpable.

"This attack is only the beginning, Witch Queen. Any village, any fae or human, who supports you, or who receives aid from you, will pay," he warns.

I was already on the edge of losing control, my emotions a swirling landscape of fury, anguish, and hopelessness. This admission sends me into a storm of rage, all other emotions eclipsed by my need to *punish*. Rational thought leaving me, I pierce one of his eyes with a small tree branch, and he screams, trying to slump to the ground, but the ivy keeps him upright. Air wraps around his throat, squeezing as if hands were choking him. At the same time, thin twigs creep into his ears and up his nose.

"Tell me what you have planned, and I'll consider killing you quickly," I say, forced boredom in my voice, though internally I'm screaming.

"I won't tell you anything," he murmurs, despite the blood running down his face.

The sword from Carex's hand flies toward the man at my command, and I will it to slice a deep gash across his stomach. Grass burrows into the wound as the rebel's screams of pain reach an inhuman pitch. I make another slice on his thigh, then have a large tree branch whip across the wound. Silent heaves wrack the rebel's body now.

"Have you changed your mind?" I ask.

"N-n-never!" he whimpers. I pierce his other eye, completely blinding him. I'm lost in the thrill of my power, lost in my righteousness. Something within me urges me on, so I flood his lungs with water.

"Laurel," Carex says sharply. "I think that's enough." Whipping around, I stare at him, letting my magic shake the ground. His eyes widen in shock and fear, and he takes a step back. "Laurel," he whispers now. "You don't have to—"

"Leave us," I command with aether in my voice, too far gone to care that I'm compelling him with the power I loathe. Carex looks like he wants to protest, opening his mouth and fighting the compulsion, but he has no choice but to turn and leave. I barely register the guilt that creeps across my consciousness, but I know I'll regret it later. My gaze finds the Prince, and I sear him with a cold look. "You too." I nod my head after Carex, but don't use the aether-voice this time.

"I believe you ordered me to never leave your sight," he says, smirk returning, though it doesn't reach his eyes. Hollow orbs stare back at me, matching my own.

"Have it your way," I murmur, not letting his absolute insolence distract me from what matters. Of course he chooses *now* to obey my order.

"Tell me what you know about the rebels' plans," I command the man, this time using the aether-voice, again pushing down the nausea I get when I remember the way it felt when it was used on me all those years ago.

"They attacked today as punishment for using your healers when they fell sick," he says dryly, not in control of his words under my influence. "We took anyone who was loyal to our cause with us before we burned the village. I know nothing more. I was told to tell you that this was the beginning."

Something deep inside me is hissing with rage, and that same feeling I had in the Council room returns. Briefly, so fast I'm not sure it's real, I *evolve* into something more, something bigger than what I am. Shaking away the feeling of losing control, I focus my gaze on the rebel to bring me back to the present.

"Who sent you?" I ask, once again using the aether to force the confession.

"I don't know. He was a fae, muscular and covered in tattoos. I've received orders from him before, but his identity has always been kept from me."

I slit his throat and release the magic holding his body. He falls with a loud thud before I will the grass to grow over him in a makeshift grave, not wanting to leave a dead body on the outskirts of this village. With the rebel dead, the weight of what I did sinks into me, and that otherworldly feeling leaves me. Sighing, I rub my hand over my eyes in exhaustion and sorrow.

Just once, I want to be the one who doesn't have to carry the emotional burden of doing what must be done. I'd love to hold my moral high ground, like Carex, would love to refuse to engage in torture and compulsion. I crave the luxury to only use my power for good. But the gods, or fate, or whatever force decides what magic we're granted made me a monster and placed me in a situation where I'm required to let that beast free regularly. I let myself sit with the feeling of self-pity for only a few seconds, before I straighten my back and square my shoulders, ready to face the world and own my fate once again.

I turn around, expecting to see the same disgust I feel about my actions reflected in the Prince's eyes. But when our eyes meet, dark green orbs stare back, steady, calm, and unphased by the violence I just displayed.

The Thayarian landscape is as abundant as the magic that runs through the heart of the kingdom. Trees, grasses, moss, vines, and flowers cover the land. The plants there have attuned to the cooler climate and stay green throughout most of the year, only dying off for about two weeks each winter—the period called Abscission—despite freezing temperatures.

A Brief History of Modern Thayaria

The stiff, formal Velmaran clothing is scratchy, but I need to look every inch a Crown Prince tonight at the Welcome Ball. I'd much prefer the clothing of a warrior or even a commoner, but we all have a part to play this evening. My tunic is navy blue, with gold embroidered suns along the shoulders and sleeves. Medals and other unearned adornments litter my chest. The fitted trousers are cream, with a gold stripe down the side. Tradition demands I wear a crown despite my loathing of it, so I place the small halo of golden suns atop my head.

I can't help but be nervous for the evening. We've spent the last week going over the plans at night in the training room. The Queen demanded I show her I could hide Fionn and Silene from another room, and at a great distance, repeatedly. *Laurel*, as she insisted I call her, was not taking any risks.

After the rebel attack on Rusthelm, Laurel became hyper-focused on perfecting every aspect of our plan, combed over every detail of the ball and the prisoner break-out, tweaking and adjusting until it met her standards. We haven't spoken of the attack since returning from the clearing, both of us exhausted and our magic spent. Nor have we discussed the otherworldly glow that had emanated from her as she was questioning the rebel sent to threaten her. She looked transcendent. When I try to bring up the attack, she changes the subject or dismisses me. When I returned, expression pale and blank, Silene held my hand as I sobbed, telling her of what had happened and of the one I couldn't save. Who had done that for Laurel? Instinct tells me she simply pushed down the horror and carried on like she has likely done her entire life.

I've spent more time with the so-called Witch Queen this week than I have since we arrived, sitting through countless planning meetings with her advisors. I've tried to charm her, making flirty remarks and innuendos, but she continues to be immune. While I can usually get a few minutes of banter out of her, she eventually shuts it down. It's incredibly aggravating. We're never going to learn about the real source of her power if I can't get her to trust me. And there is *something* different about her power. I suspected it the moment I met her in the throne room, but it was confirmed for me when I saw her glowing as she tortured that rebel.

It pains me to admit that I've fulfilled my father's request to understand what the kingdom is like and how strong she's become, though I have no intentions of providing him with that information. I'm not sure what he expected we'd find, but Laurel is strong and fully in control of the massive well of power she possesses. Even more surprising to me is how she rules, the kindness and wisdom she shows, and her unwavering drive for perfection. She's respected, revered, and has kept this kingdom together—kept this kingdom *thriving*—through three centuries of isolation. I wonder, though, if the relentless drive she has is a wall she puts up between herself and the world—her attempt to show the face of a ruler she thinks she needs to be but doesn't feel she truly is.

The desire, no—the burning *need*—to get under her skin and break that cool and indifferent mask, see the female beneath the Queen, eats away at me. I have an unrelenting urge to prod and poke at her until she cracks, even though she never does. Throughout my centuries-long life, I've seduced countless females and males into spilling their secrets with just the right balance of charm and suggestive touches. It drives me mad she won't crack, that I have no progress to show for the weeks we've been here. I'm determined to win her over to me. I just need to find the right angle.

Last night, she finally told us the full plan to break out the rebel prisoners, not trusting us with the information until the last moment.

"The palace cells are built inside the mountain, but there's a passage from them that opens on the other side of the ridge, where the rebels can meet you to receive the prisoners," she had told us. "It'll be challenging getting back from there, especially if the guards are following you, but it will also add cover. If I aerstep you back and you're immediately seen at the ball again, no one should suspect that you were with the group that went down those passages."

Fionn and Silene had to scramble all day to get the information to the rebels, meeting with contact after contact to pass the information up the chain of command, but they pulled it off. I don't blame the Queen for not trusting us with the information of the secret passage sooner, especially after Rusthelm, but it would have made planning easier.

I survey myself in the mirror and a jolt of excitement rushes through me, though I try to pretend I don't know what it's for. Fionn knocks on my door, then whistles.

"You clean up good, princey," he teases. My rude hand gesture has him laughing. The formal uniform of a Velmaran Royal Guard makes his tall frame even more imposing.

"We need to go! Stop primping and let's move," Silene calls from the sitting room.

Her small frame jitters with excitement as I exit my bedroom. Wearing a navy and gold pant suit with flowy trousers that appear like a dress until she moves, she's both regal and practical. Noticing my observation, she twirls. "I had a tailor in town make it for me this week. Rush order. It cost your father a heaping pile of gold, since we lost all of our verdes playing skran and the shop owner charged more to not pay with Thayarian currency," she says with a maniacal cackle.

"In that case, it's perfect," I tell her. "Are you ready?"

She nods. We've perfected our act since our engagement. She uses her endearing personality to get people to trust her, and by extension, me. Then I swoop in with the charm and disarming winks, and they do whatever we want them to. And if that fails, Fionn scares them senseless. It's a practiced routine that works well, and we may need to use it tonight if things go sideways. I loop my arm through Silene's, and we walk arm in arm out of the room, the perfect picture of a Prince and his betrothed, shadowed by their loyal guard.

A large open-air courtyard built into a flattened plateau on the side of the mountain hosts the ball tonight. Like everything in Thayaria, lush overgrown plants creep up the walls and across the floor, while giant planters with night-blooming flowers are scattered across the space. Lights hang across the dance floor, and beyond is a picturesque view of the twinkling city below. Dark green and crimson banners mix with gold ones to represent the two kingdoms. The effect is breathtaking, and I find myself in awe of this kingdom that I once knew nothing about.

It's early winter, so the air is biting, but fire pits dot the courtyard to help cut the worst of the cold. The smell of burning wood and the aroma of the food makes my stomach growl. Silene has acquired a large fur wrap she drapes across her shoulders that Fionn looks envious of. Velmara has a much warmer climate, so my friends must be freezing. Somehow, I barely feel the cold. I nod toward a roaring fire pit with chairs scattered around it and we make our way there to warm up.

Thayarian nobles and courtiers slowly trickle into the courtyard, unaffected by the cold. When they notice us, they give swift and shallow bows before moving away. Music filters our way from a group of musicians while servants walk around with glasses of bubbling liquid and delicate hors d'oeuvres. The menu is another blend of Thayarian and Velmaran cuisine. Fionn suggested the small fried pastry that can be found at every street food cart in the Floating Market. Velmaran courtiers would never condescend to eating what is a staple of commoner food, but the Thayarians don't know that. They love it, judging by the empty trays.

A herald bangs his staff three times, and everyone quiets. "Her Majesty, Queen Laurel Elestren of Thayaria," he proclaims. Fae and humans alike dip into deep bows and curtsies as the doors open. Fionn and Silene give me a nod, indicating they're ready to slip out during the dance between the Queen and me. As soon as they back into a corner, I concentrate on the dim light surrounding them. Pulling aether to me, once again taken aback at how much power I can draw up here in Thayaria, I will the light to render them invisible.

My focus is tested when Laurel enters the courtyard. Breath catching, I can't pretend it's because I'm nervous for Silene, Fionn, and the breakout that will happen floors below. She wears a deep crimson velvet dress the color of the thayar flower. The sleeves are long, but her perfect breasts are once again on display with a deeply cut neckline. The dress hugs her curves, emphasizing the way her hips sway as she walks, while the color of the dress brings out the reddish hue of her hair. It hangs around her in soft waves, and the desire to run my fingers through it is all-consuming. She doesn't wear the dark makeup I've come to associate with her, and I find I prefer her this way. When she reaches me, I take her hand for the dance, giving her one of my signature disarming smiles. I think I notice her cheeks flush, and it stirs something low in my stomach.

"Ready to dazzle them, witchling?" I ask in a low and suggestive tone. Her eyes heat, and another grin breaks out across my face, this one genuine.

"Have you seen this dress? I've already dazzled them. It's your turn, princeling." A deep and genuine laugh erupts from me at the confident and cocky comment.

"The dress is indeed something to marvel at," I say with a flirty wink, my meaning very clear. Rather than blushing or shying away from the compliment, she gives me a wide smile, and I can't keep my hands off her for another second. I wrap my arm around her waist and have to stifle a growl when I feel warm, bare skin meet my hand. The dress is backless. I splay my hand low across her exposed back, and her breath catches, igniting a fire in my blood. "I'm perfectly capable of dazzling, you know. I'm sure you learned *that* when you asked about me," I say with a dry smirk to hide my reaction to touching her bare skin. She rolls her eyes.

"I didn't *ask* about you. I gathered intel about a political emissary being sent to spy on me. There's a difference," she snaps, but with none of her usual iciness.

"Sure you did. And that political intel just so happened to talk about my thriving sex life. Standard procedure, I'm sure."

"Hm, I don't remember reports of a sex life," she quips back, barely missing a beat. "Just your tendency to flirt with anything that moves. It gives desperate, if you ask me." Once again, I can't stop the chuckle at the perfect barbs she lands.

"I'll admit that I'm more judicious about who I take to my bed than the rumors may suggest. If I slept with every person who wanted to get in The Shining Prince's bed, I'd have a never-ending line of return paramours, desperate for my *skills* once more."

She rolls her eyes, but I don't miss the way her eyes darken with lust for a brief moment before she darts them away from my gaze. The music begins, a traditional Thayarian waltz, and our verbal sparring takes a momentary ceasefire. I whisk her into the dance, pulling her closer with each turn while keeping my focus on Fionn and Silene moving a few floors below. When I spin her away from me, I'm rewarded with a full view of the back of the dress. My mouth goes dry at the way the fabric dips low just above her ass, accentuating the thick swell of her hips, and all thoughts of Fionn and Silene leave my head. I pull her back aggressively and her breasts push up against my chest. Her lilac and mint scent wafts over me, and I can't stop myself from taking a deep inhale as I pull her even closer. She lets out a small gasp, and a wave of pure male satisfaction washes over me.

We spin and sway a few more times before I remember that *I* am supposed to be seducing her, not the other way around. It takes immense control to ease her body away from mine to a more proper distance, though I force myself to do it.

"What do you think, witchling? Is my dancing up to your standards?" The words come out husky and low.

"It's passable," she teases, her own voice somewhat breathless. "Though I think I can give them even more of a show. Wouldn't want anyone to wonder where Fionn and Silene have gone." An airy mist wraps around our bodies, swirling as we spin. She looks up at me, and I meet those wicked green eyes with my own challenging gaze.

"That's all you've got? I can do better." I concentrate on the light emanating from the fire pits. It takes immense focus to keep the magic wrapped around Fionn and Silene as they move while pouring aether into the light from the nearest fire pit. I wouldn't have been able to do it in Velmara, but at the nexus of so many leylines, my magic is stronger. Twinkling orbs of light appear around us as we twirl, lighting up the mist. We must be glowing in the darkness, glittering with mist and fairy-like orbs dancing around us.

"Impressive party trick," she says with a wink that matches my own. I pull her closer, deeply impacted by the flirty way she turns my move against me. "And the magic around Fionn and Silene? Is it still up?" she asks, voice low.

I give her a look of mock hurt. "You wound me, Your Majesty. It hasn't slipped once."

"In that case, watch and learn, princeling." There's a mischievous glint in her eye that causes me to press her against me again. The mist around us turns to light, falling like sparkling raindrops in the night sky. In the distance, bright explosions of light erupt across the Thayarian landscape. Then misty rays dance in ribbons around us. A tendril brushes my arm, leaving a dewy drop behind. My eyes widen in surprise. She's combined the two conduits; a skill I didn't even know was possible.

The music crescendos, and I spin her away from me in the glowing orb that surrounds us, then pull her back before dipping her deeply on the final note. Her chest heaves, and I have a full view of the length of her body, breasts flattening with the position. An image of her laying on her back in bed, naked, flashes across my mind, and I nearly lose my control over the magic concealing Fionn and Silene. I pull her up to me quickly, determined to wipe the image from my mind. But then her intoxicating scent hits me again, and I sigh involuntarily, catching myself rubbing soothing circles on the small of her back. She doesn't comment on it, but her eyes meet mine with a heated look.

"Well..." she says, voice flustered and cheeks tinged with a rosy pink. I make a low noise in the back of my throat involuntarily, and I'm about to ask her to dance again when polite clapping breaks whatever spell has been cast over the two of us. I'm reminded that there are others—many others—surrounding us, and that my mission is to get information out of her through seduction. I need to leave her wanting more. I turn to Laurel, then bow deeply, before raising her hand to my lips. I brush the top of it with the lightest kiss, never taking my eyes from hers, and I swear she shivers at my touch. She gives me her own nod, the small gesture full of meaning, and we turn back to the crowd with matching plastered-on smiles.

"I'm honored to formally welcome His Royal Highness, Prince Hawthorne Vicant, Crown Prince of Velmara," she says to the crowd. "While I know this ball is coming a bit late…" Laughter breaks out across the crowd as Laurel gives them a sheepish look that says she knows it should have been sooner, "I hope tonight is the first diplomatic event of many in the history of Thayaria and Velmara. Please welcome the Prince this evening."

With that, she leaves my side and walks to join a group of her advisors. A female I recognize as Aria from the Council of Advisors walks up to me, and I put on the mask of a charming prince once again.

"Would you like to dance, Aria? Queen Laurel spoke so highly of your dance skills." She blushes, and I give her a dazzling grin.

"Yes, Your Highness," she murmurs. I wrap her up in my arms and sweep us into a quick foxtrot.

Across the dance floor, the too-handsome Captain of the Royal Guard, Carex, leads Laurel to dance, his hand wrapped around hers. A pang of what I think might be jealousy shoots through me. I've never cared whether females I'm pursuing were interested in others, never cared if another touched them. But something about seeing Laurel with the Captain puts me on edge.

I dance with Aria, then with several other females whose names I don't remember. My attention stays equally divided between Laurel and keeping Fionn and Silene hidden. Laurel floats across the floor gracefully, never turning down a request for a dance. After a second coupling with the Captain, something rears up inside of me. Before I know what I'm doing, I've stalked over to her and requested another dance, my plan to leave her wanting more entirely forgotten.

The music has slowed to a tempo that allows me to keep her close. Worry in her eyes, she asks, "Is something wrong, Prince Hawthorne? This is earlier than we expected to need to acrstep them back."

"I just needed an excuse to get away from all the female courtiers fawning over me. It's exhausting. And please, call me Hawthorne." She rolls her eyes.

"You think too highly of yourself. The females are simply welcoming you, as I *requested* they do."

"Tell yourself whatever you need to." I give her a wink, then dip her low before pulling her back close to my chest, committing the feel of her pressed against me to memory. Changing the subject before I do something I'll regret, I add, "Your magic is impressive. I understand why my father wanted me to learn more about it." She tenses, but I squeeze her tightly. "Relax, I'm not trying to get information out of you. You can keep your secrets, witchling. I'm just in awe." She gives me a look that says she doesn't believe me, eyes narrowed in skepticism and lips flattened. "Truly," I assure her, and I'm surprised at the truth of the statement. "It was not… easy, for me, learning to control the massive power I had on my own. My father isn't a light channeler, and my mother died when I was young. I had no one to guide me. I imagine it was similar for you." I'm telling her things only Fionn and Silene know, hinting at the past that has formed me into who I am today. It makes me feel untethered. Her eyes meet mine in the briefest moment of shared vulnerability, and it lights me up from the inside out.

"Yes, it was difficult for me." The words are practically a whisper, like she's afraid of admitting even this tiniest of vulnerabilities. She swallows, and my attention drags across her throat, my blood heating. "Many days it still is. There are still many *secrets*, as you say, that I've yet to uncover about myself and my magic." Her brows furrow, like she doesn't know why she's saying this.

"If you wanted to train together, I'd welcome that. Whatever secrets we uncover, I'll take to my grave." There I go again, speaking words I've hardly thought about before they cross my lips. I've always been impulsive, but being around Laurel unlocks a whole new level of rash behavior. "My magic feels new to me all over again with the strength of the aether here. It requires more finesse than I'm used to. I'm sure there's much I could learn from you. And maybe the *Shining Prince* can teach you a thing or two." I give her a grin, and this time she blushes. Those pink cheeks set my skin on fire, and I wrap my arm tighter around her. She doesn't pull away.

The dance ends too soon, and she gives me a slight bow. "Thank you for the offer. I'll consider it, Hawthorne."

An involuntary and genuine smile breaks out across my features when she drops my title, using only my name. It's a small gesture, but one that makes something in my chest dance with excitement. I bow deeply and drag myself away from her side, telling myself the energy I feel is only because I'm finally making progress in my mission here. If I can get her to train with me, I might get answers out of her. That's all the dancing butterflies in my stomach mean.

Several more females and even a bold human woman approach me for dances, and I agree to them all, charming them with winks and grins that feel hollow. I play my part well, keeping all the attention in the room on me to distract from my missing entourage. It's a role I know too intimately, used to keeping up the persona of the Shining Prince in the Velmaran court. It's never felt comfortable, but tonight it makes my skin crawl more than usual, especially each time my eyes catch Laurel watching me while I dance or flirt with another.

My senses stay honed on Fionn and Silene. While I can't sense their precise location with my magic, I do sense their movements. When they pace in the short repetitive pattern we practiced, my eyes scan the courtyard for Laurel. I find her sitting in a corner near a fire pit, speaking with Admon. I give her a nod, and her eyes tell me she understands. There's nothing to indicate she's used an enormous amount of magic, but Silene appears by my side only moments later.

"Excuse me, but would you mind terribly if I danced with my betrothed?" Silene asks my dance partner. "I've barely had a moment to speak with him this evening with all the new faces to greet, and I find I miss his company." She beams, and the female practically falls over herself in her haste to give my hand to Silene.

"Nicely done," I say low enough for only her to hear. "How did it go?" We twirl into an extravagant dance, all eyes on us, and I give her an exaggerated kiss on the cheek to cement in the party goers' minds that they did indeed see Silene and me together. She pretends to blush, giving me a shy and demure smile before answering my question.

"Perfectly, actually. The guards Laurel stationed saw the rebels at the right moment. They pursued us just long enough to justify their job but quickly gave up when Fionn surrounded them with weapons. I expect they'll be reporting to Carex shortly."

"Well done, *fiancé*," I tease. She scoffs but quickly hides the expression by touching her forehead to mine, like we're whispering sweet confessions to one another.

"Fionn's the real star of the show. He bent the metal bars of the cells faster than I've ever seen, despite his magic being dampened down in the prison. Even the rebels were impressed. They had several metal channelers with them who asked him to teach them at their next meeting."

"Let's hope this gains us their trust and that we'll be able to meet with their leaders soon. I'm eager to provide something useful to Laurel."

"Something *useful*, huh? Guess your winks and simpering stares aren't all that useful to Her Majesty," Silene goads me.

I stifle a laugh. "I don't know what you're talking about," I feign. "I simply want to secure our alliance."

"An *alliance* that gets you into her bed, you mean. You're obsessed with her. You can't keep your eyes off her. We're going to have to publicly break up if you keep staring at her the way you do." She gives me a wide smile.

"I do not *stare* at her," I scoff. "I'm just... intrigued by her. That's all. And I'm trying to get closer to her so that we can learn more. May I remind you it was our *plan* for me to use my impressively good looks to get her to open up."

She gives me a long, hard look, eyebrows raised and lips pursed. The song ends, and I dip her low before bringing her up and kissing her forehead, then tuck her arm through mine and exit the dance floor. As we're walking back to our seating area, I spot Laurel, and her eyes... For a brief moment, I think I catch hurt in them. Or is it anger? She's so hard to read, but I suddenly regret the public display of affection I just engaged in with Silene. I drop Silene's arm, but it's too late. Laurel has turned away to speak with someone else.

We attend so many of these kinds of events in Velmara that it's practically second nature to give her light kisses and pull her close. Silene's safety in Velmara hinges on our ability to convince the nobles there that we truly are engaged, despite the rumors about my mistress.

We approach Fionn, whose expression is studious, his body tense.

"All good, Fionn?" I ask. He nods. "Then lighten up a little," I tell him with a shove in the ribs. "Don't look so serious."

"The guards who saw the rebels have arrived. I'm just monitoring the situation," he growls. I put my arm around his shoulder and casually turn him away from where I see the Captain in discussion with three guards, brows furrowed.

"We don't want to show any interest in the situation. Go find a pretty female to ask to dance."

He glares at me, then turns to Silene and puts his arm out. "Care to dance, pretty female?" She giggles as she takes his arm, and they walk to the dance floor.

"That's not what I meant!"

Fionn gives me a rude hand gesture that sends Silene into a new fit of giggles. I feign annoyance but am happy to see them enjoying themselves after the events of the evening.

There's a commotion near Laurel. The Captain of the Guard is speaking loudly to her and a group of her advisors. I don't like the way he stands over her, like he's trying to show off that he's in charge. Before I can do anything about it, he stalks toward me, the group at his heels. Iron cuffs wrap around my wrists, and I look up at Laurel as she reaches me. Her face is stony and indifferent, not giving anything away.

"Prince Hawthorne, there has been a breach in palace security," Carex says. "We're arresting you and your advisors."

Velmara has the largest and most complete collection of texts on magic and the history of our
world. Scholars wishing to visit Velmara's archives are required to submit a request that
includes their research topic and justification for their visit. It is estimated that ninety
percent of requests are denied by the librarians who run the collection.

The Secrets and Stories of Velmara

I've been here nearly six weeks, and the Velmaran court still eludes me. Thayaria is
political, with countless advisors all angling for influence or higher positions within the
Council of Advisors. But Thayarian political posturing is nothing compared to the viper's
den I've entered. The Velmaran court is made up of a combination of nobles, influential
merchant families, and various courtiers who've made a name for themselves with the
strength of their magic. King Mazus has a small group of advisors who have any real power
or influence, which leaves the rest of the fae at court to their own machinations. They
claw at whatever control they can get, engaging in complex schemes to secure things like
bigger rooms, access to the King or his advisors, and party invitations.

When I first arrived, I could barely walk to the archives without a dozen fae trying to
speak with me or invite me to their next gathering. Initially, I accepted as many of these
invitations as I could, hoping to uncover more information about Mazus, Velmara, or the
thayar flower. I quickly learned, however, that the fae at court have no interest in or access

to the inner workings of the kingdom. The parties were vapid affairs, an opportunity for courtiers to share gossip and trade barbs. Once the courtiers realized I had no interest in playing their games or discussing the latest rumors, the invitations stopped coming, and I was free to spend my time dedicated to research.

The archives have been life changing. There are books on every topic, dating back thousands of years, and King Mazus has honored his word—I have unlimited access to everything. I'm sure Mazus has his own collection of volumes hidden away, but the librarians haven't denied me any section or topic housed in the archives themselves. The head librarian—Dern—loathes me, but I've found a few younger librarians who are more helpful. One female in particular, named Genevieve, has been extremely accommodating.

It's been a slow morning since I stayed up aether-knows how late reading a text I found yesterday on thayar flowers. I roll my legs off the bed, then stretch my arms above my head. The chambers provided to me have been more than comfortable. I have a large, soft bed, a massive wardrobe that my clothing only fills a quarter of, a desk, a sofa, and bathing chambers. I would have preferred a separate study area, but after discovering the lengths Velmaran fae will go to for larger rooms, I'm quite content in the smaller space.

Opening my door, I pick up the breakfast tray left there by the palace servants. Once I learned that servants in Velmara are unpaid, unlike in Thayaria, coerced into serving to pay off debts or bogus criminal charges, I insisted they provide me with the absolute bare minimum of work. The tea is tepid, but I drink it anyway, before grabbing a pastry and returning to my desk.

Last night's discovery was massive. Before falling asleep last night, I decided I needed to write to Laurel first thing this morning. I pull out a sheet of parchment and begin the missive, omitting addressing her directly and beginning with dull information to keep potential prying eyes uninterested in the correspondence.

My friend,

I'm enjoying my time in Velmara more than expected. The archives are extensive, the food is excellent, and my chambers are comfortable enough. My favorite activity outside of research is walking through the Floating Market at sunset. It comes alive at night, with street vendors selling aromatic food and the Velmaran people greeting one another outside of taverns and shops. You can find live musicians on every corner, and the commoners are welcoming and friendly. I've learned much about Velmara and its histories and culture in the last several weeks.

One particular curiosity I've uncovered recently is the history of the thayar flower in Velmara. According to an ancient text on the flower, it once covered Velmara as well but disappeared. The passage did not mention what led to its decline but presented the information as if it was well known. I've also discovered that there is a shortage of the thayar flower here in Arnia. Most of Velmara's supply is sent to the Nivan Desert to aid in trade and shipping. The aether is extremely hard to access there since it's isolated from any leylines. The courtiers complain about the shortage frequently at parties, as they often use thayar flower to enhance their own magic.

In the right hands, this information could prove useful in negotiations or in making certain demands. I'm sure you can imagine who I refer to—the sons and daughters of our great kingdom deserve a better life, and I'm determined to find the information needed to remove any complications in achieving our vision for the realm.

Your friend and ally,

Nemesia

I reread the letter twice. It's still too much of a risk, even with the vague language I've used. Assuming any correspondence I send will make its way to Mazus's eyes, I must be mindful of what I write. While we suspect Mazus knows about the declining thayar, we don't know for sure. I don't want to alert him to it, nor do I want him to guess at the rebellion in Thayaria. But if Laurel could spread rumors that the thayar flower once existed elsewhere and declined, she could curb the rebellion's recruitment efforts. With the right framing, the information might give the people less fear of the future. I sigh. It's too risky to send any correspondence. I'll have to wait till I go back to Thayaria to tell Laurel and will have to hope that until then she's able to do what she can to stop the rebellion.

A knock sounds on my door. I crumple up the letter and throw it in the trash before standing to see who's interrupted me. When I open the door, a bored-looking courtier looks me up and down, then hands me a roll of parchment. "From His Majesty," she says, then turns away.

I open the scroll, then internally groan at the invitation to dine with Mazus that evening. So far, he's rarely interacted with me. In fact, the only time I've seen him was my first day here. There was a massive spectacle of an event to welcome me. Mazus gave a long speech about diplomacy and being the light for Thayaria. It was the first time I realized how much his people believed in his *Golden King* nonsense.

The letter requests my presence this evening for a private dinner with His Majesty King Mazus, Golden King of Velmara. It also specifies I'm to wear formal attire, and that His Majesty has arranged for a suitable gown to be sent to me this afternoon. I had a feeling I wouldn't get away with leggings and tunics as a female in this country. Sighing, I decide to spend a few hours in the archives before returning to my chambers to dress and steel myself for the dinner.

"Is there anything I can help you with today?" Genevieve asks. The young librarian's mahogany and amber eyes stare down at me from where I'm seated at my favorite workstation in the archives.

"Actually, yes, there is," I tell her, though I don't actually know what help I'm going to ask for. Midnight black curls bob around her delicate features as she sits down next to me and looks expectantly at my face. She smells like vanilla and parchment, and it makes my brain turn off completely. I scramble to think of something to ask her for, hoping to keep her here. "Er, right, so, I've been reading about the thayar flower, and I found a passage last night that mentions they once grew in Velmara. Do you know of any other texts that mention that?"

Shit. That was not information I should have given her.

Her brows furrow. "No, I can't say that I do. Could you show me the book? I might be able to find other titles like it."

Digging through my bag, I realize I don't even have the book. I'm a bumbling idiot. "I must have left it in my rooms," I say with a shrug, trying to hide my embarrassment.

"Then you'll just have to seek me out tomorrow for more help!" she says with a smile. It lights up her face and makes her already breathtaking features otherworldly. My own lips lift in a grin.

"I guess I will," I say with a smirk. She blushes, and it makes my own cheeks heat.

"Anything else you need help with? I'm incredibly bored and avoiding another scholar from Delsar," she whispers conspiratorially. I can't help the chuckle that escapes me.

"Hmmm," I ponder aloud. "Maybe you could give me a tour of the archives. I've never been given one. I just showed up and started exploring." Her eyes light up at that request, and she claps her hands together.

"I would love to! I hardly ever get to give tours. Dern always gives them. He probably skipped yours because he doesn't like you very much. I don't know why, you seem fine enough to me..." She trails off, and I smirk at her cheerful honesty. Horror crosses her expression, and she claps her hands over her mouth. "I'm so sorry! I spend so much time alone that I completely forget how to speak to others. And I've always been someone who speaks without thinking. The head librarian doesn't like a lot of people, me included, so don't take it too personally."

"It's okay. I don't much like him either." She grins.

"We'll start with the oldest sections and make our way chronologically," she declares, leading the way into the darkest corners of the archives. I follow, my eyes trailing her swishing hips.

We travel through the archives, Genevieve pointing out significant books or sections as we go. When we reach a dusty and sad looking set of shelves, she turns to me in delight.

"This is my assigned section," she rushes out. "All librarians are given research areas, and we become experts in that field. Assignments only change once every hundred years or so. I've been studying Eastern Velmara for the last eighty years."

"Is it an interesting topic for you?"

"Oh yes! Eastern Velmara is fascinating. It's so different from Western Velmara and the capital. And since the Andomers—the previous ruling family—hail from there, it's filled with important Velmaran history. I was thrilled to receive the assignment." Her joyful demeanor is contagious, and I find myself feeling more at home than I have in weeks. I give her a genuine smile, and she blushes, her eyes dropping to the floor. "Sorry. I get too excited about my research. My mentor is always telling me patrons don't want to hear about it," she admits.

I take a step towards her. "Your mentor is an idiot," I assert. "And so is anyone who doesn't want to hear about your passion for your job." Her blush only deepens, prompting me to close the distance between us even more. There's a moment, so quick I could have imagined it, where I think she leans into me, lips parted. But that can't be correct, and weeks with no companionship of any kind has made me see things that aren't there. Velmaran females are known for being traditional, boring prudes, and same-sex relationships are taboo here.

"Genevieve," a harsh male voice snaps me out of my thoughts. "What are you doing? The Delsar scholar has been looking for you for an hour." She steps away from me, and I turn to see Dern, his black beady eyes narrowed in ire. "Get back to that scholar, or your uncle will hear that you're shirking your responsibilities." Genevieve shuffles past me, eyes downcast and shoulders slumped. A fierce protectiveness ignites in me at the sight.

"Excuse me, but this librarian was assisting me with something," I retort coldly.

"I don't care what she was doing. Her job today is to assist the Delsar scholar with whatever he needs, not run off with Thayarian *scum*," Dern leers. I scoff at the insult. I'm about to give him a piece of my mind when Genevieve places her hand softly on my arm.

"It's okay," she murmurs so only I can hear, squeezing my arm gently. Then she adds loudly, I assume for Dern's benefit, "I will assist you with your query tomorrow, once the Delsar scholar departs."

"I'll see you tomorrow," I say firmly, narrowing my own eyes at Dern. He only sneers at me, then turns on his heel to follow Genevieve away.

After a few more hours of getting nowhere in the archives, my mind too focused on dinner with the King, I return to my room. A long box sits on my bed, and I bristle at the invasion of my space. When I open the box, I nearly choke at the monstrosity inside. Mazus has sent me a dress. It's gold and practically transparent, with two high slits up both sides that will show off my entire bottom half. The straps are dainty and the top dips low. Embroidered suns, the symbol of Velmara, cover nearly every inch of the dress. A plan forms in my mind, and I smile to myself, looking forward to seeing Mazus's face when I appear in front of him. With that happy image in my head, I get to work preparing for the evening.

When I leave the chambers, the gown swishes over the black fighting leathers I wear underneath it. I've strapped daggers to both thighs, making sure the sheaths are low enough to be visible through the slits in the dress. While the top half of my body is still exposed, I used plants to weave between the deep vee and cover more of my chest. I also used the plants to widen the straps and left vines trailing down my arms. My hair is braided back in the same simple style I use when I train, and I'm wearing the black boots of a solider.

As I approach the King's dining room, his guards bristle when they see me. I bare my teeth, and they stare me down. For added effect, I whisper to them, "Don't forget who I serve." They both blanch, and the effect is comical in their shining golden armor that wouldn't do an aethers-damned thing on a real battlefield. They open the doors, and I enter yet another gilded room in this eyesore of a palace.

"Mazus, thank you for the invitation," I say with fake sweetness and a mocking curtsy.

He looks me up and down, frowning for only a moment before recovering. "Nemesia, thank you for agreeing to join me. I should have invited you sooner. Please, forgive me for my lapse in manners."

He sits at the head of the table and gestures for me to sit next to him. Instead, I sit at the other end, tapping into the aether so the plants at my arms move. They grow, wrapping around my half of the table and down the legs. Mazus's eyes narrow—I've clearly irked him. I stifle my smile.

"I'm so happy to see you're making yourself comfortable here in Velmara," he says pointedly.

I take a sip of the wine, then smile. "Indeed. While plants are in short supply in the palace and city, if cultivated correctly, they would be quite successful here. Hot and humid climates are perfect for many species of flora."

"I will take that under advisement, Ambassador Nemesia. Or is it General? I can never remember." I stiffen, and he leers at me. The barb lands as intended.

"Let's not pretend you don't know I'm no longer an army commander. I don't even lead Her Majesty's Royal Guard."

"What a shame," Mazus says. "While we of course don't believe females should engage in soldiering here in Velmara, you made for a *unique* adversary all those years ago. You really shouldn't blame yourself for losing. You put up an excellent fight, for a female." His eyes glimmer with malice. I only purse my lips, not allowing him to get under my skin. "Do you at least maintain your fighting skills? If you need a training space, I'd be happy to show you Prince Hawthorne's sparring arena below the palace. I can't return you to Queen Laurel weakened, after all."

I want to say no, but I wouldn't mind access to a space to train, especially if it's private. "That would be most welcome, thank you." The compliance makes me nauseous, but I endure.

He gives me a severe smile that pulls his features into a menacing expression. "I'll see that you're escorted there tomorrow." He claps his hands, and servants appear, bringing in dozens of steaming dishes. Velmaran food is rich and full of flavor, and I hate how much my mouth waters during every meal.

Once the dishes are set and we both begin serving ourselves, Mazus resumes the conversation. "Now, tell me how your research is progressing. The librarians tell me you're focused on the thayar flower and Thayarian history. Are you finding what you hoped you would find?" I take a large bite of food and chew slowly, buying myself time to think how to respond. It's no surprise that the librarians brief him on what topics I request books on, but I don't want to give him information he could use against Thayaria.

"My first goal has been to cross-check and compare the information from Thayaria's own archives with those in Velmara, hence my interest in books on the thayar and my kingdom's history. So far, the records are the same," I explain, hoping the lie is believable.

"I see. A commendable strategy," he says, "if it were true." I pause while drinking from my wine glass, then set it down and stare at him. "Nemesia, come now, let's not pretend the right hand of the elusive and secretive Thayarian Queen negotiated access to Velmaran archives and personally volunteered as the emissary simply to cross-check and compare information." His eyes are bright with knowing. "No, I think you have a very specific and critical research question."

Shit.

I switch tactics, nodding my head and raising my glass towards him in mock surrender. "You've caught me, Mazus. Well done. That doesn't mean I'm going to tell you anything more." I give him a coy look before taking a long sip from the wine, my mind racing to put together what his angle is.

"Of course not, Nemesia. As a hobby researcher myself, I understand the importance of keeping one's scholarly interests close to the chest."

Hobby researcher? More like mad aethermancer.

"I'd love to see your famed experiment room, Your Majesty."

He smiles, but it doesn't reach his eyes. "Of course. I'll arrange it before you leave Velmara." I notice he gives no firm timeline, and since we both know I could be in Velmara indefinitely, it's no promise at all. "May I make a minor suggestion in your approach? I am of course very familiar with the archives and many of the topics you may be interested in." I only nod. "Assuming that whatever you're looking for has to do with the thayar," he continues. "If that's true, then broaden your scope. Many of my best scholars argue the thayar flower has connections to the very fabric of our world. Research the history of the leylines and the aether itself. That may get you closer to what you seek." His eyes sparkle, and my stomach drops. It's an astute and poignant suggestion, but it's too on the nose. Not only has he guessed what I'm interested in, but he's determined the right research strategy before I have.

I don't let those concerns show on my face, though. "Thank you for the suggestion. I'll take that into consideration in the coming days."

The rest of the meal passes uneventfully. He asks about Laurel but politely redirects when I don't give him any information. At one point he even complains about his son Prince Hawthorne, as if we're old friends and he's sharing his concerns for the future of his only child. It's off putting, this version of Mazus, though it helps me better understand why so many believe him to be the altruistic Golden King.

As I stand to leave, he adds, "I have a few books that may be useful for your studies in my own private collection. When I have a moment, I'll look through them and send them your way. In the meantime, if there's anything else I can help you with, please send word. You're most welcome here in Velmara."

My mind races as I make my way back to my rooms. I'm confused by his motives. He wants something from me, or maybe wants me to discover something specific. My immediate reaction is that whatever he wants me to do, I need to do the exact opposite. Unfortunately, with Thayaria on the line, I don't have the luxury of ignoring good advice about my research, regardless of where it comes from.

As I get ready for bed that evening, I continue replaying every moment of the conversation in my mind, trying to uncover Mazus's aims but coming up completely blank.

The strongest of light channelers can create weapons from the light, carefully honed intense beams that will slice through almost anything. The ability is rare, and very few light channelers throughout history have been able to actually fight with these weapons. Conjuring them quickly and consistently in battle takes extreme strength and control.

The Unabridged History of Magical Orders, Volume I

The Council chamber is thick with tension. The guards on duty at the palace cells immediately reported to Carex that they saw the rebels break out prisoners, and that the rebel group knew exactly where to go. Carex acted quickly, accusing the Velmarans of aiding the rebels. When he tried to *arrest* them, I reminded Carex and the Council that, as Velmaran citizens, we weren't technically permitted to arrest them. I'm not even sure if that's true, but stating it confidently worked—a strategy I've learned to deploy well in my time as Queen. I suggested that we instead *detain* them in their rooms until we can ascertain what happened.

They are there now, with six of Carex's best guards keeping watch. Carex, Admon, Aria, Margery, Nathaniel, and several other advisors sit around me in the Council chamber, listening to the guards recount what happened down in the cells.

"There were three rebels," a guard reports. "We didn't notice them until after the prisoners had been broken out. They waited for us to make our rounds of the lower levels.

They knew our rotation schedule and waited for the exact moment we left. The bars of the cells were bent wide enough for the prisoners to walk right out. They had to have had a powerful metal channeler with them. None of the metal channelers in our Royal Guard can even make a dent in the bars in that prison with all the iron around."

"And the Velmarans just so *happen* to have the most powerful metal channeler in history here in Thayaria," Carex adds. I give him a reprimanding look, one brow raised.

"Please, continue," I say to the guard. "What happened after you found the opening in the cell?"

"We heard them running north, so we followed. The prisoners still had iron cuffs on their wrists, so they wouldn't have been able to channel. The other three rebels sent plants to bind us. Then a metal channeler took all our weapons out of their sheaths and pointed them at us. We couldn't follow, we swear. We were bound tightly and weren't strong enough to counteract their magic. But... Your Majesty, they went out through the secret passages that open up on the other side of the mountain."

I nod. "Thank you. I understand. You won't be punished for their escape." Carex tries to interrupt, but I speak over him. I won't have these guards face his wrath when I planned this heist and did indeed send the most powerful metal channeler alive after them. "You're dismissed. Take the evening off to rest." Carex glares at me. They leave the chamber, and I sigh loudly, rubbing my temples. "We'll have to cut off access to the palace through those passages. Can we send someone to blast the tunnels and collapse them?"

Nathaniel nods and leaves the room to execute my request.

"Your Majesty, the Velmarans are clearly behind this," Carex accuses, anger in his voice. He stands and points aimlessly, as if that will emphasize his point. "They have the magic to have found those passages, snuck the rebels in, and broken the prisoners out. Not to mention, I did not see Prince Hawthorne's advisors most of the night. They left the ball and only appeared later. I'm sure of it."

"I saw both Silene and Fionn several times throughout the evening, Carex," I lie. I hate it, but it's necessary. "They likely kept a low profile in order to overhear conversations between the court and gather information for Prince Hawthorne. It's what I would have done in their shoes." I deliver the last line flippantly, as if it's so obvious it's barely worth mentioning.

Carex looks me over closely, eyes narrowed. I feel his scrutiny and suspicion, but I don't break, keeping my cool mask of neutrality. He continues. "It may not have required the metal channeler to be physically present. He could have bent those cells and held those weapons from the courtyard."

I laugh, cold and sneering. "I can assure you, Carex, even I couldn't achieve that." *Not true*. It would take barely a thought from me, but he doesn't know that. I've kept the depth of my power hidden from even those closest to me—lovers and friends included—still haunted by the warnings my parents gave me as a young child. "Next you're going to suggest Prince Hawthorne used light channeling to hide them as they snuck down to the cells and back." Giving him the truth so sarcastically should redirect him.

He pauses for a moment, looking at the other advisors for help. Aria speaks up. "Your Majesty, while it appears we've ruled out the Velmarans assisting the rebels physically, we still cannot rule out the potential that they helped the rebels in other ways. They may have provided information about how to get in and out of the palace. Those passages out of the prison are a closely guarded secret amongst the Council."

Carex looks at her gratefully. "Aria makes an excellent point, Your Majesty. They may have explored the palace under cover, then passed that information to the rebels."

"And how do you suppose they would have contacted the rebels? Even our best spies haven't uncovered their leaders or meeting places. You think the Velmarans have done better in a few weeks than our spies have done in years?" I ask, desperately hoping to redirect them away from the topic of how the rebels could have found out about those passages. It's the only weakness in my plan, and I knew I'd need to be careful not to let them ask too many questions about it.

Aria considers my point carefully. "That's true. That being said, we need to be cautious. With this and the prior attack on the palace, the rebels are growing bolder."

"I too am concerned by these developments. I'm only trying to prevent further strikes," Carex says softly. The guilt in my gut grows. He's a good Captain, and this is going to weaken him politically with the other advisors. Regardless of who was behind it, the rebels breached the palace on his watch. Even if it was his own Queen who organized it.

"Carex, I will *question* the Velmarans, if that would assuage your concerns about their involvement," I offer to make peace with him.

"They will lie. It's a waste of time," he scoffs.

Admon jumps in, voice soft and intense. "I believe Her Majesty means something a bit different when she refers to *questioning* them. She has exceptional power that can make people talk with the right... *encouragement*." The idea that Admon is the one to explain that I'm offering to torture the Velmarans nearly makes me laugh at the stressful absurdity of this situation.

Carex's eyes widen, and he looks at me with fear written across his features. Despite the decades that have passed since we were together, that fear still makes my heart sink with shame. It's the real reason our relationship couldn't go further than it did. At his core, Carex is afraid of me.

Carex nods, swallowing slowly. "Yes, Your Majesty, I think that would be prudent, if you believe it won't hurt relations with the Velmarans too much if it turns out they are innocent."

I wave my hand. "I don't care what they think of my questioning. I don't give a damn what relations are like. They're only here so Nemesia has access to the Velmaran archives." As I aerstep away, I find myself questioning the truth of that statement. *Do* I care what the Velmarans think of me?

They're seated at the dining table and startle when I appear. I hold a finger up to my mouth to tell them to be quiet. Gathering aether around me, I will the air to distort our voices just slightly so the guards outside the doors can't make out our words.

Fionn stands, anger and fear in his eyes. "What the hell are you playing at, *witch*?" he hisses. "Why have we been arrested, or detained, or whatever the hell you call this?" I don't flinch at the insult, not after three hundred years of those barbs, but it still stings.

Hawthorne puts his hand on Fionn's shoulder, forcing him to sit. "What I think Fionn means, Your Majesty, is that we're confused about what's going on. Please, enlighten us." Hawthorne looks at me, the smallest hint of uncertainty in his olive eyes. Silene also looks unsure, her bubbly aura dampened. I sigh.

"I'm sorry. I swear, this was not part of my plan. I didn't expect Carex to take such quick action. I knew it was a possibility he would suspect you, but he's been trying to grab more power on the Council as of late, and I believe this is somewhat political in nature. Though I cannot fault him for his actions or suspicions. He is, after all, correct about your involvement."

"What happens now?" Hawthorne asks.

"I've convinced most of the Council that you're innocent. They believe I've come here to *question* you. Meaning, torture you for information." They visibly tense, so I quickly add, "Which is just a ruse, obviously." I can't help the small pang of disappointment that they so readily believed I had turned on them. But it doesn't matter, because I *will* have to turn on them at some point, even if it's not today.

Hawthorne smiles, always the one to project confidence for the others. "Then I guess we need to put on a bit of a show for those guards out there."

They take about fifteen minutes to really trust that I don't actually intend to torture them, but once they see it's all for show, they lighten up. We spend another hour stifling our giggles as we make nonsense noises. Hawthorne, Fionn, and Silene moan in mock pain, and I say the most outrageous things I can think of in a firm voice, knowing the guards can't hear the actual words we speak, just the tone.

"Faustus the Fighting Fae once fell while flatulating ferociously from fishy fennel fritters," I say in a menacing voice, aether lacing my words. All three fall to their knees, both from silent laughter and the compulsion of the monarch magic. Even Fionn is enjoying himself.

My eyes meet Hawthorne's, and I swear some kind of spark passes between us, like our magic is reaching out to one another. His eyes widen before he frowns, about to say something. I don't want to talk about whatever connection seems to make my magic react so strangely around him, so I decide it's time to end this. I straighten and stand tall, rolling my shoulders back.

"That should be enough. I'll return to the Council and assure them you weren't involved. You should probably look a bit nervous and broken for the next few days. I'm not known for kindness or mercy in these situations." After the words are out of my mouth, I regret them, not wanting them to know the truth of how far I'm willing to go to protect my people.

Silene and Fionn nod, but Hawthorne approaches me. "Laurel, wait," he says. I look at him, and his fingers twitch, like he's fighting the urge to touch me. The thought makes my stomach flutter. I give him an expectant look. "I just wanted to tell you, I meant what I said during our dance. I would love to train with you. I know you can channel light after tonight's little show, but I haven't seen you use any of the advanced techniques. Perhaps I could even teach you a thing or two." He winks, and I can't stop the smile that follows.

"As I said, I'll think about it, princeling." Then I disappear.

It's been a week since the ball, and I've received reports that the Velmaran ambassadors have been scarcely seen. Rumors swirl they're licking their wounds after my hour with them. What they've actually been doing is trying to get an audience with the Sons and Daughters' leadership, sneaking out using Hawthorne's light channeling to remain inconspicuous. Based on the short missives they've had delivered to me, the rebels are being dodgy about when and where they'll introduce Hawthorne to their leaders.

I've stayed away from them, preferring to get their updates via letter. I told them I was too busy to meet, but the truth is that I'm feeling too many conflicted emotions in their presence. Hawthorne was too handsome, too charming, too *perfect* at that ball, and the way my body reacted to his is not something I want to repeat. I'd *enjoyed* the way his hand had felt splayed across my bare back, had wanted to impress him with my magic. When Silene returned and I'd seen him kissing her, a host of emotions swirled through me. I cannot afford to get distracted right now with the mole and the rebels and whatever Mazus is planning.

To keep myself away, I've spent my time questioning every spy we have in our network, trying to gather any tidbit of information that might help me uncover the identity of the mole. Using the aether-voice to force them to confess, I've crossed a line I swore I'd never cross—using the aether-voice on those loyal to me. Despite the temptation to use the same tactic on every advisor until I've uncovered the mole, I *have* to keep that boundary in place, for my sense of self-worth. So far, I've come up completely empty-handed. Whoever the mole is, they're covering their tracks well. It's aethers-damned frustrating, and it's only a matter of time before word reaches Carex that I've been questioning the spy network. Though I was careful with what I asked and didn't reveal I was looking for a mole, Carex is bound to come to me with questions.

Seated at my desk with Lunaria curled up at my feet, I look out at the city from my window view, hoping to find some miraculous clue far off in the distance. The landscape is still green, but winter has fully set in. The air is frigid. It won't be long before all the trees and other plants undergo their brief period of death before re-blooming. A sharp rap on the door stirs me from my thoughts and aimless staring. I cautiously open the door, then fling it open wider when I see Admon standing there.

"Admon, I wasn't expecting you. Did I forget a meeting?"

"No, Your Majesty," he says with a bow. "I'm leaving a committee meeting and desired your company. Will you begrudge an old man a cup of tea?"

My lips form a soft smile. After the war, when I was still finding my way as a ruler and grieving the loss of my parents and my sense of self, Admon would show up to surprise me often, claiming the way my magic could heat a kettle of water made the tea better than any he'd ever had. We both knew it was his attempt to provide me with company and support without overstepping. We haven't had tea together like this in a long time. I wonder what has him reaching out in this way now—what flaw he sees in me that needs his guidance—but I welcome him all the same.

"Come in, Admon. I'll heat some water." As he crosses the threshold, Lunaria stands abruptly, eyeing Admon suspiciously. He keeps his gaze on her as he sits in a chair, expression neutral and unafraid. She's skittish around others, and the hiss she gives Admon is nothing new. Yowling her displeasure, she disappears into my bedroom.

When the tea is finished, I hand Admon a steaming cup. He takes a sip and makes an appreciative noise.

"Just as good as I remember it," he says with a smile. I only shake my head and drink from my own cup. "How are you doing, Laurel? Without Nemesia?" As usual he gets to the heart of my troubles with no preamble. I want to say I'm fine, but he knows better, so I give him the truth.

"I miss her, and I'm worried we won't be able to stop the rebels without her. I've never been any good at offensive strategies. She's the smart one."

His eyes soften. "We both know that's not true, Laurel. You're a remarkable leader, not even considering everything you've been through. You have a mind for politics that I'd say rivals any of the best political strategists out there."

My eyes sting and my throat aches, but I lock it away. He always knows what I need to hear. The recent attacks have left me feeling insecure, unsure of myself and my capability as a ruler. Not to mention all the slips with my magic and using the aether-voice so much lately. I feel like I'm unraveling. While the words don't fully reach that place deep inside me that constantly whispers that I'm not enough, they quiet the noise, at least for a moment.

"You're biased," I say when I've gotten control of my emotions again, and he smiles with a steadiness that bolsters me. We continue speaking for another hour, chatting about potential strategies to deal with the rebels, the upcoming Abscission period, and smaller topics about the kingdom. Somehow, he navigates the conversation so that I'm reminded of what a competent and capable leader I am and how far the kingdom has come in the three centuries I've ruled.

"What do you make of the Velmarans?" he asks with a twinkle in his eye.

"What do you mean? I've barely interacted with them. I couldn't possibly provide an opinion," I say as my cheeks heat. He only gives me a knowing smile.

"I've found them to be different from what I expected," he offers. "The Prince in particular is not who he's been depicted as. Much like yourself." Now his eyes practically bore into my soul, and I squirm.

"Do you think his betrothal to Miss Kalmeera is political only?" I blurt out, absolutely horrified by the question.

Admon considers thoughtfully. "The Kalmeera family is powerful in Velmara, second only to the Vicants themselves. A marriage between the two families would have political benefits for both King Mazus and Prince Hawthorne. It's certainly a carefully considered strategic match. Whether that means it's not also an engagement founded in love and affection, I cannot say. The two of them seem very close, though I rarely see any public displays of affection between them. Why do you ask?" Once again, his eyes sparkle, and I have to turn my face away from his to hide my reddening cheeks.

"Only curious, is all. Like you said, they seem close, but the Prince is a shameless flirt, and that doesn't seem to bother Silene."

"I see," is all he says, the words filled with too much knowing. "Laurel, may I give you some advice?"

"Of course." Admon doesn't need to ask to counsel me.

"I disagreed with your parents' decision to keep your magic hidden. Argued strongly with them, in fact. It was ultimately their choice, and I got behind it, as that is the role of an advisor. But it pained me—still pains me—to see how closed off and afraid of the world their warnings made you." My body is frozen, unable to do anything but look at Admon as he makes this confession. I'm not sure where he's going with it, not sure if I want to hear the advice that's coming, but I listen intently to the male who has always been my teacher. "My advice is this—don't let their warnings about what *might* happen if the world sees how brightly you shine scare you away from forming real relationships and alliances with the Velmaran Prince and his entourage. I sense something special in them, and I think you do too. Be cautious and smart, of course. But there may be a real alliance there if you set aside the stoicism and secrecy you think you have to hold on to." My mouth hangs open slightly at his words. I consciously close my jaw. What am I supposed to say to that? Admon sees right through to the absolute core of who I am, and I don't know how I feel about that. Before I can muster a reply, he stands and stretches. "Well, I've bothered you long enough for one day. Thank you for the tea."

I walk him out, my mind racing as I close the door behind him. The mist barrier pricks at my consciousness, a subtle alert that someone needs to exit or enter Thayaria. *Merchants. Good. All is well*, it whispers to me, and I grant the access needed to whoever is trying to cross the wall.

Once again, I'm reminded of the way the mist whispered to me when the Velmarans entered Thayaria. *Good. Trust. Light. Home.* Somehow, I got the feeling that it was sighing in relief as they crossed. Shaking my head, I try to push thoughts of Hawthorne and Admon's counsel aside, but my thoughts won't stop swirling. Hawthorne offered to train with me, and that could be the perfect opportunity to get to know him.

He's your enemy, another voice whispers, the one that sounds like my mother and father. *He could see too much if you train magic with him. It would put Thayaria at risk.*

But I'm curious about him, can't keep him out of my thoughts. Nemesia would tell me that's a reason to stay away, while Admon would apparently encourage it. And what if he *could* teach me something new about my magic? Could he be the key to unlocking whatever it is I need to lift the mist?

My mind made up, I walk determinedly to my desk and pen a letter inviting him to train with me tomorrow morning. I tell him to be ready after the breakfast hour in his chambers, hesitating briefly before dropping the letter into the outgoing mail pile on my desk. This is just a test, an opportunity for me to learn more about him. I'm not committing to anything. I'll train with him, but I'll be careful. I won't let him get too close or see too much of my magic. And I will *not* let him touch me again.

The origins of the Prophecy of the Thayarian Queen are unknown. There is no record of the seer who spoke it, and the earliest records are oral histories passed down through generations of Thayarian fae. There are some who argue it is nothing more than a wives' tale, a story told around the cooking stoves of females to give hope in dark times.

A Brief History of Modern Thayaria

The next morning, I'm dressed in tight leather leggings that hug my curves and a cropped deep green sleeveless tunic. There are straps that wrap around my torso to support my breasts. It's a practical choice for training, but I also know the effect it has on my figure.

He's betrothed. And annoying. And your enemy. Scolding myself, I braid my hair down my back and skip makeup entirely, but I don't change my clothes. Grabbing a black, fur-lined cloak for warmth, I aerstep to the Velmaran apartment. They're getting used to my sudden appearances. This time, they don't even flinch when I intrude on their breakfast.

Seated at the dining table, casually discussing their plans for the day, they tease one another lovingly. A familiar pang of *wanting* grips me. I shove it down, then smile at Silene, who jumped up from the table and is walking over to greet me. The guilt I felt after dressing myself only intensifies, and I vow to keep my cloak on today and to keep my distance from Hawthorne.

"How are your conversations with the rebels going? Are they ready to introduce Hawthorne to their leaders?" I ask. She beams.

"Yes! We have a time and place as of yesterday. We were so excited to tell you."

"That's excellent. Great work, really. You've had a productive week."

"So..." she says, lowering her voice, "You and Thorne are going to train today." I suddenly fear she's noticed what I can no longer pretend isn't flirting between the Prince and me. I brace myself for her to remind me of their engagement, or threaten me, or plead with me to stop flirting with him. Instead, she says with a wicked, conspiratorial grin, "Don't you dare go easy on him." With that, she practically skips back to the dining table, leaving me once again curious about the nature of their relationship.

"What was that about?" Hawthorne asks her.

"Oh, I was just telling Laurel to kick your ass today," she says exuberantly. Hawthorne bursts out in laughter, and I can't keep my eyes off him. The laugh reveals a new side of him, a vulnerability he rarely shows. Something deep in my belly turns over. "Ready to kick my ass, Your Majesty?" he asks me, a glint in his eyes.

I stiffen. "Uh... yes," I say awkwardly. *Apparently, I don't know how to interact with him if I'm not flirting.* "We have to make a stop by the kitchens first. Need to get food for lunch." He looks at me confused, brows furrowed, then gestures as if to say, lead the way. I concentrate on the aether pulsing through his body, then aerstep us both to the door outside of the kitchens. "Stay here," I tell him, walking into the humid and busy room. The cooking staff are used to my random appearances. A human woman with brown hair and freckles spots me first. She smiles, then stops what she's working on and gestures for me to follow her into the pantry. "I'd like to pack enough for two today, Sarah."

"Of course, Your Majesty." She grabs a woven basket and loads a loaf of bread, several apples, a hunk of cheese, a bottle of Thayarian ale, and two smaller containers with stew into the basket. "We also have cake today, Queen Laurel," she says with a glimmer in her eye. "Chocolate."

I giggle with glee and give her a big grin. "You know me well. Two slices of the cake, then."

When the basket is finished, she hands it and two water skins over to me. "Enjoy your day, Your Majesty."

"Thank you. You too. And you let me know if you need anything from me," I tell her pointedly, looking at the head baker who I know has a prejudice against humans. She blushes, but nods.

I find Hawthorne leaning against the wall when I return to the hallway, the perfect picture of masculine charm. His broad shoulders strain against his tunic above his crossed arms, and his assessing eyes scan up and down my body as I walk toward him. I ignore the way it makes my spine tingle, determined to keep today *flirting free*. He grins with mirth when I reach him, like he's intentionally trying to annoy me.

"Ready?" I ask.

The Prince lowers his upper body into an exaggerated bow, one of his favorite gestures of late, eyes sparkling with mischief. "Yes, Your Majesty." I roll my eyes, then aerstep us to my usual training spot, not even thinking twice about bringing him to a place that's so special to me.

When we arrive, he frowns as he surveys the environment, shivering in the northern air. "Where are we?"

"The Spined Moors—the northernmost part of Thayaria. It's sparsely inhabited, so this is where I train my magic." The wind howls, and the Prince puts his hands in his pockets, trying to disguise his discomfort. "I'm sorry, it's much colder here. I should have warned you. Here." I will the gusts to stop blowing. "Maybe stopping the wind will help."

"It does, thank you," he says as his eyes search mine. I let out my own shiver as those mossy eyes assess me, though I pretend I too am cold and rub my hands together to disguise the real reason. "Laurel, did I do something wrong?"

"Wrong? No, why would you think that?"

"It's just—back in the apartment, you were so pleasant toward Silene, and then, I don't know, it felt like you closed off when I spoke with you." There's the tiniest glimmer of vulnerability in his expression before he quickly locks it away behind a wide smile, the mask of the nonchalant prince returning. "I know I'm prone to making an ass of myself, but I don't think I did this morning, at least not yet. And *then* you didn't even laugh at my bow."

I stare at him, deadpan expression firmly in place. "You were clearly trying to annoy me. It worked." We both know I haven't answered his question, but he doesn't press it further, only widens his perfect grin. I ignore the way it makes my blood heat.

"Well, at least I annoyed you. That's always my backup plan if I can't get you to smile." He winks. I can't help the twitching of my lips at his remark. It's impossible to stay stoic around this male.

"You're a light and water channeler, is that right?" I ask, trying to change the subject back to training and magic.

"I am. But I've never been able to combine the two, like you did at the ball. It's either light or water, never both. Teach me your ways, witchling," he croons, eyes dancing with mirth. It takes the centuries I've spent as the Witch Queen to keep my lips from twitching again.

"Focus on how the two conduits are similar or how they might exist in the same space," I instruct. "Water and light are both gentle in small quantities but can also be deadly with enough volume and force. Try to connect them in your mind first before attempting to channel."

With a nod, his eyes close and his brow furrows in concentration. His lips part slightly, and the sun hits his face at just the right angle, illuminating that hard, angular jaw and the closely shaved beard that lines it. He looks... remarkably handsome. Devastatingly so, and I can't keep my eyes from scanning up and down his toned frame, admiring every inch of him. He's wearing navy fitted trousers that show off the strong muscles in his legs and backside, and an equally fitted cream tunic that strains against the muscles in his arms as he moves his hands up to conjure. A stray lock of his hair falls across his face, and I reach out to brush it away before I know what I'm doing. His eyes suddenly open with my hand in front of his face. His lips twitch, like he knows exactly what I was doing. "Can't keep your hands off me, witchling?" That cocky grin makes me clench my fists to keep from punching him in the face.

"No, I was... uh... just going to conjure light and water into my hands to see if that helps you." The excuse tumbles out of me too quickly, and I internally groan. Trying to restore some modicum of dignity to myself, I do just that, so flustered the magic sputters for a moment before two swirling balls of water and light appear in either hand. "Focus on bringing them together into a gentle mist of light," I murmur, cheeks still heated from embarrassment. That pesky piece of hair drops in front of his eyes again, but he shakes his head to move it out of the way, returning to his task without teasing me anymore. *Thank the aether.*

His attention focuses on the two orbs. The ball of water slowly moves from my right hand and covers the light, then both grow larger, moving out and away from my body until a glowing mist surrounds us. We're encased in shimmering light, and he looks every inch the *Shining Prince* in the gleam. He smiles at me through the bright mist, unadulterated joy erupting across his features. The smile resembles the ones I glimpse briefly when he's laughing with Silene and Fionn, the practiced, simpering pursing of his lips nowhere to be seen. My breath catches in my throat, and I'm frozen to the spot as his olive eyes find mine. We stare at one another, something shifting between us.

My cheeks hurt, and as I bring my hand to my face, I realize it's because I'm beaming, the kind of smile I rarely—if ever—display. It only makes me grin brighter, and now it's Hawthorne's turn to look up and down my body. His smile disappears and his expression heats, eyes burning with a fire that makes me want to squirm. He takes a step closer to me, his own large hand reaching for me before dropping it.

"Look at that. You're a good teacher," he murmurs, voice low and throaty—intimate, I think. It's the voice of a lover in the dark, praising and assessing and seductive and wicked all at once. I imagine that voice whispering dirty things to me, words I've never fantasized about as something inside my chest flutters.

"Good," I say, and the word comes out breathless and lilting. "Keep practicing."

With that, I turn, walking away from him before I forget who his father is, keeping my eyes locked on the mist barrier as a reminder of everything I've lost at the hands of his kingdom. I make it all the way to the edge of the cliff, half a mile away, before my emotions are fully locked away again behind my own misty wall.

When I return from my walk, Hawthorne is fully engaged in his training. He continues to create and destroy the phenomenon of lighted mist, losing himself in the exercises for nearly an hour, while I admire his dedicated practice. He clearly enjoys training his magic. That's something we have in common.

With nothing else to do, I run through my own magical exercises, calling aether and releasing it. All a study in measured control. Remarkably, my magic somehow feels lighter and easier to conjure today. The heaviness I've felt lately is nowhere to be seen. I chalk it up to finally having a real plan to take down the rebels. We stay like that for a while, side by side, comfortable in the silence. Finally, when it seems Hawthorne can complete the exercise with ease, I say, "Good job. You've mastered it pretty quickly."

"It's all because of you, witchling." His features beam back at me.

I blush. Trying to cover my reaction to him, I narrow my eyes and say flatly, "Are you actually combining them, or just channeling both at the same time and using their proximity to make the mist look lit up?"

He winks. "What's the difference? This is more progress than I've made in centuries. And I find that the appearance of magic is sometimes just as powerful as the magic itself." To prove his point, he surrounds us in another misty glow.

I burn away the water, leaving only a few orbs of light behind. "Because if they aren't combined, a water channeler can remove the water and expose you for the fraud you are." I give him my own wink. "It's a great start, but for them to really work together, you need to think of them as one small piece of a whole, one part of the larger aether that flows in and through everything around us."

Fuck, I shouldn't have said that.

He frowns. "Aether only flows through the leylines." The floating balls of light disappear.

I've said too much, but I have no choice but to move forward. "That's a misconception, actually. The aether flows most strongly through the leylines, but everything around us has a tiny current of aether. Well, everything *magical* around us, and that includes basically everything but humans. The aether is pure magic, and our entire world is made up of that magic."

He studies me, eyes keen and assessing. My body hums under his scrutiny. Olive eyes draw me in as he asks, "Are you... more sensitive to aether? Is that your power? Because I've never heard or read that fact, and I grew up with access to the most extensive magical library in the world."

"Something like that," I say quickly and dryly as I gesture for him to try again, desperate to divert the attention away from me and my magic. But then I remember Admon's words, his advice to let the Prince in, so I give him a small offering. "Focus on the aether in the leylines, channel it into either conduit, but then release it. As it dissipates, concentrate on what it feels like right as the aether leaves. That feeling, that exact moment, when you know the aether is there, but you aren't channeling it, is what it feels like to sense the aether in the world around you."

He closes his eyes. The surrounding light intensifies for a moment but then returns to normal. I see his brows furrow in concentration. Those mossy eyes open wide with shock, and I try not to think about how it makes his features soften. "Holy fucking aethers," he whispers.

I smile. "What, did you think I was lying?"

"I thought there was a non-zero chance you were tricking me. How—how have I never known this? Why hasn't this been written about?"

I shrug. "I can't say for sure, but I suspect Thayaria has more aether than most places, even not concentrated in the leylines. So, it would be much more difficult to sense it elsewhere. I also think it takes a powerful channeler."

"Are you saying you think I'm powerful, witchling?" he practically growls, taking a step toward me, eyes bright.

I roll my eyes, trying to cover the fact that my toes are curling in my boots. "Everyone knows you're one of the strongest light channelers in a millennium, princeling. I'm just stating a fact."

"Is that so?" His words are low and deep, and his eyes now shine with a hungry gleam. "Just so we're clear, witchling." He takes yet another step, and I'm unable to move, unable to tear my eyes from his. "I'm not *one of* the most powerful light channelers. I'm *the* most powerful light channeler in recorded history, and the records in the Velmaran archive date back an eternity. None have been born with power like mine, and were you not born at the same time as me, I'd be considered the most powerful fae to ever live. Lucky for me, that title—and all the bullshit that comes with it—belongs to you."

My back arches, my body bending in orbit around this powerful fae. The temptation to give into whatever sparks between us anytime we're near one another is overwhelming, the desire to let those strong arms wrap around me almost overpowering my senses. But then I remember Mazus and Silene and all the reasons this cannot happen, so I take a step back, the distance between us a chasm.

"I've taught you a fun party trick, now you're up. Show me your light tricks, oh *Shining Prince*," I say with a mocking tone to cut the tension.

His grin is practically feral this time, an expression I've never seen before, filled with heat and lust and primal *need*. Before I even sense the aether moving around me—something that should be impossible with my power—he wraps my wrists in ropes of light and uses magic to pull them above my head. They're firm, but gentle, and the light somehow caresses me while it binds me. He takes a step closer, and the ropes pull even tighter, raising my arms so high that my back arches and my breasts push out from my body, front and center as he takes me in. My breath catches, and the image of him using those ropes of light to pin me to my bed flashes, unbidden, in my mind. My core heats, and there's a pulsing between my legs that I absolutely do not want to think about. I push the image away, but it returns as he slowly stalks closer to me, a predatory gleam in his eyes. Our surroundings are charged with magic, and one of us—I'm unsure who—has conjured the glowing mist again. This time, it's thick, blocking out everything around us and making his eyes glow like two unholy green orbs through the haze.

He's close enough now to lean down and murmur in my ear. "How's that for a trick?" he asks, voice deep and sensual again. I swallow, my mouth dry and my lips parting as I shiver.

Feigning indifference that I absolutely do not feel, I shrug. "It's okay." Then I will the light to unwrap from my wrists and wrap around his own, pinning him in the same position. That pulsing between my thighs intensifies as I reverse the power dynamic. "Nothing I couldn't do myself," I whisper in his ear.

His pupils dilate and his jaw ticks, clearly enjoying this as much as I do. He dissolves the light pinning his arms above his head, never taking those now nearly black eyes from mine. He slowly leans in close, and the most intense and maddening smell wafts over me. Citrus, jasmine, and lemongrass. I close my eyes and inhale, and when I open them again, his body crowds mine, the large frame all I can see or sense from within the mist. The

Prince of Light leans down and whispers in my ear, his hot breath tickling my neck. "Well, then, witchling, I will endeavor to show you a *trick* you can't perform on yourself."

I try to hide my shiver at his innuendo, but he senses it. He leans in even closer to me, and our breath mingles. I can't keep my gaze from his lips. They're full and pink from the chilly northern air. It would be so easy to close the distance between us, to give in and let us get whatever *this* is out of our systems. We're completely alone out here, isolated from anyone or anything who might hear or see us. I relax into his body, letting his heat wrap around me. He inhales deeply, like he too is trying to breathe in my scent. His hand wraps around my waist and tugs me close, burning my skin, and I let out an involuntary gasp of air. He growls low in his throat as he leans into me, like he's about to kiss me, and I want to let him. My mouth parts, my body heats—

And that is the catalyst I need to pull away.

"We should eat some lunch," I say, breathless, untangling our limbs and feeling the lack of him next to me like a missing limb. I walk to my favorite flat boulder and open up the basket of food, trying to shake the way his touch made me feel. I repeat the facts that would make anything between us an impossibility. He's engaged. He's the son of an enemy who still haunts my dreams, who arranged for us to meet at the same time that the magic of my kingdom is declining. I'm using him to get what I need before I'll have no choice but to find a solution to the fact that eventually he'll go back to Velmara and could be compelled by Mazus with the aether-voice to reveal everything he's learned in Thayaria. I'm sure kissing him is *not* what Admon had in mind when he advised me to build a real alliance with Prince Hawthorne.

Taking the containers of stew out of the basket, I will them to heat, then pull out spoons and the remaining food. Hawthorne stares at me, confusion and what I think might be fear written across his expression for only a moment before he lets that mask slide back into place, where it belongs. He smirks as he sits across from me, like he's been caught trying something he knows he shouldn't do, and it angers me. It was probably all a play by him, a way to prove to me that even I'm a victim to the good looks he uses as a weapon. I must have looked so foolish, simpering and breathless by just the simple act of him getting close to me. I push down my embarrassment and let my annoyance and ire rise to the surface.

I hand him his food items with more aggression than necessary, and we eat in uncomfortable silence, though he continues to observe me like he can't quite figure me out. When we finish the stew and bread packed for us, he finally speaks.

"What was my father like, during the war?" The question takes me aback, especially after what just transpired between us. Now it's my turn to study him closely, trying to determine the motivation for the question and if there's a specific answer he's seeking.

Despite my behavior toward him the last few hours, I have to keep my guard up, though I will *try* to use the opportunity to follow Admon's advice and be more open than I would usually be.

"He was a formidable opponent. We lost. He won. I just happened to be able to kill or shove his entire army out of my kingdom before the consequences could set in." The truth, nothing more. If he is Mazus's spy, this information won't reveal anything. If he's not, the answer doesn't give him anything the rest of the world doesn't already know.

Hawthorne seems thoughtful, gaze fixed on his lap and brows furrowed. "What was he like before the war, when he was courting you?" Now I snort, trying to hold back laughter.

"Courting me? Is that the story in Velmara?"

"Yes," he says slowly, confused. "That he was courting you, and you were close to marriage, but then one night you got extremely upset and lost control of your magic. The rest... well, I guess you know the rest."

"That's not exactly how I remember it," I snap. He holds up his hands in surrender, and I take a deep breath before continuing, though it does little to calm the raging storm inside me. "I only met him once, before the war. The 'courting' you mention was a single ball. A single dance, really. He made his offer to my father that evening." Hawthorne looks stunned, and I can't help but laugh at his slack jaw and wide eyes. "There are many different sides to a story, princeling. But this is the truth. He greeted me, we danced, he made an offer to my father, who then asked me if I wanted to accept. I thought on it for a few days for propriety, but I had no interest in marrying a crusty old fae my best friend and I referred to as Mazus the Moldy."

Hawthorne sprays water out of his mouth as he erupts in a deep belly laugh. After the laughter continues for several more seconds, I can't help but join in, and soon we're both leaking tears as we cackle. Then Hawthorne says, "Mazus the Moldy," and we start the process all over again. I can't remember the last time I laughed this hard, and for this long, and I have to ignore the tiny voice inside of me that whispers that I like the way our laughs sound together. I'm wheezing by the end, unable to catch my breath from the silent convulsions in my body.

"Witchling, you don't know what you've done. I'm absolutely going to accidentally call him that in some Council meeting one day, and he's going to murder me on the spot."

"Maybe that's my goal," I say as I bump his shoulder with mine, and he beams.

"So, you met my father once, you said no to his marriage proposal. Was there even any display of uncontrollable magic by you? His so-called reason for launching a war against Thayaria."

"Nope," I say with a shrug, diverting my gaze from his. "It's certainly not outside the realm of possibility that I could have lost control, because I was overwhelmed by my power back then. I had no idea what I was doing. But the only time I ever truly lost control was... well, when I chucked thousands of Velmarans out of Thayaria, killed even more, and erected a barrier of mist around the whole country." I look down at my lap and pick at a thread on my leggings. The mood sobers.

"So why *did* he invade Thayaria, then?"

"Your guess is as good as mine. I have my suspicions, of course. But he certainly never revealed anything to me. Even at... the end... before I—you know—*did the mist.*" I wave my hand in the direction of the coast. "He maintained that I was too powerful to be left alone, that he had a 'duty,' as he put it, to unseat me. Labeled me a witch and convinced everyone my magic was immoral. I think he just didn't want to be the second most powerful ruler alive. I think—I don't know, I could be wrong about this—but I think he was afraid of the threat my power presented."

"And your parents?" he asks, tentatively. "What—"

"I don't want to talk about them," I say firmly before he can even get the full question out. I might be trying to open up, but that is a step too far. Instead, I dig in the basket, then pull out the chocolate cake as a distraction. "Enough talk of your father and the war. We have *cake* to enjoy," I say with a grin, then hand him his slice.

"Cake?" he asks, brows furrowing.

"What, do you not have cake in Velmara?"

"No, we do. You make it sound like it's more than just, well, cake." He shrugs.

"*Clearly* you don't understand the magical properties of chocolate cake. We'll finish your lessons for the day with a practical lesson. Eat the cake, that's the lesson."

He rolls his eyes but takes a bite of the cake. "It's good, I'll give you that. But I prefer frozen ices and candies much more."

My mouth drops open, aghast at his dismissal of *my* favorite food. I shake my head, and we finish our lunch in silence, though this time it's comfortable and not awkward. When I've taken my last bite of the delectable treat, Hawthorne leads me back to the unofficial training circle we've been working in.

"Can you make weapons with light?" he asks.

"I've never tried." I concentrate, then gather the surrounding light into a honed dagger.

"Good," he praises, voice low, and it lights something up inside of me. I'm annoyed with myself with how easy it is for him to affect me. "Now send it toward me." I try, but it dissipates before it makes it to him. He *loves* that. "Well, well, well," he remarks, "we've found a weakness in the witchling's magic." I roll my eyes, but he continues. "Try concentrating on the intensity of the light in as small a space as you can manage. It's similar to the concept you mentioned before. When large amounts of light are channeled into small spaces, it becomes destructive. Visualize the tiny hole you're sending it through, then blast the light into it as you move it." I try again, and this time the light reaches Hawthorne, but he easily disintegrates it. "Good. You've gotten the basic concept. Now you just need to work on the intensity and your speed and get to a point where you can consistently maintain those two things."

We continue training for another hour. Hawthorne must also have remembered his betrothed and all the history between our kingdoms, because he keeps a healthy distance between us for the remainder of the session. When we're both tired, I aerstep us back to his apartment and leave him with a promise that we'll continue with our training in the coming weeks.

Back in my room, as I wash the sweat and grime from my body, I feel airy and light. Like I could float away at any moment and lose myself in the late afternoon sky.

Raw thayar is processed in large towers by grinding the petals into a fine powder, then heating them to an exact temperature before immediately cooling them down. This process is known to increase the magical properties of the flower.

A Brief History of Modern Thayaria

"We need to get moving!" Silene says as she knocks on my door. Today I'm finally going to meet the leadership of the Sons and Daughters of Thayaria. It's an opportunity to get information for Laurel. To do something *useful* after almost two months in this kingdom.

While Fionn will carry weapons, both Silene and I will remain unarmed. I don't need the weapons, but it makes me nervous that Silene won't have that extra layer of protection. She's an air channeler of less than average strength, being part of the noble class of Velmara. I scan her small frame, looking for any sign of fear in her, but as usual, she vibrates with excitement for the adventure ahead.

The rebels want us to meet them in a village south of Arberly called Oakton. According to Laurel, it's the closest port to Arberly and is a bit larger than the port we entered through. We suspect this is where the rebellion has their base. The journey is a day's ride from the palace. Instead of taking the non-magical way, Laurel offered to provide Silene with thayar to amplify her magic enough to aerstep us there and back. As usual, it's a smart plan—it gets us there quickly while giving the rebels the impression Silene is more powerful than she is. We're going to meet Laurel in her personal chambers, where she keeps a large supply of the flower that won't be missed or accounted for. Thayar is heavily monitored in the kingdom otherwise.

I settle my magic around the three of us as we make the long trek up the stairs of the palace. I'm not sure I'll ever get used to the amount of aether I can channel here in Thayaria, especially now that I can sense it in everything around me, thanks to Laurel.

In the days since our training session, there hasn't been a single moment my mind wasn't on the elusive and alluring Queen of Thayaria. My plan was to seduce her, but somehow now *I'm* the one who can't keep my eyes off her. I know I didn't imagine the heat between us when we trained, and every day since. Aethers, I'd almost *kissed* her that day, and not in a casual, "I'm just trying to seduce her to get what I want" way. Thank the aether she pulled away when she did, or I might have done something I can't walk back from. When I'm in her presence, I lose all sense of anything outside of her, desperate to crack open that icy control she has. Every time I manage to get under her skin even a tiny bit, my body heats and my own skin tingles. I've never met a female—never met anyone—who has this effect on me. Rather than coaxing all of her secrets out of her, I'm the one spilling my guts every time she's near. It's unsettling and entirely *not* what is supposed to be happening.

Fionn grunts next to me, breaking me out of my spiraling. "These aethers-damned stairs will be the death of me," he huffs out quietly, and I chuckle. It's a sure sign that he's out of breath that he doesn't punch me for laughing at him.

"Why don't you just use your magic to make a dagger or something float, and hold on tight?" Silene suggests, and Fionn's eyes widen in glee.

"You brilliant female," he barks out before unsheathing a large dagger from his hip. He scrunches his eyes in concentration and grips the dagger tightly. Slowly, he rises in the air. Opening his eyes, he whoops with delight when he sees that it's working. My burly best friend rises maybe a dozen steps before his fingers slip and he crashes to the floor. Silene and I cackle with delight. Fionn only stands and glares at us before sheathing the dagger and stalking up the stairs once more.

We finally make it to the door of the Council chamber we came to on our second day here. Laurel's rooms are just a few paces down this hallway. When we reach the large wooden door engraved with thayars and about a hundred other kinds of flowers, I knock lightly, letting her know we're there and the hallway is clear. She opens the door, and we quickly file in.

Laurel looks captivating, as usual. She's dressed in casual clothing, hair braided back, no makeup. I can see her freckles like I did the day we trained, and my body demands that I move closer to her. As I pass her to enter the room, our eyes meet, and I swear electricity zaps between us. This keeps happening, the feeling similar to conjuring tiny bolts of lightning in my hands. But she turns as if nothing happened, leaving me wondering if I've imagined it. My body aches to touch her, but I push down the urge, finding a corner near the doorway to stand in as I survey her rooms.

Like everything else with this unlikely monarch, her chambers surprise me. They're smaller than even my own chambers in Velmara. There's a simple sitting room and bedroom beyond, but that's it. The sitting room is furnished with chairs that look like they could be older than my father, many of them fraying at their seams. As I walk farther into the room, her magnetic and seductive scent hits me—overwhelming lilac with the barest hint of mint. It invades my senses and nearly chokes me, so strong in her living quarters that I almost growl at the way it makes me feel. I take one deep inhale to satisfy whatever beast lurks deep within me, then continue scanning the room in detail to distract myself from the building heat in my core and the untethered way it makes me feel.

There's a desk that's too large for the space crammed into a corner, every inch covered in papers and books. I enjoy knowing that despite her outward perfectionism, when it's just her, she's as messy as me. A fireplace that connects to both the sitting room and bedroom roars, the warmth delicious after the cold passageways of the castle. Other than a bar cart packed to the brim with various wines and liquors, and several bookshelves equally packed, there's not much more in the room. No dining table, I notice, before I see old plates and mugs littered across the coffee and side tables.

She eats here alone.

That realization haunts me in a way I can't explain, sending ice to my heated blood instantly. I'm going to insist she join us for a meal soon. I *have* to. Laurel speaks, voice melodic, breaking me out of my silent observations.

"I keep a highly concentrated distillation of thayar in a few wine bottles. Makes them easier to store and conceal. I just have to remember which ones they are..."

Silene giggles. "What if you thought you were drinking wine from a bottle, but instead took a massive sip of the concoction?"

Laurel grins wide, and it nearly knocks me to my knees. "Thankfully, I save my straight-from-the-bottle-wine-drinking for when I'm alone. It might make me light up like a torch, but at least no one would see."

"*I* want to see that!" Silene cackles.

Laurel's lips twitch, and an odd expression crosses her features for a moment, but she only says, "Maybe someday I'll show you." Silene nods her head enthusiastically. "Here we go! Now I remember. I used the bottles that have these silly goats on them," Laurel says, pulling out an ancient-looking wine bottle from the bar cart.

"Why those?" Silene asks.

"You know, I honestly can't remember," Laurel replies, and the two of them burst into a fit of laughter. Once again, I feel a deeply seated *urging* to move closer to her, to touch her. I clench my teeth, but it doesn't stop me from casually stepping to stand by her side, pretending I want a closer look at the wine bottle in her hand. Our hands brush, and Laurel startles before stepping away to stand in front of Silene, though she looks up at me with those bright and clear green eyes. Something passes between us again, and I know she feels it this time with the way her expression twitches, but she ignores it, instead showing Silene the bottle and giggling with her over the goat printed on the label.

This is torture.

Laurel pulls a small vial from her pocket, then fills it with a small measure of liquid. She hands it to Silene, who stares at it for just a moment before throwing back her head and drinking it. She licks her lips as she passes it back to Laurel. Laurel refills the vial, corks it, and hands it back to Silene.

"It tastes better than I expected," Silene says.

"My friend...er... my advisor, Nemesia, developed the recipe herself. She brews refined thayar with sugar, honeysuckle, and lavender. It's delicious and also potent. That dose is equivalent to about four flowers." My jaw drops. Velmarans consider the petals of one flower brewed into a mug of tea to be a standard dose. Silene also looks at Laurel with wide eyes.

"*Four* flowers? This will amplify my magic for *hours*, maybe even days," Silene says, wonder in her eyes.

"I know you're going unarmed today," Laurel admits quietly. "I just wanted to make sure you would be safe. Especially if something happens and you're there longer than you expect."

Something in my chest squeezes, and I look into Laurel's eyes, trying to convey my gratitude to her. She finally returns my stare, acknowledging the unspoken words between us before looking down at her hands in embarrassment. The ice queen has a soft spot for Silene. It gives me hope that maybe—just maybe—she'll fully open up to us one day. And that maybe I won't need to seduce her to get her to trust us.

"How are you feeling?" I ask Silene to distract myself from the overwhelming desire to wrap Laurel in my arms.

"Like I could aerstep this whole fucking castle," she squeals. Laurel's lips quirk, and I meet her eyes again. This time, she doesn't look away, meeting my gaze full on. It's intimidating as fuck, and I want to run from it and drown in it in equal measure.

"Then let's go," I say, tearing my gaze from Laurel's. "We'll aerstep back to our apartment when we're done. Now that I've been to your rooms, I can flicker the lights here to signal that we're back." Laurel nods, then Fionn and I grab Silene's hands. Technically, we don't have to be touching for Silene to aerstep up, but it helps her control the magic she rarely uses. As I look up and down Laurel's body one more time, the familiar pressure of being aerstepped compresses my body.

We arrive just outside of Oakton, having picked the exact place on the map where we wanted to appear several days prior. Silene releases our hands and the three of us walk into the bustling village. The inspiration for the village name becomes immediately apparent, as it sits within a massive oak forest. Sprawling trees that are somehow still green even well into winter grow everywhere there isn't a building or road. The winter sun filters through the swaying branches high above, casting everything in a sun-dappled glow.

The buildings in the town are all wooden, likely made from the very oaks felled to make room for them. As we walk, I notice there are humans and fae living alongside one another, a rare sight in Velmara outside of the capital, but more common here in Thayaria. Children chase one another through the streets while their parents yell at them to behave. We arrive at the tavern where we were told to meet, though we're an hour early on purpose.

Silene and I enter through the front doors, while Fionn sneaks around the back to secure an exit for us just in case. It's gloomy and run down inside, nothing like the pristine and lively pubs of Arberly. A single barmaid wipes down the bar while a group of fae occupy a table in the corner, speaking quietly. Silene shrugs, and we take a seat at a table that has a view of both the front and back entrances.

The barmaid comes over, a human woman who can't be more than a few decades old. "What can I get ya?" she asks.

I give her a wide, dashing grin. "Just two ales, please," I say, winking.

As she walks away, Silene snorts. "Must you *always* flirt with every barkeep we ever encounter? What would *Laurel* say?" she asks in mock horror.

"One—yes, I must flirt with them, as it makes it easier to get information out of her when she comes back. And two—Laurel seems to pay little attention to who I do or do not flirt with, herself included." The words come out more defensive and whining than I intend, like I'm pouting that a pretty girl won't flirt back with me. It's abhorrent. I try to recover the situation. "The Queen of Thayaria is a mark, nothing more, nothing less. She's just been... difficult." The lie is as much for myself as it is for Silene.

"I think Laurel notices you flirting with her," Silene says with a knowing smile. "The two of you are blatantly obvious about your *flirting*. And we both know she's much more than a *mark*, as you say."

My cheeks heat, and I stammer out my response. "I—she's not—we're—"

Silene bursts out laughing. "I never thought I would see the day the *Shining Prince* of Velmara turns into a blubbering idiot over a female. Though I guess I've never actually seen you be interested in anyone, female or male, my entire life. It makes sense you'd be more like the rest of us when you actually care."

I'm about to retort that I have no idea what she's talking about when the barmaid returns, placing two ales on our table. I hand her a generous amount of Thayarian coin, then say, pointedly, "We're meeting some folks here in about an hour. Not sure who they are or what they might look like, but we're hoping you might know something about that." I give her another conspiratorial grin.

She looks around, then says in hushed tones, "I might know something, might not. Hard to remember after such a long shift today with barely any tips."

Silene snorts, and I give her a harsh look. Then I slip the woman a second coin. "Sorry to hear about the slow day. Maybe this will help."

She takes the second coin, putting it in the pocket of her trousers. "I'm guessing you're here for the rebels. I don't get myself caught up in none of that, but they do frequent this place since it's such a shit hole. What do you want to know?"

"When they meet, how many are usually here?"

"Depends," she says with a shrug. "Day like today, where they're recruitin', it'll probably be about two or three of them. Plus, they always keep a few outside to act as guards, case anything goes wrong."

"Thank you. When they arrive, could you give us a signal?" I ask, sliding her another two coins. She nods, then walks away.

"Hate to say it," Silene says, "but your royal coffers got her to talk, not your prince charming act."

I give her a mock sneer as I stand. "I'm going to go tell Fionn he can come in now. If the most they're going to have is a half dozen of them, we can take that and make it out, no problem."

An hour later, two males enter, and the barmaid immediately looks over at me. I give her a nod but otherwise act oblivious to their arrival. Silene and Fionn stiffen beside me.

"The one on the left," Fionn says. "He was one of the prisoners we helped escape. Laurel thought none of the prisoners were connected to leadership. I think she was wrong."

I tense as the tall fae walks toward us, recognizing Fionn and Silene. He has bright red hair and midnight blue eyes that gleam with something that puts me on alert. The fae next to him is stout and muscular, covered in tattoos, with cropped chestnut hair and matching eyes. *This must be the fae who ordered the attack on Rusthelm.* Knowing I'm in the same room as the monster who decided a village should be punished for accepting help from their ruler makes me feel ill.

"Silene, Fionn," the tall male says as they pull up chairs to our table and sit. "Thank you again for your help. I'd be rotting away if not for you." They both nod, and he turns his gaze to me. "You must be the Shining Prince, Hawthorne Vicant himself," he says with a smile that doesn't reach his eyes.

"I am," I say coolly. "Though I can't say I have the pleasure of knowing who you are."

"My name is Krantz, and this is my second, Saff," he says, nodding to the male beside him. "We are what most people would consider the leaders of the Sons and Daughters, though we prefer to think of ourselves as protectors."

"And what is it you protect?" I ask, eyes narrowing.

"Well, the sons and daughters and Thayaria, of course," he responds, as if it were the simplest thing in the world. Silene steps on my foot, and I take that as a sign to lighten up.

"Well, then, Krantz and Saff, great protectors of Thayaria, I'm pleased to make your acquaintance," I say with my most magnanimous smile. Krantz grins himself and reaches out to shake my hand. I oblige, putting the tiniest zing of aether into my grip to remind him who he's dealing with.

"We've wanted an alliance with Velmara for a long time. *We* know that your father, His Majesty the King, has spoken the truth about the *Witch Queen* for three hundred years. The outside world believed him, but here in Thayaria, her wicked magic swayed the people to her side. Only in the last fifty years have we started to see the reality of her corruption."

I hate what I'm about to say, because I've seen the truth for myself. "The Witch Queen has pulled a veil over the eyes of Thayaria. I'm here to remove it so that you can finally see."

"We knew the rumors that you were here to bring peace between Velmara and Thayaria were lies," he spits back.

"I'm no Prince of Peace, of that I can assure you," I tell him with a menacing snarl.

"I'm glad to hear it. And even more glad to hear it today, as we have an opportunity for you to hit the witch where it hurts most." His eyes are bright with malice that makes my stomach roil.

"Oh?" I feign coolness. "And what might that be?"

"We're going to attack Arberly, and we need you to help us."

My stomach drops low in my gut, but I keep my expression indifferent. "Another poorly planned attempt to strike the Queen like what my advisor saw during court? I'd rather not dirty my tunic for something doomed to fail."

His expression tightens. "No, this is nothing like that. We've been planning this for months. The attack you witnessed was merely a distraction to keep her spies sniffing in the wrong places. Had you not rescued us, we had our own plan for escape. We're going to attack the city itself and show those loyalists who live there just how vulnerable they, and their Queen, really are."

"What exactly is the target?" I ask, my heart now pumping a fast staccato.

"The target is the thayar processing tower, though the mission is to steal what we can from it, not destroy it. The merchant district is the distraction. That, we plan to leave in ruins." My mind races, trying to think of a way out of this, a way to stop them.

"What do you need our help with?" Silene chimes in, ever the strategist.

Krantz looks at her like he hadn't remembered she was there. A sneer crosses his face. "We need *Prince Hawthorne's* help to sneak us into the processing tower. It's heavily guarded, since it contains the largest supply of thayar in the entire kingdom." He looks at me. "Once we saw how easily you kept Fionn and Silene cloaked, we knew we'd found the last missing piece we needed to pull this off. My people will cause a distraction in the merchant district, while you get a small group of us in and out. It'll be simple."

I desperately want to look toward Silene or Fionn sitting next to me to see if they've determined a way to stop this. But if they had, they'd have said something. "What are you planning on using the supply of thayar for?"

Once again, he gives me that cold and calculating smile that makes my skin crawl. "Don't you worry, we have plenty of other plans in motion that will put that to use." I clench my jaw once, struggling to hide the frustration I feel.

"I'd be happy to help." I shove down my nausea.

"Excellent, Your Highness," he says, smoothly. "We leave in an hour."

*Eastern Velmara is home to a powerful family of light channelers. They have endless myths
and prophecies about a prince who will be born in a time of darkness to bring the light
back into the world.*

The Secrets and Stories of Velmara

"What the fuck are we going to do?" Fionn whispers twenty minutes later. Krantz and
Saff went over the basic details of the plan, then left us so they could arrange a few things.
We were told to wait here until they came back to get us. On the way out, Krantz pointed
to the table of fae we saw on the way in.

"Those are my men over there," he said. "They'll keep an eye on you till we come back.
Can't be too careful in these parts." I'd interpreted it for the message it was—we weren't
permitted to leave.

"If we refuse to help them, our cover will be blown," Silene says, stoically. "If I try to
aerstep to warn Laurel, they'll know. This is another test. They know exactly what they're
doing, asking us to help them again. What do you want to do, Thorne?" Her amber eyes
look to me, and I know I have a hard decision to make.

"If we don't help them now, we'll never be able to get close and uncover their plans
again. More people might die in future attacks. I don't like it, but I think we have to stay."
I don't want to make this choice, but this path is the only one that gives us any real chance

of stopping the rebels in the future. "Clearly they only care about me," I continue, and Fionn rolls his eyes. "What I *mean* is that they likely won't care what the two of you do during the heist, as long as I'm getting them into that tower. You can go with the group that's attacking the merchant quarter and do what you can to minimize the damage."

"No, we should stay with you," Fionn protests, but Silene cuts him off.

"I don't like it, but I agree with Thorne." Fionn lets out a low growl. "We can't let innocent people be injured, or worse, if we can help it. I'm still charged up from the dose of thayar Laurel gave me, and I can take a bit more. With our magic, we can get people out of the way of the worst of the violence."

Fionn tenses his muscles but nods his head in agreement.

"I may be able to hide some of the stores of thayar from the rebels to limit what they sneak out. And I can let my magic *slip* at the right time to alert the guards to their presence."

"If Laurel shows up and catches you, is she going to believe we had no choice but to help them?" Fionn asks, fear flashing across his eyes.

"She'll believe us," Silene says confidently. I'm surprised by Silene's sureness. I *think* Laurel will believe us, but I would be lying to myself if I said I wasn't nervous about it. Regardless, I nod my head in agreement with Silene, projecting confidence.

We pass the rest of the hour in nervous silence. Just before the time is up, Silene takes a small sip from the vial Laurel gave her, but she doesn't drain it. Saff walks in alone, the silent male only gesturing for us to accompany him outside. We do, then follow him through the town to a large and seemingly abandoned manor. As we enter, I keep my attention alert for any clues about whether this might be a headquarters for the rebellion, eager to provide Laurel with the information. We're led up a creaking staircase to what once was a massive ballroom. Hundreds of people have gathered inside, dressed in everything from the simple clothes of villagers to the fighting leathers of soldiers.

Krantz stands atop a makeshift stage, then clears his throat before projecting loudly to the crowd. "Sons and Daughters, for too long we have been isolated in this kingdom, cut off from the rest of the world, while the *Witch Queen* decides who comes and who goes. What's more, the very magic of our land is being drained by her Blood Magic. Our thayar blooms decline with every passing year. All because of the selfish ways of our so-called Queen."

Silene looks at me, confusion crossing her features. "Did you know that?" I shake my head discreetly.

Krantz continues. "We will not be kept prisoner in these lands any longer! Today, we strike a blow at the people who continue to believe her lies and profit from her deception.

Merchants who have access to the flower to power their businesses, all while we struggle to get by as we once did. We'll destroy their vile and corrupt district!"

The people in the room cheer loudly as I study them. I wasn't aware thayar blooms were declining in Thayaria. That information paints these people in a new light, and I wonder why Laurel kept this from us. *From me.* The rebels' fears make a lot more sense, and this situation is more dangerous than I realized.

Krantz lets the roar from the room peak and then dissipate before he continues. "And while they're busy defending our attack, the Crown Prince of Velmara, the Shining Prince himself, will aid us in a covert operation to steal a supply of thayar from right under their noses. Even Velmara recognizes the righteousness of our cause and aligns with us!"

The crowd cheers again, a deafening rally, and I stiffen. A group of fae next to me takes notice of my presence, and they whisper and point. Soon, dozens of eyes are looking my way. I bristle under their scrutinizing gaze. Krantz stands on the podium with a victorious look that tells me he knew exactly what he was doing by alerting these people to my presence.

Several other fae appear near Krantz, barking orders to organize the crowd into groups for aerstepping. Silene, Fionn, and I are directed to a group that includes Krantz. "We're going to aerstep into the merchant district first, then we'll make our way discreetly to the thayar tower," Krantz tells me.

I nod. "I'd like to leave my advisors, Fionn and Silene, with the group attacking the merchants. They're both excellent fighters with strong magic. We won't need them in our small group."

"An excellent idea, Your Highness."

We arrive on a bustling street in Arberly I recognize, lined with shops selling all kinds of goods. My gut churns with anticipation and guilt at what's about to happen, but I have to trust that Fionn and Silene can do more good than if we hadn't been here. Our group immediately breaks apart and walks off in pointed directions.

"Stick with me for now," Krantz says. "Once we get going, our people will know what to do, and we'll slip off. The others going with us know where to meet." With that, Krantz heads farther into the heart of the district. We slip into an alleyway, where a pile of *something* sits, hidden under a cloth. Krantz rips the tarp off, revealing a large pile of wood stuffed with small vials containing a deep red liquid.

"Concentrated thayar," Silene whispers, eyes wide.

Krantz grins and gives her a nod. "Smart girl. As soon as I throw this match, we need to run to the main road," Krantz says, letting the flame burn high. "If you run fast enough, you *should* make it before it explodes." His smile widens. "Bombs just like this one are being lit all over the district. Once we get everyone into the main square, we'll start phase two of the attack."

"But why are you using thayar to create bombs when you're also trying to steal *more* thayar? Isn't that defeating the purpose of the whole mission?" Silene asks, expression shocked and confused.

Krantz bares his teeth, clearly disliking being questioned by her. "Not that it's any of your business, but this bomb barely even uses one flower, and we're going to steal *hundreds of thousands.* Now, are you all ready?" He doesn't wait for a response, just throws the match onto the mound. We all run, and just as we reach the main street that runs through the middle of Arberly, chaos erupts around us.

Explosions sound from all directions. Shrieks and cries begin only a few moments later. Soon families and shop workers flood onto the main street, driven out of their homes and shops by the explosions. Their faces show confusion and fear. Dozens are injured from the explosions alone, blood dripping onto the street. A small child stands ahead of me, alone and screaming for her mother. I consider turning on the rebels and assisting the people, our plans to infiltrate the rebels be damned, but that won't help them in the long run.

Rebels emerge from the alleys, armed with weapons and magic. They attack with no warning. Bodies drop to the ground all around me, and I'm frozen in place at the escalation of violence. From what we've learned, so far there have been very few casualties resulting from the rebel attacks. Today's offensive is going to be a massacre.

Shaking all around us indicates there's another bomb coming. It pulls me out of my trance, and I use aether to create an invisible shield of light around my friends and as many people around us as I can muster. This isn't a *distraction*, like Krantz claimed—it's a slaughter.

Fionn's and Silene's eyes widen in horror. They waste very little time, jumping into the fighting but using their magic to discreetly ensure weapons don't hit their marks and blowing children out of harm's way with gusts of wind. When a large male turns his sword on a mother and her two children hiding under a barrel, a gust of air conveniently rips the sword from his hand. More and more rebels arrive, looting stores, starting fires, and causing terror wherever they go. Before I can do anything to help, Krantz is urging me to follow him down an alley that hasn't been bombed. I hesitate. It was one thing to go along with this plan when I thought the worst that could happen was property damage and a few injuries. This is so much more than that.

"Go," Silene whispers, using her air magic to carry the murmur to my ears only. "With violence like this, Royal Guards will be here soon. We'll do what we can until they arrive. Don't let these bastards get a single stalk of thayar from that tower." I lock eyes with her for only a moment before turning away, praying to whatever gods will listen that I can put a stop to this.

I follow Krantz down the alley, then over a retaining wall that brings us to a higher level of the city. We trek along a side road, and as we walk, other fae join our group every few blocks.

"Now would be a good time to hide us, Your Highness," Krantz says, almost a demand. I tune into the aether surrounding me, flowing through the light of the bright day, then bend it around the group that's now about a dozen strong. I keep us visible to one another, though that takes a larger amount of effort.

"I need to know where we're going, Krantz," I say. "I'll need to drop the ability to show us to one another soon. Point me in the right direction, and I'll make sure we're all heading that way." Krantz points to a tower only a few blocks up. I release the extra aether allowing our group to see each other, then focus my attention fully on the tower. It's hard to concentrate with the screams I can still hear from the merchant district and my doubt that this was the right decision. Taking a deep breath, I tune out the noise, mind racing to come up with a plan for when we reach the refinery. I'll need to see the storage space before I can hide any thayar from the rebels. Now that I've seen what they do with just a small supply of thayar, I'm even more determined to keep as much of it from them as I can. "To ensure I can hide us properly, I'll need to go into the building first. I can't hide this many people without knowing what the light will be like in there," I whisper, praying he hasn't been exposed to many light channelers to catch my lie. "But I should be able to keep you all hidden outside. It'll only take me a few moments."

Krantz doesn't respond for a few beats, and I fear I've made a miscalculation. He looks skeptical, eyes searching, though he can't see me. But he only says, "Okay, but be quick about it."

When we reach the base of the tower, I briefly allow the group to see one another so that Krantz can signal to them to halt. I give him a nod before walking to the front doors. There are only two guards out front, who both seem glassy eyed with boredom. I kick a stone toward the rebels, then sneak inside when the guards turn their attention that way.

There are three more guards inside, though I thank the aether that they're immersed in a game of Skran and don't notice the door swinging open and closed. Krantz explained at the tavern that the supply room is on the first floor, to the right of the front door. I head that way now, finding the door blocked by another pair of guards.

Shit.

I don't know how to get inside without them noticing. Thinking for a moment, an idea sparks. I release the aether around the rebels outside for just a fraction of a moment. Easily explained away as a distraction to the rebels, but hopefully enough to alert the guards of a strange sighting. I have to wait a few minutes before I hear another guard running toward us, shouting.

"The outside watch spotted something weird. They saw a group of a dozen fae, but then they disappeared," he calls. The two guards closest to me look at one another, clearly skeptical. "Captain says he wants everyone to meet in the entryway to investigate," the running guard says now that he's reached the pair outside the storage room.

"Fine," one says. They leave, and I thank the aether. Wasting no time, I slip into the storage room and find it filled with boxes that I'm extremely familiar with. The thayar is packed into the very crates we receive and often try to divert in Velmara. I make a quick study of the room, deciding to disguise all but the back wall, which has the fewest crates.

If I'm lucky, the rebels won't even make it here.

I slip out and head back toward the entrance, where the guards are discussing what to do. Several don't believe the outside guards saw anything, blaming it on a hangover or lack of sleep. I need them to decide to send for backup, to get more guards here, so I make a stupid decision. One that Silene would absolutely kill me for. I quickly release the magic hiding me, hoping it wasn't long enough for them to make out my features.

It works. At least four of the guards point in my direction, including the Captain. "One of the air channelers—aerstep to the palace and get backup," he orders, drawing a weapon. I quickly slink around them and out the front door while they're still looking where they saw me.

When I reach the rebels, I whisper to Krantz. "I'm back. Are you and your team ready?"

"What the hell's going on?" he growls. "The guards shouted they saw something, and they all went inside."

"I created an illusion to get myself through the doors without them noticing. Now we can all get in without their attention." Krantz seems to believe the lie. When we open the doors, a dozen guards now stand in the entryway, eyes and swords trained on the entrance. They see the doors open and shut.

"Fuck," Krantz mutters.

The guards attack, though they don't know where we are. They swing their swords blindly, injuring a few rebels, but not enough to slow the group down. Krantz, a powerful metal channeler, rips swords away from the guards. Fionn described a similar move when he saw Krantz during the initial attack.

"Magic it is, then," the Captain roars. Suddenly, dozens of vines slither across the floor, finding a few of the rebels and pinning them in place. Guards retrieve their swords from the ground and stab into the areas where the vines appear to wrap around something. As soon as the fae are hit, I release the magic around them, knowing that otherwise the guards will continue to stab aimlessly rather than look for more of us to catch.

Krantz runs toward the storage room, and I'm forced to follow him along with a few other fae who have made it out of the initial attack. When Krantz opens the door, the Captain notices and sends half of the group toward us. The rebels get inside before the contingent of guards catches up, then bar the door by bending the metal handles and wrapping plants around the tangled mess. I step into a corner, focused on keeping the bulk of the supply hidden from view.

"This is all there is?" Krantz roars. The guards bang on the door, warning that more are coming, and we should surrender now.

"Did you expect more?" I ask.

"Of course I did!" I can tell he's panicking now. He didn't have a backup plan in case they were noticed, relying too much on my magical abilities to shield them from view. "It'll have to be enough," he growls. "Everyone, grab two crates. I'll impale them on their swords, and we'll make a run for it!" I don't take any crates, since they can't see me, but I do keep the rebels hidden. I'm relying on the guards outside to stop them, so I don't have to break my cover. "On the count of three," Krantz says. "One, two..."

The doors blow apart before the rebels can make a run for it, shrapnel flying everywhere. Mist and dust obscure visibility as screams and groans sound from those injured by whatever blast that just occurred. It's chaotic, and no one seems to know what's going on. All the rebels are yelling at one another, fear in their voices now that they're injured, and more guards seem to have arrived.

The dust finally settles, and Laurel stands in the door frame.

She is all Witch Queen, terrifying and lethal. Dressed in an all-black ensemble of form fitting pants with a black corset as her top and a black cape, that same unholy light I saw at Rusthelm blazing through her furious eyes. She looks right at me as she takes several slow steps into the room, eyes narrowing in anger and suspicion. The hairs on my arm stand up with goosebumps. I'd be lying if I said I wasn't absolutely terrified of her and what she might do to me if she doesn't give me a chance to explain.

She turns in a circle, likely seeing that only the back wall of crates is visible to the rebels. I hope that's enough to convince her I'm on her side. I shake my head to silently tell her not to let on that she sees them or me, hoping I can convey everything with just my expression. They can't believe she knows about my involvement with them, or our ruse will be over before it even starts. Thankfully, she understands my silent words.

"I know there are fae in here. I can smell you, and my magic can feel you. Give yourself up now, and I'll consider a merciful punishment instead of feeding your hearts to my cat." Her words are a feral hiss, and more than one rebel trembles. I don't think she *actually* feeds hearts to that enormous beast she calls a pet, but I'm not completely sure. She certainly knows how to lean into the persona of the Witch Queen, though a voice in the back of my mind whispers that it's not a persona, just another facet of this complex female.

Krantz remains steadfast while his group falls apart with fear, many of them dropping their crates. He uses his magic to send weapons sailing toward her, but they vanish the instant they make it off the ground. As soon as her eyes lock on him, her nostrils flare. It's the only subtle sign that she not only sees the metal channeler but recognizes him as one of the rebels she allowed to escape her clutches.

"Someone else tried that trick on me, and it worked then about as well as it did now. I wonder if you're the same male who I so graciously did not kill the last time I captured you." She speaks with a quiet ferocity that makes me ache in ways that are so *not* appropriate considering the circumstances. Laurel stalks toward the group as a glowing mist appears. It covers every inch of the room, except for where the rebels stand. *Smart.* Even though she can see them through my magic, she uses the mist to expose where they are without revealing our secret. Then vines wrap around their bodies, my own included. I hope it's just a way to protect our scheme and not her actually trapping me along with the rebels. Though I wouldn't mind being trapped by her in *other* circumstances.

Shit. Focus. Get your mind away from Laurel and all the things she absolutely has no interest in doing with you.

There's a loud crash from the entryway, and Laurel's attention moves behind her for just a moment. Krantz lunges for her, pulling a knife from where it's sheathed at his side and sending it hurling toward her exposed stomach. My heart drops out of my chest and my breath hitches. I'm running for her, all sense of reason gone. I'm determined to keep that blade from even grazing her perfect milky white skin, but I won't reach her in time. The blade is spinning end over end, humming with the magic of a metal channeler.

Right as it's about to strike her, the blade diverts, likely from Laurel's own magic, and all the tension in my body releases. It's enough of a distraction that several rebels have ripped the vines off and made it out of the room, but I don't care. Laurel is safe. Krantz rolls past her on the ground, then runs out of the room himself, hands empty. They've stolen very little thayar, thank the aether.

There are now more rebels in the entryway, fighting the guards. There must have been some backup plans after all, at least enough to get the rebels out safely.

I want to stay with Laurel, but know I need to run out with the rebels. I look at her sharply, begging her to understand, before grabbing a half full crate of thayar and making my way past her. She could easily stop all of us with her magic, but she doesn't. I keep the original group of rebels hidden, and we sneak out of the tower. Once we're out, Krantz orders the others to fall back, and soon we're all running back toward the merchant district.

"What now?" I ask Krantz, keeping pace with the fleeing group.

"We have safe houses in place. You should find your people and get back to the palace before you're missed," he orders, then takes the crate from me. "We hoped to get more today, but this mission still achieved what we needed it to."

"And what is that?" I ask.

"Chaos."

When we reach the merchant quarter, Royal Guards and soldiers battle rebels in the streets. Most of the citizens have gone, hopefully to safety. Krantz and the others slip into an alley as I release the magic hiding them.

I search for Fionn and Silene, but don't see them anywhere and start to panic. Making my way toward the pub turned gambling den where we first met the rebels, I pray they hid somewhere when the Royal Guards arrived. My magic keeps me hidden as I traverse the deserted and rubble-filled streets.

My hunch was right, and Fionn and Silene are in the pub, pretending to be shielding from the attack with other citizens. Relief washes over me. I come up behind them and whisper, "We need to get out of here."

They both jump but hide the movement well. We slowly creep toward the back of the pub unseen, most eyes in the room focused on what's going on outside. I wrap my magic around them, then look at Silene, who nods. She aersteps us directly into our rooms, and we all collapse into chairs, exhausted.

"What the fuck just happened?" a familiar cold and furious voice demands from the corner.

Sidhe cats who make themselves the companion of a Thayarian royal are extremely in tune with the emotions of their chosen fae. Many Thayarian monarchs have credited their companion feline for supporting them through their hardest moments.

A Brief History of Modern Thayaria

When I get to my room, bone-weary and full of fury, I barely register the last hour. When Carex had pounded on my door, telling me there was an attack on the merchant district, all reason and logic left me. I *became* my fury, let it wash over me in a mad rage. I rushed there and aerstepped as many people as I could to safety. I wanted to obliterate the rebels attacking my city. Attacking my people. Every bit of self-control I've tried to hone over three centuries, every ounce of shame I've internalized about the nature of my magic—it all left me the instant I realized the scale of the rebel attack. I would have performed unlimited amounts of magic to stop the attack, and who knows what the result might have been. In my wrath-induced madness, I could have completely unraveled the magic of Thayaria by channeling too much aether.

But Admon had interfered, reminding me that the rebels are also Thayarians and many of them are just worried for their families. As always, his wise counsel gently guided me down the right path and back to logic. I backed off, letting the Royal Guard and army reserves handle the attackers. Thankfully, under Carex's leadership, they'd addressed the assault on the city quickly and saved hundreds of lives.

Then I got the message that the thayar processing tower was being robbed, and my ire returned in full force. When I blasted away the doors to that storage room and saw the same fae *I* was responsible for releasing, believing him to be nothing more than a farmer, I once again evolved into something more than myself, a being made of nothing but wrath. It took more control than I want to admit pretending not to see him, not to obliterate him where he stood. And Prince Hawthorne—how *could* he have gone along with this attack and not stopped this? In the room, I understood his silent plea to go along with the plan. But it doesn't mean he should've agreed to it in the first place.

My anger reignites thinking of the role the Velmarans played in this attack, and I aerstep into their apartment, not sure what I'm going to do but furious with my so-called allies. I'm ready to enact my plans to be rid of them for good. We know where the rebel base is, and I would bet we know who their leaders are. It's time to end this farce of an alliance and kill the Velmarans. I'll send their heads back to Mazus in a thayar crate. When I realize the Velmarans aren't here yet, I back into a corner, prepared to wait as long as it takes.

They appear in the room using Silene's enhanced magic, looking worse for wear. None of them jump when I emerge from the corner, demanding answers, though this time they should. "What the fuck just happened?" My voice is lethal, a blade sharpened in anger and haughty righteousness.

Silene and Fionn are covered in grime and blood, and I instantly pace towards Silene, feeling a protectiveness for the young fae that surprises me, despite my fury. She senses my distress.

"It's not mine." The usual joyfulness in her voice is gone, and I vow to not let my care for Mazus's future daughter-in-law sway me from taking the action I know needs to be taken.

"What. Just. Happened?" I repeat my question. Silene tenses, and her eyes search mine. From the corner of my eye, I see Fionn move in front of Hawthorne. I turn on them. "What. The *fuck*. Happened?" I demand. The room shakes. "Tell me now," I roar with the aether-voice, and they all drop to their knees. Hawthorne looks up at me for a long moment before speaking, staying crouched on the ground even as he explains. At least now he has the sense to cow before the roiling brutality in my voice.

"When we got to Oakton, they told us about the attack happening today and asked for my help to get them into the processing tower. It was another test. If we wanted to keep our cover, we had to help them."

"And you made that decision *unilaterally*? You decided to sacrifice *my people* without even consulting me? I'm not sure what you think it means to make kingdom-impacting decisions on behalf of the monarch, but in Thayaria we consider that treason." The words hiss out of me, my rage boiling over. How dare he decide this on his own. The room shakes again, and the doors to the patio shatter as tendrils of ivy break through them and inch toward the Velmarans, ready to shackle them.

But instead of showing fear, Hawthorne only stands and stalks toward me, his own anger visible now. In a flash, he's sliced through the ivy creeping toward Silene and Fionn with a beam of light, not breaking his stride. I don't back down either, conjuring swirling water to surround me, even though the sight of his stony face hurts me more than I want to admit right now.

"Just like *you* decided *unilaterally* to keep critical information from us," he sneers as he makes the water I've conjured disappear. If I weren't so angry, his power would impress me. He's taking my magic head on, matching my strength with his own. "Why didn't you tell us that the thayar flower is declining?" There's a severity to his tone I've never heard from him before.

My entire body tenses. I knew it was a possibility they would find out, an inevitability really, but I wanted to delay the conversation for as long as possible to avoid *this moment*. Avoid the decision I must now make. The conversation with Nemesia in Delsar replays in my mind.

And if he finds out more than he should? If he somehow sees something that puts Thayaria at risk, or discovers the declining thayar? What should I do then?

You should kill him.

Nausea and indecision wrack my body while the Prince continues his rant.

"This rebellion is about more than disagreement with your decision to keep Thayaria behind the mist." I sit in silence, my heart and my brain at war with one another. "What, now that I've pointed out your own poor decisions you have nothing to say for yourself? These people are *afraid*, and you kept that from me."

I snap, unable to keep my cool around this infuriating male and forgetting the conflict just wracking me. "So that excuses them attacking innocents and children, does it?" A wind whips around him as ivy crawls up his legs, but he doesn't balk. His lightning strikes the air above me in response, though I know it's more a demonstration that he's not afraid than any real threat to me. Somehow, even now, with both of us angry, I know he won't hurt me.

"No, it doesn't excuse it at all. But it does make this rebellion more of a threat. People will do anything when they're afraid like this. What I saw today was... unfathomable. Horrifying. And I hate that they got away with even a single petal of thayar after learning what they use it for. But you should have told me what I was walking into, the *danger* I was putting Silene and Fionn in. You let me assume they were harmless farmers playing at rebellion. Silene went into that meeting *unarmed*, for aethers-sake. We had no idea what we were getting ourselves into today." His eyes storm with fury, and I realize our bodies are only inches apart, the wind whipping Hawthorne's black hair out of place. His jaw feathers with his rage, and an involuntary desire to soothe the quivering muscle overcomes me. Instead, I step back, keeping my icy rage firmly in place.

"I won't apologize for doing what any ruler would do in my situation. I provided you with the information you needed to complete the mission. No more, no less," I say firmly, pushing down the guilt at putting Silene—putting them all—in danger with no warning. Hawthorne only scoffs and turns away from me. I'm about to follow him, to close that distance again, but Silene's hand on my arm cools my temper slightly.

"Laurel, we wanted to leave and warn you. But we were being watched. There was no way to get to you *and* keep up the ruse. It was a tough call that Thorne had to make," she tries to soothe.

I jerk my arm from her touch. I don't want to be made to feel better about this, not when I'm still so angry and so guilty and so unsure about what the right call is regarding them. Hurt flashes through her eyes, but I ignore it, not willing to examine any feelings I might have other than rage.

"You made the wrong call," I sneer at Hawthorne, who turns back to face me with an incredulous expression. More lightning streaks across the room of the ceiling, and he surrounds us in mist, making us invisible to Fionn and Silene. Once again, the casual display of so much power makes something buried deep in me respond, but I ignore it.

"I made the long-term, strategic call. You're short-sighted, Laurel, and it shows," he says with so much haughty arrogance that I want to slap the confidence off his face. The space between us has once again been closed, though I'm unsure who stepped closer. His jaw clenches and unclenches as I stare daggers into his eyes. I feel his breath dance across my face, and the sensation sends goosebumps to my arms that I ignore.

"Short-sighted? How is not wanting hundreds of my people to die and even more injured short-sighted?" I ask, my own incredulity apparent in my voice.

He rolls his eyes as energy courses between us. "If we'd left, it would have told the rebels exactly what we were doing. Not only would they have continued this attack, but they likely would have been able to get more thayar without me hiding most of it from them. They would have packed up their headquarters and moved out, returning you to exactly where you were before with no idea where they are or what they're planning. Countless more would have died. *That*, Your Majesty, is the epitome of short-term thinking." Those mossy, olive-green eyes alight with challenge as he smirks in a way that brings out his insufferable dimple. No biting retort comes to me. He's right, but I don't want to admit it. Hawthorne continues, leaning in close so our lips are only inches apart. "The greater good, Laurel. *That's* the decision I made. And if we're going to be allies, you're going to have to trust me to make those kinds of decisions."

I want to snap back that we are not, will *never* be, allies. Not with everything that's happened between Velmara and Thayaria, between his father and me. Not when even now, in this very moment, I'm debating whether I should kill him and his entourage. Instead, I turn in place and aerstep away, running from the conflict and the way it ignites my blood and my magic.

The next morning, shame courses through me at my reaction to the Velmarans. I laid in bed last night, alternating between chastising myself for what happened and replaying the Prince's words over and over again. He was right—he'd made the difficult decision I'm not sure I would have made. Not only that, but he'd kept his cool and helped mitigate the theft while silently reminding me to play pretend in the heat of the moment. He took action, something I've never been able to bring myself to do, while keeping me from ruining our only chances of learning more because of my quick temper.

Once again, someone else had to intervene to keep me from my worst instincts. Something I repaid by using the aether-voice on him and his friends, taking away his agency even though he would have happily given me the information. It was unspeakable, and every decision I've made up to this point has been the wrong one.

Time and time again, I've let the rebels get away with their attacks. I may torture those who I deem responsible for violence, but I almost always leave them alive, unable to deliver that final blow. Even when the mist prompts me to kill someone, I always hesitate until it urges me into action. On the rare occasions I do snuff out someone's life, like at Rusthelm, I feel guilt for weeks. Usually, if there's even a hint that they're nothing more than a scared citizen looking for whatever hope they can find in a troubled time, I let them walk free. And I got *played*. That red-headed fae male is no farmer, and I let out the single person in charge of the strike. He had to be, with the way the other rebels looked to him for guidance the moment I'd appeared. We could've prevented this entire tragedy had I seen through his lies and done what rulers are supposed to do.

I sit with indecision and bone-deep grief on the sofa in my sitting room, unable to bring myself to get out of my sleeping clothes or do anything other than wallow. My eyes are heavy with lack of sleep, my muscles sore from how tightly I've clenched them all night long. I know I need to apologize to the Velmarans—to Hawthorne—but the idea of facing anyone when I'm so *unsettled* makes my body shake with nerves. Examining my feelings, I try to uncover what has me feeling so on edge.

Control. I've had control over everything that touches this kingdom for three hundred years. Or at the very least the illusion of it. Knowing that someone else made a decision without me brings a tightness to my chest that I dislike. That I loathe, if I'm being honest with myself. And yet—I've had nothing *but* control for centuries, and look at where it's gotten my kingdom. Thousands of citizens opposed to my rule. A rebellion fueled by fear and hatred. Thayaria's only revenue-generating export declining rapidly. And along with it, the gut-wrenching fear that something is very wrong with the magic of our land because I can *feel* the way the aether is declining in Thayaria alongside the flower. The decline might even be my fault, a mist leeching away the magic that I can't undo, leaving me terrified I'll accidentally use the colossal amount of magic that comes second nature to me and destabilize the aether. To top it all off, we're now reliant on the kingdom who attacked us without cause for both our revenue and our wheat. My own magic—I push that thought away, not willing to examine the fear that has plagued me for the last few decades.

And now, who knows how many dead or injured from an attack that is *all my fault*. There's no one to blame but me. I let out the person who orchestrated the whole thing. I let the rebels grow this powerful. Nemesia always wondered why I was so unwilling to do anything about the rebels for so long, why I insisted they were my problem to solve. The reality is that, on some level, I agree with them. The mist *should* be lifted, our people *should* be free to travel and trade as they wish, and I'm *not* fit to rule.

You failed Thayaria yesterday. You've been failing them since you took the throne.

My breath comes in quick pants, and I can't get enough air into my lungs. My hands clench and unclench, almost involuntarily. I stand and pace back and forth, starting then stopping repeatedly. Great heaves are the only way I can breathe, and the tightness in my chest is so painful I feel like I might implode. Shaking out my arms and rolling my neck, I try to stop the rising tension in my body. When that doesn't work, I slump to the ground. The air feels thick, and I'm gasping for breath. I squeeze my eyes shut and curl my head to my knees. Tears leak down my face, and my whole body feels like it's on fire. My nails cut crescent shapes into my hands. *Just breathe.*

Lunaria nuzzles my neck, purring loudly. She always knows when I need her the most. She lays her body close to mine, and her heat seeps into my body, comforting me enough so I can calm my racing heart. I focus on the low vibrations of her purr, and it pulls me out of the worst of it.

I force myself to take a deep breath, open my eyes, and focus on what I can see around me. My desk. Breathe in. My favorite leather chair. Breathe out. This morning's tea mug.

Breathe in. A book left on the coffee table. Breathe out. A half-finished letter. Breathe in. Lunaria's glowing eyes. Breathe out.

I run through this exercise, identifying sounds, then smells. I end by standing and focusing on my body. I feel my toes curling in my boots. I feel the braid of my hair tickling my neck. Another deep breath in. Breathe out. I collapse on my sofa in exhaustion, my body tingling and shaking from the rush of emotion.

Hawthorne's too-handsome face returns to my mind. The way he'd exuded dangerous fury yesterday makes my blood heat, and it only confuses me more. I've reached the point where I promised myself I'd take action against the Velmarans. They've met the rebellion's leaders and identified a location where they meet. They've given me names and even faces of the rebellion leader and his inner circle. They've discovered the one thing I've been trying desperately to conceal. I should get rid of them now, like I always planned, like Nemesia insisted. But then that face pops into my mind again, and the idea of killing *him* makes me nauseous. But if I'm honest with myself, I never really believed I would kill them. I had alternatives I would have used, like using the aether-voice to force them to forget. Right?

That uncertainty about myself and my intentions makes me spiral again. How could I have considered killing the only three people from outside of Thayaria who have ever offered me friendship? How could I consider *not* killing them when they're my enemy, when my only true friend told me to eliminate the threat the moment they learned too much? My head throbs with indecision and uncertainty about the best course of action. Despite all my best efforts to keep them at arm's length, I've grown close to the Velmarans. I might even like them, or at least like Silene. Not to mention whatever is going on between me and Hawthorne. But he's *engaged*, to the one person I can admit I like, and I've been shamelessly flirting with him. Am I failing my people by keeping them here, by allowing them to get closer and closer to me? Should I send them back to Velmara and deal with the consequences?

There's a resounding answer that rings loudly in my head, in the place in my chest where I feel my magic.

No.

I promised Hawthorne the opportunity to prove himself to me. I owe him longer to show that he can be fully trusted. He's done nothing to make me doubt him, and all I've done is look for his flaws, for any sign he isn't telling the truth about his intentions. Despite our flirty banter, I haven't really given him the chance I said I would give him. Sure, I've let him meet with the rebels. But when it really mattered, I kept critical information from him and exploded in rage when he made the only choice he could in an awful situation.

Tears run down my cheeks again, despite doing everything I can to lock them away. I hiccup and gasp for breath. Closing my eyes, I take more deep breaths to calm my raging emotions.

When the episode passes, I force myself to move forward. After a quick bath, I dress in loose trousers and an oversized tunic, braiding my wet hair. I stroke Lunaria's head for several minutes. She slowly blinks her eyes at me, and calm washes over my tense body. When I'm done, I feel ready to face the consequences of my failure, so I once again aerstep into the Velmaran apartment.

Only Silene is in the sitting room when I arrive, and wariness makes her body tense when she spots me. "Thorne, Fionn," she calls. "Her Majesty is here."

I hide the hurt that she uses my title, knowing that it's my own fault for how I behaved yesterday. Fionn quickly walks to stand in front of Silene, crossing his arms over his chest and glaring at me. I raise my hands in silent supplication. Thorne only leans effortlessly in the doorway of Fionn's room, staring at me with a look that says I have some explaining to do.

"I came to apologize," I say quickly. "I was out of line yesterday. My guilt and fear were overwhelming, and I took that out on you. I'm sorry." Shoulders slumping, my gaze locks on my feet in shame. Warm arms wrap around me, and Silene's cinnamon scent soothes my aching chest. I stiffen awkwardly, not sure what to do.

"We understand, Laurel. Yesterday was awful. There were no good choices. For any of us," she soothes, and my arms involuntarily return the embrace. It's the first time I've hugged someone other than a lover since the war. Nemesia and I have never embraced one another, not even when she left for Velmara.

Silene squeezes tighter before releasing me, and I survey the room as she backs away. Fionn still looks pissed, his hulking frame poised to attack should I make any wrong moves near Silene. Hawthorne eyes me skeptically from the doorframe before walking closer with an unaffected grace that I could only dream of pulling off.

"You left. In the middle of our argument," is all he says when he reaches me. My eyes drop to the ground again.

"I know. I'm not good with conflict. I get angry, and that scares me, so I leave before I can hurt anyone," I admit, emotion making my throat tight, and I fear those tears from earlier will return.

Hawthorne chuckles. "You weren't afraid of hurting anyone yesterday, witchling. You just didn't want to admit that I was right." My fury returns at his arrogance, all other emotions eclipsed by my annoyance at his words. No one has ever gotten under my skin like he does. I'm trying to apologize, am practically laying myself bare, and he shoves it in my face. I roll my eyes and glare at him. Once again, our bodies are closer than I would prefer. I see the way his chest moves up and down with his breathing, the tiny gold threads interwoven in the fabric of his clothing.

"That is not—" I start to protest, but Hawthorne cuts me off.

"You know I'm right. Let this one go," he says arrogantly but firmly. Something about the earnest command in his voice makes me back down.

"Fine. Yes, you were right. Happy?" I sneer. A half smile quirks his lips as he steps closer to me and brings his mouth to my ear.

"Elated," he whispers before turning and walking to take a seat on the sofa, crossing one leg over the other, appearing completely unaffected and relaxed. Blood rushes to my cheeks as I realize he was just looking to get a rise out of me and that—once again—I fell for it. I'm even more angry that it was exactly what I needed to pull myself together. I want to snap his neck where he sits, so confident in his own smug righteousness, but all I can do is gape at him.

Silene, always one to read a room, takes my hand in hers and leads me to sit across from Hawthorne on the sofa. Fionn stands behind the Prince, unwilling to forgive me yet.

"I'd like to give you an explanation, Laurel. Now that tensions have dropped," Hawthorne says, all the seriousness from yesterday returned to his features. I only nod. "The leader of the rebellion, the one you saw at the processing tower, forced our hand." I sink further into the sofa where I sit with shame. Not only was the male I released from my cells in charge of yesterday's attack, but he is the *leader* of the rebellion. The horror of the last few years of rebel strikes could have been eliminated, if only I hadn't fallen for his act. Hawthorne stares at me with curiosity but says nothing as he continues his explanation.

"We were told about the campaign with only an hour to decide what to do, and they had us watched the entire time, as Silene said. I decided to stay, calculating in the short time we had that it was better to keep our cover while attempting to mitigate the damage. It *was* an impulsive decision, but I still believe it was the right one."

"I know," I say quietly.

"But, Laurel, I swear—" he chokes up as he continues. "I swear to you, we did not know it would be that bad. We thought it was an attack on infrastructure, that they'd destroy and loot shops to distract from the real mission. I thought Fionn and Silene could help divert the worst of the damage, and that I could keep the rebels from getting crates of thayar." His eyes are pleading, and I can see the guilt written clearly across his features, despite his surety about the decision.

"I believe you," I say, because I do.

"Do you know—do you know how many were injured?" Fionn interrupts. I hear the unspoken words. *Do you know how many died?* Despite his stony demeanor, there's an internal turmoil inside of him. I had previously misjudged him as nothing more than a burly husk, but he has a depth I should have noticed before.

"Not yet," I answer gently. "But the property damage alone is catastrophic. It will take us a very long time to rebuild, and I fear for the people who've lost their livelihoods." Fionn crumbles, and I make a note to ask Hawthorne or Silene about this later. He walks around to sit beside Hawthorne, anger and weariness gone from his features.

"I'll do what I can to help them rebuild," he says firmly, and I give him a nod of appreciation. The enormity of what rebuilding will entail threatens to break my carefully constructed calm. Before I can even process leaving again, Hawthorne is looking at me with eyes that see too much.

"Laurel, may I speak with you in private?" he asks. "Is there somewhere we can go where we have no chance of being overheard?"

After the Golden King met the prophesied Princess of Thayaria, a deep uneasiness settled over him—Princess Laurel's magic made him uncomfortable. Since she was so young, he pushed aside his worries, wanting to give her a chance to prove she wasn't the monster he feared. King Mazus agreed to court her at her father the King of Thayaria's insistence, both of them hoping he could help shape her into a force for good. Unfortunately, she revealed her vile magic and witch tendencies, and the Golden King was forced to launch a war on Thayaria to stop her.

The Witch Queen and Her Treachery

I tense at Hawthorne's request, unsure why he'd want to speak with me without Fionn and Silene present. My gaze tracks to the two of them, hoping for a clue, but they look just as surprised as me. When I study Hawthorne, the intensity in his gaze makes me agree.

"Where we trained. We can go back there, though it will be cold, so bundle up," I respond tersely. When he's sufficiently bundled in both his and Fionn's cloaks, I aerstep us back to the Spined Moors. The wind howls, and my magic can only ease it so much.

"How are you not *fucking freezing*?" Hawthorne asks the moment we appear, practically growling the last two words.

"I can warm myself up with my magic," I answer automatically, and that seems to startle him.

"But—*how*? I've never heard of anyone being able to do that. What conduit could that possibly be connected to?" Another day, another secret I've revealed to him without even thinking.

"A witch never reveals her secrets." My usual quip falls flat, but Hawthorne doesn't press it as we sit on my favorite boulder. I will it to heat a bit to cut the worst of the biting cold for him, and he studies my face for what feels like an eternity. I'm about to ask him what he's looking for, giving him one of the signature barbs we trade with one another, when he finally speaks.

"Laurel, I'd like to understand more about the declining thayar. I won't reveal any of what you tell me, not even to Fionn and Silene."

Tension rolls through my body, leaving my shoulders tight and my jaw aching with how tightly I clench it. Magic deep inside of me opens its eye, like it's waiting to see what I'll do, and the ground around us trembles. This time, I'm not sure if it's me or something else that causes the quake. I wasn't expecting this, and there's no way I'm going to discuss it with him. I open my mouth to tell him to mind his own business, but he cuts me off.

"Before you say no," he continues, voice serious and commanding, "let me remind you that Velmara is now paying twenty percent more for our thayar imports, besides buying what I can now deduce is your entire supply. Not only that, you've abandoned your wheat agreement with Delsar and now source your entire country's grain from Velmara, a deal that's contingent on you being able to continue supplying thayar. You're in a precarious situation with trade here." Is he threatening me? There are very few plants to call on here, so I gather the mist, ready to choke him to remind him who he's dealing with.

"How *dare* you threaten me," I hiss. His demeanor stays calm as he holds his hands up, placating.

"I want to understand so that I can *help* you, Laurel. This problem isn't going away without some pretty impressive political maneuvering, and even then, it's unlikely you'll fool my father. Let me be a real ally to you. *Please.*"

"Even if you *want* to be my ally, even if you have the best intentions of keeping my secrets, the moment you go back to Thayaria your father could compel you to reveal everything you've learned with the aether-voice." How can he not see the precarious situation I'm in here?

He only smirks. "First, my father cannot compel me, actually. Not without iron to weaken me. I'm stronger than him, remember?" That shouldn't send desire shooting down to my core, but I'm past the point of worrying about what my reactions to Hawthorne Vicant *should* be. "And second, I think we both know Fionn, Silene, and I won't be leaving Thayaria without a solution to that problem." His eyes burn with understanding. At least he realizes I can't allow them to leave without certainty that

Mazus won't be able to get information out of them. I may not be plotting to kill them anymore, but they won't be leaving Thayaria any time soon. It's refreshing to not have to hide that anymore.

The tension and magic building within me deflate. My shoulders slump and I heave out a great sigh. I study him carefully, looking for any sign of deceit, but he meets my gaze with an open and vulnerable look. The same energy that has always passed between us ignites, but this time it feels tentative, like even the space between us knows that we're at a critical juncture in our relationship.

Maybe it's because Hawthorne has abandoned the flirty winks and grins. Maybe it's the somber way he speaks, or the astute way he's surmised *precisely* what keeps me awake most nights. Maybe it's because I'm exhausted and still feeling the weight of my failure. Maybe it's just because I'm no better than all the other females he's used to earn his reputation. Whatever the reason, I lower my gaze and tell him the truth.

"It's been declining for some time now. It took us—took me—too long to realize what was happening, and even longer to take it seriously. It was slow at first, but the last five years have been dramatic, and this year's been the worst yet. What you saw in the tower is all that's left of our harvest, and at least half of it we owe to Velmara. Normally we'd have a dozen towers like that one filled to the brim. People who used to rely on it, especially those in rural areas, no longer have any supply. Humans who bought objects spelled to work with thayar now have their farming equipment sitting useless. Small businesses who use thayar to add efficiency to their manufacturing are back to manual labor. It's a complete disaster, and it's why I've taken so long to do anything about the rebels. The people are scared and angry. I don't blame them for joining the rebellion. They deserve better." My voice cracks, the shame and anxiety from yesterday returning. I lock it down before I bring my eyes back up to meet Hawthorne's. When our gazes meet, he sees more than I want him to.

The Prince considers my words carefully as he studies me. "Aethers, I can't believe I'm going to tell you this, but I did say I wanted a real alliance." I wait for him to continue, understanding the weight of sharing secrets. "My father's been importing more and more thayar, as you know. In the capital, he's spun a story that the Nivan Desert is expanding and getting more difficult to perform magic in, so more of our thayar imports are sent there. But the people in the desert are *also* receiving less and less of the good. The thayar shortage in Velmara is just as bad as it is in Thayaria."

That doesn't make any sense. Mazus has been doubling Velmara's thayar imports every year for decades. And I know Velmara's population hasn't increased significantly, because we monitor that closely for our protection.

"Where's it all going then?" I ask, my voice almost a whisper.

"The people of the desert whisper rumors that my father is stockpiling it deep in the northern mountains."

"Do you believe these rumors?" My mind spins with the possibilities.

"I have to. There's no other explanation for the disappearing shipments. One of my reasons for agreeing to come here, and for wanting an alliance with you, was to find out more about the flower. Understand its properties. I suspect my father's planning something big with all that thayar, some massive magical act. But I don't know what it is, and I fear for my people."

"And why is that, Hawthorne?" I ask, my voice coming out harsher than I intend. But I need answers from him. *Real* answers. If we're truly going to be allies, he needs to lay everything on the table. "Why do you fear your father? Why do you *chafe* at his rule, as you once said?" The male in front of me is an enigma. Everything about him confuses me, and this new version of him as a serious and caring ruler is the most confusing of all. It doesn't match the rumors that describe a drunk and spoiled heir, doesn't match the winking and unserious male he usually presents as. This is the male who sobbed while carrying a dead child to the forest to bury, who tenderly healed an injured family. I suspect this is the closest to the real Hawthorne I've ever gotten.

His jaw tightens, and I sense that he's debating whether to share another deep truth with me. I stay quiet, knowing it has to be his decision. Finally, he lets out a sigh.

"You know that my mother died when I was twelve years old." I only nod, allowing him room to continue in his own time. "Before she died, she discovered something about him. I don't know what it was, I only know it was massive. It wasn't until I was over a hundred years old that I found an old journal she kept, hidden inside one of my toy chests. My father packed away all the things he deemed childish after her death, along with anything that might remind me of her. Before she died, I barely interacted with my father, kept under her protection. Afterwards—let's just say the transition to being under my father's thumb was not an easy one. He was not a kind parent, to say the least. Because of that, I wasn't bold enough to seek out my childhood relics until I was much older and my hatred of him was firmly settled in place." His jaw tightens, and he puts his head in his hands. It cracks something open inside of me. The same thing that fissured when I saw him heal the family and carry the small child, but I was too wrapped up in my own hatred then to allow more than the tiniest fracture. Now, with my commitment to let him show me who he really is, it opens wide.

"I think she left the journal for me," he finally continues. "In it, she said—she said that if anything happened to her, it would be because Mazus had stopped her heart. I think he killed her. I *know* he killed her. He brushed her death off as an accident as part of magical research they both willingly agreed to, but I don't believe that for one second. Even at such a young age, I knew how much she hated him and feared his experimentation. And once I realized he killed her, all the lies he'd spun around himself unraveled." I reach for him, placing my hand on his knee. It startles me, and I quickly pull my hand back. He stares at the spot I touched him for a moment, nostrils flaring.

"I'm sorry, Hawthorne." The words sound hollow compared to his raw grief and vulnerability. I wish I were better at this, but I've had to lock so much of myself away for so long that I fear I'm not capable of true empathy.

"You should call me Thorne," he says with one of his charming winks, changing the mood instantly. I suspect he too does not like to sit in his past for very long. "You know my biggest secret, all my *daddy problems*. That elevates you to nickname status."

I laugh, loudly and involuntarily, and his eyes storm with emotion. I'm drawn into the dark green orbs that once filled my worst nightmares, but now only bring comfort and a lust I don't understand. He pulls my hand into his and gently strokes my palm with his thumb, and I don't pull away, greedy for his touch. Suddenly, I'm speaking, the compulsion to share more of myself with him overwhelming me.

"Your father... he killed my parents too. He told everyone it was me, but it wasn't. I was there when it happened. His magic was stronger than theirs. He used aether-voice to force them to impale themselves with their own plant magic while I watched. As I looked at their too still faces, sobbing and praying they weren't truly gone, he *bowed* to me. Bowed. Like he hadn't just up ended my entire world. He said, 'I'll see you again soon, Your Majesty Queen Laurel.' The way his eyes looked when he rose from that bow, full of so much glee, still haunts me most nights. Then he disappeared and left me an adolescent orphan Queen. The first time anyone called me Your Majesty, something I had foolishly dreamed about growing up, and it was *him*. After he *murdered* my parents using the aether-voice."

"Is that why you don't use the aether-voice much?" he asks, and I'm not even surprised he's noticed. I only nod as he continues to soothe my palm with soft circles.

Angry and desperate tears have gathered in my eyes, and I fight like hell to keep them from dropping. My throat burns with the effort. Then Hawthorne—Thorne—squeezes my hand, and I lose the battle. It's the smallest gesture, but now I'm crying openly, fat tears rolling down my cheeks. I haven't cried in front of another person in at least a century. He rubs my back, and I laugh at the absurdity of the situation, the noise half sob and half barking madness. He probably thinks I've completely lost my mind. I wipe away the tears, ready to explain that I just can't get over the irony of it all. To tell him I'm not insane. But then he surprises me by breaking out into his own deep laughter. It starts as a low chuckle but quickly turns into gasping belly laughs that only escalate my own outbursts.

"Why are we laughing?" he chokes out.

"I don't really know, *Thorne*," I say through my giggles, the use of his nickname sending me into another fit. He squeezes my hand again. "I think it's the only thing we *can* do. After everything, all the secrets and animosity between our countries, what we've both dealt with. The fact that we're here—in the most isolated and abandoned part of the entire Four Kingdoms—talking about all of this and freezing our asses off. The only thing left to do is laugh."

That makes him laugh even harder, and we're both in stitches. He keeps my hand in his the entire time, and I have no desire to stop touching him. I scoot closer, and he leans into me. I feel his magic like a sixth sense, calling to my own, and for once I let the door I usually keep firmly closed on my magical center crack open the smallest bit. That same *spark* I've felt between us so many times, that I've consistently ignored, flares. It's electrifying, and I want to rip open the door and let everything inside of me burst out to meet him. I'm breathless, and not from all the laughter. I revel in the feeling for a few minutes before I slowly close the door up, locking away my magic with the practiced control I've honed over centuries. All the while, we continue laughing.

"Laurel," he breathes out, and I practically shiver at the way his husky voice says my name. "You—I—" His expression heats.

"Spit it out, princeling," I tease, thinking he's going to give me some flirty remark that I'll have to meet with one of my own. But that's not what comes out of his mouth.

"Tell me you feel whatever this is between us. Tell me—tell me I'm not crazy."

Those two sentences dump ice water on whatever this moment was. I don't know what to say, don't know how to react. And that makes me close up again. Of course I feel it. The moment I saw him in that throne room, standing there like a chiseled god of light, I felt an attraction to him. After seeing how he helped heal my people with such compassion, it turned into *more*. Every time we've traded flirty barbs or longing stares, I've felt *something*. But I could pretend it wasn't real, pretend that at some point I would get rid of him and never have to confront my feelings. I locked them away, sealed shut with everything else I've buried for three hundred years. I *just barely* acknowledged to myself that I'm willing to give him a real chance to be an ally, and now this? Despite the growing trust between us and my realization that not only do I not want to kill him, but I might actually *want* the alliance he's proposed—he's still Velmaran. Still Mazus's *son*. Not only that, but he's *engaged*, for aethers-sake. And that makes me angry. I like Silene, and I won't hurt her in this way, even if her fiancé seems more than happy to. Remembering her coming out of his room, the heat fully ices over. How dare he speak to me of what's between us while he's sharing his bed with another female? That isn't fair to me, and it isn't fair to Silene.

I pull my hand from his, instantly missing the warmth, but refusing to let myself care.

"You're engaged." The words are all I manage to get out, and they come out more like a question than the reprimand I wanted them to be.

"What? Engaged? No—I mean, yes, I am—but it's not—we're not—" He sputters out his excuse, clearly believing me to be the kind of female who wouldn't care about his commitments. I've called him out on his bullshit and now he doesn't know what to say.

"And there he is, the Shining Prince I've heard so much about," I hiss. He shudders like I've physically struck him, and despite my best efforts, I cringe at the effect my words have.

"Laurel, listen." He takes my hand firmly in his, like it's a lifeline. "Silene and I are engaged, technically, but our parents forced it upon us. Neither of us has any interest in marriage to the other. We both agreed that we'd play pretend for a few years to let the dust settle before we refused the match, but it's all an act. There's *nothing* but a sibling-like love for one another between us." He squeezes my hand, but I pull it away, unsure what to believe.

It's too convenient a story. And even if that's what *he* feels, how do I know his feelings match Silene's? She's so young and could be infatuated with him. She could be pretending to pretend, hoping that one day he'll realize his true feelings for her. Even if she truly has no interest in him romantically, she'll be the *Queen* of Velmara someday. That kind of power and influence is not something to give up lightly. I may have seen a different side of Thorne today, may have enjoyed our laughter and touches and companionship, but there's a reason he has a reputation for being a flirt, and I would do well to protect my heart and my kingdom from him. *Aethers*, I've seen him flirting with most of my advisors. How can I even trust anything I feel is real and not something every person who meets him feels?

I slip on the mask of Queen again, my constant protection from the world. "We can't pursue this." It's the closest I'll come to admitting my feelings. "For so many reasons, not least of which is you're the Crown Prince of Velmara. Even if the history between our kingdoms didn't exist, you have a throne to inherit and a kingdom to rule, and I have my own. We're allies. That's it." I want the words to come out firm and harsh, but they don't. They sound kind and yearning, and I curse my stupid feelings and my inability keep Thorne at a distance.

He stares at me for a moment, and I think I see pain flash through his eyes, but it's gone too quickly. His rakish grin returns. "As you wish, witchling." A wink tells me he's back to being the Hawthorne I usually see.

"We should discuss what to do next," I say, trying to change the topic.

"Yes, what should we do next now that we both know each other's deepest, darkest secrets and you've finally admitted we're allies?" The flirty prince has returned.

I roll my eyes, relieved we've both slipped back into the roles we're comfortable in, though I have to bury my hurt that he let the feelings and heat between us go so quickly. I'm nothing more than an attempted conquest, and with the rejection, he's moved on as if nothing were different between us. I shouldn't feel this way, shouldn't expect anything different, especially since *I'm* the one who said no. But the female inside of me, the *person* who isn't a Queen and isn't the most powerful fae alive and doesn't have the weight of the world and a prophecy on her shoulders... That person wishes it could be more. Despite my hurt, this is for the best. His reaction—and my own—only prove that exploring anything between us would be dangerous for Thayaria and for me. I move the conversation forward quickly, hoping to put all of this behind us.

"I mean about the rebels. I want you to convince them to attack the palace, attack me, instead of the people of Thayaria. Tell them there are stores of thayar in the palace if you have to. I will not—cannot—have them attacking innocent citizens again. I'll set myself as bait." If the leader of the rebellion has once again clawed his way out of my grasp, the *only* acceptable outcome is for *me* to bear the consequences. I will allow no one else to pay for my mistakes.

Thorne stiffens. "Laurel," he protests, but I cut him off.

"You have only seen a *fraction* of my power, Hawthorne." Again, I think I see hurt flash through his features at my return to his given name, but I ignore it. "I'm more than capable of defending myself. They won't harm me, but I need them to think they can. We can make up vulnerabilities I have that you've discovered. We'll do whatever we need to do to keep their attention on me."

He only nods, though his expression stays wary as he looks down at me. "I'll do what I can. Their leader—Krantz is his name—something is *off* about him. He gives me a bad feeling. But I'll come up with a way to persuade him. We're allies, after all." Another wink, another sign he's put the conversation about feelings behind us, where it belongs.

"Thank you. The identity and name of their leader is more than Nemesia's and Carex's networks of spies have uncovered. And we have a stronghold. This is information we can work with."

"What I don't understand is why don't you just aerstep to Oakton now and wipe them out? You could stop this rebellion before more attacks happen."

It pains me to admit that I've thought about that very plan. "I considered it. But while the leaders of the rebellion may be corrupt, many of the people who have joined them are just scared citizens. The rebellion has offered them hope. If I kill the dozens or hundreds who are in Oakton, more will rise with even more hatred in their hearts. My actions would only make them more dangerous." He nods, and I continue, words—deeply buried truths—leaving my mouth unbidden. "But even more deadly than an ignited and hateful rebellion is a version of me who has crossed that line. I'm in a constant state of fear of who I could become if I truly let myself enact retribution." I wring my hands, unsure why I'm telling him this. "This much power... it weighs on you. I don't want to become the villain your father has painted me to be, no matter how much I might lean into that persona at times." What I don't admit, not yet, is that I also don't know how much magic is too much for me to yield without impacting Thayaria. If I slip and overdo it, the consequences could be catastrophic.

I lower my eyes, but Thorne puts his finger under my chin and pulls my gaze to his. I get lost in the verdant pools that stare back at me.

"Laurel, you are the most conscientious and caring monarch I've ever met. Granted, I've only met you and my father, but still." He grins, and my stomach flips low in my gut. I chastise myself. Thorne releases me and steps back, a seriousness coming over him again. "If you insist on this plan to make yourself bait, at least let me keep training you. Light is a powerful magic the rebels won't have. It can help you defend yourself without resorting to just... poofing the weapons and people around you."

I snort. "Poofing?"

"Yes, *poofing*." He draws out the word and flings his hand around in the air. "What you did yesterday and during the last attack. You make things disappear, which I still want to know about, by the way. And don't pretend like you didn't consider just poofing the rebels in that room when you first got there. You have brute force, but I can teach you *finesse*." His eyes sparkle with innuendo. I have so many retorts to his words, but I bury them, resolved to stop flirting and finally, truly, bury the connection between us.

"Fine," I say instead. "We can keep training. But *you* have to keep practicing using your two conduits in tandem." He salutes me to show his agreement, and I laugh again. He stands and holds his hand out to me.

"Shall we return to Fionn and Silene, who almost certainly believe we've killed each other by now?"

I nod, taking his hand before remembering the resolution I made seconds ago. Once I'm standing, I pull away quickly. Then I aerstep us back to their apartments, where Silene and Fionn still sit in their chairs, worry clearly written across their features.

"I'll fill them in," Thorne says to me. "You've had a long day. I can take it from here."

I feel dismissed, like I'm not part of their inner circle. *Of course you aren't.* But it still stings. As I turn to go, Thorne grabs my hand again. I still. "Training tomorrow, after breakfast?" he asks. I nod.

"Then you might as well join us for the meal itself." My heart skips a beat, and I aerstep back to my rooms before they can see my reaction to the simple invitation. For the first time in a very long time, my rooms feel empty.

As I lie awake in bed hours later, my thoughts drift to Hawthorne. When I returned to my rooms, I took a long bath, then curled up by the fire with Lunaria's head in my lap while I read a book, hoping to distract myself from thinking of the Prince. Once I got in bed, Lunaria stalked off to the open patio doors, preferring to prowl the palace at night, leaving me alone with nothing but the darkness and the memory of Hawthorne's eyes boring into me.

I can't stop thinking about him. His nickname. *Thorne.* His eyes—identical to Mazus's eyes and yet *so* different. The feel of his hand stroking my palm. The dimple that appears when he smiles just right. The piece of black hair that can never stay put in place. The way he winks and jokes when he wants to lighten the mood. His jawline. The serious leader I met tonight.

Fuck. You have *to stop thinking about him.*

I run through my to-do list for tomorrow, hoping that will distract me. It only makes me remember his request to train. The way his biceps flex when he spars with his light flashes across my mind. I play our first training session over in my mind, remembering the ropes of light that had pulled my hands above my head. My mouth goes dry when the same image that flashed through my mind that day reappears. Hands tied above my head with Thorne's light, pinning me in place. Him prowling toward me with the lust I see so often in his eyes. Letting go of my control and seeing what happens when that *spark* fully ignites...

My hand glides slowly down my stomach. I pull my chemise up to expose my upper thighs and the place between them. My other hand squeezes my breast as I picture Thorne's light wrapping around my body, restraining me while he touches me, licks me, *kisses* me. I imagine the firm and tentative pressure I apply to my clit are his fingers, his tongue.

I'm instantly slick, and I increase the pressure, rubbing circles around that sensitive spot, switching direction every few rotations. I pinch my nipple, and a soft moan escapes me as I see him biting down on that rosy peak. His eyes haunt my vision, and they ignite with desire in my imagination.

I slip one finger inside, pumping in and out several times before running my fingers up and over the bud of nerves. My body clenches in anticipation. Thorne slowly slips my chemise strap down, kissing the nape of my neck and down my arm. I run my hands through his hair, and he moans. I moan in return.

His words and the deep way he says my name replay in my mind. *Let me be a real ally to you. Tell me you feel whatever this is between us. Witchling. Laurel.*

The pressure builds. I'm tracing circles hard and fast now, picturing Thorne pumping his own cock next to me. In my head, he enters me, and I reach the edge. My body is warm everywhere, pleasure creeping slowly through my limbs. I don't stop, circling harder. I pinch my nipple again, bringing a biting sting to the sensitive peak. My hips lift, and I cry out as the wave of pleasure crests and washes over me.

I'm panting, thoughts still on Thorne. I roll over in my bed, curling up, and fall asleep instantly.

The Witch Queen soars across the world at night like a phantom, seeking the hearts of children to keep her blood magic powered. She can sense when a child is out of bed, for their blood pulses faster in their veins. She will smell them out, then swoop down from the sky and steal the child away in the night. She takes them back to her gothic castle, oozing with all the rotten blood that she has spilled, and they never see their families again.

Velmaran Book of Children's Stories

When Laurel appears the next morning, I'm surprised. She usually makes up an excuse to avoid seeing me multiple days in a row. I instantly jump out of my seat to greet her, but my eagerness has her shying away. So I pull back, remembering her insistence that nothing can happen between us.

Her words had flayed me open. Standing there, hair flying wildly around her face, expression open and vulnerable—I finally saw the real Laurel, finally saw the female behind the Witch Queen persona she wears so easily. But just as quickly as that delicate window had opened, it slammed shut again, and I was left reeling. I've never—not even *once*—told someone I had feelings for them. And Laurel had me practically begging her to acknowledge the heat between us. Sure, I've had lovers, females and males who I've been interested in, though not in a long time. Once I needed to rely on my charm to get secrets out of others, my own ability to lust and desire had dimmed. Somehow, without ever really trying to seduce her and everything that's happened between us since I arrived, we became allies. Tenuous allies, but allies nonetheless.

Conflicting emotions course through me as I consider the situation. On the one hand, I'm... *proud* of myself for gaining a true alliance without pretending to be interested in her. In fact, our alliance only formed once I finally opened up and showed her the vulnerable male beneath the flirty winks and smirks. At the same time, I care more deeply than I want to admit about her rejection, even if I know she's right. I've achieved what I set out to do—we've become allies in the search to uncover my father's secrets. It's unimaginable, impossible, considering the history between our kingdoms, and yet we finally achieved some kind of truce. That should be enough for me. A relationship beyond allies and tenuous friends would complicate the situation too much.

Laurel takes a seat next to Silene on the sofa, and the two laugh at something. I can't keep the genuine smile from my lips at the two of them forming a fast friendship, and I huff out a quiet laugh at the idea that Laurel thought Silene and I were really a couple, even though she had no reason to believe otherwise. They continue their conspiring, and I observe, happiness washing over me in warm waves. Even Fionn seems to warm to the Queen, his own expression light as he greets her. I clear my throat to interrupt their whispers.

"Laurel, how do you take your tea?" I ask with all the princely charm growing up in Velmara has given me. I pour the steaming liquid into a ceramic mug, waiting for her response.

Silene snorts, but Laurel responds, always one to hold on to etiquette. "As much cream as there is tea, and no sugar." I prepare the tea for her, then pass it her way. "Thank you," she says before taking a sip, and I can't keep my eyes from tracking her lips as they purse around the edge of the cup. The warm liquid makes them deepen in color, and she runs her tongue over her bottom lip. I'm transfixed by the movement, my mind imagining that tongue in other places, doing other things...

"So," Silene says with a twinkle of mischief in her eyes, breaking me out of my lust-addled haze, "what are you two getting up to today?"

"Training," we both say simultaneously, and it sounds conspicuous even to me. Fionn's eyes widen, and he smirks, while Silene bubbles with laughter.

"Hawthorne insists my light sparring skills need work," Laurel answers awkwardly.

"I believe I recall telling you to call me Thorne after *last night*," I retort back, unable to keep the sensuous innuendo from my voice, trying to get under her skin. Laurel blushes, and intense male satisfaction puffs up in my chest. As I stare at her with a smirk, her blush deepens, and my skin heats at the way it brings out her eyes. I'm overwhelmed with a desire to make her blush again and again. My body moves toward her instinctually before

I clench my fists, determined to shut down this attraction to her. There's no need to woo her. We're allies now, and while I haven't admitted the full truth about my father to her yet, she's clearly committed to helping me uncover what he might do with the thayar stores. Not to mention, at this point I'm pretty sure she doesn't practice blood magic anyway. The plan to seduce her is no more, so I *will* end this incessant flirting with her.

"Last night?" Fionn asks with mock surprise. Laurel's blush deepens, and I can sense her desire to smother the insinuation going on.

"Oh, we just shared our deepest darkest secrets. Thought it made sense for her to call me Thorne after that," I say to relieve her distress.

"A day like yesterday will bring that out, I suppose," Fionn says somberly. The mood instantly darkens.

"Twenty-four died in the attack," Laurel says softly. "Hundreds more were injured."

We all sit quietly for a moment, unsure of what to say. Fionn surprises me when he takes Laurel's hand and squeezes it, before adding, "We all did what we could, Your Majesty. Even more would have died if Silene and I hadn't been there. And we were only there because you're doing everything you can to stop this violence. You shouldn't blame yourself, like I can see you're doing." I think I see her wipe a tear away quickly, but she hides the movement so well I can't be sure.

"Yes, well," she says. "*Thorne* has agreed to convince the rebels to stop attacking citizens. To focus their efforts on the palace and on me."

"And *that* is why we need to train," I add before Fionn and Silene can object to the plan. I may not agree with it, but I feel the need to defend her now that we're with others. "What are you two up to today?" I ask them.

"We have a few sub-committee meetings this morning," Silene answers cheerily. Only she could get excited by the endless bureaucracy of the Thayarian government. "We don't have any plans for the afternoon, but, well, we thought..." she trails off, looking to Fionn.

"We thought we might go down to the merchant district and help however we can. Move families out of destroyed homes, clear rubble, whatever needs to be done," Fionn finishes for her.

Laurel swallows. I want to reach for her, but I don't. "That's very kind," she says softly. "I'm sure they can use all the extra hands. But... when will you contact the rebels next? Have you agreed to any future meetings?"

"We can stop by the granary and see if there are any messages for us. The rebels were going into safe houses at the end of the attacks. They may be quiet for a few more days before we hear from them," Silene answers kindly, keenly aware that Laurel is clearly struggling to wait for the next meeting. Laurel only nods and downs her tea.

When we finish breakfast, I go to grab the two cloaks I wore yesterday to keep warm in the frigid northern air, but Laurel stops me. "We can use the training room here today," she says. "It's getting too cold to go elsewhere. I think with the magic we're practicing, I should be okay to stay here." I hang the cloaks back on their hooks by the door, secretly relieved not to spend the next several hours freezing my ass off. "We can also walk there, if you like," she adds.

I give her a wide grin. "You are willing to be *seen* in *public* with the likes of *me*?"

"The palace is hardly public," she retorts. "But yes, I think we can be seen walking the halls of the palace together. Plus, there's something I want to show you."

I'm more than intrigued and gladly follow her out the door after saying goodbye to Silene and Fionn for the day. She leads me up several flights of stairs to a hallway of the palace I haven't seen yet. We walk to the end, then Laurel stops before a set of double doors, grinning brightly. My heart practically stops at the warmth of her expression, the genuine smile that lights her face from the inside out.

"We're almost to the Winter Solstice," she says, mischief in her eyes. "If you think it's cold now, you're going to turn into an actual glacier when Abscission begins." I raise my eyebrow, unsure what she means. "The deciduous plants in Thayaria hold on to their leaves much longer than elsewhere, because of the magic here. They do eventually die off like everywhere else, but for a much shorter period. On the shortest day of the year, the Winter Solstice, they drop their leaves, and the kingdom enters a frigid cold. Everything is dreary and gray for about two weeks, and we call that Abscission. But after the two weeks, the biting cold lessens, and the plants re-bloom."

"And what does this have to do with the roguish gleam in your eyes?" I ask, excited and terrified for whatever she's going to show me.

"Well... like I said, you don't have a very strong cold tolerance. None of you do. So, I have a... sanctuary, of sorts, for you." With that, she throws the doors wide, and a wave of warm, almost tropical air hits me. It's a balm against a cold I didn't even realize I felt so deep in my bones. I walk through the doors into a room filled with lush, exotic plants. Neon pinks, bright reds, and lime greens fill the space, tucked away under a clear dome. The flowers are unlike any I've ever seen, even here in Thayaria, and ivy that's different from what grows along the rest of the palace walls lines every surface that's not already filled with a tropical plant.

"What—what is this?" I ask.

"It's a greenhouse, kind of. It's older than our archives, so we don't know a lot about its origins, actually. I know that water from the nearby hot spring is pumped into here, but there's some kind of spell work even I can't decode. All we know is that it's self-sustaining, always warm, and has plants that don't grow anywhere else in the Four Kingdoms. It's a delightful mystery."

The humid air tickles my neck as I walk farther into the domed solarium. There's a salty dampness that comforts me, and I laugh. "This is *amazing*, Laurel." She blushes, and I take a step toward her, wanting to close the distance between our bodies.

"I thought you might want to come here to warm up after Winter Solstice," she says softly, her voice almost a whisper. Bright green eyes stare up at me from dark lashes, almost shy. When I take another step closer, she freezes for a moment before pulling back, vulnerable expression gone. "All three of you, I mean. Silene and Fionn, too. You're all welcome to use the space whenever you'd like."

"Thank you, truly," I say, then bow low, my hand fisted over my heart. "This is—it's extremely thoughtful." The longer I spend in here, the more it reminds me of Eastern Velmara, where my mother and her people hail. The humidity and lush vegetation are so similar to that oasis, it's like I've aerstepped to my maternal grandfather's estate. A twinge of sadness roils in my gut at the small reminder of her. It's not unpleasant, a cross between nostalgia and longing, but it makes me ache with how much I miss her. Even though we only spent a decade together of the three and a half centuries I've been alive, the grief at losing her has never left me, never will leave me. I can still picture the way her eyes crinkled when she smiled, can still see the exact way her mouth would purse when she was trying to pretend to scold me but wanted to laugh.

"Are you okay?" Laurel's soft voice pulls me from my walk down memory lane. She's so perceptive, this female who pretends to be so fearsome and emotionless. Her small, delicate hand lifts, like she's going to reach out and touch my arm, but just as quickly as she considers it, she clenches the hand in a fist at her side. I give her a real smile.

"Yeah, just remembering. This place reminds me of Eastern Velmara." She swallows, and I follow the movement with my eyes.

"You can come back here whenever you want. To—um—remember." Her words make her cheeks flush with embarrassment, and I can't help the chuckle that escapes me.

"Thanks, witchling. I'll keep that in mind." We stare at one another in awkward silence for a beat too long.

"Well, should we head to the training room now?" she asks stiffly.

I nod, burying my frustration. She keeps doing this. Opening up, letting me glimpse the warm and vulnerable female beneath her icy exterior, before building her walls back up. It's aethers-damned frustrating. Even if we don't give into the heat between us, I still want to build a friendship with her.

We walk side by side down and then back up more flights of stairs, to the training room. As soon as we enter, she stalks around the room in a circle, concentrating on something.

"What are you doing?" I ask.

"Building a protective shield of aether around the room. It's just a precaution in case... in case my control slips. I've never trained in the palace before. I want to make sure there's something to stop my magic from getting out." She returns to her slow walk, brows furrowed, and I study her full figure.

Aethers, she's beautiful. That dark hair paired with her creamy, plump skin makes me want to *bite* her, to wrap her up in my arms and never let her go. Her curves do something to me that no one's ever done before, and I wonder not for the first time what it might be like to see her naked. To see that heated expression she gives me when she's challenging me on her face while her breasts sway with her attitude. She's so confident and strong. And yet, there's a softness to her, a sadness, that's hard to ignore.

Something nags at me as she makes her third layer of wards on the room, a feeling about her that won't leave me be. Then, it hits me—*she's afraid of her own magic*. The realization shocks me, and I nearly laugh. The formidable and ferocious Witch Queen—feared across kingdoms, her name whispered out of concern it will conjure her, infamous for her supposed nefarious and terrible magic—is here making a shield around herself in case she loses control. The single most in control channeler I've ever encountered is *afraid* she'll lose control practicing simple sparring drills. The very fact that she can somehow build a shield of aether around us is a show of expert control.

I grieve for her. This wonderful, beautiful, insanely powerful female has been convinced she is some*thing* to be feared, rather than some*one* to be celebrated. As much as my father is envious of my power, he always sought to elevate it, even if only for his own gain. But while he memorialized my aether-blessed light and water magic through the streets of Velmara, he also spun a tale about Laurel that made her into a nightmare. Whether a small part of her believes him, or cows from her magic for her own reasons, I don't know. But she's afraid what she can do if unleashed, and I vow to change that for her.

Laurel finishes her warding and returns to the middle of the room. She must notice my staring, because she says, her tone filled with sass, "What?"

My lips twitch. "Nothing, just observing. Let's get started. Before you do any actual channeling, I want you to watch me. As you're watching, visualize yourself displaying the same power. Light channeling is the hardest for a reason. You have to *believe* the light can slice through objects, or it won't."

I drag the two massive pots filled with plants from the corners of the room to where we're standing, then close my eyes and focus on the powerful current of aether pulsing all around me. I hone that focus into the light with practiced ease, then pull it to me as an orb, making sure I extend out the movements that are so second nature to me so that they are easy for her to track. Then I guide the orb to lengthen into a sword-like shape.

It splits, and I have one in each hand. I go through a series of exercises to warm up and show her how to manipulate the light. And, if I'm being honest with myself, to show off for her.

She tracks my movements, a hungry look on her expression that eliminates all trace of the slow and patient teacher in me. It's replaced by a need to show her how powerful I really am. The light swords spear across the room in a fast beeline, then fly back into my hand. I whip them around me in fast slices and parries. One expands into a shield for an instant before it shrinks into dagger form, lightning fast. Then actual lightning-shaped spears slam into the ground, shaking the room. In an instant, all the light pulls back into a single sword, blinding in its intensity. I swing it toward the planters, slicing them in half with a sizzle.

Laurel's eyes are wide in awe, and I find heat rising to my own cheeks. "How was that for a party trick, witchling?" I ask her with a wink.

She recovers, a smirk rising to her own lips. "It was... sufficient. Though I could have done without the *property damage.*" She gestures to the planters, and I give her a sheepish shrug.

"Sufficient," I scoff. "It was brilliant, and you know it. I *know* you can't do those tricks."

"Fine," she admits, putting her hands on her hips with that attitude I was just fantasizing about. "Yes, it was impressive. Happy?" She gives me a mocking smile.

"Elated," I say with the deepest and most sensual voice I can muster, and she shivers. "Now it's your turn. Try to create a sword, split it into two, then make one of them a shield before turning it into a dagger. Don't worry about speed, just focus on form for this first try." Her brows furrow in adorable concentration, then she moves through the motions effortlessly, if slowly. "Excellent!" I clap my hands. "That was great technique. Now speed it up. Do the drill as fast as you can."

She creates the two swords again, but the light fizzles before she makes a shield. She tries again. Over and over, she attempts to move through the motions quickly, but the light always disintegrates before she can form the next shape. She stamps her foot, and my lips twitch.

"You have too much control."

She huffs. "*Too* much control? Please, enlighten me how expertise and control can somehow hinder my abilities."

"You can make the forms slowly because that allows you to concentrate on keeping the light contained. But to shift between forms, you have to let go a little. There's inevitably a moment between forms where the light exists outside of your control. The mastery comes in letting it go for that fraction of a second, then pulling it back to you." She looks distressed but only nods slowly. "Take another moment to visualize yourself doing the motions. *Believe* you can let go and still be able to pull the light back."

She closes her eyes and tries again, and this time she makes the shield, but falters when trying to make the dagger. She lets out a frustrated grunt and opens her eyes.

"That was good. Excellent really," I encourage. "It took me *years* to move between forms, and it's only taken you half an hour. It's amazing progress. Keep trying."

She practices for another hour. I give her encouragement along the way, gently nudging her to let go of the tight hold she keeps on her magic. By the end of the hour, she's able to whip through the forms quickly.

"Okay, let's try slicing through something. Er... sorry about the planters," I say, realizing there's not much more in the room for her to practice on. In an instant, the planters have been restored, as if they were never broken in the first place. I look up at Laurel, and she just shrugs.

"The benefit of *control*," she coos with a smirk, and my blood heats at the subtle challenge she offers me with her gaze. But then she shudders, and her expression turns worried. "Uh, don't tell anyone about that. Please." She must realize she's displayed yet another ability not connected to a conduit, but I don't press her on it. Internally, my mind is whirring. *What is her power? What conduit could possibly produce that result?*

"Your secret's safe with me, witchling," is all I say though, motioning for her to continue with training.

She takes a deep breath, then raises a sword of light above her head. In an impressive swipe downward, she slams it against the planters, but nothing happens, the light dissipating as it reaches them. She looks at me with confusion and frustration.

"I told you, you have to *believe* the light will slice into it. Do whatever meditative shit you need to do to believe that."

"Meditative shit?" she asks, eyebrow quirked.

"You know, your whole speech you gave me about thinking about the properties of water and light, and how they're part of the same fabric of the world. Or whatever you said. Just think about how the light is the same as the planters, so it can slice them apart." She only stares at me in challenge, hand propped on her hips again, then snaps her fingers. The planters slice in half again, but without her touching them.

"Like that?" she asks with a grin. Then she snaps her fingers a second time, and the planters are restored.

I roll my eyes. "Do it with the light," I chastise.

"Yeah, yeah. Don't watch. Go practice your own *meditative shit* in a corner."

I give her a mock bow. "As you wish, Your Majesty."

We practice in silent companionship for another hour, running through our own drills. When my stomach grumbles, I walk back to her in time to see her decimate the planters before restoring them instantly and decimating them again. I give her a slow clap. She turns, blushing again. "I told you not to watch."

"I wasn't watching till just then. I'm hungry. I need a snack."

At that exact moment, a knock sounds on the door, and Laurel startles. She crosses the room and opens the door to a human woman holding a tray of steaming food, the smells wafting into the room. She takes the tray from the servant, who murmurs something quietly to Laurel. Laurel squeals in obvious glee.

"Thank you, Sarah," she tells the woman, beaming. "You're too good to me." The woman bows, then Laurel closes the door with her foot and turns to me. "I didn't realize how long we'd been here. Thankfully, I told Sarah to bring us lunch today, so you can have *more* than a snack." I grunt, then take the tray from her and walk it to the small table in the back corner before setting out the plates and cutlery delivered with the food. Laurel picks up her plate, but I steal it out of her hands with a smirk.

"What was that screech about?" I ask as I dish out food for her, gesturing with my hands to find out which dishes she wants and how much. I enjoy serving her.

"It was not a screech," she snaps back light heartedly. "It was *an expression of joy*."

I laugh hard, and she slaps my arm. When I recover, I ask, "And what were you *expressing joy* over in such a screeching manner?" She rolls her eyes.

"There's a tavern and inn in Echosa, where you entered Thayaria," Laurel explains. "The owner's wife Mara makes the absolute *best* chocolate cake. She's in Arberly, helping her sister clean up their family's bakery after the attack, and she brought a cake to the palace for me. Sarah made sure we had two slices on our lunch tray."

"You and your chocolate cake," I mutter as I hand her a plate. She sticks her tongue out at me, and the expression is so adorable I can't help myself as I lean across the table into her space, then whisper in a husky voice, "And will you be sharing this cake with me?"

"Not if you continue to under appreciate it," she retorts. She licks her lips, and the motion ties me in knots. I reach for her hand, wanting to thread her fingers through mine, but she pulls away.

Fuck, stop hitting on her when she doesn't want it. I reprimand myself for the millionth time, vowing to keep our relationship friendly. It's not like I need a romantic complication in my life right now anyway. Or ever, for that matter. I fill my plate with the steaming rice dish, then groan at the delicious Thayarian food.

She nods at the food I just ate. "It's one of my favorites. Can I ask you something?"

"Anything," I tell her absentmindedly, and I mean it. I would confess any secret to her, tell her any information, even if it meant exposing myself and risking my safety. I'm not sure when that switch flipped on in my brain, if it was ever off at all.

"Why is Fionn so affected by yesterday's attack? Not that we all aren't, but he seems to be taking it harder, or more personally, than us." Her question surprises me. I pause for a moment. Of course she noticed Fionn's struggles. Nothing slips by her watchful gaze.

"Fionn wasn't born noble or wealthy. He's a commoner. His parents owned a fishing business. His mother was a powerful water channeler, who would sail out and catch fish for his father to sell at the Floating Market. Because of his upbringing, he cares deeply for everyday folk."

"You mention his parents in the past tense. Did something happen to them?"

I nod as I meet her penetrating gaze. "The specifics are his story to tell, but they died in a terrible accident around the same time his power manifested. Since he was orphaned and possessed the most powerful metal channeling ability in a millennium, my father brought him to live in the palace as a companion of sorts for me. He said I needed someone who matched my power to train with, and that the death of our mothers would help us bond. But it wasn't Fionn's choice. He had family, an aunt and uncle, who had taken him in. They were forced to give him over to the palace."

"That's terrible," she says, and I see genuine empathy in her eyes.

"It is. And we *hated* each other at first. He hated me for what I represented, and I hated him for his resentment of the only life I'd ever known. I found him arrogant, and I'm sure I was unbearable."

She laughs, and it makes my blood sing. "That doesn't surprise me."

"No, I'm sure it wouldn't." I grin at her teasing of me, loving the way we so effortlessly shoot barbs at one another. "But over time, we realized we had a lot in common, and our friendship bloomed. We've been inseparable ever since. Fionn entered the Royal Guard, and I immediately appointed him as my personal guard. He was with me when I found my mother's journal and has been with me for every terrible thing my father's ever done. It creates a bond."

"I feel the same way about the Chair of my Council of Advisors. Nemesia, who went to Velmara as your counterpart. She's been my best friend since birth, really. Her mother was my parents' Captain of the Royal Guard and General of their armies, so we were raised together." I remember that the Thayarian General had died early in the war, before Nemesia was appointed to the role, and I feel guilt at my connection to the loss of Nemesia's and Laurel's parents. Could Laurel ever truly forgive me for my father's sins? Will she ever be able to look past all that I represent?

"You must miss her," I say softly, and her eyes sparkle with tears for a moment, but she clears them before they fall.

"Yes. It's been difficult without her counsel." And just like that, her mask is back in place, the window into the real Laurel slammed shut. She changes the subject quickly. "What's next in our practice drills, oh great instructor?" she asks with a teasing tone not reflected in her eyes.

"Well, now that you've mastered the basics that most light channelers learn before they're twenty, we'll start some more advanced drills." I smirk.

"You said it took you years to learn how to do that!" she protests.

"It did, they just happened to be years when I was very young." She only rolls her eyes, but this time, there's a grin on her face that even she cannot shutter away.

"You've mastered the basic forms and moving between them," I explain once we've finished our lunch. "Now we spar. Fighting is a dance. You need to shift between forms on instinct. And all that shit I told you about *believing* the light can slice through things? Forget that. I don't want you nicking me." She rolls her eyes. "I assume you've been taught to fight with weapons? I haven't actually seen you use anything but magic to defend yourself."

"I was raised as the heir to a throne, forced into a war at twenty-years old, then lived in fear of another war for three hundred years. I know how to use a sword," she snaps back. I give her a half-smile to hide my own horror at her response, my grief for who she's been forced to become.

"Then use everything you've learned, but just make the weapons out of light. Light sparring is better and different, because you have every type of weapon at your disposal. A long sword can instantly become a dagger when the fighting gets close but can morph into a shield when you need it."

She nods, then creates a sword in one hand and a dagger in the other. "Let's get started, princeling," she teases, and a primal instinct washes over me, excited to spar with her. But the excitement that heats my core differs from the jolt of energy I feel when I spar with Fionn or Silene. It's a challenge and a soothing caress all at once, like there's something I've been waiting for, and it will finally click into place when we spar. I conjure a sword and dagger of my own, then launch myself at her.

She blocks me with her sword, then swipes her dagger, demonstrating competent weapons wielding. But I'm better and faster. I spin, easily avoiding her slice and moving behind her. I wrap my arm around her waist, then hold my dagger to her throat. Her ass brushes against my upper thighs, and I breathe heavily with the effort of keeping a respectable distance between us.

"You should have shifted your sword into a shield to block," I whisper into her nape, and she shivers. "It would have allowed you to use my momentum against me. Plus, we're trying to develop instinctually shifting between forms. Don't rely on the weapons as they are. Morph them into what you need." I release her, instantly feeling the absence of her in my arms, and she stalks away, her own deep breaths making her breasts lift in a rhythm that draws my eyes. I forcefully wrench my gaze to her face, which is fixed with determination.

"Got it. Ready for another round?" she asks, eyes bright.

I lunge again, this time with my dagger, trying to bring her into a fight at close quarters so I can touch her again. She lets me get the dagger inches from her midriff before her left hand makes a small shield and forces me back. Her other hand swings her sword toward me. She's taken control of the fight, and my cock twitches as I imagine her taking control of *other* situations. But I don't intend to let her keep the upper hand for long.

"Good," I tell her as I spin out of the way, conjuring two swords in either hand. I feint with one arm, and when she blocks with her sword, I bring my other arm around in a wide arc towards her left side. She instantly forms a shield in her left hand to block me on both fronts. "You're getting the hang of it! Ready for me to move faster?"

"Faster?" she gasps, incredulous.

"This is nothing," I tell her with cocky confidence. "Next lesson—don't let your opponent see the weapon you're going to use until it's too late for them to block." I spin again, lunging for her with no weapon in either hand. When I get close, I conjure a short sword. She avoids it by spinning away from me, but then I send orbs of light that resemble throwing stars toward her. Her eyes widen, and one of them hits her square in the chest.

She stumbles, hand going over her heart. She's panting, and her eyes look up at me in confusion. "Why didn't that hurt?"

"Light can just be light. It doesn't have to wound. I didn't put enough concentrated aether into it to hurt you. But you sure thought I did, didn't you?" I ask with a snicker.

"Bastard," she mutters.

"You need to shield faster. Now you won't make that mistake anymore." I wave my hand toward her. "Again."

We continue sparring for hours. She gets better but still isn't shifting fast enough to keep up with me. After what has to be the hundredth time I catch her off guard, she yells in frustration while I still have her pressed against my body. This time, I have to release her quickly, not wanting her to feel how her primal roar affects me.

"Don't be too hard on yourself. I've been doing this for hundreds of years. You won't master this in an afternoon. Plus, most people you'd be fighting won't actually be able to change their weapons out with a thought. They'll be stuck using the same thing they start with. Metal has its own challenges, but fighting another light channeler is infinitely harder."

"Then why aren't *you* using real weapons?" she snaps, clearly annoyed.

"Because I can tell the light not to hurt you if you don't shield or block quick enough. I can't do the same with a metal weapon. This is the safest way to train." She only huffs. She knows I'm right but doesn't want to admit it. "Let's take a break. We've been going for hours. You must be exhausted."

"And you aren't?"

"Hate to break it to you, witchling, but I grew up training with Fionn. He's the only one who can really tire me." As if my words conjured the bulky male, he and Silene enter the training room.

"Damn right," Fionn says smugly. "Thorne here tries so hard to beat me, it's cute."

I roll my eyes. "I can beat you sometimes." Fionn only huffs a grunt. "Should we give Laurel here a demonstration?" I ask, and he smiles wide. Two swords from the training rack fly across the room into his hand.

"I thought you'd never ask," he says, then barrels toward me.

Thayarian tradition demands that during the Winter Solstice, fae and human alike spend the day in rest. No work is done, even to cook. Thayarians are encouraged to spend the day with their loved ones.

A Brief History of Modern Thayaria

The two males blur in my vision as they whirl around the room. They lunge and parry, spin and duck. Thorne wasn't kidding when he said the sparring we did was nothing compared to sparring with Fionn. The warrior somehow looks even more massive as he swings his blade over and over again. Thorne blocks every blow with practiced ease, but I still stand erect, anxiety coursing through my veins. At one point, Fionn summons every weapon on the rack and has them all diving at Thorne, who blocks them with shields of light that appear around him. Thorne sends his own weapons hurling at Fionn—arrows, throwing stars, orbs—all made of light. But Fionn easily dodges or blocks them with the two blades he keeps firmly grasped in his hands.

Silene stands beside me, looking bored. "It gets a bit tiring eventually, trust me," she says. I laugh, but only for a moment before my eyes lock back on the two males weaving and bobbing around one another. If I'm honest with myself, I have eyes for only *one* of those males. Thorne's muscles tense with every swing of his sword. My eyes track a bead of sweat rolling down his face toward his full lips, and I almost trip over myself as I lean forward to be closer to him.

Thorne summons more lightning bolts. They crack into the floor around Fionn, who dodges them and laughs. "I can see those coming from a mile away, friend," he roars at Thorne, before sending a dagger zinging towards Thorne's chest with aether-honed precision. My breath hitches, and I clutch my hand over my chest, feeling my heart beating wildly. It's too similar to the moment Nemesia was almost killed by Mazus's assassin in the war tent all those years ago. Silene notices and places her hand on my shoulder.

"Are you okay?" she asks.

I nod, taking a deep breath. "Yeah," I respond. "It just reminds me of a moment I don't care to remember."

Silene seems to understand. "Alright, boys, that's enough," she calls out. The whirling ball of light and metal they had become slows, and they look over, both panting and smiling widely. Thorne's eyes immediately find mine, and he frowns.

"What's wrong?" he asks, but Silene cuts him off.

"We're just tired of watching the two of you show off. I for one am ready for dinner." With that, she hooks her arm through mine and marches me toward the door. I give her a look that I hope conveys my gratitude. Fionn and Thorne pick up the room, then follow us back to their apartment.

The dinner tray's already been delivered to their rooms when we arrive. Silene unhooks herself from my arm and prances over to her and Thorne's bedroom, hollering that she's going to change, and we better not start dinner without her. It's a good reminder of the reason I won't explore my attraction for Thorne. If they're just friends, as he says, why does she sleep there? Why does she keep her clothing there? Of course I know that many sexual partners don't have rules of monogamy in their relationship, and maybe that's the situation with Thorne. But if that were the case, why not tell me that instead of some lie about there being nothing between them? Does he consider sex to be so insignificant?

"Stay for dinner," Thorne says, his low voice startling me. I hesitate, not wanting to intrude. I'm about to decline when he adds, "Please. Fionn and Silene might have an update from the rebels."

He knows how to convince me. "Fine, I'll stay," I say with a long-suffering sigh I don't really feel. He grins.

"What did you think of today?" he asks.

"It was a good lesson," I respond genuinely. "I haven't learned something new with my magic in at least a hundred years."

He smiles wide, and this one is the real Thorne, not the winking and smirking prince. "Pretty soon you'll be sparring with me like Fionn does. I'm sure of it."

"As loath as I am to compliment your massive ego, that *was* impressive. I can't imagine ever being able to fight like that."

"You'll get there, witchling." He nudges my shoulder. "You have more power than the two of us combined. You just have to learn to let go and let your instincts take over."

"I'm not entirely sure that's wise." What I don't say is that the idea of totally letting go terrifies me. If I could put up a mist barrier that can't be undone when I was untrained and barely coming into my power, what horror might I unleash with three hundred years of deepening my well of magic? If I let go, I might destroy my kingdom. Might destroy the *world*.

"And why is that?" he asks, eyes wholly focused on me with an intensity that makes me squirm. Lunaria could pounce on him right now and he wouldn't notice, his gaze so focused on me.

"Because with power like mine... It's important that I stay in control. Letting go could cause real damage." It's all I can admit to, the tiniest peek at my true feelings. But even these words are hard to whisper, a confession I didn't know I needed to make. Relief eases across my chest, a weight lifting.

He leans forward to whisper in my ear. "I disagree, witchling. But there's time for me to help you see that letting go doesn't mean losing control entirely." I can't hide the shivers that rack my body.

"Alright, let's eat," Silene exclaims, returning from their bedroom and immediately filling a plate with food.

Thorne motions for me to go first, and I quickly put distance between us, especially after seeing Silene once again leave their shared room. After filling my plate with food, I make a point to sit beside Silene at the small dining table, not wanting the feeling Thorne's presence brings me. He's forced to sit across from me, and I quickly realize dining with his eyes lingering across my body, tracking every bite of food, is no better than sitting next to him. It might be worse.

"Did you make it to the granary?" I ask Silene and Fionn to distract myself from the way his attention makes my pulse thrum.

"We did," Silene says through bites of food. "They left a message for us that basically said to lie low through Abscission, whatever that means, and to meet them in Oakton once the blooms begin again. Does that mean anything to you?" I laugh as a piece of bread falls from her mouth.

"You're quite the lady," I tease, and the room erupts in laughter. It warms something up inside of me, and for a moment, I can forget Thorne's drifting gaze and bask in the glow of friendship. When we finally ease back into a comfortable silence, I explain to Fionn and Silene what Abscission is.

"So basically, we won't really communicate with the rebels again for several weeks," Silene says when I'm finished, and I nod.

"And you won't have any sub-committee meetings either during Abscission," I tell her. "The kingdom pretty much shuts down. Everyone sleeps in, spends time with family, and rests."

"That sounds like a great tradition," she remarks excitedly. "I'm *finally* going to read some of those saucy books you loaned me." Thorne chokes on his water, looking at me expectantly. Heat rises to my cheeks.

"What? I just gave her a few romance books from my collection," I deflect.

"Saucy?" he asks, eyebrow raised.

"They're just really... exciting," I respond, and Silene and Thorne both break out laughing again.

"What will the people in the merchant district do?" Fionn asks, and the mood sobers. I take a swallow of wine before answering.

"We have a little less than a week to get them into temporary shelters," I explain. "Once Winter Solstice and Abscission arrive, it'll be too cold to do much else in the district. My advisors' number one priority is finding them a place to stay until we can rebuild their homes."

"Where will they go if they don't have family to stay with?" Fionn's eyes are bright as he listens intently to my words.

"Here. The palace is deceptively large. There are entire wings under the mountain that aren't in use. We have more than enough rooms for displaced families. The real challenge is getting them cleaned and properly set up in time."

Fionn looks thoughtful. "You'll house them here? What if there are rebels among them? It could be another trick, to sneak inside so they can launch another attack."

"That's a risk we'll have to take," I say somberly. I considered the very question, worried we'd have another attack inside the palace. "It's the best option with the timeline we have. I have to trust that the rebels will honor this kingdom's most sacred tradition and rest for the next few weeks. Besides, I won't leave my people without shelter, no matter the risk." Fionn gazes at me with a look of newfound respect, and the approval of this warrior lifts something inside of me.

"We'll help prepare rooms," Silene says cheerfully. "I can sweep dust with my air channeling. And Fionn can help move any furniture with metal in it. Thorne, well, I'm not exactly sure how he'll be able to help, since light doesn't really do much and he hates any kind of physical labor or cleaning..."

Thorne scoffs and looks offended. "One—may I remind you I'm also a water channeler, and water is typically very useful when *cleaning*. Two—I don't hate physical labor or cleaning. I just prefer not to do it if I don't have to. With the number of servants always swarming me in Velmara, setting them a cleaning task was sometimes the only way to get a moment of peace and quiet."

We all laugh at his expense, Thorne included. The dinner passes in camaraderie and laughter, and I find myself more excited for an Abscission than I have been in a long time.

The next week passes in a frenzy of cleaning, moving furniture, and hauling boxes of belongings into rooms in the palace. All three of the Velmarans are true to their word, working tirelessly alongside my advisors and me to prepare comfortable lodging for those without alternative shelter. Silene even convinces me to throw a Winter Solstice dinner and invite everyone staying in the palace. She takes on most of the planning, becoming fast friends with the advisors and servants she works with. Silene probably becomes fast friends with everyone she meets. After six days of hard work, we successfully get everyone settled.

On the morning of Winter Solstice, I wake up in my bed, the air cold even to me. As usual, Lunaria prowled outside overnight, so I left the balcony doors open, and the frigid air makes my breath come in puffs I can see. I'm covered in a multitude of blankets and furs, and I loathe the idea of getting out of bed, so I use my magic to start a fire and heat the room.

Thankfully, it's Winter Solstice, which means I get to laze around with the rest of my kingdom and do absolutely nothing. I have complicated feelings about this day, though. I love the Thayarian tradition of rest, but each year it reminds me of my loneliness. I've spent a few Solstices with lovers, but usually it's just Nemesia and me, since both of our parents died in the war and it's incredibly uncommon for fae to have more than one child. We always build a massive fire in my room and lay in my bed together reading all day, eating whatever pastries or other sweets we can pilfer from the kitchens. I notice her absence even more deeply today as I lay alone in my bed, realizing I have no one to spend the day with. I wonder not for the first time what she's doing. If she's safe. If she's happy.

Spotting Lunaria fast asleep at my feet, I channel a gust of wind that shuts the balcony doors. That startles her, and she stretches before gingerly making her way to my side and curling up next to me.

"Late night?" I ask. She only nuzzles closer to me. I grab the book on my nightstand, excited for a morning of reading about Cairn and Stella, the characters in my most recent saucy book.

An hour later, the room has warmed and Lunaria's body heat seeps into me. I'm sweating, so I throw the blankets off, which disturbs my cat. She gives me a grumpy look before leaping from the bed to her pallet in the corner, where she falls back asleep.

"What a drama queen," I mutter under my breath. I stretch my arms high above my head, releasing the pressure in my shoulders and back, then step out of the bed to make myself a cup of tea.

Just as I'm settling onto the couch in my sitting room, there's a knock at my door. I'm not expecting anyone, so I step cautiously toward it. I pool light in my hand, then open it a crack. Thorne stands there, alone, grinning from ear to ear. He notices the light in my hand.

"I'm glad you're taking precautions to defend yourself with what I taught you," he says.

"Why are you here?" I ask, opening the door fully. Thorne's eyes widen, and his gaze tracks up and down my body. Heat builds in his expression, his jaw going slack and his eyes dilating. "Hello? What are you doing?" I snap.

Thorne startles. "Well—uh—" He coughs, and I cross my arms over my chest in impatience, which only makes his gaze darken. "Uh, in Velmara, the Winter Solstice..." He moves his eyes to stare at something over my shoulder. "We celebrate by exchanging gifts. Silene has sent here me on strict orders to bring you with me."

It finally hits me—I opened the door in my chemise, a short length of gauzy and nearly transparent fabric. I want to hide myself in shame. My mortification forces me to wave Thorne in before quickly turning and grabbing a robe draped over the couch. Thorne says nothing, though his gaze returns to my face now that my body is covered.

"In true Silene fashion," he continues, "she's somehow managed to organize a dinner for hundreds of people while also finding time to shop for gifts and help move said people into the palace. I'm merely a messenger, witchling. But I fear if I return without you, Silene may lose that chipper personality she's so known for and rip my still-beating heart out from my chest. She's learned a thing or two from the Witch Queen while in Thayaria." He winks in that classic Thorne way.

Panic grips my gut. "But, I don't have gifts for any of you. I—I didn't know. It's not something we do here in Thayaria," I confess.

"You've already given us our gift." When I look confused, he continues. "The greenhouse. It's the best gift we could've asked for in this arctic wasteland. You weren't kidding when you said it would get cold."

"The cold gets worse," I tell him absentmindedly, my mind racing. The greenhouse, while a gift of sorts, is not sufficient. "Come in and sit down for a moment," I tell him before racing off.

I gather the things I need, stuffing them into a bag, then rush to my closet. I dress in warm trousers and a long-sleeved tunic, buttoning it up over my cleavage to make up for what he previously saw. Grabbing my bag, I motion for us to leave, then follow Thorne down the endless staircases.

"I can aerstep us," I say grumpily. "I hate these stairs. I never take them."

His lips twitch. "Silene also ordered me to take the long way to make sure she had enough time to get everything in place. Also, you do live at the top of these stairs. In a giant palace with endless rooms to choose from. This seems like your own fault."

"In case you haven't noticed, I'm a super powerful *witch* who can magically appear anywhere I want in an instant. Where I live doesn't matter," I quip back.

"Except when faced with the unstoppable power of one Silene Kalmeera. She's a force of nature. In a tiny little fae body," he says, and I can't stop the deep belly laugh that erupts from me.

"That she is," I say with real fondness when I finally stop laughing, and his eyes are bright with amusement. We walk down the endless stairs, trading flirtatious barbs despite my resolve to be nothing more than allies. Maybe the flirting is harmless, anyway. It's not like he doesn't flirt with everyone else around him. I'm no different than everyone else.

When we come to the wing of the palace with the greenhouse, I'm surprised when he leads me there. "We're meeting in here?" I ask, but he only smirks before throwing the doors wide open.

Silene has transformed the room. Plants line the edges of the space, stacked neatly together but not overcrowded, their vibrant hues popping against the dreary landscape beyond the glass panels. In the newly cleared area is a giant rug with brightly colored poufs that match the brightness of the exotic flowers around them. A pile of gifts sits in the middle of the rug, and there's a spread of pastries off to the side with several pots of tea.

Silene is bouncing with excitement. "Happy Solstice, Laurel!" she squeals before rushing over and giving me a tight hug. I still for only a moment, surprised by the contact, but then easily wrap my arms around her to return the squeeze. She takes my hand and leads me to a pouf. "When Thorne showed me the greenhouse, I knew we had to have our Solstice morning celebration in here. It feels so much like Velmara. It was such a thoughtful gesture." The genuine warmth in her expression makes me smile.

"I wish I'd known you guys exchanged gifts. I would have prepared..." I say, but Silene cuts me off.

"Nonsense. You've already given us something wonderful. The gift of home on a holiday is more than we could have asked for."

"Agreed," Fionn adds. The giant male sits on a pouf next to me, his long limbs awkwardly curled up next to him. I have to stifle giggles at the comical sight.

Thorne appears at my side with a cup of tea, lightened with just the right amount of cream. I take a sip, and sigh. It's perfect. No sugar, the right ratios. Then I realize the servants aren't working this morning, so they shouldn't have my favorite cream for tea. "You have cream?" I ask, incredulous.

"Thorne had the servants bring extra the last few days so we could save up enough for you since you need so much of it in your tea," Silene tells me with a mischievous look I don't understand. Thorne blushes, and the sight... It melts my insides to see the usually cool and collected charmer blushing.

"Thank... uh... thank you," I manage to get out. The gesture is so thoughtful. It sends me spiraling, especially the fact that Silene is aware of it and seems *in* on it. Maybe she just appreciates seeing her betrothed show the kindness she clearly values so much. A small, hopeful voice whispers that maybe they don't have feelings for one another, that the betrothal really is just political, like Thorne said. I smother it. Even if that's the case, it doesn't change the situation we're in. Now is not the time for me to entertain such distractions. I'm hosting a ball tonight in the palace because *hundreds* of my people lost their homes only days ago. I shouldn't be worried about males who are shameless flirts and likely only want me for the conquest it would be.

Thorne sits next to Silene with the tray of pastries in his hands. He takes one, then passes it to her. When it reaches me, I'm delighted to find my favorite sweet bread on the tray. "Where did you get the pastries?" Now Fionn blushes.

"There was a baker whose shop wasn't impacted by the attack and who took in as many displaced people as he could," Fionn says. "I bought out his entire shop yesterday. It seemed like the least I could do." Once again, the hulking male surprises me with his gentleness.

"Time for gifts!" Silene cheers. She grabs a parcel wrapped in black paper ornamented with thayar flowers and hands it to me. "Open it, open it!" I peel the paper back and frown at the compact silver box in my hands. Opening the lid, my confusion grows when I see what's inside. I look up at Silene. "It's a travel makeup container," she informs me. "It has dark kohl, dark red lipstick, eye paint—everything you need to transform into the Witch Queen on a moment's notice. I noticed how much you rely on the makeup when you're in public. Now you can carry that little mask with you for whenever you need it."

I swallow down the lump in my throat. It's extremely thoughtful and affects me more than I can say. "Thank you," I whisper.

Silene moves on to watch Fionn and Thorne open their gifts from her. An extremely well-made dagger for Fionn with thayars carved into the hilt, and a pair of silk lounge pants for Thorne. I catch myself analyzing her gift for Thorne, wondering if it's the gift of a lover or just a friend, before I scold myself for caring. *It doesn't matter what his betrothed got him. Focus on helping your people.*

I don't get to watch Silene open her gift from Thorne, because Fionn hands me a small package. I'm surprised. I assumed only Silene would give me a gift. The box reveals a set of small and very sharp metal pins.

"These are popular in Velmara with female metal channelers, and I found a blacksmith here who would make them for me. You pin them into your sleeve, so that you always have a weapon on you. With enough force, these sharp little things can do serious damage to an enemy. You need that protection on you at all times, queenie." His smile is mischievous, revealing a side to him I've never seen. And the nickname—it hints at an acceptance of me by the warrior that I didn't know I desired.

Overwhelmed by a second thoughtful gift, I stifle the emotion surging through me. "That's so kind, Fionn. I'll wear them every day," I promise, and he beams.

All three of them have considered me in every aspect of their plans for this day. It makes me uncomfortable while also lighting up something inside of me I thought I buried long ago. The more time we spend together, the more *open* I am with them, and that's dangerous, for them and for me. Despite the casual way Thorne invited me here today, I sense the significance of spending this day together. If I let it, today will solidify our alliance—our budding *friendship.* Is that what I want? Do I actually care for these Velmarans, or am I simply feeling vulnerable without Nemesia? Before I can even consider the question fully, I know the answer, and that scares me.

Determined to ignore these feelings, I reach for my bag, pulling out the lump of ore I'd nabbed for Fionn before leaving my room, and hand the hunk of metal to him. He looks at it a few moments, brows furrowed, before thanking me politely. I laugh.

"You don't even know what it is."

"It's, uh, a rock. It's a great gift," he says sheepishly, and I burst out laughing.

"If that's all it was, it would be a terrible gift. It's not just a rock. It's ore refined with thayar petals and stems. It makes the metal even more sensitive to the aether and fluid in its shape. A skilled metal channeler can shape it into different weapons instantly, like how a light channeler can shape their weapons. Thorne won't be able to beat you ever again with this in your pocket." I give him a conspiratorial grin.

His eyes widen, and he looks at the gift with a new appreciation. He closes his eyes, and the metal slowly shifts into two daggers, then a short sword, before morphing back into a misshapen hunk.

"This might be the best present I've ever received, queenie," he says with wonder in his voice that's so unusual for the warrior, and my heart squeezes. I leave him to test out the properties of the gift.

"Silene, I have something for you," I tell her. "It's not much, but I couldn't just let my gift be a warm room with some plants." I hand her the book. She flips through it and her eyes light up with glee.

"What is it?" Thorne asks.

"It's a biography of the first female General of Thayaria. She was a formidable warrior, but also a brilliant strategist. Nemesia never shuts up about her. And she also happened to be fun-sized like Silene."

"There are actual war strategies in here!" she exclaims. "And fighting techniques for someone with a smaller stature. Thank you!" I smile as she starts reading immediately, then I stand and walk to the bar cart in the corner to refill my mug with more tea.

"I have a gift for you as well," Thorne says from behind me, and I jump. He's so good at sneaking up on me. He hands me a small parcel wrapped in cream and navy parchment. My heart flutters at the sight of his signature colors. I set the mug down on the bar cart, then tentatively take the gift from him. I open it to find a delicate and finely crafted gold necklace of a lightning bolt. I look up at him expectantly. "Channeling lightning is the hardest of the light magic because it's so unpredictable," he tells me, eyes locked on mine in an intense gaze. "It requires the wielder to give up control, to trust that even if the path it takes down from the sky isn't what we would have imagined, it will still strike where we want it to." I swallow, keeping my eyes on his handsome face. "May I?" he asks, gesturing to the necklace and then my neck. I nod.

He takes the necklace out of my hands, then stands behind me. I feel his breath on the nape of my neck as he gently moves my hair to the side, and my back arches toward him just slightly, something akin to lightning striking in my core. He brings the necklace over my head. As he clasps it, he continues his explanation, voice a delicious low tenor.

"The sun is the symbol of my father, of the throne of Velmara. But the lightning bolt is also a reminder to him and to everyone in Velmara that the real power lies with those who channel true light. Those who oppose his rule wear a lightning bolt as a small act of rebellion." His hands rest on my shoulders now, thumbs rubbing gentle strokes across the fabric of my gown. He leans down and whispers in my ear. "I wanted you to have this lightning bolt to remind you to let go and to bring a piece of resistance against my father with you wherever you go." I shiver as he moves away, feeling the absence of warmth where his hands once were. I touch the necklace, and I swear it sparks under my fingers. Thorne turns me to face him. With slow, intentional movements, he takes my cup from the table, fills it with tea and cream, then hands it back to me, his gaze never leaving mine. "Happy Solstice, witchling," he says, practically a growl. I'm speechless, so touched by his gift that I have no words.

I remember the gift I found for him and awkwardly walk away, muttering "stay here." I grab my bag, then cross the room toward him, where he stands leaning against the wall with that effortless grace I've grown so accustomed to. "My gift is really just a loan, because you have to give it back." He raises an eyebrow, and I hand him the ancient and massive book on thayar.

"This is Thayaria's oldest and most comprehensive text on thayar flowers. Well, it's a copy that I had made so I could annotate it. I read it often. Every day, pretty much, and centuries of my notes on the flower are in there, along with places where I've added information from my experience with the aether and the flower. I thought... I thought maybe you'd like to read it to see what your father might be up to. Fresh eyes and all that. It seems silly compared to your gift, but it's all I had in my room at the moment..." My cheeks heat, voice rising higher and higher as I speak.

He cuts me off, placing his hand on my arm. The touch burns deliciously where his fingers trail over my skin. "It's perfect. I'll read it thoroughly and treat it with care. And I cannot begin to tell you how excited I am to see notes from a young Laurel. Thank you for trusting me with it."

I look into his eyes, and they bore into me. He always seems to see right down to my very core. It's infuriating. It's thrilling. It's *everything*. I can't look away, and it's only when Fionn makes a pointed cough in our direction that I realize we've been standing there, staring at one another for who knows how long. I shuffle back to my pouf and sit down, eyes decidedly *not* on Thorne as he returns to his own seat.

There are many traditions and myths about the Winter Solstice. Each kingdom has their own practices, from resting for two weeks to exchanging gifts. One of the most beloved of Winter Solstice legends is that of fae mates, who are compelled to give their mate a Solstice gift that once belonged to them. Some trinket or object that holds significance or meaning, given to the fae's mate for safekeeping. Many young lovers will practice the tradition on Winter Solstice, lost in the myth's romanticism. But fae mates, if they ever existed, are now nothing more than fables told to spark joy on a holiday.

The Legends of the Fae, Volume III

In the early afternoon, I return to my room to prepare for dinner. After running a bath, I set my travel makeup and metal pins on my vanity. But I keep the necklace on as I dip into the steaming water. I run over every moment with Thorne, still so confused by him. One moment he's flippantly flirting, treating me no differently than every other female he's encountered in Thayaria. Then in the next moment, he's looking at me with a deep longing that goes beyond simple attraction. His relationship with Silene is so baffling. He clearly cares deeply for her, but whether that's as a friend, a lover, or something in between, I cannot sort out. He says they're just friends, but with everything the rumors say about him, how could I possibly trust that? I stay in the bath until the water turns tepid, staring out at the barren landscape through the window, lost in thought.

Lunaria startles me out of my stupor, stalking into the room and staring at me as if to say, time to get moving. I get out of the tub, dressing myself in a simple silk gown that hugs my body, the color matching Thorne's eyes. I keep the lightning necklace on, adding only a set of simple earrings and black elbow-length gloves to complete the look. My hair hangs long and wavy, front pieces pulled into a twist that keeps it out of my face, and my makeup is light and airy.

When I aerstep into the massive dining hall that's rarely used, it too has been transformed by Silene. In addition to the overgrown vines that line the palace, there are lights everywhere. Glowing strings swoop down from the high ceiling, while gossamer navy fabric drapes under them. The effect is that when you look up, it's like you're looking up at the night sky. Twinkling lights also hang down the walls, interspersed with the creeping ivy.

A single long dining table runs down the length of the space, decorated with more lights and arrangements of cut flowers from the greenhouse. Bright yellows, pinks, reds, and blues are interspersed with dark green, giving the decor a look that is wholly at odds with how Thayarian affairs usually look. From the front of the room, smells of garlic, onion, meat, and freshly baked bread waft from a buffet table lined with covered dishes. The cooks are dressed up though, socializing and drinking like everyone else. Silene must have organized it this way so everyone could take part.

Across the room, Thorne speaks with Aria, his prince charming act out in full force. His eyes twinkle with mirth as he says something to her, giving her a smirk that I'm all too familiar with. He's clad in a navy suit, perfectly tailored to show off the hard lines of his body. Aria's hand is on his arm, and she laughs brightly, leaning into him. He winks. Hot jealousy spikes through me, and I stalk toward them.

"Thorne," I say, placing my hand on his shoulder. "Thank you for coming tonight." Aria looks at me with the briefest flash of annoyance before she bows.

"Your Majesty," she says, "what an excellent idea the Velmarans had for this Winter Solstice. I dare say His Highness must have had a hand in these arrangements. The Velmarans are known for their own lavish dinner parties, I hear." She flashes a pretty grin at Thorne, eyelashes fluttering, and it makes my magic rear up with ferocity. I crush it, not willing to let the room shake with my power and give away my feelings. *You like Aria. She's a good advisor.* The reminder doesn't help the feeling of my skin crawling.

Thorne looks my way, lust briefly flashing in his gaze as it drifts across my body, landing on the necklace. He grins at me, an intimate, half twist of his lips, like there's a secret between us, before he turns back to Aria. A satisfied warmth creeps over my body, calming my magic.

"Oh, I had no hand in this whatsoever," he admits. "I confess I usually hate the Velmaran dinner parties. It's all to the credit of my advisor, Miss Kalmeera. And, of course, Her Majesty. This wouldn't have been possible without Queen Laurel's agreement to Silene's schemes. You should extend your praises to them." I can't help but note that he referred to Silene as only an advisor.

"I see," Aria says, realizing Thorne has dismissed her. "Well, I will go find Miss Kalmeera and offer her my thanks."

When she's out of earshot, Thorne turns to me. His eyes slowly travel the length of my body, like he's drinking me in, and it sets my skin ablaze. "You look stunning," he growls. I blush. "And my necklace suits you."

"*Your* necklace?" I ask, confused. Thorne looks sheepish.

"Well, uh, it was mine. But I wanted you to have it."

"Why?" My eyes search his, but he's spared from answering by Silene's appearance at our side.

"Laurel, we're about to start. Do you want to say anything?" she asks. I nod, then leave with her to address the room, mind still whirring from Thorne's revelation and the way it stirs something inside me, something that feels ancient.

"Welcome to the first Winter Solstice dinner," I say loudly to the group gathered for the dinner. "While the circumstances that led to this event were deeply upsetting, I'm happy to have this opportunity with all of you. As we dine tonight, please remember the lives we lost last week. Remember their families. Enjoy tonight and know that you're welcome here in Thayaria's palace. It's your home as much as it's mine. And please, join me in thanking our Velmaran emissaries, whose idea and planning led to this evening." The crowd of human and fae, children and adults, bow to me, then clap for the Velmarans, and the sight is remarkable. I'm overcome with the vision of a future where dinners like this are common in Thayaria, both at the palace and around the kingdom. I raise my wine glass. "Happy Solstice!" I toast. The crowd echoes my toast, then breaks into the murmur of conversation.

Servants dressed in their own fancy gowns and suits uncover serving dishes with food before returning to the party, and Silene shoos people to go make plates.

"Your Majesty, you look beautiful," Carex says as he approaches me.

"Thank you, Carex. And thank you for coming tonight."

"I wouldn't miss it. My parents are here as well. We decided to have our family dinner here instead of at their home."

"That's wonderful. Please, tell them Happy Solstice from me," I say, then turn to make a plate, but his arm reaches out, halting me.

"Laurel, can I speak with you for a moment?" I look down at his hand wrapped around my wrist, gripping tightly. He removes it quickly. "Sorry," he mutters. "Please, can we speak privately? Just over in that corner." I nod and follow him there. "Laurel, I know you've been spending more time with the Velmarans. The Prince especially. My Royal Guards reported you spent an entire day with him in the training room the day after the attack."

I'm shocked at the boldness of his statement, surprise quickly turning to anger. "Excuse me? May I remind you they are *my* Royal Guards, as I am the titular *royal*. You are simply their Captain, who serves at my pleasure. And who I spend my time with is none of your concern. What *concerns me*, however, is that you appear to be spying on your Queen. Receiving *reports* about me."

Carex blanches, and he stammers his apologies. "Please, forgive me, Your Majesty. It was a series of poorly chosen words. It's only that the guards informed me, as they were concerned for your safety. I assure you I'm not having you watched." I study him closely, suspicion building. He now has access to Nemesia's network of spies and informants. And he campaigned fiercely to be sent to Delsar for the Forum of Royals. Our relationship gave him access to many of the inner workings of the government, decades before he was an official advisor on my Council. Could he be the mole? "I wanted to speak with you because I need to share critical information," he continues. "I've been trying to get a meeting scheduled with you since the day of the attack, but you've been busy helping prepare the palace. The guards who went to the thayar tower that day described seeing a fae who matches the description of Prince Hawthorne. It was a brief glimpse, as if *light shielding* failed for just a moment. I think he was there during the attack and is working with the rebels. We need to question him." Carex's eyes bore into me, concern and something else lingering in them.

This presents new challenges. I won't be able to hide my partnership with the Velmarans for much longer if the rumors of this spread. I carefully consider my next words. "Thank you for the information. I'd like to think over the best approach for investigating this. Let's not worry about it during Abscission." Hopefully that buys me some time to squash these rumors. He nods, looking like he wants to say more, but I cut him off. "Now, I should sit with the people." I turn and walk away.

As I approach the buffet to fill my plate, Thorne leans against the wall next to it, arms crossed. Something about his posture is off, not giving off the usual vibes of effortless nonchalance. When I enter the buffet line, he follows behind me.

"*Why* is the Captain of your Royal Guard grabbing your wrist?" he asks icily, his eyes containing no trace of the flirting male I'm used to seeing. "I could see it from here. And he used your given name." He clenches and unclenches his jaw. "Is everything okay?"

"Carex and I have... history. We used to—we were together. Lovers," I joke. The muscle in Thorne's jaw feathers. "He occasionally blurs the lines between advisor and monarch. He was informing me the guards spotted you at the tower during the attack. Descriptions made their way to him. We need to be careful."

"Lovers?" he asks sharply, and his jaw clenches again.

I laugh. "I tell you that my advisors are warning me you're involved with the rebels, and *that's* what you focus on?"

"They can't prove it, and as long as I'm not spotted again, it will pass. It was a brief sighting, and in a very confusing and highly emotional moment for them." He waves as if this is trivial compared to his real question. "How long ago did your *history* end?" I study him for a moment, electricity sparking through me as I consider whether Thorne might be jealous. But surely he's not. That seems like a stretch, especially for someone who flirts with everyone. And then I feel confused again, remembering that I chose not to pursue anything with him, and for good reason.

I roll my eyes to hide my conflicting emotions as I fill my plate with dish after dish. "A long time ago, Thorne. And it's none of your business. He wanted more from me, but he couldn't handle it. And I wasn't ready for that commitment. He was afraid of me and still is. It never would have worked out. End of story." I pause. "*Why* am I telling you this? It's *so* not your business." He only shrugs and winks. I sigh. *Aethers, this situation is weird.*

"If he grabs you like that again, I want you to spear him through the middle with light," he commands, that serious, unflinching leader emerging in his tone and expression.

"Noted."

The Solstice dinner passes in joyful celebration. The people open up over the course of the evening, and I speak to many of them about their lives and what they lost in the attack. Though it breaks my heart, I feel hope—for the first time in a long time—that we'll be able to rebuild and stop the rebellion. I wish Nemesia were here. She'd love seeing the people brought together like this, even though she'd pretend she hated the party. I smile inwardly thinking of her dressed up in a gown for a fancy dinner. She'd probably wear her fighting leathers underneath it, knowing her.

"This was a wonderful idea," Admon leans over and says to me, interrupting my thoughts of Nemesia. I can't help but agree. We clink our glasses together in a toast, and his eyes twinkle in a fatherly approval that makes me pull my shoulders back proudly. When dinner is over, Silene stands from her seat next to me.

"I hope you all enjoyed the delicious food. I certainly did. Now, we dance!" With a dramatic hand gesture, several advisors escort musicians into the room. They set up and begin with a lively tune.

Silene walks along the table, encouraging people to get up and dance. She's asked to dance by practically every male in the room, but she turns them all away, preferring instead to run around chasing children while they scream with glee. Thorne and Fionn, on the other hand, are each led to the dance floor by females, though Fionn doesn't look happy about it. Aria has her hand wrapped around Thorne's, and she laughs at something he says. Steaming jealousy rears its head inside of me again. Silene seems oblivious, content to let her fiancé dance with a gorgeous and lust-filled female. Maybe they really are just friends.

"Laurel, would you dance with me?" Carex asks, startling me from my brooding. Although I want to say no, I need to distract myself. Taking Carex's hand, he leads me to the dance floor just as a slow and traditional Solstice dance begins. Carex wraps his arm around my waist and pulls me close as we sway to the music.

"This reminds me of our first Solstice together," he says, voice low. "I think it was this very song that we danced to that night."

We had danced to this song, alone in his parent's home in Arberly after they'd gone to bed. We'd been courting for several months but hadn't gotten serious until that night. It was the first Solstice I spent outside of the castle. At the time, I was so captivated by Carex's handsomeness that I barely remembered the steps to the dance. He smiled every time I blushed, and we ended the night whispering our feelings for one another in front of the fire, kissing and fucking like adolescent fae experiencing their first relationship, even though it was hardly the first time for either of us.

"It was this song," I say, smiling at the memory, cheeks heating.

Carex's hand tightens around my waist, and he pulls me closer, placing his forehead on mine. "Laurel," he breathes. "I've missed you."

"You see me every week," I respond as I pull my head back, knowing that's not what he means.

"I see the Queen every week. I haven't seen Laurel, *my* Laurel, in a long time," he whispers. "But something about you is different. In a good way. You seem lighter, happier. More open, despite everything going on." His hand splays across my back, fingers lightly exploring, trailing closer and closer to my ass. I stiffen.

"Carex—don't. We agreed. We both wanted to move on. We couldn't give each other what we needed." I repeat the words we'd said.

"What if—what if I don't? Want to move on, I mean. All I ever wanted was for you to open up to me, to the world. That's what I needed from you. Maybe now you're ready to give it to me. I know you didn't think our relationship was over for good back then. I certainly didn't." His gray eyes are shining and hopeful. When it ended, there *was* a part of me that had hoped he'd change his mind, hoped he'd give me a reason to try again. I've imagined countless conversations like this one over the last several decades.

Now those thoughts have been consumed by others that are decidedly *not* about Carex. Thoughts about someone who's equally unavailable, but who's undoubtedly the reason for the change Carex has noticed in me. I almost laugh aloud, realizing Carex wants me now that someone else has brought out what he never could.

"I don't think it's a good idea," I say slowly, but Carex interrupts me.

"Why not? Lots of fae couples go through up and down periods. My own parents have had three different marriages, and they've ended things temporarily in between them each time, but always decide to come back to one another. We can have a whole new relationship. We're different people now, just like my parents." He pulls me tighter, and I feel smothered.

"We're not them, Carex." I try to pull out of his grasp, but he grips me tighter. I push against his chest, my eyes blazing with anger, and he releases me, but keeps my hands firmly grasped in his.

"Laurel," he pleads. "Think about this night. This song."

Now I'm fuming, and suspicion about the song causes me to rip my hands out of his. "Did you set the musicians up to this? Tell them to play this song?" He doesn't answer, but his sheepish look and flushed cheeks are all the answer I need.

"We were so good together," he whispers in a desperate attempt to keep me here.

"We actually weren't, Carex. We didn't end only because of *me*. And you're still the same male you were then." I will a small orb of water to collect near his face, not even honing it into a dagger, and Carex's eyes widen in fear. "Exactly," I say before turning from him.

He grabs my wrist again, this time tightly, forcing me to face him. "Please, help me understand—"

"I was hoping to have the pleasure of dancing with Her Majesty," a familiar and comforting voice says behind me. Thorne angles his body between Carex and me, his scent washing over me and drowning out everything else.

"We're still dancing," Carex sneers with the sheerest mask of polite courtier.

"Doesn't look like that to me," Thorne hisses, taking my arm and removing Carex's hand from my wrist before placing his hand on my shoulder. "Your Majesty, would you like to dance with me?"

"I would, thank you." In an instant, Thorne has wrapped me in his arms and spun me away. As we turn, Carex returns to my line of sight. He looks furious, eyes narrowed, shoulders tense, hands balled.

"What happened to running him through the gut with a light spear, witchling?" Thorne growls. I laugh.

"I would have, but *someone* interrupted before I got the chance," I tease. Thorne shrugs.

"I'm not sorry. I don't take kindly to males touching females when they don't consent. Daddy issues, remember?" he says with a wink. I want to press him, to ask about what his father did to his mother, but I drop it. Not here, where he's the Shining Prince, with no worries or fears. I know better than anyone the need to separate the vulnerable person behind the mask from the public face we wear.

"Thank you," I murmur. He only pulls me closer, the heat of his hand through the thin silk of my dress both deliciously warm and scalding hot. As we perform the movements of the dance, my body heats, and not from the activity.

"Let's go outside," I say, surprising myself. "I'm hot and want to cool off."

"Can't say I disagree," he growls with a devilish glint in his eye. I can only roll my eyes at him for what feels like the millionth time as we walk to the small terrace built off the side of the palace. As soon as we walk outside, the frigid air cools my flushed cheeks. "Fuck, it's cold. I know I say that literally every time we walk outside. But *fuck*," Thorne says, exasperated and shivering, though still looking every inch a prince.

"You're so whiny," I tease, even as I wrap him in a warm magical embrace.

"Thanks," he says, and I give him a flirtatious wink. Suddenly, snow begins to fall around us in thick, dense flakes. Thorne's eyes light up as he stares up at the sky. "Is this snow?"

"What do you mean, is this snow? Of course it is!"

Thorne shrugs. "I've never seen it. Doesn't snow in Velmara."

My jaw practically drops to the floor. "Seriously?"

He places his hand over his heart. "I swear it on what little honor I have. Which is practically none. So you'll never know, I guess." He winks.

I giggle, the sound so unfamiliar to my ears that I almost choke. Thorne smirks at me like he knows the effect he has on me, but it sends me spiraling. Am I just another pretty face among a sea of beautiful females? Do I look just like Aria does when she's near him, fawning and blushing every time he looks my way? I study him closely, looking for answers I know I won't find. When he notices, his eyes turn serious.

"What was all that about, anyway? With Carex? Is he still talking about the guards seeing me? It didn't look like a conversation between advisors to me." He says the words with forced nonchalance, like he's making a joke with a friend, but I can see his tensed shoulders through that tight suit jacket.

I smirk. "Not your business."

"But I gave you such a pretty necklace. Doesn't that at *least* give me the honor of being the friend who you tell all your boy troubles to," he says with a mock pout, flecks of snow turning his hair and beard white, and I can't help the laugh that escapes me.

"Fine," I say, groaning. "He wanted to resume our former affair."

Thorne's eyes dilate and his nostrils flare. "And I'm assuming you don't want to, judging by how quickly you tried to get away from him."

"Not even a little. I told you, he's afraid of my magic. Afraid of me. I can't be with someone like that."

"Good, witchling. You deserve someone who will worship you, who thinks your magic is just one of dozens of things they find incredible about you. Don't settle for anything less." The heat in his gaze lights me up inside, and I even catch myself studying my skin, wondering if I might be actually glowing. I'm not, but the spark inside of me doesn't go out. For once, I step closer to Thorne, not the other way around, and I think I hear a low noise in the back of his throat.

"Laurel," he breathes my name like a prayer, like a lifeline in the dark. His eyes are searching, darting across my face with all the fae senses he's honed over centuries. Before I know what's happening, his arm wraps around my waist, pulling me into him, and I don't protest.

"Thorne," is all I manage to whisper out. Somehow, he moves us up against the wall of the terrace, placing one arm above me so that all I can see is *him*. His tall and muscular frame is so much more pronounced this way, crowding my space and towering over me. It's dark outside, but the light floating our way from the ballroom makes his features glow in a hazy brilliance.

He dips his head so our foreheads are touching, mirroring the movement Carex had forced on me only minutes ago. But this time, I welcome it. Slowly, gently, like I'm a wild animal that might spook if he's not careful, Thorne brings his hand up to caress my face. His hand is massive, practically cradling my entire head in his palm. His thumb strokes over my lips, and an involuntary moan, so quiet I could almost miss it, escapes me. Or maybe it was him? I'm unsure, too wrapped up in his heated gaze.

His head leans down, and time stops. He's going to kiss me. I *want* him to kiss me. I think. But maybe I don't? I'm so unsure, still so tangled in knots when it comes to him. His reputation, his betrothal, the way he winks and simpers with every female around him. His kingdom. His *father*. I should stop this, but I don't. When I feel his hard body press against my own, my resolve falters. Would it be so bad to give in to the attraction?

Just for one night. So what if I'm just another conquest of the Shining Prince? I'm sure it would be electrifying, sure his experience makes him a skilled lover. Surely one time wouldn't hurt anything.

My own body leans in, and I'm going to meet his lips with mine, going to—

"Laurel? Hawthorne? What are you doing out here? It's freezing!" We jump away from one another as Silene's bouncing form prances over to us, breaking whatever spell we'd been under. I should feel relief, but as I turn my back on Thorne, all I feel is yearning need.

The fae tell many stories about the origin of our world. One of the most popular usually
follows this structure: our once united world was torn apart long ago by a terrible and
immense display of power. When all seemed lost in the Great War, the witches sealed
away the darkness. Kingdoms disappeared, and families lost their loved ones to the other
side of the world. The act cost the witches more than their lives, and the world as we know
it was born from their sacrifice.

The Legends of the Fae, Volume II

There's a knock on my door, and I groan. It's the Winter Solstice, and I fully intended
to keep my own kingdom's traditions by not doing anything today. I close my eyes,
content to ignore whoever it is. The knock sounds again, more insistent in its pounding.

"Coming," I yell at whoever's disturbing me. When I open the door, a servant stands
there holding a box wrapped in gold paper with a gold bow on top. She bows.

"His Majesty King Mazus wished me to deliver this Solstice gift to you." Her eyes dart
around as if Mazus will appear at any moment. Taking the giant gift, I thank her before
shutting the door and lugging it to my desk. There's a note attached to the bow on top.

Dear General Nestern,

You may not be aware, but it is tradition to exchange gifts on the Winter Solstice here in
Velmara. As I had promised you a selection of books from my personal collection, I thought

presenting them as a gift on this holiday seemed appropriate. Please accept these rather interesting tomes as an extension of the friendship I so wish for Velmara and Thayaria. Happy Solstice!

His Royal Majesty, King Mazus, Golden King of Velmara

I roll my eyes despite my excitement and eagerly unwrap the package to find four books inside. Scanning the titles, I'm surprised by what I find. *The Secrets and Stories of Velmara, Blood Magic Through the Ages, The History of the Aether,* and a book title in Old Fae. I think it loosely translates to *The Legends of the Fae.* Why would Mazus send me these books? Once again, his motivations are unclear, and it brings an uneasy feeling to my gut. Under any other circumstances, this *gift* would be the best I'd ever received. But anything I discover in these books will serve Mazus's aims, and that can't be a good thing.

I scan the book titles again, lost in thought. My attention snags on the book on blood magic, and I open it, scanning the table of contents. It appears to be structured chronologically, detailing what various scholars thought about blood magic at different points of history. Sighing, I close the volume. Maybe the gift isn't as helpful as I thought.

Over the months I've been here, my frustration with the archives has been slowly growing. Every book seems to be an anthology or review of *other* literature, but those primary research texts don't exist anymore. I have to trust that what I'm reading is an accurate summary of those earlier works, and when you're dealing with history this ancient, so much can get lost in translation or through the bias of the scholar reviewing the literature. Every day I wake up, do a bit of training in the underground cavern Mazus made available to me, then head to the archives, where I sit for hours and hours reading anthologies of other research. My life unfortunately consists of very little outside of that—I'm relentless in my desire to find information to help Laurel and Thayaria.

After my dinner with Mazus several weeks ago, I shifted my research to the history of leylines as he had suggested, though the same challenge remained. Based on the breadth of writings available in the archives, I've confirmed what I already suspected—leylines reflect the magic of our world, and the presence of thayar flowers in Thayaria is because of the numerous leylines that cross the kingdom. The thayar flower seems to be directly related to the magic of our world. I've also ascertained that several leylines used to cross the Nivan Desert but disappeared inexplicably. This explains why thayar flowers used to be present in Velmara but disappeared when the leylines did. These revelations are concerning for many reasons, not least of which is that it could indicate the magic coursing through Thayaria is declining. That the decline in thayar blooms is the symptom, not the cause. The history is ancient, dating back thousands and thousands of years, so it's hard to decipher what's real and what is only speculation. Several texts even used different names for the kingdoms of our realm. I've yet to work out which name corresponds to which modern kingdom name.

My eyes catch again on the book in Old Fae, and hope rises in my chest that this might be a primary or original work of research. I open the dusty and massive volume, eyes blurring at the tiny characters. *This is going to be challenging.* I pull out a sheet of parchment to use as a scratch pad while I translate. The table of contents reveals that the book is structured around various topics, from the origins of the fae to ancient religion. A section on mates catches my attention, and I furrow my brows, flipping to that part.

I can translate about every fifth word and groan at my rusty translation skills. I'll need to get an Old Fae dictionary from the archives, which means I have to leave my room on the Winter Solstice. Laurel would be outraged. We spend nearly every Solstice together, holed up in one of our chambers reading and eating sweets, refusing to leave or even change out of our night clothes.

A thought crosses my mind, turning around my sour mood. The Velmarans celebrate this holiday as well, which means the librarians won't be working today, and I might be able to slip in and have the archives completely to myself. Mazus didn't set any parameters about when I wasn't allowed there—he had granted *full access.*

After dressing quickly, I make my way through the deserted castle to the wing dedicated to the archives. When I arrive, the doors are shut, and I worry they've been locked for the holiday. With a gentle push, however, they glide open easily. The massive entryway is eerily quiet compared to the usual noise of at least a dozen librarians walking about to direct patrons to the right section. The high ceilings are capped by a massive stained-glass dome that covers the entryway, letting in soft light that paints the marble floor in hues of red, yellow, and green. As I walk across the floor, my steps echo in the cavernous space.

Turning down the corridor that leads to the language section, I scan the paintings on the walls that I've never had the luxury to observe before, too caught up in my research to wander. There are depictions of the rolling golden plains of Velmara, and surprisingly, a painting of what must be Thayaria with its verdant and mountainous landscape. I check all the other artwork, but no other kingdom is represented, though there are several more paintings of Thayaria.

Lost in thought about what that could mean, and remembering Lobelia's strange comment at the Forum about returning Velmara and Thayaria to allies as they once were, I crash right into another person.

"I'm so sorry," Genevieve says from where I've knocked her to the ground. I offer my hand to help her up, and her soft skin momentarily distracts me from my whirling mind.

"No, no, it was completely my fault. I wasn't paying any attention to where I was going." She grins, and it lights up her whole face.

"We're both at fault then, because my nose was in a book," she says as she bends to pick up the book she dropped when I smacked into her.

"Why are you here in the archives instead of celebrating the holiday?" I ask, and her cheeks flush slightly.

"I don't have family to celebrate with, and I love the archives on holidays when it's completely empty. There's nothing to do but read at my own leisure." I hide my surprise that she has no family and change the subject, not wanting to pry.

"I hope it's okay that I'm in here. I was also hoping to find it deserted." I give her a mischievous look that brings another radiant smile to her face.

"Well, Dern wouldn't like it, but he isn't here!" she exclaims brightly, and I laugh.

"I don't want to get you into any trouble—"

"You won't. It's not really a rule, just the result of his stubbornness and prejudice. Can I help you find anything?"

"Actually, yes. I'm looking for an Old Fae dictionary so I can refresh my vocabulary of the language. It's been a while since I read anything in it."

Her eyes widen in surprise. "You can read Old Fae?"

"Not well," I admit. "But enough to translate with the right lexicon nearby."

"This way," she says with a quick pivot on her heel. I trail behind her through several corridors and rows of books before she stops in what looks like the oldest and dustiest corner of the entire place. Her brows furrow in concentration as she scans the book titles, and she bites her bottom lip in a tantalizing movement.

"Here it is!" she exclaims in triumph, eyes shining brightly as she hands me a massive and crumbling tome.

"Thank you," I say, and we stand awkwardly for a few beats. "Would you like to read together?" I ask to break the silence.

"Oh, I wouldn't want to disturb you," she says, though without much resolve.

"Nonsense. It's a holiday, and I would love the company. It's a bit lonely here on days like today."

Her expression softens. "I can imagine how hard it must be to be in another kingdom, away from your family and friends, on days like today." The compassion and understanding in her voice makes my throat tighten uncomfortably, so I turn away before she can notice.

"Do you have a favorite reading nook?" She gives me the most ornery grin I've ever seen.

"Follow me, Ambassador."

She leads me to an area of the Archives I've never been, even during her tour, then up a winding spiral staircase. When we reach the top, my jaw drops. There's a small platform tucked right where the stained-glass dome meets the walls, somehow invisible from the entryway. It's only about twelve feet in either direction, but a worktable with chairs along with several hanging hammocks create the coziest looking alcove I've ever seen.

"This is amazing," I mutter. Genevieve beams at me, her expression so unguarded and open it takes me aback.

"Not many know about it, and the rest of the librarians would *never* be caught using such a small space as their office. They all prefer the larger, ground-level offices, but as soon as I discovered this space, I knew I had to claim it."

Light dances across the alcove in more intense colors this close to the stained-glass dome, and the heat from the windows warms the room to a perfect temperature. When I'm done gaping at her office, we both set up—me at the table so I can spread out my books and Genevieve in one of the swinging hammocks. I get to work translating, and she loses herself equally in whatever it is she's reading.

After an hour or so, she stands, stretching her arms above her head in a way that I try not to notice shows off her figure. Padding over to sit across from me, she places her elbows on the table and her head in her hands, looking at me with an innocent curiosity.

"Can I ask what you're translating? There aren't any Old Fae books in the archives."

"His Majesty provided me with several books from his personal collection. As far as I can tell, this book is a collection of stories about the fae."

She claps her hands in delight. "That is a most high honor from His Majesty!" Her entire body quivers, clearly excited to simply know someone who's been granted access to Mazus's personal collection. "Would you permit me to examine the books? Only when you are done with them, of course."

I smile at her enthusiasm, noticing the way it makes her features even more radiant. Internally chastising myself for getting distracted by a pretty face, I respond, "Of course, I'd be happy to share them with you when I'm done. In fact, you can look at the others while I'm busy translating this one." I nudge the three books toward her.

Genuine thrill crosses her expression. "Thank you." She picks up the book titled *The Secrets and Stories of Velmara* and immediately dives into reading. Studying her, I wonder whether I can trust her with my concerns about Mazus providing me the books. It would be helpful to have another person reviewing the contents of them with skepticism.

"What do you think of King Mazus?" I ask, hoping to ease into the conversation carefully.

Her brows furrow. "What do you mean?"

"I don't know him very well," I say slowly. "I was... *surprised* to receive these books from him. I'm just curious about him, I guess." Hopefully that is open ended enough.

"We are taught from an early age about the Golden King. He's ruled Velmara for hundreds and hundreds of years, and the kingdom has prospered under his leadership," she responds by rote. The words sound rehearsed, and her eyes almost look distant, like she's dissociating from what she says.

I press further. "That doesn't sound like an answer to my question." I keep my expression cool, giving nothing away as I stare at her. Her shoulders tense for the briefest moment. There's something here.

"As one of the youngest librarians, I'm often assigned the task of documenting the King's speeches or other informational materials. I file them away in the section on his rule and cross-check his words against information in the archives." Her eyes are filled with meaning, but I don't understand what she's trying to tell me. I'm about to ask her to speak plainly when she abruptly changes the subject. "Would you like some tea? I'd like to go make myself a cup." Before I can even answer her question, she's gone, slipping down the stairs in a blur. The conversation clearly made her uncomfortable, but for what reason, I can't say.

When she returns, two mugs of steaming tea in her hands, I don't continue the conversation. We sit side by side in silence, each reading one of Mazus's books. Genevieve takes furious notes as her eyes dart across the pages of the book on Velmara. After only an hour, she's filled pages and pages with her scribbles. I want to examine them, curious what she's found that's so noteworthy, but I leave it be. I clearly spooked her with my questions about Mazus. There's more to what she said, but I need to probe delicately.

When the setting sun makes the light dance across the table in a soft glow, we both simultaneously decide to leave at the same time, turning to one another and speaking over one another.

"We should—" Genevieve says.

"Well, it's getting late," I say.

She giggles loudly while I let out a soft chuckle, then we stand there awkwardly, unsure what to say. The moment stretches with tension, though it's not unpleasant. A million possibilities expand before us as we stare at one another, a question hovering in the space between us, though I'm not sure what it is. Is she—Could she be—

"Would you like to walk through the gardens of the palace?" Genevieve finally asks, interrupting my thoughts, eyes bright. "They are beautiful at sunset and will be as empty as the library." I can't keep the soft and warm smile that breaks out across my face. Something about Genevieve brings out a gentleness in me that I'm not sure I've ever shown anyone, wasn't even sure I possessed.

"Yes, I'd like that," I answer softly before following her out of the library and through the halls of the castle.

"Did you always want to be a librarian?" I ask a half hour later as we stroll through the manicured garden built in the center of the Velmaran castle. The garden's nice at this time of night, with perfectly trimmed hedges and trees lining a sandy path. Only a few flowering bushes add any color to the space. It's nothing compared to the lush gardens and verdant landscape of Thayaria.

"Oh, no, not at all. I'm part of the Kalmeera noble family." I raise my brows, recognizing the name as the most powerful and wealthy family name in Velmara. "My mother was the sister of Silas Kalmeera. She married my father, another distant Kalmeera cousin, when she was only forty years old. She died giving birth to me at forty-two, bringing great shame to my family. My father married another Kalmeera cousin and left me to be raised by my uncle Silas and his wife. Silas' daughter, Silene, is one of the ambassadors who went to Thayaria, actually. She's much younger than me." She delivers the information straight forward, with that same bright and cheery energy she always has, as if it's the most natural thing in the world to tell a practical stranger about her family history. I recall the brief meeting with her cousin as I left Thayaria, and I can't believe I didn't put the connection together before. They look remarkably similar. "Anyway, I was raised to be a wife and a mother, as all noble females are. But since my mother died in childbirth, there was a fear I would inherit her weak constitution. Silas struggled to betroth me. So he gave me to the archives instead." She says the last part as if it's the best thing to have ever happened to her, and I can't help but agree with the sentiment.

"And do you like your life as a librarian?"

"I do, very much," she says with a soft smile, eyes distant as if, even now, she's thinking about the books she wants to read. "I much prefer it to being a wife to some male I despise." I snort in laughter, and she gives me a conspiratorial grin.

"In Thayaria, females are valued for more than their childbearing. Many female fae choose to stay unmarried." Genevieve looks at me like I've grown two heads, and I laugh. "It's true. We even let females and human women serve as soldiers or Royal Guards." Her expression is incredulous.

"I enjoy my life as a librarian..." she says slowly. "But I've always wondered, if other opportunities had been available to me..." she trails off, not willing to say the words aloud. It breaks my heart a little. Genevieve is clearly someone with a deep well of energy and intelligence, two traits that would have opened many doors for her in Thayaria. "Do you enjoy being an ambassador?" she asks, though I get the sense it's not to change the subject, but to simply continue the conversation.

I consider my answer for a moment. "I don't know that I'm serving as a true ambassador. I've spent almost all of my time in the archives, which I love. I'm enjoying whatever it is I'm doing here in Velmara," I answer honestly, and she laughs, a bright and almost chirping melody.

"That's good, then. And the archives *are* wonderful." We settle once again into companionable silence as we follow the winding labyrinth of the path.

As we walk, we occasionally bump into one another, one or both of us unable to walk in a straight line. Every time our hands or arms brush, a warm tingling sensation gathers low in my belly. I'm lusting after this cheery, bright, and open female. I'm not one to shy away from my sexuality, but here in Velmara, where roles for women are so dictated by society, I don't dare pursue it. Even if she were interested—which is very unlikely, considering the way Velmara frowns upon relationships between females—it would put her in danger. And the thought of that is intolerable to me.

So we continue walking, chatting pleasantly about some of our favorite books and places in the archives. I tell her more about Thayaria, about the way the landscape is covered in foliage and so unlike Velmara. She listens with rapt attention, filing the information away, her mind a natural fit for the life of a scholar. Despite my earlier curiosity about her notes on Mazus's book, I forget about them, caught up in the fast friendship forming between us. If I'm honest with myself, it's refreshing to have companionship after so many weeks alone.

When the sky is inky black, we finally head back inside the palace. "Thank you for walking with me," Genevieve says with a gentle smile that's soothing. She radiates calming energy effortlessly, a balm to my weathered soul.

"Thank *you* for inviting me." My words are quiet and slow, so unlike me.

"Good night, Nemesia." With that, she turns down the corridor to my right and leaves me standing there staring after her. The soft and gentle way she said my name repeats in my mind as I walk to my own room, and for the first time since I've arrived in Velmara, I don't feel alone.

The Golden King and his son, The Shining Prince, stand together as a beacon of light against the darkness of Thayaria's Witch Queen. With King Mazus watching over Velmara, its children are safe from the evils of the Witch Queen, as long as they mind their parents and teachers. But the poor children of Thayaria are enslaved, forced to work for the Witch Queen or provide her their blood. One day, King Mazus and Prince Hawthorne will defeat the witch, and the children of Thayaria will be safe and happy once again.

Velmaran Book of Children's Stories

We pass the rest of Abscission splitting our time equally between our apartment and the greenhouse, reading, playing Skran, and talking late into the night. Laurel joins us most days, though she spends nearly all of her time with Silene. It's almost like she's avoiding me. The two of them giggle side by side, reading romance books or playing pranks on Fionn and me. At one point, they convinced Fionn to walk under a swirling ball of water. Once he was under it, Laurel had it collapse over him, drenching him in water filled with glittery strings of a slimy substance that stuck to his skin. When he turned and looked at them with incredulity on his face and covered in glitter, they burst out laughing and didn't stop for a full ten minutes. Fionn just stalked off to his bathing chamber without saying a word.

Laurel also trains with me every few days, slowly improving but still struggling to let go and let the light do what it will. Today, I attempted to teach her to create lightning, hoping it would be an exercise in letting go, but she failed spectacularly. Her drive is impressive—once she's determined to learn something, she doesn't stop until she masters it. Equally impressive is her impatience. Not one used to struggling with magic, Laurel gets easily frustrated when she can't do something immediately.

Despite the additional time we're spending together, it's awkward between us after the Solstice dinner. I *know* she was going to kiss me that night, know that if Silene hadn't interrupted us, we might have done more than kiss. I can't get the feel of her body pressed against mine out of my head, those soft curves brushing against me. I want to get her alone again even as the thought scares me. The second Silene appeared, Laurel ripped herself away from me and has somehow ensured Silene or Fionn or both are present when we're together, even when we train.

After today's session, where I had to physically drag her out of the training room to get her to stop practicing, I glimpsed her clutching my lightning bolt necklace. The sight sent hot desire shooting through every inch of my body, and I couldn't stop the image of her naked, wearing nothing but that necklace, from barging into my thoughts. Even now, laying alone in my room late at night on the last day of Abscission, my mind wanders to her.

I think about her more than I want to admit. She haunts my dreams, those heart-shaped lips trailing down my body, full breasts cupped in my hands, reddish hair creating a cage around my face as she rides me. Her body is so different from what I'm used to. The fae, especially females, are lithe and willowy, bodies drawing a straight line. Small breasts, small ass. But Laurel—those curves. I'm tantalized by her cleavage and her round backside. Seeing her immediately ignites my blood, and my eyes find her in any room. Even when I don't have her in my line of sight, I *feel* her, keenly aware of her presence like a sixth sense. When she smiles, the world stops around me, and when she laughs, bright and melodic, I cease breathing.

If I'm being honest with myself, the energy that pulses between us makes me uneasy. I don't know how to be the kind of male she deserves. And, aethers, she deserves so much. Everything that's been taken from her, everything that she's had to endure for *so long*—all at the hands of my own aethers-damned father—is incomprehensible. She should be with someone smart and capable, who can rule at her side and share her burden. I can't be that for her. I've only played pretend at spy, pulling together a small network of allies in Velmara who've achieved little. *I couldn't even stop my own father from secreting away the entire country's supply of thayar flowers.* I'm not worthy of her, and she was right to shut down pursuing anything between us. There's too much history, too much baggage, for us to be anything more than allies.

And yet, when I'm with her, all of that shame and loathing and worry disappears. I get too caught up in poking at her, trying to see which comments or grins make her laugh, or shiver, or open up. It takes so much energy to keep my hands off her, and I fail more often than not. But I'm still trying to respect her reasons for not wanting to act on this attraction, reasons that the rational part of my brain agrees with, even if other parts of me don't.

Attraction. I laugh out loud. What courses between us is so much more than attraction, so much more than lust. There are many beautiful females in Velmara, all eager to catch the attention of the Shining Prince. None have ever set me on *fire* the way Laurel does, like I'm a light burning brighter and brighter the longer I spend in her presence. I'd be lying to myself if I said I didn't enjoy flirting my way through most situations, but what I do with Laurel is so much more than flirting. My magic becomes easier around her, too, something about her nearness allowing me to tap into the aether with a stronger and deeper connection.

A soft thud on the small balcony outside my room startles me. Looking over, two bright yellow orbs stare back at me. *Laurel's cat.* When I open the door for the feline, she stalks inside. I stay frozen, unsure what to do about the enormous, wild animal in my room. Her sleek body pads toward me, sniffing first my feet, then my legs, then my stomach. My heart beats quickly in my chest, and I regret opening the door for her. She rubs her head against my palm, and on instinct I scratch it. Yellow eyes close in satisfaction, so I increase the pressure. Sitting down on the foot of my bed, I run both hands down her body.

"You're just a regular house cat, aren't you?" She responds by purring loudly and jumping onto my bed to lay her head in my lap. I continue scratching her, as I'm not sure what else to do, and I certainly don't want to anger what is one of the most terrifying beasts I've ever encountered. We sit like that for several more minutes. With no warning, the cat stands up, stretches, and jumps through the open door. She's disappeared before I can even stand. I chuckle as I shut the door behind her. Cats are all the same, no matter the size.

That night, after my usual inappropriate dreams of Laurel, I dream of an old fae female. She stares at me with haunted yellow eyes, and is saying something to me, but I can't understand her. She has long black hair that reaches past her waist, and sharp nails that resemble claws. I get the sense that she's desperate to tell me something, but I can never hear her or speak back to her. When I wake in the morning, the image of her distraught expression lingers.

"Are you almost ready?" Silene asks as she pops her head into my bedroom. I straighten my tunic, push my hair back from my face, and turn to Silene, whose shit-eating grin gives me pause.

"What?" I ask, cheeks heating for no reason. Absolutely no reason at all.

"Nothing. You're just taking a lot of time with your appearance for a day of hard work cleaning up the merchant district. I wonder why." She delivers the last line in a sing-song voice before she skips away. Rolling my eyes, I follow her out of the room.

"She's right, brother. You've got it bad for Laurel," Fionn remarks with a smirk.

"I do not!" I snap, but that only causes Silene and Fionn to trade a look and burst into laughter. I storm past them and walk out the doors of the apartment. Once I'm in the hallway, I yell back at them. "Let's go! These buildings aren't going to clean up themselves."

We make the trek down into Arberly and to the destroyed merchant district. Now that Abscission is over, Fionn committed all three of us to help with efforts to clean up and repair the destruction from the rebel attack. Not that I mind. Fionn converses with several fae and humans who are in charge of the cleanup. They direct us farther into the district, to a stretch that was completely destroyed and needs to be fully cleared away before rebuilding. We immediately get to work, Fionn hauling giant beams of metal away with his magic while Silene follows behind him to blow away any remaining debris. I stick to physical labor, picking up what I can and carrying it to the giant burn pile that's carefully maintained.

After several hours of back-breaking work, we've cleared our stretch enough for me to wash it down with water. I focus on the aether pulsing strongly around me, and it helps me find the dozens of barrels of water placed throughout the district for this purpose. A tidal wave crashes down over the area, washing away dirt and debris.

"Impressive," a familiar feminine voice says from behind me. Turning, my eyes instantly find Laurel, surprisingly clad in a modest purple gown. Though I can't say I dislike the scandalous dresses she likes to wear when she's playing a scary witch, I like this look on her too.

"I'm glad you've finally realized I'm impressive," I quip back with a wink. She rolls her eyes.

"I'm going to the school today to speak with the students there. I thought you might like to come with me. There are still a few light channelers who would love a few tips from you." Her open expression makes my heart flip.

"Lead the way," I say with a grin before yelling back to Fionn and Silene about where I'm going.

The school mirrors the palace in that it's also built into the side of a cliff, with training platforms carved out along the ridge. Margery, the advisor I recognize as the Minister of Education, greets us at the front doors before leading us to a massive meeting room where hundreds of students have gathered, eager looks on their faces. When Laurel enters, there's a shuffling as students and teachers stand to bow, but she waves them off.

"Please welcome Her Majesty Queen Laurel," Margery says and begins clapping, giving the audience an alternative to bowing. Laurel's cheeks blush. I love seeing this side of her—the shy and reluctant leader who cares deeply for those she serves.

"Thank you," Laurel says to quiet the applause. "I'm also joined today by a special guest, His Highness Prince Hawthorne of Velmara." Awkward applause and murmuring breaks out, the students unsure what to make of my presence. "Prince Hawthorne, would you give the students a demonstration of your light magic?" There's mischief in her eyes. I nod, and the room erupts in blinding light as several awes sound throughout the room. I bring the light into small orbs that whizz around the room, playfully dancing around the students. Then the light rushes forward toward me and collects in a massive long sword that I swing around my body. The applause that breaks out this time is fervent, and Laurel's eyes sparkle with a plan well executed. I give her my own appreciative grin. "Thank you, Prince Hawthorne," she says. "As you can see, the Prince has a very rare and unique power. He'll be taking those of you with light channeling abilities for a private lesson later. But first, what questions do you have for me or Prince Hawthorne?"

Dozens of hands raise, and I can't stop the grin that spreads across my face. The students are eager to learn and clearly adore their Queen. Laurel fields their questions expertly, turning a few over to me. Most are some version of how we learned to use our magic, what our training looks like, or how they can learn to make swords with their magic.

"Is it true that you have an affinity for every conduit?" a very young student asks Laurel, awe in her eyes. Laurel stiffens for the tiniest fraction of a moment, so quick few would catch it. Rather than answering the question, she quickly displays magic using all conduits. Water streams through the air, sliced by a metal dagger she pulled from her waist. Plants crawl through the windows, illuminated by orbs of light. She finishes the demonstration with a gentle breeze of air. The students applaud, eyes wide in fascination and bodies moving with uncontainable energy from their excitement.

It's a smart way to evade the question.

"One last question," a beaming Laurel tells the group, and she calls on a student no older than ten in the front row.

"Now that Prince Hawthorne is here and things are better with Velmara, does that mean the mist will come down?" The student asks the question innocently, clear enthusiasm written across her features. But Laurel visibly tenses, her entire body on alert, and several of the teachers exchange worried glances with one another. Margery steps in, clearly trying to avoid what seems to be a tense and politically charged topic. It's the rebels' most prevalent point of contention with Laurel.

"I think we're actually out of time—" Margery says to smooth over the situation.

"It's okay," Laurel says to stop Margery, voice quiet. Her gaze lands on the student, who now looks fearful at the reaction of the adults in the room. Laurel smiles kindly and walks to kneel in front of the small fae girl. She takes the child's hands in hers, speaking to the room loud enough for all to hear but never breaking eye contact with the girl. "I would love nothing more than to bring the mist down for Thayaria. But we must be careful. Prince Hawthorne is my friend, but I still don't trust the rulers of the other kingdoms. I hope that someday Prince Hawthorne and I will open up Thayaria's borders together."

Something in my chest flips when she says we're friends, but it's quickly replaced by the weight of her next words. *I hope that someday Prince Hawthorne and I will open up Thayaria's borders together.* I sense the trueness of that statement. It's a promise and a prophecy spoken by lips I think about too frequently.

Laurel stands, and the room stays eerily quiet. "Thank you for having me today," she says, and they applaud softly. Margery takes over, directing the students back to their classes and asking the light channelers to stay. Laurel inches closer to me, and my body reacts instantly. I close the space between us, our arms grazing as we survey the room. For a brief moment, our hands even brush. "Thanks for coming today," she says softly, leaning closer to me.

"Of course, I wouldn't have missed helping my *friend*." I give her a wink, and she rolls her eyes, a practiced exchange between the two of us at this point.

"Don't make me regret saying we're friends," she says sternly, and I chuckle.

"I wouldn't dream of it, witchling. I'm happy to be your friend." She stares at me, but I meet her scrutinizing gaze. After what feels like an eternity, she nods, and I release the breath I'd been holding. "Did you attend this school?" I ask, nodding to the room.

"I did, though not for very long," she admits.

"Why is that?"

"Once my parents realized how powerful I was, they pulled me out. They didn't want me to hurt anyone, and they wanted to keep my magic a secret. But I didn't mind. I was lonely here, and I never knew if it was because I was the Princess and the other students were intimidated by me, or whether I was just unlikable. Even though I became even lonelier when I had to spend my days with Admon as my teacher, I was happy not to have to find out the real reason my only friend was Nemesia." The admission seems to shock her, because her eyes widen in surprise and I can see her physically shutting me out like she has many times before, turning her body away and slumping her shoulders. Before this moment can get away from us, I offer my own story, determined not to let this moment of vulnerability slip through my fingers.

"We have that in common, you know. I told you at the ball how lonely it was for me to be the only light channeler. It was also lonely to be more powerful than any of my tutors, more powerful than my parents. I didn't get to go to school, even for a short time. Fionn was my only companion, and it took us years to become friends." I watch her closely for her reaction, and for the briefest moment, she seems to open up. Our eyes meet. Something intangible passes between us, an energy with a low and slowly humming frequency, so unlike the typical charge between us.

"I'll see you back at the merchant district," is all she says before turning and walking away, and I sigh at her dismissal. I spend the next hour with a group of four light channelers, walking them through similar exercises that I've been teaching Laurel for the last few months. Their progress is not as quick as hers, but the teacher, a metal channeler, promises to continue using these same drills with them. He seems relieved to have the guidance.

"Where do these students come from?" I ask the instructor as the students practice conjuring light into small, concentrated orbs and releasing them. "I thought light affinity only existed in Eastern Velmara, with my mother's people. I was shocked to learn of light channelers here in Thayaria."

The instructor nods. "Indeed, these are distant relatives of yours. When the barrier went up after the war, many Velmarans were trapped here, and most were too afraid to declare their heritage and ask to be sent home. Several families were from Eastern Velmara, and these are their offspring." He smiles.

His words give me pause, adding to my complicated feelings about the relationship between Velmara and Thayaria, and the lengths Laurel felt she had to go to in order to keep her kingdom safe from my father. The thought of my family, distant cousins though they may be, stuck here without a way home makes me grieve in a way I don't fully understand. Her words from earlier echo through my thoughts once more, and I vow to make them true.

"Thank you for letting me come today. If you'll have me, I'd love to visit again in a few weeks to see their progress."

"We would all enjoy that."

When I return to the merchant district, Fionn and Laurel are using their magic together to haul metal beams into place for the frame of a new building. They've made amazing progress while I've been at the school. Not only have they cleared the rubble of four more structures, but they've built a new frame and a second is going up.

"Steady, almost there, queenie," Fionn coaches Laurel. Fionn looks like he's straining, but Laurel remains as cool and unaffected as ever—she could likely perform the task on her own. When the beam is in place, Fionn melts the ends of it with his magic, then has it rapidly cool against the connecting beams. It leaves the frame sturdily secured. Several of the fae and humans helping with the rebuild cheer for Fionn, and he grins.

Striding up beside Laurel, I whisper, "I think *someone* is hiding the real depth of her power, witchling." She blushes.

"I don't know what you mean," she returns, eyes bright.

"Mmmhmmm," I growl. "At least Fionn is getting to use his magic."

"Exactly. It's clearly important to him to feel useful, especially here. With the citizens. He deserves their cheers." She's not wrong, and for what must be the hundredth time, I'm taken aback by her thoughtfulness, the way she can read a person so easily. I step into her body but stop myself from wrapping my arm around her waist like I want to out of respect for her request to not pursue anything between us, even *if* she clearly almost broke that rule herself.

We're *friends*, and that is enough for me. I think.

"Watch this," she says, nodding her head to the five fae who have gathered around the new frame of the building. The branches of a massive oak tree nearby stretch toward the structure. Limbs weave themselves between the metal beams, growing quickly in a crisscross pattern. When an entire section is fully covered, the leaves die off, leaving only the wood from the tree wrapped tightly between metal beams. A fae chops the tree each place it connects to the building, and the branches that had stretched out return to the tree. Several humans climb up on the structure and begin sanding down the woven wood until it's smooth. They repeat the process again on the next structure.

"That's incredible," I whisper, and Laurel gives me a wide and genuine smile. "And so efficient."

"Thayarians are powerful plant channelers, and we use that in as many ways as we can," she says, genuine admiration for her people clear in her expression. We stand together while the build team covers the structure in wood and sands it down. Fionn and Silene join us, the same awe on their faces.

"Imagine if we could do this in the Floating Market," Fionn murmurs. "Merchants could replace the worn wood every year to keep the buildings safer and more secure."

"All you need is a few plant channelers and the right materials," Laurel tells him. "You can even bring in a potted tree if there are none nearby. Something that's water resistant."

"If there are light channelers here who got stuck after the war, there are certainly plant channelers in Velmara who are afraid to identify themselves," I say, and Laurel shudders. Silene grips her hand, always aware of the comfort others need, and I regret my words. Of course they make her feel guilt—I should have been more careful.

Fionn coughs, then adds, "We'll have to try it when we get home. Whenever that is." Laurel only nods.

Desperate to change the subject and bring the smile back to her face, I bump her with my hip. "I'm sure Laurel is ready for us to depart any day now."

She opens her mouth to speak, but closes it again, before looking between the three of us. "You know," she says, "I'm actually not. I can't even jest with you. I've enjoyed getting to know all three of you." Her cheeks redden at the admission, and I smirk, though internally my organs feel like they're exploding. Her small admission lights me up with hope and longing.

"We're irresistible, we know," I tease, trying to break the tension for both her and myself. Laurel and Silene both snort, then link arms and sashay away together.

"Those two are trouble," Fionn says in mock seriousness before grinning at me.

"Trouble is an understatement."

And in the final days of the rift, a prince will be born with the ability to see through the darkness. The truths he will discover will tear down that which never should have existed. His light and his blood, when joined with the other's, will open the gate that brings in the light.

The Secrets and Stories of Velmara

After two weeks of constant rebuilding, the merchant district has reopened in small pockets. Yesterday, Fionn, Silene, and I attended the grand reopening of an art studio. Silene has made numerous friends throughout Arberly, to no one's surprise. The human woman who owns the art studio had personally invited Silene to attend, and when we'd arrived, Silene bounced off to mingle with the dozens of people she's met these months. Fionn and I were left to admire the art on our own, and he stayed grumpy and silent while I charmed a group of females with stories about Velmara's Floating Market.

After the event, Laurel stopped by our apartment and left Silene a small vial of thayar concentrate to get us in and out of the village for our meeting with the rebels today. Hopefully that's all we need it for.

"Ready?" I ask Silene, who's less bubbly this time using the thayar than the last time, before we knew what was waiting for us in Oakton. She nods and grabs Fionn's and my hand. Pressure, then we stand in front of the manor. It still looks abandoned—the rebels have done a good job hiding this place.

Our goal today is to convince Krantz that attacks on civilians are too risky for him, and that Laurel and the palace should be his focus. I also want to find out any information I can about the manor that seems to serve as the rebellion headquarters. A human woman, who looks to be in her mid-thirties, approaches us. She has mousy brown hair, blue eyes that look kind despite her participation in the rebellion, and a short but curvy frame. Fionn stiffens beside me.

"Hello," I start to say with a bright smile that shows my dimple, but she cuts me off, as unaffected by my charms as Laurel.

"Follow me," is all she says in a quiet and gentle voice before turning back toward the manor. I look at Silene and Fionn, then shrug. We follow her into the decrepit building and up two flights of stairs. She stops in front of a door. "Krantz told me to bring you here when you arrived. He's away, but you're to wait in his office until he's back. It will probably be half an hour." With that, she opens the door and gestures us into a room painted bright white. It's clearly used frequently, filled with furniture and stacks of papers, and Krantz has tried to make it look less crumbling than the other parts of the manor. As we walk in, she gestures to a couch and two chairs, before leaving and shutting the door behind us. As soon as it's closed, I use my light magic to search for any light coming into the room from unexpected places. When I determine we're not being watched, I jump up to examine the massive oak desk that fills half the room.

"What are you doing?" Silene hisses.

"She said it would be half an hour before he's here. I'm going to snoop through his desk for information," I tell her, lifting a stack of papers from one corner and flipping through them.

"What if this is another test of loyalty?" she whispers. I shrug.

"I'll put everything back exactly as I left it. Plus, I scanned the room. There are no peep holes. And if it's a trap, I'll just own up to it and tell him I wanted to know what he was up to so I can report back to my father. I'm persuasive." I give her a confident wink. Silene sighs but resigns herself to my antics as she usually does. Everything on the desk is just correspondence with other rebels, or ledgers of food supplies, so I move on to the drawers. I find a book with what appears to be the name of every rebel who has joined, and while that could be useful, it would surely be missed, so I put it back. At the bottom of the desk is a locked drawer, and I smile. "Fionn, come unlock this drawer for me." He frowns but does as I ask. Kneeling down on the ground next to me, he closes his eyes and concentrates. I hear a click, and the metal locking mechanism has popped open. "Thanks," I tell him with a cocky grin before sliding open the drawer.

It's more organized than any other drawer, with folders containing documents, each one labeled with the subject of its contents. Mostly letters, though these are more sensitive in nature. There's a missive from a potential secondary leader in Echosa, detailing their recruiting efforts. There are also ledgers of thayar supplies. I hand that to Silene.

"Memorize this," I tell her, knowing she has the best ability amongst the three of us to remember random facts and figures. I keep flipping through the folders, finding nothing else useful. In the last folder, I find a single sheet of parchment. It's a letter from an ally in Velmara, providing information to the rebels about the thayar flower. I take in the words quickly, excitement that I might've found something that could truly help Laurel.

The sons and daughters of our great kingdom deserve a better life, and I am determined to find the information needed to remove any complications in achieving our vision for the realm.

My heart stops when I read the signature at the bottom.

Your friend and ally,

Nemesia

I read the letter a second time, my eyes stopping on the harsh lines that make the signature at the end. This can't be true.

"What is it?" Fionn asks, taking the letter from my hand. "Nemesia... isn't that..." I nod. Silene looks up from where she is still scanning over the thayar supply notes.

"Nemesia, Laurel's friend?" she asks.

"I believe so, based on the contents of the letter. But it could be a forgery. Laurel could probably confirm the handwriting. We need to take it back with us."

"We can't. What if it's found missing? We would be the first suspects." Silene's eyes widen in fear.

"I don't give a fuck," I spit out. "If they confront us, we own up to it and make an excuse, and if they don't believe us, we fight our way out and be done with them. At this point, we've found their leader, we've found their headquarters, and this letter tells us who their informant has been. That's good enough. Laurel needs to know if this is true."

Silene weighs my words. "This might not even be a real letter. Your feelings for Laurel might—"

I cut her off. "I don't have feelings for Laurel." *Liar.* "But even if I *did,* this would still be important to show to her. I'm not negotiating." My voice comes out harsher than I mean for it to, but I don't back down.

Silene only raises her hands in submission. "Fine, take it. But you have to be the one to tell her."

Fuck, this is bad. This will devastate Laurel. She's spoken little of the friend turned advisor, but I can sense the closeness of their bond. I fold the letter up carefully, then tuck it into the inside pocket of my cloak. Silene returns the thayar ledgers, and Fionn locks the drawer again. We sit in silence until Krantz arrives. When he opens the door, he gives us a threatening smile, something about his facial expressions *off* from the last time we saw him, like his skin is stretched tighter across his face.

"How was your Solstice and Abscission?" he asks as he seats himself at his desk.

"It was restful, thank you. Velmaran tradition only celebrates on the day of the Solstice itself, so we were pleasantly surprised to find we had two weeks to do nothing but relax, among *other things*," I explain lazily, insinuating I had many affairs over the course of the holiday period. The mask of the charming and pleasure-seeking prince is firmly in place.

Krantz grins wide. "Excellent, excellent. I've heard rumors you've been seen rebuilding the merchant district. Why is that?" His gaze is cold and calculating, turning quickly from comradery to accusation.

Silene and Fionn stiffen beside me, but I keep my cool. "The Queen asked us directly for our assistance. Surely you can understand we were required to help her to maintain our cover."

Krantz waves me off. "Yes, yes, of course. What do you think of Queen Laurel? Have you grown close to her?"

Even I can't keep my brows from furrowing at this strange question. "I wouldn't say that I've grown close to her, but I am attempting to maintain my position as an ambassador," I say slowly, unsure what kind of answer he's expecting. Krantz's expression darkens for only a moment before he smiles again and changes the subject.

"And what was the palace like after our attack?" His eyes look predatory, and I carefully consider my words.

"It was somber, to be sure. We don't interact with many who live there, but we attended a Solstice dinner with those who were displaced by the attack." He hangs on my every word, manic interest in his eyes. "I must tell you, I fear you harmed your reputation by attacking citizens." I say the words slowly, as if I'm just considering them now.

"And why is that?" His gaze is intense.

"Just the whispers at the palace. Many say you're only interested in causing terror, that you don't actually care about undermining Queen Laurel's rule, since you've yet to attack her directly. I overheard servants just the other day saying you hadn't attacked because you're afraid of her."

"I'm not afraid of that *bitch*," he spits, though there's also a twinge of excitement in his tone. It's strange, and once again I find myself uneasy in his presence. "Of course we want to attack the palace and the Witch Queen directly. But we haven't been able to get enough information about her habits to plan an effective attack. And the palace is hard to infiltrate unless there's a public event."

I pause, pretending to think hard about his conundrum. Then I break out into a massive grin. "Perhaps we can help with that."

He grins back. "Perhaps you can, Your Highness. Our alliance is proving to be more and more fruitful." I want to squirm at the way his eyes alight with malice, but I hold myself steady.

"What information do you need?"

For the next hour, we discuss the various details he wants us to uncover. Nemesia's letter burns my skin where it rests against my chest, but I keep my mask and focus in place. Krantz wants details of Laurel's daily routine, how her advisors who don't live at the palace get in each day, any additional secret passages we might know of—all the typical things someone would want. I lavish him with promises of information and vows to work together to bring down the Witch Queen. Fionn and Silene stay silent, playing their roles as advisors well. We agree to meet here again in two weeks' time to exchange any information we collect. Krantz assures me that he has no current attacks on civilians planned, and I leave feeling as if I've accomplished Laurel's wishes. Even if I know the additional information I uncovered will bring her more than she may be prepared to handle.

When we arrive back at our apartment in the palace, I immediately will light to dance across the ceiling of Laurel's rooms, hoping she'll see the signal quickly. My mind races with how best to relay the information, and where to do it. I pace in our sitting room, running through every possibility.

"I'm going to go find her," I tell Fionn and Silene when she hasn't arrived after twenty minutes of waiting.

"Give it more time," Silene says soothingly. She places her hand on my forearm, quieting my pacing. "She may have meetings or other things going on. You know she wants information on how the meeting went. She'll come." Silene leads me over to a couch, and I sit, pulling the letter out and reading it again and again. I search for clues that it's not what we think but come up empty.

After another hour, Laurel finally appears, looking somewhat disheveled but still glowing with an ethereal beauty I am as drawn to as ever. I stand abruptly and walk to her. "Is everything okay?" I ask.

"Yes, there were just some families who wanted to speak with me from the merchant district. Have you been waiting long?" she asks.

Before I can answer, Silene cuts in. "No, Laurel. Thorne is just on edge today. Don't mind him." Laurel stiffens, eyes searching mine. She's too sharp, too watchful, to keep anything from, even for a moment.

"What happened?" she demands.

I reach for her instinctually but pull back. Lowering my voice, I say, as calmly as I can, "Everything's okay, but we found something you need to see."

"Show me then," she snaps, clearly concerned. I sigh.

"Not here," I say. "We should go to the northern moors. I can handle the cold. I'm already dressed in two pairs of pants from our travel to Oakton." I give her what I hope is a reassuring and self-deprecating grin.

She studies me for another moment, then shakes her head. "No, it's too cold, even for me. Why can you not tell me here? It's secure and private, if that's what you're worried about." I exchange glances with Silene, which clearly agitates Laurel even more. "Just tell me," she orders. Silene steps toward her, placing her hand on Laurel's shoulder.

"I think you should go to the greenhouse with Thorne. Fionn and I will stay here," Silene says softly. Laurel nods. Before I can prepare myself, I'm squeezed with a familiar pressure, and Laurel and I appear in the greenhouse, still set up with poufs from our Winter Solstice morning.

"Tell me what's going on before I force you to," Laurel practically growls, shoulders tense and eyes searching. I pull the letter from my pocket, clutching it tightly.

"When we got to the manor in Oakton, we had some time alone in Krantz's office. I searched his things. We found several items of note, but this..." I hold up the paper. "This was too important to leave there. We knew you would need to see it with your own eyes." I hand her the damning letter, heart aching. She snatches it from my hands, her eyes ablaze with annoyance and worry, then looks down. I watch as her expression slowly shifts from the haughty frustration of an impatient Queen to the sorrowful grief of a betrayed friend. Her eyes move furiously across the page, repeatedly, always stopping at the end for several beats before restarting. With each reread, she slumps in on herself, shoulders dropping and back hunching. "The handwriting..." I say slowly. "We weren't sure..." I trail off, unable to say it aloud.

"It's hers," she says with the practiced coolness I've come to expect.

"Laurel," I say softly, taking a step toward her.

She holds up a hand. "Don't. I need to stay in control right now." I halt mid-stride. Her eyes are predatory, resembling the giant feline she keeps as a pet. "Nemesia warned me of a mole on the Council of Advisors before she left. Someone passing information to the rebels. It's why I haven't told them about working with you to infiltrate the rebels." The confession, though something we'd already guessed thanks to Silene's intelligent observation, still shocks me. Not that she has a mole, but that she's actually revealing it to me. She finally trusts me enough to share. The situation dampens the satisfaction I feel.

"There haven't been any leaks since she left, have there?" I ask her slowly.

"No," she says, voice steely. "But she told me not to trust any of them, not to share any information…" Her voice quakes for just an instant, but then her features harden as she expertly pushes down her emotions. "It was to keep her own involvement secret. If I wasn't sharing anything important, it meant I wouldn't question why more leaks weren't happening."

"It could be a mistake, Krantz could be deceiving us somehow," I say, trying to find any reason her best friend has not betrayed her.

But Laurel only shakes her head. "No, it all adds up. She was the mole all along." Her voice shakes. "She desperately wanted to go to Velmara, and she convinced me it was to find information to help Thayaria, to help me… She insisted she go alone, pretending it was because she didn't want to put anyone else at risk. But it was to hide what she was really doing there. She went to Velmara to aid the rebels, not to aid me." Her voice cracks, and she finally displays emotion, tears welling in her eyes.

"Laurel, please," I say again, pleading with her for what, I don't even know. She suddenly collapses to the ground, and I can no longer keep my resolve to stay away. I cross the room in two strides, then sink to the floor with her. She's clenching and unclenching her fists, clearly trying to fight the emotion building up inside of her.

"We should go somewhere else… my magic…" she whispers.

"Shhh," I soothe. "You won't lose control. You're not going to hurt anyone." I wrap my arms around her, and that's the last thing she needs to let go. She sobs into my chest, gripping my shirt so tightly I think she might rip it off me. Stroking her hair, I kiss the top of her head, shocking myself at the intimacy of the gesture. But once I've done it, I can't stop, placing light and gentle kisses into her hair, across her forehead. She doesn't stop me, doesn't protest. Just continues crying, holding on to me like I'm the last person she has left in the world.

We stay like that for several moments. I slowly stroke her hair, her back, but stay silent, offering comfort but giving her space to process. When she finally stops crying, she immediately stiffens and jumps out of my arms, putting distance between us again. I want to sigh, but I keep it in. Now is not the time to think about the constant dance she does between vulnerability and standoffishness. I feel her absence deeply, and a small part of me cracks apart at her refusal to let me help her. I stand, but keep my distance, unsure how to help.

"I want to spar," she says resolutely. "Will you spar with me in the training room?"

I nod. "Lead the way." In this moment, I'll agree to anything she asks of me. I only wish I knew what was going on inside of her head. She aersteps us to the training room that's now become a sanctuary for me, as it's one of the few places I get to interact with her regularly.

"Weapons *and* light," she grunts as she walks to the weapons rack. I start to protest, but she only repeats herself, aether lacing her voice. "Weapons and light." I select a short sword, while she picks up a dagger. We walk to the middle of the room and both conjure our light weapons of choice. "I want to go full out," she says somberly. "No holding back. Spar with me like you spar with Fionn. I have a weapon. I'll be capable."

I hesitate, not sure it's wise with her current emotional state. But then she murmurs the word *please* with so much vulnerability and raw pleading, and I can't deny her. I nod, and before I've finished the gesture, she leaps toward me, swinging her light sword with a ferocity I haven't seen from her yet. Her dagger whips toward my face, and I have to dodge to keep from being hit in the eye with it.

I smirk. "Bring it on, witchling."

The mythical mating bond between fae is nothing more than a story, a tale woven to satisfy the romantic tendencies of fae and mortals alike. And yet, its staying power throughout history tells us that there is something to be learned from these tales. Love, the kind that is destined and often tragic, excites the mind. But those who fall prey to believing in these myths will find themselves heartbroken, unsatisfied with the life they've been given.

The Legends of the Fae, Volume III

I spar with Thorne, weaving in and out of his reach, the light and metal responding to my every thought. I'm so angry, so devastated, and that makes it easier for me to channel larger amounts of aether. In this moment, I don't care what happens if I lose control, so I press forward with every ounce of magical and physical prowess I possess. Laurel is no longer here, all that remains is the aether that courses through my veins.

Thorne matches me blow for blow. At first, he goes easy on me, but when it's clear I'll slice him in half if he falters, he pivots into full intensity. If either of us slips up, we could seriously injure the other. There's a thrill in it that makes my blood heat and my center thrum with need. I let it wash over me, drowning out the sorrow and soul-deep grief I'm running from.

Thorne grunts as he swings his short sword down toward my head. I block the blow with a shield of light, then throw him off me. This dance we're in sets me on fire and I lose myself in the flow of it. We thrust in and away from one another in a measured rhythm. Sweat drips down my back, but I ignore it. There's only me and Thorne, and the magic that lights the room around us. I'm so honed in on the pulsing beat of the spar that I have no idea how much time passes. It could be hours, minutes, or days. All my focus is on Thorne and staying in this moment with him.

He jabs his short sword toward my stomach. I pivot to dodge it, but he's able to spin himself behind me. A dagger of light presses against my throat, and Thorne tuts in my ear.

"This is exactly what tricked you last time, witchling," he whispers, pulling me closer to him. The vibration of his voice sends shivers down my spine. I feel every inch of him pressed against me, and his labored pants heat the nape of my neck. It's similar to the night of the Solstice dinner, when I decided to give in to the aching need I feel around him before Silene, of all people, interrupted us. I want to press my backside against him and arch my back so my face is closer to his. Just like that night, I'm desperate to let the heat between us play out, consequences be damned. But I won't—can't—let him get under my skin, not right now. So I stomp on his foot, then whirl away, sending another dagger from the weapons rack hurtling toward his too handsome face, but he blocks it with ease. "I know you can do better than that," he taunts me, eyes sparkling with mischief and thrill. If I looked in a mirror, I'm certain my eyes would match his.

"Just giving you a little break, princeling," I taunt with a husky and breathy lilt to my voice that I've never heard before.

He advances on me, so quick I struggle to block each blow as they come hurtling toward me. Light sizzles across his skin, bathing him in an otherworldly glow that sends my blood racing through my veins. He glistens with the lightest sheen of sweat. His cheek bones look like daggers, and his biceps bulge with each movement. I swipe my short sword but can't follow through with the movement because of my screaming muscles. I'm tiring, but his stamina has been honed from centuries of practice with Fionn. I think he's going to swipe with a long sword made of light, so I block that, but he slices across my upper arm with his short sword instead. I can't block the movement in time, and blood drips out of the wound.

"Fuck, that hurt," I say, dropping my weapons and placing my hand across my arm.

I expect a biting retort from him, a tease about the tiny cut, but he's silent. I look up from my bleeding arm and his pupils have dilated. Two inky black orbs with just a sliver of olive green around them stare back at me with an intensity that makes me squirm. His nostrils flare and his face locks in an expression of shock and awe. He drops to the ground on both knees and places one hand over his heart.

"Laurel," he whispers my name like a prayer, like it's the last word he'll ever utter.

"What the fuck? Does my blood smell or something?" He looks up at me, eyes glistening with tears and confusion. I'm totally at a loss. "It's okay, it'll heal. The sting's already gone," I say to console him. I didn't mean to make him so upset with my outburst of pain. My fae healing abilities are already closing the wound together, though blood still drips down my arm.

Thorne just keeps staring at me in what seems like wonder. After a few more beats, he seems to decide on something. Standing, he takes a deep inhale, body shivering, then picks his short sword back up. His eyes return to normal, but he still looks off.

"I drew blood, witchling. It's only fair you do the same," he teases with an attempt at a roguish grin that doesn't meet his eyes.

"I don't understand."

"It's okay. You will. Just spar with me again. Draw blood. *Please*." He whispers the last word, almost a plea.

"Thorne, tell me what the fuck is going on. Is this some weird chivalry thing? I don't need to draw your blood to get back at you. It's already healing. No big deal." He only conjures small balls of light that whip toward me. I block them with my light shield, growing annoyed. They keep coming, an onslaught of tiny little pricks that don't hurt but aren't painless either. I quickly move from annoyed to angry. "What are you doing?" I ask, real ire in my voice now.

"I'm sparring with you until you draw my blood," he growls, low and primal, then lunges at me.

I react instinctively, blocking his blows and becoming lost in the fight once more. We spin around one another, resuming the careful dance we know so well. He conjures lightning bolts to spear down from the ceiling at me, but I dodge them easily by tapping into the aether. I'm able to sense where they'll strike. Swords and light clash, and the room becomes a cacophony of flashing lights and singing metal once more. There's something feral about him; he stalks me like a predator. But there's also unmasked lust in his eyes, a fury of attraction that he doesn't try to hide. His jaw clenches and unclenches, and every so often I notice his nostrils flare as he takes deep inhales.

"Is that all you've got, witchling?" he taunts. "I thought you wanted to go all out. I could do this all day and not even break a sweat." I bare my teeth and growl at him in a primal fury, the noise surprising me. But he only laughs. "There she is." His eyes light with glee. "Let go and *fight me*." He growls the last two words, matching my intensity. It only heightens the feral beast inside of me clawing to be let out.

I focus on the leyline running almost directly under this training room, pulling the energy of the aether into me. I lift every weapon off the rack and send them flying toward Thorne along with small discs of light. They hurl end over end in his direction, and his eyes widen in shock and surprise, but not fear. Never fear, not with him. Even as there are dozens of weapons spinning his way, his mouth quirks in a half smile. Inches before the weapons reach him, all but one tiny dagger halts in midair. It slices across his arm in the exact place he wounded me, drawing blood but not cutting too deeply. Thorne laughs, loud and boisterous, his expression filled with something I don't understand. I'm about to demand he tell me what's going on, why he insisted I draw blood only to laugh at me, when his scent hits me.

Citrus, Jasmine, and Lemongrass—the same thing I've smelled every time he's gotten close to me, every time our bodies have pressed together. But now it's unmistakably threaded with something else, something new. I can't place it, but I know it means Thorne is *mine*. I want to bite him, possess him. *Claim* him.

I press my hand over my nose and shudder, looking across the training room at him. He's on his knees again, one hand placed over his heart and the other reaching out to me.

"Laurel," he whispers again, and now tears flow freely down his cheeks. But he's not in pain or upset. I think these are tears of *joy*.

"What—I don't—I don't understand," I finally manage to choke out.

"But you do," he soothes. "Look inside yourself. Find the source of your magic and listen to the aether that courses through your blood. It will tell you what you already know." He keeps staring at me with a soft expression, one that I've *never* seen on him, even in his most vulnerable moments.

Trembling, I close my eyes and take a deep breath, following his instructions. Thorne's scent invades my senses, as it grounds and centers me. I first focus on the aether pulsing through the leylines around me. I use that to guide me to the aether in the room. I can sense Thorne's presence as a being made of aether, can feel exactly where in the room he is. *That's new.* I take that awareness and apply it to myself. I feel the aether mingling with my blood, with my muscles and tendons. I follow it down into the center of myself, where it converges around my heart. There's a tight ball of aether humming inside of me. It's a chaotic and swirling mess, but I let my awareness focus fully on it...

Realization slams into me, knocking me to my knees. Tears stream down my face now, and I can't stop them, but I keep my eyes shut tight. I *feel* Thorne slowly move to close the distance between us, then take my hand. He strokes my palm gently with his fingers, waiting for me.

"When you're ready, open your eyes," he says with so much gentleness it nearly sends me spiraling again. I breathe him in one more time before I open my eyes and stare into those deep green pools that have become so familiar to me these past few months. Eyes that, impossibly, no longer haunt my dreams.

"How?" is all I can say, and he laughs, beaming at me.

He shakes his head, his expression one of awe. "I don't know, witchling. I just know what my heart, what my soul and my magic, tell me. What I should have realized the moment we met. Somehow, impossibly—"

"We're *mates*." I finish for him, shivering when I utter the word, unsure whether in elation or dread. He wipes a tear from my cheek, then cups my face in his palm. "But—but mates... mates aren't real," I whisper, tears continuing to stream down my face. "They're fables, silly stories we tell children." Thorne doesn't falter, just continues staring at me with that look of pure adoration that makes me uncomfortable.

"All fables come from somewhere. Think about it, Laurel. You're the most powerful fae in a millennium, maybe ever. I'm the most powerful light channeler to exist, as far as anyone knows. There are prophecies about you, maybe even some about me. If any two fae were going to somehow turn myth into reality, it's us."

I open my mouth, then close it. I have nothing to say. Shock and fear run through me in equal measure. I can't process this, not right now. Not when I just found out about Nemesia. My breathing comes in fast pants. *Not now, not here.*

I stand and pace away from Thorne. *From my mate.* I try to take deep breaths, but they won't come. My chest is heaving, and I bring my head to my knees to try and gain some control. Thorne doesn't hesitate. He's up and by my side in an instant, rubbing soothing circles across my back that I both crave and abhor at the same time.

"Talk to me. What's going through that mind of yours?" His voice is still steady, calm, like all I have to do to make this all okay is open up and tell him what I'm feeling.

I stand and face him, my breathing still ragged. At least this explains the unbearable attraction I've felt for him, why I've been compelled to open up to him again and again. It explains the constant game of catch and release we've played with one another, neither of us able to truly stay away from the other. But the information is too much for me right now with everything else I'm carrying. And nothing about our situation changes with this discovery. He's still Mazus's son, Crown Prince of Velmara, the Shining Prince. And I'm still the Witch Queen, a figure reviled by his people and feared across the Four Kingdoms for good reason. Despite what Nemesia has done, I cannot forget that she believed Mazus *wanted* Thorne and I to meet. And Thorne, he's—he's betrothed to another.

Any hope I had before this moment collapses into a pile of ash. Yet another fucked up way the universe has decided to play with me and the prophecy about me. I meet my mate, the person who's supposed to fulfill the prophecy alongside me, and he's not only my enemy but engaged to someone else. Engaged to the one person who has helped to fill the void Nemesia's departure left. Engaged to someone I consider a friend, who I've been too cowardly to ask directly about her feelings for Thorne and the crown. Not because I'm worried she'll say she's in love with him, but because I'm worried she'll say she's *not*.

I don't want this, not if I have to sort through these emotions and complications to have it. Even if I *did* want this, even if there was a *thread* of excitement about the idea of being tied to Thorne in this way, I'm not ready to open myself up to this level of intimacy, not ready to admit that I've developed feelings for Mazus's son. I still don't even know the true reason Mazus sent him here. For all I know, Mazus sent him because he *knew* we were mates and wanted us to discover it for some fucked up reason.

I need to scream, need to erupt. I turn my eyes on Thorne, who still looks like he's the happiest male who's ever existed. I steel myself for what I have to do.

"You're betrothed to Silene," I tell him with the iciness I've perfected over centuries of being the Witch Queen. It's not the only reason I'm running, but it's the only one I can say aloud. "And you're the son of my enemy. I won't destroy Silene's chance to become Queen of Velmara, and I won't make myself vulnerable to Mazus in this way."

Thorne's eyes widen in shock. He tries to protest, but before he can get anything out, I aerstep away. I don't want to hear his excuses, don't want to hear him say he'll break things off with Silene. *Or, even worse, hear him say he won't.* I leave and don't look back, because my control is slipping, and I have to get away from it all.

When I arrive in the cave, I barely make it two steps before I'm screaming in fury. My wrath repeats back to me in hollow echoes. I scream again, trying to release the pent-up frustration of the last few hours, the last few months, my entire life. There's so much buried inside of me, so much hurt and longing and need, that I feel like I'm going to explode. I scream and scream into the void, desperately seeking relief. When that doesn't help, I collapse in anguish, all the emotions and fears I'd been pushing down for so long leaking out of me. My pulse races, my breathing quickens. I try to maintain control of the aether coursing through my blood, but it demands to be released. With a roar, I unleash myself.

Energy erupts in arcs from my body, shaking the cave. Rocks crash down around me, but a shield of light I instinctively wrap around myself protects me from the falling debris. Moss expands and covers an entire wall, then the ceiling. Water droplets gather into massive orbs before falling to the ground with splashes that soak everything around me. A wind whips through the cavern, churning up dust and rocks that orbit my light shield. I think I glimpse lightning forking across the tall ceiling but am so absorbed by my pain and grief that I can't say for sure. Like so many times before, my magic feels heavy, like if I make the wrong move, it will completely consume me. I walk the precipice of madness, one heartbeat away from letting *Laurel* disappear. I'm not sure who would take her place behind my eyes.

I exist in that liminal state. Time doesn't pass. There will be no beginning or end to my desperation. Tears stream out of my eyes before collapsing on the ground in a puddle.

Eventually, I burn myself out. The magic falters, then stops altogether. I lie down on my side, curl in on myself, and stare out at the darkness that surrounds me, wishing that I could just disappear.

The origin of the myth of fae mates is unknown. Most scholars agree it is unlikely there is one singular origin story that inspires this longstanding legend. Like most fables, it is an amalgamation of several tales that over time converged into one story. The nuances of each tale are, unfortunately, lost to history.

The Legends of the Fae, Volume III

She left. She left, and I don't know how to find her. *My mate left. My Mate. Mate.*

I pace across the training room, barely coherent. I need to see her, need to touch her. *Claim her.* Snippets of our conversation weave in and out of my consciousness. I replay her face right before she disappeared. Grief, fear, rage. It's so at odds with how I felt in that same moment that I'm lost. I don't understand what's happened, how this could've gone so wrong.

Fury and fear and joy bring a deep uneasiness to my gut. My blood races. Her scent lingers in the room, and I can't get enough of it. I take a deep inhale, breathing in her smell of lilac and mint. It calms me, allows me to focus. I need to find her. I have to convince her that there is *nothing* between Silene and me, even though I've already assured her of that. I have to somehow find a way to get her to overlook who my father is. *I. Have. To.*

With one last inhale, I leave the training room to seek her out. I make the miserable and endless trek up the stairs to her room, pounding on the door, but she doesn't answer. I consider breaking down the door, but some inexplicable sense tells me she isn't there, so I walk back down to the greenhouse. She isn't there either. I have no choice but to return to the apartment and enlist the help of Silene and Fionn. As I walk through the door, my mind races over how to explain to them I *know* Laurel is my mate, when such a thing isn't supposed to be real.

They're seated at the dining table, playing a game of Skran. Silene looks up at me, then does a double take. "Went that bad?"

My mouth goes dry. *Where do I even begin?* "You could say that," I start slowly. "There's something I have to tell you, and I need you to believe me. *Please* believe me." The words are a plea, full of emotion I don't know how to express. Silene's brow furrows, and Fionn raises an eyebrow. They set down their cards, waiting for me to continue. "Laurel—she wanted to spar after I told her about Nemesia. I guess she just needed to get the frustration out, or lock it away, I'm not sure."

"Makes sense," Fionn murmurs, and Silene gives him a look that tells him not to interrupt again.

"We were going all out. She was ferocious and—and *brilliant*, making all the right moves. So, I pushed harder. But then she tired, and I accidentally sliced her arm. And when she bled..." I take a deep breath. "When she bled, and the scent hit me, I had this *knowing* wash over me. Laurel is, we're—Laurel is my mate," I finally finish in a furious rush of words. They both stare at me, confused. "I swear it's the truth. We both felt it, both *knew* what it meant," I explain, a silent plea in my shaking voice.

"Okay..." Silene says slowly. "And Laurel felt this too?" Her expression is one of studious caution, while Fionn just looks worried.

"Yes. I pushed her to draw my blood too." I let out a chuff remembering how easy it had been to work Laurel up to fight me. That same satisfaction I've felt from the very beginning every time I can get under her skin washes over me briefly before I shut it away and focus on finding her. "And as soon as she scented my blood, she knew." Fionn now looks suspicious, while Silene's expression has shifted to unreadable.

"And where is she now?" Silene asks.

"I don't know!" I growl. "She aerstepped away. She thinks we're really engaged, even though I've told her we don't want it." Silene's jaw drops open, but she lets me continue. "She said she couldn't take away your chance to be *Queen*, as if you're interested in that at all. And she said—" I deflate thinking about those final words she uttered. As much as I want this, as much as it makes complete sense and like everything in my life has finally *clicked*, she's right. I'm still her enemy's son, and this would give him one more thing over her. "She said she doesn't want to let my father have this connection to her. Another way to make her vulnerable. Then she left." I'm shaking now, with need or fear or anger, I'm not sure.

"She'll come back. Just give her time," Silene says quietly, rubbing my forearm in support. I yank it away from her.

"No!" I roar. "You don't understand, I *need* to find her. I know this sounds unbelievable, but I can tell that she's not okay. I think—I think she's in danger. She needs me." The last sentence is a whimper.

Silene and Fionn share a look, and Fionn tags in. "Thorne, brother, if she left, she probably needs some space. Probably needs to process whatever's going on between you two."

I growl again and stalk away. "If you won't help me, then I'll figure something out myself." I grab a cloak, resolved to walk outside in the freezing temperatures until I find her.

"Wait," Silene calls. "Of course we'll help. Just, take a minute. Let's go over what we know. We need a plan." I reluctantly stalk back to the table and sit down, putting my head in my hands.

"You're not yourself, Thorne," Fionn says suspiciously. "Are you sure..." he hesitates, like even he doesn't want to say his next words. "Are you sure this isn't some *magic* by Laurel?" He whispers, like he's afraid of the very idea.

Ire builds in me, and I erupt. "How dare you! After all we've seen from Laurel, you still believe her capable of witchcraft?" Light curls in my palms, and I'm about to launch myself at Fionn when there's a faint scratching noise coming from my room. We all turn toward the sound.

Realization washes over me as I remember my previous visitor, and I run into my room and open the door for the black feline, who rushes into the sitting room. Silene shrieks and Fionn hisses. I wave them back, then look at the creature. Her eyes convey fear, and she's agitated. She paces back and forth, and if I wasn't sure that Laurel is in trouble before, I am now.

"How do I help her?" I ask the beast, searching her golden eyes. She stalks toward Silene, then stands at her side, looking back and forth between us. "I don't understand," I tell the feline.

"I do!" Silene yells excitedly. "She means me. I can aerstep you to her. We just need to sneak into Laurel's room and snatch more elixir."

"But I don't know where she is!" I huff out in a frustrated grunt, desperation threatening to take over. Silene's brows furrow for a moment in thought.

"You said you can feel that something is wrong. That she's in danger. Can you feel where she is? Would you be able to point to it on a map?" She's so clever, and I want to wrap her in a bear hug.

I close my eyes, then seek out the bright light that is the core of my power. I can feel the way it's changed since the mating bond. Where once it was static, an immovable and steady orb of light, it now pulses like a beating heart. It expands and shrinks, moving erratically. I hone every bit of myself onto that vibrating orb.

First, I feel Laurel's pain. Her grief. It nearly knocks me to my knees, and I ache in ways I can't explain knowing that she's feeling such deep emotion and I'm not there to share her burden. But then I feel the creeping cold that surrounds her, threatening to wink out her aether-force. *Where are you?* There's a tugging on that bright orb, like a thread pulling me to her.

"Get me a map!" I bellow. Silene and Fionn scramble, opening up our hidden compartment in Silene's dresser to pull out the map of Thayaria Laurel lent us. Fionn spreads it out along the dining table, keeping his distance from the cat who still lurks along the edges of the room. I close my eyes again, and Laurel's energy is easier to find this time. It guides me to an area due north of Arberly. There's a vastness around Laurel, and when I spot caves identified on the map, I immediately know she's in them. "There."

"You're sure?" Silene asks.

"As sure as I can be," I tell her and shrug.

"Works for me," she chirps back. "Now we just need to get into Laurel's rooms."

We bundle ourselves up for the foray outside, then sneak out of our apartment and start the endless trek up to Laurel's room. *I can't believe I've done this twice today.* Laurel's cat stalks alongside us, hurrying us along every time we slow. When we finally reach the top, I bend the surrounding light to hide us. As we approach Laurel's door, I stiffen. Carex stands there, knocking.

"Laurel, please let me in. I want to apologize for the Solstice dinner," he says to the empty room beyond. The cat pads up behind him and he jumps when he notices her. She growls, low in her throat. Not loudly, but enough to warn him away. "What are you doing out here, Lunaria?" he asks, trying to pet her head, but she pulls away, hissing. A pang of jealousy zings through me at his knowledge of the cat's name. It represents history with Laurel, an openness between them I long for. Before I know what I'm doing, I let out my own growl.

Carex's eyes widen and immediately search the hallway. He draws a sword, and ivy vines curl toward us. "I know you're there, *Prince*," he spits. The vines inch closer, about to reveal our hiding place.

"We're here to meet with Her Majesty," I tell him casually after I release the magic cloaking us. It takes every ounce of court training I possess to keep the intensity and deep-seated need out of my voice. "She requested we come to her rooms."

"Is that so?" he asks, his expression pulled into one of hate. "If that's the case, then why hide yourself with your magic? Last I checked, you're free to roam this palace, and if Her Majesty summoned you, there should be even less need to remain unseen."

He's going to make this difficult, and I don't have time for that. "Force of habit." I try to say the words casually, but they come out imposing and sneering.

"I don't believe you. What's more, Laurel isn't even here. Why would she summon you to her rooms if she wasn't going to be there? Why summon you to her rooms at all?" He advances toward us, sword raised and ivy creeping with him.

"Maybe she's just ignoring *you*," I respond with a haughty air while picking lint off my tunic. I want to spear him through with lightning, like I told Laurel to do if he ever touched her without her permission again, but I hold it together, just barely.

"I don't think so," he snarls. "Return to your rooms. I'll inform Her Majesty of this when she returns."

"And what if we don't?" I hiss, unable to stop myself from rising to his challenge.

"I think you know what will happen." He sends a vine shooting toward me, but I block it easily with a shield of light.

"There are three of us here, Carex, and only one of you," I growl menacingly. "We aren't here to do anything nefarious. Laurel trusts us, and she can fill you in later. *Step. Aside.* I don't want to hurt you." I actually *do* want to hurt him, but only the smallest sense of how Laurel might react to that stays my hand.

"It's Her Majesty to you," he snaps. Carex bares his teeth, then lunges toward me with his sword. Before I can react, Fionn has ripped the blade from his hands. It throws Carex off balance, and he stumbles. Fury flashes in Carex's eyes, and he responds by wrapping ivy around Fionn's legs. The vines trip the warrior, and Fionn crashes to the ground. Carex plucks his sword back from Fionn.

"Oh, you shouldn't have done that," I tell Carex with a vicious smirk.

"Why, because you're going to blind me with your light?" he asks in a mocking tone, as if my magic is nothing more than a glare that might make you want to cover your eyes. I'm losing my control, and I want to show him exactly what my power can do. Before I can respond or act, Fionn regains his footing and launches himself at Carex. Carex is better in hand-to-hand combat than I would have guessed, but after a few minutes of trading blows, Fionn has him in a headlock.

"No," Fionn says to Carex in a bored voice. "Because I don't like being swept off my feet." Normally I would laugh at the unexpected joke from Fionn, but I'm too focused on Laurel to appreciate it. Carex spits at me, and I punch him in the stomach.

"Knock him out," I instruct Fionn. Carex's eyes widen.

Silene yells, "No" at the same time that Fionn says, "Gladly." Fionn takes the end of Carex's sword and knocks him in the head with it. The male slumps, and Silene sighs.

"That's going to be a problem," she says. I shrug.

"We'll deal with it later. Let's bring him into Laurel's room so no one sees him."

Fionn hauls Carex over his shoulder, then stalks to the door. The metal lock clicks open and Fionn prowls in, barely breaking his stride. As I walk into her room, I realize for the first time that she doesn't have guards. Has never had guards here. It should have occurred to me before.

The room is empty, but I'm overwhelmed by her scent—it nearly knocks me to my knees. Even though I've been here before, the realized mating bond heightens every sense. I see evidence of her life spread corner to corner—empty mugs, half eaten pastries, discarded clothing, discarded correspondence. Dust and crumbs and litter. The space is so *lived in,* and woven throughout every inch of the room is that intoxicating smell. I let myself drown in it, my body tingling as I take in deep inhales.

Silene's movements near the bar cart bring me out of my haze. She quickly retrieves the bottle of concentrated thayar, pours herself a measure of the liquid, then downs it. She unrolls the map and focuses on the spot I identified, looking at me for confirmation that she has it right. I nod.

"Ready?" she asks. Fionn and I take her hands for the third time that day, and we aerstep away.

The cavern is much larger than it looked on the map. I illuminate the space by pulling light in from the opening several paces behind us and amplifying it. I don't see Laurel, but I can feel my pulsing magical center practically jump out of my chest when I look to the north.

"You should go back," I tell Silene and Fionn. "Thank you for getting me here."

They exchange a look. "No, we won't leave you," Silene says resolutely. "She might not be here. You'll be stuck in this frigid cave with no way back."

"She's here, I know it. Please. I need to do this alone," I implore. "If I'm not back in two hours, come for me. I'll make sure I'm in this same spot." They both look uneasy.

"Thorne," Fionn protests, but I interrupt.

"Please," I whisper. I look them both in the eyes, pleading with unspoken words.

"Okay," Silene whispers, tears gathering in her eyes at the intensity of the last half hour.

"Take this dagger," Fionn says as he hands me the blade. "It will make it easier for me to track you if you aren't here." I nod.

"We're coming back in exactly two hours," Silene promises. I take her hands in mine and squeeze. She wipes her eyes, then takes Fionn's hand. They disappear, and the cavern is eerily silent. Turning north, I let the tugging in my chest lead me toward my mate.

The bond directs me down a passageway that narrows quickly. I bring light with me in dancing ribbons to illuminate my way. I take several turns, always following the tugging in my chest. Aether gathers thickly here, and I wonder if this is some kind of nexus for the leylines. Strange markings line the walls, indiscernible shapes that slowly morph into clearer carvings. Massive beasts soar through the air. Creatures that resemble Lunaria look up at them from the ground, while figures with pointed ears hold swords as if ready to battle. If I wasn't in such a frantic rush, I would have stopped to examine them more closely. They don't resemble any ancient markings I've ever seen.

The thumping in my chest grows stronger as both my heart and the magical bond dance at the nearness of Laurel. The passageway opens up to another massive cavern with clear signs of her magic. Moss covers every inch of the walls and ceilings, and massive puddles of water pool every few feet. I scan the space, eyes searching desperately for her. At the farthest end from me, massive rocks form a circle, like they fell from the ceiling but were blocked by a shield. I run toward the rocks, and when I'm halfway across the space, I see her laying in the middle of them, body curled in on itself. I'm sprinting now, jumping over fallen debris and trying not to slip on the wet moss.

"Laurel," I scream. She doesn't respond. Panting, I increase my speed. When I reach her, I instantly notice how pale her complexion is, like all the color has leached out of her. Shaking her, I whisper her name like a prayer. "Laurel. Laurel, please wake up. Please, Laurel. Please." Tears run down my face as it becomes clear she's not responding. I cradle her in my arms, wishing I hadn't sent Silene and Fionn away. It will be two hours before I can get her to help. "What's wrong with you?" I ask, voice cracking, knowing she won't answer. I close my eyes, seeking answers in the jittering ball of light in my chest that our mating bond has ignited. My eyes open in stunned shock when I sense that she's quickly draining of aether.

Desperate to save her, I lay her down on the cold floor. Coaxing the aether whirling around us into a blazing mass, I will it to become a healing light. I'm drawing up more aether than I ever have, and a quiet voice in the back of my mind whispers I shouldn't be able to control this much magic, have never controlled this much magic, even here in

Thayaria. But I ignore that voice and keep growing the orb of light at my fingertips. When I've channeled as much aether as my body can stand to hold, I slowly—so slowly—lower it over Laurel's body, shaking with the strain of controlling it. I watch in awe as it spreads to cover her entire body. The light—my light—caresses her, lapping at her curves and face gently. When she's fully wrapped in my light, I concentrate on the aether.

Fill her, I command.

For a moment, nothing happens. But then, with a brilliant flash, color returns to her cheeks and she takes in a gasp. I stumble, my magic draining out of me in a way I've never experienced before. But I don't care, because she's awake, and I scoop her up into my arms, squeezing her middle in elation even as I sway with burnout.

The gods were angry with the fae. They decreed that, in punishment for their magical crimes, mates would be trapped on opposite sides of the world. Those fated for a mate bond would feel its absence their entire lives, not understanding the persistent ache they feel deep in the core of their magic.

The Legends of the Fae, Volume II

"Laurel," I sob, holding her to me as tightly as I can. Her body molds to mine, head nestled perfectly under my chin. She relaxes into me, and I stroke her back in a gentle caress, whispering her name like it's the lifeline that will tether her to this realm.

"What—how are you here?" she asks, almost dreamily.

"It's a long story, and we have some things we'll have to deal with when we're back. But we can worry about that later." I'm so relieved that I found her, that I *saved* her, that I nearly collapse over her body. I pull her closer, my lips grazing across her forehead gently. It's the wrong move. She jerks away from me, and I nearly weep.

"Thorne," she croaks.

I interrupt. "Laurel, please listen to me." I grab her hand, trying to anchor her here and prevent her from leaving again.

"I can't," she says, tears gathering in her eyes. But she doesn't release my hand. I grab her other hand, a silent promise that I won't let her go this time. Staring into her captivating green eyes, I squeeze her soft skin.

"Silene and I have spent every minute of our engagement the last year trying to get out of it," I rush out before she can get away. "If you believe nothing else I tell you, believe that. What I told you before was the *truth*. And I can assure you that Silene has no interest in being Queen. But you don't have to take my word. Speak with Silene. She will tell you the same." She tries to protest again, but I rush onward, determined to get this out before she can object again. "My father—aethers, Laurel, I know. I *know*. My father is the vilest male to ever live. I hate him with the same intensity that you do. You think that us being mates makes you vulnerable to him, and it might, but it also makes you stronger. We're *mates*. We're the two most powerful fae alive, and together, we have *so much* more magic than him. Don't you think there has to be a reason for a bond like this to emerge in the world after all this time?"

Her eyes glimmer with the tiniest spark of hope. It's the same window I've seen open so many times before it slams shut again, but now it's cracked, and that gives me the confidence to continue. My body shakes, knowing I need to tell her how I feel. It scares me, being this open and vulnerable. But if anyone in all the Four Kingdoms deserves this, it's her.

"I find you to be the most alluring female I've ever encountered. My mind doesn't wander to you, because you're *always* in it. I feel it when you walk in the room, sense you when you aren't near. The mating bond is hard to believe, but so is the fact that I didn't guess what we were to one another right away. You're in my dreams every night, and every morning I fight to stay asleep to keep you with me for just another moment. For the longest time, I tried to deny what I felt for you. Tried to convince myself that I wasn't seeking you out at every opportunity. My whole *being* orbits around you, and it has since the moment I met you. Please believe me, witchling." As always, her expression is unreadable. I pull her hands to my chest, stroking gently over her thumbs. "Say something, please. Let me into that unreachable mind." The words are a plea.

"But—you and Silene. I've seen her come out of your bedroom," she finally says.

I furrow my brow in confusion. "My bedroom?"

She nods. "The primary bedroom in the apartment. The large one. With gold everywhere."

I burst out laughing, then reach up to wipe a tear from her face. I brush back her hair, then hold her face in my hands. "Laurel, witchling, all this time, did you think she and I were sleeping together, even though I told you there was nothing there?" Another nod, her eyes wide. "I let Silene *choose* her bedroom when we arrived. Fionn too. Silene being

Silene, she picked the biggest one, which is well and good because I loathe the color gold. I ended up in the green one. It—it reminds me of you." Her eyes search my face for any sign of deceit. I hold her gaze, letting the vulnerable truth show in my eyes.

"You flirt with Aria. Aethers, I've seen you flirt with *Carex*. You flirt with practically *everyone*," she says, another challenge, her voice a whip. My stomach sinks. She's right. It's the only way I know how to keep up appearances, to make people underestimate me. It's how I've stayed *alive* being more powerful than my father.

Shame and guilt lacing my words, I respond. "I know. But I don't—it means *nothing* to me, Laurel. It's a fucked-up habit I learned to make my father think I'm not a threat. Or, it started that way. Now—I don't know. But it's always been different with you." She again searches me, her lingering gaze flaying me open.

"Your father—" She chokes the final word, and the same force that's driven me since the day we met takes over. I pull her back to my chest and rub her back.

"You have no idea how much I *wish* you didn't have to be mated to The Golden King's son. I wish we were just Laurel and Thorne, two ordinary fae who found each other and get to live out their happily ever after. I would trade all my magic for you to have that dream, because it's what you *deserve*. I don't know what it means, and I don't know what my father will do with the information, but we'll figure it out together. We're *friends*, like you said. Allies. *Mates*."

"You don't want to be mated to me," she whispers, voice shaking. And here I think is the real truth of why she ran from me. She believes she's what my father has painted her to be. "I'm the *Witch Queen*. Terrifyingly powerful. A monster. And don't say I'm not. You don't know what I've done, what I'm capable of." She shudders, trying to pull away. I let go of her middle so I can look at her face but place my hands on her hips to keep her close, tracing circles across the soft flesh.

"There's no part of you that scares me," I whisper, the words an oath now and for the future. "I think—I think we're mated because we're both terrifyingly powerful, as you put it. We're made for each other." I bring her closer to me, our knees touching.

She closes her eyes and breathes deeply. When they open, her pupils have dilated, inky black orbs staring back at me. She brings her face closer to mine, breathing quickly with flared nostrils. She's all primal fae now, and I don't dare move. She gently brushes a single finger across my cheeks, my lips. I stay still, afraid I'll spook her if I shift even an inch. Her hand lands on my chest.

"This is confusing," she whispers, and I bark out a laugh.

"Immensely confusing. But I'd like to figure it out together."

She nods. Body trembling, she stands, taking my hand in hers. "Follow me."

"To the ends of the world," I murmur. She blushes, and I squeeze her hand tightly. I follow her through another passage, this one leading east. We descend deeply, though I keep a soft glow of light around us. The air grows thick with humidity, and the temperature warms. We emerge in a smaller cavern than before, with lower ceilings and moss growing thickly. She leads me along the edge of the space, hand firmly in mine. When we stop, she turns to me with her lips pulled into a mischievous smile, then looks out to the middle of the cavern. When I illuminate the space, I see deep pools of water, steam rising from them in curling tendrils.

"The hot water in the palace comes from deep in these caves. There are several hot springs buried in this mountain. This one doesn't feed into the palace pipes. It's a well-kept secret for the royal family of Thayaria," she explains. Without warning, she pulls her tunic over her head, and my mind shuts off entirely. Her full breasts are wrapped in a thin, lacy, bandeau, nipples peeking through the fabric. Milky white skin curves down from her breasts, her soft stomach breathing gently in and out. My gaze tracks to where her leggings meet her skin on her waist, then down the swell of her thighs and hips. A growl tears out of my chest, and it makes Laurel's eyes heat. "Easy, princeling. That mating bond's got you feral," she teases. Eyes locked on mine, she pulls down her leggings, exposing her thick thighs and rounded ass, more of that tantalizing lace covering her. But I don't mind, completely satisfied with the view I'm getting. My mouth goes dry, and her verdant green eyes sparkle with mirth. *She knows what she's doing.* When she pulls her long auburn hair out of its braid, my knees go weak.

Laurel turns, giving me a full view of her backside, before gingerly stepping into the water. She walks down the stairs carved into the rock, and all I can do is stare as her hips sway. When she's fully submerged, she turns her head to look over her shoulder at me. "Aren't you coming?" Then she dives, disappearing into the steamy black water.

I undress quicker than I ever have, ripping my tunic and trousers off my body, only leaving my tight undergarments on. I splash into the water, and she swims away from me.

"You do remember that I'm from a kingdom known for its oceans and beaches, right?" I ask, swimming after her quickly. Just when I think I've caught her, she aersteps across the pool, giggling. I growl. "And that I'm also a water channeler?" She squeals as I bring her to me on a quick current. She crashes into me, and I wrap my arms around her waist, letting the water carry us to the shallow edge of the pool. I press her up against the wall, my body humming with the feel of her. Skin to skin, there's nothing but a small length of fabric between us. I bring my lips to her ear. "You can't run from me, witchling." My voice is seductive and demanding.

When she shivers, I tighten my grip on her, and she lets out an exhale that's part sigh and part moan, the ends of her long hair floating around her, and her body glowing from the soft light hovering above us. I bring my lips close to hers, an inch away, then cup her ass. She wraps her legs around me, and my twitching cock fully hardens. She smirks, but I bury my face into her neck, breathing in her seductive scent.

"Laurel," I sigh. She's a goddess, and I will willingly worship her. My hands knead her ass in soothing circular motions. Her head drops back, and she arches her pelvis into me. I groan low in my throat. I want her *so badly*. But I know I have to go slow, have to let her be in control, or she'll run again.

Her head lifts and her eyes meet mine, and there's a new kind of heat in them I've never seen. "Kiss me," she demands, breathy and pleading, squeezing her hips closer to mine. That's all the encouragement I need.

I crash my lips onto hers, demanding and punishing. She returns in equal force, tongue sweeping my mouth and hands scratching down my back. I grind my hips into hers, the friction laying kindling to my passion. Her hot center brushes against me through her lacy underwear, and I close my eyes in concentration to keep from taking her right here, right now. She moans, and it ignites me. With another crushing kiss, I bite her lip, and it makes her growl low in her throat, though she doesn't break the kiss. The noise sparks the embers of my magical core until it's a blazing flame.

We're both desperate now, hands moving furiously over one another, exploring. I angle her so that I can deepen the kiss, and she moans again. Sucking her tongue as I pull back from her lips, I lick up the column of her throat, making her shiver. One hand finds her breast, and I cup it in my hand through the bandeau, ready to rip the flimsy piece of fabric off her body. My exhale comes out like a feverish sigh as I squeeze her breasts like I have in my dreams every night since I met her in that revealing black dress.

"Thorne," she moans my name, and it undoes me. I sweep one hand under her knees, the other behind her shoulders, and carefully cradle her close to my body. I walk her up the steps and out of the water before setting her down on the ground. I'm going to take her, right here, on the hard rock floor of the cavern. She sits there, body dripping water off her curvy figure, and stares at me with pure lust in her eyes. Male satisfaction courses through me, and I can't wait to make her moan my name again, can't wait to have her *undone* in my arms. That need to break her icy exterior takes on a whole new meaning when she's sitting there practically naked. I want her screaming in pleasure, letting go of her control because of the way *I* make her feel. I kiss her again, this time slow and sensual, but when I pull back, her expression is guarded once more, uncertainty written clearly across her features.

"Thorne, I—we don't know—we don't know anything about the mating bond. What might happen if we..." she trails off.

"What might happen if I fuck you?" I finish for her. She swallows, then nods, uncertainty in her gaze. "Are you saying you want to wait?" I ask.

"I am," she says, resolutely.

Laurel

It is a widely held belief that the fae species first lived in Thayaria before migrating to other parts the world. Buried deep underneath the mountains of Thayaria are endless unexplored cave systems, and prior to the isolation of Thayaria, scholars were eager to explore the thousands of runes and drawings etched into those caves.

A Brief History of Modern Thayaria

"We don't know how any of this works," I slowly explain to Thorne. It takes more willpower than I want to admit not to straddle him where he sits, water glistening off his toned and naked body. I've imagined him shirtless and naked so many times, and yet, nothing compares to the real thing. I shake away the lust addling my brain and continue. "Until a few hours ago, I thought mates were a myth." He nods thoughtfully. The second I said I wanted to wait, he honored my request and pulled away, keeping his hands and eyes away from my naked body.

"Of course," he says resolutely. "We'll take it slow, figure this out one step at a time. Whatever you need." He looks at me with so much understanding, like he can see through all of my blustering and excuses and knows that it's fear that keeps me from going further with him. I almost cave right then and there and give in to the months-long need that's been burning in me, but the news of Nemesia's betrayal still rattles in my mind. There's just too much information for me to process right now, especially with my emotions in the fragile state they're in, and I'm grateful that Thorne seems to understand that without me having to say it. We have to take this slowly and carefully, with research and consideration of the facts.

He gives me a cocky grin, breaking me out of my thoughts. "I still can't believe that you thought I was *sleeping* with Silene. After telling you there was nothing between us and shamelessly flirting with you! I can't decide if I'm offended you think of me as the kind of male who would do that, or elated you think highly enough of my ability to seduce two females." I blush, embarrassment washing through me for believing the worst of him. I too can see through Thorne's blustering, and I can tell this hurts him more than he wants to admit. If I'm honest with myself, though, I'm not sure I ever *truly* believed it. I used it as an excuse to avoid confronting my complicated emotions about Thorne, and I want—*need*—him to know that.

"Thorne, I—forgive me. It was an easy excuse I used to keep you at a distance. I had a million opportunities to ask Silene, and I didn't take them." I lower my head in shame, but he forces me to look at him. He breaks my somber mood with a cocky grin.

"I know, witchling. You were so overwhelmed by your attraction and feelings for me that you had to pretend I wasn't available to prove to yourself you could still be the big, bad, scary Witch Queen." He says the words light-hearted, like they're a joke, but we both know he's struck right at the heart of the issue.

Suddenly, I remember something he said before, my lips pulling into a wide grin. "Wait... if you're sleeping in the green room, and Silene has the primary bedroom—that means, Fionn..." I burst out laughing.

Thorne looks confused. "What?"

"Fionn's bedroom," I say between pants. "It's the one we prepared for Silene based on what we were told by the Velmaran palace she would like. They sent us specifications for all of your rooms, actually. The room Fionn chose is completely pink, like, everywhere. The bedspread is floral, but the walls and all the furniture are *pink*." I cackle in laughter at the image of the massive male sleeping in that pink room.

Thorne grins from ear to ear, and he laughs next to me, the sound a beacon to my frayed heart. "I'm so glad you told me that, witchling. I'm going to tease him so relentlessly."

"How have you not noticed? Have you never been in there?"

"He's not exactly the most forthcoming person in the world. It took him decades to tell me about his parents. And he always keeps the door closed. Now I know why." We laugh together for another few beats, the sound bolstering me to face everything I've learned today.

"So..." Thorne says, eyes boring into mine, the same color as the dark green moss that covers the walls of the cavern.

"So," I say back, feeling slightly awkward and suddenly becoming *very* aware of the fact that I'm practically naked sitting next to him.

"What do we do now?" His lips quirk in a half smile, a genuine and open expression on his face. It's the version of Thorne that makes my chest tug.

"Well, I think we should go back to the palace and speak with Admon. If anyone's going to have information about mates, it's him. Now that I know…" I trail off, not wanting to say the words aloud. I swallow, and his eyes steadily gaze into mine, patient and waiting for me to continue. "Now that I know Nemesia is the mole on my Council, we can trust Admon with this information," I finish softly.

Thorne's expression shutters with compassion and understanding but not pity. Thank the aether it's not pity. "I'm so sorry, Laurel." He takes my hand and squeezes. "Why didn't you tell us you had a mole on your Council?" There's no judgment in the question, just simple curiosity.

Guilt rears its head in my chest, but I stand my ground, knowing I made the only logical decision available to me. "I'm the Queen of Thayaria, and you were—are—the son of my enemy. Of course I didn't tell you. I didn't know why Mazus sent you, and I didn't want you or anyone else finding out about a breach in my inner circle."

His eyes flash with hurt for just an instant before he locks it away. "You're right, I get it. But is that—is that still all you see me as?" The question is haunted, pleading and grieving all at once, and now I feel guilt for an entirely different reason.

"No," the word rushes out of me. "I don't really know how—what I feel—right now. There's a lot that I'm trying to process, and I don't do that easily. But you're more than Mazus's son to me. Much more. And you have been for a while." He smiles, the gesture soft and vulnerable, and I allow myself to give in to the urge to lean closer to him.

"Silene figured out you had a mole immediately, anyway. We knew." He smirks with not an ounce of shame. I'm not surprised, but I pretend to be and swipe an arm at him playfully. He catches my wrist, turning my palm face up and stroking gentle caresses over it. "So we go speak with Admon, hope he can give us some information. I can live with that as our plan." He flashes me a dazzling smile, one that makes my chest tighten. "I guess we need to get our clothes back on, though I would be perfectly happy if you stayed in just that." He winks, and I blush while rolling my eyes.

"Let's get dressed." I will the water to evaporate off both of our bodies, and Thorne stares at me in awe.

"Your magic never ceases to amaze me." I say nothing, just pull my tunic over my head, then re-braid my hair.

When we're both fully dressed, Thorne says, almost shyly, "We may need to make a few stops before we discuss things with Admon." I raise an eyebrow. "Well, first, we have to tell Silene and Fionn that we're back, otherwise they'll be barging back here to pick me up. Silene aerstepped me here." I realize I hadn't asked how he'd gotten here, simply accepted his presence as if he belonged at my side. "And for Silene to aerstep me here, we had to break into your rooms to get thayar elixir for her. Which would have been completely fine, except Carex was there, and he found us out and tried to fight us. Well, he tried to fight Fionn, actually, and you can probably guess how that went..." Thorne trails off, finishing his rambling. He's flustered, and I like it, but I pretend to be exasperated.

"What happened?" I ask with a groan.

"We just knocked him out." When my eyes widen, Thorne continues. "He's just unconscious. He's fine. Probably. But we should check on him, especially since we left him in the room with your terrifying cat, and she didn't seem to like him very much."

"Lunaria has never liked Carex," I say, remembering the way she would hiss at him every time he was near me. We had to meet at his townhouse in the city to avoid her for any sleepovers.

"She has good taste, then," Thorne says smugly and with the barest hint of jealously that I can finally admit gives me a feeling of satisfaction.

"Are you ready for this?" I ask him softly. My eyes convey the real questions I'm not capable of speaking aloud. *Are you ready to have to explain to people why we think we have a connection only told in myths? Are you ready for everything this might entail?* Thorne takes the hand he's been delicately cradling, then turns it so he can weave his fingers through mine.

"I'm ready." His voice is full of unspoken meaning, confidence in whatever the future may bring. I wish I had his same surety. I only nod. Then I take a deep inhale, filling my nose with his calming scent, and aerstep us into the Velmaran apartment.

Fionn and Silene jump when we arrive. Shoulders hunched, hands clasping and unclasping, their body language gives away their nerves. Silene crosses the room quickly, wrapping me into a tight hug as she sobs into me.

She doesn't let go as she says, "I'm so glad you're okay. We were so worried. About both of you. Thorne said you were in danger." When she releases me, her eyes are red, and her face is splotchy. She wipes away her tears, sniffling. "He also said you thought he and I might be really engaged. That *I* might want to marry him so I could become Queen or because I *liked* him that way." She shudders. "That would be the most disgusting thing I've ever done, for so many reasons."

I take her hands in mine. "Are you sure? Even if you don't actually want the love part of a marriage. You would be Queen of Velmara someday."

She laughs, bright and merry. "I have literally *zero* interest in ruling over that den of vipers back in Velmara. I hate it there. I hate the nobles. I hate my family. I'm even dreading going back to the heat after the coziness of the cold here. I don't want to be Queen, and I will marry Thorne over my dead body."

Thorne nudges my shoulder playfully, murmuring, "Told you so." I stick my tongue out at him, and he wraps an arm around my waist, tucking me into his side.

Silene squeals. "You two are so adorable. *Mates!* I can't believe it! What was it like, the realization?" She looks dreamy eyed, and I chuckle.

"To be honest, it was extremely confusing and weird," I admit. Thorne laughs deeply, and it makes me nestle in closer to him.

"That's just because of the way it happened," Silene coos. "You two have been obsessed with each other since the moment you met. We could both see, couldn't we, Fionn?" He grunts in agreement with her.

"Fionn, Laurel gave me some very *interesting* information while we were in the caverns discussing the sleeping arrangements in this apartment," Thorne says, a mischievous glint in his eyes. Fionn stiffens. "Could we take a peek in your room, brother?" Thorne asks.

"I'd rather you didn't," Fionn responds coolly. Thorne rushes toward the bedroom door, but Fionn is faster. Fionn blocks Thorne, wrapping him in a headlock. Giggling, I blow a gust of air at the door, and it swings wide open. Fionn looks at me in betrayal, but I shrug.

"Sorry, he's my mate. I think I have to pick his side in these situations? Though I'm not exactly sure." Silene giggles and Thorne beams at me before walking into the very pink room. Silene follows, and she and Thorne erupt in laughter.

"It's the closest bedroom to the outside door. What it looks like is irrelevant," Fionn grumbles. Thorne and Silene only laugh harder.

Taking pity on him, I say, "I can have servants come in and redecorate." He shrugs, like he doesn't care either way. Remembering Carex, I sigh. "Should we go take care of the Carex situation?" Fionn looks sheepish.

"Sorry, queenie," Fionn says with a smirk. "In my defense, he attacked first. And Thorne was in pretty bad shape. We needed to get him to you as quickly as possible." Thorne blushes, and I find that I like the look of him squirming.

"I wasn't *in pretty bad shape.* I was just a little worried," Thorne grumbles.

"A little?" Silene teases. "You almost attacked Fionn, and you growled at us no less than three times."

Thorne pulls at the collar of his tunic. "It was a very confusing situation. Emotions were running high."

"They were," I say, an apology in my gaze. He meets my stare, accepting the offering and understanding my silent words. *I'm sorry for leaving.*

"I'm going to hurl if you two keep staring at each other like that," Fionn murmurs. "Go take care of Carex." We both smile. As I take his hand in mine, I'm struck with a deep urge to never let go.

It's remarkable how little we understand about the aether and the rivers of magical current that circle our world. Despite millennia of research, its mysteries still baffle our best scholars.

The Unabridged History of Magical Orders, Volume I

Carex is still unconscious, slumped against a chair, when we arrive in my rooms. Lunaria sits across the room from him, eyes homed in a predatory gaze and body tensed as if she's ready to pounce. But when she sees Thorne, she stretches lazily, then rubs against his legs until he scratches her head. My mouth drops open in shock.

"What?" he says, noticing my dumbfounded look. "She likes me. She even visited me once before. And then tonight she showed up and helped us figure out how to find you." Something light and airy fills my chest.

"Lunaria has never tolerated anyone other than me," I explain. "The only other person she's allowed close to her is Nemesia, and they still kept out of each other's way most of the time."

"I'm your *mate*," he says with a low, sensual growl, and the word sends flutters to my stomach. "Maybe she senses that somehow."

I only nod, determined not to give in to the desire burning through me when my ex-lover is lying unconscious at my feet. Taking a bottle of strong liquor from the bar, I unstopper it and hold it under his nose. He jumps back into consciousness, eyes confused and searching.

"What... Laurel—you're okay, thank the aether," Carex pants, clearly confused but trying to pull his thoughts together quickly. "The Velmaran Prince—he was here, and I think he was trying to break into your rooms. He was up to something. He and his so-called *advisors*... we fought... and then—where am I?"

"I *was* trying to break into her rooms," Thorne replies from across the room with more haughty arrogance than I've ever heard come from his lips. Carex stiffens, then looks from me to Thorne.

"It's okay, Carex," I say. "I was in some trouble, and Thorne was only trying to help me. He did, and all is well now." Carex looks like he doesn't believe me, lips pursed in a half-sneer. He stands, swaying with what is probably a concussion. He and Thorne stare each other down with looks of mutual loathing.

"Thankfully your *meddling* did not prevent me from saving Her Majesty," Thorne spits at Carex with a formal and princely air.

"I'm sorry you were injured," I say to appease Carex as I turn him toward the door. "Please, go see a healer right away. And I'll speak with the Velmarans about their *tactics* for aiding me. While their intentions were in the right place, their actions were questionable." Carex hesitates at the door, not wanting to leave me alone with Thorne. "All is well, Carex. Please, go," I say gently. He looks like he wants to say something more, but with a growl from Thorne he turns and leaves, closing the door behind him.

The instant Carex is gone, Thorne's at my side again. He presses me against the door, one arm up and body crowding mine like the night of the Solstice dinner. This time, I feel no conflicting emotions, able to fully appreciate the feel of his hard, strong body pressed against mine.

Thorne leans down and whispers in my ear. "Are you really going to *speak* with me about my tactics, witchling? I can think of much more exciting things for you to do with your mouth." My blood heats, imagining some of those very things.

I lean into him, eyes ablaze. "As long as you are sufficiently *punished*, the method means little to me." The words surprise me. *Who is this person flirting with Thorne, because it can't be me. I'm not this witty.* His eyes widen, and unbridled lust rips across his expression. He snares me between his arms and crushes my body with his.

"I have been very *bad*. Very bad indeed. I'm afraid I'll need *hours* of punishment." My skin is on fire, my breath coming quickly. I lick my lips, and Thorne's eyes trace the movement with predatory intent. I can't keep a shudder of satisfaction from washing over me. An arm wraps around my waist, and he spins me quickly so that he's behind me. His hands caress my hips slowly and with the awe of a male starved for touch. One hand leaves my hip and slowly wraps up in my hair, pulling my head back with a gentle tug. It's exhilarating. "Do you know how my cock *ached* every time this ass pressed against me in training?" he murmurs, grinding into my backside and increasing the pressure of his tug on my hair. I can feel the way it affects him, hard length pressing into me, and my thighs clench with need. "I would wait for just the right moment to get the upper hand on you, every day looking forward to pressing my body up against yours." I let out a whimper, and his other hand leaves my hip to cradle my breast. He circles my nipple with his fingers, while his other hand continues to tug my head back into him, forcing me to arch my back toward him in pure need.

"Laurel," he growls in my ear, and my toes curl. Every nerve in my body is alight, anticipation making me hot and flushed. Now I'm the one grinding against him, and I can practically feel the smugness enter his body. He presses once more into my ass with that hard length. "When you decide you're ready to accept this, to lay claim to me, I'm going to take you from behind so hard you won't remember your name." Lightning sparks in my core, but he releases me. "But not until you're sure." With that, he walks away, casually trailing his hand over the back of the leather sofa. Chills race along my body in his absence, and my need demands that I push him down on the chair closest to us and ride him until we both forget who and what we are. But my rationale wins out, and I take a few steadying breaths. "Ready to go speak with Admon?" he asks, eyes shimmering with playfulness and the satisfaction of winning whatever game we're playing.

"I—er—I need to change." It's an excuse to get a moment to collect myself alone in my closet, to pull myself together and attempt to get a handle on this bone deep need. He merely sits down in a chair and picks up a book I left on the side table next to it.

"Take your time." He waves at me, casual and effortless, like we've had a hundred interactions just like this one. For once, I appreciate his ability to command every room he's in instead of feeling jealous of it. And there's a tiny voice in the back of my mind that whispers to me what a powerhouse the two of us could be together. I push it down, determined to find out more information about the mating bond before I make any rash decisions.

In my closet, I take a few more deep, steadying breaths, then dress in a fresh pair of tight leather leggings with tall, leather, heeled boots. My black tunic is sleeveless and deeply cut. I shake my hair out of its braid, leaving it loose and wavy around my shoulders. I dab my lips with red lipstick. *Two can play at this game.*

When I return to the sitting room, Thorne looks me up and down, gaze heating. "Ready?" I say, challenge in my eyes. He continues staring as a cocky grin spreads from ear to ear, like he knows exactly what I'm doing and loves every minute of it.

"Lead the way, witchling."

"Explain to me the moment you say you knew you were mates," Admon gently says in his comfortable rooms next to the palace library. We barreled into his room during his dinner, claiming we were mates and asking him for whatever information he might have. The old fae had graciously let us in and offered dinner or drinks, the very picture of nobility. When we declined refreshments, he slowly seated himself across from us and started asking questions, a genuine sense of curiosity lining his queries.

"I realized first, after I drew her blood. As soon as I scented it, this bottomless awareness washed over me, like she was the answer to a question I'd been asking all my life," Thorne says, wonder back in his gaze as he looks over at me. How can he feel so calm and in awe when he talks about it? I'm baffled. My instincts—the voices that sound so similar to my parents—are screaming at me to run from this bond, to not let Thorne in.

"Was it the same for you, Laurel?" Admon asks, breaking me out of my spiraling. Admon's eyes twinkle with knowing.

"No," I say slowly. "Thorne had to guide me there."

"There?" Admon asks. "Is it a place?" His curious observation remains focused on me, parental in his attention.

"In a way, it is. I have this source of magic, buried deep within me, that I only really realized existed today, though I think I might have sensed it before. Especially since Thorne arrived. And when I focus on that source, I feel a swirling around it, like something's trying to get in. That source whispered to me what we were." Thorne looks at me with his brows furrowed. Admon notices.

"Is it a different experience for you?" Admon asks Thorne.

"The whispering is the same," Thorne begins. "That's how it started, right when I scented her blood. And I feel a source of magic too, something that I never realized I had. Now that it's changed, I can remember feeling it my whole life. But the form of the source has changed for me. It used to be almost like a rock of light. Static and unmoving. Now, it's constantly churning, and I feel a cord connecting me to Laurel."

Admon frowns, lost in thought. "You do not feel such a cord?" he asks me. I shake my head.

"The cord, or thread, or whatever it is. It's what helped me find Laurel after she left," Thorne adds. "I focused on it, and it helped me find Laurel. The whispering intensified as I got closer to her, telling me she was in danger."

Admon looks sharply at Thorne, concern for me written clearly across his features. "She was in danger? How so?"

"I don't understand it," Thorne says slowly, brow furrowed in concentration and eyes wandering, like he's remembering the moments in the cave. "When I reached her, it was like all the aether was being sucked out of her. I somehow knew if I didn't do something, I was..." Thorne chokes. "I was going to lose her." His eyes drop to his lap, expression shuttering with grief. I stare at Thorne and the raw emotion on his face. I don't understand how he could have such deep *feelings* so quickly.

"And how did you save her?" Admon asks.

"I pulled as much aether together as I could into the surrounding light—more aether than I've ever controlled—and had it cover her body with healing power," Thorne says matter-of-factly, as if that's a totally normal thing to do. "Then I willed the aether to disperse into her, willed it to fill her back up." Now it's my turn to stare at Thorne with awe and confusion.

"How long did it take her to recover after you pushed the healing aether into her?" Admon asks, still showing signs of concern that make me nervous.

"Not very long. Just a few seconds." Thorne squeezes my hand as if to assure himself I'm still there.

"Then we're very lucky indeed that your magic worked so quickly. I've never heard of such a thing. This was incredibly dangerous, Laurel," he chastises, and I lower my head in shame. "You know better than to isolate yourself when you're feeling out of control with your magic." His words are stern, the voice he used when I was young and he was my teacher. I pick at my nails, too embarrassed to meet his eyes. He's right—one of the first lessons we ever had was the importance of finding someone to help me if I felt like I was losing control. "I'm glad you're okay," Admon adds, voice tender.

A strange feeling crawls along my skin, like my magic is trying to tell me something. The whispers that come from the source of my magic start up, but they're incoherent. Admon abruptly stands, then walks out of the room. I look at Thorne, who just shrugs at me. We wait in silence for a few minutes before Admon returns, carrying a massive book. He thunks it down on his dining table. As he cracks the pages open, dust shoots in all directions.

"This is an ancient text we have on the fables of the fae," Admon informs us. "It details all the myths of our kind, and I remember there is an entire section on fae mates. There may be some truth to these tales. At the very least, it's all we have."

I stand behind him, looking down at the characters written across the page. "What language is this?"

"It's a character-based language the earliest of fae used. Some might describe them as runes," he explains.

"I saw runes like this scratched into the cave wall," Thorne adds.

"I would expect so," Admon says with a knowing smile. "The fae have been in Thayaria for a very long time, as far as we know. And the earliest of them used those caves."

"Can you read it?" I ask Admon.

"I can, though my ability is only rudimentary. Nemesia would be more competent." I stiffen, thinking of my *former* sister and advisor. Now that the initial shock of her betrayal has worn off, all that remains is icy rage.

"Nemesia is no longer welcome in Thayaria," I order sharply.

Admon's eyes widen in shock. "Why not?"

"Thorne discovered correspondence between her and the leader of the Sons and Daughters. She was revealing information to him about her research findings in Velmara. She's betrayed us." My voice is steady and cool, the practiced ruler making an appearance, but inside I'm in turmoil. Thorne finds my hand and squeezes it before releasing it again.

"If that's true, then I'm sad to hear it. Nemesia is my friend," Admon says, though the words don't quite reach his eyes. *Maybe he doesn't believe it.* "Well, we'll have to proceed with my basic understanding. It may take me some time to find the right passages and translate them." I deflate. I hadn't realized how much hope I'd placed in Admon knowing the answers, in him being able to tell me what to do. He seems to sense my distress. "I will translate as quickly as I can, Laurel." I only nod, not trusting myself to speak.

"We'll leave you to it, then," Thorne says confidently, like he senses my distress and wants to get me out of there as quickly as possible. He takes my hand and leads me out of the room. Admon bows, but I barely register it. We walk hand in hand back to my rooms.

When we're safely tucked away into my sitting room, Thorne hesitates, then says, "Laurel, I think we should talk about what's next."

"What do you mean, what's next?"

"We're mates. We want to jump each other's bones, but you want to wait to do that, which I completely respect. I understand why you need more information—you're not completely impulsive, like me." He nudges me with a half-smile. "But I'd like to get to know you better while we wait." Vulnerability, hope, and longing shine in his eyes, no trace of the confident Shining Prince in sight.

I swallow, palms sweating. "And how do you propose we do that?" My voice is tentative, uncertain.

He smiles, the mischievous look that makes my skin prickle back in his eyes. "We do what any two people do when they're exploring a romantic relationship. We talk, we go out on the town, we have meals together. We just already know we have a soul-deep connection."

His sureness about the mating bond scares me, so I tease him. "Are you asking if you can court me?" My smirk is plastered on my face, a shield against my feelings.

But Thorne responds seriously, eyes locked on mine in a look I can't pull away from. "Yes, Laurel, that's exactly what I'm asking."

"Okay," is all I can say, breathless, and he grins.

"Tomorrow night, then."

"Wait, what? Tomorrow night? What are we going to do?" I ask, incredulous.

"For once in your centuries-long life, Laurel, you're going to have to let someone else make the plan. Be ready just before the dinner hour." Then he takes my hand in his and lifts it to his lips slowly, pressing the gentlest of kisses into my palm. He gives me a wink before walking out the door.

Mates are said to be a blessing from the gods. Very few fae get to experience the sacred joining of their aether-heart *with another's. Blood is, naturally, the conduit of realization for two fae, though many mates have reported feeling a deep connection to one another prior to scenting the blood of their mate. It is tradition to draw the blood of your mate, a symbolic gesture that shows no other will draw their blood again, because they are now under your protection.*

The Traditions of the Fae

Instead of working in the crowded and noisy archives, Genevieve lets me use her office to study every day. It reminds me of my small reading nook in the Thayarian archives and is hidden away from the prying eyes of the other librarians. That fact also seems to be a reason Genevieve likes it so much as well—she's an outcast, even amongst them. But it never appears to affect her. She's always happy, always grateful for the life she was forced into for no reason other than her own mother's death delivering her and the whims of the males who control her fate. When I work here, she brings me tea and snacks throughout the day on her breaks, and we talk until she realizes she's late and dashes away again. During one such break, we're drinking steaming cups of tea when she asks me about the books Mazus gave me.

"Have you found anything interesting in the books from King Mazus? The one you're translating, or any of the others?"

I consider my words carefully. I like Genevieve. We've formed a fast friendship, and I want to trust her, especially after all the small cracks I've seen when she talks about Mazus. But I've also seen how brainwashed the Velmaran citizens are when it comes to the Golden King.

"Many interesting tidbits, though nothing that's sparked my own particular interest. One of the stories about the fae says that we're the descendants of a powerful group of goddesses."

Genevieve laughs brightly. "What a fun story," she giggles out, and the way it makes her cheeks flush and her eyes brighten overwhelms me with a need to touch her. I lean into her warm amber gaze and place my hand over hers on the table. Her eyes cut to mine, a question in them. Before I can say anything, she stands and straightens her gown, though I swear her fingers linger on mine for a moment before she fully pulls away. "I need to get back to covering my section. There's a Reshnar scholar here. The King himself granted the request, so I should check in on him." She turns her back to me.

"Wait!" I say, and she turns, eyes sparkling. "Would you like to join me for dinner this evening? I'd be happy to let you look through His Majesty's books after." I don't know what's come over me, but I don't want her to go—I want her to stay here with me. The prospect of beautiful company after so much solitude both excites me and makes me cringe at my lack of restraint. I find her stunning, something about her quiet yet exuberant demeanor intoxicating. And the questioning look in her eyes when our hands touched... Could she—I don't let myself finish the thought.

She blushes, and it lights me up with excitement for what might be. "That would be wonderful." Her eyes are bright with what I swear is longing, and there's a small spark between us. Despite my earlier decision not to pursue anything romantic with her for her own safety, something about that look in her expression makes me waver in my resolve.

"It's decided then. I'll find you when I'm done here for the day, and we can retire to my room for dinner." I emphasize the last word, suggesting dinner is the furthest thing from my mind. She blushes again before walking down the spiral staircase, and my chest flutters.

What would Laurel say, seeing me flirting with Velmarans? Practically inviting one to sleep with me?

Shaking my head to clear the thoughts of Genevieve from it, I open the massive Old Fae book and the dictionary I've been using to translate. My vocabulary has improved quickly, the knowledge refreshing from the depths of my memory. I started translating the section on fae mates two days ago, and I return to that section now.

Reading a passage about how mates discover one another, through blood, I catch the word used in the book's title, though here it makes little sense to be translated as *legend*. I wrack my brain, searching its depths for alternative translations. I flip through the dictionary for the character in question, then scan through the various translations to the common tongue. Legend, myth, fable, story, and tradition are all listed as viable translations. *Tradition.* The word stands out to me, making the most sense in the context of the passage. *Does that mean the title of the book is The* Traditions *of the Fae?* That puts the volume in a whole new light.

Does that mean fae mates could be real? Or were real, at some point?

I keep reading, unsure how to feel about this new information and constantly asking myself why Mazus would give me these books, as I have every day since I received them. The passage continues, explaining that when the mating bond is accepted by both partners, their magic *changes*, though the text doesn't explain exactly how or what this looks like. According to the book, many famous fae mates of the past decided not to accept the bond, worried about the change to their magic. Even the simple fact that the book casually references infamous mated pairs is revolutionary, solidifying my suspicion that mates are more than myth.

My mind wanders to Laurel and the prophecy about her. Realization hits me like a punch in the gut. I practically run down the spiral staircase, through the archives and to the section on Thayaria, looking for an Old Fae version of the prophecy. Finding it in an older book I scanned several days ago and deemed useless, I take it and hurry back to Genevieve's office. Panting from the sprint, I compare the Old Fae word that has for centuries been translated as *lover* to the word used for mate in this text, my mind whirring with possibility. My suspicions are correct—the words are the same.

The last line of the prophecy should read *Blood to blood, the Queen and her fated* mate *will unite what has been torn apart.*

Why would Mazus give me this book? Is this even the section he wanted me to read? Does he *want* me to give Laurel this information? I consider writing a letter to Laurel that makes it appear I haven't found anything useful, just to throw Mazus off my trail when he inevitably intercepts it. But that could also be what he wants. There's no good option for how to proceed, and I slam my fists onto the table in frustration. I know that I'm playing a game with Mazus, but only he knows the rules and which pieces are on the board.

Mind ruminating, I pass the rest of the day tediously translating the text, taking copious notes that fill dozens of rolls of parchment. When the light becomes too dark to see, I consider lighting a lamp but then remember the dinner with Genevieve. Despite my eagerness to keep translating, desperate for every morsel of information on mates, I won't stand her up. I pack up my things, taking extra care with all four books Mazus provided, then stalk down the staircase and through the endless rows that make up the archives until I find Genevieve shelving books from a cart. She notices me and smiles tentatively across the hall at me, though there's something in her expression that seems off.

When I reach her, I notice her eyes are puffy and her cheeks are flushed, as if she's been crying. I'm about to ask her what happened when she quickly speaks, like she knows I've noticed and doesn't want me to ask.

"I have to finish shelving these before I can leave for the day, or the Head Librarian will never let me hear the end of it." Her voice is lifeless, so unlike her usual tone. Something is definitely wrong, though she clearly isn't ready to talk about it.

"Then let me help you," I say softly, giving her the emotional space she so desperately wants. I take a book from her hands and intentionally brush my fingers over hers in the movement. She shivers, and I smile internally.

"You don't have to—" she starts, but I cut her off.

"It's no problem. I know these archives well by now." Scanning the title of the book in my hands, I find its place on the top shelf before filing it away. We make quick work of the cart, finishing in about a quarter of an hour. As we walk back to my room, she steals glances my way, and I make excuses to bring my body close to hers or brush my hands over her fingers. The dinner tray sits outside my room, and Genevieve frowns.

"The servants should have brought that in for you. Anyone could walk by and poison your food," she huffs, concern in her voice. I laugh as I pick up the tray and lead her inside.

"I told the servants to leave my food there. I like my privacy, and I don't want to create more work for unpaid labor. No one is interested in poisoning me."

Her brows furrow. "But... they are *servants*. Of course they should be unpaid. Their payment is paying off debts or giving back to the community for their crimes," she says slowly, not understanding my own distaste for the practice.

I shrug. "In Thayaria, we pay our servants, and we pay them well. It's considered an honor to serve in the palace, but it's also a lucrative career, and the wages they earn can support an entire family. If the servants here were paid, they could pay off their debts just as easily with real coin and potentially have some left over to make a life for themselves," I lament to her. She seems to consider my words, so I leave her to ponder. Setting the tray on the small dining table, I uncover the dishes while Genevieve looks around my room with more confusion.

"Your chambers are so small! Surely someone made a mistake by giving you a single room. I would expect the Thayarian ambassador to have a whole suite."

Again, I only shrug. "I don't mind," I tell her, though she seems unconvinced. "Plus, a larger room would surely come with nobles and courtiers trying to position themselves close to me to somehow sweep the rooms out from under me. I spend most of my day in the archives, anyway. All I need is a bed and a place to eat." I gesture for Genevieve to sit across from me at the small table tucked into a corner, and she does. She delicately lays a napkin across her lap, then serves herself a small portion of food. I frown, realizing she has the manners of a noble. I should have realized sooner that she was from a noble family. "How was your day?" I ask, hoping to probe more about what had her so upset now that we're away from the library. She launches into a story about the Reshnar scholar.

"He's awful and acts so entitled because the King invited him here. I spent the entire day running across the archives to fetch books for him because he was too lazy to get up himself and retrieve them. And then at the end of the day, he had the audacity to try—to put—" She trails off, and I study her blushing face closely. Unease builds in my gut, along with hot, churning anger.

"What happened?"

"Well, you know how males can be," she says, the flippancy in her voice not matching the horror and grief in her eyes.

"Did he touch you, Genevieve?" I ask, my voice low and filled with fury.

Her eyes dart to the floor. "It's nothing I'm not used to. It shouldn't have bothered me." I reach my hand across the table and grab hers, stroking soothing circles with my thumb.

"That's bullshit. You are not an object for males to do with what they please. What happened?"

She wipes her eyes quickly. "He grabbed me from behind while I was shelving and pulled me tightly against him. His breath was so hot on my neck, and I felt—he ground against my backside." She's bright red now, cheeks aflame with embarrassment and shame. My blood boils. Living at Laurel's side the last three hundred years has isolated me from the realities of the world. I'd forgotten what it meant to be a vulnerable female in situations where males have more power. I lift Genevieve's chin to lock her eyes on mine.

"I am so incredibly sorry that happened to you, Genevieve. It isn't okay, and you have every right to be affected by it. How much longer is he here?"

"Just one more day," she admits, eyes filling with tears.

"Would you like me to sit downstairs in your section tomorrow?"

"You don't have to, really, it's okay. I shouldn't have bothered you with this. Like I said, this happens a lot. It's not the first time..."

I squeeze her hand tightly. "Genevieve, I would not offer something I'm not willing to give. I'm furious that this has happened so frequently to you that you think it's normal. If you want me there, I'll sit at the same aethers-damned table as him with my daggers and plants on full display, if that's what you want. I will tie him to his chair with vines, wrap his dick so tight the blood can't flow there." She laughs, and relief washes over me.

"Yes, I would like that." Her voice is soft. "For you to be in the section. Not to tie him up. Or do *other things* to him," she says with another giggle. I only nod stoically, like a soldier taking orders from her general.

"Was there anything about your day that was good?" I ask, hoping to lighten the mood, and she smiles again. A bright, genuine quirking of her lips that makes my breath catch. I serve us both the steaming dishes from the dinner tray as Genevieve tells me of her most recent research project on Eastern Velmaran flora. Her passionate explanations last the entire dinner. I listen quietly, noting the way her lips quirk or her eyes squint when she's trying to remember something she read.

When we finish dinner and clear the table, I spread out Mazus's books across it. After what happened to her today, our evening is only going to comprise dinner and companionable reading. Genevieve flips through each of the books before deciding to return to *The Secrets and Stories of Velmara*. She pulls it to her and immediately begins reading. I smile at the clear scholar she is. We read in silence, though she makes small tuts and murmurs as we read, little noises that make my chest warm.

After at least an hour spent translating across from her, she gasps. I'm instantly behind her, crouched so that I'm at eye level, curious at what surprised her.

"What is it?" I ask, my breath in her ear sending shivers down her entire body. Her throat moves with a deep swallow. I track the movement like Lunaria tracks her prey, but I stay silent, letting her soft and delicate smell wash over me.

"Librarians are assigned a research area that we must become experts on. Mine is the history of light channeling and the Andomer family, hence my interest in the plants of Eastern Velmara, where the Andomers are from. I just read a section that it says—contradicts..." She's flustered and can barely get the words out. I squeeze her thigh reassuringly. "It contradicts what's in our archives," she finally says, slowly.

"Tell me." My voice is all commander, but she doesn't flinch away. I stand and slowly make my way back to my seat, my gaze never leaving hers.

"Well, you may not know this, but the light channelers were the original rulers of Velmara. Many suspect it's why King Mazus married Esther Andomer, to strengthen his own claim to the throne. And it's why my uncle betrothed his daughter to Prince Hawthorne—he wants the Kalmeera family to be associated with the Andomers. He doesn't care about the Vicants. Everyone knows the Andomers have the real power." This is new information to me. I didn't know there was a line outside of the Vicants that ruled Velmara. My mind races with the implications. Genevieve continues, her voice unsure and questioning. "The passage I just read indicates that the Vicants, King Mazus's line, forcibly took the throne from the Andomers in a great civil war a millennium ago. But all of the texts in the *archives* say that the Andomers willingly stepped aside when they tired of ruling, believing the Vicants best suited to leadership."

"Power is rarely given up willingly." My voice is low, and she nods. "I don't believe for one second that a ruling family just decided to hand over their throne one day, especially one with what is considered the most powerful magical ability."

"Now that we're discussing it aloud, I can't believe how silly it sounds," she admits, blushing deeply with embarrassment. "I wonder how the Vicants defeated the Andomers. Air channeling is powerful, but almost nothing can defeat light magic."

"What indeed," I murmur, mind racing.

"This is—this information... Is everything in the archives a lie?" she asks, eyes wide with an emotion I can't place. Without thinking, I'm back at her side, turning her chair outwards so I can kneel in front of her.

"No Genevieve, not everything there is a lie. But history is written by those in power, and King Mazus and his line have been in power for a very long time. Victors tell the story they want to tell, and I suspect Mazus has a prolific pen." I take her hands in mine, and she doesn't pull away. Her skin is so soft, and her hands feel so small in mine...

"I feel so foolish." Her words bring me back to the present. "But there are *hundreds* of books that all say the Andomers willingly stepped down from ruling and preferred to settle in Eastern Velmara peacefully."

"Don't feel foolish." I stroke my thumbs across the tops of her hands, comforting her practically second nature to me. Her gaze darts down to where our hands meet, studying them, then rises to meet mine. Lust heats her gaze, and I know I've read the situation correctly, even if I'm still not sure it's safe for her to pursue this.

I want to kiss her bright pink lips, run my mouth over her flushed chest. But I remember what happened today, and I won't take advantage of her vulnerability. I gently run my hand over her wrist, then squeeze her hand tightly before releasing it and standing. She looks at me with a small smile, biting her lip as she gazes up at me through thick lashes. Her amber eyes bore into me, conveying her longing and need. But today was a hard day for her, so I return to my seat. I ask her to tell me more about Eastern Velmara, and even though she continues to look at me with heat in her expression, she excitedly returns to telling me about the mystical and lush part of Velmara that runs the entire length of the eastern coast of the kingdom.

The Kalmeera family name has been respected throughout Velmara for thousands of years. Known for their practice of wedding the females of their line much earlier than tradition dictates, Kalmeeras are highly sought after for the Sons of Velmara. Some say their proclivity for producing multiple children comes from this practice, as well as the way they raise their females. Kalmeera males, on the other hand, are praised for their wit and intelligence. Many of the notable royal advisors throughout history have been from this noble family.

The Secrets and Stories of Velmara

When I wake the next morning, my body aches. Thorne's revelations about what happened to me in those caves confuse me. *Why had the aether been draining from my body?*

I wonder if that's why my muscles are so sore and why my joints screech when I lift my body into a sitting position. Lunaria is curled up at my feet, and I think I remember her sleeping there through the entire night. That's rare, and yet another sign I'm still healing from yesterday. Any time I've ever truly been injured, Lunaria hasn't left my side. I try to delicately shift my body so as not to disturb her, but it doesn't work. At my tiniest movement, her ears perk up and her eyes open. She stands and pads over to me on the bed. Her massive frame bends over me, sniffing every part of my body before satisfying herself and leaping from the bed to curl up in her nest in the corner.

I sigh as I stretch my arms above my head. I want to tell my Council about Nemesia today, and my stomach churns with anticipation. I barely eat my breakfast, instead downing six cups of tea, which only serves to further agitate me with anxious energy. I also want to tell them I've been working with the Velmarans to infiltrate the Sons and Daughters and ask them to help me fight them. For too long I've stayed my hand, only acting in defense when the rebels made moves against my people. But today we start our offensive campaign. If they have Nemesia working with them, they're more dangerous than I could have ever imagined.

I'm nervous though, and I don't want to admit defeat and ask for help. They're my advisors, but I've always kept them at a distance, allowing them to run the day-to-day of the kingdom and offer me their opinions. For three hundred years, I've presented myself as a calm and capable leader, who takes advice but never *seeks* it. The very idea makes me nauseous. I've pretended to have all the answers for so long, even when I didn't have them, that I don't know the first thing about where to begin. At first it was a necessity, the only way to quiet their fears and take control of the Council when my parents died and a young, inexperienced, female took over. Over time, it became the only acceptable part to play around them. Somehow, I need to not only tell them about Nemesia but explain without revealing too much about why I trust the Velmarans implicitly. Why I trust Velmara's *Crown Prince*.

I try to ignore the movement around the source of my magic. It dives in and out, and I have this *longing* to let it in. Whatever *it* is. But until I know more, I cannot—will not—act on this strange bond with Thorne. Thayaria hasn't survived three hundred years under my rule because of my rash or emotional decision making. My duty is to act strategically, carefully considering well-researched information. This will be no different.

Even if a small part of me wants to run down to Thorne right now and ride him until I forget my duty and our connected pasts.

"Lunaria, what am I going to do?" I whisper to the sleeping feline. She opens her eyes, then gives me a look that tells me I already know what to do. "You're no help," I hiss. She merely closes her eyes and hides her head under her enormous paws. An idea strikes me, and I pen a letter to Silene, asking for her to visit my chambers alone to discuss the strategy with my Council. I could easily aerstep down to her, but I'm nervous about seeing Thorne, so instead I will the paper to appear in her bedchamber where I know only she will find it. Less than twenty minutes later, there's a knock on my door.

"Hi," Silene huffs out the moment I open the door, and I can't keep myself from grinning. "You wanted to see me?" She says the words tentative and excited, like she can't believe I'd call on her now that Thorne's my mate. I open the door wide and gesture her in. When we're seated, me in my favorite chair and her on the sofa, she's practically bouncing with excitement. Hiding my smile at her reaction, I explain why I asked her to come here.

"Thorne told me you guessed I had a mole on my Council." She nods and gives me a sheepish grin. "I want to tell my Council about Nemesia and working with you three..." I trail off, realizing that other than Nemesia, she's the only other person I've ever sought help from. Her amber eyes only stare back at me steadily. "I'm not sure if it's the right decision. I think it's time to go on the offensive with the rebels, but I don't want to harm my people. What's your advice?" Her eyes widen in surprise.

"Me? But—why me? Why not Thorne?" Even though she knows she's the better strategist of them, she still doubts herself.

"You're the smartest of all of us. Myself included. I'm lucky to have you as a friend and ally." I say the words gently, hoping I can convey the truth of my sentiment. She blushes but then sits up straighter in her chair and pulls her shoulders back. She nods like she's ready for battle. "What do you think about telling the Council? Is it the right move, politically speaking?" Her brows furrow in concentration.

"Do you really think Nemesia is the mole?" Her words are quiet, questioning, like she knows the way they'll sting. Some part of me, deep down, wants to scream *no, she couldn't possibly have betrayed me.* That same part of me that still doesn't believe it's true. But I must bury that voice.

"I don't know how I could possibly believe otherwise. The evidence is too damning." My words are short and clipped.

"Well, here's what we actually *know.* The letter wasn't addressed to anyone in particular. It only said *my friend.* It could just as easily been meant for you. Or another person on your Council." My nostrils flare, not willing to accept this version of the story.

"Then how would the rebels have gotten the letter?" I snap, immediately regretting it. But she doesn't flinch away from me, understanding my outburst is a coping mechanism to deal with my emotions. *Just like Nemesia always understood.*

"I'm not sure, but there are several possibilities," she says slowly. "The actual mole may have intercepted it and placed it there for us to find. Or the rebels intercepted it and kept it because of the information it contained. All I'm saying is, we should be careful about assuming we're in the clear with the mole. There could be multiple, or this could somehow be a trick we don't yet understand." She's right, and I sigh at the complicated situation we've found ourselves in. Every time I think we've found answers, it only creates more questions and raises the stakes of failure.

"What do you recommend, then? With the Council?" She goes silent for a few beats, lost in thought. Her eyes track quickly side to side, like she's visually playing out every possible path forward to determine which has the best outcome.

"You should still tell your Council about Nemesia. Tell them you've been working with us and you're bringing us together to fight the rebels. In the background, the three of us will keep watch and try to see what information we can gather. We're pretty good at getting information out of people when they think they're flirting with Thorne or teaching a young and inexperienced female about politics." She grins for a moment, but then her eyes widen. "I'm sorry. I shouldn't have suggested that. Thorne doesn't have to—" I hold up my hand to cut her off, hiding the hot spike of jealousy boiling in my veins.

"It's okay. It's a good strategy. I knew you'd come up with something brilliant." My words are true, even if I hate the idea of Thorne flirting with my Council. "The three of you might find something useful. If there *is* another mole on the Council, someone may have heard or seen something, even if they haven't put the pieces together about what it means."

She looks unconvinced. "But, what about you and Thorne? Don't you want to tell your Council about the two of you being mates?"

I laugh, a lifeless chuff. "Absolutely not. Until I know more about what this means, the only person I'm telling is Admon. You and Thorne will have to continue your charade. He and I will... Well, we'll keep everything a secret." She stares at me, and I know she can see through my words and flippancy, but she doesn't press it, only nods and moves on with planning.

"We should plan an attack on the rebels and strategically leak information to different parts of the Council. Then, Fionn and I can use our in with the rebels to see if any of that information has made its way to them. That could help us narrow down who might be involved, and whether they're working with Nemesia. Even if all that happens is the rebels distance themselves from Fionn and me, it might signal that someone has tipped them off that we've been working together, and we'll know there's at least a second mole."

I nod, surprised by the relief I feel to have another person guiding me. Silene is *so* intelligent, and I should've consulted her sooner. "And what about—" I start, afraid to even say this aloud for how weak it will make me sound. "What about hurting innocent civilians? I don't want to become even more of a monster in their eyes." The words are soft, tentative. Her amber eyes glow with understanding of everything I can't say aloud, of the fears and insecurities that I truly am the Witch Queen they whisper about.

"Laurel, there are always casualties in war. And make no mistake, this is a war. The rebellion has attacked you directly, has committed acts of domestic terrorism so severe they deserve to be punished. But I promise you, we'll limit the worst of it." She smiles at me and then jumps up from the couch and wraps me in a tight hug. It takes me by surprise, but this time my arms instinctively wrap around her with no hesitation.

"Thank you," I murmur, and there's so much meaning in those two words. *Thank you for being my friend. Thank you for filling the hole Nemesia left. Thank you for understanding me.*

She squeezes me. "Good luck with the Council. You'll do great, I know. Let me know how it goes." With that, she turns and practically skips out the front door.

When the time for the Council meeting arrives, I take a deep breath, then walk down the hallway to their meeting chambers. Every advisor is here today, answering my last-minute summons. They all bow, and once I'm seated the rest of the room follows, chairs scraping against the floor.

"I have upsetting news to share today," I tell them, my voice steady. I feel them lean in with interest, and I scan every single advisor, looking for the smallest sign that something's amiss. My eyes meet Carex's gaze, who seems to hang on my every word. "I've discovered evidence that suggests Nemesia is working with the Sons and Daughters of Thayaria." Dozens of eyes stare at me with nothing but shock and disbelief. Murmurs break out, but I silence them with a raised hand. "The leader of the rebellion had in his possession a letter in her handwriting and with her signature," I continue. "She passed him information she discovered in Velmara."

"Your Majesty," Carex interrupts, and I bristle. "I mean no disrespect, but how did you uncover this letter? Our spies couldn't uncover the identity of the leader, much less his or her location." Maybe it's because he interrupted me, or maybe it's because he's been irritating me lately, but I narrow my eyes in anger before speaking with dangerous calm.

"Spies that I will remind you were hand selected and trained by Nemesia herself before she turned them over to you in her absence." The murmuring in the room breaks out again.

Carex only bows his head slightly. "Of course. But then, how did you find this?" I steel myself for what I'm about to tell them.

"I've been working in secret with the Velmarans," I admit, and chaos erupts in the Council chamber. All the advisors are speaking at once, some to me, some to each other. They're shocked, angry, and uncertain. But none of them display anything I wouldn't have expected except Admon, who doesn't seem surprised in the least, though I suspect that's because of what I told him about Thorne and me yesterday. I simply sit in silence until they quiet again. "I suspected a mole on this Council," I disclose. "Nemesia herself brought the accusation to me and advised me not to disclose any sensitive information while she was gone. It was a convenient way to ensure I didn't uncover that in her absence, there were no leaks. I'm deeply sorry for my suspicion of all of you." Dozens of angry eyes glare at me, and I know I've broken trust with many of them. I'll have to deal with those consequences later.

"Your Majesty, you acted in the best interest of Thayaria with the information you had," Admon offers, though I know it won't undo the damage I've done by lying. I give him a thankful smile anyway.

"The Velmarans were approached by the rebels and brought that information to me. They offered to pretend to seek an alliance with the rebellion in order to discover their leadership and movements. They were successful," I explain.

"Your Majesty," Carex interrupts again, and now the interruption feels targeted. I'm trying to get all the information out, but he keeps adding his own commentary. I want my advisors to speak up, but not when I'm in the middle of revealing important information. "If the Velmarans are the ones who procured this letter, how are you so certain of its authenticity? I think I speak for all of us when I say that I doubt their trustworthiness." Murmurs of agreement break out across the room, and after Carex's display at Winter Solstice, I want to rattle him with my magic a little. But I don't, knowing now is not the time and place for such personal feelings and actions.

"I can assure you, I've reviewed the letter myself," I challenge. Adding, *as I would have explained if you hadn't interrupted me,* in my head. "I'm certain she wrote it. What's more, the Velmarans have proven themselves trustworthy allies. They're not aligned with the Golden King. If you don't trust them, then trust me." If Silene's suspicions that there's a second mole on the Council are true, this is a dangerous admission. But the time for secrecy is over. The only way we'll defeat the rebels is with the full strength of the Council.

Hesitation fills my advisors' eyes, most of all Carex's. His hatred of Thorne goes beyond dislike or distrust of Velmara. But Carex doesn't continue to challenge me. Instead, he offers, "Of course, Your Majesty. You have our unyielding trust. If you find them worthy allies, then so shall I." Flowery language that doesn't match his eyes.

I look around the room, staring into the eyes of every advisor to convey my certainty in my position, and again looking for anything useful that might indicate whether Nemesia had allies on the Council. When there are no more challenges, I continue.

"I'd like to create a small sub-committee focused on offensive strategies intended to root out and ultimately quell the rebellion. For too long I've left them to attack at will, without hitting back. That ends today. All three of the Velmarans will be members of that sub-committee." Thankfully, this seems to please the advisors, who have collectively pushed me to take action against the rebels for years. Multiple heads nod in agreement and murmurs of relief break out.

"Excellent, Your Majesty," Admon remarks, clapping his hands together. "We shall make your intentions realized." He takes control of the discussion of who will take part in the sub-committee and ideas for how to strike against the rebels. I simply sit and listen, trusting Admon to lead the conversation. After twenty minutes of nominations and voting, the members comprise Admon, Carex, Aria, Margery, and three other advisors, plus the Velmarans. Admon offers to organize the first meeting by the end of the week. Before the Council dismisses, I offer them final words, letting the tiniest thread of aether seep into my voice.

"Nemesia is no longer welcome in this kingdom. If she appears at any port, she is to be arrested and brought to the palace cells immediately. Send the messages out." They all nod before taking their leave.

Carex hangs back, and I groan internally. I move to a corner of the room, pretending to look out at the city of Arberly from the floor-to-ceiling windows in the Council chamber, hoping Carex won't follow. But he does, coming up to stand next to me, his arms crossed and shoulders tense.

"Did you want to discuss something further, Carex?" I ask without meeting his gaze, pretending I don't know exactly what he's going to say. He doesn't hesitate at all, his words rushing out as if he can barely contain them.

"Aethers, Laurel, what's going on with you and the Velmarans? After everything that's happened, how can you trust them?" His words are harsh, anger written across his features. My own temper rises to meet his.

"Please, do tell me how *I* should feel after everything that's happened to *me*," I snarl, finally turning to meet his gaze. "Enlighten me on *everything* that's happened and how that somehow means my instincts and decisions should be questioned." I lose a bit of my control, not because of my anger, but because of the hurt I feel that Carex of all people wouldn't trust me. That he would use my past and history against me like this. With the wound that is still gaping at Nemesia's betrayal, I'm even more sensitive to Carex's barbs. The lights in the room flicker slightly at my slip, and I take a deep breath to wrap a fist around my magic. Even through his ire, Carex's eyes widen in fear, still afraid and unable to meet my challenge, so unlike Thorne.

"Laurel, that's not what I meant. I've only ever wanted the best for you." He deflates. "I love—I *loved* you, Laurel. For decades. I just..." His outrage fully fades. "I just don't understand. He's the *Prince* of Velmara. The son of King Mazus. How can you trust him so easily? It took you *years* to tell me anything about the kingdom. You would shut down if I even mentioned the Council or your rule. And now, in just a handful of months, you've brought him into secret political schemes? Not only that, but you *lied* to me. He *was* at the tower that day, and it was the Velmarans who helped the rebels escape. I don't get it. How could you trust him so easily and keep me out of your schemes?"

My temper dissipates. For the first time in years, I *see* Carex and understand him. My heart aches for what might have been, for his sake. His issues with Thorne make sense. The two of us certainly haven't kept our raw lust hidden very well. If the roles were reversed and he had not only lied to me but mocked my rational assessment of a dangerous situation like I've done to him multiple times, I'd be incredibly hurt. Carex has patiently waited all these years, hoping I would open up to him, probably working himself up in the Council so he had a reason to be involved in running the kingdom organically.

But what he doesn't understand, can never understand, is that our issues didn't stem from just me. Fear of my power and the way he's always clung to a vision of me that isn't reality stunted us before we ever even began. He might love Laurel, but he doesn't love the Queen of Thayaria, much less the Witch Queen, and as much as I wish I could separate the two, I will always be both.

"Carex," I say softly. I don't want to tell him, don't want to take this risk. But he needs to hear it from me, before Thorne in his jealousy and male pride reveals it. More than that, Carex needs to let me go, and I need the Captain of my Royal Guard to trust the Velmarans. They'll have to work together to stop Krantz and the rebels. Hopefully revealing the information will help him understand. "Thorne is my *mate*." His eyes widen. "I know we've always been told they aren't real, and it's something I'm still figuring out myself. But it's true."

His shoulders slump. "Are you sure about this?"

"I am. And I want you to know, it's not just that fact that made me trust Prince Hawthorne and his advisors. They are good people, Carex. I kept them at a distance initially, but time and time again, they've proven themselves to me. Please, give them a chance." The words are a balm to my frayed heart. I didn't realize how much *I* needed to admit to myself that my interest in Thorne and the friendship I have with Silene and Fionn has nothing to do with the mating bond. Carex only nods, eyes filled with too many emotions for me to decipher. "I know I don't need to tell you this, but this is to be kept secret," I order. "Other than the Velmarans, only Admon knows. I'm still processing what this means and what I want to do about it. I'd rather not do that with nobles and courtiers breathing down my neck."

"Of course," he says, hands over his heart. "I'll try to give them a chance, Laurel. I swear I will." For the first time in months, his expression is open and genuine, and I feel content I told him this information, that I finally put the relationship we had behind us.

Carex leaves, and I take a moment to look around the Council chamber, looking for clues I know I won't find. I made it through the meeting, but that doesn't mean I'm not still reeling from what I had to reveal and feeling emotionally raw in the aftermath. Nemesia ran hundreds—thousands—of Council meetings in this room, standing confidently at the head of the massive round oak table. Mugs and loose papers litter the room, and I react to the normalcy they represent. The room should be charred, broken, dark—anything that symbolizes the inner turmoil I feel thinking about her counseling me after she'd already become a betrayer. When was the last time she was here as my friend? *After which meeting did she decide to betray me?*

I can't believe she was *never* my friend. I know that not to be true, not after the childhood we spent together and the bond forged in the shared trauma of the war. Was it something I did? Did she lose confidence in my ability to lead this kingdom? It's the only explanation that makes any sense. She knows I'm not the person the rebels have painted me to be, who Mazus has painted me to be. She chose what she knows is a lie over her oldest friend, likely because she knew I wasn't capable of saving Thayaria. That's why I feel so unsettled—it's not the betrayal, per se, it's that there must have been some moment I didn't catch when she lost faith in me. What if that happens with the Velmarans, or Admon, or the Council? Will I even see it?

The questions swirl, threatening to consume me. I have to find a way to move forward, have to find the strength to push through the hurt, like I always have. But this time, without the foundation of my friendship to Nemesia, it's even harder to push everything down and pretend like I'm not dying inside. I cross the room and stand at the door. With a deep breath, I glance around one last time before closing the door on both the room and my pain.

The former Queen of Velmara, Esther Vicant, was known across the realm for her ethereal beauty. Daughter of the infamous Luxar Andomer, the third most powerful fae in the kingdom of Velmara after the King and his heir, Esther met a tragic end. Her untimely accident left the kingdom of Velmara grieving her loss. Centuries later, she is still considered the standard of beauty for fae females in Velmara.

The Secrets and Stories of Velmara

I take extra time dressing that evening for whatever Thorne has planned, my stomach dancing with nerves. After trying on at least six different gowns, I decide on a deep olive-colored chiffon dress. As I survey the dress in the mirror, I realize this is the second time I've unconsciously selected a dress that matches Thorne's exact eye color. The thought should scare me, but I find that it doesn't, and I like the way the dark green brings out the bright green of my own eyes. I keep my hair loose and only apply the lightest tint of makeup to enhance my features, no sign of the Witch Queen costume. The only jewelry I wear is Thorne's lightning bolt necklace, a gift that becomes more and more precious to me every day.

When I'm finished getting ready, I observe the full effect. I've always been unsure of my appearance, have always questioned whether my curves made me beautiful or blemished.

Thorne's own father had found me wanting, claiming I wasn't half as beautiful as his first wife, Thorne's mother. Would that impact Thorne's view of me?

I've seen depictions of the former Queen of Velmara. She was flawless, tall and lithe like so many fae females. Delicate features, elegant and airy in appearance, with dewy skin that practically glowed from the inside out. Her long, toned and tan legs are on display in every picture I've ever encountered of her, peeking through high slits on her clothing. And I couldn't be more different—shorter than most fae, with wide hips, full breasts, and thick thighs. Even my stark white skin, that won't tan no matter how long I'm in the sun, is unique. For so long, it didn't matter to me, because the *Witch Queen* is supposed to be different, exuding confidence and a sensual demeanor, not bothered by things as petty as appearances. But *Laurel*—I'm not exactly sure how the female beneath the cold mask feels about not being the right body type to be beautiful.

A knock at the door startles me out of my thoughts. I take one last look in the mirror, smoothing the chiffon and pulling the neckline of the dress lower to show more cleavage. I know my breasts affect Thorne, so I rely on that feature, hoping he'll overlook everything else about me that's different from how females are supposed to look. I cross the room and open the door.

Thorne leans against the doorframe, arms confidently crossed, the very picture of a debonair prince. Not for the first time, I'm reminded of how different we truly are. My mate is effortlessly casual, suave, and comfortable in his own skin. I could never pull off the grace he so easily embodies, nor am I naturally likeable. He's dressed more formally than usual, a crisp navy suit with cream accents—his signature colors. No gold, no tie to Mazus and Velmara. His hair is slicked back, though pieces fall in his face as always. Those eyes, that I once thought defined Mazus and the entire kingdom of Velmara, openly drift up and down my body, taking in every part of me. I immediately feel the need to look away, to suppress my attraction to him and hide how his assessing gaze affects me, but he catches the movement and lifts my chin so I'm forced to meet his eyes.

"You look stunning, Laurel," he says resolutely, like he's trying to speak it into my very being. I feel my cheeks heat and I want to look away again, but his fingers keep my gaze locked on his. Gently, he caresses my lips with a finger and cups my cheek. "Aethers, you're so beautiful." Satisfied he's praised me enough, he lets go of my face before threading his fingers through mine. "Ready for our date?" he asks with his usual devilish grin, though there's something in it that's reserved only for me, like a secret between the two of us that no one else knows about. It gives me butterflies in my stomach that are not wholly unpleasant.

"How can I be ready, when I don't know what we're *doing*? Also, you better not be expecting me to walk down all these stairs in this dress." His lips twitch in amusement.

"Wouldn't dream of it, witchling. You can aerstep us to the outskirts of Arberly, to the path from the palace into the city." I keep his hand in mine as I take us there. The foliage has already started its regrowth, and the early blooms of flowering trees and shoots of spring flowers line the path. The air is still quite brisk, but I don't feel its chill, too heated from being in Thorne's presence. He wraps my arm in his and leads us into Arberly, though our fingers stay threaded even in this gesture, like he can't bear to let me go.

"Where are we going?" I ask, impatience to know the plan seeping into my tone. He smirks.

"Right now, we're just strolling through town. Enjoy the moment, witchling."

"Fine," I say with a huff, and he laughs.

"You truly never give up even an inch of control, do you?" The words are chastising, but he's smiling like he likes it.

"No, because I'm the Queen of a mysterious kingdom and most people are terrified of me, even when they know I'm not what the stories whisper of me. Really gives me the upper hand," I say, baring my teeth in a mock hiss.

"Your Witch Queen act won't work on me. I've seen you giggle while reading romance books. Or, to use your term, *saucy* books," he quips, then pulls me closer into his side. He stops us, turning me into him. He pushes a piece of my hair behind my ear, and the touch makes me shiver. He leans in, whispering with a throaty growl. "I can assure you that when *I* have you like those romance books you read, giggling will be the furthest thing from your mind." My skin tingles and my thighs clench together with need. An image of his face between my thighs, hot breath tingling across my skin, crosses my mind unbidden. My toes curl and my mouth goes dry. I lean into him, desperate for more of his touch, for a kiss, but he turns us back to the path with a smug look of satisfaction. "What's your favorite place in Arberly?" he asks, changing the subject, though I can tell it's his own kind of challenge. He wants to see if he can rattle me. I won't let him win, won't let him see he got to me with his deep voice and insinuating remarks, so I swallow down my lust and answer the question.

"Easy, all the bakeries."

Thorne barks out a laugh. "You and your chocolate cake addiction," he murmurs. "Anywhere else?" I consider his words, wondering what to tell him. The honest truth is that I don't have a favorite place in the city, and it spills from my lips like it always has with him.

"I don't spend a lot of time in Arberly, to be honest. I keep my distance. I don't want to scare my people, and it's better that way."

"I disagree," he says immediately and resolutely, and I'm shocked by his bluntness. "Your people have more than just respect for you, Laurel. They *admire* you. Just look at the way the children reacted to you when we visited the school. They weren't afraid—they were curious." I lower my eyes, unsure what to make of his statements, but he stops us and again raises my chin to meet his eyes. When I shy away from the truth, he forces me to see, insists I keep looking. Not even Nemesia had the sheer force of will to do that. He continues his speech, eyes locked on mine. "I've been in the taverns and shops. Have heard the people speak of you, heard their praises for the programs you've implemented in Thayaria. I think they would welcome your presence more often. Just look at how successful the Solstice dinner was." My throat tightens with emotion for an instant, but I push it away.

"I'll consider it," is all I say, but he simply nods and continues our walk.

"Do you have a favorite place in Thayaria that isn't the palace or Arberly?" He is insistent with his questions tonight, but I like it. This time, the answer comes easily.

"The valley on the other side of the mountains that circle Arberly—Moormyr, it's called. It's still the most beautiful landscape I've ever seen," I say with a small smile, thinking of the rolling fields of thayar flowers that always fill me with so much awe and wonder. Thorne smiles, like he can sense the way they bring me happiness.

"What makes them so special?" He rubs circles on my knuckle, the touch automatic from him, like he can't help but find new ways to touch me, to comfort and soothe.

"The lush green fields dotted with the deep crimson of the thayar flower, circled by white mountain peaks. When the thayar is in full bloom, you won't see anything but red for miles and miles. It's extraordinary."

Thorne smiles down at me. "That sounds special. I hope I can see it sometime."

"There's a festival held there on the Spring Equinox. I haven't gone in a long time, but I used to go every year with my parents. Maybe... maybe we could go this year." I say the last sentence like it's a question, soft and tentative, worried about what he might think of me trying to make plans for us so many months in advance. He only squeezes my hand where it rests in his.

"I'd really love that, Laurel," he says, eyes shining and intense. It's too much for me, too close to being what I'm so afraid of, so I ask him a question to give me time to think and process.

"What about you? What's your favorite place in Velmara?"

"Eastern Velmara, where my mother comes from. It's almost as green as Thayaria, but more tropical." His eyes look off into the distance, like he's picturing it even now. "Waterfalls everywhere. I haven't spent a lot of time there, but every time I do, it makes me feel closer to her."

"What was she like, your mother?" I ask. He pauses, and I'm afraid I've stepped too far. "I'm sorry, that was really personal. I—"

"It's okay. I love talking about her—no one asks about her anymore, and I wish they would, if only to give me an excuse to remember her. I was just thinking of what to tell you," he says gently. "She was so kind, and fiercely intelligent. I think that's what you would have most appreciated about her. I thought she could read my mind, because she always seemed to know what trouble I was about to get into before I did it. But then she would tell me to go do it anyway, just to be careful." I chuckle, and he looks down at me with his own smile. "She always encouraged me to read and do extra research in the archives. So naturally, I did the exact opposite."

I laugh brightly. "She sounds wonderful."

"She really was," he says, eyes bright. "She would have loved you." I scoff, but he squeezes my hand. "I really mean it. She would have been shocked by the mating bond, of course, but she would have been so happy I found someone like you. Someone who sees through my antics and doesn't put up with my bullshit." My cheeks flush, even as I smile. "That necklace was actually hers, you know." He nods to the lightning bolt necklace resting on my collarbone. The necklace that I haven't taken off since the day he gave it to me. "Her father gave it to her when she married my father. She used to tell me she wore it to remind her of me and my lightning power. I found it among her things when I finally searched through them, hidden away with the diary that revealed the truth of her death. It was only then that I learned more about the symbol and what it meant that she wore this necklace every day." I gently touch the jewelry, feeling unworthy to wear such an important piece of Thorne. He must sense what's going through my head, because he covers my hand with his where it rests against my neck. "I wouldn't want that necklace to be anywhere else but right there. And neither would she. It belongs on you, on my mate." His words are gentle and soothing, and they crack something open inside me I'd been trying to keep at bay.

"I'm still having trouble believing it's all real," I admit, the emotions flooding me, making it hard to say anything else.

"I know." He smiles. "And it's okay that you need time to process this. Maybe it's just the impulsive streak Silene always says will get me in trouble, but I'm not struggling at all. Just last night I remembered the way the mist reacted to me when I entered Thayaria. It caressed my face, I swear. Fionn and Silene teased me so much about it when I told them. I thought it had done the same to them. I was sorely mistaken." His smile and corresponding dimple take my breath away.

"I forgot about that! I felt a weird zap of energy when you entered that I'd never felt before. I just thought it was because my enemy entered." I give him a wink, and he lets out a deep and full laugh. We continue down the path in silence, brightly colored buildings now on either side of us as we enter the city proper. When we reach the bustling streets, he takes my hand and has us walk single file so we can weave through the crowds of people making their way home for the day. But even as we weave and bob, he never releases my hand. Eventually, we stop in front of a red storefront in the merchant district. It's been restored already, though many buildings around it are still under construction. Thorne leads me through the front door and into an empty cafe.

"This is Mara's family bakery," he explains, and my eyes widen in delight. "Silene and Fionn have been helping them rebuild their store. When we asked if we could use it for a private dinner with the Queen, they practically jumped through the ceiling. And since Mara was still in town, I asked her to whip up an entire cake just for you." Thorne's eyes sparkle.

"How did you know who Mara even was?"

"When Sarah brought the cake that day we trained, you mentioned Mara and her family's bakery. I remembered. It was easy enough to seek Sarah out and ask her how to find the baker who makes your favorite chocolate cake. Then I connected the dots between the family Silene and Fionn were helping and your Mara." He shrugs, like it's the easiest thing in the world. "We have more food than just cake," he says with a grin, gesturing to a small table in the room's corner laid with dishes of food and candles.

He pulls my chair out for me, his hands lingering on my shoulders even as he moves away to his own seat. Sitting across from me, he pours a cup of tea, adding the perfect amount of cream, and hands it to me. My heart squeezes at the small gesture. When we each have a plate full of aromatic food, he starts his questioning again, and I realize that this really *is* a date. I don't know what I thought it would be, or why I'm surprised, but the normalcy of spending time with Thorne in this way is striking. We could be two regular fae, learning more about one another, just like he said he wished we could be yesterday in the caves.

"How did you end up with Lunaria?"

I chuff. "I was training in The Spined Moors, more inland than where we've visited. I felt her presence and was absolutely terrified. She stalked me for hours before I finally glimpsed her. When I realized what was watching me, I aerstepped to the coast, but she followed me there. Every day after that for a month, whenever I would train, she would just appear. If I moved locations, she would follow me. Eventually, I worked up the courage to pet her, and she let me. I asked her if she wanted to come home with me, and I just somehow knew her answer was yes. So, I brought her back to the palace, and she's been with me ever since." He looks at me with equal parts incredulity and awe, like I'm the most interesting person in the world.

"I can't believe you just brought one of the most fearsome wild animals in all the Four Kingdoms home with you after petting her one time." His eyes convey both terror and humor.

I shrug. "That's the best part of being so powerful. I'm usually pretty sure I'm the real predator in any situation." I say the words as a joke, but I watch his face for any sign of fear or recoil. His expression reflects nothing but respect "Did you ever have any pets?" I ask, trying to distract myself from the feelings building in my chest.

"Other than Fionn, no." I roll my eyes.

"How are Fionn and Silene taking everything? Do you think they really believe us?" I ask.

"Silene does. She's still sighing in hopeless romanticism every half hour." I chuckle with the image of a dreamy eyed Silene. "Fionn is harder to read. I think he's still skeptical but trusts me to make the decisions that are right for me."

"I'm envious of the family you've found with Silene and Fionn," I say quietly, thinking of the loss of my own found family. Thorne takes my hand.

"They see you as their family too, you know. Silene especially." Once again, emotion tightens in the back of my throat, but I push it away.

"Don't do that," Thorne says.

"Do what?"

"Push away your emotions. I see you push it down, try to hide it away. *Your feelings are safe with me.* You don't have to be the stalwart leader, or the Witch Queen, or whoever the fuck else the world expects you to be. Just be Laurel. The good, the bad, the emotional... I want every part of you." My throat clenches and I let the mask crack just a little. He strokes my fingers as I wonder what the catch is. Wonder what flaw he might have that will bring this all crashing down. The smallest flutter of hope ignites in my chest. "How are you feeling today about Nemesia?" he asks, and a hollowness returns to my gut thinking about her.

"I don't know. Betrayed? Angry? Hurt? It's still so hard to believe. I told the Council today and put the order out for her arrest if she enters Thayaria."

"And how did the Council take the news?"

"They were shocked of course, but the topic of conversation focused primarily on *how* I received the information." Thorne's shoulders tense, waiting for me to continue. "I told them of our alliance and scheme. Many are furious that I lied to them. I suspect there will be more to deal with on that front later. For now, the three of you are going to work with seven of my advisors to plan our next move on the rebels, while secretly looking for any information that might tell us if Nemesia was working alone."

He nods. "It's a good plan."

"It was Silene's," I admit, and he chuckles.

"Of course it was. Is that why she mysteriously disappeared this morning and wouldn't tell us where she was going?" I laugh, and a warmth builds in my chest that she would keep my request secret from them and only between us, like I'm just as much her friend as they are.

"Yes," I say with a sheepish look. "I asked for her advice today. She agreed it was time to tell the Council everything and hatched this plan for me in about five minutes."

"I continue to be amazed by how forthcoming you are with your advisors. My father would never tell them his plans so openly, even in a scheme to draw out a mole."

I shrug. "I was crowned when I was twenty years old, with no experience or knowledge of what I was doing. I've had to rely on advisors my entire life. I learned the lesson too many times that I don't always have all the answers, even if I need to pretend I do. Listening to others is a critical part of ruling. Even if there is another mole on the Council, there're dozens of advisors who *are* loyal."

He brings my hand to his lips and kisses it. "Many would have done differently in your shoes, even at twenty. You're remarkable." An emotion I can't place swims in his eyes, but I shy away from it, dropping my eyes to our hands again despite his request not to push away how I'm feeling. He only lifts my chin with two fingers as he's done so many times before, meeting my gaze with a probing stare. "During your rule, as you've been setting up the Council of Advisors and creating hundreds of programs for citizens and training your magic and doing all the incredible work I see you do regularly—what in all of that makes you happy? When are you the happiest, Laurel?"

His question takes me aback, and not just because no one has ever asked me it before. I've never asked *myself* the question. Happiness is for normal people, not for leaders running an isolated kingdom because of their own failure. Words pour out of me, unbidden, like they always do when he gets me alone and asks me these impossible questions.

"I didn't have time to be happy—*don't* have time to be happy. I'm too busy trying to be the leader Thayaria deserves, too busy trying to solve every problem that arises. There's so much work to do and too many people who depend on my decisions. The weight of it—" My words break off. Thorne remains silent, a steady presence as I sort through the emotions bubbling to the surface after he's flayed me open. "It's a lot of responsibility to bear," I finally say. "I have to be strong. Happiness is optional." Thorne's lips purse and his eyes turn downward, the expression too close to pity for my liking. He opens his mouth and I'm sure is about to tell me my answer is bullshit or, even worse, to tell me how sorry he is for the life I've led, and I don't want either of those things from him. So, I pull a page out of his own book, changing topics rapidly with a fake grin and a wink I know he sees through. "No one feels sorry for the Witch Queen." His expression remains studious. "Where's this cake? I've eaten enough regular food," I say with enthusiasm.

He laughs, playing along with my silent plea to leave our feelings behind us, then stands to retrieve the cake from behind the counter. He sets it in front of me, then hands me a fork. "It's all yours." I dive in.

When we finish our dinner, we take the long walk back up to the palace. Thorne continues to pepper me with questions about small and big things, though nothing quite as harrowing as the question about happiness. When I can get one in, I ask him questions too. The walk passes too quickly, and suddenly we're at his apartment door. I stand there awkwardly, not sure what to do from here.

"Normally I'd walk you to *your* door, but as you're the one with aerstepping powers, I can't really do that," he says with a sheepish quirk of his lips, and I laugh.

Holding my hands, he brings me to his chest, wrapping me up in his strong body. I tuck my head under his chin, and he murmurs contentedly as he strokes my back. I could stay here forever, and despite how uncomfortable I feel with the emotions Thorne brings out in me, when I'm wrapped in his arms, inhaling his scent, my mind quiets.

With a squeeze, he releases me, then kisses the top of my head. "Goodnight, witchling," he says, then enters his apartment and closes the door, leaving me aching for his presence.

Many stories of the early fae refer to a source of magic that each fae has deep inside themselves. There are various terms for this source, but the most common is the aether-heart. *Early fae believed that in addition to their physical heart, they possessed a magical heart, made of the same aether that courses through the leylines of the world. Fae of today do not possess such a source, and it is impossible to know whether the* aether-heart *is fable alone or whether it has disappeared from the fae people over time.*

The Legends of the Fae, Volume II

"The rebellion's primary headquarters are an abandoned manor in Oakton," Silene tells the Council of Advisors four days after my first outing with Laurel. We've spent every evening together since, talking, laughing, and stealing glances at one another when we think the other isn't looking. My body *burns* deliciously when she's near, leaving me frigid in her absence. But if I don't move slowly, she may bolt, both metaphorically and literally, with her ability to aerstep great distances at any moment.

"What do you propose, Miss Kalmeera?" Admon asks Silene.

"We attack there, scatter them. From what I've observed, many members of the Sons and Daughters are just normal villagers. Some from Oakton, some from surrounding villages. They'll run back to their families at the first sign of trouble."

Laurel leans casually against a window in the back of the room as Silene leads the meeting, expression blank, listening intently but revealing nothing in her features. It takes the centuries of control I've honed like a blade at my father's side to stay seated and keep my gaze from her luscious body. She doesn't want to reveal anything about our connection, even accidentally, to the Council. She says it's so that Silene and I can better uncover information within the Council, but I know there's more to it. I'm content to wait as long as it takes.

"How do we know when there will be a large gathering of rebels at the manor?" Carex asks Silene.

"We don't, but we actually don't want there to be a lot of rebels there when we attack," she responds, the smallest ounce of haughtiness seeping into her tone, so subtle only those who know her well would catch it. She knows about Laurel's past with Carex and dislikes him on my behalf. I can't keep my lips from twitching with a smirk—she's a great friend.

"And why is that?" Carex demands. I clench my fists. I *loathe* this male. I can't believe I tried to flirt with him when I first arrived, even if it was just a ploy to get close to Laurel.

"The attack will scare away the less committed rebels, whether we kill many or kill a few. We're better off not risking inciting rage further by killing someone's mother, or father, or child because they happened to be in the wrong place at the wrong time." Silene's response mimics Laurel's cool confidence. The two of them together will be an unstoppable force. Carex looks like he's about to say something, but Laurel steps forward to support Silene, clearly as annoyed as I am by Carex's continual questioning.

"Silene's right. We should keep casualties to a minimum. They're still citizens of Thayaria." There's no room for argument in her voice, and I *love* seeing this side of her. Not quite Witch Queen, but not the Laurel I know either. This is the Queen of Thayaria, the female who has strategically protected her isolated kingdom for three hundred years.

"I agree with Her Majesty and Miss Kalmeera," Admon offers in support. The ancient fae has yet to find any useful information on the mating bond in his texts. I'm impatient, but only because I know Laurel needs information like she needs chocolate cake and aether.

"And what if we arrive and the rebels have a large contingent who return with force?" Carex asks, haughty arrogance in his voice that makes me want to wrap my hands around his neck.

"We offer them a chance to lay down their weapons and surrender," Laurel says calmly.

"And if they refuse?" His tone implies that Laurel doesn't know what she's doing, and my blood *boils*. How dare he question her like this in front of others? How dare he imply she's anything less than the seasoned leader she is? My fury on her behalf is misplaced, however, because the Queen of Thayaria responds, and she takes care of his questioning with only five words.

"I show them no mercy." The ruthlessness she embodies makes my blood heat for a different reason.

We spend the rest of the meeting discussing the plans to storm the Oakton manor. I offer little to the discussion, content to let Silene and Fionn shine. They're both in their element. Silene offers strategies while Fionn provides the tactical advice to execute on those strategies. When we've confirmed final plans, the Council adjourns, but I hang back, desperate for any extra moment with Laurel. To my disappointment, both Carex and Admon remain as well. I nod to Silene and Fionn, giving them the signal to leave and use the gathering of the advisors in the hallway to probe for information under the guise of gossip.

"Prince Hawthorne," Carex says as he approaches me, and I narrow my eyes at him. "I wanted to—um—apologize for my treatment of you these past months. I'm sure you can understand how my mistrust of Velmarans may have led me to make assumptions about your character that were unfair. Laurel has assured me of her trust in you." I want to rip out his tongue for using Laurel's name and not her title, but I quell my rage. This is a peace offering, and I will play nice, for Laurel's sake. When he sticks out his hand to shake mine, I merely stare at it. Some things are a step too far.

"Apology accepted, Captain," is all I say before walking away, leaving him alone with his hand held out. My eyes catch Laurel's, and I swear I see the corners of her mouth tick up, but she keeps her expression neutral as she speaks with Admon. After a few beats, Carex bows to Laurel, then leaves.

"Your Majesty, Your Highness," Admon says with a respectful nod. "I've found something that might interest you. Would you like to speak here?"

Laurel's features instantly sharpen. "No. My rooms," she says, then strides from the room. The Queen is so different from the female I know as Laurel, and sometimes it throws me off, though not in a bad way—I like the surprise. This is one of those moments. I look at Admon and shrug with a grin, then follow behind her.

Lunaria is lounging in a patch of sunrays that beam down from a window set high in the wall when we enter Laurel's rooms. The cat raises her head lazily until Admon follows in behind me. She leaps to her feet, and a deep yowl emits from low in her throat.

"Oh, go," Laurel shoos. The cat holds her ground for another moment before slowly backing from the room, yellow eyes never leaving Admon, who looks deeply uncomfortable by the interaction. "Told you she doesn't tolerate anyone but Nemesia. Her liking of you is very out of character," Laurel says with a sly smile.

When we're all seated, Laurel and I pressed close together on a sofa and her hand in mine, where it always belongs, Admon recounts the information he's gathered.

"It's difficult to translate, and I haven't made out all the characters, but I believe I have enough now to understand the meaning of a story about mates recounted in the tome." I can practically feel Laurel's anticipation crawling across my own skin. But she only nods for him to continue. "This story details an unusual mating bond between a male fae and a female witch. At least, that's the closest translation I can find to the character that describes the female. It seems to be a magical creature that is not fae. Likely just an embellishment to the story, since it's a book of fables." Admon seems to become lost in his own thoughts.

"And why is this story of interest?" Laurel prompts, sharp but not unkind.

"Ah yes, well, in the story, the mating bond is described similarly to how you both discussed yours," Admon continues. "Discovered when blood has been spilled and connected to the magical source of each partner. In the story, the fae and witch must accept the mating bond, and once they do, their *aether-heart*, as I believe it's translated, changes to incorporate features of their partner's *aether-heart*."

Laurel is thoughtful, and I wait for her to speak first. What Admon described seems similar to what we've experienced. My *aether-heart*, if that is what it's called, has changed dramatically. Where once it was immovable, now it whips and roils with a fierce energy that *feels* like Laurel, despite the cool exterior she so often portrays.

"Does this fable explain how the mates accepted the bond?" Laurel finally asks, expression guarded.

"I'm afraid not. All I've translated so far is that story and a short passage that explains some of the common elements included in all stories about mates. There's always an *aether-heart,* there's always some change to the fae as a result of accepting the bond, and the mates get to choose whether to accept or deny the bond. What that acceptance looks like seems to be unique to each individual story." The idea that Laurel could choose to deny the mating bond makes my chest ache, but I stay silent. Laurel lets out a frustrated sigh. "I'll keep translating," Admon promises. The old male looks at Laurel with the love of a parent, clearly wanting to help her with this. He hesitates, like he wants to say something but isn't sure if he should. "But, Your Majesty, if I may speak plainly..." he finally says.

"Yes, of course, Admon," Laurel says.

"It seems to me that Prince Hawthorne may have already accepted the bond, based on how he described his experience. His *aether-heart*." His words ring true, and I nod.

"It's definitely changed, and it... it feels like you," I say, locking eyes with Laurel. I want to smile, but her expression gives me pause.

"How can you possibly know that?" she demands, somewhat sharply, but I don't flinch. I just keep meeting her gaze, unwavering in my certainty.

"It's just an instinct, like the mating bond itself. But I know it's right." Her eyes stare at me, searching my expression like she always does, looking for any sign of deceit.

"Your Majesty," Admon interjects, "based on your description, I think you have not yet accepted the bond. You mentioned a swirling energy trying to get in. My guess is that energy is the bond, waiting for you to accept it. I imagine if you rejected the bond, that energy would go away, and if you accepted, your *aether-heart* would change." Laurel practically shudders, and it breaks my heart just a little, but I keep my expression neutral. I won't pressure her—she needs to decide for herself if she wants to take this leap with me.

"I see," is all she says, her voice quiet and thoughtful.

Admon clears his throat again, then stands. "I'll send word if I find anything else." The male has ascertained that the two of us need a moment alone. With a bow, he leaves the room, and I instantly wrap Laurel's hands in both of mine.

"Talk to me Laurel. Tell me what you're feeling," I whisper, unable to stay silent. I drop my chin to her shoulder. She stalls, looking everywhere but at me. I only squeeze her hand, giving her time.

"Do you really think you've accepted the bond?" she finally asks, pulling back from me so she can search my face.

"I do," I soothe, steady in my resolve.

"But... How? How could you accept something so *massive,* so *life changing,* in an instant?" Her voice cracks just slightly, and I know this is hard for her. This is the same female who has shuttered herself away from the world, away from any companionship beyond the best friend who has now betrayed her. She practices her magic in the most isolated part of the entire Four Kingdoms so that there is no chance of her losing control. She plans down to the most insignificant detail. Of course she's struggling to accept this. I'll do whatever it takes to show her she can trust me, that I'm a safe place for her. I take my hand from hers to wrap my arms around her middle, snuggling her against me where we sit on the couch.

"Because it wasn't in an instant. I've felt that bond since the moment I met you, even without knowing what it was. I've watched you, gotten to know you, seen your love for your people and your desire to be a good ruler." I squeeze her tightly. "When I said you were the answer to a question I've asked my entire life, I meant it. Something about you feels right. Realizing what you were to me was simply a moment of clarity in what has been an aethers-confusing several months." She laughs, bringing a lightness to my body instantly, but it doesn't last. She stands, walking away from me to stare out the window.

"I'm not like you," she says, voice emotionless. "I'm not—I don't easily accept others into my confidence. And the ones I have accepted either end up dead or betraying me..." She says the words quickly, like they're just a fact, but her voice cracks, and that sound has me on my feet and moving to stand beside her again. But I don't touch her this time, just give her my presence as she continues. "Thorne, I'm not good. I care for my people, yes, but I—the *things* I've done to protect Thayaria..." She's lost in her own thoughts, *finally* revealing her emotions, so I stay silent, even if what she tells me breaks my heart. Her expression steels, like she's going to tell me something truly terrible. "I planned to *kill* you when you finished getting me information about the rebels. I don't know if I would have, but I still planned—" The way her voice cracks tells me the risk she doesn't accept this bond is low. She cares for me, she just needs time to realize it. "And you don't even know—don't understand. My power, it's... my power is different. It's not good. *I'm not safe.*" Tears build in her eyes, but only a single teardrop escapes. I wipe it away, keeping my gaze locked on hers. While my curiosity about her power has plagued me for months, I don't press it. It's torture not wrapping her up in my arms.

"I understand why you would've planned to kill me. It was the smart decision, one I know that had our roles been reversed, Silene would have advised I do to you." I give her a nudge and a grin. "Laurel, I told you before—there's no part of you I fear. But let me amend that statement. There's no part of you I don't admire, that I don't respect. And there's no part of you I wish you to hide from me. I want to see every side of you, Laurel, even the parts you can't bear to look at yourself."

"What if I'm too afraid to show you?" she asks, so much vulnerability in her voice it makes me ache. I take both of her hands in mine, then cradle them on my chest, next to my aether-heart.

"You aren't, of that I'm sure," I whisper. "I know there's nothing you're too afraid of, even if you yourself don't believe that yet. It might take you a month or a century to trust me enough, but I'm patient. I'll make every day another opportunity to *prove* to you I'm worthy of your trust, that I'm worthy to stand by your side. And even if you never accept the mating bond, I'll still choose you. You can let that light swirl around your *aether-heart* for eternity. I'm not going anywhere." The words are truer than she knows. Even if she accepts the bond, I'll spend every day we're together trying to be worthy of her, even if I never achieve it. Lunaria appears, rubbing her body against Laurel's legs until she lets go of my hands and pets the massive cat. I laugh at the intrusion in such an intense moment, but it seems to calm Laurel, so I'm happy to let Lunaria into our space. "All I ask, Laurel, is that you don't give up. That you keep chipping away at that stony exterior and let me in a little at a time. It doesn't have to be every day, and you will inevitably put walls back up even as you drop others. But can you promise to give us a real chance?" I ask, holding my breath for her answer. She nods, and I release a sigh.

"Yes," she says, breathy, like a confession. I can't stop myself, and my lips crash onto hers. She meets my passionate embrace, wrapping her arms around me. I'm vaguely aware of Lunaria padding away, but my focus on Laurel is singular. I cup my hands under her ass and lift her, carrying her to the desk in the corner. With a blink, she removes everything from the top with magic, and I chuckle even as I continue my frantic kissing. I place her gently, so gently, on the desk. Then I rip open the top of her dress in one furious motion, exposing her perfect breasts.

The world around me disappears. I've imagined this moment, dreamed of exposing those perfectly blush nipples, so many times. But now that it's finally here, I can't believe I ever tried to construct the perfection in my mind. Nothing compares to reality, and an involuntary groan escapes me as I hold their weight in my hands. Laurel runs her fingers through my hair, and I bring my lips to her chest. I kiss my way across each breast, then suck one nipple into my mouth and bite down gently.

"Thorne," she moans, and it nearly undoes me. I bring the skirt of her dress up to her hips, running my palms across the soft and delicate skin of her thighs. Thank fuck she's wearing a gown today. She dips her head back, and I tease her with light touches on her inner thighs that move closer and closer to where I know she's already wet. She moans again. "Please," she whispers, but I hold back from giving her what she wants. I stroke my thumb across the barrier of fabric of her undergarments, but I don't move them to the side. She arches her hips toward me in a demanding motion. With a final sensual kiss, I lower her skirt, taking my time stroking her legs as I do. "Thorne," she whimpers, the word a plea, but I hold my ground. I bring my mouth close to her ear.

"I want you to be sure, witchling," I whisper, and she shivers. "Of us, and of the mating bond. When you're ready, I promise you our joining will be *electrifying*." I help her from the desk, then patiently wait for her to change into leggings and a tunic for a training session.

"They're asking for a route into the palace," Silene tells Laurel, Fionn, and me several hours later. After the meeting with the Council, Silene and Fionn visited the granary to check in with the rebels. They were trying to discover whether the rebels discovered the letter we stole. Instead, they'd received a message from Krantz, detailing plans to attack

Laurel and the palace. I guess they don't suspect us, at least not yet—not a promising sign that Nemesia isn't the mole.

It feels like eons have passed since I promised Laurel I would help convince the rebels to attack her instead of her people. So much has changed between us, and I'm even less interested in enabling her to put her life on the line than I once was.

"And they plan to attack in three weeks?" Laurel asks, wholly unphased by the news that the rebellion is planning an attack on her.

Silene nods. "That's what they said. They also mentioned a backup plan, but it's less than ideal, so they'd like us to sneak in three dozen rebels. And said that once we sneak the rebels in, we should make ourselves scarce." Laurel's calm somehow makes me more agitated.

"We obviously can't help them," I say with a voice that leaves no room for argument. "We need to cut our losses and move on. We've gained what we needed to." Silene and Fionn both look like they're about to agree, but Laurel cuts them off.

"No. If they can't get in here, who knows what they'll do to Arberly or the nearby villages. We'll let them attack, but in a controlled way." Every nerve in my body protests the plan. "There are many servants' entrances. You can tell them about one of them. We'll let them in, but I'll be ready for them." I dislike this plan, and I'm about to look to Silene for help to convince Laurel that this is madness when my friend adds her own twist to the scheme.

"Good point. We should rush our plans to take out their headquarters in Oakton and do it at the same time," Silene adds, and I slump in defeat. "It will probably be empty while they attack the palace, and we can send a group to the manor. We'll collect all the information we can from it, then burn it to the ground. It only brings our plans up by a few days, and this way we won't have any unnecessary casualties." I don't like this, and my agitation throws me off. I'm not used to getting so worked up, but the thought of Laurel putting herself at risk makes my skin crawl.

"If the timing of our attack on their manor coincides, the rebels will know we're working with you. Our ruse will be over," I offer, clawing for any excuse not to move forward with this plan.

"As you said, Thorne," Laurel says coolly, challenge in the gaze she lands right on me. "We've gained what we needed to. Time to cut our losses. Might as well go out with a bang." Her smirk is wicked, and if I weren't panicking for her safety, I'd growl back my own flirtatious barb.

"I think Laurel's right," Fionn says gruffly, and I give him a look of betrayal. "A lot of the rebels are just common folk, pulled into something they don't understand. We shouldn't punish them, at least not without a warning first." *Of course he would take the commoners' side.*

Laurel gives him a grateful nod. "We can tell the Council tomorrow morning and complete our plans." No. No, no, no. This isn't safe. I can't allow Laurel to put herself at risk like this.

"Laurel, can I speak with you privately, please?" I ask, trying and failing to keep the tension out of my voice. She follows me into my bedroom in the apartment. "I don't like this," I growl, my voice low. "It puts you in unnecessary danger. I know you haven't accepted the mating bond yet, so you don't understand the... *primal urge* I feel to protect you." She puts her hand on her hip, expression haughty and fierce.

"I'm the strongest fae to ever live, Thorne. I think I'll be okay," she snaps.

"*I* know that, but the mating bond doesn't," I practically choke out.

"I will always be a target. If it's not the rebels, it will be your father. If it's not your father, it will be the Queen of Delsar. If you truly intend for this to work between us, you're going to have to learn to live with my being in danger." Her eyes are bright, and it drives me mad. I understand her reasoning, but the protective urge is overwhelming. I swallow once. Twice. Then I take a deep breath, pulling myself together.

"Okay," I finally say. "But I want to be by your side, hidden." She starts to protest, the attitude I love so much rising to her expression. I know what she's going to say, so I hold my hand up. "Please, Laurel. I know you can protect yourself. But I *need* to be there."

I can feel the weight of this compromise between us. Me accepting her exposure; her accepting my protection. She studies me, and for once I understand the thoughts running through her mind—she also realizes how important this moment is for us.

"Fine," she says, and I loose a breath I didn't know I was holding.

I give her a giant cocky grin. "You won't even know I'm there, witchling."

The witch's great power was consuming her, becoming too much for her to bear. Those closest to her from the coven searched high and low for a solution to stop the madness they were glimpsing. No solution presented itself.

Unknown Story, Unknown Origin

"Follow me," Genevieve says, taking my hand in hers. I follow her through the bustling crowd of the Floating Market. I'd mentioned to her my love of the district at night, and she'd insisted on bringing me to her favorite places in the humid and damp bazaar.

We weave in and out of stalls where merchants sell silk scarves, roasted nuts, magical objects, and everything else imaginable. Despite the Market's position atop the salty water of an inlet on the coast of Arnia, the wooden walkway is sturdy beneath our feet. The sun has just started its descent in the sky, deep orange in the haze of the briny air.

"Where are we going?" I ask. Genevieve only turns her face back to me, joy written so clearly across her open expression, and smiles.

"We're almost there," is all she says before tugging harder and increasing our pace.

We near the end of the pier-like structure that halts abruptly at a cliff that soars a hundred feet above the water. The crowd has thinned significantly this far away from the hub of the market, and less than a handful of patrons stroll the walkway. When we reach the mass of rock, Genevieve jumps, grabbing a rope ladder expertly hidden in the crevices of the cliff. Her eyes are bright, and without speaking, she climbs.

"What are you doing?" I hiss, my heart rate skyrocketing.

"I'm going to our final destination. We need to hurry. Start climbing." Eyeing the flimsy ladder skeptically, I pause before sighing and beginning my ascent, limbs shaking involuntarily. Genevieve climbs quickly, her short frame scaling the cliff fully before I'm even a quarter of the way up. Black curls peep over the edge at the top as she peers down at me. "Come on!" she yells. "You're going to miss it!"

"Miss what?" I yell up at her.

"The view!" she cheers before disappearing from my line of sight. I move my legs and arms quicker, focused on not looking down. I've never been particularly fond of heights. Especially not while attached to a fraying piece of fabric turned into a makeshift support system. When I finally reach the top, I roll my body away from the edge, remaining prone on the ground as I wait for my racing heart to still. Genevieve nudges me gently with her shoe. "Just a few more minutes of walking and we're there."

Standing to follow her on shaky legs, the adrenaline still coursing through me, we walk a few more minutes along the edge of the cliff. I keep several feet of distance from the sheer drop on the other side. Noticing my breath quickening, I realize we've climbed even higher and now stand on the highest point of the shoreline for miles around. A few other couples sit spread out along the smooth rock. Genevieve finds us a private location before flopping down and patting next to her.

When we're both seated, I survey the view. Cobalt sea wraps around most of the view, the ocean turning more green-gray with each minute of twilight that passes. The sun almost reaches the horizon, and a vibrant explosion of tangerine, peach, and blush ripples across the sky. The fluffy clouds that perpetually surround Velmara light from within with the color of apricots. The smallest sliver of moon appears in the sky directly above us, and Genevieve sighs next to me. Her sweet scent wraps around us, and I can't help but let out my own contented sigh. Genevieve speaks softly, explaining the significance of the location.

"When my father still lived in Arnia, before he remarried, I had a nursemaid turned governess who was common born. She used to bring me up here in the evenings to watch the sunset and to distract me from the fact that my father wasn't around, even at night after his responsibilities had ended. I always felt like I was in the middle of the sky. We'd lay here until the sun had fully set, then she'd aerstep us home so we didn't have to make the long trek down the ladder in the dark. But we always climbed up. She said that I needed to learn that not everything required magic." The setting sun paints her face in a golden glow as she tells me the story. "I haven't come back up here in years. It's just as breathtaking as I remember it."

"What happened to her? Your governess?"

Genevieve swallows, turning eyes filled with grief upon me. "When my father remarried and gave me over to my Uncle Silas, she tried to sneak us both away. Silas was unkind to both of us. She feared for me and hatched a plan to take us deep into the Nivan Desert. Silas caught us and killed her on the spot."

"How old were you?" I ask, afraid of the answer.

"Twelve." Indignation fills my chest on her behalf. How dare her uncle murder the only parent she ever had right in front of her? If I ever meet the male, I may not have the willpower to bite my tongue. Or quell my magic. My shoulders tense with rage, but Genevieve strokes my shoulder and turns a small smile my way. "Don't be sad, Nemesia. She would have been so happy I found someone to share this secret place with. And she wouldn't have cared that you were Thayarian." She smirks, and I can't help returning the smile. "Is there somewhere like this in Thayaria? A secret place you'd show me if we were there instead of here?" I consider the question for a moment, knowing any answer I could give would inevitably be tainted by some trauma I've experienced.

"My favorite place in the palace is the archives, but they would underwhelm you after a lifetime spent in Velmara's archives." She starts to protest, but I laugh and cut her off. "They would. Velmara's archives are a hundred times what Thayaria has. Maybe more." I look down at my hands, deciding to open up and tell her about my *real* favorite place. "My family kept a cabin deep in the mountains to the east of the capital. Even after my parents died, I would go there every few months just to sit with the quiet. It's very different from here. You can barely see for all the trees that cover the landscape. It's eerie to some, but I love the feeling of being surrounded by the wild. Where you feel like you're in the middle of the sky here, I feel like I'm just another tree there, part of a larger ecosystem that's bigger than any of my problems. Part of a forest that will remain long after I'm gone."

She studies my face quietly, eyes searching. For what, I'm not sure. "You must have had the weight of many problems on your shoulders there," she finally says. Her honesty cuts like a knife. She's so quick to spot the truth of my feelings. But somehow, her calling them out so openly and directly makes them easier to talk about.

"Not so much in recent years. But after the war with Velmara... I disappeared into that cabin for far too long. Left my friend to deal with the aftermath on her own. I couldn't bear the weight of my guilt. My mother had always taught me that *the* most important battle strategy is knowing which you can win and which you can't. Laurel—the Queen—and I, we forgot that lesson after our parents died. And it cost us *everything*." My eyes drop to the ground as I think about what that *everything* entailed. Our childhood and young adulthood, the safety of the kingdom, thousands of Thayarian lives, our sense of hope for anything good in the world. Our ability to form meaningful relationships with anyone but each other.

Genevieve's soft hand wraps around mine and squeezes.

"You were so young," she soothes, but I scoff.

"Laurel was younger. And hadn't received nearly the education I had. I've always wondered... if I hadn't gone to that cabin—if I hadn't left her—would she have retreated so far into herself. When I finally came back, she wasn't the same female I knew. She was cold, calculating. Strategic to a fault at times. And instead of trying to help her find her way back to herself, I mimicked her stoicism, though I couldn't pull it off like she did. We became an impenetrable force, open only with one another. Neither of us able to move on from what happened. And now, three hundred years later, I've left her with no other confidants." A sob chokes in my throat, and Genevieve rubs soothing circles on my back. Even now, with a female who has experienced more trauma than anyone should have to, I suffocate others with my grief. Shame courses through my body, making the sobs worse. "I'm sorry," I murmur, and Genevieve lifts my chin, so similar to the way I had in my rooms when she'd told me of the Reshnar scholar.

"You have nothing to apologize for. I think you've been carrying this for a very long time. It's good to let it out." She smiles, and my heart squeezes in awe of this brave and open female. I wrap my arm around her and pull her in close to me, despite the risk of being so openly affectionate in public. She leans in, and the scent of parchment and vanilla wafts over me. It feels so much like home that my body aches to wrap myself around her and never let go. We finish watching the sunset, then lay on our backs to wait for the sky to fill with stars. When there's no light but that from the moon, she shimmies away from me and stands. "Time for the main event," she says with an excited mischief lacing her voice. I stand beside her and panic floods my system thinking about climbing back down the rope ladder in the dark.

"What do you mean? How are we getting down from here?" I ask, the fear in my voice obvious. She laughs.

"Not a fan of the climb?" I shake my head. "Lucky for you, we aren't going back the way we came. Unlucky for you, the only way back inevitably involves heights." With that, she turns and begins walking away, and I have to walk fast to catch her.

We stumble through the darkness for twenty minutes, rapidly dropping our elevation. Orbs of light twinkle in the distance, and the faint sounds of water splashing and people yelling tickle my ears.

"Where are we going?" I ask. She just wraps her hand in mine and keeps walking. The movement feels right, like we should never walk unless it's hand in hand.

The light grows brighter, and a cliff about thirty feet above the water appears. A stranger stands at its edge, soaking wet from head to foot in a short linen swim dress. The brightness allows me to see Genevieve's face, and her eyes study me for a reaction. I scan the cliff again, just as the female from before leaps off the cliff into the dark water below. I abruptly stop.

"No," I say involuntarily and pull my hand from Genevieve's.

"Yes," she says with a smirk, grabbing my hand and tugging me forward. I follow, despite my blood beating a fast rhythm in my veins. We reach the cliffside, where a dozen fae swim in the water below. Another rope ladder hangs from the cliff, and several people climb it, presumably to jump again.

"No, I can't—I don't like—we have to jump?" I ask, body deflating.

"It's either this or climb back down the rope from earlier. It's really fun, I promise. You'll be safe." I swallow, then search the ground for grass, a shrub, a small flower—anything I can grow to ease me down the cliffside. But Velmara isn't known for its smooth, rocky cliffs without reason.

Genevieve pulls her dress over her head, and my mouth goes dry at the nearly sheer shift she wears underneath, her small frame on full display. Then she turns back to me with a question in her eyes before pulling my tunic over my head. Lust heats her gaze when she exposes the bandeau I wear underneath. I've never been shy about my body or my sexuality, but now I shiver under her heated gaze.

"Do you want to stay in your leggings? Or take them off?" she asks quietly with a deep swallow. Her delicate throat moves with the motion, drawing my attention down to it and then farther down to the small, pert nipples that peek under her chemise.

"I'll take them off," I say with a husky voice, not recognizing myself. She nods, then helps me pull the fighting leathers off my body, fingers lingering over my skin as she pulls them down. I stand there in only my undergarments, unaware of our surroundings, attention focused solely on Genevieve. She scans my body, and I grin, confident in the line of my feminine figure toned with muscle. "Like what you see?" The words come out of me unbidden, and I tense. We've *definitely* flirted, but never this openly, especially not in public. I scan our surroundings. Thankfully, we're still alone up here. I'm about to apologize, or murmur some excuse, when her lips part and she exhales with a breathy sigh that *almost* sounds like a moan.

"I do." Her eyes meet mine, gaze unflinching. She's confident, no seed of doubt in her words or posture. I swallow, and that makes her break out in a cocky grin of her own. "Ready to jump?" I freeze. I'd somewhat forgotten about the reason we were undressing in my lust-addled distraction. While I fight the urge to run back away from the cliff edge, she picks up our clothes and places them in a basket that she lowers down toward the water. "No turning back now," she says with a glint in her eye. "Our clothes are at the bottom. Unless you want to stay standing up here half-naked, we have to jump in the water."

"I wouldn't mind staying half-naked," I involuntarily murmur, and her cheeks turn pink. But she takes my hand and leads me to the very edge of the rock. I look down and pale, trying to take a step back, but she holds me firmly in place, deceptively strong for her small stature. My palm sweats in hers, but she strokes my thumb.

"I've got you," she soothes. "On the count of three. One. Two."

Pulse racing, I close my eyes.

"Three!"

My thighs coil, and I lift myself up and out over the edge of the bluff. We both free fall, but Genevieve's hand never leaves mine. Air whooshes around me, and the white-blonde tendrils of my hair slap my face. An involuntary shriek leaves my lips, and Genevieve giggles in the air beside me. For a moment that could be seconds or hours, we fly through the air, adrenaline pumping through my veins as I face this fear with a female I've come to care deeply for at my side.

We slam into the water, the brisk, salty waves washing over us as we sink below the surface. Bubbles float around us as Genevieve hauls me upward, cresting the surface before me.

"You did it," she cheers and wraps her arms around me. As I tread water, I pull her into an embrace, and her arms circle my neck. We stare at one another for a beat. Her tongue brushes over her lower lip, and I track the movement. She wraps her legs around me, then leans in—

Someone yells at us to swim away from the landing spot so another can jump. Smiling, we both swim toward the sandy beach that was hidden behind the cliff face.

"We could have walked down to this beach all along!" I chide, but she only grins with an roguish glint in her eyes.

"We could have, but that wouldn't have been nearly as much fun."

Once we reach the beach, we quickly pull our clothes over our wet bodies and walk back to the castle, our hands brushing every few minutes. When we reach the wing where the archives and my room are located, I don't hesitate, pulling Genevieve toward my room. She doesn't protest, only gives me a suggestive look that has my body tingling. We missed the dinner hour, so a food tray filled with enough for two waits for us when we arrive. *Someone has noticed our frequent shared dinners.* I vow to consider the implications tomorrow, not wanting to ruin this perfect evening with my paranoia.

The room is dark when we enter, and I quickly light the sconces and candles, then throw her one of my tunics and a pair of leggings to change into. They swallow her, and the sight sends my blood racing. As soon as she's clothed in the dry tunic, Genevieve sits at the table and starts eating directly from the serving dishes, not wasting time making a plate. I chuckle.

"I'm starving," she explains with a grin. I only pick up a spoon and dip it directly into the bowl of spiced rice, then groan when it reaches my mouth.

"I'm starving too," I say with my own grin.

We finish dinner that way, eating with no propriety. Genevieve seems to enjoy the spectacle greatly, and I realize it must be because, to her, this is a great rebellion for a female raised by the Velmaran nobility. To egg her on, I dip a finger into the pudding and lick it off, and she squeals in delight before dipping her own finger in the bowl. We scrape it clean.

"Thank you for tonight," I say softly. "It's nice to take a break from all the books. Even if I had to literally jump off a cliff to get away from them." I give her a smile that she returns with her own sly grin.

"It was my pleasure." She bites her lip, tantalizing me. I swear she was leaning in to kiss me in the water, but I don't know for sure. And this is *dangerous* here. We stare at one another, the tension in the room coiling around us, thick as mist. "Kiss me," she finally says, breathless, eyes wide, and the small amount of control I had disappears.

I walk slowly to her side of the table, then angle my body behind her and gently sweep her black curly hair off her shoulder. Leaning down, I place the gentlest kiss to her neck, just below her ear, and she shudders. I kiss my way across her collarbone and up her jaw, delighting in the way she reacts to every one. When I reach her lips, I don't kiss them. Instead, I take her hand and tug her from the chair, then sit down and guide her to straddle my lap.

"Is this what you want?" I ask, my voice low. "Are you sure?" I have to give her another chance to say no, to walk away from something that might get her fired from the archives, or worse. But there's no hesitation in her expression, only heat and need gathered in those amber eyes.

"Yes," she whispers out, eyes darkening with desire.

I lean in and kiss her soft lips gently, and she moans. When I cup her breast through the tunic, she lets out a breathy sigh, and that seems to unlock something in her. She takes control, grinding her hips into me, kissing me with a demanding intensity that I match. My own hips arch up to meet hers, and I bring my hands down to cup her backside.

She removes my tunic, lifting it quickly above my head and throwing it across the room. With feral delight in her eyes, she undoes the clasp holding up the bandeau covering my breasts, then stares down at my chest as she continues to grind on my hips. There's a hunger in her eyes, like she's been waiting for this her whole life. I let out a moan, removing her own tunic and bandeau so that we're both topless. She leans in for another kiss, and the soft brush of our naked breasts has me clenching my thighs in desire. *I need more of her.*

I lift Genevieve from the chair and carry her to the bed, slowly removing her leggings so I can take in the sight of her. She blushes under my gaze, her confidence from earlier gone now that she's so exposed. But something tells me she doesn't want me to coddle her, doesn't want me to proceed carefully and gently.

"Touch yourself," I command, and her heated expression tells me my hunch was right. She does as she's told, bringing her fingers to the apex of her thighs, wet with desire. As she circles her center, she keeps her gaze locked on me, my boldness unlocking her own.

"Take your leggings off," she orders, and I'm happy to comply. Even as she touches herself, her eyes stay focused on me. When she lets out a delicate whimper, I can keep my hands off her no longer. Lowering my body to cage hers, we lose ourselves in the passion of kissing and limbs and darkness.

MAZUS

My eyes scan the ground far below, my vision excellent in this form. My armies—fae and human alike—train in their hidden camp in the northern mountains of Velmara, oblivious their King flies hundreds of feet above them.

Consume. Devour. Take.

The urge to swoop down and feast on their bodies, on the aether-force of the fae and the flesh of the humans, rips through me. For a brief moment, I almost give in, almost lose control... Grinding my teeth, I bank hard and turn back towards Arnia.

Landing in a clearing just outside the city, I fight with my frame, forcing the transition to fae. *It's getting harder and harder.* Brushing the thought aside, I aerstep to my suite in the Velmaran castle. The cold white tile on my bare feet cools the blood pulsing through my veins, and I drop to the ground and press my face against the floor.

After a few moments, I channel aether into a gentle and cooling breeze, allowing its magic to stabilize my pulsing skin. With a deep breath, I finally feel more fae than beast. I take one more inhale before standing and stalking to my study. A new letter sits in the basket reserved for incoming correspondence. Recognizing the seal, I open it swiftly, eyes hungrily taking in the update from my Thayarian contact.

Your Majesty,

Things are still progressing according to your plans here in Thayaria, though slower than we had both hoped. Laurel and Thorne have finally discovered the mating bond; however, based on their scents, one or both have not yet accepted it. I also don't believe they have been joined, and the research you provided me explained this conjugal step is critical in strengthening the bond and subsequent magical alterations. They have not announced the mate bond broadly, though whispers run wild through the Council of Advisors about how close they have become.

I know you have been hesitant to loop me into your plans with the Thayarian rebels, but I fear they will become a hindrance soon. I urge you to inform me of your intentions so that I can properly guide their strategy and direct the Council in ways that will help them, and you, achieve the right ends.

I will write again as soon as I have significant updates to share, as you know as well as I that these letters are dangerous and challenging to get out of Thayaria and into your hands alone.

Sincerely,

Your Faithful Ally

Rage rises within me, risking losing control of my fae form again. I crumple up the paper in my fury and toss it into the fireplace. *That stupid boy can't even get his own mate to accept him. What an imbecile.*

But I've been patient, waiting centuries to enact my plans. I can wait another few months.

Sitting at my desk, I read through the remaining correspondence. An update from the Head Librarian of the archives tells me Nemesia has taken the bait. I pen a letter to her, an invitation to another dinner, loathe as I am to spend more time with the churlish female. I need to make sure she's finding what I want her to find in those books, and nothing more. The Head Librarian also mentioned a budding romance between Nemesia and one of the younger librarians that could prove useful.

With my correspondence read and responded to, I aerstep to my research room below the castle, though very few of my experiments live here anymore. Most are housed deep in the northern mountains now, supported by my supply of thayar and closer to the leylines running through Velmara.

I pick up a vial of dark crimson liquid, then carefully pour a single drop of it onto a clear glass plate. Picking up another vial, I pour a second drop onto the plate, then close my eyes, whispering a spell. The two drops light up with an unusual glow, then slowly inch closer to one another until they combine into one large glob. The light brightens, and I smile wide...

"It's getting stronger," I say aloud, eyes alight with a manic and feral gleam.

Dual channelers are rare. They typically only occur when two powerful family lines with different magics intentionally ally themselves through marriage, with the explicit purpose of producing strong heirs. Common births of dual channelers are nearly unheard of, and as such, most dual channelers are well-known across the realms.

The Unabridged History of Magical Orders, Volume I

Thorne continues to *court* me, even as we prepare for an offensive attack on the rebels. We train together. We have meals together. We go on walks just to have an excuse to talk to one another. I feel myself letting him in more and more, and it's both terrifying and exhilarating. He told me that all I had to do was keep letting down walls for him, one brick at a time—asked me to promise to try. But what I didn't say, what I desperately wanted to admit, is that I'm *exhausted* from the effort of keeping those walls up for three centuries. I fear that once I crack one stone, the whole fortress will collapse, and I'm not sure if he's ready for that outpouring of emotion from me.

One night, he insisted on bringing me to a tavern for a pint of Thayarian ale. The patrons were nervous around me at first, but after a joke from Thorne and his announcement that the next round of drinks would be on me, the mood lightened. I envy his ability to charm any room he walks into, to light up whatever he touches. And when that light focuses wholly on me, I forget everything else around me.

After Thorne extracted himself from the dozens of fae who wanted to speak to the charismatic *Shining Prince*, we drank in a corner with Fionn and Silene, playing Skran and talking till early in the morning. Thorne's intolerance for Thayarian ale had him stumbling to the castle, insisting I was the most beautiful creature he'd ever seen. I feigned smirking disinterest, but the raw compliments lit me up from the inside out.

Today, the rebels will attack the palace. Fionn and Silene are helping them sneak in and will tell them I'm in the throne room with some advisors. While they make their way to my trap, a small group of trusted soldiers led by Carex will storm the rebel stronghold in Oakton. Unfortunately, none of the planted information we strategically leaked to the Council seems to have made its way to the rebels, signaling either Nemesia *was* working alone, or her counterpart has been too smart to share anything more.

Standing in my closet, I consider my appearance for the attack. I have a part to play, so I don the dark makeup and even darker clothing of the Witch Queen. The dress I select is a two-piece black velvet number. The top is long-sleeved, with a square neckline and hem that stops just below my bust. The skirt rests at my natural waist, with a sleek line that hugs my curves before flaring out. Several inches of my stomach are on display, and I've braided my hair in an intricate design that circles my head.

Thayar and laurel crown resting on my head, I survey myself in the mirror. The female staring back—the Witch Queen—is becoming unfamiliar to me after the months spent with Thorne, Silene, and Fionn. Lunaria rubs against my legs, startling me from my observation. I scratch her head until she purrs deeply, then aerstep both of us to the throne room antechamber, where Thorne awaits us.

The moment he sees me, his eyes hungrily track up and down my body, lust instantly darkening his eyes.

"Aethers, Laurel. You're going to be the death of me. The Shining Prince will be taken down by the Witch Queen after all, through tight dresses and crimson lips." He gives me a sly smirk. I bare my teeth in mock ferociousness, and his smirk turns to a full out grin. "You look similar to the first time I met you," he adds softly, threading his fingers through mine and bringing our foreheads together. The irony of the moment isn't lost on me. "Are you going to bewitch the throne room in the same way?"

"Yes," I breathe out, and the word sounds more seductive than I intend. He squeezes my hands, then releases me and pulls away.

"Don't make it too dark, or I'll lose the ability to stay hidden," he reminds me as he cloaks himself with light.

I nod, then will the room beyond us to dim. I gather the water in the air in an eerie mist, then stretch the plants across the tile so that they slither in serpentine spirals. Even though Thorne hides himself with his magic, I can see him clearly. A muscle in his jaw tightens, and his hands clench and unclench. We walk through the door of the antechamber together, Lunaria close behind. Thorne stands just beside me as I sit on the throne, body angled toward me in an athletic stance, as if he's ready to jump in front of the throne at any moment. Lunaria lays at my feet, tail swishing with interest and eyes glowing.

We wait several minutes, the anticipation building. I know that the longer they take to arrive, the more time Carex and his team will have to search the Oakton manor, but I'm anxious for the meeting to begin. Despite Thorne's protests, there are no Royal Guards here, so the silence in the room is oppressive. While we wait, I take deep calming breaths to center myself within the aether. I need to stay in control during the attack—I cannot slip and use too much aether. After another ten minutes, Lunaria yowls, alerting us to their approach, and I subtly put up a strong shield of light magic around Thorne to keep him safe.

The rebels blow the doors open with a magical explosion, then barge in. Their leader, who I now know as Krantz, stands in the middle of the group of three dozen fae, protected by those in front of him. *Coward.* Several others have his bright red hair—it's a family affair, apparently. I wait for their dust to settle before sealing the doors closed behind them with a strong gale, winding plants through the handles so they cannot escape. All at once, the group tenses, noticing that I'm here alone and there's no exit for them. Krantz only snarls.

"Now, now, there was no need for that," I coo. "The doors were unlocked, and I was waiting here to greet you." Three dozen apprehensive eyes glance around the room, though Krantz only pulls back his shoulders in arrogance. "Did you think I wouldn't know when you breached my palace?" I ask, mock pity in my voice. "Oh, you did. How unfortunate for you." I smile, wide and feral, as I let loose a wave of energy that shakes the room. Bits of rock and debris fall from the ceiling, not enough to hurt them but enough to make them duck out of the way and break their tight formation.

Krantz snarls, stepping to the front of the group. "It doesn't matter. There are dozens of us and you're alone," he spits, clearly trying to rally his team after my magic rattled them. He takes another step toward me, and Lunaria hisses.

"I'd be careful not to get too close to the cat. She's got a temper. And very big claws," I mock. Krantz sends at least a dozen hidden daggers whipping toward me, and I will them to break apart into tiny pieces. "I believe that is now the *third* time you've tried that on me. Hopefully third time's the charm, and you've finally learned you won't get a blow in that way." Krantz's eyes widen, and his jaw opens slightly, realization dawning across his features. "Ah, yes, I see you're realizing that the Prince did not hide you as well as you thought during that little attack on the thayar tower. If only he were as powerful as me, but alas, you allied yourself with someone whose magic is as apparent to me as your fear."

I hate mocking Thorne's incredible magical strength like this, but I need to keep his cover in case we need to use him with the rebels again.

Krantz bares his teeth at me, and the other rebels with him fan out in a semicircle around me with practiced movements, like they've drilled this repeatedly. From the corner of my eye, I notice Thorne's body tense as he watches Krantz with predatory intent. The posture matches Lunaria, who now stands, her graceful body angled and on alert.

"It's only fair that I trick you," I continue, "after you put on such a good performance when I had you in my cells. Here I thought you were a farmer, just trying to protect his family. I won't let you out of my clutches again."

"I *am* trying to protect my family, and all of Thayaria, from your wicked *blood magic*," he jeers. "Witch!" He spits at my feet, but the ire in his voice doesn't match his eyes, confirming my suspicion that he's using a convenient narrative rather than possessing any real belief that I'm a witch. All the rebels with him spit at my feet and hiss, raising swords over their heads in a pitiful semblance of a battle cry.

I only smirk, then will all of their swords to fly out of their hands in an instant. All but Krantz cower back in fear. When I stand, they back up, inching farther away with every lazy step I take down the dais. I'm eager for a fight with the bastard who's slipped from my clutches not once, but twice. Vines inch along the ground with me as I delicately make my way across the marble floor, my steps echoing loudly. A foot away from Krantz, I stop, though he doesn't flinch when my vines reach him and crawl up his legs.

"Your arrogance will be what brings you down," Krantz says with a quiet fury. With those words, the rebels snap into action, despite their fear, and magic of all kinds whips around me. The swords were clearly a distraction, and this is their code phrase, but my surprise only lasts for a beat before I spring into action, blocking their attacks with light shields that Thorne taught me to use.

Water honed into blades whip toward me, guided by currents of air. Daggers pulled from hidden locations spin end over end, guided by magic that ensures they'll hit their mark—me. I could halt the rebels where they stand, make them unable to move. I could make their hearts stop beating in their chests, but I don't. Centuries of keeping my magic secret prevents me from taking the easy way out, not to mention my fear that any large expenditures of aether will disrupt the balance of magic in Thayaria.

Instead, I block and dodge, sending elemental, conduit-based magic hurling toward them. Tiny discs of light, water blades, and reclaimed daggers fly from my hands. Thirty plus fae fight me alone, and I hate to admit it, but I might not have been able to keep up had it not been for Thorne's training. I move easily between shields and weapons of light, adding in other elemental magic as I dance across the throne room. Vines catch five of the attackers unaware, stealthily wrapping up their legs and bringing them down.

Their screams fade to muffled cries as the sprigs lock them in place and wrap around their mouths.

When a large, hook-nosed male nearly the size of Fionn gets too close, I'm forced to turn my back on him to get away, and a small female uses the opportunity to trip me. I fall to the ground but jump back up quickly, cursing my long velvet skirt. The hook-nosed fae pulls me into a headlock. I slam my elbow into his groin, then spin when his grip loosens. I kick him in the chest into Lunaria, who pounces on him, gouging his eyes out with a single swipe.

The closeness of the encounter rattles me. I use the brief respite to rip off my skirt at my knees, giving me more freedom of movement. When another fae nearly pulls me into his grip, I unleash the ruthlessness lurking just below my skin. I choke those trapped by plants by sending vines down their throats and up their noses. I rip air from the lungs of the three fae closest to me, but one of them is an air channeler and reverses my magic quickly. In normal circumstances, they wouldn't be able to overpower me, but between maintaining the shield protecting Thorne, the vines pinning down a dozen rebels, and the magic I'm using for hand-to-hand fighting, my magic is being pulled in too many directions.

Only two dozen fae remain, though I can't be sure. Magic continues to batter my shields from all angles, and Lunaria can't keep herself from the fight, her protective instincts making her absolutely feral. She swipes fae across the chest with her claws. The deep gouges slow them down but don't stop them entirely. Thorne stands anxiously next to the throne, desire to intervene written clearly across his expression. Several times he steps toward the fight with light gathered in his hands, only to step back. I need to focus, keep my attention away from him, but he's like a beacon to my magic with all that aether gathered around him.

A blonde female uses her speed to slice Lunaria's side. It doesn't bother the cat at all, likely a shallow cut, but I scream in fury, the room shaking with my ire. My eyes lock on Thorne's, communicating my desire to him instantly with no words. He nods. I see a subtle ray of light appear at Lunaria's side, lapping against the wound gently until it's healed.

My brief focus on Lunaria and Thorne costs me, and Krantz has moved in closer, a dagger in each hand. I will them to crumble, but they don't. Surprise crosses my features, and Krantz smirks. "Some of us have our own secrets, *witch*," he hisses before swiping the blade toward my stomach. I block the blow, but just barely. Krantz whips around me, slicing my arm. It's the first time anyone other than Thorne has spilled my blood in a very long time, and I erupt in fury.

"Get on your knees," I bellow with the aether-voice, this time with no guilt at using the magic. Krantz hesitates for a moment, like he's somehow immune to the voice, before dropping to his knees. Something about the movement looks voluntarily, unlike the stilted movements of those around him. About a dozen pairs of hate-filled eyes stare up at me from the ground as I walk slowly toward the group.

"This isn't the last time you will see us," Krantz hisses.

I'm about to command them to turn on one another, compel them to slit each other's throats, my loathing of using the aether-voice in that way be damned. I hesitate for barely a breath, calculating the benefit of keeping them alive for questioning or killing them now. Before I can act, those left alive disappear. They've aerstepped out of the palace.

I roar with rage. Thorne appears at my side, magic burned away.

"I hesitated," I scream, hating myself. "I could have killed them in an *instant*, could have ordered them to turn on one another, ordered them to stop breathing. But I hesitated to *plan*, to determine the perfect course of action, and they got away." I sink to my knees in anguish, my failure closing in on me. A too familiar weight settles on my chest, restricting my breathing. Thorne sinks to his knees beside me as I try to catch my breath through the panic-induced shortness of breath.

"You can't blame yourself," he says gently, rubbing my back. "They brought enough air channelers today that their plan was clearly to leave if they lost." Lunaria nuzzles her nose into my thigh, and I frantically check the spot where she was cut, but she's fully healed. Relief makes me breathe out deeply.

"Thank you for helping Lunaria." I rest my head against her side, letting her intense purring soothe my nerves. "And thank you—thank you for staying out of the fight. I can't imagine that was easy for you."

His hands clench, and his eyes harden. "No, it wasn't."

The room is littered with dozens of bodies, blood spewed across the floor and dripping from all the water left behind from the fight. "We should get help to clean this up," I say with a sigh, standing.

"Can't you just do your poofing trick?" he asks, and I can't help the small laugh that I let out.

"No. It's a long story, but once a fae has died, the aether leaves their body. My magic only works when aether is present." It's too much information, practically a confession about my magic. But Thorne doesn't pry, and I'm not panicked about the slip.

"Maybe you should get cleaned up first?" he suggests. "You're covered in blood, like literally every inch of your body. And you ripped off your skirt, which makes you look a bit unhinged. The smeared red lipstick and smudged kohl doesn't help with that either. It's *sexy as fuck*, but a little scary." He smirks, and I howl with laughter, clutching my side from the stitches.

"I don't think anyone has ever told me I looked unhinged," I say between gulps of air.

"That's what mates are for, witchling." He shoves my shoulder with his in a gesture that feels so natural, like we've been doing it for centuries.

Rolling my eyes, my magic gathers to aerstep us to my rooms, when I realize the rebels may have gone to the manor, where Carex and his team are sitting targets. "Oakton," I whisper. "We need to help them." Thorne's eyes widen in realization, and I aerstep us to the manor in Oakton, not worried about blowing Thorne's cover this time. My focus is singular—catch the rebels who got away.

Confused expressions line the faces of Carex and his dozen guards as they stare at the manor when we arrive, though they jump when they notice me.

"What's going on?" I demand, walking up to Carex. His gray eyes scan up and down my body in shock, and he takes a step back when I reach him. Beside me, Thorne makes a low noise in his throat. Carex bows, but keeps his narrowed eyes locked on Thorne.

"Your Majesty," Carex says tightly. "You should step away from the Prince." Now Thorne's low noise turns into a full out hiss.

"Tell me what's going on. Now," I command. Carex swallows and adjusts his grip on his sword.

"The manor is abandoned, Your Majesty. There is no one inside. There are also no signs that *anyone* has been here recently. No furniture, no paperwork, no signs of life at all. The information that this was a rebellion headquarters appears incorrect." Carex settles his hardened gaze onto Thorne, and I can see the mistrust bubbling in Carex again. The two males stare one another down, tension buzzing between them so thick I can almost see it. I step in before they come to blows.

"Did you check every room?"

"We did, Your Majesty. They either knew we were coming and cleared out *very quickly…*" He says the words mockingly, implying it's an impossibility. "Or—were never here in the first place."

"Say what you mean, *Captain*," Thorne growls with princely haughtiness, eyes narrowed. I turn on him.

"You're not helping," I hiss. "Go take a walk." He does, finding a group of three guards to converse with. The moment he's gone, Carex relaxes his tense shoulders and steps closer to me.

"Laurel, there were *no signs* of *any* activity in that manor. You must know what this means," Carex murmurs. I ignore his implication.

"Burn it down," is all I say before walking away from Carex. I won't entertain his prejudice toward the Velmarans. He tries to protest, but I hold up my hand to silence him and don't say a word. Blanching, Carex gathers several guards, and together they throw flaming torches into the windows of the manor. Air channelers provide encouragement for the flames, and soon the entire estate is blazing.

"What's going on here?" a human woman asks behind me. She's come from the village, and four others stand grouped behind her, likely sent to investigate the glowing flames that appeared in the sky. Her face lights up in fear when I turn toward her, and she takes several steps back. I realize I look like a nightmare, covered in blood and clothing ripped. Thorne returns to my side, placing a hand on my lower back in silent support. "Your... Your Majesty," she says, bowing quickly. The others around her drop into deep bows.

"This manor is a known location of rebel activity," I announce in a loud voice. Their eyes don't widen in shock—they knew about the rebels here. "They planned the attack on Arberly's merchant district in this very manor. Planned the attack on Rusthelm. Dozens of innocent citizens died because of their actions, not to mention the hundreds who were injured. They attacked children running in the streets looking for their parents. The Crown will not tolerate this." Using the newfound power Thorne has taught me, I command the sky, and cracks of lightning spear the manor. It explodes in light, and the faces of the villagers illuminate with reverent trepidation. Thorne squeezes my hand and leans in close.

"Nicely done, witchling," he whispers in my ear. I shiver at his closeness. Only a few feet away, Carex stares at us, eyes alight with ire.

"If you hear of any other rebel activity, please report it immediately. Oakton could be the next village the rebels go after," I warn as I study their faces. Resolve crosses several expressions, and I feel confident we've made a difference here today, despite not being able to take out Krantz and his leaders. Turning away from the departing group of villagers, I find the Captain of my Royal Guard.

"Carex, leave a few guards here to monitor the fire to ensure it doesn't spread," I order. He nods before jumping into command. When everything is settled, I aerstep Carex, Thorne, and the remaining guards to a small receiving room on the bottom floor of the palace. The guards immediately return to their posts, leaving Thorne and I alone with Carex.

"Laurel," Carex starts, still staring daggers at Thorne. I interrupt.

"I'm going to go clean up. Meet me in the Council chambers with the rest of the rebellion sub-committee," I order. Carex only nods, his face white as a sheet, as Thorne takes my hand, and I aerstep us away.

Twenty minutes and a quick bath later, Thorne and I sit in the Council chamber, awaiting the other advisors to debrief today's events. He disappears behind me, then reappears with a steaming cup of tea for me. I nearly groan at the aroma wafting up toward me.

"You're perfect, princeling," I moan with exaggerated sarcasm, even though I mean the words. He only winks, and I take a sip. It instantly soothes the nerves of the last several hours. Thorne grabs my hand under the table, absentmindedly threading his fingers through mine, stroking my thumb in gentle circles.

We sit like that in an easy silence for another twenty minutes. When I finish my first cup of tea, he simply asks, "Another?" When I nod, he stands and makes a second cup before returning to his seat and grabbing my hand again.

Fionn, Silene, and Admon enter the chambers, followed by Carex, Aria, Margery, and the other advisors assigned to tackle the rebel problem. Carex is still tense, his eyes roiling with a building storm. Once everyone sits at the large circular table, I brief them on what we discovered at the manor, and Carex has barely let me finish before he's spewing vitriol. His eyes don't leave Thorne, and the hatred I see in them has taken on a new level.

"This was an excellent excuse to get your best soldiers and the Captain of your Royal Guard out of the palace while *you* were attacked, Your Majesty."

"I'll say it again, Captain. *Say what you mean,*" Thorne growls, and I think I sense the barest hint of aether in his voice, but that can't be true. Only sitting monarchs can use the aether-voice. I'm too distracted by the thought that I don't step in before Carex makes his accusation.

"The Velmarans have betrayed you. This was a trap set by them. There's no other explanation."

The room erupts in chaos. Fionn stands abruptly, and Silene has to hold him back from Carex. Several of the guards draw their swords and point them towards Fionn, Silene, and Thorne, Carex included. Half of the advisors look like they're frightened, and the other half have their own magic swirling in their hands, ready to attack. And Thorne—Thorne has subtly pushed my chair back from the table and behind him, cooly and effortlessly angling his body in front of mine while making it look like he's only leaning back in his chair in nonchalance. Together we make the perfect picture of royal indifference, unbothered by the chaos of the room.

"Those blades are awfully close to being pointed at me," I say coolly. Carex immediately lowers his weapon, and the guards follow his lead, their gazes dropping in shame. "I've stated numerous times to this Council, and to you specifically, that the Velmarans have my full trust. Sit," I command. I stand and pace to the front of the room, taking control of the meeting, an unusual occurrence. "Did the rebels tell you anything that might explain this when you let them in?" I ask Fionn and Silene.

"No, nothing," Silene says, and Fionn nods.

I continue my line of reasoning. "While it's strange that the manor was abandoned, it could also be a coincidence that the rebels moved their stronghold before we attacked. It may also have been strategic on their part. They had a very clear escape plan today. I would not be surprised if they decided disappearing was in their best interest prior to launching an attack on me." What I don't say is that the rebels could also have been tipped off that we were coming by someone in this very room, or at least another councilor. Nemesia may not be working alone after all. Carex looks like he wants to protest, but Admon jumps in instead, ever the diligent supporter.

"What happened during the attack, Your Majesty?" His voice is soft, kind, and curious, and it makes the tension in the room dissipate slightly.

"It went as expected," I explain. "They were very prepared. I killed about two-thirds of them, but the rest escaped by aerstepping away the instant it became clear they lost. I also revealed to them that Prince Hawthorne lied about concealing them from me during the heist on the thayar tower. We've likely spoiled the ruse with the Velmarans."

"If I may, Your Majesty," Silene says, her use of my title startling me. But she's right to use it here, when tensions are so high. I nod. "They may have also discovered the letter we stole and made assumptions about what that meant about our intentions. I think they may have left the manor weeks ago, as soon as they suspected us, and used Fionn and me one more time to find a way in before revealing that they knew we weren't on their side. Their preparation today also tells me this is a possibility. They probably knew they were walking into a trap but were willing to risk it for the opportunity." I study Silene closely. Surely, she's also put together the connection about the rebels being tipped off. She must have a reason for trying to make it appear like their disappearance from the manor was the result of the missing letter.

"Sound reasoning," Admon praises. I sigh.

"For now, this is enough," I say, despite my disappointment at letting Krantz get away a *third* time. "I'll consider the situation carefully. We'll meet again in a few days to plan our next move, if we have one." Carex again tries to protest, but I shoot him a look that says I'm not in the mood, and he finally relents.

The group disperses, but Thorne stays at my side. Fionn places his massive body directly in the path Carex would need to take to reach me, arms crossed and staring daggers into Carex's back as he leaves. Silene quickly steps to my side, concern in her eyes.

"Are you okay? After the attack? Were you or Thorne injured?" Her features are etched, and I soften at her genuine interest in my well-being.

"I'm fine, and so is Thorne. Lunaria took a very shallow cut, but Thorne healed it instantly. Other than frustration that the rebels got away, I'm well." I look around the room to see if we're alone. When I spot none but the Velmarans, I ask Silene about her strategy in a hushed voice. "You put the pieces together, right? About the rebels being tipped off?"

She gives me a triumphant smile. "Of course. It's obvious there's someone else on the Council feeding them information."

"Then why did you bring up the letter?" I ask. Again, that sly and winning smile breaks across her features.

"Because I wanted to make whoever it is think we aren't on to them. Clearly, they spotted our strategic leaks and didn't spill those but still told the rebels we were coming. Let's see what happens now that we pretend we believe the letter caused the relocation." I nod, and I want to ask her who she suspects, want to ask her about Carex. My suspicion of him is only growing, but I'm not ready to make that accusation aloud. We'll need to proceed carefully around him. I sigh involuntarily, rubbing my temples from the headache forming. Silene hugs me.

"Will you come have dinner with us tomorrow? We have something special planned," she asks. Thorne's eyes widen at her, but she keeps her focus trained on me.

"Of course." She practically leaps with excitement before prancing away, hauling Fionn behind her as she leaves the room.

Hours later, Thorne and I are together in my sitting room, the late afternoon light spilling over us as he attempts to cheer me up by teaching me various small magic tricks—the kind that children learn to pass the time and show off for one another. My failure to take out the rebels made my chest tight, and as usual, Thorne immediately noticed and whisked us into my rooms to "hang out," as he had so casually said.

He creates animal shapes with light, having them dance across the ceiling while I laugh in delight. He scoffs when I immediately master the ability to make light shoot out of my eyes in rounded beams. We end the session in stitches as we shoot huge balls of light at each other that do no damage. It's friendly and normal, though I can't shake my feeling of disappointment.

Thorne takes my hand when he senses my mood shift again. "What's going through that mind of yours, witchling?" he asks, a familiar phrase at this point. I don't know how to answer him, don't know how to explain that sometimes it's all just *too much* to process and think about. And lately, that *too much* feeling has only grown with the flower declining, then the rebels, then Nemesia. I say the only thing I know with certainty.

"I need to get out of this palace." My voice cracks with emotion.

Thorne is instantly up, my hand in his. "Take me with you," he implores. "Please." Without answering, I aerstep us away.

Laurel

Any magic practiced without the aid of a conduit for aether—water, plants, air, metal, or light—is considered witchcraft and is forbidden. The most well-known witchcraft is blood magic. Blood magic refers to the act of using blood, typically fae blood, as a conduit for the aether. Very little is known about blood mages, but most scholars agree that the use of blood unlocks powerful and nearly limitless abilities, especially when combined with spellwork. For this reason, blood magic is an abomination, an evil practice that is illegal in all kingdoms of our realm.

The Unabridged History of Magical Orders, Volume I

We step into a clearing in the southernmost tip of Thayaria. It's much warmer here, only a half day's sail from the coast of Reshnar. The hotter temperatures mean the foliage has almost fully regrown after Abscission. Towering maple trees create a canopy over the small glade, and bright pink, white, and red azalea bushes bloom with tiny flowers in a circle around us.

"Where are we?" Thorne asks, eyes vivid with wonder.

"This is where my mother grew up. Humans live all over Thayaria, but they're most concentrated on this small peninsula. My mother grew up in a small home built in this clearing. She planted these azalea bushes as a child—they were her favorite."

"I always forget that your mother was raised by mortals. What happened to her home?"

"It fell apart. My parents were well into their third centuries when they had me. Structures built by human hands aren't meant to last more than a few hundred years. It was gone before I was even born. But my parents kept this clearing undeveloped so my mother could come back here. Some of my earliest memories involve running around this little circle, my mother chasing me." I smile, lost in the memory, and Thorne wraps his arms around my waist from behind. These small moments of physical intimacy are becoming more and more familiar between us.

"It's beautiful here," he whispers in my ear, then kisses my neck. I arch my back into him, and he tightens his grip.

"There's a small estate just over the hill there. It looks over the sea. My father built it for my mother, who loved this region and spent most winters here, where it was warmer. She never adjusted to the frigid air of Abscission in Arberly. They used to hold court for humans at the estate."

"Do you come here often?"

I shake my head. "Not as often as I should. I haven't been able to bring myself to hold court at the estate—it reminds me of them too much. But I also can't leave it to rot, so it sits here empty," I admit, though I leave out how I feel like the estate has become a ghost, reminding me of my parents and hollow of the life it once had. Unwrapping Thorne from my body, I take his hand and lead him to the stone path that will take us to my parents' second home. "There are human servants who maintain the estate. It's a way for me to employ as many humans as I can in the region to bolster their economy," I explain to him as we walk. "I suspect we're going to surprise, and potentially terrify, a few of them."

"Good thing I can charm anyone," he teases, and I roll my eyes.

When we arrive at the home, my breath catches at the beauty of the grounds, despite the hundreds of times I've visited. The front of the main house comprises four massive floor-to-ceiling windows facing the sea. Lush green grass covers the grounds that decline slowly to a small, private sandy beach. The barrier of mist that circles Thayaria is about a half mile out from the beach, allowing for enough space to swim. In the late afternoon light, the house sparkles from within.

Turning to Thorne, I watch as his eyes dart from the house to the beach and back again. "Ready?" I ask. He nods.

We walk in through a side door and down a marble lined hallway to the main entrance of the home. The foyer is made of the same dark green marble of the palace throne room, a massive black iron chandelier lighting the room. Matching staircases lead up to the second floor on both sides of the foyer. Instead of heading upstairs to the main living area, I release Thorne's hand and walk quietly toward the kitchen, where I know most of the servants are gathered.

When we enter the warm and lively galley for the estate, a dozen humans startle at my presence. Many of them have never met me. Their nervous glances tell me they're uncertain what to make of this surprise visit. The main housekeeper, Meera, an older woman who travels to Arberly once a year to update me on the status of the estate, smooths her skirts and dips into a deep curtsey, and the rest of the servants awkwardly follow her lead.

"Your Majesty," Meera says calmly. "What an unexpected but delightful visit from you. Welcome back to Eless Estate. How can we assist you today?"

"Thank you, Meera," I tell her with a reassuring smile. "I'm showing His Royal Highness, Prince Hawthorne of Velmara, some of my family's favorite places." Hawthorne bows deeply in respect of the humans, and it warms that place in my chest I'm learning is reserved just for him. The expressions of the humans are split equally between fear and awe.

"We've heard of the ambassador from Velmara even all the way down here," Meera says with the smile of a courtier. "I'm happy to see the Prince has been a trustworthy emissary." I inwardly applaud her careful navigation of a situation that must feel extremely uncomfortable for the humans here.

I smile. "Yes, he's proven to be a true ally of Thayaria. Please, don't fret over our presence. You can prepare my suite and the guest room down the hallway for the Prince. Other than troubling you for dinner, which we'll take in my suite, you may continue your usual routine. We'll be on the terrace." Meera nods in acknowledgement, then quickly sends various servants off to complete preparation tasks.

Thorne follows closely on my heels as I lead him up the stairs and out a set of double doors to the second-floor terrace. It faces away from the sea but overlooks the misty rolling hills of the southern part of Thayaria. One side has a pergola covered in fragrant wisteria, the other side lined with padded outdoor furniture. I flop down onto a chair. Sprawled across the chaise lounge, the sun beams down from low in the sky, and I feel that first warmth of spring begin to unthaw my bones. Thorne pulls a chair up close so that he can hold my hand.

"Do we care if the servants see us being affectionate?" he asks with a teasing tone that doesn't meet his searching eyes. It's a fair question, one that I'm not sure how to answer. I think for a moment.

"The servants here are from families who have served the Elestrens for centuries. I believe they're trustworthy. And their eyes are very sharp. They'll likely suspect either way. So no, we don't care." The admission is exhilarating.

"In that case," he says with a sparkle in his eyes. "Scoot up." I lift my back, and Thorne steps his long legs over the back of the chaise so that he's seated behind me, my back nestled against his chest between his legs. I instantly clench my thighs, need coursing through me. When he runs his hand down my braid and loosens the weave, I think I might light on fire.

Thorne shakes out my hair. "Much better," he growls, running the strands through his fingers. When the silky locks bore him, he moves his hands to my shoulders and massages the knots out of my neck. I moan in appreciation. "I must know—what do you think the temperature of the sea water is right now? Swimmable for a Velmaran with very little cold tolerance?" he asks, and I laugh.

"I should've known you'd be drawn to the water."

"I love the water, especially the open sea. It's one of my favorite places to think."

"I prefer my water heated. A hot spring or a bath."

He laughs at that remark. "I've noticed, witchling," he murmurs in my ear, and I shiver.

"To answer your question, I think the water might still be too cold for a Velmaran. But us Thayarians love the bite this time of year, so maybe you need to try it out anyway."

"Only if you come with me," he whispers, and I swallow before nodding, imagining us taking a dip in the frigid waters in nothing but our undergarments.

We stay there until the sun sets, trading flirtatious comments and toeing the line of propriety with our touches. Meera arrives and clears her throat, causing me to practically leap from the chair in my embarrassment of what she's seen, despite my earlier statement to Thorne.

"Your Majesty, Your Highness," she says with a small dip of her head. "Your rooms are ready, and dinner will be served soon."

"Thank you, Meera," I tell her, my cheeks heated. She walks away with a mischievous smile on her face, like she knows exactly what's going on and plans to tell the entire staff. I sigh, and Thorne takes his time standing, stretching his arms over his head.

"Shall we?" he asks. I nod and lead him back inside and down the left hallway, stopping at a door carved with azaleas.

"This is your room," I inform him, though I instantly regret my words when I see the way his face falls.

"And would you like me to go there now?" His voice is tentative and uncertain, so unlike the male I know him to be that it gives me butterflies. Without thinking, I shake my head, and he gives me a dazzling grin that takes my breath away. "Lead the way to *your* suite, then, witchling."

We walk to the end of the hall, to a set of wooden double doors carved in intricate designs of thayar flowers, laurel wreaths, and mountains. I push them open, bracing myself for the suite that's filled with too many memories. Several rooms make up my parents' former apartment. A sitting room with a small dining table, two offices, a bedroom, and a bathing chamber. I swallow, unable to hide the nervous energy this place brings to me.

"These were my parents' rooms. I've had them completely remodeled and redecorated, but it's still hard for me to be in here sometimes." The admission should shock me, but at this point I'm desensitized to the way Thorne's presence makes me open up parts of myself I thought were long buried. He only kisses my hand.

"Why not stay somewhere else? I'm sure the servants could prepare other rooms."

"Because I—I think I'd like to make happy memories here," I whisper. "I used to love sneaking in to snoop through their offices. My father kept a small jar of my favorite candy he would always hide in different places in his office for me to find." I smile at the memory. "And this small balcony over here." I gesture to my right. "This is where I read my first *saucy* book, in the summer sunshine. I remember being so worried my parents would step away from their work and look over my shoulder." Thorne laughs, deep and throaty. "I modeled my bathing chamber in the Arberly palace off the bathing chamber here, when I renovated the rooms usually reserved for the Chair of the Council of Advisors."

"I *knew* you couldn't have been staying in the royals' suite," he says loudly, as if I've answered a question he'd been pondering for months.

"I don't use their suite at the palace. It's... it's where they died," I whisper again. "So, I've always just used the rooms down from the Council chambers." He touches his forehead to mine.

"I'm in awe of you, your strength and your resilience."

"Thorne..." I sigh his name. "There's—there's something I need to tell you. That I *want* to tell you, but that I'm terrified to trust you with," I admit, my heart racing.

"Whatever it is, it won't change how I feel about you. That I can promise. And you can take all the time you need," he promises, squeezing my hands. I nod, looking into the pools of olive and mossy green staring back at me. There's a knock on the door, and we both jump. I clear my throat.

"Come in," I say with a voice that sounds guilty. So much for keeping this from them. Meera, along with several other servants, brings in endless trays filled with steaming food, laying the dining table with the spread. "This is incredible. Thank you. Please, take the evening off. We have everything we need." Meera nods, and the servants leave quietly. "I'm actually starving," I tell Thorne, grateful for the distraction and the excuse to stall. He looks me over carefully but says nothing.

I load up a plate with the aromatic and delectable food, then go to the patio to watch the rest of the sunset. Thorne follows and creates several glowing orbs of light that bob around us. When the sun reaches the horizon, it lights up the mist barrier, making the sea look like its glowing pink and orange.

"The mist is beautiful at sunset," Thorne remarks in awe, finishing his dinner. "I see why you keep it up. Besides the protection, of course." He winks. I take a deep breath. It's now or never.

"I can't lower it," I croak out, desperate for him to know my secret, even while every molecule in my body fights this admission. His eyes widen in shock.

"What?" he whispers.

"When I put it up, I wasn't fully *aware.* I was grieving my parents and knew I was losing the war. I went to your father. Offered to marry him, practically begged him to end the war. But he refused. He told me I'd missed my chance and sent soldiers to slaughter my remaining army. I got there just as an assassin sent a blade hurtling towards Nemesia's chest, and I knew it wouldn't miss. I lost control, and I barely remember what happened. I just know I wanted it all to end, wanted my people safe, and the Velmarans gone. I—to be honest, I didn't really even want to live anymore. I thought if I just hurled every bit of magic out it might stop your father, even if it killed me in the process. I passed out, and when I woke up several days later, there was a barrier of protective mist surrounding the kingdom. *No one,* not even Nemesia, knows that I can't lift it. I've pretended all this time that I just want to keep it up for the safety of the kingdom. But no matter how hard I try, no matter how much magic I hurl at it, it won't lift." The words rush out of me, and my hands shake at finally—finally—telling someone this truth. My eyes dart back and forth between the ground and Thorne, wanting to know his reaction but afraid of it all the same. He only continues to stare at me calmly, thoughtful and silent, so I continue.

"It's why I've spent centuries training my magic. Practicing control. I never want to lose control like that ever again. I *won't* lose control like that ever again. Because my breakdown has *trapped* my people here for centuries." I taste salt in my mouth, surprised that tears run down my face, but I ignore them. "The thayar flowers are declining because the magic of Thayaria is declining. I can *feel* it. And every single day, I ask myself if it's because of the mist. If the massive amount of aether it takes to keep it up is draining my kingdom of the magic that runs through it. It's the only logical explanation."

Thorne stands, and I tense, unsure what he's going to do. He walks around the small coffee table, then drops to his knees in front of me. Taking both of my hands in his, that beautiful, handsome face stares up at me with *so much* compassion and adoration in his eyes that I can't bear to look. My eyes dart to the ground, undeserving of this male who sees the best in me. He gently grips my chin, bringing my gaze back to his like he's done so many times before, forcing me to face my demons with him.

"Laurel," he breathes, "you were *twenty* years old, young even by human standards. Still a child by fae standards. Fate, or the gods, or a prophecy—whatever determines these things—blessed you with an indescribable amount of power and very little guidance in how to use it. Your parents had been murdered, your best friend on the verge of death. You should not—*cannot*—blame yourself for this, yet I've seen the guilt you wear for the months that I've been here. I see the fear you have of your own power. You may play dress up as the villain my father created, but you are no more villain than I am. Even if the mist is responsible for the flower declining, *it's not your fault.* If anyone is to blame, it's my father."

I know I need to continue, need to tell him *all of it*, but I'm shaking with fear. Once he knows this last secret, I'm sure he'll walk away from me, walk away from the mating bond.

"There's more." My words are the smallest whisper, so quiet I'm not sure I've even said them aloud. He only squeezes my hands. My breaths are coming quickly now, and I realize I'm panting with anxiety as the tears flow freely. "My magic..." I start, struggling to say more. I pause to pick at my fingernails, at a loss how to explain something that only my parents and Admon ever knew. "My magic is different," I finally say, and Thorne laughs.

"That much is obvious, witchling," he coos, and for once the nickname makes me wince, too close to the truth. I take a deep, steadying breath, letting Thorne's scent wrap around me and provide the comfort I need to continue, even if he may not be here when I'm done telling him.

"Channelers need a conduit for the aether. Water, plants, air, metal. *Light.* When a fae performs magic without the use of one of those conduits, we classify it as witchcraft. Spells fueled by the aether in blood," I explain. He nods with a look of confusion. He knows all of this already. *I'm stalling.* "I'm no blood mage, Thorne. I swear that to you." My lips tremble, and I look to the sky, seeking anywhere to look but his eyes. "But my magic is just as *perverse*. I don't need a conduit. Whatever I will, whatever I desire, can simply happen, as long as aether is present. I try to limit my magic in front of others and only perform what could be done through conduits, but sometimes I slip. Like the poofing trick you've seen so many times. If I wanted to, I could stop the heart of every magical creature around me with a single thought, could freeze their limbs so they can't move. I could will the aether that creates the world to simply cease." I try to huff out a laugh, but the noise is hollow. "If witchcraft is practicing magic without a conduit, then I am indeed the *witch* your father has made me out to be. My magic is vile and perverse. *Corrupt.* At least blood mages need blood to perform magic. At least they have boundaries around what they can perform. I have no such limits. I'm an *abomination*." The words shudder out of me for the first time in my entire life, my deepest secret and most honest truth, and I brace myself for his rejection.

Thorne stands and walks to the edge of the balcony, bringing me with him. He scoops me into his arms, then leaps off the second story to the ground below, using his fae strength to soften the landing. I yelp, and he chuckles, but says nothing. Murky confusion makes my thoughts slow. Is he going to take me somewhere to kill me, rid the world of my vile magic? The voice that sounds like my parent's whispers that this is what they always warned me about. *If you tell anyone about your power, they'll kill you, Laurel. You must keep it a secret, always.*

He cradles me against him, and I let him, not wanting to let go of the moment. I'm sure that everything's about to come crashing down in the worst possible way. He picks his way down the stone path, back to my mother's clearing. The sun has fully set now, and the stars are blurry spheres in the sky, mist blocking their piercing light. The moon emerges from behind a cloud, and I let out an involuntary gasp. It's a rare blood moon. The last one to shine over Thayaria occurred on the date of my birth. The light has an eerie red glow as Thorne carries me through the ring of azaleas and across the glade.

When we reach the middle, he sets me down on my feet. Nerves wrack my body, and I fight down the urge to run away. *If this is my end, then it's one I deserve.* Thorne drops to his knees before me. Everything goes silent around us, like the stars and moon, cicadas and owls, hold their breath in anticipation of Thorne's next words. Mist gathers thickly around us, so that all I can see is Thorne kneeling at my feet. I'm not sure whether I'm creating the mist or whether it's a natural phenomenon, but it casts everything in a reddish hue. I'm holding my breath, not ready for Thorne to speak, and yet desperate to hear his deep voice.

"Laurel Elestren, Queen of Thayaria, Mate of My Aether-Heart," he murmurs reverently, still kneeling in front of me. "You're the furthest thing from an abomination I could ever imagine. Both of my hearts ache to hear you say such things about yourself. Our *actions* define our character, Laurel, and for three hundred years you've done everything you can to protect your people, even painting yourself a villain to the rest of the world to keep curious minds from trying to enter the mist for fear of you. You make hard choices every single day that protect your soul from corruption, unlike my father, who is the real abomination. Your magic does not define you, and it certainly doesn't make me desire you any less. Fuck, Laurel, your power is sexy as hell." Tears flow down my cheeks again, though I'm not sure they ever stopped. I drop to my knees, matching his pose. Taking his face in my hands, I bring my lips to his, softly, trying to convey so much with that one kiss. It's wet from my tears, slow and soothing. When we pull away, he wipes my cheeks delicately and smooths down my hair, then laughs. "I have to tell you, witchling, your secret wasn't all that secret. I'd already guessed it," he teases with a wink, and I smack him across the chest. "Maybe not the *full* extent, but I knew you could control magic without a conduit." I give him a shy smile and he pulls me into him, holding me close before coaxing me to sit on the ground, legs tucked underneath me. The hum of cicadas returns. Owls hoot, and the mist clears. I laugh loudly, and soon Thorne joins me.

"Why are we laughing?" I ask, and he shrugs, the moment so similar to the first time we admitted secrets to one another that it sends goosebumps up my arms.

"Because we're deranged, both of us." That makes me laugh even harder. Thorne suddenly goes serious. "Since we're trading secrets, I have one more to tell you." I wait for him to continue, nervous about what he'll reveal. "I haven't told you this, but it's only because you've been so secretive and defensive about your magic. I swear. I wasn't trying to hide anything of myself from you." Thorne takes a deep breath. "I think my father is an *actual* blood mage. That's the secret I believe my mother discovered about him, and how he killed her so easily. When I came here, I had my own plans... I wanted to get close to you to discover how blood magic worked, to uncover a way to stop my father. That was my real motivation for wanting to become allies. And I—I thought I could seduce the information out of you." He gives me a sheepish look, though there's fear and anticipation in his eyes.

I still. The news should make me question Thorne immediately, should make me question the relationship we've slowly built these last months. And aethers, *of course* Mazus is a blood mage. It makes so much sense. But I'm surprised to find that the information doesn't change anything about how I feel about Thorne. I trust him, implicitly, and I'm not exactly sure when that change occurred. I open my mouth to tell him that, but he continues on, words frantic, like he might lose me if he doesn't get everything out.

"Please believe that very early on I realized you weren't a blood mage. I think my desire to be close to you was never *really* about discovering more about your magic, though I used that as an excuse for myself initially. The moment I met you, I was desperate to see you again, to get to know you. And *aethers* Laurel, you seduced *me*. There was not a single moment that I was in control of my reaction to you." His eyes are beseeching, and I decide to put him out of his misery.

"I believe you," I say quietly, and he offers a slow and tentative smile, squeezing my hand tightly. "But let's promise to each other now, no more secrets." The words are a vow I don't fully understand. Thorne nods somberly and reaches out his hand.

"No more secrets." He shakes my hand, like we're sealing a deal. Suddenly, the source of my magic—my aether-heart—grows hot and bright. I clutch my chest, gaze locked on Thorne's concerned eyes. "Laurel," he yells, wrapping me in his arms tightly before pushing my shoulders back slightly so he can examine my face. "What's wrong?" Panic laces his voice, but I can only laugh. His brows furrow in confusion and fear, hands stilling on my shoulders.

"Thorne," I whisper. "I think—I know—I just accepted you as my mate. I can feel you, in here." I point to my chest. "My aether-heart is usually chaotic, but your presence is... *soothing*. It feels calm, like it's wrapped in a soft, glowing blanket." Thorne's eyes brighten, and now tears build in his eyes.

"Are you sure?" The question is so tentative, somehow conveying understanding if my answer is no. I swallow, nerves and butterflies and fear and a thousand other emotions running through me. *You could lie.* I could wait a little longer, really examine whatever's changed deep inside of me. I could plot and scheme and control every aspect of telling him about us. Admon still hasn't found anything useful that might tell us about what it could mean. The words are on the tip of my tongue, but then I pause. Every moment between us flashes across my mind. Every cup of tea he's made, every time he's opened himself up to me, every time the heat between us has felt unbearable. Fingers brushing across the lightning bolt necklace he gave me, my smile is so wide it practically hurts as I nod my head.

"I'm sure." The barely held back tears gathering in his eyes lose their battle and stream down his face. Strong arms wrap me around my middle, hauling me to my feet and then squeezing even tighter when we're standing. My own tears leak slowly down my cheeks as Thorne caresses my back and then my hair. He finally releases me from the hug, though his big, warm hands wrap around mine as he stares into the center of me, all the way down into my aether-heart.

"My Queen," he whispers, kissing the top of my head, my forehead, my eyelids, my lips. "My mate. *My Laurel.*"

The witch and the fae fell madly in love, despite all the warnings about what might happen if they gave in to the bond fate made for them. The Mages, that ancient sect of ichor-worshipping fae, were displeased by the power the witch and the fae could command once they were united. It launched a war that would change the very fabric of the world for millennia.

Unknown Story, Unknown Origin

I aerstep us back to the suite at the estate, and a feral energy consumes us both. His hands explore every inch of my body as he kisses me with a fierceness that makes me moan, a low and humming noise from the back of my throat. The sound causes him to take my face in his hands and angle me to deepen the kiss. I don't know where one of us begins and the other ends, our bodies are so intertwined with one another.

"Laurel," he groans between kisses. I only pull him closer, unwilling to break the current of energy thrumming between us. After months of holding back, I *finally* allow myself to touch him, unrestricted, and I can't stop now that I've opened that flood of need. My hands explore every hard line of his muscles, noticing the way he flexes under my touch. He pulls back from me and gives me one of those classic Thorne grins, dimple exposed, and I can't keep my lips from kissing that tantalizing spot where his cheek hollows out. His resulting moan is reverent, and his hands take their time as they smooth up and down the curve of my waist.

When his hands finally still, they grip my hips firmly, not hurting but giving me the delicious feel that I'm *possessed* by him. I hum my satisfaction against his mouth, and he only grips me tighter, fingers digging into my love handles. I need to see more of him, need to explore every inch of his hard body.

Tentatively, I grab the bottom of his tunic and break our kiss to look up at him, a question in my eyes. The burning inferno that is his expression tells me I can do whatever I want, but I wait for him to nod. I slowly inch his shirt up his chest, hungrily taking in his tanned and toned stomach. When I reach his collarbone, he takes his hands off me for the briefest of moments to rip the shirt from his body, but I whimper at the loss of his touch. His resulting smirk tells me he knows exactly what I'm thinking and that he *likes* it. He drinks me in hungrily with his eyes.

"Your turn, witchling. Take off your clothes." The primal demand in his voice makes my skin prickle and my thighs clench together, but we haven't spent months delighting in the game of catch and release with one another for me to give in so easily. I give him my best haughty expression, pure mirth in my eyes.

"I don't take orders from *princes*. I'm a *Queen*." His eyes darken with need.

"You wicked little thing," he says slowly as his lips spread wide in a grin. "Witchling, *please* take off your clothes." I shiver at the way he says *witchling*, deep in his throat. But I only shrug, like I'm considering his request. He grips my waist again and hauls me to him, devouring my mouth with another breathtaking kiss. When he breaks the kiss and I whimper, he gives me a challenging look that says he thinks he's won this round, but I'm not giving him the satisfaction. At least not without a little more torture.

"I am feeling rather warm." I give him my best impression of a flirty Thorne wink, and it makes him chuckle as he cups his hands on my ass. I untangle myself from him, then slowly ease my leggings down, then my undergarments, never taking my eyes from his. My agonizing pace is intended to taunt him, and it works, if his feathering jaw is any sign. My tunic is long and covers most of my delicate parts, which makes Thorne growl in frustration. He tries to pick up the lacy fabric of my undergarments, but I will them out of existence the moment his hands clasp around them, earning me another growl.

I turn my back on him to walk to the bar cart in the corner, emphasizing my swaying hips with each step. I intend to pour myself a glass of wine, but within seconds firm but gentle hands have me by the waist, spinning me so that I have to look into his pupil-blown eyes. He kisses up the column of my throat, moaning with each press of those full lips to my now-glistening skin. Just like in the hot spring, he weaves his fingers through my hair so he can pull my head to the side and lean down to whisper in my ear.

"I like you teasing me. But just know, witchling, that *I can give as good as I take.*" A delicious warmth crawls up my body, and I close my eyes with a small sigh. With that, he releases me, backing himself up a few paces and staring me down with a smirk. My body aches for his touch, and he knows exactly what he's doing to me.

Keeping my gaze firmly on his, I delicately unlace the tie at the top of my tunic, exposing a small bit of cleavage. Then I sweep my hair off my neck and arch my back in the movement, knowing exactly what it does to my neckline. My fingers graze delicately over the hem, about to tease him more, but Thorne's impatience gets the better of him. In an instant, he's in front of me. He rips the tunic and the bandeau underneath straight down the middle, exposing all of me in seconds. A noise that's half yelp, half moan escapes me, but Thorne's lips crush mine in an all-consuming kiss, stifling the sound. He kneads both of my breasts while I run my hands across his smooth, hard chest. When we break apart again, I'm about to make a biting comment about how I won, but his words still me.

"Aethers, Laurel, you're perfect," he whispers in my ear, sending shivers down my spine. Suddenly, the game we're playing is over, and only pure, raw need remains. The small of my back presses against a wall as Thorne leans over me, but I'm not exactly sure how we got there. *Did I aerstep us without realizing it?* But then Thorne is kissing my neck and my collarbone, and I don't care about anything except the feel of his firm body against mine. *My mate. My mate. My mate.*

He cups my ass, lifting me, and I wrap my legs around him. I'm completely naked, but the fabric of his pants blocks the friction I desperately crave. He growls my name, and it sends a wave of hot, slick pleasure shooting across my skin. If I wasn't already wet for him, I would be with the deep and longing way his voice comes out. Pinning me between the wall and his body, he brings both of his hands to my breasts, giving them a firm squeeze that melts my insides.

"I could fuck you for a century and I wouldn't tire of these," he groans, sucking one nipple into his mouth and swirling his tongue across the hardened peak. I let out a deep sigh of pleasure. He squeezes my other nipple between his fingers in response, and the combination of pain and pleasure lights me up. Literally. My body glows with a soft radiance that I've *never* experienced with another lover. I've never had this happen to me at all. My shocked expression quickly turns to lust once more as Thorne growls deeply, the vibration against my nipple sending a fresh wave of need racing through my body. "You're glowing," he whispers, bringing his forehead to mine.

"I don't know what this is," I admit. He only murmurs as he lavishes kisses up and down my neck once again.

"I don't care what it is," he says between brushes of his lips. "You look like a goddess." In another instant we're at the sofa, but I've lost track of what my magic is doing or not doing. Thorne sets me down gently on the cushion, then splays my legs wide with his large hands. He stares at the apex of my thighs with a hungry gleam in his eyes, like he can't wait to devour me. "You're so fucking wet for me, witchling," he murmurs. I tremble under his lust-filled gaze, suddenly self-conscious. I cover my breasts with my hands and slowly bring my knees together, but Thorne uses a rope of light to bind my wrists and pull them above my head like he did that day on the moors. He forces my knees open with his palms, laying me bare. When he speaks, his voice is so gentle it makes something inside of me crack open even wider, heart aching at the tenderness.

"I promised you I wouldn't take you until you were sure about us, sure about the bond. We can still walk away, Laurel. I want to fuck you with my mouth so bad it's consuming me, but I won't. I'll help you dress, then I'll go back to that separate room you had prepared for me. It doesn't matter that you've magically accepted the mating bond. If you desire it, we can continue our slow courting. I'll wait however long you want to take this next step. Just say the word."

Aethers, this male. I have no hesitation. Not anymore, not after telling him the things I've been afraid to tell anyone else for three centuries. His acceptance of those deeply-buried secrets has removed any lingering doubt.

"I want you. I want *us.* I want to be fucked by my *mate,*" I say with my aether-voice, commanding him to take me. He lets out a feral noise that's half moan and half feral howl.

"Then you better use all that power of yours to conceal the noises coming from this room and set up a protective barrier, because I don't plan on stopping until you're screaming my name with magic laced through your voice and losing control." The words are a demand, and this time, I obey without hesitation. I close my eyes, sealing us in and locking the doors. Then I weave a barrier around both the room and the empty estate for good measure. With the right protections in place, I raise a brow, challenging him to make good on his promise.

He's on me in an instant, dragging my hips down to the edge of the sofa and tugging my hands farther up above my head with his light. He gently strokes my inner thighs, but instead of pulling away when he gets to the apex like he has every other time, he lets his hands move where I want them to, stroking me in maddening circles. It's barely the ghost of a touch, so soft that I push my hips farther into his hand, demanding more pressure. He only smirks at me. One finger, then two, pump in and out of me, and I squirm at the pressure, desperate for his fingers to return to *that* spot. Thorne only places a hand on my abdomen, locking me down so that I can't move. He plans to take his time, and I'm not sure my body can wait.

Ribbons of light appear around us. They tease my nipples while Thorne uses his fingers, and the sensation is—I have no words to describe it. Needy whimpers escape me involuntarily as I buck my hips, but Thorne continues his gentle caress. It's hard to remember to breathe with all the different ways he's touching me. With no warning, ribbons and fingers swap places, and Thorne squeezes my breasts firmly with his warm hands while a beam of light teases between my legs, gently swirling and pulsing with pressure that is both punishing and delightful. His magic is playful, working me up only to back away right when it finally feels just right. I close my eyes at the sensations, but he barks my name, a commanding noise that has me tingling.

"Laurel. Keep those eyes on *me*." My eyes snap open to find his locked intensely on my face. I haven't seen this side of Thorne yet, haven't seen the male who can command every movement I make with just a few words. There have been glimpses, mostly when he lets the mask of the Shining Prince slip and the true leader beneath shines through. But this is different, and I can't get enough of it.

He removes his hands from my breasts for just an instant so he can bring his lips to mine in a demanding kiss that has me losing all sense of myself. My magic hums at the surface of my skin, desperate to be let out, but I somehow push it down and keep it at bay. Like he senses the last bit of control left in me, his fingers return to my clit, and he finally—*finally*—gives me the pressure I'm craving. He rubs me in hard and fast circles, and I cry out, my words incomprehensible. He only laughs, keeping that steady pace unwavering and his gaze firmly locked on my face. Somehow, his fingers know exactly the right rhythm and pressure I like, and heat builds low in my stomach.

Just when I think I can't take anymore, he lowers his head and blows cool air across my sex, and I shudder in pleasure. He grins wide and feral, then lowers his mouth. The anticipation alone undoes me, and my hips thrust upward to meet his lips. He chuckles against me, and the vibration feels *so good*. But then, Thorne's tongue licks up and around my sensitive spot in slow, sensual strokes, and I realize I didn't know what *good* felt like.

"Aethers, you taste good," he groans, but I can't respond, too lost in the feel of him and taking the brief relief from his touch. "You can't fathom the number of times I've dreamed about this, wondering what you would taste like. I don't think I'll ever get enough of you." Without hesitating, Thorne lowers his head again, returning to that maddening swirl of his tongue. This is incredible, unbearably pleasurable. He licks one more long stroke before clamping down on my bud and *sucking*. An animalistic need courses through me, and I fist my hands in his hair and tug firmly.

"More," I pant, my voice pleading, and another satisfied chuckle creates maddening vibrations that nearly send me over the cliff of my pleasure. I hold him to me, not letting him move his face away from between my legs, but I don't think he minds as he gives me exactly what I asked for. Never taking his mouth from me, tendrils of light dance in and out of my center, filling and releasing me over and over again, all while he continues the perfect rhythm of his tongue.

The tension builds, coiling low in my gut. I writhe in pleasure, but Thorne just tightens the light restraints holding me in place, adding a band of light over my lap to keep me from moving my hips. It brings me even closer to the edge, unable to release the pressure that threatens to erupt out of me. I have the vague sense that the room has filled with a misty light, and Thorne chuckles when a vine crawls all the way across the room from the window and laps lazily at his abs. I've lost some of the control I had clamped around my magic, but I can't bring myself to care.

"Thorne," I moan, my words a plea for him to bring me over the edge.

"Come for me, witchling," he growls. Then he lifts his head, and I let him, though I keep my hands in his hair. His mouth glistens with my wetness, and his full lips are vibrant red. "Come for me, Laurel. I want to watch that beautiful face of yours come undone."

Ribbons of light hold me down but also stroke across all my sensitive areas. Thorne rubs circles on my clit with one hand, the other absentmindedly caressing every inch of my exposed body. The pressure builds and builds, and when he thrusts a wide ribbon of light inside of me and has it stroke the *exact* spot that I like, I erupt. With a scream, the tension crests in me, and every muscle in my body clenches in pleasure. The room shakes around us, and anything metal not bolted down hovers in the air. The mist in the room intensifies, and a bright light flashes. It's not until the tension slowly releases from me that I realize the brightness was me, lighting up like a beacon in the night.

I take deep breaths, slowly trying to come back to myself after what may be the longest and most intense orgasm I've ever had. Thorne doesn't release me, slowly stroking my clit once, twice, my entire body jerking at the pleasure. When I finally collapse against the sofa, every muscle in my body limp, he lets my hands drop to my side and sits next to me.

"I told you it would electrifying," he says with a smirk and a wink.

Scholars, historians, and religious leaders alike have written volumes about the Prophecy of the Promised Thayarian Queen. There is much interest in understanding what the "powers of old" refer to. Some believe it to be a reference to the old gods, others believe it refers to a time when the fae were more powerful. But no topic is as hotly debated as the fated love the prophecy promises.

A Brief History of Modern Thayaria

Laurel lays on the sofa, her smooth, milky flesh flushed with satisfaction. Her body still glows with a soft light and her hair floats around her with magic, like she's hovering in the air. It's ethereal, otherworldly. She looks like a *goddess*, and she finally let me worship her in the way I've ached to since I first laid eyes on her. The months of bone-deep *need* to get under her skin, to unravel that collected demeanor, finally ease, though only slightly. I have a feeling it will take months or even years of seeing her come undone to finally soothe that desire to a burning ember. But it will still burn, no matter how many times we're joined.

The taste of her still dances on my tongue, and I can't get enough of the smell of lilac and mint that hovers in the air around us. There's something about her scent that's shifted slightly. It's still Laurel, still the smell of my *mate*, but it's even more intoxicating than before. There's a spiciness to it now that heats my blood, and I know that I'd be able to track her anywhere she goes by following that scent. My cock *aches* to be inside of her, but I'm content with what she's given me tonight. The sight of her so completely relaxed next to me is almost as good as my own release, though I don't know if I can wait too long before I'll need to taste her again.

She sits up, breasts swaying with the movement and eyes sparkling. I growl when I notice her hard nipples, blush circles surrounding them. I *need* to put my hands on her. But when I try to, she binds them behind my back with her own cord of light, and my cock twitches. I enjoy teasing her, like bossing her around and shredding that control she so carefully maintains. But the thought of *her* ordering *me*, taking her pleasure from me, is equally, if not more, intoxicating. I want her so badly, but I know she needs to take her time, so I don't let myself hope we might do more tonight.

"My turn," she says, voice low and husky, and everything around us—the mist still lingering from her outburst of magic, the ivy that's creeped in through the windows and under the balcony door, the debris of metal objects that litter the floor—disappears. All I see is Laurel, the way her verdant eyes track my movements with the same hunger I feel. She wants *more*, thank fuck. I don't dare breathe, not wanting to jinx this moment. Without warning, she aersteps us to the bedroom, not releasing the bindings around my wrists. A massive four-poster bed sits in the middle of the room, curtains hanging loose around it. Laurel pushes me against it, releasing me for an instant before binding me again, this time tied tightly to the columns of the bed.

"You're *dirty*, witchling." The delight is clear in my voice, and she gives me her own wicked smirk, the gesture bringing me immense pleasure. What I don't say is that I'm coiled so tight with need I might explode with magic like she did.

"We're only just beginning," she whispers in my ear, sending shivers down my spine, and now I know I'm not going to be able to stay in control of my magic or my release. Keeping her gaze locked on mine, she slowly unbuttons my pants and pushes them down to my feet along with my undergarments, freeing my aching cock. I sigh in pleasure, the strain against the fabric of my clothing finally gone. I step quickly out of the pants gathered at my feet, aching for her to touch me. She traces one finger from my collarbone all the way down my chest, then drops to her knees. I swallow, my mouth dry and my body humming with need. Wrapping her delicate hand around my hardened cock, she looks up at me through dark lashes with those piercing green eyes. I drop my head back, eyes closed, and moan my pleasure. "Keep those eyes on me, princeling." She mimics my words from earlier and I snap open my eyes, looking down at her just as she licks up the length of my shaft. Another noise escapes me, this time an animalistic yowl, and her lips quirk before she laps up the bead of liquid gathering at my tip. With one singular motion, she pumps once and then brings my cock into her warm mouth, moving in and out with a maddening slowness that makes me shiver. I want to touch her, to wrap my hands in her hair. Even though I could easily unbind myself from the ropes of light, I don't, letting her claim me the way she let me claim her. My hips thrust into her involuntarily with need, but she only takes me deeper, swallowing the movement.

"Fuck, Laurel," I groan. She responds by caressing one of my balls, and the movement sends me spiraling in a wave of pleasure. I take that as a sign of encouragement, and thrust my hips harder, fucking her mouth with reckless abandon. Her bright green eyes flutter up to mine, and I nearly come at the sight. Every time she shifts, her breasts sway, and it drives me mad. My thrusting intensifies, but she doesn't waver, even as her eyes water. I'm losing myself, lost in the feel of her around me, pushing deeper and deeper as she moans around me. Fuck, I won't last much longer.

She must be able to tell I'm unraveling, because she pulls back with a soft smile, wiping her mouth over the back of her hand. Then she licks me from navel to chest before placing soft kisses over my neck and the sensitive tip of my pointed ears. Without warning, she sucks my neck so hard it'll leave a mark, and I growl in pleasure at the thought.

She releases my wrists from the ropes of light binding them, and I'm instantly on her, unable to keep my hands off her for even a second in my freedom. I scoop her into my arms and lay her out on the bed, but as soon as I try to lower myself over her, she wraps her legs around my hips and flips us so that she's on top, smirking at my shocked expression.

"I told you, it's my turn," she murmurs, a predatory glint in her eyes, and it nearly undoes me right then. Like a phantom of my dreams, she kisses the hollow of my throat, her pert nipples skimming across my skin as she makes her way down my chest and stomach, kissing every inch of me she can reach. It drives me mad, the slow way she's taunting me, but I wouldn't dream of rushing her, wouldn't dream of rushing *this*.

Sitting up, her eyes alight with glee a second before a warm, teasing wind dances across my shaft. I let out a gasp, and that only encourages her. Somehow, I feel her hands touching me in multiple places, though I see them resting lightly on the sides of her wide hips. Those phantom hands massage my shoulders and delicately trace the lines of my abs. When they squeeze my shaft and pump up and down in a steady rhythm, I buck my hips and let out a groan. That only makes Laurel chuckle in satisfaction, those haunting green eyes shining with delight.

"Witchling," I moan. "You're going to make me come without even touching me. That just seems wrong. Let me. Inside. You." I mean for the words to come out teasing and cheeky, but they're breathy, practically pleading. With an unholy, feral grin, she crawls above me, her long hair caging me. When her face is right above mine, she slowly lowers her hips, guiding my shaft inside her hot, wet slit. Her eyes never leave mine, the look on her face possessive. I moan at the perfect feel of her as she drops inch by inch, taking my large girth without hesitation. "That's it, nice and slow," I encourage. The way her nipples harden and her eyes heat tells me she likes the praise, so I keep going. "You're doing so well. My good girl." At that, she shivers, the movement wracking her whole body in a way I can't wait to see again. She keeps going, not stopping the tantalizing drop of her hips. When she's fully seated, we both let out moans, grinding our hips in circular movements. I want to touch her clit, want to pull out so I can thrust back into her. But she's in control, and there's too much pleasure in that thought to take it from her. "You were made for me," I murmur.

Instead of responding, she lifts herself and slams her body back down on mine. An involuntary noise makes its way out of me, and I bring one hand to her hip and the other to her breast. Her head dips back, hair cascading down her back and breasts swaying.

"That's right," I whisper, voice low. "Ride me. Fuck me, witchling. Take what's *yours*." Her smooth thrusts get faster, and her breaths come out in pants. She bites her lip, and the sight makes me thrust up into her so deep she lets out a groan of surprise. Moisture glistens across her stomach and collarbone in the soft glow that surrounds us. My power has a mind of its own, caressing her body with gentle ribbons of light. She moans at the touch, and any hope I had of keeping my hands, or my magic, to myself disappears. I squeeze her nipple and her hip in unison with my hands, the pressure causing her to increase her grinding to a punishing pace.

"Thorne, I'm close. Please," she whimpers, practically begging me to help her finish, and that's the sign I need to bring those ribbons of light to her clit, stroking her again and again with my magic while keeping my hands on her hips to guide her up and down my body. Those incredible tits bounce up and down with the movement, and I'm transfixed at the look of her astride me. I never want to leave this position, her body hovering above me, hair fanned out around her. Her cheeks are flushed bright red with exertion, and I have to focus to keep myself from cresting that wave with her. But I'm not done, and I won't come until I've brought her to climax at least a few more times.

I can tell she's reaching a fever pitch, her hips rocking back and forth so quickly she practically vibrates. She's also glowing brightly again, as sure a sign as any that she's close. It's remarkable, and I hope she always lights up like this when we make love. I replace my light with my thumb on her clit, pressing hard just as I thrust up into her, and that does it. She comes again with a small breathy noise, this time not an eruption but a gentle wave, and it's just as beautiful. The walls of her pussy flutter, squeezing my cock and nearly finishing me. I stroke her through her crest, waiting until her hips are jerking with overstimulation before I remove my hand from between her thighs.

As soon as she's wrung out every drop of her pleasure, I'm moving, swapping our bodies so that she lays prone beneath me. Rising to my knees, I kiss her neck with a hungry need, then suck deeply to leave my own mark just under her ear. I think she likes it too, because she brings her hand to my cock and strokes again. I'm on fire, my body thrumming with electricity, and lightning strikes across the ceiling. It lights up the room in flashes as I continue to explore her satiated body with gentle caresses. I *need* to be inside of her again, but I want to give her time to come down, so I gently lift her naked, curvy body and carry her to the wall, something about pinning her against it the sexiest thing I've ever seen. I kiss her slowly, tenderly, letting her know without words how much I worship her.

"You're bewitching, Laurel," I murmur as I smooth back her hair from her face and take it between my hands. She looks so stunning, the glow of exertion making the freckles that dot across her nose stand out. I kiss each one I can find, and she laughs, so bright and melodic that it warms everything inside of me.

"That tickles," she whispers, dropping her forehead to mine. I only lay another kiss across her brow, then angle her head so I can kiss her deeply, my tongue sweeping across every crevice of her mouth. The soft and gentle kiss quickly turns heated, and without warning she wraps her legs around me. "Fuck me again," she demands, and I oblige.

With a punishing thrust, I enter her, and she cries out in pleasure. I keep up the rhythm, slamming into her harder and harder as she moans in ecstasy. The feel of her tight walls around my cock is intoxicating, and I lower her body so that I can reach even deeper.

Her hands claw my back, drawing blood, and I see the moment the scent hits her. Her body goes preternaturally still, and she tracks me like prey, scanning every inch of my body as it continues to thrust in and out of her. All of that passion and need homes in on one singular focus. *Me.* Eyes dilated, she bares her teeth.

"Mine," she growls, the sound so unlike her but thrilling all the same. I push deep into her, holding the position. She cries out my name, circling her hips to feel every angle of my cock deep inside her. I shift, somehow getting even deeper, and that unlocks something wild inside of her. She claws at me, the momentary pain blissful as she soothes her magic over every scrape of her nails. Pupil-blown eyes bore into me as she grinds her hips in rhythm with mine. Then, so fast I can barely track her, she bites me, right above my heart. The gesture sends an electrifying shock through my entire body, and small sparks of my magic dance between us, like tiny lightning strikes connecting our bodies. I bleed from the wound, but she laps up my blood with her tongue, sighing contentedly as she does. "Mine," she says again, this time softly, eyes returning to usual now that she's claimed me.

As Laurel returns to herself, I lose every inch of control I possessed, a feral beast locked deep inside of me unleashing itself. In an instant, we're against the bed, and I've bent her forward, her elbows resting on the mattress and her ass in the air. I lightly slap one curvaceous cheek, watching for her reaction. She moans in satisfaction, turning back to me to nod her consent. I slap her again, this time with more force, and she lets out a high-pitched whine for more.

"I told you that when you claimed me, I'd take you from behind. And I intend to honor my word, witchling," I whisper in her ear before I thrust into her with a roar. She screams my name, and it sends me into a state of ecstasy. I keep pounding into her, and every time I do, she cries in pleasure, begging me to bring her to release. She pushes her hips back into me, trying to force me deeper, so I stop and gently guide one leg to rest on the bed, then the other. When she's on the mattress on all fours, I haul her backward and push her head down so that she's even more exposed to me. Then I enter her again, and the position allows me to push so deep inside her she lets out a low, surprised grunt, the breath knocked from her. As I hold the deep position, I growl out the words I now know she loves to hear. "Good girl. My good Laurel." My hands wrap her hair in a fist, gently tugging even as I keep the other hand on the back of her neck to keep her gently pinned in place.

Without warning, I pull out and slam into her again, and this time every thrust inside her is euphoric. Her body shakes with need, incoherent screams and moans coming from her now. Pressure builds in my spine as a thick mist gathers around us, my magic completely uncontainable. The room flashes again with lightning. It feels like we're fucking in a thunderstorm. I know I'm close, so I remove my hand from her head and bring my fingers to her clit, no magic, gently stroking while I continue my demanding rhythm. There's nothing between us now, no magic aiding our pleasure, no smirks or winks hiding what we truly feel. Just our naked, glistening bodies pressed to one another, open and raw in our need.

The thread of light I feel inside my aether-heart pulls taut between us, telling me she's close to her peak. With another roar, I push as deep as I can, my release erupting out of me at the same time Laurel squeezes with her own orgasm. The room flashes blindingly bright, and there's a cracking noise behind me I ignore. We slowly grind against one another, wringing out our pleasure.

When we're fully spent, I gently turn her around to face me, my hands rubbing up and down her arms to warm her pebbled skin. "Laurel." I say her name like a prayer, going to my knees in front of her. She shudders. Keeping my eyes locked on hers, I bring my lips to rest just above her heart, swirling my tongue across the swell of her breast. I gently caress the curve of her body, resting my hand on her full hip. "Mine," I whisper softly. Then I bring my mouth down and bite her, firmly, drawing blood. She moans. When the scent hits me, I instantly harden, wanting to fuck her all over again, but I stop myself. I want to savor this moment with her, want to take in every detail of our joining and what feels like the cresting of the mating bond.

Slowly, I will aether to lap against the wound with light, healing the cut but leaving the scar. I do the same to my own wound. Then I place her hand over my scar and put my hand over hers.

"Mates," I whisper, and joyful tears build in her eyes.

"Mates," she sobs, and the word obliterates my control. I crowd her body with mine, and we're frantic for one another once again, skin and magic clashing in a heated fury.

In the quiet after they accepted the mating bond, the witch and the fae fell even deeper into their magical connection. But it was a momentary respite, their fate marching ever closer.

Unknown Story, Unknown Origin

I lose count of the number of times we come together. As soon as a passionate round ends and we settle into one another, curving our bodies together, another spark of need ignites. We fuck on every inch of the suite, moving from the bedroom to the sitting room to the office, leaving a hurricane of destroyed furniture and general disarray in our wake. Our power is uncontrollable, aether exploding out of us in waves. Through it all, we don't hurt one another, subconsciously protecting the other from the force of our magic.

We orgasm together again in the bathing chamber, Laurel pressed against the vanity and my eyes watching every movement from the mirror, hungry for whatever glimpse I can get of her as she comes. When we're done, I stare at our reflections, matching marks over our hearts, hair tousled and unkempt. Words can't describe the way Laurel looks, standing there with her hair hanging over her breasts, leaning on my body for support because of how satiated and relaxed she is. She meets my eyes, and I beam at her.

"You're so perfect," I murmur, kissing the top of her shoulder, the words not enough to convey the deep well of feelings I have when I think of her.

"You're not too bad yourself," she teases. "But we'd both be more perfect if we bathed. We stink of sex." I growl, the idea of her washing my scent off sending a possessive ripple through me. Laurel seems to understand, and I'm grateful that we're going through the confusion of the mating bond together. "We can fuck again immediately," she soothes, eyes bright. "But I need to relax my muscles for a minute and clean myself up." Suddenly, worry for her consumes me. *Have I hurt her?* I've been demanding and exacting, without once thinking about how that might make her sore. Again, she seems to know my thoughts before they fully form in my mind. "You didn't hurt me. I wanted every backbreaking thrust. Trust me." Her eyes light up. "But I do want to soak for a minute, and this is my favorite bathtub in the entire kingdom."

I look at the tub that's big enough for four fully grown fae, dominating the bathing chamber. Laurel pads over to it, hips swaying, and channels steaming water to fill the tub. Then she walks to a built-in wardrobe and pulls out two plush robes and various soaps and creams. She dumps several of them into the running water before lowering her body into the mound of bubbles.

"Are you going to join me?" she asks, invitation in her eyes, and I'm in the tub in a flash. An involuntary moan escapes my lips at the steaming water that instantly releases the tension in my neck, arms, and legs. I lean my head back.

"This bathtub *is* divine," I sigh, and she chuckles with an *I told you so* look in her eyes. When the water level sits a few inches from the lip of the tub, I grab Laurel and bring her to rest between my legs, massaging her shoulders. She lets out her own contented sigh, and the sound settles something deep inside of me, like her satisfaction is my own. I press more kisses to her shoulders, then wrap her up in my arms. "Can we stay here for another week?" I ask, and she bursts out laughing.

"While I'd love to, I promised Silene I'd join you guys for dinner tomorrow night. She said she had some big surprise. And the idea of disappointing Silene upsets me way more than the idea of disappointing you." I huff out a laugh.

"On that, we can agree. If Silene has a surprise, then it's something enormous. She's incapable of small gestures." I don't tell Laurel the reason for tomorrow's surprise dinner, not wanting to ruin our moment. She smiles, a vulnerable and open quirking of her lips, and the sight steals the air from my lungs, the sensation not unlike the one when Laurel does it with her magic.

"When we go back to the palace," she begins, tentatively, "would you consider announcing to the Council that you and Silene aren't really engaged? We won't tell them we're mates, but I don't want to hide my relationship with you. Or at least, I don't want others to think I'm desperately flirting with a betrothed prince. We don't have to confirm anything about us yet, but I'm sure they're whispering. Let's at least let them know our flirting is wholesome." I can sense Laurel holding her breath, but the worry is entirely unnecessary. I kiss the top of her head.

"First, how dare you say our flirting is wholesome. I don't do anything *wholesome*." She laughs, and it eases the worry in her gaze as I intended. "And second, nothing, and I mean *nothing*, would bring me more happiness, Laurel. I want to hold your hand whenever I'm in your presence, and now that you've accepted the mating bond, I think it's going to be extremely hard for me to keep my hands off you, anyway."

She grins. "It really is unlike anything I've ever experienced," she admits. "I love Silene like a sister, but there's a part of me that wants to rip out her throat when I remember that she's pretending to be engaged to you." I bark out a laugh, and she grins.

"I love your dark possessiveness, witchling." My voice is low and full of need, and her hips arch into me. My cock is instantly hard, pressing into her ass. "But if we talk about that much longer, you won't get the soak you deserve. Dip your head under the water." She obeys, and I pump out what I think is hair-washing soap. "This?" I ask, wanting to be sure. She nods, so I lather the sweet-smelling soap into her hair, making sure I scrub every lock. I massage her head, and she moans in satisfaction.

"No one has ever washed my hair before." The comment is quiet and innocent, and pleasure jolts through me at being able to care for her in this way.

"I'll wash your hair every single day, witchling, if that's what you desire." And I mean it. I would do anything for this female, for my Queen, my mate. I have no intention of ever leaving her side again, my father and his plans, my throne, and Velmara be damned. *If Laurel isn't with me, I won't step foot on Velmaran soil again.* "Dunk," I order, preparing the conditioning treatment she points to as her head dips below the water. When she reemerges, I run it through her long reddish strands, letting it soak in. "Is this what makes your hair so shiny and soft?"

"Exactly how much time have you spent studying my hair?" she teases.

"More than is entirely appropriate," I tell her. "Especially for someone who was supposed to be engaged to another and an ambassador from an enemy kingdom." Her melodic laugh lights me up inside.

"I could tell. That's why I always wore it down unless it was impractical not to." Her smirk is intoxicating. I lean down to whisper in her ear.

"I knew you like my hair too, ya know. That little piece that always falls in my face. I might have intentionally coaxed it to fall a time or two."

She turns around in my arms, expression incredulous. "You depraved, deviant flirt!" she teases as she lightly slaps my chest. Our laughter makes the water slosh out of the tub, but neither of us care as the laughter quickly turns to slow, sensuous kisses. This time there's no hurry, no need to even have sex. We sit in the bath, pressing our bodies together and exploring one another slowly.

We finish the bath, and Laurel wraps herself in a thick robe, then hands one to me. When we're seated on the bed, I comb her hair for her, and she closes her eyes in bliss. When the knots are all out, I realize she's fallen asleep. I slowly lower her to the bed, then cover her with blankets. Crossing to the other side of the bed, I crawl in behind her, cradling her body in mine.

We wake late the next morning, still in our robes. I don't know who woke first, only that my eyes opened from slumber at the same time Laurel's did. We were instantly on one another, needy and frantic in our joining.

"What do you think Silene has planned for tonight?" Laurel asks when we manage to pull ourselves into a semblance of normalcy, resting her head in my lap while I sit against the headboard.

"I have no idea, but considering it's my 350th birthday, I would imagine she went all out." My grin is teasing and knowing.

"What?" Laurel sits up, eyes churning with an emotion I can't place. "Today's your birthday?"

I shrug. "Yeah."

"Why didn't you tell me? I wouldn't have brought you here, wouldn't have stolen you away from your friends." She stands from the bed and paces. I stand too, unwilling to stay away from her side for even a moment. I grab her hand and pull her to my side, preventing her from continuing her anxious pacing.

"Are you suggesting you think I would have rather spent the night playing Skran with Silene and Fionn instead of endlessly fucking my mate for my birthday?" I ask, wrapping my arms around her body in a tight embrace. "Are you serious? This is the best birthday ever, and it's only just started." She blushes.

"I don't have a gift for you. Do you give gifts for birthdays in Velmara? I don't even know!" She sighs.

"I'm regretting telling you it's my birthday, witchling. Accepting the mating bond is—it will be the best gift you ever give me." I hug her tightly, trying to calm the whirling anxiety I know races through her veins. She relaxes into me and calm settles over her. I release her, then take her hand and lead her into the nearly destroyed sitting room to look for breakfast, famished after our all-night workout. "Thank the aether there's a breakfast tray here," I say as I grab a slice of sweet bread and stuff it in my mouth. She examines the destroyed room—plants creeping in from the windows, bookshelves destroyed, all the curtain rods on the ground. I spot the moment she realizes servants came into this room to deliver breakfast. Her cheeks blush deeply.

"We, uh, we really made a mess last night," she says. I only wink at her with a satisfied smirk. She rolls her eyes, then snaps her fingers and the room returns to the pristine condition it was in last night. "I wish I had thought of that last night," she murmurs, and I can't help the chuckle that escapes me.

I start to make her a cup of tea, realizing as I pour the water that it's tepid. "Tea's gone cold." She grins, and suddenly the water in the kettle is steaming again. "I could get used to this limitless power of yours," I tell her, then pour cream into the steaming mug before handing it to her.

"How do you take *your* tea? You're always making mine. I've never noticed what you make for yourself."

"Hate the stuff. I think it tastes like burned water." She nearly spits out the tea she just took a drink of in her laughter.

"First, you don't get why chocolate cake is the best food ever, and now you don't like tea? How can you possibly be my mate?" she teases.

"More for you," I growl, and I can see her body tense with need at the throaty noise. I scoop her up again, unable to keep my hands from her, breakfast forgotten as we find new ways to learn one another's bodies.

While mates are said to be random, at the discretion of the gods or fate, certain pairings appear to be part of the very fabric of our world. Thayarian rulers often find themselves with a Velmaran mate, specifically a powerful light channeler, and often the strongest light channeler alive during their rule. None know why fate favors these matches so frequently, and neither the Andomer nor the Elestren lines have ever offered their own explanations for the phenomenon.

The Traditions of the Fae

"Can we have *dinner* again tonight?" Genevieve asks me suggestively after lunch as I settle back in for a long afternoon of research. Even though I love her office, I try to spend some of my time out in the archives so people don't grow suspicious of where I am. Her eyes are bright with mischief and lust, and it stirs my own desire. She's proven to be an excellent lover, despite her lack of experience. Teaching her new things has been more exhilarating than I expected. There's an urgency to her need, like she feels she needs to experience everything before it slips away from her.

"I'd like that," I say with a knowing smile, and she blushes. "I have a few more texts to show you, as I'd like your opinion on their meaning," I add loudly to protect our cover of researcher and librarian, though I'm not sure anyone cares what Genevieve does with her time. She's as forgotten as the books deep in the archives detailing royal coin balances throughout the centuries.

"Yes, I would be happy to *assist* you," she says, the innuendo clear, and my thighs turn slick. Genevieve walks away, hips swishing in her gown. I stare at her ass until she turns the corner.

Brushing aside images of what I want to do to her tonight, I return to the text I've been reading all morning, *The Secrets and Stories of Velmara*. The section where Genevieve found the information about Mazus's line—the Vicants—forcibly taking the throne from the Andomers has proven most illuminating. Not only did the Andomers rule Velmara, but they have their own prophecies about a prince who will bring light in the darkness, uniting peoples or realms, depending on which oral history is being detailed. It could be an iteration on the prophecy of the Thayarian Queen, derived from the same stories but branching at some point in history for different peoples. But they're not *quite* similar enough to make that likely.

The Andomer line is strong, and this prophesied prince is supposed to be the strongest among them. I can't help but draw connections to Prince Hawthorne, who's rumored to be the strongest light channeler at least in living memory. Laurel has never given much credit to the prophecy so many believe is about her, so I've rarely studied it, not wanting to poke a still-sore wound. But if Hawthorne is the Prince of Andomer in the prophecy, and Laurel is the Queen of the Thayarian prophecy, then the two of them are surely connected in some way. I told Laurel I suspected Mazus wanted her and Prince Hawthorne to meet, and these revelations only heighten that suspicion.

I'm pondering the possibility that the prophecies about Laurel and Prince Hawthorne are connected when a servant arrives with a roll of parchment, sealed with Mazus's signet. Sighing, I take the missive from her and open it. Mazus has requested my presence in three evening's time for another dinner and has apparently already dispatched servants with my attire for the affair, indicating this is not a request but a summons. Not that I had any delusions otherwise.

I return to my research, frustrated that I'm beholden to the King's whims, but with a renewed sense of urgency, hoping to find something useful by the time we meet. I return to translating *The Traditions of the Fae*. It's been slow work, and I've had to take breaks from it to maintain my sanity. I've been working on the section on fae religion, but after reading more about Prince Hawthorne's potential significance in Andomer lore, I decide to return to the passages on mates, a question percolating in the back of my mind.

This book is the closest I've come to a primary source, detailing the traditions, customs, and stories of the fae at the time it was written. I have no idea how old it is, though it must be ancient to discuss mates as if they exist. I slowly comb my way through a history of prominent mated pairs, unsure if the names are significant. Feeling like this is unproductive, I skip ahead through the six pages of recorded names. If there are *this* many recorded names, mates cannot have only ever been myth. But why they've disappeared from our world is still a mystery. The old fae character for Thayaria catches my attention, and I stop to translate the passage that mentions my kingdom.

I double and then triple check my work, heart racing. According to the passage, Thayarian rulers once frequently found themselves with a Velmaran mate. Specifically, with a powerful light channeler, from the Andomer line, as a mate. The pieces are slowly coming together, and they paint a troubling picture.

Laurel and Prince Hawthorne must be mates. And while that would normally bring me joy at the thought of my best friend—my sister—finding the great love she's always been promised, the fact that Mazus gave me these books means he must also know. He intentionally sent the Prince there for them to discover their connection, though for what end, I cannot say. And while the stories about Prince Hawthorne paint him as a powerful but unintelligent flirt, what if he knows and is working with Mazus? He's the *son* of the Golden King, after all.

Laurel is in danger. That thought echoes nonstop through my mind as I continue my frantic translation. I don't know how much time passes, only that I must keep going, for Laurel's sake. I startle out of my research haze when Genevieve approaches my workstation.

"Nemesia," she says, eyes smiling. "You've surely lost track of time. I haven't seen you take a break all afternoon."

The fact that she's been observing me doesn't go unnoticed, but I'm too frazzled by my discoveries to comment on it. I consider canceling our dinner plans in order to continue the research but decide against it when I see the excitement written so clearly across her features. It physically pains me to leave the research behind, but Genevieve has become a priority for me. She's had so few give her any attention or care her entire life. I won't break her heart.

"It was a productive day for me," I admit, though that's as close as I can come to the truth of what I've discovered, what I fear. "I'm grateful you pulled me out of my studies, as I might have been here all night if not for you. And I'm still eager to discuss the earlier matter with you over dinner this evening." Meaning fills my eyes, and I love the way she drops her eyes to the ground as she blushes.

Once I've packed up, we walk side by side to my room, hands brushing but not daring to clasp together. Dinner is forgotten the moment we close the door behind us, clothes and undergarments hitting the floor in a frenzy. Genevieve has grown bolder these last weeks, and she pushes my naked body onto the bed, spreading my legs wide as she brings her mouth to the apex of my thighs. Normally I'm a very giving lover, preferring to take care of my partner before myself, but I know Genevieve craves the ability to be bold, to be in control, so I let her do whatever she wants. I moan as her soft lips bring me to climax, and as soon as my pleasure finishes its crest, I grab her body and push her to the mattress. She makes the sweetest breathy whimpers when she comes, and now is no different.

"Nemesia," she groans when I pull my mouth from between her legs, and I wrap her up in my arms and press a kiss to her temple. We lay there naked in my bed, trailing soft touches over one another's bodies as we discuss our days. "What did you discover today?" she asks, and I know she's genuine in her curiosity about my research. I hesitate, worried revealing the information about Laurel and the Prince might put her in danger.

"I don't know if I should tell you," I start slowly. "For your own protection. What I found, what I suspect, could expose you to danger." Even this admission is a risk, but if I'm honest with myself, I want to tell her, want to share this burden. Her soft brown eyes study mine, expression firm and decided.

"I want to know anyway." I start to protest, but she holds up her hand to silence me. "I know you're here looking for something important. And I know that even if you and His Majesty pretend at cordiality, there's still tension between you and between Velmara and Thayaria. What is it that could be so dangerous?" I'm about to refuse, to tell her the risk is too great, when she surprises me. "I've also discovered something that may be dangerous, in the book you lent me from His Majesty's collection."

"Tell me," I command, all General in my voice. But Genevieve only smiles, unaffected by my imposing tone.

"You first," she whispers, rubbing a circle around my exposed nipple. I drop my head back at the sensation and close my eyes, loving the way her soft skin feels on mine.

"Not fair," I grunt, but she only laughs, pressing a kiss to my forehead.

"Open your eyes." I do. Her warm amber eyes bore into me. "Tell me, please." The request is so gentle but filled with so many unspoken words. She wants me to trust her, wants me to open up. It's a choice I have to make, one that I'm not sure I'm ready to make. She's been the best thing about Velmara, and I care for her. I don't want to put her in danger, but I don't think I can bear the look of hurt I know will cross her face if I don't reveal this secret.

So I tell her everything. The discovery that mates may be real, my suspicions that Laurel and Prince Hawthorne are mates, that Mazus likely knows and sent the Prince there for that purpose. My worry about his motivation for wanting them to connect with one another. The fear that the Prince is working with his father and hopes to use the connection to crush Laurel. I let my loathing of the King bleed into my voice for the first time since coming to Velmara, but she doesn't shy away. When I'm finished, she sighs.

"I used to believe the Golden King was truly a hero, someone who desperately tried to save the people of Thayaria from their terrible ruler. But as the years have gone by, I've seen his propaganda machine at work, seen the way the histories are rewritten for storage in the archives. I've been skeptical of him for years, but after I discovered that the Vicants took the throne by force, it was like all these disparate facts I'd been holding finally came together. I've read through *Blood Magic Through the Ages* no less than four times, and it—it tells a story I'm afraid to say aloud." Her lips are trembling, and her body shakes. I wrap her in my arms, kissing the top of her head and stroking her hair.

"It's okay. Please tell me. Your secret's safe with me," I soothe. She takes a single deep breath before spilling what she's learned.

"There's a passage that mentions that blood magic is an inherited trait. Not just anyone can practice it. You need an affinity, just like with any other conduit, though the power is extremely rare." My mind races to fit the knowledge into what I already know. "It also said that the blood mage lineage originally came from Velmara. I think—based on what I've read... It seems to be unlikely that the Witch Queen—that Queen Laurel—would be a blood mage. King Mazus must have made that up."

I laugh aloud, and it startles her. "Sorry, but of course Laurel isn't a blood mage. I already knew that," I tell her gently. She blushes in embarrassment.

"Of course you did. I didn't mean, didn't—"

"It's okay," I say, relieving her from her adorable discomfort with a squeeze. She blushes again but then turns somber.

"Nemesia, there's more." Her expression is grim once again. "This is just a hunch, there's nothing in the text to confirm it. But it talks about how the blood mages were a powerful family in Velmaran history, second only to the Andomers. The family isn't named, but the only other magical line that would make sense..." She trails off, clearly afraid to speak the words aloud.

"The Vicants," I finish for her, and she nods, eyes wide. My mind swirls, the information unlocking the final piece of the puzzle for me.

"We both wondered what could take down the Andomer line, what could steal a throne away from a family with the most powerful conduit in the Four Kingdoms. I think we have our answer." She whispers the last words, so afraid and yet so courageous for putting these pieces together, for not ignoring the obvious truth sitting in front of her. Most people are content to believe the lies they're told, to go along with the status quo for fear of the unknown. But not Genevieve. The world has used and abused her, shown so many times that adherence to the way things are is the only way to keep her safe. And yet, still, she fights back.

"Listen to me, Genevieve." The army General is back in my voice. "You must not tell this to anyone. Don't even reveal that I let you read through these books from Mazus. He clearly wanted me to come to these conclusions on my own, despite how dangerous they are for him. I fear there's more going on here than we've uncovered." She nods, eyes wide in fear. "I'm having dinner with him in three days. I'll use the opportunity to see how he tries to goad me, and then I'm going to leave Velmara. I've discovered everything I need to, and I must warn Laurel before it's too late. Will you—will you come with me?"

I shock myself with the request. I've *never* taken a serious lover, preferring casual one evening affairs or clear physical-only relationships. Boundaries between my sex life and my personal life have always been firmly in place, a necessity considering my position in Thayaria. And even though I know I'm not *in love* with Genevieve—not yet, at least—I know that she's the first female who's ever made me care this much. She's the only person who's been able to crack me wide open and start healing all the parts of me I've hidden away. The promise of what we might become in Thayaria, away from Velmara's rules and customs, gives me so much hope for the future. It ignites something in my chest, making me hold my breath as I wait for her answer.

She hesitates, clearly unsure how to respond. I can understand her fear—her entire life's been spent in the archives. Not to mention, she's been pulled into a scheme to leave by someone she trusted before, with her governess, and it cost her so much. Leaving must be a terrifying prospect for her, but she nods in agreement, and I release a sigh of relief.

"Meet me in my room the night I dine with Mazus. Pack a bag, but pack light. Until then, we shouldn't be seen together." She only nods. I give her one last squeeze, then return us both to a sitting position. "You shouldn't stay here tonight. Go back to your rooms and make a point to not be seen in my company for the next few days."

Genevieve dresses quickly, and with a brief kiss, she departs. I only hope I can get us both out according to plan.

I pass the remaining days pouring through the books Mazus gave me, trying to get every possible detail locked away in my memory in case the books don't make it out with me. I plan to pack them into a bag, but I also want to be prepared if something goes amiss. I've found an air channeler willing to take a significant bribe to aerstep us back to Thayaria. Once the dinner is over, I need to collect Genevieve, then get us safely to the Floating Market. True to her word, Genevieve stays away, and I don't see her at all, not even in the archives.

When the evening of the dinner arrives, I dress in the scrap of fabric Mazus sent as my gown, this one even skimpier than the first. Like before, I wear fighting leathers underneath and use ivy vines to weave more coverage over my chest and arms. I sheath multiple daggers to my person, both visible and hidden. I spent the afternoon in my room, packing a single bag with my belongings and the books I hope to smuggle out with me.

Genevieve is supposed to meet me in my room and stay here until I return from the dinner with Mazus—she should be here by now. As I pace back and forth across the floor, anxiety courses through me about what might have kept her. She's never been late before, but she could also just be struggling to sneak away undetected. Did she decide she doesn't want to come after all? After five more minutes of pacing, I can't delay any longer and have to leave without our plan fully in place. I leave the door unlocked so she can enter my room when she arrives. *If* she arrives.

When I approach the doors to Mazus's private dining room, I'm escorted in by several guards in golden armor. Mazus isn't here, but servants have already set out food on the table, so I make myself a plate, hoping it irks him when he arrives. I've taken my first bite when the Golden King strides in, adorned in cream clothing covered in gold embroidery. I don't stand at his arrival and a deep sense of satisfaction courses through me when I see how his jaw clenches at the disrespect.

"Nemesia," he says, splaying his arms wide. "I'm so glad you've made yourself so at *home* here in my palace." He sits down and servants rush into the room to fill his goblet with wine and serve him food. "I trust you've found the books I had delivered useful?"

"Indeed, I have. Thank you," I say, then take another bite of food, and I can tell it annoys him. I elect to keep up the strategy of saying very little. Let him show his hand first.

"And what have been your most exciting discoveries?" He can't drop the subject, a sure sign these books were sent for a specific purpose. I take another bite of food, chewing slowly, then swallow several gulps of wine before I set my fork down and stare at him.

"Why don't you just tell me what you're hoping I found, and we can skip the part where we dance around one another," I say with an edge in my voice. Mazus laughs, but it doesn't reach his eyes.

"You remind me of my son. Thorne also has little patience for my schemes. Perhaps that's why Queen Laurel has grown so close to him. He reminds her of you. Or is it the other way around? Hard to say, when magical bonds are involved." His eyes swirl with knowing. I keep my expression neutral, not rising to the bait. *Let him wonder what conclusions I've come to.*

"I haven't had any correspondence with Her Majesty, so I can't comment on whether she and the Prince have become close. You seem to be better informed than I. Though I'm happy she's getting to know the emissary. That was the whole point of the arrangement, was it not?" I raise my brow, challenging him to reveal more.

"I've received word that the two have been *extremely* close, as I had hoped." I want to roll my eyes, but I keep my face stoic.

"Why did you hope for them to grow close?" I ask nonchalantly. He grins, seeing through my facade.

"Now, now, you can't expect me to answer that truthfully," he says with a sarcastic sneer.

I shrug. "Not really. I don't actually care. I'm happy Laurel has found a *friend* in my absence. Life has been hard on her, after you convinced everyone she was the villain in the story."

"And you believe she is not?"

I nearly choke on my wine. "We both know there's only one villain in the story of the war between Thayaria and Velmara, and it's not Laurel," I spit, cursing myself for letting him get under my skin. He only grins.

"Let me let you in on a little secret." He leans in, pure malice in his eyes. "Villains, heroes, it's all irrelevant. What matters is power, and what you do with it. I'm a hero because I made myself one with the power I claimed. Laurel is the villain because I said she was one. If she wanted to change the narrative, she should have fought harder, should have *won*."

"You think highly of yourself for a man who inherited a stolen throne, won a war against a twenty-year-old newly crowned monarch, and can only single channel," I respond coolly. The remark has the intended effect. His eyes widen in anger, and he stands. *So, he didn't intend for me to find out about his blood magic. Just the mates.*

He laughs maniacally. "I can assure you, I'm more than a simple air channeler. And while I may have inherited my throne, I've had to keep it, had to expand my power and influence, and I've done that all alone."

I slow clap. "Very good, Mazus. I'm sure your parents are *so* proud. Are we done here?" His eyes light up with something I can't decipher, but he waves his hand.

"You're dismissed."

I leave the room quickly, mind racing and eager to return to my room and get out of Velmara with Genevieve. My steps echo loudly in the castle, eerily quiet for this time of day. When I get to my room, I stop in my tracks. The door is ajar. Surely Genevieve wouldn't have been so careless as to leave it open. I unsheathe a knife, walking slowly towards the open door.

"Genevieve," I call out, but don't get a response. I enter the room, and it takes my brain a moment to process what I'm seeing. Genevieve has been tied up and gagged, and both

Mazus and a man I recognize as Silas Kalmeera are standing over her. Mazus must have known my plans and aerstepped here immediately.

"So glad you could join us," Mazus says, a haughty glint in his eyes. Silas just sneers at me.

"Neme... rrrrnnn!" Genevieve tries to yell through her gag, though it comes out as a muffled grunt.

"Let Genevieve go. This has nothing to do with her," I say, raising my knife.

"Oh, but you see, it does," Mazus says. "As soon as Silas offered Genevieve a place in the family again, if only she would reveal what the two of you had discovered, she spilled all your secrets immediately."

Genevieve's eyes go wide, and she struggles against her bonds, and my heart feels like it's dropped to my stomach. Words I cannot decipher come out as murmurs from her gagged lips as she fiercely shakes her head side to side. I look back and forth between her and Mazus, completely lost. Why send me the books if he didn't want me to discover something? Why bribe Genevieve to reveal our research in books *he* lent me? I want to run, but I need the books, must risk everything to bring them back to Laurel. I lunge for my pack, scooping it into my arms and drop it behind me. In response, Silas holds a knife to Genevieve's throat.

"Don't move, girl, or I'll slit her throat," he growls. "Now that I know what an *abomination* she is, having intimate relations with another *female,* I'm looking for any excuse to exterminate her."

I'm taken aback by the vitriol in his voice. While I intellectually knew that Velmarans looked down on relationships between females, experiencing their hatred firsthand is an entirely different experience. Genevieve's amber eyes stare up at me, shining with tears and shame that breaks my heart. She struggles against her bonds again, but Silas only presses the knife deeper into her neck. A bead of crimson blood tracks down her throat.

"In Velmara, females serve *one* purpose—to produce strong heirs," Mazus lectures calmly, as if we are old friends and he's politely answering a question I've asked him. "Any deviation from that is met with punishment. As a member of a powerful noble family, Genevieve has already brought shame upon her family by being deemed unworthy of marriage." Silas growls in agreement, and Genevieve drops her head to her chest in defeat. "When the Head Librarian reported your *relationship* to me..." Mazus and Silas both look at Genevieve in disgust. "I immediately informed Silas, who determined it was time to end the shame she has brought upon the Kalmeera family."

"No!" I scream, but Mazus rips the air from my lungs. I clutch at my throat, trying to breathe before I pass out and leave Genevieve vulnerable and alone. He releases his hold on me, and I take in a deep gasping breath, then launch myself towards Silas and Genevieve. Mazus steps into my path, dagger pressed against my stomach.

"Now, now, *General*," he coos with mock sympathy. "You're in Velmara, and we do things differently here. You wouldn't want to start another war over a disgraced librarian." I stiffen, then slowly back my body away, using the movement to cover the growing plant inching toward Mazus from the corner of the room. "Good," he soothes. "Now, return the books I loaned to you, and I will personally aerstep you back to Thayaria. We can forget this whole thing ever happened."

"Never," I snarl, willing the trailing plant to curl up Mazus's legs and pin him in place. He looks down at them, then breaks into a deep laugh.

"You stupid girl," he sneers. "You really think this can hold me?" In a flash, the plants wither, as if they're rotting from the inside out. "I tried to be nice, offered to send you back to Thayaria safe and sound. But now," he shrugs, as if he's not responsible for his actions. My lungs freeze again, and a dagger flies through the air toward me.

Genevieve screams through her gag. I try to duck out of the way of the blade, but my muscles have completely frozen. The dagger scrapes my shoulder, cutting deep but not delivering a fatal wound. It'll heal in a few hours, but I don't care, my focus is singular. *Get to Genevieve.* My vision swims with black spots from the lack of air, and I fall to my knees. Genevieve's wails reach a fevered pitch.

I try to claw my way to her but only fall forward on my face. The familiar pressure of being aerstepped tingles across my back. My eyes lock on Genevieve's, and she nods her head, answering my question. I try to yell at her, to tell her not to do this, but I'm still mute from Mazus's magic.

"Silas, stop her," Mazus hisses. In his fury, he must lose focus on the magic pinning me in place. I can breathe, and the air comes rushing back into my lungs. I grab my pack, intending to cling to her so she can't do this, so we can both get away. But before I can reach Genevieve, or even say anything to her, I'm disappearing from the room.

Genevieve is an air channeler, a powerful one at that, and she's aerstepping me away. She kept this secret from me, allowing me to believe she had very little magic. We never discussed our magic, I realize. The last thing I see before I wink away is Silas slicing her throat, blood pouring down her slender frame, eyes unseeing.

The cells of the Thayarian palace are one of the strongest prisons in our world. Built atop an iron floor, even the water that seeps into the damp dungeon is laced with iron, the only substance known to nullify access to the aether. Most fae and other aether-made creatures cannot access the aether from within the cells, even without the iron cuffs typically placed on those kept there. Only the strongest fae can overcome its effects.

A Brief History of Modern Thayaria

Water drips from the ceiling in a torturous rhythm. The iron shackles around my wrists pinch my skin and rub blisters. The cell is dark and damp, and the cold seeps into my bones through the scrap of silk Mazus had required I wear to our dinner. Unfortunately, the magic nullifying effects down here mean the deep gash on my left shoulder isn't healing, and I can barely move that arm with the way the cut makes it ache. I've never been a prisoner in these cells before—they're horrific. When Laurel realizes what's happened, several Royal Guards might lose their lives. I can't say I'll be upset by their deaths after they roughly seized me and brought me here after Genevieve aerstepped me to the port at Echosa.

Pain shoots in my chest at the thought of the sweet female I'd begun to care deeply for. Even though she betrayed me, in the end she lost her life trying to protect me. The way her usually vibrant face looked after Silas sliced her throat, those eyes completely hollow of the life I cherished, flashes across my mind. Deep breaths do little to ease the stab of grief, but I choke back my tears. I won't cry, not down here, not until I'm out of here and know that Laurel is safe. Then I can lock myself in my family's cabin far from here and grieve Genevieve the way she deserves.

As soon as I landed at the port, I walked through the mist. Years ago, Laurel somehow spelled the magical barrier to allow me to come and go as I pleased, even though I rarely use the ability. Unlike many others, I didn't need to wait for someone to collect me and quickly made my way into Thayaria. But not twenty minutes after I settled in by the fire at The Emerald Shell, soldiers arrived and arrested me. Mazus's books were taken from me, and an air channeler aerstepped me directly into the palace cells. Carex arrived shortly after, giving me no information other than my arrest was on Laurel's orders. His eyes held pity in them.

Surely Laurel had not ordered my arrest, or if she had, it must be part of some scheme I don't yet understand.

After what feels like hours, footsteps echo off the rock hallway, the only noise I've heard since arriving other than the drip of water. I stand and smooth the pitiful excuse for clothing I'm wearing, ready to laugh with Laurel at whatever's going on and tell her everything I've learned. The movement of my left arm makes me wince, but I ignore the stabbing pain, resolved to show Laurel the calm and put together demeanor she expects from me. But when she arrives, the Velmaran Prince at her side and expression cold and filled with fury, no amount of resolve can keep the emotion and panic from my voice.

"Laurel, thank god you're here. I have so much to tell you. What's going on?" Her face hardens and she bares her teeth, only adding to my confusion.

"Why don't you answer that question first? Why are *you* here?" she demands. I recoil from the ire in her voice.

"What—I don't—Laurel, I escaped Velmara. Barely. I need to talk to you. Privately." There's pleading in my voice, a crack in my exterior. Laurel doesn't seem to notice, too consumed with her fury. My eyes dart to the Velmaran Prince next to her, and I try to convey with my eyes that he should not be part of our conversation, whatever scheme she's playing at be damned. Prince Hawthorne stiffens by her side, subtly shifting his body to stand in front of her. *So, they have grown close, as Mazus said.*

"Traitors are not afforded a private audience with the Queen," Laurel hisses at me, and my mouth actually drops open in shock.

"Traitor?" I whisper, my brows furrowing. Is this what Mazus wanted Hawthorne to do? Did the Prince grow close to Laurel so he could somehow convince her I'm a traitor? She's too smart to fall for something like that, too calculating and distrusting. "Laurel, there's been a mistake. I don't know what you think you know—"

"I don't *think* anything," she snarls. "I saw the evidence with my own eyes. Tell me, when exactly did you start working with the Sons and Daughters of Thayaria? Was it you who has been leaking information that bolstered their recruitment efforts? You who told them all of our plans?"

I'm speechless. I open and close my mouth, unsure how to even respond. The rebels—how could she possibly think I would work with them? That I would betray her? Some scheme is at play here. Either Laurel is trying to convince the Prince she thinks me a traitor, for what reason I can't say, or the Prince has actually convinced her I'm one. I wrack my brain, trying to weave pieces together that just don't fit. I debate playing along, but the situation is too urgent.

"Laurel, please," I plead, but she cuts me off.

"Save your breath. You'll rot in here while I determine what to do with you." Then she turns on her heel and marches out. Carex gives me another pitying look before following her, but the Velmaran Prince hangs back, leaning toward me in the cell. His eyes are dark with a protective anger.

"Whatever lies you're trying to spin in your mind right now to get out of this, save your energy. I've spent centuries at the Velmaran court. I can spot a lie from a mile away," he whispers, his voice pure venom. Then he too turns on his heel and stalks away, leaving me reeling.

Three days pass in complete solitude, kept company only by stoic guards and the occasional servant bringing me meals. I try and fail to summon the aether, over and over again, even though I know it's completely impossible. At some point, a healer comes and tends to my shoulder, removing the ache but leaving a numbness in its wake. In the prison's silence, all I can do is think of Genevieve—her smile, her laugh, her unbridled love for research. The way she blushed when we did something she'd never done before. How even after everything she'd been through, she'd still known *I* needed to *jump*, and not just off the cliff into the Velmaran sea. Her amber eyes and black curls haunt me, both awake and dreaming. I lose my resolve to wait until I'm closed away in the cabin to grieve for her. Sobs wrack my body in an endless cycle of desolation and longing and pure, aching sadness.

I should've known our affair wouldn't be a secret with all the eyes Mazus had on me. I was a *fool* for forgetting where I was. I want to be angry with Genevieve for betraying me to Silas, but I can't. She'd lived her entire life at the mercy of others, contained within whatever cage her closest male relative had built for her. I don't blame her for jumping at the chance to improve her station.

When I'm not thinking of Genevieve, I pick through every detail of my last days in Thayaria before leaving for Velmara, trying to discover the action that's been interpreted as traitorous, but come up blank. The longer I go without answers, the more my confusion turns to anger. It consumes me. Either Laurel believes the worst of me without even hearing my side of the story, or she's made me a pawn in some larger strategy without consulting me and left me here to rot.

I saw the evidence with my own eyes, Laurel had said. *What am I missing?*

Carex visits on what I think is day three, though he provides no information about what made Laurel think me a traitor. Doubt clouds his eyes as he questions me about my involvement with the rebels. Whatever evidence Laurel thinks she has, I can tell Carex doesn't believe it. But he's too loyal to her, too *in love* with her to ever go against her wishes. What a useless excuse for a male. If only he could have seen that what Laurel needed was someone to challenge her, maybe they would've stood a chance.

Laurel finally visits once I've lost count of how many days I've been in this underground hell. I don't bother standing this time, my fury burning too hot to even look her in the eyes.

"Come to make baseless accusations again?" I spit. Her eyes widen for an instant before the cold mask I know so well returns. Not once in three hundred and twenty years has that mask been turned on me, and it both breaks my heart and enrages me in equal measure. "Or are you here to secretly torture me, like you've done to so many other prisoners down here?"

She flinches, and I know the blow lands as I intended. Laurel has never let go of her guilt, even as she holds onto the rage that drives her down here in the first place, stuck in an endless cycle between the two. The mask returns, though I can't help but notice her eyes show regret and sadness.

"I'm not here to torture you," she croaks out. "I'm not—I don't—I don't even know why I'm here," she admits, and I study her closely. Dark circles line her eyes, just like how I left her. But there's also a lightness to her I've never seen before. She practically floats as she paces, wringing her hands. I wonder whether she and the Prince have discovered the mating bond yet. *Would they even know what it is?* "Nemesia, how could you?" she asks, mask cracking to show the vulnerable female beneath.

"I don't even know what you think I've done, I swear that to you. I'm your friend—your sister. That hasn't changed," I tell her, my voice losing some of its edge. "There's so much I need to tell you, Laurel. I—the books. I had books with me, but they were taken. You *must* get them to Admon, he'll know how to read them." Regardless of what she thinks I've done, those books cannot fall into the wrong hands. She only studies me closely.

"Admon has had the books since the day you arrived," she acknowledges curtly, and some of the tension I'd been holding releases. Admon will be able to gently explain the mating bond to her, of that I'm sure. "The letter—we found the letter you wrote to the rebels, telling them that the thayar flower once existed in Velmara before disappearing," she continues, accusation back in her voice. "You told them of your research in the archives." Bright green eyes bore into me. I furrow my brows.

"I didn't write any letter to the rebels, but that information *is* accurate. There's so much more to it than that..." I say, wondering whether this letter was forged with early discoveries I made. I walk through my early time in Velmara, before Mazus gave me his books. Realization dawns on me. I quickly stand and stalk toward her, pressing my body against the bars of the cell. "Laurel, that letter, did it mention the Floating Market at sunset?" I ask, frantic. She nods. "I wrote that letter for you but decided not to send it. I'd completely forgotten about it until now. Mazus must have found it and gotten it into Thayaria somehow." My voice is pleading as pieces click together in my mind. My anger is gone, replaced with worry for her. Mazus clearly has a contact in Thayaria. It would be so easy for Prince Hawthorne to gain her trust, then give her this letter that Mazus sent him.

Now her brows furrow. I can see her mind racing, eyes darting back and forth as she considers my words. I also see the moment she decides she's not ready to believe me. She shakes her head, backing away.

"It's too easy a story," she whispers. "You would know what was in the letter, could easily have just spun this tale. There have been no other leaks in your absence." Her features harden. "When you're ready to tell the truth, send the guards for me. Until then, enjoy your cell."

With that, she disappears, not even bothering to walk away.

Iron is poisonous to fae. Without quick action, an iron wound can fester and make even the strongest fae very ill. Deep cuts or prolonged exposure will kill. It takes incredible amounts of aether to heal an iron wound. Healers treating those inflicted by iron should expect weeks of depleting their power stores to aid their patient.

A Practical Guide to Magical Healing

We're in the greenhouse at Thorne's request. He's been experimenting with his light the last several weeks to see if it will influence the exotic plants here, exploring some hunch he's yet to tell me about. As we walk around the room, he points out every plant in painstaking detail, not missing one tiny leaf that may have changed with his magic. As it turns out, the plants have thrived under his radiant tutelage. At least four that have never flowered before now display bright, unique blossoms, and even more have grown larger or brighter. It's like they needed his power to fully mature.

When Thorne brought me in here, his eyes filled with pure joy, my heart—both of my hearts—had squeezed tightly. Despite the bone deep ache I've felt since the moment Carex informed me that Nemesia had been captured at the port in Echosa, Thorne somehow makes me smile. Since I've accepted the mating bond, my magic feels lighter, easier to carry. My *aether-heart*, the source of my magic, is soothed in a way I didn't know was possible, a way I didn't know I needed. I'm steady and grounded with Thorne by my side, despite everything closing in on me right now.

We still haven't made any progress in finding the rebels after their disappearance from the throne room, nor have Silene and Fionn been able to contact them. It's like the rebellion has completely disappeared from Thayaria. Not to mention, Nemesia's reaction to the accusation that she was the mole isn't sitting right with me. She looked utterly lost and confused in those cells, devastated when I accused her of being a traitor. Silene's suggestion that the letter we found was intended for me but intercepted by the rebels has replayed in my mind at least a dozen times.

I've only visited her once since we brought her to the palace cells in the two weeks she's been imprisoned. I'd had to tap deep into the cold and heartless Witch Queen persona to stop myself from aerstepping her away from the cells and into my sitting room, where we could pretend everything was back to the way it was before she left for Velmara. I ordered her to be left alone and well cared for, not able to bring myself to have her tortured for information. I saw a cut that had festered on her arm, and sent healers to mend her, but otherwise have kept my distance, despite my near constant worrying about her. Nothing makes sense to me anymore *except* Thorne, and the irony of that is laughable.

"Where have you gone, witchling?" Thorne's soft and amused voice breaks me out of my spiraling, and I look up at him with a soft and sad smile.

"Just thinking about Nemesia." It's all I can say aloud without breaking down, but he understands. Thorne wraps me tightly in his arms and places a kiss atop my head. Tears gather in my eyes. "What if I got it wrong, and I've left my best friend, my only family, to rot?"

"Then we'll fix it. If she isn't the mole, then she's still the same Nemesia you know, and the two of you have a bond strong enough to survive this."

"I think I should move her out of the cells," I whisper, afraid to admit what feels like weakness in me. "She can still have guards posted in a low-level room, but I can't bear the idea of leaving her down there any longer, even if she is the mole. The Council will be in outrage though."

Thorne chuckles and pushes me away from him slightly so he can look into my eyes, his warm hands placed solidly on my shoulders. "Laurel, you are their Queen. You rule by committee most of the time, and that's admirable beyond belief, but you shouldn't shy away from making the decisions you feel are right out of fear of their reaction. Trust your instinct. And if any of them push back, I'll spear them through with light and drown them on dry land." He gives me an unholy smirk, filled with the promise of violence I know he's capable of.

I laugh aloud. "Look at us now. I'm the charming courtier trying to make everyone like me, and you're the menacing brute force who will kill any who opposes you. Our roles have reversed."

"What can I say, spending time with the Witch Queen has changed me." His wink makes my thighs clench. I love it when his flirtation turns wholly on me. I bite my lip, and he growls, pulling me close again. "If you keep looking at me like that, I can't be held responsible for my actions," he whispers in my ear, nipping it with his teeth. The move sends shivers down my spine.

"Maybe that's what I want," I coo in a husky voice, arching my back to press my breasts closer to his broad chest. He trails his finger down the column of my neck.

"If I recall," he murmurs, "you were just complaining yesterday that I'm ruining all your favorite garments with my impatience to get you naked."

He's right. Since I accepted the mating bond, our need for one another has been uncontrollable. We can barely spend any time alone without ripping off our clothes, no regard for where we are. Silene's been the one to handle getting out the word to the Council that she and Thorne's betrothal was a sham, whispering it into the right ears. It's a cover we desperately needed with how much additional time we've been spending together, often in compromising positions. Yesterday, we were nearly discovered naked in the Council chamber while waiting for advisors to arrive for a meeting. Thankfully, Silene once again saved the day, having the foresight to speak loudly to Admon before they walked in together, buying us enough time to dress. While I'm sure my advisors have their suspicions about us, I certainly don't want to confirm them via accidental nudity.

Evenings are a different story. Regardless of whose bed we're in, gone is the savage and wild lust. Instead, Thorne makes love to me gently, slowly. We explore one another, our sighs filled with emotions we haven't yet expressed. I tell him stories of my life, and he offers his own. And when we finally fall asleep, it's in each other's arms. I'm the happiest I can ever remember being, despite the Nemesia-shaped hole that consumes me when I'm not with him.

I mock pout, and Thorne's pupils dilate. "Why can't you simply unlace my gown or pull the skirt up, instead of ripping open the front of whatever I'm wearing?" I ask him with a smirk. He returns it with his own, then peppers kisses over my collarbone and neck.

"Because. If I'm going to fuck you. Witchling. I need it to be with your breasts. Cupped. In my palms," he says between kisses. I moan.

"Let's try it, just this once," I breathe out, then lift my skirt to my hips. To entice him, I wrap one exposed thigh around his waist. He takes the bait, lifting me fully, and I wrap the other leg around him as he carries me to a worktable in the back corner. Plants cover the table, but in a blink, they disappear and reappear in neat lines several feet away. Something prickles in the back of my mind, but I push it aside, lost in my lust for Thorne. He sets me down gently, tucking my skirt out of the way before he unbuttons his own trousers. My already wet center pulses, and I can't pull my eyes away from his cock.

"Like what you see?" His voice is low and gravelly, and it sends electricity shooting through my veins. I only nod, unable to speak. "Keep those eyes where they are. I want you to watch as I push into you." I do as he commands, practically coming undone as his length slides into me. Fully seated, he slowly pulls back out, and we both watch as our bodies come together. He slams into me, and my eyes roll to the back of my head.

"Thorne," I sigh, and he growls, hands coming to my breasts and kneading them through the fabric of the gown. He lets out a frustrated sound.

"This is the only time I will ever agree to this," he pants. "We'll get you infinite gowns. We'll order a dozen replicas of each one."

I let out a laugh that quickly turns to a moan when he conjures light to touch my clit in soft strokes. The surrounding air becomes almost unbearably humid, water dripping down my back. Thorne lights up the steam in the air around us, surrounding our bodies in a soft glow. My own body hasn't radiated light since the first night we came together, but one or both of us is always letting our magic out unbidden when lust overtakes us. The plants suddenly seem to glow on their own, and my eyes widen. I meet Thorne's gaze, and he seems as incredulous as I am as he continues his even rhythm of thrusts. The greenhouse has transformed into a lush and tropical oasis, light and water dancing around us as we reach our climaxes. With a mutual roar, we crest that wave together. Our panting slowly evens out, though Thorne keeps his forehead pressed to mine as he caresses my hair and places kisses atop my head.

Slowly, so slowly, he pulls out of me. I stand and adjust my dress.

"If our clothes stay mostly on, we can do that a lot more often, princeling," I say with a wicked grin.

"Still not worth it," he murmurs, squeezing my nipple teasingly. The sensation lights me up with need all over again.

"What is it with you and my breasts?"

"Are you kidding? Isn't it obvious?" When I shake my head, he laughs in delight, cupping them both through the dress again. "Your breasts, Laurel, are exquisite. Have you never noticed how different you are from other females? They're slim and lithe. No curves or breasts to speak of. I love everything about your body." He growls the last sentence, and my toes curl. Of course I've noticed how different I am. How could I not? But to hear Thorne *praise* that difference, to find it attractive... The desire to run from this feeling is strong, but I push it down, deciding to sit with the feelings of delight and fear and *something else*, however uncomfortable. I survey the greenhouse. Misty steam has fogged up the glass panels that make up the dome. Even if someone walked in here, I'm not sure how much of us they'd even be able to see. Soft light glows around us, though I can somehow sense that Thorne is no longer controlling the light. The plants also glow with a luminescent shimmer. "Your magic is incredible, Laurel," Thorne remarks, but my brows furrow, finally having the clarity of mind to process the magic we see.

"This isn't me," I say slowly, and now Thorne's brows scrunch together.

"Then how—" he starts.

"I think," I interrupt. "I think it's some kind of reaction to your power. It *feels* like you, but I can also tell you aren't using your magic. It's unlike any power I've ever encountered." He surveys the room with renewed interest, closing his eyes and taking a deep breath before responding.

"This place has always reminded me of Eastern Velmara, where the light channelers come from. What if..." He trails off, lost in thought.

"What if what?"

"What if this place was meant to be some kind of replica? Of Eastern Velmara? I think I knew I was connected to this greenhouse in some way. It's why I started experimenting on the plants." The implications of his theory are too massive for me to consider right now, only minutes away from lust-addled fog.

"We need to speak with Admon." Thorne nods his agreement. I look around the greenhouse one last time, marveling at the otherworldly feel it has to it, before taking Thorne's arm and aerstepping us to Admon's chambers.

We knock on Admon's door, but there's no answer, which is unsurprising, since it's the middle of the day and Admon is a busy man as the now permanent Chair of the Council of Advisors. Just as I'm about to aerstep us back to my rooms, Admon appears at the end of the hallway, slowly walking toward us.

"Your Majesty," he says with a bow when he reaches us. "I did not expect you. Did I forget a meeting we had scheduled?"

"No, no," I say to the old fae, feeling guilty for appearing without notice at his door. "Thorne and I just wanted to discuss something with you. But we can come back at another time. Give you more notice."

"As it happens, I have something I'd like to discuss with you as well. So the timing is fortuitous." He smiles, then leads us into his sitting room. I heat water in his teakettle, then make myself and Admon a cup of tea before settling down into a leather sofa by

Thorne. I give him a wink at the frown I see forming on his expression and instantly know it's because I did not let him make the tea for me.

"Admon," I say once he's also settled, "what did you want to discuss?"

"I've just come from visiting Nemesia." I tense. I hadn't explicitly forbidden anyone from visiting her, but I didn't expect that she would have visitors. "I confess my own curiosity about what she may have learned from the Velmaran archives drove me to her. I've visited a few times. I hope I did not misstep. I assure you, Your Majesty, my intentions were scholarly only." Thorne rubs circles on my thigh, and I relax.

"It's okay." I trust his intentions implicitly. "It's good that you're attempting to extract information from her. Though we should consider anything she tells us carefully, as she could be lying." I'm not ready to voice my doubts about Nemesia aloud to anyone but Thorne, even Admon.

Admon looks thoughtful. "That is, of course, a possibility. But I've spoken with Nemesia at length about her time in Velmara, her escape, and what she uncovered."

"Escape?" I ask, fear for my friend cutting through all the layers of emotional detachment I'm trying to maintain.

"Indeed," Admon continues. "Nemesia discovered a great secret, and King Mazus killed someone she'd grown close to before attempting to capture Nemesia. Thankfully, the librarian who was killed was a powerful air channeler, and she aerstepped Nemesia to the Echosa port just before she died. I believe Nemesia feels immense grief over the loss of the librarian." My mind is racing and my stomach churns with too many emotions for me to unpack right now.

"What was the secret?" It's all I can get out amid the flurry of feelings roiling through me.

"She says she won't tell anyone but you. Even now, Nemesia demonstrates her stalwart fealty to you and to Thayaria. I must say, I struggle to believe Nemesia betrayed us," Admon says gently. "She's always been so loyal to you, and the knowledge she revealed to me matches the books she brought with her. She insists the letter you discovered was meant for you." I crumple in on myself, those words from Admon the final nudge I need to change my approach with Nemesia.

"Admon," I sigh out, rubbing my hands over my face in exhaustion. "I'm going to have Nemesia moved to rooms on the lower level of the place, right above the prison. The iron below will still somewhat affect her, and I'll station guards, but..." I remember Thorne's words, his encouragement to own my decisions. "I want her moved today." My words are resolute.

"I think that's a wise decision, Your Majesty," Admon counsels with a smile, and my shoulders rise in pride at his praise. Thorne nudges my arm to silently communicate *I told you so*.

"You do? Why?" I ask.

"Beyond my hesitation to believe she's betrayed you, Nemesia is a quicker translator than me. If we have any hope of finishing the translation of the Old Fae book she brought with her, we need her working on it. I truly believe there are critical answers in it. If you still doubt her, I can spot check her work to ensure it's a truthful interpretation of the text."

I nod. "Coordinate her move. And inform me if there are any rumblings on the Council about the decision." My voice reminds me of my mother, and I smile inwardly.

Admon nods. "Now, what is it that led you and Prince Hawthorne here today?"

I'd forgotten that Thorne and I had our own set of questions for Admon, so wrapped up in my thoughts of Nemesia. I struggle with where to begin, looking to Thorne for support. He jumps right in.

"The greenhouse reminded me of Eastern Velmara, though the plants are not the same," he starts. "I've been experimenting with exposing the plants to my light magic, and they've had an incredible response. New blooms, larger leaves, growing taller and wider."

"By new blooms, he means plants I've never seen flower have suddenly sprouted breath-taking blossoms," I add, and he grins. Admon only continues to look on with interest.

"I was showing Laurel, and we... uh... I..." he trails off, remembering what *exactly* led to our discovery.

"He showed me the progress he's been making on combining light and water channeling. He lit up the greenhouse in a misty glow," I finish for him. Admon has a gleam in his eye that tells me he knows exactly what we were doing, and I'm completely mortified, but continue anyway. "The plants themselves started glowing and continued to do so even after Thorne stopped channeling. Even the light and mist remained. And the magic... it felt like him." Admon's expression looks far away, like he's remembering something from a long time ago. He shakes whatever it is from his mind and smiles inquisitively.

"That is curious indeed. I'll stop by the greenhouse today and take a look. I suspect the answers we need are in the books Nemesia brought with her."

"Let's get Nemesia moved to new rooms, and then she can begin translating," Thorne says excitedly to me, threading his fingers through mine. "You can speak with her about what she may have learned, and we'll figure out together what we believe." I squeeze his hand in appreciation of his support, so unused to having someone to rely on.

As we're walking out the door, Admon calls out to us. "I'm happy that the two of you have both accepted the mating bond." My brows furrow.

"How did you know?" We hadn't yet told anyone other than Fionn and Silene.

"I can just tell from seeing the two of you together. You're glowing," he responds with a smile.

The next day, Nemesia is set up in rooms just above the palace cells, the iron from below still making any fae on that level uncomfortable and dampening their power. Thorne and I agreed he'd come with me to speak with her, but that he'd stand back and allow me to do the talking. It's a small but important moment as we learn to navigate our life together. I consider donning the Witch Queen persona, but the effect would be moot on Nemesia, who has so often seen that mask. Instead, I opt for soft leggings and a navy tunic, braiding my hair back in its classic style. At Thorne's insistence, I wear daggers on both thighs. We both know I won't need them, but the mating bond requires these small compromises to settle the persistent desire to protect.

Thorne brushes a piece of hair off my face, then squeezes my hand in my bedroom before we aerstep to Nemesia's door. Four guards stand at alert, barely reacting when we arrive. They all bow quickly before one of them pulls a key from his belt and unlocks the door. Thorne and I enter, hand in hand.

Nemesia doesn't look good. White-blonde hair hangs in matted clumps around her face. Her eyes are hollow, very little emotion reflected in them as she sits in a leather chair by the fire. Her clothes are still dirty and soiled from the weeks she spent in the cells. A twinge of guilt stabs my gut.

"Have you not been provided with clean clothes and water for washing?" I ask, sternly. Nemesia doesn't even look up at me, just continues staring into the fire that warms the room.

"I have. Don't feel like cleaning up."

"And why not?" I ask, shocked at the person who sits before me. She only shrugs, and I look at Thorne, suddenly lost for what to do. He squeezes my hand, encouraging me to trust in my own instincts. "You will clean yourself up before speaking to your Queen," I command with the aether-voice. Nemesia stiffens, clearly trying to fight the compulsion, but eventually stands up and walks toward the bathing chamber, eyes burning with fury and hatred. For once, I don't feel guilty using the aether-voice in this way. Something tells me Nemesia may not have washed up without it.

I seat myself by the fire while I wait for her. Thorne finds a beverage cart and makes me a cup of steaming tea. I smile when he hands it to me, grateful for this silly and small thing he always insists on. Rather than sitting beside me, he takes up a place against the wall behind me, leaning against it with his arms crossed. If I wasn't already completely enamored with him, I would be after this. As always, he's so beautiful it nearly takes my breath away, and the way he can pull off disinterest impresses even me. I sense that a subtle but strong shield of light surrounds me where I sit on the couch, invisible to all but myself. Just like me, he can perform incredible feats of magic with no sign of it in his expression.

When Nemesia returns from the bathing chamber, clean and in fresh clothes, she looks closer to the female I know, though her eyes are still haunted, and her frame is too thin. She collapses into a chair, and I study her for another moment before speaking. Something's changed in the weeks she was in the cells. She was angry with me when I visited before, pleading that I had made a mistake. Now, it seems indifference has settled over her. That bolt of guilt shoots another strike through my body.

She notices me staring at her, and says, voice a sarcastic sneer, "Happy, Your *Majesty*? Am I clean enough to be in your presence now?" I ignore the barb.

"You told Admon you discovered something you would only share with me. I'm here now. What is it you wanted me to know?" Nemesia's eyes quickly dart to Thorne, uneasiness crossing them. "A lot has happened while you've been away. Thorne and I are… allies." I opt to save the more unbelievable information for another time, still not sure I can trust her. "I trust him with any information you have to share." She hesitates, staring between the two of us, scrutinizing us with those empty and hollow eyes.

"I discovered interesting information about the myth of fae mates while in Velmara. Would that be of interest to either of you?" I stiffen, instantly understanding what she's looking for. She knows mates are real, suspects Thorne and I are connected in that way, and wants to determine if we know before she says anything more.

"It would, yes," I say with a nod, the closest I'm going to come to admitting the truth. Nemesia nods, indicating she understands what I'm saying and the relationship between Thorne and me.

"Mazus knows. About the two of you, and your connection. It's why he sent Prince Hawthorne here," she finally admits, emotion returning to her somber eyes, body straightening itself to resemble the female I know. "Beyond that, I know nothing more of his motivation. I've already translated the section on mates from the book in Old Fae I brought with me. I wasn't able to bring my notes with me, so I'll have to copy it all out again to share it with you."

"Why would you help us?" I ask, my voice tentative and questioning, seeking any clue in her expression or answer to help me determine whether I can trust her.

She deflates once again. "El, you *must* believe me. I did *not* send that letter to the rebels. I intended it for you. I don't know how it got to the rebels. They must be working with Mazus." Her eyes are pleading.

I believe her, despite my desperation to hold her at arm's length until we can prove without a doubt that she's not working with the rebels. The realization makes me question my sanity. Am I so desperate for my old friend that I'll believe anything to erase the months of heartbreak and betrayal I've felt? I fear that my trust will be misplaced. Fear it will be a mistake I deeply regret. But Nemesia has been by my side my entire life—if she wanted to betray me, it would have been so easy in the early years, when I was a complete mess after the war. Even if her opinion of me has recently changed, I just can't believe she would work with the rebels. But I'm not ready to admit this to her.

"So Mazus knows that Thorne and I are mates," I say, and her eyes widen. She understands the statement to be the closest thing to an olive branch I can give her right now, and I think I see her lips quirk just slightly. She nods. "Is that the secret you would only tell to me? You should know that Admon also knows. We turned to him for answers. Carex knows as well." Thorne stiffens behind me, and I realize I hadn't told him that Carex knew about us. I inwardly smirk at the alpha-fae jealousy I'm going to have to deal with later but turn my attention back to Nemesia.

"No, that's not the secret, though I had no intention of telling anyone but you of Mazus's knowledge." She takes a big breath, releasing it in a sigh to steel herself. It's a mannerism I'm familiar with, and it brings me a bit of relief to see her returning to her usual self. "I believe Mazus is a blood mage." Her words are firm, confident. Both Thorne and I tense, and Thorne walks to my side, our arrangement forgotten, though I can't blame him. This was not the news we were expecting. Nemesia gives him a suspicious look but continues. "Blood magic is not what we've always been told it is. You must have the affinity, just like any other conduit power. You can't just decide to practice blood magic; it has to be something you're gifted with. And the blood magic line comes from Velmara. I believe..." she trails off, and I give her an encouraging nod to continue. Thorne sits next to me now, hand in mine and body leaning in toward Nemesia. "I believe Mazus descends from this line. What's more, I discovered information that says the Andomers, the light channelers—your mother's line," she says with a nod to Thorne, "once ruled Velmara, but were forcibly overthrown by the Vicant line, the blood mages." Thorne's coloring has gone pale, and I can see the gears turning in his mind.

"I was always taught that the Andomers tired of ruling, so they peacefully handed over the throne," Thorne says, clearly realizing the absurdity of the words as he says them. Nemesia doesn't tease him, simply nods in understanding.

"Did you find any proof that Mazus is actively practicing blood magic?" I ask, but Nemesia shakes her head.

"No. Once I suspected it, I decided I needed to get out. What's strange is that the four books I arrived with were not in the archives. Mazus had them sent to me from his personal collection. I still don't understand why he allowed me to find this information. It was too strange, so I had to flee. I tried to bring the librarian who helped me back to Thayaria too, but she... Mazus..." Nemesia's voice cracks, and I almost reach for her, but I hold back, still wary.

"Admon told us," I say instead, offering her the compassion of not having to recount the story. I decide to speak with her about this again at another time, suspecting the librarian was more than a friend. But I know better than most that some wounds have to scab over first.

"There's more information about mates you should know," she says, changing the subject. "According to the Old Fae book, Thayarian rulers used to always have an Andomer light channeling mate. Even then—whenever *that* was—no one knew why. It just always happened, and it was usually the strongest among the light channelers who mated with the Thayarian monarch." Thorne's hand tightens around mine, and I grip it back tightly.

"The greenhouse," he whispers, and I turn to look at him.

"What do you mean?" Nemesia asks. Thorne looks at me, seeking my blessing to take over the conversation, and I give him a nod.

"The greenhouse here in the palace. It reminds me of Eastern Velmara, and it struck me as a strange feature here. But it was practically life saving for my friends and I during Abscission, and I've been drawn to it. What if it was created specifically for those Andomer mates? To help give them a piece of home."

"That's a very real possibility," Nemesia murmurs, lost in her own thoughts.

"And it explains the reaction to your magic," I whisper softly as I squeeze Thorne's hand, but Nemesia overhears.

"His magic?" she asks. I quickly explain what happened earlier, leaving out the more intimate details. Halfway through recounting the story, I realize I probably shouldn't be trusting her with this information. But old habits die hard, and for over three hundred years, I told her most things, if not everything. "The greenhouse must be reacting to Andomer light after centuries or even millennia of it missing," Nemesia offers, expression thoughtful, like there's more she isn't saying. "I'll keep reading the books. I can make you a translated copy of the section on mates. I haven't even read through two of them yet." I nod, then stand to leave, but Nemesia's expression goes hard, and I pause. "Laurel, you should make the Council believe I'm still a prisoner." Her voice is steely.

"You *are* still a prisoner," I add, eyes narrowed, though the words don't come out with the intensity I had hoped for. Nemesia only rolls her eyes, and I have to stifle the smirk that rises to my lips at seeing my old friend before me.

"There's still someone on the Council who betrayed you out there. Even if you don't believe me, for the sake of Thayaria, proceed as if there could still be another mole. Let them think your suspicions lie fully with me."

I nod, then leave, unsure who is friend and foe in this palace.

Some mated pairs have reported being able to use their mate's power after accepting the mating bond. These reports typically align with powerful fae pairs. Scholars disagree whether this phenomenon is real or whether the presence of one's mate simply unlocks additional conduit affinities in a fae.

The Traditions of the Fae

"I still don't know what to believe. My heart tells me to trust her, but I fear that's exactly what she's hoping for," Laurel confesses after our discussion with Nemesia. We're in my mate's rooms tonight, and I watch her with focused intent as she undresses and pulls the plait from her hair.

Unable to keep my hands off her, I quickly appear behind her with barely any memory of taking the ten or so steps between us to reach her. Taking the braid from her hands, I slowly unwind her silken hair, breathing in her addictive scent as it washes over me. When her hair falls down around her shoulders, she turns in my embrace, pressing her body against mine. I'm instantly hard, though that isn't surprising. The slightest touch or graze of skin from her turns me on these days. And when we aren't together, I'm on edge, needing to get back to her as soon as possible.

She pries herself from my embrace, hips swaying as she walks naked to the bathing chamber. My gaze trails after her, hungrily drinking in the curves I've come to know so intimately the last few weeks. From the doorway, she pauses and looks at me over her shoulder with mirth, knowing the effect she has on me as she stands there in the nude. Her full body and wide hips are hypnotic, and I lose all sense of reason or conscious thought when she's undressed. A low, needy groan escapes me, but Laurel only winks and turns back to resume her nighttime routine. I love the bathing chamber she washes her face in now, and we've had countless couplings in her massive bathtub, modeled after the one in the Eless estate. When she returns from her closest, she's clad in a nearly transparent lilac chemise, and I hum in appreciation of the sexy garment, then wash my own face before changing into a pair of soft sleep pants and turn back to the bedroom.

Laurel and Lunaria are snuggled up together on Laurel's massive bed, and I grin at the pair. The giant cat's purring is so loud I can hear it from where I stand across the room. I crawl into bed beside them, stroking Lunaria's sleek body.

"Of all the surprising things that have occurred between us, Lunaria allowing you to touch her might be the most surprising of all," Laurel teases.

"I think she liked me before you even did." The cat slowly closes her eyes before opening them again in acknowledgement. Laurel laughs, and the sound lights up what I now know is my aether-heart. The laugh jostles Lunaria, and the cat jumps from the bed in protest of our movement. With a look back at us, she disappears through the cracked patio door. "We *have* to build some kind of cat door for her before next winter. I cannot stay in here with that door open." Laurel lets out a low chuckle, but I see through it to the emotion she tries so hard to keep hidden. There's a nervousness to her at my statement, like she isn't sure whether she's afraid or excited by the prospect of me still being here next winter. I wrap her in my arms and haul her body close to mine, her backside pressed against me, then place a kiss on top of her head and inhale her scent. Laurel needs to be *shown* that I'll be here, not told. All I can do is hold her close and breathe my intention into every exhale. "For what it's worth, I think you're making the right choice moving Nemesia out of the cells and trusting her to translate the book for us," I murmur gently, returning to our conversation about the best friend, turned traitor, turned potential friend again. Laurel sighs.

"I hope I don't regret it. This whole situation has been confusing. I think your father's planning something massive, but I have no idea what it is," she says ruefully. I turn her to face me and thread our fingers together.

"I *know* he's planning something. Giving Nemesia those books, sending me here knowing that we're mates... and if Nemesia is to be believed, working with the rebels—none of it makes sense, but we're going to figure it out together. We haven't even put Silene on the case yet. Give her a few days and she'll have it all uncovered."

Laurel smiles. "I feel guilty. I haven't been spending as much alone time with Silene since we bonded. We need a girl's day."

"Silene understands." I stroke her thumb with mine, the incessant desire to touch her, to soothe her, even stronger than before the mating bond clicked into place.

"To be honest, I think I've pulled away from Silene since we found that letter. I think—I think a part of me is afraid of being betrayed again." I study her closely. Long auburn hair flowing freely, face free of makeup, vulnerable emotions raw and exposed—she's never looked more beautiful to me. If I could have her just like this every day, I would. But that would mean we aren't the people we are, and I also wouldn't change one thing about my mate.

"It's normal to feel that fear. You just have to recognize it and not let it control you. Spend some quality time with Silene tomorrow at the Spring Festival." We're attending the traditional Thayarian event that marks the beginning of Spring tomorrow, at my own insistence. I want to do things with Laurel that aren't plotting and scheming and worrying. "She was made for dancing in fields of flowers with children running around her." Laurel chuckles warmly, and it shoots pleasure through me.

"That's an understatement," she says, placing a delicate kiss on my lips before staring up at me with those bright green eyes from under dark lashes, snuggling her body closer to mine. Her pink lips pull into a shy smile, and the freckles that dot her cheeks stretch with the movement. I see the smallest lines of wrinkles at the edges of her eyes. There's no sign of the Witch Queen here, or even the serious but caring Queen of Thayaria. In this moment, the only person with me is Laurel—*my* Laurel—my mate, the other half of my whole.

"You're so beautiful," I whisper, tracing my fingers across her cheekbones and over her lips, wanting to study every inch of her face and commit it to memory. She blushes, lowering her eyes, afraid of the emotions I wear so openly. But how could I not? How could I be anything but completely besotted with this incredible female? Even before I knew she was my mate, Laurel saw me in ways no one else ever could. She enabled a version of me I'm proud of—the kind of male who fights back against injustice, who protects the innocent, who helps *lead* change instead of hiding in the shadows hoping things will get better. I may have talked about resistance in Velmara, but it was Laurel who showed me what effective action looks like. We challenge one another, take delight in the delicious tension that comes between two evenly matched powers. She's stronger than me, but just barely, and neither of us gets to experience the thrill of knowing another person can match us blow for blow very often, both physically and intellectually. She cares so deeply, even as she locks her true self away. I want to spend every waking moment inhaling whatever parts of her she trusts to give me.

Before I know what I'm doing, I take her face in my hands, placing kisses atop her nose, her cheeks, and her lips in reverent worship. It matches my response the night she accepted the mating bond, and that feels fitting for what I'm about to blurt out.

"I love you, Laurel Elestren," I say on an exhale, surprised by my confession but knowing the truth of it. "You *are* my aether-heart, the air that I breathe and the magic coursing through my veins. Without you, I'd still pretend to be the Shining Prince, charming and flirtatious, unserious and unbothered by anything or anyone. You unmasked me, allowed me to be the male I always believed myself to be, always wanted to be, but feared revealing. You light up my entire world, witchling." I place a kiss on her forehead as she stares at me with a shocked stare. "I also want you to know that I love the *Witch Queen* too, because she's a part of you. I love your soft parts, but I also love all those hard angles and vicious barbs. I love watching you take control of a situation, love you seeing you claim your power and show your strength. I love you when you show your enemies mercy, and I love you even more when you don't. There is *no part of you* that I don't love." Her mouth parts slightly, and she takes a deep swallow. She starts to say something, but I place a finger over her lips.

"I know you aren't ready to say it, my love. *My Queen.* You've experienced so much loss, cut yourself off from *feeling* for so long. I will spend every day I'm at your side working to pay back to you everything you endured at the hands of my father. *I* will break the cycle of violence and hatred my father and all of Velmara have created for you. I know how challenging it is for you to access emotion. Everyone you've ever loved has died, betrayed you, or been afraid of you. *I know you*, Laurel. If you take a week, a decade, or a century, I'll be by your side, loving you. Even if you can never say it, I'll still love you. You are my home and my purpose, the person I want to wake up with every morning and hold in my arms every night. I love you, and I need you to know that, can't go another moment without telling you." The smile on my face stings my cheeks, but I ignore the feeling, too happy to care.

Laurel's eyes are wide with emotion, delicate tears gliding down her rosy cheeks. I pull her to my chest, stroking her hair, the joy I feel unmatched by any other happy moment in my life. We lie down together, Laurel wrapped tightly in my arms and her scent surrounding me. As we drift off to sleep, I try again to commit her to memory—the feel of her pressed against me, the way her smell mingles with mine, the small noises she makes as she drifts into unconsciousness. I dream of her, knowing that even in my sleep I'll love this female in this life and the next.

"Laurel, my love, wake up," I whisper in her ear when the sun breaks the horizon. She murmurs something incoherent, then snuggles farther down into the blankets, pressing her body closer to mine. I moan at the feel of her ass firm against me. "Witchling, you have a girl's day to get to, and if you don't stop tormenting me with that delicious backside of yours, you'll never make it," I growl as I kiss up the column of her neck. She wakes, and the scent of her arousal hits me immediately. Another growl lets out from low in my throat, and she wiggles her hips against me again. "You're torturing me," I complain.

She turns in my arms, breasts pressing into my chest, and I squeeze her waist tightly. Green eyes light up with delight as she looks at me, and that's the only sign I need to ravish her. In a blink, she's under me, breasts flat and nipples peaking through her sheer nightdress.

"Thorne," she murmurs. Her clothes disappear, and she lets out a surprised gasp before I silence her with my mouth on hers. I run my hands up the curves of her body until they cup those irresistible tits, fingers pinching her nipples as she moans into my mouth. "I lose control of my magic around you," she breathes out. "I don't even remember willing my nightdress to disappear."

"You can *poof* away your clothes any time," I huff out before ripping my own pants off. When my length presses into her, Laurel's eyes darken with a hungry lust. "Put my cock in your dirty mouth, witchling," I command, and she obeys, moving her body with fae speed to switch our positions and bring her lips to my shaft. She licks up the column, and I moan. When she takes me deep in her throat, I nearly come, but resist, unwilling to finish without her. My hands weave through her tantalizing hair, guiding her up and down in a steady rhythm.

She nips the top of my cock with her teeth, sending shivers through me, and I can't wait another moment to be inside her. I guide her body to rise and sit on mine, groaning with pleasure when I enter her.

"Fuck, witchling," I murmur, but she only smiles, devilish with glee. She moves slowly up, letting me inch out of her at an agonizing pace, then slams her body back down with her own moan. Repeating the motion, I crawl closer to release with every dip, knowing she does too. When I get dangerously close, I will my light to stroke her in the hard and fast circling I know she likes, and she lets out a feral scream that undoes me. We roar our climaxes together.

When she drapes her body over mine in satiated bliss, breasts tickling my chest, I harden inside her again. We're on the balcony suddenly, and plants creep their way over the railing to bind her hands behind her back. Confusion flashes over her features briefly before disappearing as I suck her nipple into my mouth and nip it lightly. We're exposed here on the balcony, and a fae with particularly strong eyesight could see her naked body from a courtyard or terrace of the castle. The thought makes me irrationally protective. Mist gathers around us, shielding our bodies from view. *Thank the aether for Laurel's magic.* Within the hazy fog surrounding us, I take my time worshiping her. I kiss between her breasts, up her throat, nipping her ear in a way that makes her shiver with satisfaction.

"Laurel." Her name is a sigh. My hands cup her ass as I lift her to me, clinging tightly like I'll somehow lose her if I let go. Our foreheads touch, and she gives me another of those soft smiles I love so much. "I love you," I whisper, then gently thrust inside her, slowly, reverently. We find a slower rhythm, hands exploring one another like it's the first time. "I love you. You're mine. And I'm yours. And you're perfect. *We're* perfect." The words are a soothing murmur, the backdrop of my worship of her. I can't get enough, can't get close enough to her. Deep within me is some *feeling* that we'll be parted, but that must be the mating bond. To soothe it, I pull her even closer, wrapping her hair in my hands and gently tugging her head back so I can kiss her deeper.

"Thorne," she moans. "I..." she trails off, unable to say the words I know she feels.

"Shhhh..." I whisper. "It's okay." I trail kisses over every inch of her as we both ease into our climax this time, moans soft and gentle and filled with emotion neither of us can fully express.

When we finish, we make quick work of bathing and dressing for the festival, running late for our meeting time with Fionn and Silene. Laurel wears a soft pink cotton gown that brings out the rosy hues of her skin. The square neckline accentuates her breasts, and the ruching along the bodice has her curves on full display. She starts to braid her hair back.

"Will you leave it down?" I ask, and she smiles. Air swirls around us, wrapping around her hair and leaving it flowing down her back in soft curls.

"Silene taught me that trick," she says with a smirk, and I chuckle.

"Then I'll have to thank her, because you look ravishing." She blushes before slipping on delicate pink shoes.

Laurel didn't want to go to this festival—she hasn't gone in over three hundred years. The last time she went was with her parents, and just five years later, her people were slaughtered in the very place where the festival is held. The Battle of Moormyr, named after the valley called Moormyr, is known throughout the Four Kingdoms as being a dark day for Thayaria, regardless of which side of the story you hear. It's challenging for Laurel to be in that valley without remembering the war that cost her everything. She'd told me all of this in the early light of morning a week ago, wrapped in my arms.

"How are you feeling today about the festival?" I ask as I pull a cream tunic over my head. She shrugs, trying to fake nonchalance. Even with me, after months of letting me in every day in small ways, she still defaults to hiding her emotions. "Really?" The skepticism is apparent in my voice, and she sighs, her shoulders dropping as she releases the tension of keeping her emotions at bay.

"I'm nervous," she admits. "Not just to be back in Moormyr after all this time, but for the risk of a rebel attack. I know we've kept my attendance as secret as possible, and I know there will be as much security as we can possibly provide... But I fear if they know I'll be there it will lead to more innocents being injured or killed. Aethers, we're not even sure if the rebels realize yet that you were working with me the whole time. They could attack just to get back at us, especially since you were the one to redirect their attacks away from villages and citizens. I can't help but feel like this is a terrible idea, and I'm not sure if the pain low in my gut is a premonition of violence to come or simply my deep anxiety." I pull her into my arms.

"We are the two most powerful fae alive. We'll keep your people safe." I keep her firmly pressed into my chest, kissing the top of her head and trying to will some measure of comfort through the kiss. She sighs contentedly.

"I hope you're right." I give her a wide, mischievous grin.

"When have I ever been wrong, especially about you and me? And our *magic?*" She rolls her eyes, but I don't miss the way the comment makes her cheeks flush with desire, even after weeks of fucking at every opportunity we get. "Let's go dance in the field with children and pick flowers and whatever else we do at this festival." Now she laughs, and warm male satisfaction spreads through my body. I love making her laugh, love easing her worry. She takes my arm in hers and aersteps us to pick up Silene and Fionn. When we reach the apartment, they're ready, giving us knowing smirks when we mutter our excuse for being late. Then Laurel aersteps all four of us to the valley and festival.

We stand at the top of a hill, looking down on the celebration below. Laurel tenses for just a moment, eyes unfocused, likely recalling another day standing in this exact spot. I watch as her eyes find every single Royal Guard stationed around the valley, assuring herself of the security of the event. While I wait for her to be satisfied there are enough guards, I look out at the breathtaking sight before me. Snow-capped mountain peaks surround the valley on all sides, sharp ridges eventually softening to rolling green hills. The ground is thickly carpeted in thayar flower, the crimson petals swaying gently in the breeze. There are tents set up along the entire perimeter of the valley, and fae and humans alike enjoy the warm spring air. Children chase one another through the fields of flowers, their mothers' calls to be careful ignored. A large tent at the farthest end of the valley appears to be hosting a Skran tournament, and music filters through the air, mingling with the sounds of the revelers.

"It's so beautiful," Silene says, eyes wide with wonder, and Laurel smiles. Arm in arm, the two of them make their way down the small hill to Moormyr, Fionn and me in tow. When we reach the floor of the valley, it's easier to see that the tents circling it belong to merchants and vendors of all kinds, selling everything from steaming and fragrant food to jewelry, clothing, and artwork. Silene and Laurel have already pranced away, and I'm happy they're spending quality time together, even if being away from Laurel makes my skin itch.

"I guess it's just you and me today, brother," I say to Fionn, who laughs before leading me to a stall selling what looks like Thayarian street food. The smell is divine as we approach, and Fionn orders one of everything on the menu, insisting I'll love it all. Apparently, he's tried them all in Arberly these last months while I've been preoccupied with Laurel. When the food arrives, I nearly groan at the look of roasted meats skewered on sticks and fried stuffed dough. Fionn murmurs an *I told you so* as my jaw drops open, mouth watering. Food in hand, we find a makeshift tavern, where tables sit amongst the flowers. Seated and with ale in our hands, we dig in, both of us groaning at the taste of Thayaria's rich and unique food.

When I've eaten so much I can barely even sip my ale, I survey the festival and bathe in the warm spring air, the sun beating down on me and making my magic feel alive. There's an area for dancing, with live musicians playing an upbeat jig. Revelers swing one another around with abandon, not worried about knowing the right steps. The people seem happy and carefree. There are several competitions set up across the valley as well—arm wrestling, axe throwing, and even basket weaving. There's something here for everyone. And even though they're very subtle, I also spot the groups of Royal Guards that walk the perimeter in plain clothes, eyes scanning while they pretend to make conversation with their companions. Despite what I told Laurel, today *is* a risk, and I'm as nervous as she is, but for her sake. I desperately want today to be perfect for her, want her to make new memories in the location she once told me was the most beautiful place she's seen in all the Four Kingdoms.

When we finish our food and drink, Fionn is unsurprisingly interested in the axe throwing contest, and he unfairly uses his magic to make every axe land in the exact bullseye, delighting the spectators and winning the grand prize—a laurel wreath. I can't help but chuckle at his massive form preening around the festival with a crown of laurel on his head.

Eventually, Silene and Laurel find us. Silene is breathless with excitement as she shows us everything the two of them have bought—rings, necklaces, gowns, slippers, makeup, trinkets—it's an impressive haul. Their arms are full of bags that hold their treasures, and I take as many of them as I can, offering to carry the weight so they don't have to. Silene has even had a small child braid her dark curly hair and weave thayar blossoms throughout it. She's the epitome of a spring goddess, delighted by the festival and its attendees.

Laurel pulls out a small package and hands it to me. I have to drop the many bags in my hands to accept it.

"What's this?" I ask, and she grins.

"I felt bad taking your necklace from you. I thought I should replace it."

I open the package and inside is a ring made of a dark green substance, with thayar flowers and lightning bolts engraved all around it. It's a beautiful piece of jewelry, given by a beautiful female. I take it out of its box, and Laurel places it on my second finger.

"Are you proposing, witchling?" I ask with a dazzling grin I know shows my dimple and drives Laurel mad. She blushes deeply.

"I—No, it's a gift. I mean, not that I wouldn't—I would marry you, in the future. If you wanted. I mean, when we're ready..." she trails off, and I laugh deeply.

"Relax, witchling," I say, taking her out of her misery. "I'm only teasing. But when you're ready to ask the question, I know what my answer will be." I place a quick kiss on her temple, and her blush deepens.

"It's made of the same marble that the floor of the throne room and the foyer of the Eless estate is made from. It also covers the floor of the royal chambers in the palace, where my parents—their suite. The marble is harvested from the caves where the hot springs are and there are many legends about its magical properties. It's not as significant as your necklace, but I thought it could give you a piece of Thayarian history and lore wherever you go." Her eyes are bright with meaning, and I know this is her way of showing me she reciprocates my feelings, even if she's still not ready to say it aloud. I wiggle my fingers on the hand where the ring is placed at her.

"I'll never take it off." She smiles again, this time no hint of a blush or lowered eyes in sight, just pure joy that lights up her face. She takes my arm after I'm loaded down with bags again, and together we walk next to Silene and Fionn, browsing shops and talking to one another. The people notice Laurel, bowing or curtseying as she passes by. I can tell it makes her uncomfortable to be so revered by her people, but I try to encourage her to take it in stride, reminding her that their reaction is a form of excitement at seeing their Queen.

Fionn finds a weapons maker that empties his pockets, and between his weapons and the additional purchases Silene has made, Laurel has to aerstep all our bags and weapons back to the palace because we can no longer carry them all. Once we're relieved of the burden of our purchases, the four of us make our way to the dance floor just as the sun sets. The children have all been sent home, and the atmosphere of the festival takes a noticeable turn. In the shadows of twilight, revelers abandon the propriety of the day, drinking copious amounts of ale and engaging in more sensual activities on the dance floor.

"How late does this thing go?" I ask Laurel, who grins.

"Till sunrise tomorrow morning," she explains, and Silene cheers while Fionn groans. "We don't have to stay all night. We can leave whenever we want to."

"We're staying all night!" Silene remarks with glee, dragging Fionn to dance with her. Laurel grabs two cups of faerie wine for us, and we nurse them slowly while watching the dancing, the alcohol making me feel lighter. When a song I know from Velmara starts, I drag Laurel to the dance floor with me, and we wow the other revelers with a display of magic while we perform the steps of the sophisticated dance. By the end, Laurel's cheeks are flushed and she's grinning wide, unbridled joy on her face.

The music switches to a somber and sultry ballad, and I sweep Laurel up in my arms and spin her around. The people around us pair up, and soon we're surrounded by couples swaying to the music. Laurel looks up at me, full lips pink and cheeks rosy. She's breathtaking, and I lower her into a dip, taking her by surprise. It reminds me of the first time we danced, at the Welcome Ball. Just as they did then, my eyes hungrily take her in. She laughs as I pull her up to my chest, and just as I'm about to drag her away to a dark corner to ravish her luscious body, there's a loud and violent explosion across the meadow.

The witch and the light bringer were each the half of a powerful whole—the witch's raw power a question, the light bringer the answer. Without the shared burden of a bond, the power would have corrupted the witch's mind, making her go insane, as so many others before her. But with her light bringer by her side, she saved the realm from the beasts above.

Unknown Story, Unknown Origin

Screams and moans fill the Valley of Moormyr after the explosion. I push Laurel behind me amidst the chaos, angling our bodies away from the sight of the explosion and wrapping a shield of light around us both. Eyes trained to the opposite side of the valley where people run from, both Laurel and I miss the bomb that detonates right by the dancing area. We're knocked to the ground, and only my light shield protects us from flying debris. More shrieks pierce my ears as I try to make sense of my surroundings, never taking my hand from Laurel's.

I light up the meadow with magical orbs to help us see the attackers—and the damage.

Dozens, maybe more, are injured or worse, though water and plant healers have already reached them and are quickly trying to heal those who can be saved. Fionn and Silene slowly make their way toward us through the running and screaming, but their progress is slow. Another explosion shakes the ground, this time from right beside us. Laurel is ripped from me, and the mating bond explodes in fury. I roar, and my light is so bright across the sky it's blinding. Lightning crackles in the sky above, though I won't allow it to strike the ground until I know where Laurel is, too afraid I'll hit her in my heightened emotional state.

My eyes frantically scan the ground around me, and I finally spot Laurel twenty paces away, still lying prone on the ground. With a single step, I'm by her side. Nothing will keep me from her, not the rebels and not the limitations of my magic. I offer my hand, and she grips it tightly as she stands. For a second so quick I almost miss it, she looks up at me with confusion, brows furrowed in deep thinking. But with another round of screams from a smaller explosion, she shutters it away behind a look of pure venom. Laurel is gone, and in her place is The Witch Queen.

We turn together to survey the scene. The valley is in absolute chaos now, and people are panicking as they try to escape, running over one another as they look for a safe route out. Royal Guards have unsheathed their hidden weapons, and some are trying to quell the chaos while others make their way toward their monarch. Around the ring of the festival, shadowed figures appear.

"It must be the rebels," Laurel whispers, true fear in her voice. "I *knew* this would happen. We have to protect these people." Without warning, Laurel jerks her hand out of mine and aersteps away, reappearing in the very center of the valley, her body lit up with an ethereal glow. Something in my chest breaks open at her disappearance, and I break into a run, desperate to be by her side again. "Silence," Laurel commands with the strongest aether-voice I've experienced yet. The valley around us goes completely still as her words ring in my head, and I'm taken to my knees along with everyone around me. "You will not harm the innocent here today. If you're an air channeler, gather as many with you as your magic will allow and aerstep to safety."

Slowly, people wink away, but it's not enough. There are hundreds of Thayarians left, terror written across the faces of those nearest me. Royal Guards who took a first round of citizens out of the valley return for more, but they barely make a dent. We're far from Arberly, and the magic it takes an average magic user to aerstep that great a distance limits the numbers they can bring alongside them. The shadowy figures that line the perimeter return to their slow march inward, and I can tell they plan to circle us. I order the handful of Royal Guards near me who can't aerstep to focus on the attackers and spread the word. They hesitate for only a moment, unsure whether to take orders from a foreign prince. I repeat the order, voice allowing no room for argument, and they obey.

Across the meadow, Laurel wars with herself, chewing on her lip in a gesture so subtle I'm the only person who would recognize it. But I've studied her face closely for months. I know she's trying to determine what the right strategy is, running through endless possibilities in that brilliant mind of hers. Once again, with barely a thought, I'm by her side, wrapping her hand in mine. Her eyes widen in surprise, but she shuts it down to focus on the attack.

"Get Fionn and Silene," I tell her, and she nods. They appear at our side, windswept but otherwise okay. "If the four of us go after the rebels and try to lure them into a fight away from here, the Royal Guards can use the distraction to get everyone to safety." My voice is strong and confident. Laurel looks like she wants to protest, but I cut her off. "Even if they aren't here for you, they won't be able to resist the opportunity to attack you if you engage them in a fight, especially the strongest magic users. Some of the combat fighters might stay, but your guards can take them."

Silene nods her agreement. "It's a good plan. We'll lure away as many as we can and then take them on in a fight once we're isolated enough that there won't be casualties." Laurel's face hardens.

"No, the three of you should stay here to help the Royal Guard. I'll lure the rebels away alone. I won't put you three in unnecessary risk. I can take them alone." Her words are clipped, like she doesn't even want to take the time to utter them in her impatience to release her fury on the rebels attacking. But the thought of her going after them alone makes my heart race. This is different from the throne room attack where we used her as bait. That was a controlled environment. We have no idea how many of them there are, how many might wait in the shadows to come after us as soon as we turn our backs.

"Laurel, other than you, Fionn and I are the next two strongest fae *alive*. Silene is as skilled a fighter as Fionn. We'll be okay. You don't have to do this alone. We're stronger together." I keep the pleading from my words, trying to sound like the equal partner she deserves her mate to be.

She hesitates, uncertainty and the desire to do everything herself as clear to me as the mating bond. Her eyes flash to Silene, who resents Laurel's protection. Silene has spent her life training, trying to compensate for her less than average magic. She won't be left behind, but Silene can tell Laurel that herself.

"I'll be fine," Silene says firmly. "Plus, I have a small amount of thayar concentrate left." She pulls a vial strung on a leather cord around her neck from under her shirt. "It's a small amount, but enough to give me a few hours of a boost."

Finally, Laurel nods, and Silene downs the small bit of elixir. Explosions and the sounds of hand-to-hand fighting continue to ring out around us as we strategize our attack. Thankfully, my order to the Royal Guards seems to have made the rounds, because they've set up their own perimeter around the valley, fighting the rebels that continue to advance inward.

"Look over there," Fionn says, nodding his head toward a stream entering the valley from a canyon carved into the mountain. Dozens of rebels gather there while their lower ranks continue the assault on the valley proper. Laurel nods, staring into each of our eyes for a brief moment before taking my hand and aerstepping all four of us to a shadowy crevice near them.

Fionn takes control of the tactical operation. As he makes quick hand gestures to signal the plan, Laurel only nods, shockingly letting him become the de facto leader. If we weren't in a life-threatening situation, I'd smirk. With a count of three, Fionn and Laurel step from the shadows and instantly disarm the dozens of rebels around us, dropping their weapons at our feet. Silene and I stroll out and we all arm ourselves, though Laurel and I only take one blade each, reserving our other hand for light weapons.

The rebels stand their ground, attacking us with magic. It causes enough commotion that dozens more rebels abandon their posts around the perimeter of the valley and run to help the group assaulting us. *Our plan is working.* Laurel and I trade off shielding our small group to conserve our strength, and together the four of us advance. Our shields are impenetrable. Not a single plant, drop of water, gust of wind, or dagger reaches us. The onslaught grows, nearly three quarters of the attacking rebel force now gathered before us to take us out. I scan their faces, looking for Krantz, but he's nowhere to be seen. *Coward.*

"Forward ten steps," Fionn commands, his voice strong yet not loud. We follow his instructions, advancing as a unit as he counts out the steps we've taken. It puts us in a perfect position for Laurel to use the plants that grow along the stream to bind the rebels closest to it. At the same time, Fionn sends a slew of weapons from the pile he and Laurel created hurling into the group of attackers. They break their formation to dodge the onslaught, and Fionn's face breaks out in a satisfied grin. "Another ten steps," he orders, and again we advance.

As we make our way into the heart of their formation, shouts ring out, and the rebels abandon their attack and run. We give chase, following them up the canyon, keeping as close to the stream as we can. I hurl daggers of light toward them as we pursue, Laurel and Fionn doing the same with their respective magic. When several of them trip, I know Laurel has used her plant channeling to drop them, even while maintaining a shield and weapons made of water and light. Despite her endless well of power, if she tries to keep up using this much aether for what could be an hours-long fight, she'll burn out. I put up my own shield, yelling at her to drop hers and conserve her strength.

Silene quickly dispenses of the rebels who fell, slicing their throats with brutal efficiency. Despite our quick scrambling, we lose sight of the rest of their contingent and are forced to stop to regroup in a small clearing of trees.

"They're gone. Let's cut our losses and get the people back there to safety. We did what we set out to do by forcing them to run," I say, but Laurel growls in frustration.

"We need to find them and take them out!" she hisses through gritted teeth.

I'm about to reassure her we'll search for them tomorrow, when arrows fly toward us. One catches me deep in the thigh, but I barely feel it as I race to cover Laurel with my body. I'm struck in the shoulder and in my lower back before Laurel's magic wipes out the arrows still flying and the archers with one blood-curdling shriek. I grunt in pain before standing and helping Laurel up.

Fionn and Silene have both also been struck, though the arrows seem to have only skimmed across their flesh. Laurel's okay, and that releases some of the tension coursing through my veins. I rip out the three arrows, hissing in pain and realizing the actual tips remain inside my flesh, then stalk toward Fionn to heal him. When I hold my hand against the wound on his outer arm, I can't feel the magic rise to my call. I realize my access to the aether has diminished. I try to conjure light, but it sputters.

"Iron arrows," Fionn hisses before walking away to survey Silene's injured arm.

Laurel growls behind me, the sound animalistic and so unlike her, and I turn to see a group of fae led by none other than Krantz advancing toward us with weapons and magic. Laurel aersteps to my side, bringing Silene and Fionn to us in the same movement. Her eyes rove over the wounds on my shoulder and thigh, and she bares her teeth, a low hiss coming from deep in her throat. Her eyes are pure black, filled with a feral rage, and I understand. Had our roles been reversed, and she was the one losing blood right now, I'd be lost in the primal urge of the mating bond.

As Krantz and his group of dozens of fae surround us, Laurel replaces my light shield with her own. It's so thick it lights up the entire canyon around us, as if it's daytime. Weapons and magic slam into it, but it doesn't budge. She tries to heal the wound on my shoulder, but it won't work until the iron barb has been removed. She roars out in frustration, completely lost to the fury incited by an injured mate.

"I'm okay," I soothe, trying to break through the animal-like rage that's consumed her. "Let's aerstep away and focus on helping the valley." She makes a low gravelly noise and only shakes her head.

"Krantz," she growls, and I know we won't be able to convince her to leave when she has the opportunity to take him out.

"I've got him, queenie," Fionn says, wrapping his good shoulder around mine to support my sagging weight. Laurel hisses when he touches me and conjures a dagger made of ice that she presses against his throat. There's nothing in her eyes but a beast. Fionn falters for only a moment, and I give him credit for staying firmly by my side despite the lethal look she gives him. He's come a long way since we arrived in Thayaria. I take her hands in mine, stroking soft circles over her thumbs.

"I'm okay, witchling. Fionn is my friend. He won't hurt me. Turn that sexy rage the other way." I give her a wink and a half smile, trying to use the irreverent and cheeky tone I know she loves so much to break through the mating bond. Her eyes lose some of their blown-out inkiness, and a small sliver of green rings them. She slowly backs away, keeping her eyes locked on mine as she crosses to the other side of the thick shield she keeps up around Silene, Fionn, and me. As soon as she's outside of it, water and wind join the swirling mass of light that protects us.

She turns back to the rebels, thankfully at the exact right moment to see weapons hurtling her way. They wink out of existence, and she stalks toward them, a predator caging her prey. Lightning cracks down from the sky in an astonishing display I've never seen her manage, branching out in all directions. Right before it strikes, the small group of rebels disappear, reappearing ten feet away. Krantz laughs coldly.

"Impressive, Witch," he says with a hiss. "But I told you I had secrets of my own. You didn't expect a powerful dual channeler from amongst your *commoners*, did you?" Laurel is completely still, eyes narrowed on Krantz in a rapacious stare.

"I'm going to kill you," she spits with the icy rage of the Witch Queen of legend. Krantz only sneers.

"I've heard that before, and yet here I still stand." He brings his arms wide, cocky smirk on his face. "I see Prince Hawthorne was never on our side. Can't say I'm surprised. But you wound me, Your Highness." Krantz places his hand over his heart in mock offense. I only bare my teeth at him, though even the small movement makes my vision swim from the pain.

Laurel shoots light daggers at his chest, but he evades them by aerstepping away and using his own sword to block, leaving his people behind to be struck with her magic. Several of them drop to the ground with grunts of pain. With a growl, Laurel creates a massive cyclone of air that she sends spinning toward Krantz and his group, but he uses his own air magic power to smother it. With a whistle from Krantz, dozens more rebels surround us on all sides, emerging from deep within the forest. This was a trap, and we fell right into it, surrounded now by at least a hundred fighters. Fionn grunts next to me, the same realization dawning on him.

"Go. Help her, please," I beg him. Despite losing his magic from the iron-tipped arrow that skimmed his shoulder, Fionn is still a formidable warrior, and the wound is shallow enough that he can still fight with full physical strength. I won't leave Laurel defenseless, and while I'll fight until I drop, I can feel my body losing its battle with the iron coursing through my veins. Fionn releases me and I stagger but remain upright. He crosses the thick shield and runs stealthily into the copse of trees surrounding us, swords in both fists.

Without his support, the pain from the gash in my leg nearly overwhelms me. My eyes water and a wave of nausea makes me sway on my feet. I'm about to drop, but Silene scoops her shoulder under mine, supporting my weight despite her small frame. I try not to place all my weight on her, but a shooting pain down my leg forces me to slump. I take a deep breath, wanting desperately to pull myself together to help Laurel.

Grunts from the shadows sound out, and I know Fionn has started his covert campaign. The noises embolden Laurel, and lightning strikes again at the same time that she launches herself forward into Krantz, light sword in one hand and a steel blade in the other. They fight in close combat, a whirl of blades and magic flashing with light as Laurel's lightning strikes around them. I wince every time a bolt hits the ground, worried she'll lose track of the magic and zap herself. But my fear is unwarranted, for Laurel fights as well as any Andomer light channeler who's been training for centuries. She moves through her forms with expert precision, shielding one moment and parrying with a light sword the next, all while maintaining the shield around Silene and me. Pride radiates through my chest even as I clench my hands in fear for her.

But Krantz is a strong fighter as well, and he uses Laurel's rage against her. It's obvious to an observer that he's slowly edging her toward a group of rebels. Silene's gasp tells me she notices it too.

"Laurel!" Silene screams, but Laurel is too far gone in her fury to hear her. Krantz's strategy is successful, and now at least ten rebels surround Laurel, and she has to fight off their magic in addition to Krantz's. The shield around Silene and me drops, and I sag in relief that she's got her focus entirely on protecting herself.

With the shield down and our attention firmly on Laurel, vines creep from the forest beyond and slowly wrap their way around our legs, pinning Silene and me in place. There's a plant channeler hidden away somewhere that Fionn hasn't taken out yet. A sprig of ivy squeezes my wound, and my body shakes involuntarily with the pain. I'm feverish now, the iron arrows still lodged in my wounds leeching away my aether-force. I moan in pain, and slump farther onto Silene, who lets out her own grunt. Fionn notices from the other side of the clearing and runs in our direction, striking down every rebel who stands in his way.

When he reaches us, he slices through the vines holding us and lifts me off Silene, who looks like she's about to collapse. Her hand goes to her stomach, where crimson blood has soaked through her tunic in a deep arrow wound I didn't initially see. She's as injured as I am.

"Silene," I cry, but she waves me off.

"I'll be okay. Go help Laurel, Fionn. Krantz is baiting her," she commands, no room for argument in her voice. Fionn hesitates, eyes unsure as he looks between Silene, Laurel, and me. But it's moot, because before he can act, we're circled by rebels who have been aerstepped by Krantz to surround us. Iron-dipped swords point at our hearts. From across the clearing, Krantz laughs again before he aersteps to stand right in front of me, leaving Laurel swinging her sword at empty air.

She spins around and screams, eyes narrowed in a feral gleam. Her hair is matted with sweat, and blood has turned her pink sundress deep red. There are scratches across her arms and chest, but her blood has not been drawn. If it had, I would know. More rebels appear from out of nowhere to surround Laurel, engaging her in a furious hand-to-hand battle, making it impossible for her to aerstep to us.

"Not so cool and collected when your *mate* is at risk, are you?" Krantz sneers as he looks over his shoulder at her, and my stomach drops out of my body. *How does he know?*

I see the same question written across Laurel's expression for a moment before it fades behind a wild gleam. With a roar, she reaches out her fist and clenches it, and the six fae surrounding her drop dead where they stand. She's winked out their aether-force, and Krantz doesn't look surprised in the least.

I take stock of my surroundings, trying to figure out how to get us out of this mess. The rebels have separated me from Fionn and Silene, who now stand huddled together with no less than six iron-dipped swords pointed at them. I can't see the number of fae behind me, but there are at least four in front besides Krantz. Without Fionn's or Silene's support, my entire body throbs with pain, and I can feel the sweat leaking down my face and back as I try to bear the convulsions now wracking my body. I shift my weight to stand on the other leg, but it doesn't help. Instead of giving into the tempting bliss of unconsciousness, I keep my eyes locked on Laurel forty paces away from me, where she continues to fight off three and four attackers at a time, chest rising and falling with her heavy panting. She's powerful, but even she cannot keep this up alone, especially not while she's in a blinding rage and hurling whatever magic she can at her assailants.

Another wave of pure agony washes over me, and I lose my battle to stay upright, dropping to the ground. Krantz uses the slip to advance toward me, and that's a mistake. I watch as all reason leaves Laurel's eyes and the only thing that remains is a terrifyingly powerful female whose mate is threatened. With an unholy snarl from Laurel, Krantz and everyone around him freeze, unable to move. *Laurel's magic.* She's stopped the aether from coursing through them, rendering them completely immobile. Fionn's and Silene's eyes go wide, unaware of the true depth and nature of her power. But I know, and I also know how much she fears the impact using this much aether will have on the magic of

Thayaria. It's a testament to how lost in the mating bond she is that she's willing to risk exposure and her kingdom's magical stability.

She aersteps to me and drops to my side, taking my hand in hers as she helps me stand, eyes completely black with rage once again. She scans every inch of my body, taking in each wound and the scent of my blood. With a deep inhale, her eyes blow out further, and she hisses.

"It's okay," I murmur. "Let's get Fionn and Silene and get out of here." My words ease the edge of her wrath, bringing a semblance of logic back to her. She nods, thank the aether, and I feel the tingle of magic along my spine that tells me we're about to aerstep.

Suddenly, Krantz breaks through Laurel's hold. It's impossible, and yet, he seems as sure of himself as ever. Laurel freezes, but only for a moment before she's up again and stalking toward him. She smirks at Krantz, but then her face falls. True fear enters her eyes, and I don't understand what's happening, but I can't focus with the waves of pain that continue to wash over me. I drop to the ground once more, vision blurring. I catch a look of pure glee on Krantz's face as Laurel backs slowly away from him. His eyes make a quick calculation, darting around the glade, and before either of us can react, every fae surrounding us has disappeared, Silene and Fionn included. I vaguely hear Laurel's cries of desperation and rancor before I lose consciousness, the pain from the wound finally overtaking me.

Laurel

It is said that blood mages can create potions and spells for other magic users, though this has never been confirmed. Whether this is because it is not true, or because blood mages are so infrequently willing to share their magic, this scholar cannot say.

Blood Magic Through the Ages

"Guards, guards!" I scream in panic as we arrive in my rooms. Thorne is dead weight, and it takes all my strength to slowly lower his large body to the ground without hurting him or myself. His blood covers us both, the scent tinged with the acidic rancor of iron. The two guards Thorne insisted I keep at my door rush in and look upon the bloody scene before them, eyes wide with confusion and fear. I'm grateful for their presence at this moment, even though it had annoyed me to no end when Thorne had declared I must have guards for my rooms. "Get me Admon and your Lieutenant Captain," I order with my aether-voice.

They pale, though one of them breaks through the order long enough to say, "What about Captain Carex, Your Majesty?" I snarl, and they look terrified, but I don't care. Not right now.

"Carex should be considered a traitor to the crown. He's not to be informed of our arrival," I hiss with the aether-voice again. He's the only person who could have betrayed our secret to the rebels, the only person other than Admon who knew of the mating bond, and I trust Admon implicitly. I will not risk Carex gaining any additional information.

The guards nod and leave, eyes glassy with the compulsion of the aether-voice. I turn my attention back to Thorne. Lunaria appears at my side, nuzzling my thigh before considering Thorne. Her yellow eyes study him while she sniffs his wounds, hissing at whatever she smells. Her reaction only makes the terror I'm barely holding at bay seep out of the walls I keep firmly in place around it. My breaths come in deep pants as I try and fail to heal his wounds with every magic available to me. Soothing water, warm light, and medicinal plants gently cover his wounds to no avail. Sobs wrack my body, but I keep going, hurling every bit of magic I can at my mate, despite feeling the shakiness of burnout quickly approaching. I lost all sense of self in that fight, completely at the whims of the mating bond, and thus did nothing to conserve my power.

Lunaria pads to the wine shelf and yowls loudly. I look on in confusion as she paces back and forth in front of it, clearly trying to tell me something. Before I can determine what she means, there's a knock at the door, and I yell for whoever it is to come in, hoping it's Admon. The only Thayarian I truly trust anymore opens the door and his face goes white. Admon quickly walks toward Thorne and me and Lunaria hisses at him before she disappears.

"What happened?" he asks, voice filled with concern.

"The rebels. They attacked the festival. We went after them, but they got away. I only managed to get Thorne and me out. He was hit with three iron arrows," I explain, breathless and fearful.

"What about Fionn and Silene?"

Grief wraps around me like a blanket. "The rebels took them," I whisper, tears running down my cheeks. I wipe them away. "Can you help me heal Thorne faster? He and I can go after Silene and Fionn, but we have to heal him first. I can't—I need him." The last words come out a whimper, and were they in front of anyone but Admon, I would cringe with the vulnerability I've displayed. But Admon has been by my side through so many tragedies, has provided the comfort of a parent even as I grieved the death of my own mother and father.

Admon looks at Thorne's wounds, then shakes his head. "I'm afraid these wounds are beyond my abilities. Nemesia may be able to help, but it would take several days of being removed from the iron influence for her to recover the strength. Thorne *will* recover, it will just take some time. Remove the iron still buried in his wounds, then set him up with the palace healers."

I stand and pace back and forth across the room, a frustrated cry rolling from my dry throat. We don't have *time*. I need to go after Silene and Fionn *now*, but I don't want to do it without Thorne by my side. It's a testament to how deeply he's carved into my very being, that rather than rushing off to fight the battle alone, I pause so that I can bring him with me. I give him one more look before resigning myself to doing it alone, letting out a deep sigh.

Despite Admon's presence, Lunaria returns, pawing at the wine rack. It finally dawns on me what she's been trying to tell me. "You brilliant creature," I murmur, rubbing her head. Admon looks on, an emotion in his eyes I can't place.

I take the now opened bottle of thayar concentrate from the rack, pouring two small measures. Crouching next to Thorne, I dump the contents of one down his throat, then close his mouth and hold his nose to force him to swallow. He begins to glow. Taking a deep breath, I pull a dagger from my side and dig into the wound at his side to remove the arrowhead still lodged there. His body reacts to the pain by clenching and sweating, but he doesn't make a sound. That silence forces me to move faster. *You will not lose him.* Hands covered in his blood, I rip the arrowhead out of his thigh. Then I gently lift him on his side to pull the arrowhead from the wounds in his back and shoulder. As I lay him back down, his body glows brighter, and I can tell that the light wants to heal him but can't break through the poison of the iron.

I look at the second dose of thayar concentrate, pausing for a moment to evaluate whether this is a good idea. Who knows how much aether I'll channel with thayar concentrate coursing through my veins, but it's a risk I must take to save my mate. Admon understands what I plan to do.

"Your Majesty, are you sure this is wise? Have you ever taken thayar concentrate before? Do you know how it will impact your power?"

"Nope," I say with a forced irreverence that would make Thorne proud. And before Admon can convince me not to, I down the concentrate.

My body heats from the inside out, and I can feel myself sparking with energy. The light in the room becomes blinding, forcing Admon to shield his eyes, and I realize it's because I'm glowing so brilliantly. Power like I've never experienced slams through my body, knocking me flat on my face. I take a deep breath, forcing myself to exercise the control I've honed over centuries. Though it's difficult, I wrestle the aether pulsing through me into my firm grasp, then focus my attention on Thorne. A thread connects his body to mine, so clear with this boost in magic that a sob of relief pushes against my throat. As long as he's tethered to me, I know he'll live.

I place my hand over the wound on his thigh, and I swear the blood that coats my hands—Thorne's blood—shimmers, but I don't stop to consider what it could mean. I surround the wound with the strongest water, light, and plant healing magic I know how to conjure, somehow also knowing through some deeply seeded knowledge that I can coax his own light to follow my command to heal him. I pump aether into him, praying the extra power I gave him with his own dose of concentrate will also aid in quick healing. Skin slowly stitches itself back together, and I cry out in joy. Then I flip him over and heal the wounds in his shoulder and back, repeating the process of gathering as much aether as I can and guiding it into him through every conduit available to me. When I lay him back down, color has returned to his face, and the fevered sweat that dotted his brow is gone.

Slowly, Thorne opens his eyes, though he has to immediately close them again. "You're glowing like a star, witchling," he rasps out, and I huff out a small chuckle, not quite ready to laugh at his usual quips until I know for sure that he is okay.

"Look down at yourself, princeling," I murmur. His eyes widen at his own ethereal glow as he lifts his hand and turns it over to observe the effect. He closes his eyes again, slumping from the exertion of raising his arm. Even though I know it will take him more than a few minutes to fully recover, panic rises to my throat, but I push it down. With a deep breath, Thorne's brows furrow in concentration for a moment before the light making him glow winks out.

"What happened?" he asks, and my heart breaks. I don't want to recount the last several hours, don't want to admit I'm the reason his best friends aren't with us.

"The rebels attacked us at the festival," I start, but he cuts me off.

"I remember all of that. What happened to make me glow and you shine like a fucking sun?"

Now I can't help the barking laugh that escapes me. "You passed out from your wounds. I gave us both doses of the thayar concentrate to heal you quickly. I'm not exactly sure how long I'm going to look like this, but it might be awhile..." I trail off.

"Fionn and Silene? Did they..."

"They took them," I whisper quietly. The memory of our enemies disappearing with our friends makes my heart skip a beat. I continue with steely resolve, no room for argument in my voice, "We'll get them back."

"I have no doubt about that, sunbeam," he says as he stands, keeping his eyes closed to protect them from my burning light. I guide him to sit on the couch, not caring one bit about the mess of the blood that still covers him. "But before we do that, let's see if we can get that light of yours under control. Close your eyes, take a deep breath, then imagine yourself as a candle or an orb of light. Physically picture the image in your mind." He waits a few moments before continuing, "You got the mental image?" I nod. "Good, now envision yourself blowing the candle out, or covering the orb with a bowl, whatever makes sense."

I concentrate on the candle in my mind, then imagine a great wind sweeping through and blowing it out. I slowly open my eyes, and the room has returned to its usual brightness.

"I did it," I exclaim, and Thorne opens his eyes with a grin.

Admon claps. "Excellent work, Your Majesty. Can you tell me what happened now?" Thorne and I together relay the events to Admon, who furrows his brows. "They knew you were mates? Who else knows?"

"Carex," Thorne and I snarl together, aether in my voice and another hint of it in Thorne's, causing Admon to take a step back from the force of our magic-laced words.

"Surely you don't think he betrayed your secret?" Admon asks. The deep lines of his face pinch together in worry, and his eyes are unseeing as he thinks through all he's learned.

"I don't know what I believe anymore," I say with a sigh. "But if Nemesia is innocent, then that leaves someone on the Council who knew about me using the plant channelers to help coax the thayar populations. Until I can question him myself, arrest him and keep him in his rooms under guard. I've learned a lesson with Nemesia, so I won't have him sent to the cells without proof, but he will not leave this palace until I know more. Thorne and I are going to go get Fionn and Silene."

Admon bows. "Of course, I'll have him detained." His eyes bore into me, fear written clearly across them. "Be careful, Laurel. I'm not sure we've discovered every facet of the situation yet. I fear there's more to this that we're not seeing." I nod curtly, and he turns to leave, Lunaria tracking his every step with the focus of a feline.

"Where do you think they've taken them?" Thorne asks, his own worry apparent now that we're alone. I squeeze his hand in reassurance.

"I recognized several of the fae from a tavern I visited on my way to the Forum meeting. In Echosa. There was open distaste for me when I walked through the tavern as well. They must have a second headquarters there." Thorne's eyes light up with knowing.

"The documents we went through in Krantz's desk mentioned Echosa frequently," he relays.

"Then let's go find the Echosan rebel base and get our friends back," I say with a menacing smile.

"You're sexy when you're angry," he says, the words hollow with our family taken. "But we should wait until the morning." I start to protest, but Thorne adds, his words firm, "It's dark outside. I won't be much use to you until daylight. I want to get them back as desperately as you do. I can barely stand the thought of leaving them there even a minute longer than necessary. But we need to be prepared, especially if it's just going to be the two of us. Not to mention, I'm still sore from my wounds and you used *a lot* of magic during that attack. We should rest here for a few hours and let the thayar concentrate fully restore us, then depart as soon as the sun rises."

Although I want to argue, I know he's right. Plus, even though my magic is stronger with the concentrate running through my veins, it's more unpredictable and harder to wield—not a great combination for stealth.

"Fine," I relent. "But we're leaving the moment the sun's on the horizon." He nods, and I take his hand to lead him to the bathroom. I gently wash the blood from his body, fussing over him as he protests. I wash myself quickly, then we both collapse into bed for a few hours of restless sleep.

"Have you heard of any places the rebels might have gathered? An abandoned manor or other place they might hide?" I ask Mara and her husband early the next morning. When we'd arrived at The Emerald Shell at sunrise, only a single maid had been awake, just beginning her task of cooking breakfast for the overnight guests. She paled when we demanded she wake the owners immediately but did our bidding asking no questions. Though it's a risk, I trust that Mara and her husband are loyal to the crown and not working with the rebels. It's early enough that none have come down for breakfast, so we can hopefully slip in and out of Echosa unnoticed. Mara's husband shakes his head, but Mara looks at me, fear in her eyes. "Mara, if you know where they might be, please, tell me. They have Fionn and Silene, who worked so tirelessly to help build back your family's bakery in Arberly," I implore.

"There's an old house about an hour away, if you're traveling by foot," Mara says. "Due north of here, completely isolated. It used to belong to a wealthy family who abandoned it to move to Arberly. My parents were friends with them. I don't know if there are rebels squatting there, but it's the only structure I can think of near Echosa that could hold them."

I take her hands in mine. "Thank you, Mara. I will make sure you're not connected to this in any way. You have my full protection."

She nods, and Thorne and I hurry out the back door of the tavern before I aerstep us north as close as we can get without being seen. We walk for about twenty minutes before we spot the old house in the distance, hundreds of makeshift tents surrounding it on all sides. It's much smaller than the estate in Oakton, probably causing the need for so many tents.

"How's your magic?" I ask Thorne. "If I aerstep us closer, can you keep us hidden?"

He gives me a cocky grin. "There's plenty of light, witchling. You get us close, I'll make sure we aren't seen."

I nod, feeling Thorne's magic wrap around me with a loving caress before I aerstep us several yards closer. We watch in silence as the house wakes up. There's a clear guard rotation, the morning shift relieving those tasked with keeping watch overnight. Humans emerge from the tents, and I bite back a scoff that the fae get to sleep in the house while the humans are relegated to tents.

"I think we found the right place," I whisper. Thorne nods. I can still see him using my own magic, though I'm not sure if he can see me. "Am I invisible to you?"

"No," he murmurs close to my ear. "I can choose how the light bends and make it so that we can see each other even while we remain hidden to others." His magic finds new ways to impress me every day.

"Let's walk inside carefully. Take stock of the situation and see if we can find where they're keeping them before we launch an assault. Follow me." Slowly, we make our way through the rows of tents, stopping and starting every few steps to avoid crashing into someone. It's agonizingly slow, and I want to just aerstep us inside the house. But without knowing the layout, the risk that I would drop us right on top of Krantz is too great. When we finally make it to the front door, we pause for a moment to let a human man walk through it before quickly following him, so we don't have to reopen and close the swinging door. I take a deep breath on the other side, steeling my nerves.

Once inside, the manor buzzes with activity, making it even more difficult to stay unnoticed. Despite being invisible, if someone walks into us, we'll be just as exposed as if we'd waltzed in. Hugging the walls, we slowly inch down the hallway. Rebels polish weapons and inspect supplies in almost every room. A human woman walks around dishing out porridge from a steaming pot, and young women and females run around gathering laundry and picking up discarded dishes. *Of course Krantz would have the same backwards views about females as Mazus.*

As we follow a pretty young human woman, no older than twenty-one, carrying laundry, she stops abruptly, and I almost crash into the back of her. A male has walked out of a room ahead of us, and the terror I see on the woman's face makes me angry on her behalf. She tries to turn, but the male spots her, a menacing smile breaking out across his face.

"Hazel," he murmurs low as he stalks toward her. I take a few steps back, knowing we should turn and leave but not able to. To his credit, Thorne stays by my side, letting me lead our recon mission.

The woman's eyes drop to the ground and her shoulders slump. The fae male reaches her, pinning her wrists tightly in his grasp so that she's forced to drop her laundry. He pushes her against the wall and fondles her breasts. Disgust and shame cross her features, but she does nothing, likely too used to the abuse to stand up for herself. The male unbuttons his pants, and I've seen enough. I freeze his limbs and force the air from his lungs. Thorne tenses beside me, knowing we're about to be discovered and preparing himself for the fight. Hazel's body is freed, and she stares in shock and fear around her, not understanding what's caused the fae to halt his assault and go red in the face from lack of air. Instead of screaming for help, she darts away, and I let out a sigh of relief as I allow the male to breathe again, though I don't release his limbs.

"Nicely done," Thorne murmurs in my ear, and I can't stop my jaw from dropping open in shock. I expected him to chastise me, to tell me we don't have time for this or express disgust that I would take away someone's agency in this way, but he doesn't. Instead, he conjures a dagger of light and steps up to the male before slicing him across the throat without hesitation. The male slumps, and Thorne catches his body, angling him so that not a single drop of blood falls to the floor. With strength that makes me weak in the knees, Thorne hauls the man's body into the room he exited and drops him unceremoniously. Thankfully, it's an empty laundry room. "Can you lock it with your metal magic?" he asks as he returns to my side. I do as he bids, my body humming in appreciation of Thorne. Something about seeing him so willing to kill, with no hesitation, deepens my feelings for this male. It's not the violence of it, but rather the knowledge that he can share the *burden* of the crown with me. For the first time in my entire life, someone killed for me, *spared* me the act that darkens my soul each time I must do it. "Let's move quickly, before someone finds him," is all he says, grabbing my hand and walking us away.

We continue our search, looking through every room on the first floor, finding nothing, before moving to the second and third floors. The upper levels are even more crowded, and it's slow work, our bodies ducking and pressing against the wall every few minutes to avoid detection. After searching every inch of the manor and finding nothing but rebels, we return to the small laundry room where we stashed the dead male.

"Where are they?" I whisper in frustration, running my hand through my hair. Thorne keeps his cool, thinking through what we might have missed. Something prickles my awareness, like the feeling I get when someone needs to enter or exit Thayaria. But it's muted, and I can't quite pinpoint what I'm feeling. I close my eyes and extend my awareness to the mist, but nothing's out of the ordinary. I shake it away, focusing my attention instead on the mission at hand, though a feeling of dread continues to fill my stomach. "Let's look again, and this time keep our eyes open for a hidden door or anything we missed," I offer.

Thorne takes my hand and leads the way out of the room. I lock it behind us again, then we slowly make our way back down the first level hallway. It's too crowded now, the house filling with more and more rebels. We can't navigate this, and I'm about to aerstep us out of the house to regroup when I hear a human woman say, "I'll take this food down to the prisoners." My eyes dart toward the voice and I see a large guard grunt and pass a tray of water and bread to a human woman with blue eyes and mousy brown hair. She's curvy, like me.

"I know her," Thorne whispers quietly in my ear. "She was at the Oakton manor and escorted us to Krantz."

We follow her closely, surprised when she heads outside. She walks to the back of the manor, to a set of external cellar doors she opens with a grunt before carefully making her way down the steps and into the dark space of the cellar. I can't believe we didn't think to check the back of the house. We follow her down the stairs into the cellar, and as soon as we're fully in shadow Thorne's magic disappears, though it's dark enough that I only see a faint outline of him. We're making hand gestures, trying to align on a plan in silence, when the woman speaks to someone, and we freeze.

"I'm getting you out of here."

"And why would you do that, you traitorous piece of shit?" Fionn hisses back, and relief washes through me that we found them and that he's alive.

"Because I stopped believing in the rebel cause after the attack on Arberly," the woman whispers quietly. "That wasn't political protest, that was violence against the innocents, motivated only by a desire for power." I glance at Thorne, who gives me a shrug. We silently decide to stay where we are to see how this situation plays out.

"What's your plan?" Fionn asks the woman skeptically. "The iron arrow barely scratched me, so I have enough magic that I healed a bit before they locked us back up with iron. But my friend took a direct hit, and she's unconscious. We need to be aerstepped out. She won't be able to run."

Hearing that Silene is gravely injured brings out Thorne's rash side, and he jumps out of the shadows, wrapping Fionn in a tight embrace. I have no choice but to follow, and my eyes immediately stop on Silene's too-pale body. She's chained to the wall with iron shackles and slumps on the ground, the rise and fall of her chest barely visible. She's not in good shape, and a gentle probe with my magic tells me there's no chance I'll be able to heal her here.

"Your-your mm-m-majesty," Fionn and Silene's would-be savior mumbles, eyes wide in terror at my sudden appearance. I hold up both of my hands in supplication, praying I can keep her from bolting in fear.

"We're only here to save our friends. I heard your conversation with Fionn. If you truly wish to help, I'll take your partnership gladly and will consider you a friend to the crown when this is over." Hands trembling, she nods, then realizes she should bow, so she attempts a feeble curtsy. I think I see Fionn's lips twitch.

"Yes, Your Majesty. I'm here to help," she says, voice feeble.

"What's your name?"

"Allyssia," she responds.

"Then, Allyssia, do you have keys to the iron chains? We'll need to get them out before I can aerstep us away."

"I don't have them, but I know where they are." Fionn rolls his eyes and tries to say something, but I hold up my hand to stop him.

"Take us there. Fionn, we'll be right back. See if you can at least get Silene to drink some of this water while we're gone." Reluctantly, I leave Silene behind as we follow Allyssia out of the cellar. At the top step, I grab her arm to stop her. "He can use light channeling to make us invisible," I explain, nodding my head toward Thorne. "You should loop your arm through mine to stay close to us."

Allyssia nods and links her arm through mine. Together, the three of us make our way back into the manor. She leads us up the main staircase to the second floor, then turns right and walks down a long hallway that ends in a locked door Thorne and I had unlocked and relocked earlier. I see her fumbling, likely trying to find her key to the door. I squeeze her arm to signal I can help, then force the metal in the lock to move, squeezing again to tell her she can open the door. Thankfully, she understands, and we quickly sneak into the office.

The room is small, with a too-big desk and several chairs surrounding it. It looks like a meeting ended abruptly and everyone left quickly. There are papers everywhere, and a crate in the corner contains stolen thayar. Thorne releases his magic, and Allyssia goes straight to the desk, searching through each of the drawers frantically.

"I know he keeps the keys in here, I just don't know exactly where," she murmurs, and I'm about to step in to help her when she holds up a ring of keys and grins in satisfaction.

"Great work," I whisper. "Let's get out of here."

There's a noise on the other side of the door, and Thorne's eyes meet mine quickly before he conceals us again. I reach out and find Allyssia, then pull her to me and try to aerstep us out of the room. But just as the tingling sensation reaches my neck, it fizzles out, like it's been doused with water. Thorne senses my fear, and our eyes lock. I mouth *I can't aerstep* to him, and he slowly guides Allyssia and me to a corner of the room, placing his body in front of ours and conjuring a dagger of light, all while keeping us hidden. I try one more time to aerstep as the door clicks open, and once again am met with resistance.

Krantz walks in, and he looks more unkempt than I've ever seen him, even when he was in the palace cells. His eyes are bloodshot, hair greasy. He walks to his desk and sits down, placing his head in his hands and sighing. He stays like that for a few minutes before looking back up and sorting through the papers that litter the top of the desk. I spot a drawer that Allyssia left open and tense, praying he won't see it. I don't want to have to fight our way out, not with the shape that Silene is in and whatever is preventing me from aerstepping. Unfortunately, the gods have never answered my pleas.

Krantz notices the open drawer and immediately looks up and scans the room. He walks to the crate of thayar, plucking a stalk out of the box and chewing on it. Then he pulls a small vial out of his pocket and shakes out a few drops of a dark red liquid into his mouth. His pupils dilate, and an eerie *wrongness* settles over him.

His gaze immediately falls on us, and his lips lift in a menacing smirk. "I thought we might be seeing you today, Queen Laurel."

Very little is understood about blood magic, which leads to the fear surrounding it. Stories would have us believe those who practice it are limitless, their magic restricted only by their own imagination. One of the famous blood mages of our past—known only by the ominous pseudonym Feerdax—is believed to have been able to change his form at will. From young to old, male to female, even fae to animal.

Blood Magic Through the Ages

Thorne tries to keep himself between Krantz and me as protection, but I make a point to step in front of him. A low growl from deep in his chest tells me how he feels about it, but I ignore him.

"How are you able to see through the Prince's magic? And why couldn't I aerstep out of here?" I ask Krantz, not really expecting him to answer.

"I told you I had secrets of my own, *witch*." The aether rolls through his body in a chaotic wave. He's like a magnet for all the aether around us, sucking the room dry of the magical current somehow. I *feel* Thorne's magic also being drained, so I put up the strongest light shield I can manage. It stops the draining, and Krantz snarls.

"INTRUDERS," he bellows, and I don't waste another minute. I grab Thorne and Allyssia's hands and make a run for it. This time, I let Thorne lead the way, and he slices through every single rebel who tries to stop us with ease. Once we've made it down the hallway and to the first floor, I grab Thorne and Allyssia and attempt to aerstep again. This time, it works, and we emerge on the lawn in front of the cellar, and I re-conjure my shield.

The rebels aren't far behind, pouring out of the house. Krantz and at least six dozen fae fighters run toward us, weapons and magic flying. Thorne takes over shielding, giving me time to evaluate the situation. Taking a deep breath and closing my eyes, I concentrate on the currents of aether flowing around us. It gathers together in crimson pools, sparkling brightly where each fae stands. Where Krantz stands, the aether has turned so deep red it's almost black, and all the red mist around him is being sucked into his orbit. I will the aether to halt, then open my eyes.

I've successfully frozen all the rebels, with the exception of Krantz. Whatever he consumed, it prevents me from controlling him. He looks around at the immobilized rebel army and grins wide.

"What was it you once said to me? Something about trying the same trick twice?" he sneers before sending dozens of swords hurtling into our trio. Thorne reacts instantly, blocking them with his light shield and bringing about half down to the ground. I obliterate the other half, but it pulls my concentration from stopping the flow of aether in the other rebels. They resume their advance toward us. Allyssia whimpers with fear.

"You focus on Krantz," Thorne commands, "I'll take on the rest of them."

"Are you sure?" I ask, concern evident in my voice.

"Doubting my abilities, witchling?" Thorne asks with a mock shake of his head. Even in the throes of battle, he finds a way to be cocky. I roll my eyes.

"Fine. Allyssia, get back into the cellar, and work on getting Fionn and Silene free. I'll provide cover. Free them both, send Fionn to me, then stay down there with Silene. The sooner Fionn is fighting with us, the sooner we can get out of here." The woman looks terrified, but nods. "I'll come get you when it's safe. On my count. Three, two, one, go!"

She races away from us, back to the cellar, and I break away from Thorne to shield her with light. A few rebels try to hurl magic into her, mostly spears of water, but the light protects her from their blows. I'm impressed that she doesn't falter, just keeps running even as magic darts her way. Once she's down the steps, I plant myself in front of the cellar doors, forming an imaginary line the rebels will not cross with my friends vulnerable behind me.

Quickly scanning the field for Thorne, I find him grinning wide as he slashes through three rebels with a light sword. None can break his impenetrable shield, even as they try running into it six males at a time. Sometimes I forget how powerful he really is. *He'll be fine.*

Krantz stalks my way, daggers and swords rotating around him in a swirling orb that acts like a shield. By now I've figured out that he's a dual channeler—metal and air, a rare combination—and I regret not looking into his family history. Most dual channelers descend from powerful families, but Krantz seems to have come from nowhere.

"I'm not letting you leave here alive, witch," he snarls, and I nearly laugh aloud at the hubris a little potion has given him. I can't halt him or will him out of existence with the magic protecting him, but I can still do quite a bit of damage, especially with traces of the thayar concentrate still coursing through my veins. But I won't lose myself to rage this time like I did last night when Thorne was injured. Despite centuries of training and practicing control, everything I'd learned left my consciousness when I'd scented his blood tinged with iron in the clearing. The mating bond had blinded me, and I vow to keep my cool today and make smart decisions about my magic.

I conjure a sword of light in one hand and a dagger in the other, then advance toward Krantz, keeping my awareness on that cellar door. For good measure, I will a barrier of light, water, and wind to form just before the doors for an added layer of protection.

"How would killing me help your cause, Krantz?" I yell over the sounds of Thorne battling others around me. "I thought the Sons and Daughters wanted the mist barrier removed. I have to be alive to do that."

"What we tell the masses and what we really want are two different things. Surely you know that better than anyone," he says as he lunges toward me with his own sword. I deflect the blow, parrying with my own sword that he blocks with a strong current of air.

We circle one another.

"What is it you actually want, Krantz? Me dead, got it. But after that? You'll still be stuck in Thayaria with a barrier of mist around it and no way in or out." I take control of several of the weapons that circle him and shoot them down toward his body. He diverts all but one with his magic, but one is all I need to slice a deep gash across his upper left thigh. He doesn't even react.

"Power," he growls, then charges forward. I wait until the last millisecond before stepping out of the way, slicing through his back as I pivot. He snarls, whipping around quickly. Both his thigh and back have already healed thanks to the supercharged fae abilities combined with the thayar flower and whatever was in that vial. "If you're gone, with no heir to replace you, I'll take over Thayaria with the help of some friends. Of course, I'll make it look like a democratic election, make the people think we're following in the footsteps of Reshnar."

I engage him in an easy back-and-forth parry, blocking his blows with little effort. I'm a better fighter than him, but his quick recovery time makes it challenging to get any kind of upper hand. We trade blows while I evaluate what to do next, keeping him engaged in conversation so he doesn't turn his sights elsewhere. All the while, I maintain a strong shield in front of the cellar doors and around myself.

"Is that all? Power?" I let the disappointment and sarcasm ring out in my voice as I block another blow and slice him with a beam of light. "Here I thought you were truly an interesting and worthy opponent. Instead, you're nothing but a backwoods magic user trying to be more than he is." Krantz growls, and I've clearly struck a nerve, so I keep pressing. "What, did the kids at school not like you very much? Did the females not fall over themselves in awe at your dual conduit affinity?" The ferocity of his blows increase, and now the tables have turned. Last night, he got under my skin, but tonight, I'm coming for him. Miniscule orbs of light rush him, too many for him to block them all, and his body is covered in tiny cuts when they reach him. He falters, and I slice the backs of his knees with ice as I deliver the final, stinging verbal blow. "Poor, sad Krantz. The male who had to start a rebellion just to stroke his own ego."

He hisses at me from the ground, still healing, and I can only laugh. All this time, I worried about taking the leaders of the rebellion out, worried that *I* was the real villain in the story. But all along, Krantz was an ego-bruised male playing insurgent to make him feel better about his lot in life. I stalk toward him, ready to take him out, but he recovers, launching into his own offensive again. It takes me by surprise, and he slices my arm. I *feel* Thorne's growl from across the yard, but I trust him to stay focused on his own task. With barely a thought, I'm healed.

"I'll let you in on a little secret, Krantz," I hiss as we trade blows with our metal weapons again. "Those who play the game only for the satisfaction of winning it almost always lose. You need real motivation, not just a hollow drive to escalate your own status. Even now, seeds of disquiet are building inside your movement. I've seen it with my own eyes. Not everyone will follow you blindly as you slaughter innocents. Not to mention, a kingdom that's stuck behind a wall of mist with no way to export or import goods won't survive for very long." He's too winded from the fight to react, though I'm barely out of breath thanks to Thorne's incessant training. I search my awareness to find Thorne through the mating bond, checking in that he's okay.

He's singled-handedly reduced the number of rebels down to only three dozen, but that second sense I have for him tells me he's tiring. A wave of his scent washes over me, his blood dripping from a small nick the male he's currently sparring with delivered. I snarl involuntarily, and the distraction costs me. Krantz gets in a blow with the back of a sword to my stomach, knocking my breath from me. He slices my thigh before I can shield again, and Thorne's own snarl sounds as the scent of my blood reaches him.

I jump up, hissing at the pain in my leg, even as it stitches back together. I will the smallest bit of light to heal it. Then I take a deep breath, calming my mind and taming the wild beast within that roars at me to go to Thorne. Spears of light fly at Krantz, this time from Thorne, and Krantz drops his weapons to dodge the blows. I give Thorne a look that tells him to focus, and he only winks at me before spinning and slicing the hand off an attacker, just before their sword reached him. I'm forced to return my attention to Krantz, even though I could watch the effortless way Thorne fights all day long.

Frustration and anger are written clearly across Krantz's expression while he tries and fails to get through my shield. He bares his teeth and hisses, then turns his back on me and aersteps to Thorne, catching him off guard and burying a dagger in his gut. Thorne falters, his hand coming to cover his stomach as he drops to the ground. I don't think Krantz has been using an iron blade, or the small knicks he's got in on me would have nullified my magic, but the uncertainty makes me panic.

"I tell you repeatedly that I have secrets, witch, and you continue to underestimate me," Krantz says coolly while he keeps a hand on Thorne's nape. "If I take you out, let's just say I have a plan for keeping Thayaria together. It will *thrive* without you." Krantz smiles from across the yard, raising his sword and slicing Thorne on the thigh, right where the iron arrow hit him. Thorne winces in pain, and I scream my rage, but mine is not the only scream I hear. Fionn has arrived, and he's all lethal warrior as he surveys the scene. I aerstep him to my side, never taking my eyes from Krantz.

"Let's take this bastard down, queenie," he roars, and I nod. Thorne has put up a shield to protect himself and stands, but Krantz and the remaining rebel fighters are pummeling him with magic and blades. Krantz's strategy is clearly to target Thorne to get under my skin and force me to lose myself again, but I push down the urge, keeping a tight fist around the mating bond and its demands.

Fionn grunts, and at least half of the remaining weapons in the field have flown hundreds of yards away. What remains are now pointed directly at Krantz, who laughs.

That feeling of *wrongness* surrounds me again, and with Fionn at my side, I feel confident enough to close my eyes once more. The churning black mass around Krantz has grown, and red currents of aether flow into him faster than before. Thorne is particularly impacted, the aether that courses through him dimmed significantly. Fionn is also being drained. I have to find a way to stop Krantz, have to find a way to keep him from bleeding my mate and my friend dry of their aether-force.

When I open my eyes, Thorne has dropped to the ground again, and his shield dims. Fionn's brow is damp with sweat. *Krantz's magic is affecting them.*

"I need to keep my eyes closed so I can focus on Krantz," I tell Fionn. "Can you cover me and keep Thorne protected for a little longer?"

Fionn clearly doesn't understand my request, giving me a strange look, but he agrees anyway. "I got this."

I close my eyes again and focus on the swirling black mass around Krantz. It's made of aether but has been corrupted. I attempt pulling it away from him, willing the aether to bend toward me, but it resists. As I pull, it only gives slightly, like a jammed door or a stuck lever. The effort makes me lightheaded. It won't budge, and I huff out my frustration, trying to focus through the dizziness that overtakes me.

I open my eyes again, and returning to the world of sight helps steady me. Once corrupted, it appears it stays under his command. I don't want to think about the implications of that for Fionn and Thorne, whose aether still flows into Krantz in red streams, or for the magic of Thayaria. I have to stop it from reaching him in the first place. I close my eyes again.

Instead of pulling the aether to me, I attempt sending my own pure aether into the mass surrounding him. I worry it will just make him more powerful, but I have to try something, so I keep a firm lock on the pathway that connects me to the current of aether around me to ensure he only gets the small amount I'm willing to give him. The bright crimson of my aether moves toward the maroon-black mass where he stands. When the streams collide, red appears to battle back the black, and the mass surrounding Krantz is encircled with a red glow. The aether I sent into him is absorbed back into the ground, not corrupted.

I sigh. Of course the only way to stop him would be to do the one thing I've spent decades avoiding. I do one more test, this time with a larger amount of aether. Once again, red and black fight for dominance, and as my crimson stream wins and returns to the ground, Krantz's unseemly swirling mass actually shrinks.

Encouraged, I take a deep breath and center myself, letting the feel of my feet on the ground steady me for what I'm about to do. Then I outstretch my arms, palms facing down, and pull massive amounts of aether from the closest leylines and direct them into Krantz. A tidal wave of scarlet crashes into him, and even though I can't see him, I can tell he falls to the ground at the onslaught. The black mass circling him dissipates, lightening to red, before also flowing back into the world around us. He's still pulling from everyone around him, but it's at a much slower rate.

I do it again, and this time I hold nothing back. I've never tested the limits of how much aether can flow through me, but today I'll find out. With a cry to the sky, I fully open that mental valve that has always kept the aether flowing into me at a trickle, allowing myself to become the conduit through which the aether flows. The second it slams into me, I gasp. I collapse to the ground as the aether threatens to consume me. The torrent is overwhelming, hard to redirect, but with another infernal cry, I coax it into Krantz, drowning the black mass until nothing but the usual glow of red surrounds him. Then I grit my teeth and close off my access to the aether once more, my body trembling with the effort. I lie there on the ground, eyes closed, too shaky to stand. It takes me several minutes of deep breathing to recover, and I'm grateful Thorne and Fionn have the fight so firmly under control, or I might not have been afforded the luxury of laying still for so long.

Finally, I open my eyes and stand, and the cacophony of the battle slams into me all at once. Fionn has left my side and is fighting Krantz hand to hand a few paces ahead of me. Krantz seems frantic to get to me, eyes wild and more animal than fae.

"Bitch," Krantz spits. He knows what I've done to his magic. Fionn sends a dagger flying into Krantz's gut, and blood pools out of him, the smell foul despite the disappearance of his vile magic. I wrap his arms in cords of light, bringing him to his knees. He struggles against the bindings, but without his *secret* magic, he's no match for me.

"Go help Thorne," I order Fionn, who immediately follows my command. They take out the remaining dozen rebel soldiers together with ease.

"It's over Krantz," I tell him, and he spits at my feet. I sigh loudly, then check my nails. "You have two options. I can kill you slowly, torture you with water and plants in your lungs—it's a specialty of mine—before I force the information from you anyway with the aether-voice." I give him a wink. "Or, I can kill you quickly, which I'll only do if you tell me who on my Council you're working with. Your choice."

"I won't tell you anything," he growls, and I shrug.

"Not the choice *I* would have made, but I did give you the option," I say before ripping the air from his lungs. At the same time, I will the grass under him to lengthen and wrap up and around his body, squeezing tightly. I leave him like this until his eyes water, then release the air back into his lungs. He heaves in a breath as he gives me a look filled with hatred. I only smirk before sending grass up his nose and water down his throat. I pick up a dagger from the ground with my magic, using it to make small slices over his arms and face. Tears stream down his cheeks. "Because I'm such a benevolent Queen, I'll give you a chance to change your mind," I coo, pulling all my magic back.

"The one. You least. Expect," Krantz says between gasps for air.

"Be more specific," I order, bringing an orb of water to his face in threat.

"You'll find out soon enough," he hisses. Then, before I can stop him, he uses the last dregs of his magic to pull the dagger I was using to him, slicing his throat before slumping to the ground with a gurgling noise. I sigh in frustration, then use my power to stop his heart, if only to spare myself from listening to him slowly die.

"Laurel," Thorne says, and I freeze. Panic washes over me, fear that Thorne will only see a monster when he looks at me now. He's seen me kill, but I've been brutal the last two days.

"Thorne," I say, "I can explain…" He just wraps me in his arms, crushing his lips to mine in a kiss that tells me how relieved he is that I'm okay, that we both made it through this fight relatively unscathed. Releasing me from his lips, but keeping me pinned to his chest, he stares down at me, and pure, male lust fills his eyes.

"Aethers, you're so *fucking* hot when you go all evil Witch Queen," he whispers, and both of my hearts practically explode with emotion for this male, finally believing the words he whispered to me in the dark only two nights ago.

Allyssia stayed by Silene's side during the fight, getting her free of the iron and even forcing some water into her unconscious body. I do what I can to heal the infection that's started spreading from the wound, but it's not enough, not without thayar concentrate and the shakiness I still feel from my battle with Krantz. Some of the color has returned to her face, but we need to get her to a healer.

"Would you like to come back with us, Allyssia?" I ask. "My earlier promise still stands. You've helped my friends and stood up to the rebels when it mattered most. Any past crimes are forgotten." She blushes, then curtsies, a bit more coordinated this time.

"Yes, Your Majesty," she says. "I would like to go back to Arberly. But—I—"

"What is it?" I ask, gently.

"I don't have any family, friends, or anyone else to take me in," she says, eyes lowered in shame. "I've lived with the rebels my entire life. I… I might need a place to stay for a few days until I can figure out what to do." A small tear runs down her cheek, but she wipes it away quickly. I think I see Fionn stiffen beside me.

"We'll find you rooms in the palace. You can stay as long as you need," I promise, and that sends her over the edge, sobs erupting out of her. I freeze, unsure what to do and uncomfortable with the emotions of others, but Fionn steps to her and wraps his massive arm around her shoulders, walking her a few paces away.

Shock must show on my face, for Thorne laughs and says, "Underneath that massive frame is a heart of gold."

I nod as I survey the house and all the gore around us. Most of the rebels at the manor either died or fled. The only people remaining are children and those forced here either by a family member or their own desperation. Thorne took over communicating with them, seeing the way I slumped after the battle and knowing I needed him. He told them that if they abandoned the rebels, there would be no punishment for them, and his words felt right. We still need to hunt down those who escaped who *are* complicit, but we can deal with that another day.

"Krantz said the mole is the person I least expect," I whisper to Thorne, unable to keep my worries hidden from him any longer.

"What do you think that means? Could it be Nemesia, after all?" he asks.

"I don't know. I've made so many missteps in judgment, I don't know what to think." He threads his fingers in mine.

"We'll figure it out together," he says, eyes bright. I place a soft kiss on his lips before he gives me another tight hug and places his chin on the top of my head. "I love you," he whispers as he rubs soothing circles on my back. I want to say it back, want to aerstep us to a private corner of the woods and show him how much he means to me as I finally whisper the words that have been on the tip of my tongue for weeks, well before he admitted his own feelings to me. But Silene still lies unconscious before us, and we need to get her to safety. There will be time now that we've cut off the head of the rebels. Plenty of time for me to tell Thorne how I feel and show him he's well and truly *mine*. I give him one last squeeze before releasing him.

"Let's go," I say loudly enough for Fionn to hear me. Thorne lifts Silene's body gently from the ground, then nods at me. Fionn and Allyssia return to our side, and I aerstep us back to the palace.

The witch goddess made the ultimate sacrifice to save her people and the world she and her sisters had so lovingly created. Despite the light bringer begging her not to do it, not to sacrifice herself, she had no choice but to slice their forearms. She used the blood of herself and her beloved to end the Great War before she lost herself to the brutality of her magic.

Unknown Story, Unknown Origin

We arrive in the healer's quarters in the palace by my design, where Silene is immediately handed off to a group of powerful fae I trust to keep her alive and safe. After the healers remove the iron arrowhead from her stomach, Thorne, six healers, and myself weave magic over her body to stabilize her. It doesn't wake her, but it returns her skin tone to her usual golden hue. She looks as if she could be sleeping. I'm a bit surprised that with so many of us I'm not able to heal her after I did it with Thorne so easily, but it must be because Thorne is so much more powerful than her and his own magic aided in the process. I want to immediately go get more thayar concentrate and use my enhanced magic to help her, but even I know that isn't wise considering how much magic I've expended today and the exhaustion I feel. To do that again, I need to be fully in control—I can't risk another moment like at the Battle of Moormyr. But after seeing the way the aether returned to the ground after channeling so much of it to defeat Krantz, I'm feeling relieved. For the first time in a very long time, I have hope that maybe the declining thayar isn't my fault after all.

After assuring the healers I'll return to help heal Silene myself as soon as I'm able, I aerstep Thorne, Fionn, and Allyssia to the Velmaran apartment so we can clean up and regroup. My body protests with every step I take, craving a nap and a cup of tea to celebrate our victory. Fionn and Allyssia move near the fireplace to speak in low voices, so Thorne pulls me into his room. The second the door closes, he's wrapped me in his arms before I can even take my shoes off.

"You're so sexy when you fight," he whispers into my hair before pulling it aside and kissing my neck. The words lack their usual flirtatious zing, and I know he's trying to use the irreverence to help us both decompress. I let him make his way across my collarbone, up the other side of my neck, and to my mouth. He parts my lips with his tongue, devouring me with his full lips.

"Mmmmm," I moan. "You're pretty sexy yourself. You've officially completed your mission as my ally, princeling. You helped take down the rebellion. Guess it's time to send you back to Velmara." He laughs deeply, the noise vibrating my chest from his proximity. It sends a delicious warmth through me.

"And how does it feel, witchling? To have formally allied with me and to have taken out one of your enemies?" he asks as he continues to find areas of my body to touch and soothe. After today, we both need the comfort of physical touch, assuring each other that our mate is well and whole.

I pretend to think for a moment, scrunching my nose, and it brings his lips back to mine once more. When we finally part, I whisper, "It feels like this." Then I wrap us both in warm and calming light, using tendrils to caress his face and backside, earning me a low hum of pleasure. Thorne moves us to the bed in a flash and is pulling my shirt above my arms when a prickling on the back of my neck gives me pause. It's the same feeling I had when we were in the laundry room at the rebel stronghold, like someone's entering the mist. Another check in tells me all is still well. But I'm not convinced.

"Wait," I say, and Thorne immediately releases my shirt.

"What's wrong?" he asks, concern crossing his eyes.

"I don't know, exactly. Something's off in the palace." His brow furrows as I close my eyes to try and understand the uneasiness I'm feeling.

Someone bangs frantically on the apartment door. Our eyes lock for only a second before we're both up and moving back through the sitting room. Thorne answers, revealing a harried Carex, face ashen and body trembling. Tension visibly coils in Thorne's shoulders, so I intervene before Thorne kills him with the same brutal efficiency he displayed today.

"What do you want, Carex? How did you get out of your rooms? You were supposed to be under guard," I demand. I don't want Thorne to kill Carex—not yet, at least—but neither am I pleased to see him.

"Your Majesty, you must come quickly. It's—I can't believe—how—why—You must hurry," he sputters, sounding like a madman, his eyes wild.

I place my hand over his arm to calm him, shock and worry churning low in my gut. Thorne takes up a defensive stance beside me. "Carex, tell me what's wrong," I urge at the same time Thorne hisses, "Spit it out." The magic of the aether-voice lingers, though from which of us it came I'm unsure of.

"King Mazus... is... *here*. In the throne room," he finally says, and all the color drains out of Thorne's features as my heart drops out of my chest.

"That shouldn't be possible," I whisper, and Carex shakes with fear.

"How did this happen?" Thorne barks out.

Carex only shakes his head. "I don't know. Admon came to my room and asked me to accompany him somewhere. I swear I didn't want to go, didn't want to disobey your orders. But Admon insisted. Said it was urgent. Then he led me to the throne room, where Mazus already was, sitting on your throne. Then Admon told me to find you."

Suspicion twists through my gut like a serpent. I'm worried this is a trap Carex has laid. But if it's not a ruse... The risk is too great to ignore. Krantz's words echo through my mind, and a sinking feeling enters my gut. *The one you least expect. You'll find out soon enough.* I meet Thorne's eyes, and I can feel through the bond that we've come to the same conclusion.

"Stay here," Thorne says to me with a voice that once again flickers with the aether-voice, but I ignore it as I let out a haughty laugh.

"Absolutely not."

He only sighs. "Knew you'd say that. Didn't really expect you to listen to me, but I had to try."

Fionn whispers with Allyssia, but he finishes and comes to our side. "She'll stay here for now," he says, nodding to the woman. "I'm coming with you." His tone leaves no room for argument, so I nod.

"Get Nemesia, and meet us in the throne room," I order Carex. If Mazus wants a fight, I need every powerful ally I have at my side, even ones I'm still not sure about. Taking a deep breath, I look into Thorne's green eyes once more, letting them give me strength, before willing the aether to take us to the male we both hate.

When we arrive, Mazus sits on my throne, out of place in the dark and moody room in his bright gold attire. He smiles as we step cautiously into the room, eyes matching my mate's, and it makes me want to hurl. Admon stands beside him, and my heart sinks. *The one you least expect.* The male who has watched over me like a father for the last three hundred years has betrayed me. It's the only explanation for why he would be standing here, why he would have released Carex from his rooms and told him to find me.

"Welcome, Laurel," Mazus says with mock cordiality. He nods to Thorne. "Son."

"What are *you* doing here?" Thorne says with a lazy drawl, crossing his arms and feigning nonchalance. His ability to look unruffled right now is impressive.

"I thought I'd pay you two a visit, congratulate you on discovering a mating bond," Mazus says, and I stiffen. I'd barely had a moment to process the news Nemesia had brought about Mazus's knowledge of our mating bond. And now he's here, aether-knows for what purpose.

"Consider us congratulated and honored by your *magnificent* presence," Thorne says with a smirk and an obnoxious and exaggerated bow. "We're absolutely beyond honored by your presence." He says the last words sarcastically. It's been months since I've seen this side of Thorne, the smirking and lazy prince, who makes his way through every interaction with flippant and brazen remarks, as if he hasn't a care in the world and fears nothing. Mazus only bares his teeth.

"I wouldn't be so cavalier, son. You haven't heard what my mating present is yet." I keep my features schooled in a neutral expression, but inside I'm screaming, completely rattled by this whole interaction.

"You know what," Thorne says, tapping his chin and looking around the room like he's trying to find something. "I think we're out of room in the palace for even a single additional gift." My lips quirk at Thorne's comments, and it bolsters my own haughty resolve.

Mimicking Thorne's irreverence, I add, "I think you may be right. Thanks for the greeting and gift, but we're all set."

"What happy news, then, since I intend to *take* as my gift," Mazus says, eyes feral with delight. Without warning, Thorne is ripped from my side, appearing next to his father and bound in slimy black ropes that look suspiciously like the mass that had surrounded Krantz.

"Thorne!" I cry out, then turn my gaze back to Mazus. He only smirks, and the expression is so like Thorne it makes me nauseous. With a blood-curdling shriek, I hurl as much aether as I can at the ropes like I had with Krantz, but this time the black mass doesn't dissipate. If anything, it squeezes Thorne tighter. Panic briefly flashes across his eyes before he gains control over his features again, looking bored and uninterested in what's taking place. For added effect, he even picks at his fingernails, while I completely fall apart inside.

I close my eyes to evaluate the aether around Mazus, and my suspicions are confirmed when I find a web of pulsing onyx surrounding him, at least ten times the size of what Krantz had accumulated and somehow darker and inkier. It makes me lightheaded to look at, and I'm forced to open my eyes again. I try sending small streams of light to probe the ropes holding Thorne, looking for any weakness, but it does nothing.

Mazus makes a tsking noise.

"Unfortunately for you, Laurel, the only magic that might help you break those bindings is entirely unknown to you. What a shame you and Thorne never explored the true power of the mating bond," Mazus simpers.

"What do you mean?" I hiss.

"Do you want to tell her Admon, or should I?" Mazus asks the old male. Admon's eyes meet mine, regret and something else I can't place clearly written across his expression, but I only bare my teeth.

"How could you?" I snarl, and he gives me a pitying and regretful look that only angers me further.

"It was the only way," Admon says with the same gentleness he's always shown, though his eyes are sad and resigned. My ears ring with fury and my vision swims. How *could* he, after everything we've been through, everything he's seen me endure?

"Yes, yes, it's the only path, you've consulted the stars. No one cares, Admon. Tell her what you know about mating bonds. What you *failed* to tell her before," Mazus hisses, though it comes out gleeful. Admon's eyes continue to express deep regret, but I don't care. *He will pay for this.* I hurl a dagger of light toward Admon, but Mazus disintegrates it before it reaches him, a power he shouldn't have. "Tell her," Mazus commands with the aether-voice, the words reverberating through the room.

Somehow, Admon remains standing while everyone else in the room but me and Thorne drop to their knees. When he speaks, his words quiet and scholarly, it's like we're back on the moors and he's explaining a concept about the aether to me.

"When mates bond, they typically influence one another's power in some way. Sometimes they each gain each other's conduit affinities, sometimes they just both grow stronger. But there are *certain* mating bonds that are part of the very fabric of our world, blessed by the aether or by some long-lost gods. When those bonds form, one mate accesses a deeper well of power than before, while the other mate acts as an anchor to protect them from losing their mind. It's a magical insanity, of sorts—it's complicated." Finally, Admon looks flustered, like he doesn't know how to explain. But his words horrify me. What they imply... Finally, with a swallow, Admon continues. "Their blood—the mates' blood—can create frighteningly powerful spells." Admon finishes his speech tentatively, as if he's not sure he got it right. He looks to Mazus, who only cackles.

The shimmering blood. Memory slams into me as I recall the way Thorne's blood had shimmered after he'd been injured, while I was healing him. My mind is reeling, and there's a lot to process right now. Pieces are clicking together even while new questions form. Mazus breaks me out of my spiraling with his grating tenor.

"You see, Laurel, by forcing you and Thorne together, I've unlocked new facets of power in you both. Your power will slowly drive you insane without your mate by your side, while Thorne's blood... Well, let's just say it will be extremely useful to me." My eyes meet Thorne's and all traces of the Shining Prince are gone now, the fear and horror displayed transparently on his face. He tries to scream something to me, but Mazus wraps more shadowy ropes around his mouth. I run toward him, determined to claw him out of those ropes if I must, but the strongest barrier of air I've ever experienced throws me back at least ten feet. Fionn's at my side instantly, offering his hand to help me up. He tries launching any piece of metal he can find in the room at Mazus and the barrier between us and Thorne, but they disintegrate while airborne.

"Like that little trick? Does it seem familiar? Krantz told me *all* about it in the letters he smuggled out with the thayar shipments," Mazus sneers. Suddenly, Krantz sits on the throne where Mazus previously was. My eyes search the room for the Velmaran King, but he's nowhere to be seen. Krantz laughs, an eerie and maniacal sound. "Do I look familiar? I told Hawthorne Thayaria wasn't as inaccessible as he thought. I've been in and out of your kingdom countless times," Krantz says.

"I don't—I don't understand," I murmur. The eerie laugh from Krantz returns, before he somehow shifts his body back into Mazus, so quickly I almost miss it. I swear his eyes become yellow slits for a brief moment, but I'm too confused to process the information.

"I can shape shift, Laurel. It's not that difficult to figure out. But then again, you've never been very bright, have you?" Mazus sneers.

"But, Krantz... I killed him," I murmur.

"Oh, Krantz was a real person. It was him who you imprisoned, who attacked you multiple times. The only time I impersonated him was the brief little conversation I had with Hawthorne at the estate. I needed to be sure you got Nemesia's letter, and I wanted to check in on your mating bond myself. Krantz and I had a deal that if he killed you, I'd make him ruler of Thayaria. Of course, I had no intention of getting rid of you, at least not until you accepted the bond, but it gave you and Hawthorne a common enemy. I should thank you for killing the rat. He was becoming a problem for me. Getting too wrapped up in his own ego."

The room spins around me as my magic expenditure from earlier and the sheer shock of what's happening catch up to me. Too much information is being revealed to me, when all I can focus on is Thorne. He's trapped by his father, who's revealed his intentions to steal him away from me. Everything in the room fades around me as I stare at my mate, mind frantically reeling for any plan that will save him. Thorne struggles against his bindings, trying desperately to get free. I sink to my knees in horror and despair.

Nemesia appears at my side and lifts me from the ground with steady hands. It's like the moment at the Battle of Moormyr, when she had helped me stand to face Mazus. Three hundred years later, we're still locked in a battle we can't win, once again at Mazus's mercy. I desperately want to collapse, curl in on myself, and sob. But I don't. I pull my shoulders back and squeeze Nemesia's hand once, the only apology I can offer her right now for everything I put her through. I instantly recognize her brand of powerful plant magic, trying to penetrate the invisible wall between us and Thorne, but it doesn't work.

"I can assure you, General, this is not a fight you'll win," Mazus says to Nemesia, who snarls at him with her own grief-laced fury.

"So, it was you who gave them the letter stolen from my room? How did you even enter Thayaria?" Nemesia asks, confirming what she'd told me. I'll have so much shame to unpack later, but right now I can't think of anything except Thorne, can't bring my thoughts to wander anywhere but my trapped mate and how I'm going to save him.

Mazus only shrugs. "I hoped that by convincing Laurel you betrayed her, it would push her into Thorne's arms. From what I hear, it worked. And as for *how*, let's just say only the tiniest drop of blood can unlock many doors that once seemed sealed shut."

"If you do this, if you take him, it means *war*," I snarl with the aether-voice, but Mazus is unaffected. I lock that information away for later, unable to examine it now.

Mazus only laughs at me. "Oh, you stupid female. *The war never ended*. I just took my time between battles, honing my strategy until it was perfect. I thought I needed you, but turns out, I had the solution all along. I just needed the mating bond to officially snap into place so I could swap your blood for his."

"But you didn't plan for me to escape with your books. You can take him, but we still have the histories," Nemesia hisses. This time, Mazus practically cackles, the infernal sound echoing hollowly through the room. The hairs on the back of my neck stand as tears of laughter gather in his eyes.

"This is why we don't allow females into positions of power in Velmara. You're so feebleminded. I *let* you escape. *With* the books. Last I had heard from Admon, these two idiots hadn't accepted the mating bond yet. I needed you to come back with the books to provide the same information Admon already had to protect his cover, and I hoped the presence of her best friend would help Laurel accept Thorne."

Nemesia stills, predatory gaze focused on Mazus. "And Genevieve?" she asks, a quiet intensity in her voice.

His eyes light with menacing delight. "She didn't betray you, or at least not on purpose. We gave her a truth serum that forced her to reveal everything. I needed to be certain before you left that you'd made the right connections."

"But... you... you *killed* her," Nemesia chokes out, her arms circling her own waist. The move is vulnerable, heartbreaking, and something I've never seen my stalwart friend do. Mazus only shrugs.

"I didn't care whether she lived or died, really. I would've been happy sending her back here with you. But her uncle had tired of her. It was a convenient excuse for him to do something he's wanted to do for a century but couldn't act on out of propriety. Your little relationship allowed him to kill her and save face with the many Kalmeera relatives he has." Nemesia drops to the ground, completely defeated, her eyes staring off into nothing. Once again, there's no one left to save me and my kingdom. I repeat the mantra I've repeated to myself nearly every day for three hundred years.

You are the last defense against Mazus. There is no one coming to save you. You must always save yourself.

I grind my teeth, strengthening my resolve and amending that mantra. He will not get away with this.

He will not take Thorne.

Closing my eyes, I focus on the nexus of four leylines that meet under the palace. I unstopper my connection to the aether, like I did only hours ago when battling Krantz. But this time, instead of just letting the aether flow into me, I *pull* on the current as hard as I can, absorbing every drop of the life blood of the world into my body. I shake with the effort of holding that much power at once without releasing it, and my brow heats. When I open my eyes, I'm glowing as brightly as I had when I ingested the thayar concentrate, and this time with no magical boost.

There's a hunger in Mazus's eyes, unbridled lust for my power. Despite the similarities between him and Thorne—the same eyes, the same jaw, the same nose—Mazus possesses none of Thorne's warmth or charisma. With a roar that somehow reverberates with the aether-voice, I hurl every bit of magic I possess at the wall keeping me from my mate, my will entirely focused on freeing Thorne. I let aether run into and out of me, becoming my own leyline. The world seems to bend around me, and now I'm no longer pulling aether, but it's still being forced into me in a torrential surge. I lose control over it, and now all I can do is exist while magic courses through me. My eyes sting, my vision blurs. I vaguely hear screaming, and I think it's Nemesia begging me to stop. Or maybe it's Fionn. The gentle and soothing murmur of Admon washes over my awareness, and it only drives me forward. The *thing* inside of me that has briefly opened its eyes on a few occasions now wakes up in a furious rage. Whatever has made me feel like *more* than myself not only blinks its eyes but completely overtakes me.

I *become* the aether, and my consciousness rises out of my body. Everything goes quiet and still, and I nearly sigh in relief at the calm that settles over me. I float over the room, surveying the scene with detached observation. Laurel—me—looks so incredibly broken. So does Nemesia. My spectral gaze finds Thorne, still fighting like hell to free himself of the bonds that won't break, not without our blood. I swoop down to caress his face, even in this liminal state feeling the soul-deep thread that binds us. His nostrils flare, like he can sense me.

"I'll be okay," he whispers, or maybe thinks, since his mouth is still gagged with Mazus's vile substance. I'm not sure how it works in this form. "Let me go. You're killing yourself." I don't want to let go, would rather stay here by his side in my final moments than return to my body and face a reality where he's gone. I know what being in this state is doing to me, but I can't bring myself to care. "Live to fight another day, witchling. Please," Thorne begs. The raw ache in his voice—his thoughts?—slams me back into my body, and the chaos and noise of the room erupts around me.

Once I'm corporeal again, the desire to let go of the aether fills me, but I can't break free of it. It continues to surge through me, unrestrained. My palms are sweaty, and I slip in and out of consciousness. Thorne's words repeat through my mind. *Live to fight another day, witchling. Live.* With an otherworldly and determined roar, I find the tap on my magic and slam it shut, hurling every bit of aether that remains in my body at Mazus and his wall, before collapsing in a heap on the ground.

Despite knowing what's inevitable, I look up at the invisible wall that shimmers with Mazus's dark magic, hoping that it will drop. The barrier wavers for a moment, but holds, and I deflate.

Mazus laughs, a deranged sound that makes his eyes flash yellow again, as tears stream down my face. I leap up and run at the barrier, getting hurled back, but I don't stop. I'm not ready to accept defeat, not ready to accept what I know is going to happen. I keep running at it over and over again, screaming, shrieking, while Mazus looks on with euphoria.

Eventually, Nemesia, Fionn, and Carex restrain me. It takes their combined strength to hold me back, and even then, I blast them away from me with a force of magic that flings them to opposite corners of the room. A quiet voice whispers that I should check if my friends are okay, but I ignore it, too consumed with terror at losing my mate. Thorne thrashes in his bindings, clearly using every bit of strength he possesses to free himself, despite the words he whispered to me when I was in his mind.

"I tire of this pitiful display of affection. We're done here. Enjoy losing your mind," Mazus jeers.

I panic, remembering just two nights ago, when Thorne had professed his love for me, and I hadn't said it back, even though I knew I felt it. Even though my aether-heart had screamed at me to tell him, to let down that final wall to this brilliant, beautiful male, I had remained silent. And at the festival, I planned to give him that ring and tell him then, but my words had failed me. Just hours ago, I wanted to whisper it to him in the quiet moments we had after the battle with Krantz, but decided to wait until there was more *time*.

And now my time has run out.

Thorne peeled away the calloused exterior I've worn for so long—too long—revealing a joyful, confident, compassionate female beneath, and I was too cowardly to give him those final, all-important words. I collapse, grief and rage washing over me in equal measure. I'm sobbing now, a black hole, everything I am caving in. My eyes meet Thorne's one last time.

"I love you," I whisper.

But he's gone before the words make it out of my lips.

"I love you, I love you, I love you," I scream to the void, because Thorne is gone, and he can't hear me.

Want more Laurel and Hawthorne? Keep reading for a bonus chapter that takes place between 44 and 45.

LAUREL

Many Velmarans were trapped inside Thayaria after the war. Most were there visiting relatives or exploring the once beautiful Thayarian landscape. The Witch Queen rounded them up and keeps them locked away in dank and dark prisons, using their blood when she needs to cast another corrupt spell. It is for this reason that the Golden King continues his quest for peace with Thayaria. He wishes to return home the lost and broken Velmaran souls, or whatever remains of them after 300 years of torture at the Witch Queen's hand.

The Witch Queen and Her Treachery

The last twenty-four hours have been unbelievable. I have a mate, who I willingly told my darkest secrets to, and nothing bad happened. Not only did Thorne accept me, he *worshiped* me. I've had lovers. Many, in fact. But none have brought me as much pleasure as my mate. When I'd bitten him, it was like some beast hidden deep inside of me had reared its head and opened its eyes for the first time.

We'd aerstepped back to my rooms, where Lunaria looked up with what I swear was a knowing smirk. I chuckle, while the giant cat only padded over to Thorne and *licked him.* Groomed his hand, actually. Thorne wanted to go change before the dinner, understandably, so I aerstepped him to his apartment door and then came back here. Without him by my side, I'm antsy.

You need to pull it together.

There's a knock on the door. When I open it, Silene jumps into my arms in a hug, her breath coming in huge gasps. "Thorne just told us you accepted the mating bond, and I had to run up here immediately. I'm so happy for you." She beams at me, and I return her hug with my own tight squeeze.

"Why didn't you tell me today was his birthday?" I chastise.

"I didn't want you to get all weird about it and in your head." Her words are matter-of-fact, and she shrugs. "You retreat when you think you shouldn't be part of our little group, and I knew Thorne would want you there."

"I — do I do that?" She only gives me a look that tells me I absolutely do. We both burst out laughing.

"I had something made for you for tonight. Thorne is going to *lose it* when he sees you." She shoves a garment bag in my face that she had apparently dropped the instant I opened the door. I unzip the bag and my mouth falls open. "I had that seamstress who lost her shop in a fire make it. Paid triple for it with Mazus' gold." Her eyes sparkle with mischief as she takes the bag from me, then pulls out the most beautiful gown I've ever seen.

Cream and navy, with only small hints of gold, it represents Thorne's colors. The bodice is a structured cream corset, with translucent sleeves dipping off either side. The stitching is gold, but thayar flowers, laurel wreaths, and lightning bolts have been expertly woven into the details, nearly impossible to spot except with careful attention. The a-line skirt is navy, with a long bow the trails dow the back. It's unlike anything I've ever worn or owned.

"Can I help you get ready?" Silene asks, excitement in her eyes. I can only nod, my adoration of this tiny ball of kindness in a fae female body too much to express in words. She uses air to curl my hair, something I've never seen before. The trick gives my hair a blown out, voluminous look, with soft waves framing my face. "Doing it this way protects your hair and keeps it shiny," she explains.

Then she does my makeup with her own kit, painting my face in soft pinks and lilacs, the kohl a soft brown rather than a harsh black. The effect makes my green eyes pop. Pink lips and cheeks complete the rosy look. Once I'm dressed, I survey myself in the mirror, awed at the effect light makeup and lighter colored clothing has on my appearance. Thorne's lightning bolt necklace is the only adornment I wear, and it rests in the hollow of my throat.

"I don't look like myself." Seeing Silene's face fall, I add quickly, "But in an amazing way. I love it. Thank you." She nods with a small smile. "Don't you need to get ready?"

"My gown is in the same garment bag. I'll get ready here, if that's okay. Then you can aerstep me down, because I do *not* want to walk down all those steps in formal clothing."

As she digs in the bag to pull out her own dress and additional makeup, I consider the freindship we've developed. It's nice to have a friend who likes makeup and dressing up. Not that I always want to preen with my female friends, but I do enjoy some of the more feminine things Silene takes her own delight in. Nemesia — well, that isn't what Nemesia likes. I don't want to think too deeply about her, so I return to studying Silene.

She makes quick work of making herself presentable, blowing out her own hair with the same air magic trick. The effect is jaw-dropping on her, long locks shining in voluminous waves that reach the middle of her back. It's the only time I've ever seen her hair not coiled tightly, and while she's always one of the most beautiful fae I've ever known, the look makes her look otherworldly. She does her own makeup a bit darker than mine, accentuating her olive skin, and her gown is a shiny cream and gold mermaid cut. Jewels cover every inch of fabric.

"You look stunning, Silene," I tell her. She grins wide, mirth dancing in her expression.

"These males won't know what to do with us."

As we stroll into the Velmaran apartment, Thorne's scent immediately washes over me. My thighs turn slick, but I push down the overwhelming need. I can't see him, but I can *feel* that he's in his room.

"Alright, boys, your girls have arrived," Silene calls out in a sing-song voice. "Come lavish us with praise." Fionn steps out of his now redecorated room, wearing a dark green pantsuit, hair slicked back.

"You look nice," I tell him, and he nods. I'm about to tease Fionn for the formal wear when Thorne steps out of his room, and everything around me disappears as my vision tunnels in on him. He wears his own navy suit, with a cream shirt and cream tie. Small gold accents shine brightly, but are minimal. His moss-colored eyes meet mine, and his lips curl into a smile that takes my breath away. That stubborn piece of hair falls into his face as usual, and I grin.

"Laurel," he breathes, instantly at my side. "You... you look... wow. You are *exquisite*." I blush. His fingers thread through mine, the move so familiar to me now that my own fingers slip into his without even thinking. He kisses me on the cheek, and I can't keep my body from pressing into his. One of us groans, but I'm not sure who, too lost in the feel of him by my side once again.

"Aethers, it's getting worse," Fionn huffs.

"What is?" Thorne asks absentmindedly, eyes still trained on me with glassy-eyed lust.

"The two of you. Your longing stares. It's disgusting," Fionn complains. "Can you try to act normal for *one* night?" Thorne gives me a conspiratorial smile and wink, then turns to Fionn.

"Brother, when you find your own mate some day, I give you permission to engage in longing stares," Thorne croons while Fionn rolls his eyes.

"Leave them alone, they're *adjusting*," Silene chides, then claps her hands together. "Are you ready for the surprise?" We all nod. "Laurel, could you please aerstep us to the heart of Arberly? The main square in the city will do nicely."

I give Thorne a curious look, and he shrugs, before we're all stepping into the bustling city at night. Lights are strung up in criss-crossing patterns over the square and down the streets leading from it. Fae and humans jostle about, on their way to dinners or family or other evening activities. As we follow Silene down the street, the eyes of my people widen when they see us. Some bow, some stare, but all mutter "Her Majesty" as we pass. Not

Witch Queen. I don't spend much time in Arberly, but I realize now that Thorne was right on that first dinner we had when he started courting me. My people do want to see more of me, and they aren't afraid.

Silene stops us in front of a restaurant with a golden awning and big windows. When we enter, wait staff immediately greet us with bows and escort us to a back room. When we're seated at a private table, my curiosity gets the best of me.

"What's the surprise, Silene? Is it just dinner and a night on the town?"

"As if I would just do a regular dinner on Thorne's *birthday,*" she tells me, rolling her eyes teasingly. A fae couple walks into the room, and they bow, looking nervous. Silene stands and gives them both hugs, like she's known them for years, then turns to us. "This is Cecil and Maeve. They own this restaurant. I visit it frequently because their food is delectable," she chirps. "Cecil and Maeve are Velmaran. They were in Thayaria visiting family when the mist barrier went up. They remained here, building a life for themselves and building this restaurant. Once they told me their story, I knew I had to have them cook dinner for Thorne's birthday. Traditional Velmaran food!" she claps her hand in excitement.

I'm speechless, my body weighed down with guilt and grief. I knew it was inevitable there were Velmarans trapped here, but I'd never met any. They look at me nervously, and I realize they're probably worried I'll throw them out of Thayaria or do something even worse for the simple fact that they're Velmaran. The guilt and shame at what I've done and the environment I've created for these two closes in on me, my breathing becoming short. Then, Thorne's warm hard finds my leg under the table. The feel of him relaxes me, and I'm able to speak.

"I'm deeply sorry for your experience," I say, trying to soothe their nerves. "Had I known, I would have done what I could to get you back to Velmara. I hope you're happy here in Thayaria, and I'm honored that you'll be sharing Velmaran culture with me." They smile, and Cecil steps forward.

"Please don't be sorry, Your Majesty. We love our life in Thayaria. We've built a family here these centuries. It feels more like home than Velmara ever did. Though we do miss the food." He blushes slightly.

"We're delighted to have the opportunity to bring the Velmaran ambassadors a small piece of home for Prince Hawthorne's birthday," Maeve adds, jumping in to help her blushing husband. With that, they leave, and Silene returns to her seat.

"Silene, wow, this is amazing," Thorne says. "Thank you for such a thoughtful celebration. Even if my birthday is definitely not worthy of such a meal."

"I can't wait for this food," Fionn says excitedly, and we all laugh.

My mouth waters when the first course comes out, a meat dish in a creamy tomato sauce. Thorne tells me it's his favorite, and Silene cheerily informs us that everything on the menu will be his favorites tonight. After the first bite, I moan in delight, and Thorne's eyes light up at the noise. He squeezes my thigh under the table again, this time for an entirely different reason, rubbing circles up and down the inside of my leg. I can barely contain the shivers that wrack down my spine at his touch, but his casual and confident demeanor never falter, even when my breath hitches as he inches closer to my new favorite place for him to touch.

We spend the evening eating delicious food, drinking copious amounts of wine and Thayarian ale, talking, and laughing. One of Thorne's hands is always touching me throughout the evening, like he can't bear to break that physical connection between us. I'm grateful for that, because I feel the same way. When Maeve brings out the desert, a chocolate cake with candles lit on top of it, I clap my hands in delight. Silene beams.

"Thorne's life includes you now," she says. "So the food that represents home *must* include chocolate cake." Thorne blows the candles out, then leans down and whispers in my ear.

"I agree with Silene. You are my *home*, even if that means the desert at every meal for the rest of my life is chocolate cake. It's my favorite because it's *your* favorite." His fingers tap a rhythm on my exposed shoulder, the small movement sending need coursing through me. "I can smell your arousal, witchiling. Have been able to smell it all night." His voice is low and full of promise. "It's fucking distracting, and the best thing to ever happen to me. I want to smell you like this at every dinner for the rest of our lives, even if it drives me mad with need." I blush, clenching my thighs. He only smirks, that dimple I love so much making an appearance. Fionn rolls his eyes and Silene stares at us dreamy-eyed.

When dessert is finished, we thank Cecil and Maeve. Thorne passes them a massive bag of gold as we leave the restaurant.

"So, what now?" I ask, and Silene grins.

"Now, we go back to the apartment, change into more comfortable clothes, and hit the town. We're doing a tavern crawl!" she says with delight dancing in her eyes. Fionn and Thorne cheer, and I'm sure I've missed something. Thorne notices, and immediately brings me into the loop.

"Our favorite activity in Velmara for birthdays is to walk this one street in Arnia that has over twenty taverns lined down it. We have an ale at each place before we move on to the next one," he explains.

"And that's it? You just get drunk one stop at a time?" I ask, confused.

"That's *it? That's it?*" Fionn says, aghast. "Thorne, your mate is clearly confused." Thorne laughs and wraps his arm around me, pulling me closer to the side, and I relish the heat that seeps into me from him.

"It's more fun than you think, I promise," he tells me, kissing the top of my head. I shrug, happy to be included regardless of the activity. I aerstep us to their apartment, and Silene surprises me with a set of leggings and a tunic that she somehow swiped from my closet without my noticing. Grateful for her thoughtfulness, I change in Thorne's room, taking my time while I'm naked to torture him. As expected, he can't keep his hands off me, and I'm wrapped in his arms the second my clothes are fully removed.

"I'm suddenly no longer in the mood for a tavern crawl," he says, low and teasing, hands delicately stroking near the apex of my thighs, but I bat him away.

"It's your birthday! We're going. I want to see what this is all about. Plus, you're adorable when the Thayarian ale hits you," I coo, and he sighs dramatically before releasing me with a light slap on my ass.

When we arrive at the first tavern, Silene orders us a round of drinks, and Thorne and Fionn race one another to down the ale. Fionn wins, and then he and Thorne look at Silene and I, as if to say, your turn. We take the bait, and I beat Silene easily. We repeat the same game at each tavern, until eventually we realize I'm the better match for Fionn, so he and I pair up as the first drinkers each time. In the fifth tavern I finally beat him and Silene erupts in loud cheers. Thorne beams at me, wrapping his arms around me and burying his face in my neck for a little too long, the ale clearly affecting him.

At the sixth tavern, Silene announces she's done drinking, so Fionn and I split her drink. At the eighth tavern, Thorne's slurred words are nearly impossible to understand as he recites awful made-up poetry to me, so we cut him off. With the birthday boy inebriated past the point of coherence, we decide to call it a night. Fionn laments the effect Thayarian ale has on Thorne as we walk home, practically dragging Thorne between us.

"In Velmara, he can make it to all twenty taverns!" Fionn complains loudly, the ale impacting him more than he realizes. He hiccups, and I cackle.

"None of you can handle Thayarian ale," I say, but the words come out sloppy, and I realize I'm also completely wasted. Telling no one what I'm doing, I aerstep us back to the apartment, and Fionn immediately vomits on the floor.

"Can't do that, queenie," he mumbles. I giggle, then will the vomit away. Fionn stares at me in wonder.

"Goodnight, everyone," I say, about to aerstep back to my rooms, but Thorne tugs me into his room before I can get away. Fionn and Silene simply call goodnight to us from the sitting room and disappear to their own spaces.

"Stay here," Thorne pleads, arms wrapped tightly around me. "I need you here, with me. Or we can go to your room, but we stay together."

We haven't talked yet about what things will look like now that we're officially mated, but when I consider it, I don't want to be away from him either. Instead of answering, I slowly remove my tunic and leggings, eyes locked on his, revealing the lacy undergarments Silene also stole from my room earlier in her infinite wisdom. Thorne's eyes darken, and before I realize what's happened, we're both laying in his bed with only our undergarments between us. Like last night, my magic seems to be out of my control around him, aerstepping us places without my knowing. But as Thorne twines our legs together and plants sloppy kisses across my shoulders and collarbone, I forget all about my concern that I don't have control over my powers.

"Witchling, the things you make me think about," he murmurs into my hair, squeezing his arms tightly around my waist and hauling me as close to him as possible.

"You don't have to just think them," I coo, ready for another night of passionate love making. But when I turn in his arms to face him, he's already fallen asleep, arms remaining locked firmly around me. I smile at his sleep-softened features and nestle my head into the crook of his shoulder, breathing deeply. As the smell of him—the smell of my mate—washes over me, I drift off into a deep and contented sleep.

Several hours later, he wakes me with soft and gentle kisses peppered up and down nearly every inch of me. Desire shoots to my core immediately. We've both recovered from the affects of the alcohol and are alone for the first time since last night's frenzy, and the need has returned with an intensity that matches the first time we came together. When it's clear that I'm awake and very much on the same page as him, Thorne rips my bandeau down the middle, the cool air hardening my nipples and making me arch my back into him. He buries his face between my breasts and sighs contentedly, like he could stay there, breathing me in, forever.

But he's kindled a burning fire in me, one that won't be satiated with his face resting on my chest. It needs to go *other places*. I grind my hips up into his, silently communicating with him to get moving, and he chuckles.

"You're so demanding, witchling," he coos as he raises his head to meet my eyes. The mischevious glint in those mossy irises tells me I'm not getting what I want anytime soon. A whimper escapes me, but that only intensifies the unholy look in his eyes. Without warning, caressing bands of light lick at my wrists and ankles, before wrapping around them and spreading me wide in four different directions. My legs he brings upwards, exposing every inch of my pussy. His hands trail from my breasts, down the curve of my waist, before settling under my ass. Reverently, he cups my backside, lifting my hips to bring my center to his mouth. "How wet for me are you, *mate*?"

I whimper again, unable to stand the torturing way he growls *mate* into me. Slowly—achingly, unbearably slowly—he licks up my slit, growling in satisfaction at the pooling slickness he finds there. I buck my hips when he reaches my clit, expecting him to clamp down and suck, or at least give me *some* friction. Instead, he pools away, laughing at my neediness.

"Thorne," I moan. "Please."

"Please what, *mate*? I want to hear you say it."

"Please touch me." My words are breathy and pleading.

"Is that all you want? For me to touch you?" He rubs circles along my upper thighs where he still holds me lifted to him. Small sparks of electricity dance across my skin where he touches me, not strong enough to hurt, but enough to electrify my need. My back arches involuntarily, every inch of my skin on fire with desire.

"No. Make me come. Please. Now." The last word is demanding, laced with the smallest hint of aether-voice, and Thorne laughs again.

"Whatever you wish, my queen." He's on me lightning fast, his mouth sucking while his fingers pump in and out. In this position, with my hips so starkly elevated and my limbs spread wide, every sensation sends waves of pleasure washing over me. My eyes close, and unlike last night, he lets me keep them closed, content to let me focus only on the sensations of him touching me. When he uses his light magic to make electricity zap my nipples, the pain delicious, I cry out.

"Shhhhh, witchling. We wouldn't want our friends to hear us," he teasingly chides. I hiss, not liking the idea that anyone else hears us. I immediately put up a sound shield around us.

"Problem solved, princeling," I coo with every bit of sensual and seductive prowess I possess. "Now get inside me and fuck me like I'm your fucking *mate.*"

Now it's his turn to moan, and I watch in fascination as the pupils in his eyes blow out. His clothes disappear, like I've *poofed* them away, as Thorne would say. Though I don't remember willing that with my magic. It doesn't matter though, because seconds later he lowers my hips and releases me from his bindings. He pulls me up, then sits on the edge of the bed and guides me to straddle him. My legs wrap around his middle as I slowly lower myself so that he's fully sheathed inside me. We both groan in pleasure at the feel of how perfectly our bodies fit together in practically any position.

His hands find my waist, holding on to me as I rock my hips back and forth. My head drops, hair swinging down my back as we move. We're both moaning incoherently now, lost in the feel of one another. Unable to keep from touching my breasts for very long, Thorne's mouth lowers to my nipple and sucks hard. It only encourages me to move faster, my thrusts becoming frantic as he bites down. I rest my hand over the scar of my bite mark above his heart, and he releases my nipple to lavish delicate kisses over my matching scar. All the while, his hands squeeze my love handles, guiding me to move faster and faster. Tension coils inside of me, so tight that I know I'm going to erupt with this orgasm.

"Thorne," I cry. "I'm going to come. Hard."

"I've got you, witchling. My mate, my queen. Let yourself unleash." His words are so gentle and tender. It fills me with a sense of safety and calm. Slowly, he moves one hand from my hip and brings it to my clit, pressing just lightly enough to bring me over the edge.

My eyes roll back in my head and I *shriek*. It's a wild and feral sound, filled with so much aether I'm not sure how Thorne stays upright. But he holds me tight through my release, placing a shield of light around us so that nothing gets destroyed with the raw aether I release at the peak of the sensation. I feel him clench inside me, my squeezing bringing him over the cliff with me.

We pant when it's over, our foreheads pressed together.

"Good girl," he whispers as he runs his warm hands up and down my shoulders. He's still inside me, and when the walls of my pussy clench at his words, I feel him harden again. We both laugh, equally exasperated and pleased with the constant ache this new bond gives us for each other. He picks me up, my legs still wrapped around his waist, and lays us both down on the bed. We spend the rest of the night in the same feral passion as the night before, until we both collapse in exhaustion as the sun rises.

ACKNOWLEDGEMENTS

I read a lot of books, and I'm one of those weird readers who reads the acknowledgements every time (except if you leave me on a terrible cliffhanger! So, if you're actuallly reading this after that ending, you're a better human than me). Author acknowledgements always say some version of the same thing — blah, blah, blah, this book wouldn't be possible without all my people. I'll be honest, I've been skeptical of that. Skeptical of the outpouring of love from authors to what seems like an endless list of supporters. Now that I've written a book, however, I have an acute appreciation for this outpouring of thanks.

The reality is, the human creative process is not achieved independently. Creativity seems to be a sourcing of ideas from some larger collective, a participation in an iterative process that may start in my mind but certainly can't be finished there. Every single aspect of getting this book into your hands involved help — from the truly incredible beta readers who gave me invaluable feedback, to my indie author friends who answered all my silly questions about the publishing process or recommended vendors, to the awesome community on bookstagram and booktok who helped hype the book and me. As I write this, I genuinely don't even know where to begin to thank the dozens of people who brought Witch Queen together.

In many ways, this book is a love letter to bookstagram (sorry booktok, no shade, it's just not where I started my journey). I have built such an incredible community over the last 2+ years, a community I barely knew existed and absolutely couldn't appreciate how much I needed when I made my first book review post. It's bookstagram that reinvigorated my love of reading, bookstagram that introduced me to the genre of fantasy romance and the concept of an independently published author. Bookstagram introduced me to almost every single beta reader for Witch Queen (except for my close friends and family who read it), and it's where I sourced every vendor — from the editors to the artists. Ultimately, the bookstagram community is what inspired me to write a book in the first place, and gave me the confidence to keep going until it was published.

Thank you so much to my incredible team of beta readers. If they have a book social media, you should absolutely follow them.

- Ali / @aliduggan901

- @thedishwithlish_

- Allie

- Becca / @rebecc_3

- Bri

- Caitlin

- Caitlin (of the sister-in-law variety)

- Cortni

- Dan (of the friend and not husband variety)

- Heidi / @essentially_heidi

- Hollie

- Jess / @jdemchuk

- Joanne / @bookscatsandtats

- Julia / @juliallovesbooksandcoffee

- Kara

- Katrina / @bookish_kat_reads

- Lindsey

- Nicole / @bookloveaholic

- Rebecca

- Siobhan / @siobhan.taylor.library

Thank you to Mel at Made Me Blush books for the developmental editing, and to Lindsey with PineCorn Publishing for the proofreading and for catching all the times I forgot the eye color of a secondary character. Thank you Whitney Law at New Ink Services for the stunning chapter headers that appear in the print version of The Witch Queen, and to Selkkie Designs for that incredible cover and for answering the MILLION of questions I had about cover design and print formatting. Thank you to my incredible Street Team and ARC readers, who have supported this book with just a description and had no idea if it was any good but were excited to give me a chance anyway.

And to once again participate in another author acknowledgements cliche, I have to say thank you to my incredible husband, Dan. Our lives completely changed when I one day decided, literally completely out of the blue while in the bathtub, that I might want to try and write a book. I had never once in our entire relationship expressed interest in being in author or writing a book. In fact, when you met me while I was in grad school, I think I might have said something like, once I get my master's I'll never write anything ever again. Thank you for picking up the slack in all of our house chores, for entertaining yourself alone while I spent entire weekends writing, and for letting me read the book aloud to you on every single road trip we took in the fall of 2024. Sorry I didn't dedicate this first book to you, but the series dedication is all yours.

ABOUT THE AUTHOR

Alexandria Arden, or Alley, has been writing since she was young. Somewhere between the self-consciousness of her teenage years and the soul crushing experience that was grad school, she stopped writing creatively, convincing herself that the thing she loved doing as a child just "wasn't her skillset."

Cue the pandemic and the rise of popular Fantasy Romance books. Alley rediscovered her love of reading and stories. Throughout that process, she started an Instagram account and podcast dedicated to talking about books. She's built an incredible community of readers and authors alike, and it was this community who inspired her to revisit that childhood passion of writing.

Alley lives in Salt Lake City, Utah with her husband and the true love of her life, her cat Willow. When she's not reading or writing, Alley can be found working in her yard, starting a house project she can't finish, or complaining while hiking in the Wasatch mountains. Alley is most active on her Instagram accounts, @alexandriaardenauthor and @alleycatsandbooks